SCHEMERS, LOVERS AND SURVIVORS PROWL THE HOLLYWOOD JUNGLE

CHRISTIE LARSEN
The first female president of a legendary film company, she would risk the scandalous exposure of her most personal secret to retain control of United Cinema.

SIMON and GUY MacLEOD
The blue-blood brothers who run Wall Street's most powerful investment banking firm—one willing to risk everything for the beautiful studio executive he loves ... the other willing to destroy anyone, including his own brother, to gain ownership of United.

JO CARO
She bedded the rich and powerful to win a position of influence at United. But now treachery offers her far greater rewards.

STAVROS LENNOS
The Harvard-educated front man for the ruthless Lupo family and one of a new breed of Mafia kingpins, he not only wants dominion over the troubled studio ... he wants its beautiful, strong-willed president as well.

IRENE LARSEN BENTLEY
Christie's beautiful, scheming mother, a rich theatrical producer, she has to choose between her own ambitions ... and the daughter she has one last chance to love.

Other Avon Books by
Davidyne Mayleas

BY APPOINTMENT ONLY
THE WOMAN WHO HAD EVERYTHING

Avon Books are available at special quantity discounts for bulk purchases for sales promotions, premiums, fund raising or educational use. Special books, or book excerpts, can also be created to fit specific needs.

For details write or telephone the office of the Director of Special Markets, Avon Books, Dept. FP, 1350 Avenue of the Americas, New York, New York 10019.

NAKED CALL

DAVIDYNE MAYLEAS

AVON BOOKS ● NEW YORK

If you purchased this book without a cover, you should be aware that this book is stolen property. It was reported as "unsold and destroyed" to the publisher, and neither the author nor the publisher has received any payment for this "stripped book."

NAKED CALL is an original publication of Avon Books. This work has never before appeared in book form. This is a work of fiction, and while some portions of this novel deal with actual events and real people, it should in no way be construed as being factual.

AVON BOOKS
A division of
The Hearst Corporation
1350 Avenue of the Americas
New York, New York 10019

Copyright © 1991 by Davidyne Mayleas and William Mayleas
Cover art by Walter Wick
Published by arrangement with the author
Library of Congress Catalog Card Number: 91-91762
ISBN: 0-380-75688-9

All rights reserved, which includes the right to reproduce this book or portions thereof in any form whatsoever except as provided by the U.S. Copyright Law. For information address International Creative Management, Inc., 40 West 57th Street, New York, New York 10019.

First Avon Books Printing: July 1991

AVON TRADEMARK REG. U.S. PAT. OFF. AND IN OTHER COUNTRIES, MARCA REGISTRADA, HECHO EN U.S.A.

Printed in the U.S.A.

RA 10 9 8 7 6 5 4 3 2 1

NAKED CALL—A Wall Street term giving a buyer an option to buy a given amount of a given stock at a given price at a given time. If the price of the stock does not rise to the given price, the buyer of the naked call loses the money he paid for the call.

OPEN CALL— A Hollywood term inviting all actors—with or without credits and/or agents—to audition for a part in a motion picture. If the actor does not get the part, he loses the money and time he spent preparing for the open call.

Prologue

1990

THE LAUGHING child-woman glittered and slithered her way through the party, a mixture of innocence and seduction in a white peasant dress, white flowers in her long, blond hair, a flower in her hand. When she smiled, a tooth was missing—a baby tooth.

"Hey, kid, come sit on my friend's lap," a black-haired, young soldier called to her. He was a blooded soldier, proud to be there . . . only admitted because he had killed two men in the service of the Family.

"On your lap?" the child-woman flirted.

"On his lap . . . Mr. Lapidus."

The girl wrinkled her nose at the sight of the man in the wheelchair. "He's too old. And he can't dance. I can't dance with a wheelchair."

The man in the wheelchair was frail and old. "Get rid of her, Tito," he rasped.

"Mr. Lapidus, she's a kid. She'll learn."

"I'm too old to wait. She learns now. Or she doesn't . . ."

"Hey, kid," Tito yelled to the back of the blond child. "Get your ass over here."

The blond nymphet turned and stuck her tongue out at Tito.

"*Che stupido!*" the black-haired man yelled. "I'm sorry, boss. I'll get her and . . ."

". . . dispose of her." The eyes of the old man were blank. Dead. "Come back when you're finished with her. I'll pick another."

The party was in full swing, swirling around, noisy with voices and music. A tenor stood at the far end of the bar singing Sicilian folk songs, while two big-breasted young women dressed only in skimpy panties were passed around the small dance floor from man to man. The black-haired soldier lunged after the young blond girl who was seated at the bar. When he took the girl's arm, she was agreeable, thinking he wanted her for himself. But when he shook her violently and dragged her toward a window, she started to kick and scratch and yell. The other girls paused in their eating and drinking and dancing for an instant to watch. Then they turned away, stone-faced.

The soldier held the squirming, screaming girl by the scruff of her neck and opened the window with his free hand.

"Boss?" he said to the man in the wheelchair.

"Hang her... upside down," the old man said quietly.

The soldier did as he was told. The child dangled helplessly over the concrete patio thirty feet below, her full skirt billowing about her face. All that covered her nakedness was a pair of lace panties.

"Drop her," the voice commanded.

The girl shrieked, "Noooo!" as she tumbled through the air. Then silence.

The soldier turned back to the room and scanned the party. The old man in the wheelchair would select another girl. Which one this time?

Suddenly Angelo Lupo shouted, "Stop the fuckin' film! Turn on the lights and rerun the opening." The screen went blank and the lights in the ceiling brightened. Lupo seethed as he waited for Pepe to rewind the film. He'd told him to rerun the opening because he must remember the credits—the names of those responsible for this insult to his honor. Disgust contorted his face as the first credits appeared. "AEREO UOMO Presents *The New Mafiosi*... Starring..." The credits slid by, dripping red blood. Behind the credits were quick cuts of scenes in black and white, showing a teenage prostitute getting paid by a drunk conventioneer... a middle-aged lawyer being viciously beaten by Mafia enforcers for not paying the interest on a loan... a twelve-year-old kid pushing crack to another kid in a school yard...

NAKED CALL

Angelo Lupo shouted again, "Stop the fuckin' film! Turn on the lights." He faced Moshe Cohen and asked softly, "Now tell me, old friend, why did you want me to see this piece of shit?"

"You are angry, Angelo."

"You are not?"

"No. I am never angry when someone gives me valuable information. I listen." The old man gasped for breath.

"They make me look like a fool. A Pig! I never had a birthday party like that. And you—you never bothered the girls. They make you a dirty old man."

"In my life I have been many things. Once a brave, young lover. Now a dirty old man. And you have been a fool, Angelo. Sometimes."

"*Maledetto!* Only you can say that to me."

"I say it. The picture is important. It tells a story about us to millions of Americans."

Tony the Trunk squinted. His deep-set black eyes all but disappeared. "Moshe, what are we talking about?"

Moshe Cohen propelled his wheelchair across the room to the bar. He poured a glass of Perrier water, swallowing it quickly. Although quite old, with a thin, small-boned body shriveled by his ten-year battle with emphysema, he was in complete possession of his mental faculties—which were as young and sharp as ever. He gazed at Angelo Lupo, thinking that his closest friend still had something in him of the swaggering, old-style, Family Don. Tony the Trunk thought he was invulnerable, immune from the perils of ordinary mortals. He wasn't. He must pay attention to the new winds abroad in the world or his days were numbered. Moshe leaned slightly forward.

"Who taught you to make business loans?"

"You did."

"Who showed you how to get into legitimate businesses?"

"You did," Tony said with respect.

"And what kind of companies do you control?"

"Soft drinks, wine, whiskey, a fast food chain, a pizza chain." Lupo gave Cohen a sly look. "Wall Street. Investment banking. Where the money is."

"You've made a beginning. There is much more to do.

But first you must concentrate on the media."

"The media concentrates on us. They concentrate on us too damn much. The media hates us."

"Nothing is more likely to dispose them in our favor than the threat of losing their jobs." Cohen's tone was softly sardonic. "And how do we accomplish that?"

Lupo smiled. "We have the money. We buy a newspaper. A television station . . ."

"Later. You start with a movie studio."

"I don't want to make movies. I don't like actors. I know too many actresses already."

"You liked *The Godfather*."

"Puzo understands our family life."

"But you don't like this new Godfather trash. Do you?" Cohen asked politely.

Lupo shook his head decisively. "No. I'll buy that film. If they won't sell it, I'll destroy it. And the producer."

A wave of chilling anger came off Cohen. "If you do that, you do it out of weakness—not strength. That is dangerous. Yes, try to buy the film. If they will not sell, then you wait. The movie will open and it will close. It's garbage. But that must be the end. For the sake of the Family's future you will buy a studio." His voice became gently persuasive. "A movie studio is immediately profitable. In a studio you can launder many millions of dollars while learning the business."

Lupo nodded. "You have always had vision."

"When a story about the Family is offered, our studio will buy it. If it pleases us, our studio will produce it. If not, the story will be buried."

"The public will think better of us."

"No—they will continue to fear us. To hate us. But they will respect us. We don't live by the rules of their world. Those rules are set by other men of power who make rules for their own benefit. The powerless they eat up alive. But we refuse to be eaten. For we, too, are men of power. We will show that in our movies."

"I will call Bruno. You like him. He lives in Hollywood."

"No. Bruno is a smart talent agent. He handles actors.

Actresses. Makes deals. But not this kind of deal. Call Stavros."

Lupo had been listening carefully, weighing his friend's advice. "Stavros was always your favorite," he said. Then he asked, "You've been thinking about this a long time?"

Cohen smiled. "Yes. Ever since Bruno telephoned me."

"He telephoned you? He thinks you're an actor?" Lupo pretended to laugh.

"He told me there is great interest in Hollywood in a screenplay—that's what he called it—a screenplay."

"A screenplay?" Lupo frowned. "Why did he call you?"

"Because the screenplay is about me." Lupo's mouth opened as if he wished to speak. Then he closed it and swallowed. Cohen continued. "The working title is *The Gangster*. And the gangster is . . . me . . . Mosh Cohen."

Lupo lost his temper. He cursed the movie business, the actors, actresses, Hollywood. He cursed in the strong Sicilian dialect with words that more vividly expressed his fury than English could. When his rage finally exhausted itself, he spoke with controlled disbelief. "*The Gangster*? They call you—Little Mosh Cohen—a gangster?"

"Don't misunderstand, Angelo. They will not use my name. Only my life, as they see it. An alternate working title is *Mob Boss*."

Lupo blinked. Then he slowly shook his head. "No. If there is ever a film made about you, our studio will make it. You are a great man. The film will tell the truth about you to the American public." For a very heavy man, Lupo moved across the room with surprising speed. He picked up the telephone. "I will call Stavros now."

PART ONE
1991

Chapter 1

CHRISTIE LARSEN tilted back the brown corduroy recliner and swung her legs onto the footrest. She stretched contentedly in her comfortable khaki pants and loose sweatshirt. As she watched the NBC nightly news, she sipped a glass of chardonnay and admired her new high-resolution TV set. It gave her a brighter, clearer picture than she'd ever before seen on TV, almost as clean as the picture one saw in a movie theater. The shade of purple in Tom Brokaw's purple power tie was exactly the same shade of purple he saw when he chose the tie at Brooks Brothers. She looked closer. Once high-resolution TV reached the American public, TV makeup artists would have to be as careful as movie makeup artists. They'd missed Brokaw's ears.

Oblivious of the news, her son was focusing his attention on the drawing pad on his lap. With quick, deft strokes of his crayon he was finishing a jungle scene: a drawing of a stately lion, full grown and powerful, his mane blowing in the wind, standing over the carcass of a giraffe.

The drawing caught Christie's attention as completely as if it was a brilliant moment on a movie screen. Tommy was as gifted as his drawing teacher insisted. The sketch was no childish crayon scribble of a jungle, but a scene from reality conveying a strong sense of the splendor and terror of Africa.

Tommy had a real talent. Perhaps one day he would be an artist or a set designer. Or a boat designer like his grandfather.

Abruptly, the boy glanced up from his sketch pad. "Mom, can we go to Africa on my birthday?"

"Not this year." Christie smiled at the almost-eleven-year-old.

"On a safari?"

"It's possible."

"Maybe you'll shoot a movie in Africa. If you do, could I go along?"

Christie nodded.

"Okay. If it happens, remember you promised." He went back to his sketch.

Christie watched him draw. Where did he get his ideas—a lion after a kill? Then, as if in answer to her question, the words of Tom Brokaw caught her full attention. Her face paled.

"... the FBI revealed today that, in their continuing investigation of organized crime, they obtained a court order to tap the phones of two alleged high-ranking Mafia figures, Paolo Galeffi and Alberto Rizzio. Mr. Galeffi and Mr. Rizzio have been arrested on charges of drug dealing, loansharking, and prostitution. What came as a surprise was that the name of Stavros Lennos arose several times in the course of their conversations. Rizzio stated at one point that they'd been ordered by the *Capo di Tutti Capi*—the Godfather—to stay away from the Lennos operation, to let him alone. He was highly respected." Brokaw raised a quizzical eyebrow to the camera. "Today, there is widespread speculation in the financial community as to the possible connection between the Greek-born Stavros Lennos, financier and well-known specialist in leveraged buy outs, and the Mafia. How deep into the heart of the financial community has the Mafia penetrated if Stavros Lennos has connections to organized crime?"

Christie's eyes wandered to Tommy's sketch. Africa wasn't the only jungle. Hollywood and Wall Street were jungles. The whole world was an untamed jungle. Tommy knew it in his bones. As she did. All that was missing from the so-called civilized world were the dense forests, the untouched grassy plains, the heat, the lack of indoor plumbing, and primitive living conditions. Predators were everywhere. Christie stared at her son's sketch. The wildlife of Hollywood and Wall Street was merely a free translation from Africa.

She thought about the dinner party Louis planned for tomorrow evening. Maria would give Tommy dinner while

NAKED CALL

she would dine on wine and blood. Louis Levy and Stavros Lennos would be at each other's throats. Two jungle animals in action.

His name was Michael F. X. Riordan. F for Francis. X for Xavier. Michael Francis Xavier Riordan; a name to be reckoned with, even in Greenwich, Connecticut; a pillar of society, a deacon of the All Saints Episcopal Church. Although in his late fifties, on some mornings he woke with an erection. This was such a morning. With mild distaste he glanced at the woman sleeping beside him. Dear Jane, his second wife, her sleeping mask askew, was snoring lightly. No sense waking her. She didn't want him. The idea of being wanted made him think of Sonny. His erection grew harder. He pulled on it once, twice, three times. And stopped. Horny teenagers masturbated. Michael Francis Xavier Riordan did not. It was time for his shower.

Every morning—including weekends—he took a shower at the same time. 7:30. He ran the shower for a minute, making it comfortably warm, then stepped into the stall, closed the glass door, and let the water caress his body. After soaping himself, he rinsed off, turned the water to ice cold, and watched his cock dwindle away.

After toweling off, he studied his naked body in the full-length mirror. Two weeks on the sands of Laguna Beach ... even he was tanned, one among many tanned, beautiful bodies. He had watched the volleyball games on the beach, picnicked on the beach. Two weeks in Laguna Beach and he felt human again. Ready for another Southampton summer and Dear Jane, for managing the Riordan Trust, for being a credit to his heritage, his fortune, and the Union League Club. His skin glowed with a golden tan. It was only when he was naked that an observer might see where the real Michael Riordan began. And ended. In contrast to the tan, his skin from his paunchy waist to his flabby thighs was milky white. The milky white color was the permanent stamp of his boxer shorts bathing suit and boxed-in life. No bikini bathing suit for Michael. His dignity was skin deep. And when Sonny whipped him with a sensuously soft leather whip, it stung but left no marks on his skin. The memory made him smile. It was time to shave and dress for breakfast.

Saturday mornings he arrived at the breakfast room promptly at 8:45. Punctuality was another of his virtues. Michael Riordan reached for the large glass of orange juice in front of him and the five letters on top of the newspaper. He enjoyed reading his mail with his juice and first cup of coffee.

The letter on top was from Pauline, his older sister who lived in Paris when she wasn't living in Rome or on the Riviera. Alexis was doing an exhibition of her paintings. Michael must fly over for the opening and the fabulous party afterward. Leave DJ home. Michael poured a second glass of juice. Maybe he would have gone if Dear Jane hadn't already booked them solid for that week.

There were four more letters to read—one caught his eye. The handwriting was jagged, bold. Unfamiliar. Usually he recognized the handwriting on mail he received at home. Bills and business mail went to the office. Perhaps it was someone he'd lost touch with.

He slit the envelope and reached inside to pull out the letter . . . and found something else. Three snapshots clipped to a piece of paper.

Michael Francis Xavier Riordan was suddenly ice cold, yet wet with perspiration. His heart beat violently, his blood pressure went through the ceiling. He didn't have to look at the snapshots to know what they showed. Up to this minute he hadn't dared think about it. Or admit it. But it had to happen. The second shoe dropping . . . it was fated . . . inevitable, ever since Stavros Lennos made him an offer. He'd almost had Lennos thrown out of his office. That thug! Perhaps he should have been more polite.

Michael's eyes blurred. He felt dizzy. He might keel over—faint. He didn't. Men don't faint. He forced himself to look at each snapshot. His hands trembled. He closed his eyes tight, then opened them. The snapshots didn't disappear. They were as bad as he expected. Worse. They were in color.

In one he was entangled with Sonny . . . his prick was up Sonny's ass. Christ! The camera made the KY jelly on his condom glisten. In another he was lying on his back with Sonny's mouth on his prick, his hand on Sonny's head pressing his head downward. Then there was the snapshot of Sonny poised over his naked body holding the silky soft, black leather whip.

Michael almost threw up his orange juice. He felt choked. He opened his mouth, gulping in air. In the silence he heard his heart drum.

Later, seated in the library, the snapshots safe in his jacket pocket, a semblance of his calm regained, he waited for Louis Levy to pick up his private line. When Louis did, he said quietly, "Louis, I've made my decision."

"Michael?"

"Yes. I must sell my United Cinema stock."

They got to you, Louis thought. The lousy bastards. Blackmail. You poor S.O.B. "Okay, Michael. I understand."

"What do you understand?" Riordan asked, sounding a bit too frantic.

"Take it as a figure of speech," Louis said gently. "If you want to sell, I'll buy you out. It was nice having you aboard."

"At fifty?"

"That's the price we agreed on the last time we spoke."

"Good enough. I'll have Jim Scudder of Scudder & Havermeyer contact your lawyers," Michael F. X. Riordan said. "By the way, Louis, have you met the bastard yet?"

"I haven't had the pleasure. He's called twice but I've been tied up. I'll get back to him shortly."

"Do it, Louis. Now that you own all the stock, he'll live on your doorstep. And I admit I'd enjoy having you meet him. I'm moderately curious as to your opinion. He's actually attractive." Awkard pause. A small stutter. "I . . . I mean if you're looking to cast the new criminal type. Let's say, a well-educated sadist."

"Sounds interesting."

"He is. Have him to dinner. See the animal up close. He'll think you're eager. You might find it amusing. A once in a lifetime experience."

"Dinner? That is an original idea, Michael. Why didn't you have dinner with him?" Louis saw no reason to mention that he'd already invited Stavros Lennos to dinner.

"Well, you see . . ." Words stuck in Michael's throat. He ransacked his brain for a reasonable reason.

"Because of Jane?" Louis decided he shouldn't have asked.

"Yes. Actually, Jane is the reason I have to sell you my stock. You know how she is."

"Jane wants you to sell?" Louis asked too innocently.

"No . . . not really . . . I mean if she ever heard of Lennos' offer . . . you know . . . the Mafia connection."

"Ah." Louis was understanding.

"Yes." Michael clung to his brainstorm. "The Mafia terrifies her."

Crap! You're scared shitless, Louis thought. Jane would cream in her panties if she met a Mafia *capo*. "Women are like that."

"Jane is high-strung."

Louis helped along. "How is her analysis coming?"

"You do understand, Louis. Jane is paranoid. I mean she's loaded with free-floating anxieties. She'll start thinking there's a killer in every closet. Her psychiatrist would never forgive me."

Louis felt he deserved a little fun. "Of course, we know she's not in danger, Michael. If anyone is, it's you. But even you're safe. They don't mix business and blood."

Michael pulled in his stomach and breathed deeply. "Tell that to Jane. I can't argue with her when she gets her mind set."

"She's your wife. You know her best."

"Have him to dinner." Michael forgot Jane. "I wonder if he eats with a knife and fork. Or simply rips the meat with his teeth."

"I'll keep you posted on his table manners," Louis promised.

"Do that. Oh! Jane looks forward to seeing you over Labor Day. She wants to hear all about Hollywood and the movie business. She's crazy about the movies. And, Louis . . ."

"Yes?"

"She'd be pissed if she knew I sold you my stock in United Cinema." He cleared his throat. "Even though it was for her own good."

"I won't mention it."

"Right on. We'll see you over Labor Day. Good-bye, Louis."

"*Ciao*, Michael." Slowly Louis Levy hung up the telephone. The poor slob. All the money in the world couldn't change his sexual hang-ups. Imagine, a bisexual Riordan. Louis shook his head. Somehow that bastard, Lennos, had found out.

Christie Larsen glanced at the digital clock in the dashboard of her car. Although she'd left home in plenty of time to drive to Louis' villa in Pacific Palisades, she was fifteen minutes late. It had rained and the freeways and Pacific Coast Highway were clogged. Without stopping, she waved to the guard at the wrought iron gate and drove up the cobblestone driveway leading to the area reserved for guest parking. As always, her eyes widened with admiration as she spied the house. Built in the early twenties, with borrowings from the Spanish and the Italian, the house had a definitive style of its own. Christie called it California Mediterranean. She loved the house for its graciousness and dreamlike quality. It was unlike any of the homes she'd been to for parties or business conferences in the years she'd worked in Hollywood. There was nothing formal, ostentatious or forbidding about it. Designed to take full advantage of its spectacular location high on a cliff overlooking the Pacific ocean, the house had been tastefully restored with no regard for expense. The main building, with its red-tiled roof, white stucco walls, and brown shutters, was U-shaped. The spacious courtyard was alive with colorful flowers, a stone fountain, and a lily-choked pool that evoked a charming old world flavor. The air itself was filled with memories. There was an aura of mystery about the house, as if time had stopped and the garages still held Daimlers and Packard convertibles and the rooms echoed with jazz. At any moment, Jean Harlow and Clark Gable might step through the French doors that opened out of every main room into the courtyard.

She pressed the bronze knocker, and a bell rang softly in the house. While she waited, she thought with mild irony about her appearance. She didn't shine or shimmer with the same wattage as the ghostly women of the past who drank champagne in this house. She had dressed in the new Hollywood mode, expensively informal. White silk pants, a silver lamé tank top, ropes of silver jewelry, and one serious nod to true glamour in her silver fox cardigan. She felt herself tense, thinking about the evening ahead. Louis had primed her for this dinner party, underlining its importance in a hand-scribbled memo. But why? Louis disliked the man intensely, took pleasure in not returning his calls. Even before the FBI announced the results of their wiretap, he had suspected Lennos' underworld connections. Why this sudden hospitality?

Lei, the Vietnamese majordomo who managed the sizeable establishment, opened the huge door.

"Welcome to our home, Miss Larsen."

"Thank you, Lei. It's always lovely to be here."

Silent as a shadow, he led her through the reception hall with its tall, slim, carved wooden columns painted to imitate marble and the hand-painted ceiling depicting a pale blue sky and drifting clouds. Christie was again keenly aware of the splendor and revelry of the house's past. When they arrived at the glass-enclosed patio with its awesome view of the Pacific, Lei announced her arrival, took her fur cardigan, and disappeared. Christie noted that the combatants were resting in their corners, having already felt each other out in Round One.

". . . at another time, Louis," Stavros was saying, "I wouldn't presume to make an offer. But times change—so here I am. Speaking as—let's say—a friend."

Louis looked up from the papers he was reading and chuckled. "We're not friends, Stavros. We may end up enemies. I'm undecided. Your persistence intrigued me. So I'm being hospitable. Extending to you the courtesy of a gourmet dinner while not permitting your numbers to annoy me. Don't push your luck."

"I thank you for dinner. It's hard to find good French cooking even in those restaurants that claim the finest chefs." Stavos was congenial and not intimidated. "But I suggest that you don't push your luck. Take my offer seriously, Louis. You need my help."

Louis slouched in one of the bamboo patio chairs and glanced occasionally at a sheaf of papers while sipping a

Tanqueray martini. Like Christie, he was dressed in the casual uniform of evenings at home in Southern California—a beige silk shirt, open at the neck, beige slacks, and soft leather sandals—ready to wage war.

Stavros Lennos leaned against the well-stocked apothecary bar. By contrast, he was the East Coast executive personified, dining out. He wore a black, gabardine, three-button suit, a white shirt with a button-down collar, a red tie, and shiny black shoes. Gucci. His square, chunky body was typical of many Europeans, but somehow his face didn't match. It was an aristocratic face, thin and aquiline with high cheekbones; yet for a face so finely drawn, the mouth was strangely vulnerable. His thick, curly brown hair was cut short, drawing attention to his deep-set brown eyes. They held Christie for a moment . . . ruthless . . . arrogant . . . with a minor physical quirk that actually worked to his advantage. His right eye sometimes wandered abnormally to the right of his normal line of vision, the eyelid drooping slightly. The effect was distracting, menacing, . . . making him look even more like a hungry predator.

He was sipping one of Louis' twenty-year-old scotches, and as Christie entered, he smiled. They'd met once at the studio and Christie had disliked the man on sight. But she recognized his magnetism.

"Hello, Christie," Louis said, ignoring Stavros. "You're late." The comment was made without criticism. "Take these." He assembled the papers on his lap, returned them to their folder, and extended the folder to Christie. "Look at the numbers. Tell me what you think. This new breed of Mafia front man is offering me a piss pot full of money. He wants to buy United Cinema. Save my skin, he says."

"Good evening, Louis," Christie said, gazing at her boss with undisguised affection. Then she glanced at Lennos. Why was he here? How seriously did he take this meeting? Did he realize Louis had no intention of selling United? That this was an exercise in make-believe? She studied Louis. He was a short, thickly made man who had a sure-footed, young, muscular walk and a face that even in repose showed great energy. He wore his years well. His black hair did not have the flat look that a Grecian Formula type dye job would give it. It was naturally black and showed few signs of grey. Though he was almost eighty, she'd grown accustomed to his eternal youth, to thinking him young... even a stud. Tina confided he was the best—better than any jock she'd had—or did she have a father complex? Maybe a grandfather complex? Christie slipped the folder under her arm and continued to the bar.

Louis smiled good-naturedly at Lennos. "Christie is a natural with numbers. Better than I am. A computer mind. It will save us time if she goes over them."

Christie almost laughed. More sheer nonsense. Numbers talked to Louis. He'd taught her everything she knew about movie business bookkeeping.

Temporarily distracted by her appearance, Stavros said, "Good evening, Christie. What can I get you to drink?"

He was acting as though he, not Louis, was the host.

"Good evening, Stavros. Thank you, but I can pour my own gin."

Stavros left the bar and walked to the glass wind break. He stood with his back to the room, staring at the ocean as it reflected the red of the setting sun. Christie poured herself a snifter of Beefeater gin and gazed at his back. There was nothing subtle about the strength of that body. It went with the territory that was Stavros. But there was something stiff, almost military, about his posture, and Christie thought with amusement that he was probably the only Greek who couldn't dance.

Louis was speaking again with mild scorn. "For the sake of discussion, tell me, Stavros, why should I sell the studio to you? Money? I have enough pots to piss in. What else do you offer?"

Stavros turned away from his study of the sunset. "A long, productive life for United Cinema. One day in the near future, your bankers will feel anxious. They'll look at the studio's line of credit and find it inconvenient. Awkward. They'll do a rain dance when you call." He smiled. "But if you accept my offer, United Cinema will never face a financial embarrassment—"

Louis interrupted. "United has never been a financial embarrassment! Our bankers have never been anxious. Or have you something else in mind? Is this some kind of threat? I don't like threats."

"I've threatened nothing. I've offered you a great deal of money for your stock in United. Plus a financial package that will keep the studio secure. The studio you've spent your life building."

"You're damned right I've given it my blood and guts. And I haven't busted my balls to have a Mafia front man say he'll do me a favor by buying it. What a crock of shit!" Momentarily, Louis' heavy, black eyebrows contracted in a thick frown that vanished as quickly as it appeared. He gave Stavros a comradely smile. "My boy, you've made a mistake. Any deal you offer will be open to public scrutiny. So don't try to muscle me. Or I may file a complaint. Then you're in deep shit. You'll never pass the smell test at the SEC. Big Brother is watching you, Stavros, and—lest we forget—so is the FBI. In no time they'd have you by the short hairs. Abracadabra—pffft! You're out of my life." Louis brimmed with good will. "I am not a corporate pantywaist who craps in his boxer shorts at the sight of you."

Stavros listened patiently. Christie had the impression that Louis' language vaguely irritated him. She was only half right. It was the mother tongue of the gutter. He'd heard it so often from his uncles and cousins that he accepted it as he would any industry buzzwords.

"Louis, you're making the mistake all entrepreneurs make. Because you own the company and have made it successful, you think you can do no wrong. You can."

"I won't. I've managed United's financing for fifty years. Maybe I'll try for another fifty. You have nothing to offer me." Then abruptly, like a bird swerving in midair, Louis changed his attack. "Or to offer Christie. I don't own all the stock. I forgot to mention that she's also a stockholder. You'll need her blessing, too. And she has no taste for this sale."

Christie didn't react. Her eyes never left her glass of gin. But she felt like a juggler who had let an orange drop. What should she say? Or shouldn't she say? What was she missing? What was Louis up to now? She owned no stock in United Cinema.

"I thought Michael Riordan was the only other stockholder—"

Louis interrupted with the warmest smile imaginable. "Where did you get Riordan's name?"

"I take the fifth Amendment. My sources are confidential." Stavros returned to his seat, all the while watching Christie.

Their eyes met... she looked away first. She poured more gin and walked to a patio chair set next to Louis, sinking into it gratefully. She opened the folder Louis had handed her and stared in amazement at the spread sheet. Their five-year cash flow and P & L projections? She glanced at Louis. He'd seen it and said nothing. She'd do the same. Someone took a bribe... someone would be fired.

Louis leaned back in his chair, solid and relaxed, even sleepy. Christie admired his performance.

"What else do you know about United?" Louis asked.

"Quite a bit. I make it my business to know everything there is to know about a company I'm thinking of acquiring."

"Very sensible."

"Self-protective."

"And Riordan's name came up?" Louis might easily have been reasoning with a retarded child.

"Riordan's name is one of those confidential matters that becomes less confidential when one is interested."

"And can bribe well."

"The cost of reliable information, like the consumer price index, is affected by inflation." Stavros stared back with faint amusement. "As I understand it, Riordan owns thirty-three percent of the company. Courtesy of his father—the senior Michael Riordan, who sowed his wild oats in Hollywood. Senior was your angel. A Broadway metaphor. Worked with you... drank... whored. And in the spirit of camaraderie saved your hide financially when *The Queen of Hearts* bombed. For that bit of good will, you sold him thirty-three percent of the stock in United Cinema. For a mere ten million dollars. Generous. It wasn't worth a plugged nickel."

"Then. It is now."

"By a factor of thirty."

As she listened to the thrust and parry, Christie's eyes were fixed on the numbers. She held back a smile. Point for Louis. Stavros was not omniscient. Louis told her this morning he'd bought out Michael Riordan's position. He was now sole owner of United Cinema. Stavros' sources suffered data lag.

Louis sipped his martini. "You have a nice sense of history, Stavros."

"It's essential. History so often repeats itself." Stavros moved from his chair at the bar to sit opposite Louis and Christie. "Later, Riordan Senior returned to the banking business in Philadelphia to manage the family fortune. When he died in an ice boating accident, Michael Junior inherited—along with other uncountable assets—his father's United Cinema stock."

Louis stretched his legs, seeming to grow more relaxed. Interpreting his body language, Christie went to red alert.

"Since you know so much, you know that Michael feels as I do. United Cinema should remain a privately held company."

"That's in character. His family fortune is in a privately held trust. Unfortunately the Riordan trust is not for sale." Stavros rubbed his knuckles against his chin. "Once we settle on the terms, I'm sure Michael will cooperate."

"If he will or won't is irrelevant. I'm not fond of hypothetical questions." Louis was testy, again on the attack. "I've decided. I won't sell United. So the question of what Michael will or won't do is moot."

"You won't get a better offer."

"I don't want a better offer. Yours or anyone else's." Louis turned to Christie. "Did the numbers tell you anything I don't already know?"

Give the devil his due. "Stavros doesn't think small. Based on our projected cash flow and P & L, he's offering you six hundred and fifty million for your two-thirds of United Cinema." As she said the words she told herself Louis didn't need the money. He wasn't greedy. Why should he sell? She prayed he wouldn't. She tried to read his expression.

"I've heard enough. More than enough. I'm bored with the bullshit. Pack it in, Stavros. Talk to me about Dietrich. Or Garbo. We'll look at *Ninotchka* after dinner."

"Louis, your last release was *The Royals*."

The truth hurt. "Not as good as *Ninotchka*. But it got five Oscars."

"It wasn't *Ninotchka*."

Angry and offended. "If you mean it wasn't a classic..."

"I mean you're as good as your last release. *The Royals* wasn't a classic. Or an also-ran. What it was, was a box office bomb. Over budget by ten million." Stavros sounded genuinely regretful. "Next time you go to the well, you may find the well dry. Your bankers will be gasping for air when they get a look at your P & L. And your projected cash flow."

"My bankers forgive and forget. They remember *The Cuckoo Clock*. Grossed over one hundred and fifty million." Louis tried on for size a deep, comfortable breath.

"No one's questioning your talent. But that was '87. What have you done for them lately?"

"*Wild Cat* goes into national release in the fall. It's a winner," Christie said heatedly. "Scary, gory, and gorgeous. A real Hitchcock."

"It makes me sick. Too much blood." Louis made a face. "But the public will lick it up."

Stavros nodded. "Tina Traymore is the star—that blonde wipes her nose every thirty seconds. Coke is rotting the cartilage."

"There's a drug counselor on the set with her," Christie pointed out.

"Who keeps her well-supplied with drugs."

"High quality stuff. Better than the street shit she was buying. Or crack," Christie countered.

"Better if she took nothing. My sources tell me she's developing a taste for heroin. Oh?" Stavros raised his eyebrows. "Your drug counselor hasn't informed you?"

"You bastard!" Louis was furious.

"Please, Louis. Nothing arrived at the Traymore dressing room but a plastic packet of white power. The powder puts on weight. That's all. Out of consideration for you I insisted the boys give her sugar."

"Go to hell!"

"If the banks knew... need I say addicts are not bankable?"

"When *Wild Cat* is released we pack her off to a drug rehab. The Betty Ford Institute or some such place."

Stavros took no notice of Louis' baleful stare. "If I had control, she'd be free to commit suicide . . . after the picture is released . . . on her own time. She should never have been cast in the first place. A drug program won't help. It's in her blood. Her mother . . . her sister. Why use a star who is a born addict? The beaches are full of blonds."

"She's a fine actress!"

"She's also an example of loose management. United needs a return to the efficiency of the old studio system."

Louis hissed, "I am the studio system. I invented it before you were old enough to get an erection. Fuck off!"

Christie winced inwardly. Each man was right. But if she didn't know who was who, Louis sounded more like the Mafia than Stavros did. Maybe it was atavism—a reversion to ancestral type. Given Louis' East Bronx and garment center origins, he and Stavros probably had much in common. So the personality interchange was natural.

"Tina Traymore aside, I've a more important question. Why Marconi?" Stavros asked in a level tone. "Another great talent? A genius? Maybe. But will the genius director bring *The Feathered Serpent* in on time?".

Louis didn't ask how he knew about *The Serpent*. "You have your sources. You tell me."

"My sources are not in Marconi's head. They know as little as you do. Though I do have friends who could persuade your genius to meet the shooting schedule—if you were inclined to cooperate." Stavros didn't say it nicely. The first hint of the Mafia *capo* was in his tone.

Listening to him speak—rough, almost gritty, not entirely civilized beneath the cultured veneer—Christie heard Stavros' true voice. It dovetailed with his family history. Louis had filled her in after their first meeting. Orphaned at birth, he was brought to the United States and raised by his mother's Italian family—big in the tombstone business. Legitimate. Their money was earned by selling tombstones and caskets in Queens and later, Brooklyn, the Bronx, and Staten Island. From carved stone tombstones, the family branched into concrete. Their concrete mixing trucks were seen on almost every big construction project in New York: the Lupo

Concrete Company. Their Mafia connections were never proven, and their impact on real estate eventually reached well beyond cemeteries and concrete extending into the construction business, building the government-funded 608 apartment houses on which hundreds of millions of dollars were made. Usually legally. Stavros' relatives owned a number of choice parcels of Manhattan and Queens real estate. In keeping with the family's prosperity, brains, and ambition, Stavros went to Harvard, later the Harvard B School and the London School of Economics. He never married but was often seen at New York social events with women of impeccable credentials. Now, at forty-five, his origins were well-camouflaged. Until the FBI report, his name was seldom linked with anyone whose reputation was not beyond question. His hands were clean of drugs, pornography, prostitution, and loan-sharking. His turf was business, and his life devoted to taking over the country. Lawfully when possible. Or when necessary, with the aid of ancestral connections.

"Give my regards to your friends," Louis said scornfully. "Tell them to go to hell. I know Marconi. I know what he can do. He'll bring in a winner! People waiting in line to see the film."

"Your bankers agree. They think he's bottom line insurance."

Louis' face was still, but his eyes sparkled. "Crap. When it comes down to pay dirt, the bottom line is me. Me, Louis Levy. That's who they depend on. Not Franco Marconi. Not Tina Traymore. That's my gift. I'm bankable."

Stavros slowly shook his head. "Today you are bankable. But not tomorrow. It seems I will have to make myself more unpleasant than I want to. The fact is, Louis—you are too old." He paused, sipped his scotch, allowing time to let the words sink in. "You're in good shape for a man your age. And in another art form—painting, music, writing—you would have years. Picasso did. Casals did. Michener does. But Hollywood has its own timetable. In Hollywood you are not a fair-haired, boy genius. Or a middle-aged genius. You are a John Huston type genius." Stavros smiled sympathetically. "Like Huston was, you, too, are a vintage genius. An antique. Almost eighty. In the eyes of your bankers, eighty is a very old man." Stavros looked at his scotch.

Christie saw that Louis was winded. For an instant she was doubtful. Was he too old? She stared at him hard—Buddha-like face, round with slanting eyes. It had something of the unlined agelessness seen in Asians but rarely in Europeans. No. Louis looked nothing like his seventy-nine years. But she understood Stavros' point. For the first time since she'd known Louis . . . the God's honest first time . . . Louis' age worried her.

When Louis found his voice, he said firmly, "Stavros, I plan to live forever. I've discovered the secret of immortality."

"I believe you. But will your bankers? Soon they won't be able to get insurance on you. Not when you're eighty."

"They don't need it!" Louis said, outraged.

"They need it. Suppose something happens to you?" Stavros asked as sincerely as an insurance salesman. "Not death but maybe a stroke? Even a small stroke could put you out of commission." His expression was kind, commiserating. "Long enough to cost millions. If the banks have invested fifty million on your signature, what do they do without insurance?"

Sheer hate twisted Louis' face. "Are you finished?"

"You have an answer?"

"Louis Levy, age seventy-nine—in perfect health! Full of energy! Should I need a sudden vacation, United has many competent people to fill in while I swim and sun. Executive producers. Christie, for instance. Ezra Stone. In a privately owned company the owner takes the risks—takes the bows. That's me—the owner!" There was both fury and condescension in his voice. "United is owned by me! And me—Louis Levy—has made Christie president. The announcement is being prepared." Louis gave her a spotlight smile.

Christie flushed. "President? President of what?"

"Of United Cinema, funny face. It was you, Ez Stone, or Rudy Bingham. Mannie Wolf, maybe. But you've got a better numbers mind than Ez. Rudy adds on his fingers. Mannie's fantasies are all about bean counting. All numbers—no people. United needed someone creative who can also add and subtract. I selected you."

"Thank you, Louis." Christie could hardly believe what she'd heard. Louis had told her his decision last week. Sworn her to secrecy, stressing the confidentiality of the promotion. He wanted time to smooth ruffled feathers... Ezra... Rudy... itching for the post. This was his first mention of Mannie Wolf. But why tell a stranger? Lennos?

"How do you like the title?"

"Who wouldn't like it?" She tried to sound as enthusiastic as she'd felt when he first told her.

"Speech! Speech!" Louis applauded.

"Uhm... four score and seven years ago... our forefathers..."

"Fine! Fine!" Louis chortled. "Champagne at dinner! We celebrate!"

Christie licked her lips. What was Louis doing?

"That's what I mean, Stavros. I own United. I call the shots."

"We will drink to your promotion, Christie," Stavros said smoothly. "Should I take over United Cinema, working with you will be a pleasure. But Louis..." He gave Louis a look of infinite patience. "Bright and beautiful as she is, Christie isn't bankable. Her track record is good but—be realistic—not long enough. Could she get—for the sake of discussion—a line of credit for a hundred million dollars? No. A nice gambit, Louis, but it won't play. And, as I said, you won't play, either. Christie is too young. And you're too old. Although I know your life signs are remarkable." He shrugged, conveying his message almost apologetically.

"You've gotten to my internist?"

"I stay in touch. So do the banks. They learned some hard lessons backing vintage geniuses."

"Get the fuck off my back!"

Louis said it with such ferocity that Stavros blinked. But he continued stuffing his truth down Louis' throat. "If you die in the saddle, Louis, United Cinema, your brain child, may become only a memory. A golden oldie."

Stavros stopped speaking. Silence, like dust, lay over the room.

Louis' fingers drummed on the arm of his chair. At last

he turned his head slightly and asked, "If I sold you my stock, you'd take the company public?"

The standoff was over.

Christie caught her breath. Was he taking Stavros seriously? Did his age actually worry him? Was that what this evening was all about?

"Yes." Lennos nodded. "With public money, United Cinema, which you built single-handedly, will have the funds to make better pictures than ever before."

He developed the theme of movie making with genuine feeling—so sincere, full of emotion. Christie almost believed him . . . almost threw up. The thought of Lennos owing United Cinema made her sick to her stomach. Given his history, Stavros could trash the studio, dispense with filmmaking entirely—stage sets, sound sets, the back lot, personnel, everything—sell off the premises as real estate. For a shopping mall—no. There wasn't enough real estate for a mall. Not enough parking space. Maybe a small condo complex? No! No real money in that. So why the hell did he want it? The film library. Worth hundreds of millions—was that all?

She must have asked her question out loud, for he answered with good humor. "On my honor, Christie, we'll go on making movies. Great ones. If for no other reason than to keep the film library stocked."

Louis was weary. "I'm sure you'd keep the library stocked."

As though by some prearranged signal, Lei was standing at the door of the patio smiling at them.

"Ah, here's Lei."

"Dinner is served," Lei said in his French-accented English, and vanished.

"I'm hungry," Stavros said. "Business talk always makes me hungry. Think about what I said, Louis."

"I'll think about it," Louis muttered.

"I'd like an answer by the end of the week."

"You'll get one when I'm ready."

"It's fortunate that I'm a patient man."

Louis rose and started toward the door of the patio. "Come along, Madam President," he said to Christie. "Put the papers in your briefcase." Then he turned his sharp eyes on Stavros and asked, "Have you contacted Michael Riordan yet?"

Momentarily, Stavros almost lost his balance on his skateboard. "It was an exercise. You're the controlling stockholder, so he doesn't matter."

"He matters. If he sold you his stock, you'd be better positioned to put the screws on me." Louis laughed dryly. "Good move, if it worked." He walked toward the French doors leading to the dining room. "Leave Michael alone, Stavros. I bought his stock. What worked with Michael won't work with me. I'm not open to blackmail."

Stavros took the news in stride. "Blackmail is useful only with those who have something to hide. Although, in truth, doesn't everyone?" He shrugged and smiled as if to say, even you. Instead he said, "Even I." With the implied threat hanging in midair, he slipped his arm through Christie's and guided her into the candlelit dining room.

Chapter 2

ALTHOUGH JEFFREY Moore's name was on the door of the brokerage house, Maxwell, Gluck & Moore, and Stavros Lennos owned no stock in the firm, Moore knew who was the boss. Maxwell & Gluck had been a small, regional investment banking house located in Los Angeles. Through a series of seemingly providential coincidences, Stavros Lennos and Jeffrey Moore became friendly. When Moore took over as the managing partner of Maxwell & Gluck, Stavros Lennos became a subordinated lender to the new firm—Maxwell, Gluck & Moore—to the tune of fifty million dollars. Maxwell and Gluck soon retired.

Aside from Stavros' use of the firm to park stock in a company he was secretly acquiring, the terms of his arrangement with Moore were legitimate. He asked for a reasonable rate of interest on his fifty million dollar loan—no more and no less than other firms paid subordinated lenders—and a suite of offices consisting of a large corner office for himself and a smaller but comfortable outer office for his secretary, Rita Solieri . . . his cousin on his mother's side.

After a brief meeting with Jeffrey Moore during which they'd put off a decision on Moore's ambition to open a New York office, Stavros swiveled his chair about so he faced the window. He leaned back and rested his feet on the windowsill. Los Angeles—from Century City to Santa Monica—embraced him. Stavros saw nothing of its hungry vitality—his eyes were turned inward. All he saw was the tanned, tough face of Louis Levy—a stubborn mule. Hell would freeze over before he heard from Louis.

Deep below the surface of his anger a process of weighing, appraising, considering was going on. His mouth was tight and twisted. Questions . . . no answers. How did he get to him? What button must he push? What had he missed? Louis Levy . . . Levy? All at once, as if answering some inner call, he heard again the soft voice of the mentor of his boyhood years—the man who long ago taught him how to think—come back to show him how to think about Louis Levy.

"Is he a brave man?" his teacher would have asked.

"He's a brave man," Stavros silently replied.

"How is he brave? Is he afraid to lose money?"

"No. He's a gambler. He'll risk his own money. Your money. My money. Widows' and orphans' money."

"Does he care what people think of him?"

"No," Stavros answered. "He thinks most people are fools."

"He can take psychological stress?"

"Yes. A great deal."

"All kinds?"

"Yes. Money pressures and more."

"Such as?"

"Contempt. Hate. Hysteria. Anger. Tears. Pleading."

"He's not emotional?"

"Not at all. He pretends."

"Has he ever loved anyone?"

"Besides himself? No. Yes. His dead wife and their daughter. Also dead."

"Can he take physical stress?"

Stavros' eyes narrowed. "He's never been tested. He missed the wars." Stavros was silent for a moment, then added, "He doesn't like the sight of blood."

"Well?" his mentor asked.

"Yes, I see," Stavros said, grasping the iron in the logic. He bowed his head in respect to his mentor. "Thank you." These were the first words he said aloud.

It was a typical summer morning in Los Angeles. The clouds had burned off by 8:30, leaving an easily observable layer of brown smog between the Angelenos and the sun. Christie parked her Cadillac one space away from the entrance to the two-story concrete and glass corporate headquarters of United Cinema. The space was reserved for her, her name painted in large, white, capital letters on the concrete tire guard. The studio occupied one corner of the huge Burbank lot. NBC, Universal City, Warner Brothers, and the Disney Studios also used the Burbank lot. The guard at the front door waved, calling, "Good morning, Miss Larsen."

"Morning, Tom."

"Going to be a hot one."

"The radio says it's over 100 in New York. We could do worse."

"Tell me about it. I grew up in Queens," he said to Christie's retreating back.

Christie wore fitted tan safari pants and a lightweight safari jacket. Under the jacket was a white, cotton, man's type shirt, except for its pleated front and pearl buttons. She owned three marvelous Armani suits that had cost thousands of dollars and were much admired by Christie and by Christie watchers. But sometimes Louis Levy had to remind her to wear one when they had an important meeting, or she might show up in her old faithful working clothes. Christie loved fashion, and her taste was impeccable. But she thought no more about her clothes than she did about her beauty. She wore very little makeup and often brushed her red hair

NAKED CALL

without looking in a mirror. It was the same with her success. She seldom noticed how voices changed when speaking to her. In a way, she had a one-track mind. She never thought about herself—about the impression she made on other people. She had too many other things on her mind ... budgets, actors, stories. Movies, movies, movies!

Christie walked across the hall to the elevators. The guard at the gate had long since pushed the button announcing her arrival to everyone in the building, and the executive elevator was waiting. In seconds the doors opened on the second floor, the executive floor of the building.

The decor of the second floor was a startling contrast to the exterior of the modern building. The carpet was deep and earth-toned. The walls were paneled in rich oak. The lighting came from elegant bronze chandeliers that were hung at twenty-five-foot intervals along the entire length of the hall. The only evidence that it was the headquarters of a film studio stood in the middle of the corridor. Three kiosks were lined up like soldiers, one under each lighting fixture, and each displayed bold, colorful posters advertising United Cinema's latest releases.

The hall was lined on both sides with offices, each with a bronze plate next to the door on which an office number, a name, and a title were etched. It was impossible to determine the power of the occupant of the office from the sign. Inside the offices, the furniture was not much more informative. The desks, chairs, bookcases, credenzas, everything, were clean, Danish modern. Lots of teak. Only the framed plaques, prizes, and awards on the walls gave one a clue as to who could do what to whom at United Cinema. Louis Levy believed in "go," not "show." At the end of the hall were a pair of double doors leading to Louis' secretary's office and, finally, his private office. There was no identifying bronze plate next to the double doors. No title, no name, no number. Anyone visiting the head of United Cinema was expected to know that Louis Levy was the CEO and where his office was located. If they didn't know, why were they on the executive floor?

Christie's office was the last one on the right-hand side of the corridor, closest to Louis Levy's office. When Christie entered her outer office, a small, slim woman was busy fixing a pot of coffee. At the sound of the door opening, she glanced around.

"Good morning, Christie," she said with easy familiarity.

"Morning, Nan," Christie replied. "Have the exhibitor contracts for *Sweet Cheat* arrived?"

"They're on your desk." Nan Grey had a naturally sweet voice that rose to a birdlike chirp when she was excited. "Your messages are also on your desk. And Mr. Levy has called twice. He's anxious to see you before the meeting starts. He wants to know what you've decided to do."

The possibility that Louis Levy had actually allowed her to make the final decision in a matter as important as *The Feathered Serpent* made both women smile. They both knew that hers was the final decision... providing Louis agreed with her.

"Did he give you any hints about my decision?" Christie asked.

Nan shrugged her shoulders. She was a small, plain woman. But her plainness was an appealing contrast in a world of tall, leggy, tanned beauties. Nan loved working for Christie and going to movies. In that order. "You don't need any hints," she said, laughing. "You know how to read his mind."

The cast assembled for the Tuesday story meeting in Louis Levy's office included Christie, the two writers—a husband and wife team—Addie and Art Grossman, the director, Franco Marconi, and Linda Loomis, Louis' secretary. Linda was seated well out of the way, next to the rosewood etagere that displayed Louis' taste for porcelain dogs, birds, and fish. The etagere also emphasized Louis' taste for success, as proven by the eleven Oscars that United Cinema had won for Best Film over the last forty years.

Louis was seated behind his gargantuan walnut desk with his jacket draped over the back of his desk chair. Christie sat at the far end of the mahogany conference table and waved everyone to their seats.

"What the fuck are we doing here? I thought *The Feathered Serpent* was set. Cast in granite," Franco Marconi said petulantly. The meeting was a pain in the ass.

"You're scheduled to start production two weeks from Monday," Louis pointed out, his eyes scanning the walls where posters announcing the most recent films made by United hung. *The Challenger*, *Simple Simon*, *The Royals*. All good films, if not equally good money-makers. "The script is in better shape now."

Addie and Art Grossman relaxed and sighed in relief.

"Much better. Except Louis and I keep asking ourselves if it's worth doing," Christie remarked offhandedly.

There was a moment of shocked silence, then a babble of questions from the writers. They had identical pained expressions on their faces, as though they were being crucified.

Marconi considered her gravely, a woman who had committed a mortal sin. "What do you mean, if it's worth doing? You're damn right it's worth doing! I'm directing it. It will win five Oscars." He used his eyes to nail her to the back of her seat.

"I know," Christie said patiently. "Movies are a director's medium."

"Fuck other directors—they're my medium. I understand what's natural to the eye. I have an instinct for spatial relations. I despise the shot for the shot's sake. But my shots are unforgettable."

"We know . . . you are the consummate artist. Responsible only to your own conscience." Christie's smile was sympathetic and pure hokum. "But this story requires more than whippy camera work or the high refinement of Eisenstein cuts. It has strong characters with something to say. The dialogue must explain to the viewer what the characters are thinking. They can't just mug for the close-ups."

Marconi glared at her. He had wild, curly black hair and a beard to match, and his ears looked as clipped as a show dog's. His eyes, too, were curiously atavistic, a shrewd, watchful brown—at the moment glowing with fury. "My close-ups reverberate! People stare—or gasp—and look away. I am not afraid of my audience. I honor them!" He paced the floor, waving his arms.

It was a fine tantrum in the best Franco Marconi tradition. Christie watched with amusement. Fellini couldn't have performed better. Franco was an old hand at the Hollywood game. He meant to keep the film alive, come hell or high water. And he knew how to fight... when to apple polish and when to ass kiss. He'd learned a lot kibitzing his father's poker games. He was old Hollywood and his entire family—all his relatives—had made their living doing one thing or another in the movie trade since *The Birth of a Nation*. Stuntmen, dialogue coaches, make-up artists, wardrobe keepers, actors, set designers, production assistants, directors. They'd worked with Valentino... Chaplin... Garbo... Gable... Cooper... Garland... and others through the years. Eventually it was Franco's turn. He was in his late twenties before anyone realized he would amount to anything more than a good guy to get drunk with—wonderful company—if you could stand the pace. He wandered into writing by accident. But he was born to be a film director—won two Oscars plus the Screen Directors Guild award. Now, in his forties, he was one of the hottest directors in the business.

"I can do anything. Drama. Westerns. Mystery. Sci-fi. Romantic comedy..." He ranted on.

Finally Christie interrupted. "We know, Franco. You're a genius, but the dialogue—"

"What the fuck if the dialogue is lousy! Writers always need help. That's a director's job! I'll teach them. I've done it before—I'll do it again!" The matter was closed. He sat down.

"Yeah, what the fuck!" Addie exclaimed. She loathed all directors and didn't care who knew it. "To hell with the dialogue. Franco will shoot around it. The film will be new—a fucking innovation! Imagine!... A Silent Movie!" She took a deep breath and turned to Christie and Louis. "What's wrong with the dialogue?" she asked. "I thought it was pretty goddamn good."

"I can't put my finger on it," Louis said from the protection of his desk. "Christie and I worked past midnight the last three nights trying to figure out what was wrong."

"That sex scene between the General and the English cunt is great! What's eating you, Christie? Not getting laid enough? If you need to be serviced, don't be shy. You don't have to rely on your trusty vibrator. I'm still available." Franco was permitted the crack because he was Franco.

Christie smiled faintly. "Very generous of you. As Louis said, it's hard to put one's finger on the problem. One way to say what's wrong is that I wouldn't want to spend United's money to put Meryl Streep in it. Or William Hurt."

"You mean it isn't a cultural event?" Art sounded offended. He was a veteran of the business, a recognized intellectual of the second rank.

"She means it would be throwing good money after bad," Louis explained.

"Try to be specific, please," Art said. "What is it you don't like? Is it the dialogue? Or something else? How about the plot structure? The scenes?" He looked from Christie to Louis, his voice querulous.

"The first thing you must understand is the kind of story we want." Christie's manner became that of a teacher conducting a class. "It's lyric. But raw. Primitive. Passionate. About a man and woman locked in a power struggle. Sexuality is the way it's expressed."

"We thought we had them. Dead on. We're open to all suggestions." Art crouched as if ready to spring. "Aren't we, Addie?"

"All ears," Addie nodded.

"Fine," Christie said. "The story we want is the novel. It's about a highly sensual, instinctive way of life. The old, old way. This isn't about romance. It's about a woman obsessed with the idea of dominating the man sexually. But he can't be dominated. He symbolizes the sexual supremacy of the male."

After a half hour of heated discussion about Christie's proposed changes in the script, Christie looked at the writers. "Have I said enough? Do you want to take another crack at it? Or should we call in someone fresh? We don't have a lot of time to get this script into shape."

"This is a quality picture," Art said uncertainly.

"You bet it is. We're taking a real flier," Christie said. "They'll either line up at the box office or it'll bomb."

"If it bombs, it's your asses that'll be in a sling." Franco enjoyed needling the writers. Any writers. "I've got two Oscars on my mantelpiece. You got zip. This could make you. Or get you a table at Morton's next to the good paintings. Siberia!"

"Well?" asked Christie gently.

"We'd like another shot at it," Art said.

"You, Addie?"

For a minute she said nothing. She had the stoicism of all wage earners. This was a nice studio to be associated with and besides, they needed the money for the new house in Malibu.

"Yes. We'll do it up gorgeous," Addie said.

Franco gave them a nasty look and rose, kicking his chair away from the table. "Now that you've all kissed and made up, I'll light candles for the final script, so you don't end up with a story about a little girl whose best friend is a dead mouse."

Addie's eyes followed him with hate. When he reached the door she called, "By the way, Franco, your fly's unzipped."

He looked down in sudden embarrassment, then looked up at Addie. "Cunt!"

"Hey, Franco, we'd like to catch your act with the goat in Tijuana. When's the next show?" Art called happily.

Franco slammed the door.

"I think that's a wrap," Christie said.

The writers thought so, too.

"I'll have Linda type her notes and send them to you," Christie said, glancing at Linda Loomis.

Addie nodded, but she had a mind like flypaper. Every word Christie said would cling to it. "Thanks," she said. Art smiled. At the door, Addie turned abruptly. "Hey, Louis," she called out. "What's this about your selling United?"

"Horse shit," said Louis.

"Good!" said Art. "We feel at home here. We know all the phone numbers by heart."

"Forget it," said Christie. "Will you have a rough draft by next week?"

"Why not?"

"This is the tenth time this month someone has asked me about selling United," Louis complained.

"It's something to gossip about. In bed, on the bidet, in the Jacuzzi. At the Polo Lounge where jackets are required. Hollywood invented the rumor mill." Addie rolled her eyes.

"Don't believe any rumors you don't start yourself," Christie said.

"Nice," Art smiled. They left the conference room. As soon as they were gone, Linda Loomis stood up, bowed her head, and left, deferring to the confidentiality of any meetings between Mr. Levy and Miss Larsen.

Christie thought how she'd known and liked the Grossmans for years. They were smart, funny, generous, and respectable professionals with not too many pretensions. Some said Art was the baggage and Addie had the talent. Others said he was the brains and she took dictation. Christie didn't know and didn't care. But the fact that at fifty, Addie refused to have a face job and Art wouldn't have a hair transplant or at least wear a rug seemed proof positive to everyone that the two were quirky.

"A good meeting," Louis said gruffly.

"They can do it." Christie slouched in her chair. "They've a gift for plagiarism."

"That's why we chose them," Louis said and grew silent. His strong face was relaxed but anger showed in his eyes. "What did you think of the bastard?"

"Lennos? Only the devil and John Huston could have invented him."

"Good casting."

"I think killing is his way of making love. Of course he wouldn't actually soil his hands. That's for the soldiers. You really want to talk about him?"

"Not this morning. I'm booked." Then, peevishly, he asked, "He couldn't be spreading that rumor about my selling United?"

"It would work against him."

"So who the hell is talking it up?"

"Ricky Bruno. Who else?" Christie tilted her chair back on its rear legs.

"Damn it, you're right. You mean I sweated those eighteen holes for nothing? Filling his ear with all the offers I'd turned down."

"He didn't believe you."

Louis looked away, his grieved eyes gazed fixedly at a point in space, the way people do at funerals and weddings.

"That agent has the worst slice and the biggest mouth in Hollywood."

"You're the one who taught me—never complain, never explain, and never expect to be believed. You broke all your own rules. Bruno got suspicious."

"Why didn't you talk me out of seeing him?"

"You're joking. That was the week Michael F. X. called."

"The first time," Louis said with sudden savage intensity. "When Stavros offered to buy his stock."

"There was no holding you."

Louis' face darkened. "Okay. You're right. You've picked up a bad habit. You're not supposed to be right when I'm wrong."

"I'm getting out of here," Christie said. "I've a production meeting with Ezra."

"When's Tommy's birthday?"

"This Thursday . . . the twelfth."

"Who does he look like? Not you. Not Barry."

"He looks like my father." The minute Christie said it, she wished she hadn't.

"You never talk about him, Christie. I didn't know you had a father."

He'd caught her off guard once. Not twice. "I wasn't hatched, Louis. Are you seeing Gil Murphy this morning?"

Louis grunted. "Don't change the subject. Your father must have been a handsome man."

"Almost as good-looking as you, Louis," she said sweetly, fluttering her eyelids. "I can hear Gil panting at the door."

"Would you like to come by with Tommy on Sunday and split a birthday cake? Also ice cream and junk candy?"

"We're going to Lake Tahoe for the weekend."

"Get out of here."

"Yes, sir," Christie smiled, saluted, and about-faced.

He watched her walk toward the door. "Linda wants to see you," he said softly.

Christie turned. "About what?"

"Ask her. I'm not her secretary."

Christie made a face and left.

Linda was not in her office, but Rosalie, her assistant,

NAKED CALL

came waddling in after Christie. Rosalie had the face of an angel and wore queen-size pantyhose.

"Christie! Linda's waiting for you in your office and would deeply appreciate your going there immediately, because she should be back here to audit a meeting between Mr. Levy and Mr. Gilbert Murphy."

"Why is she waiting for me in my office? What's wrong with this office?"

"Nothing," Rosalie said. "A package arrived while you were in the meeting with Mr. Levy. Linda didn't know how long that would take and she thought it would expedite things if she took it to your office and left it there. But she's still there. I suppose she didn't want to leave it with Nan. Please, Christie, go to your office and send Linda back posthaste so she can take Mr. Murphy into . . ."

"Mr. Levy, posthaste. Okay." Christie left Linda's office.

"Hello, Christie." A pleasant English voice interrupted her thoughts as she strode down the corridor. Gil Murphy, the breezy English director, the new boy genius from London, had arrived for his meeting with Louis.

"Hello, Gil." She paused and smiled briefly. "How are you?"

"Looking forward to working with you, Chris."

"Likewise I'm sure. Good luck with our friendly neighborhood monster. He's expecting you. You've a short wait in Linda Loomis' office. But she'll be with you in a few minutes to escort you into the *sanctum sanctorum*."

Gil amused her more than most. She liked his boyish grin; he had the sort of face that would still be boyish in his fifties. She liked his innocent air, his curling, foppish beard, his entire look calculated to a millimeter to distract one from his shrewd numbers mind, his canny instinct for the main chance. He'd be easy to work with because he was smart.

"Thank you, Christie. A little luck never hurt. You won't be at this meeting?"

"No. There'll be other meetings."

"Many meetings I hope."

"Many. See you." She smiled again.

Gil almost gasped as he watched her. It was a smile

that started sweet and could break your heart or break you. Like most men, he just liked to look at her. He'd met her first at meetings and now, watching the grace of her movements, he saw afresh her narrow waist, her high breasts, her long, supple legs. What a star she'd make! The real thing—in the old sense. They'd just put the camera on her and let it roll. Instinctively, she'd fuck the camera. He felt punch-drunk with lust. Then he steadied himself... dismissed his X-rated impulses. He needed all his brains, all his force of nerve when dealing with Louis Levy.

As Christie hurried into her office, Nan greeted her with a warm, puzzled smile.

"Linda's inside waiting for you."

"Gotcha," Christie said, opening the door. There was Linda Loomis, seated on a chair, with a two feet by three feet by five inches wide, carefully taped carton leaning against her knees. When she saw Christie she sighed with relief.

"Thank heavens you're here. I'll leave this in your hands personally." Linda rose gingerly so as not to tip over the carton.

"What is it?"

"A birthday present for Tommy. From Mr. Levy."

"Louis never mentioned it."

"Mr. Levy said that I was personally responsible for seeing that you received this package. Now it's your responsibility to see to it, personally, that Tommy receives his birthday present from Mr. Levy."

Christie stared at the carton. "Linda?"

"I've guarded it with my life since it arrived."

"You are not answering my question," Christie said. "What is it?"

"It's for Tommy. He'll love it." Linda's tone was evasive.

"Not if I don't give it to him. And I won't give it to him unless I know what Louis Levy is giving my son."

"I can't tell you. You'll see when Tommy opens it." Linda Loomis gave her a beggar's smile. "It's a surprise."

"Letter bombs are also a surprise."

"Oh, Christie! Mr. Levy would never—"

NAKED CALL 41

"Never! What I'm saying is I don't like surprises. I . . . want . . . to . . . know . . . what . . . it . . . is."

"Christie—Miss Larsen—Christie," she moaned. "I can't tell you. It's a surprise. Tommy will be thrilled. Mr. Levy bought it especially for him." She stood up. "I have to go to my office where Mr. Murphy is waiting."

"If you don't tell me what it is, I won't take it home to Tommy."

"If I tell you, Mr. Levy will fire me."

"You're caught between a rock and a hard place," Christie said firmly.

The gray-haired woman gazed at Christie with pleading affection. "If I tell you, will you promise—will you swear—not to tell Mr. Levy I told you."

"I swear in blood."

There was a moment of silence. "All right." Linda's resistance collapsed. "It's five of the original drawings Walt Disney did of Mickey Mouse."

"The Disney drawings!" Christie gasped. "I was with him at the Northbie auction. They cost twenty-five thousand dollars."

"I know," Miss Loomis said primly.

"I can't take them."

"You must!" Linda was horrified. "If you don't, he'll think I was undiplomatic. That I handled it poorly. You know how mad he can get. He really could fire me . . . again."

"Why didn't he give them to me himself?"

Linda fumbled. "Giving presents embarrasses him."

"Taking them embarrasses me. Especially when they cost—"

"Christie! It's only money. Mr. Levy has piles of money. He'll be offended if you refuse." Linda was breathing hard. "Years ago he didn't bid enough to get the Judy Garland shoes, the red ones she wore in *The Wizard of Oz*. He never forgave himself. They went for only $15,000. So he meant to get these and give them to Tommy. He said he never makes the same mistake twice."

"$25,000. That's enough for a down payment on a house."

"But he'll blame me. He may cancel my vacation. I was

going to Paris. Worse! He'll make me his executive assistant. Then I won't get overtime pay. He'll think of something awful. You know how he is. If you don't take them, I could end up having to eat lunch in the executive dining room. Every day!"

"The world is full of blackmailers," Christie said soberly.

Linda Loomis threw her arms around Christie and hugged her. "Thank you, dear. You won't regret it. Tommy will love them." She turned to the door where Nan was standing. "I gotta go. Mr. Murphy is never late. He's like taxes." She rushed out of the office, afraid that Christie might change her mind.

By the time Christie arrived home that evening, it was late, and the fog was gathering in the canyons that cut through the Hollywood Hills. She pushed the electronic gate opener that operated the security gate and maneuvered her car up the driveway to the garage. After turning off the motor, she sat back for a moment and gazed at her surroundings. Although most senior executives in Hollywood would have only been content with a house in Bel Air or—at the least—Beverly Hills, Christie remembered too clearly her struggle to survive when she first arrived in Hollywood. So the house in the Hills suited her fine. It satisfied both her taste for comfort and her reluctance to splurge in an industry that often played Russian roulette with careers. One day you were the powerful president of a studio and the next day you were an independent producer. The stock excuse was, "I needed space to be more creative. Now I can make my kind of movies." In other words, you were out on your ass.

Entering the house, she gazed around. It was ample for Tommy, for Maria Lopez—housekeeper and baby sitter—and herself. It was her first real home on the West Coast. She found it after the armistice with Barry had been signed, ending their futile, dispiriting war. She went her way, he went his. Barry—her soul-damaged husband. Possibly he loved her. As best he could. He may even have loved Tommy—but his love was lethal. A child exposed to his chaotic, drugged-out, bisexual lifestyle would be permanently at risk. She'd thanked all the fates when Barry vanished from the face of their earth. Tommy was less than a year old at the time—too young to be tainted by his father's corruption. When he grew older he only occasionally asked questions about his father. Christie was prepared—improving on the truth, with bright, white, and sensible lies, dishonesties that Tommy accepted. She hoped. Walking softly through the house, Christie glanced at the TV set. Unexpectedly, years later, she'd seen a bright, toothy smile on the TV screen. Barry Easton. The new host of a popular TV game show. She wished him luck—and was afraid. Every time she saw the show listed in *TV Guide* or noted his face or name in a tabloid featuring what-the-baby-sitter-saw-through-the-keyhole, she crossed her fingers. The sleaze factor sold copies, and Barry was a role model sleaze. All the sly insinuations about his naughty-naughty excesses rang true. She knew firsthand. Her single wish was that he had forgotten her. Forgotten Tommy. Mentally she lit candles. Hopefully he had suffered a benevolent amnesia. Barry mustn't get any ideas . . . like joint custody. Christie closed her eyes. Opened them. She was crazy. Barry was past history. Knock on wood.

She opened the door to Tommy's room and leaned the carton holding the Walt Disney drawings—that cost twenty-five thousand dollars—against Tommy's bureau. She gazed at her sleeping son and thought of all the things she tried to do for him. She wanted him to have the time to store up security—the kind of security that comes from the long, golden celebration of a safe childhood. A growing up such as she never had. One filled with summers and winters of unquestioned certainties . . . and no fear at night. Night was only a time of stars and a coming home to love and sleep. She wanted Tommy to have it all—faith in tomorrow and the strength that faith could give him for facing the risks of manhood. Thinking about the childhood she never had, she felt a rush of emotion, not only tender but savage. Nothing bad would happen to Tommy. She'd see to that.

Chapter 3

CHRISTIE'S WEEK rushed by in a haze of activities—meetings with writers, agents, actors, actresses, every breed of talent in the Hollywood zoo whinnying, braying, hooting. So many names, so many faces, so many voices—pitching, pressuring, coaxing. She read production proposals, treatments, attended production meetings, screened rushes, calmed directors, watched the rushes in the projection room, checked two screen tests—a character actress and a boy—gave visiting bankers the red carpet tour. By week's end she was lightheaded with fatigue. She worked with the competence of a computer, all the while picturing candles on a birthday cake. Watching Tommy take a deep breath and go whoosh!—the candles blown out. Kids laughing and shouting—at the party that would never happen. No games. No ice cream. No party. Ever. It wasn't Tommy's and her way. They never celebrated his birthday on his birthday. How could they? By a prank of the calendar his birthday seemed destined always to fall in the middle of the working week, or on a weekend when Christie would be in the middle of a production crunch. Invariably she would be in a meeting until midnight, or be visiting a location shoot.

Yesterday—technically, another birthday—was another subversive trick of the calendar. She'd been scheduled for a dinner meeting with Gil Murphy at LAX—Gil was off to London's West End to work up the project Louis had okayed. Tommy was asleep when she opened the front door. "Happy birthday, Tommy," she hummed. And stopped. After all, what's in a number? Only astrologers and Social Security cared. Tommy and she juggled dates. Every year he was born whatever day he blew out the candles. This year it would be on Saturday. They would celebrate under

NAKED CALL

the trees with a birthday cake from The Killer Cookie and fish from Lake Tahoe fried over a camp fire.

When Louis called her office late that Friday afternoon, she almost told Nan to say she'd left. She didn't. Today he needed comfort. A safe, sympathetic ear to dump on—to camouflage his pain with talk about *Wild Cat*, *The Feathered Serpent*, Marconi, Gil Murphy, Stavros, or anything that came to mind. The chanciness of the movie business, which he often said wasn't rational, like the soap business. The process of creating, producing, and distributing a successful movie was a mystery that could not be quantified. Important producers could suddenly lose their smell. A successful movie—unlike soap—was a mysterious equation, exempt from logical analysis. Louis counted himself one of the few who had mastered the entire equation. But even his power was elusive and ephemeral. On particular days he felt it ran through his fingers like sand escaping. This was that kind of day. She'd seen it coming all week.

When Christie entered, he looked up, frowning. He had been reading a glossy, colorful annual report.

"Stavros sent this to me. Trans-Western—General Movies' parent. They own airlines, rental cars, insurance policies—I may vomit. Can't you see a rental car vice president in charge of making a movie?" Louis was picking up the thread of a dialogue about Stavros Lennos that they'd had on and off throughout the week.

"Sony owns Columbia."

"I hate electronics. What do engineers know about gaffers? A lap dissolve? Music? A telephoto lens? The report's a threat. The bastard—he's warning me of a fate worse than death. I could become a corporate acquisition—a cog in a cog—unless . . ."

"Unless you clasp him to your heart." Louis showed signs of wear. The youthful look had worn thin at the edges and there were lines etched in his forehead. There was a long pause before Christie finally said, "I don't know what Lennos is after. What the hell does he really want?"

"To make movies."

"Movies?"

"Movies. Think about it." Louis was positive.

"Movies? Oh. I see." Slowly the pieces fell into place.

"Movies are the laundromat. I should have guessed."

"I did. I didn't at first. Then I did. It's the only reason that makes sense. Hundreds of millions of tax-free dollars—mostly cash—from drugs, gambling, loan-sharking. Where do they hide that kind of cash? Studio bookkeeping is a Byzantine maze . . . a crock of shit. Perfect for Lennos. A custom-made washing machine. Better than hiding the cash in Swiss bank accounts." An unfamiliar feeling of fright stole over Louis, and he choked it off with a major effort of will. "I admit the prick has a very inventive mind. He had Michael by the balls."

Christie waited for Louis to say more. He didn't. She sensed his restraint—an edgy guardedness. He wanted to say more, but couldn't. Why? What was he afraid to talk about? Michael Riordan? "You said Lennos used blackmail on Riordan. How? Riordan is one of the richest men in the country. Comes from a long line of sanctimonious Yankee thieves. But his money is legitimized by over 200 years. It's so old, so hallowed, it's way beyond any ambitious Attorney General's criminal investigation. It's described in the history books as one of the great American fortunes. Tell me, how can Michael Riordan be blackmailed?"

Louis smiled at Christie. "You're too realistic about our American myths. You don't see the Riordans riding off into the sunset . . . their eyes full of noble dreams. You're right. They rode off into the sunset to steal . . . to loot . . . to rape the nation. But Michael F. X. is a mutation. An off horse. A very proper, honest billionaire. Committed to respectability and good deeds. Unfortunately, Michael has a dirty little secret. He's AC-DC. The poor bastard. He thinks he's a disgrace to the Riordan name."

Christie was intrigued. "I'll bet it wasn't Michael who told you."

"No way," Louis snorted with amusement. "He doesn't know that I know. Hollywood has its own gutter grapevine. My sources are as good as Stavros'."

A momentary silence settled between them and unconsciously Louis put his hand on his chest, comforted by the steady thump of his heart at work. "Fortunately I'm not open to blackmail. I've nothing to hide."

"From the world or yourself."

NAKED CALL

Louis gave her a startled look. "What do you mean?"

"Nothing," Christie floundered. "That wasn't a question. I was thinking out loud. You have nothing to hide..."

"... from myself or anyone else," Louis filled in a shade too vehemently. "A damn good thing, too. Stavros is no ordinary Mafia *capo*."

"He's no ordinary anything. He's efficient, organized, brilliant. No threats. No time wasted breaking fingers or knee caps. Only the appropriate thumbscrews are used. He knows exactly which nerve to pinch to cause terror."

Christie glanced at the small brown grocery bag on Louis' desk. This was a ritual—the real reason for their meeting. Their talk filled the void. Postponed his misery. Every year at this time she'd seen the same kind of small brown paper bag on his desk. Linda Loomis had made the purchase at some grocery store. Inside the bag was a candle set into an ordinary water glass half filled with wax. On the glass was a label with Hebrew letters. For no reason she could explain, the sight of the brown bag gave her a sinking feeling. She looked away. Even looking at the bag seemed an intrusion. She tried to concentrate on the subject at hand.

"Did you tell him I owned stock to smoke him out?"

"Yes. To see if he'd come up with Riordan's name. He did." Louis glanced at Christie with fondness. He liked the way her subtle mind quickly picked up cues. Even those he missed. "I've taught you well."

"You told him you were making me president to test him?"

"To see if he already knew."

"There are leaks in the company," Christie said.

"It's a sieve. Someone gave him our last P & L and our projected cash flows. The same someone might have found out about your promotion and told him. Only a few people knew. People I trust. But I may be misplacing my trust. For instance, does Linda think her bonuses and pension are enough?"

"I'll vouch for Linda," Christie said.

"I'll vouch for you. And myself."

Christie's affection for Louis filled her eyes, but she wasn't deceived for a moment by his words. His suspiciousness was a well-developed muscle. He could even be suspicious of her, although not without causing himself some pain. "I think the news of my promotion surprised Stavros."

"I think so, too."

The intercom buzzed. It was Linda.

"Guy Macleod is calling you from New York, Mr. Levy."

Louis looked at Christie. "Macleod. One of Wall Street's finest." A flicker of bravado crossed his face.

"A persistent suitor."

"I seem to be in demand. Okay, Linda. Put him on." Louis held the line.

Louis and Macleod talked only moments. Guy Macleod would be in L.A. on business and would like to set up a meeting. They made an arrangement to have breakfast toward the end of the week. When Macleod was settled in the Bel Air, he should call Louis' secretary and firm up the day.

After Louis hung up, he explained to Christie. "Michael Riordan called him. They're old schoolmates from Choate. Michael told Macleod I might be in the mood to sell. Macleod says he's prepared to raise his offer."

"Michael had no business—"

"Easy, Christie. I won't sell to Macleod. Stavros scared the shit out of Michael. The poor guy thought he was doing me a favor."

"What do you think of Macleod?" Christie tried to sound offhand. At the fringe of her consciousness she heard a warning, drifting like the hum of a bee. Guy Macleod? Why did she know the name?

"He's old family. Old money. Well-educated. Well-bred. Absolutely unscrupulous. Like Stavros, a bird of prey." Louis' lips twisted in a nasty smile. "No, I'm wrong. Unlike Stavros—Guy is scrupulous. An Anglo-Saxon tradition. But his scruples rest on a very simple premise. Whatever he does is right."

"To put it another way, it's the other bastards who are unscrupulous."

Louis nodded. "Always. Macleod is merely fulfilling his destiny."

"Why see him?"

"I think it's the way a woman keeps love letters from a man she doesn't care for. He could be someone to buy her dinner on a cold, rainy night."

"An extra string in your bow?"

"Just a hunch—he might be useful. He is a money man."

"It's possible," Christie humored him. She wanted to leave, but the need to say something about the candle had become an uncomfortable necessity. At last she said, "Today's the day, Louis? Isn't it?"

"Yes." His voice seemed to come from a long way off. "Tonight I light the Jahrzeit candle."

This ritual was Louis' only concession to the religion of his ancestors. The candle in the glass of wax that orthodox Jews burn once a year in memory of a loved one who had died on that day. Every year at this time, April 13th, Louis would burn a candle for his daughter, Jessie. The sight of it always reminded Christie of her own losses.

"I wish Episcopalians had something like that. I'd like to light a candle for my father," she said softly.

Louis glanced at her in mild surprise. "In the ten years we've worked together you've never told me about him. Or your mother. Your family. All I know is you had one."

"I don't talk about them. But you don't talk much about Jessie, either. Or Hazel." The best defense was a good offense. "And I understand."

"There's nothing to say about Hazel. She died in childbirth. And Jes? I light a candle for the peace of her soul. What can I say about my daughter? Do you want to know what she was like?" The rugged cut of Louis' features seemed to blur and for an instant he couldn't meet Christie's eyes. Instead he gazed around the office, ranging from floor to ceiling as though looking for something—a place to rest.

"Don't talk about her, Louis. It makes you unhappy. I don't have to know anything." She despised herself for upsetting him. "It's none of my business. Not anybody's business."

"There's not much to say. She died."

"As we all will. As my father did."

"She was so young when she died." His mouth became

thin. "And the years pass so fast. If she'd lived she'd be older than you are today."

Christie wished she hadn't brought his daughter up, with all the implicit questions that seemed to turn his soul to salt. "I heard she was very beautiful."

"What else did you hear?"

Christie felt herself sliding on slick ice. "Just that she died of some illness. Pneumonia I think."

"Pneumonia," Louis said dully. "They didn't have the right drugs."

Christie knew he was lying. His unwillingness to talk was like her own—A fear of opening old wounds over which scar tissue had formed.

"She was beautiful," he continued suddenly. "And wild. I don't think I was a good father."

"I'm sure you were a wonderful father."

"I tried. Believe me I tried. I gave her everything. And all my love."

"It sounds to me as though you gave her enough."

"No. I was generous with everything but my time. I was never around. I was busy running United. That took all my energy. Every hour, every day and night. I was a lousy father."

"I don't believe that."

"I wasn't strict enough. A beautiful, young girl needs discipline. I loved her too much to discipline her."

"There are worse sins than loving too much." Christie gazed at him with compassion and tenderness.

"I indulged her every whim. Not just out of love but because I was guilty. I knew I was overdoing it but I wanted to make up for not being around more." He was a criminal confessing... to a judge who wouldn't judge him.

"I'm sure she knew how much you loved her."

"I don't know what a girl understands. I do know a girl needs a father." At these words he looked away. "Or a mother. I should have remarried. I was too selfish and there were too many broads climbing all over me. So I didn't."

"Stop it, Louis!"

"Sorry. It's the season to be sorry for oneself."

"I'm sorry I brought it up."

"Did your father indulge you?"

Christie laughed a low, gentle laugh. "If he could have, he would have. Just like you."

"You always look so sad when you mention him."

"We've both had losses, Louis. I think it's one of our bonds."

"What was he like?"

Christie said nothing for a moment, lost in a scene from her past. The memory, the sorrow, the shadow of it absorbed and silenced her. Finally she said, "Someday I'll tell you all my dirty, little secrets." She made an effort to laugh.

"I didn't mean to press you. I apologize," he said gruffly, embarrassed by his own emotion. "But you mean a lot to me. And on an evening like this..."

"Don't apologize. You've been wonderful to me." Her eyes probed the sad, patient face of the man who had treated her almost like his own daughter for so many years.

"You're a survivor. Jessie wasn't." His grief was old.

"That only means I was lucky to meet you."

They had an extraordinary moment. "Someday you can light a Jahrzeit candle for me."

"You'll never die," Christie said with a trace of a smile.

Louis looked at her with gratitude. "That's not what Stavros thinks."

"What does he know about fancy fucking?" She walked around the desk and kissed Louis lightly on the forehead. There was only one more thing to say. "If you should need to talk to me, or want company tonight, just telephone. I'll be home with Tommy. Which reminds me. He's spent the week copying and recopying those drawings you gave him."

"I'm glad he likes them," Louis said. "And thank you for the offer."

"You're welcome, Louis."

Christie sat at her desk thinking about Louis. About how much he loved his daughter. About what a wonderful father he must have been to Jessie. Probably he was overindulgent. But to err on the side of love was a blessing. She thought how different her own life might have been if Louis Levy had actually been her father. A beautiful home.

Good schools. Fine clothes. Piano lessons. Drawing lessons. Trips to Europe. Maybe a year off from college to live in Italy.

She shook herself, feeling disloyal and disgusted, and riffled through the telephone messages Nan had stacked on her desk. A call from a writer. A call from Financial. Mannie Wolf had retired and the new treasurer, Harry Weiss, wanted a meeting. A call from an agent. A call from the Marketing Department. A call from Jo Caro. A call from her accountant, Gene Morgan. A call from a real estate broker. A call from Stavros Lennos. A call from a French agent—she blinked. A call from Stavros Lennos. She picked up the pink message slip and read it slowly. "I fly back to Manhattan tonight. Can you have a quick drink? I've greetings from Roger Tysen." Then the number of the Bel Air. Christie frowned—Roger Tysen. Who was he? Suddenly she began to shiver violently ... Roger Tysen! She almost sobbed as she collapsed backward into the chair. What right did he have coming here to haunt her ... intruding into her life? How did Stavros know him? Very slowly, she pressed the intercom button and told Nan to get Lennos at the Bel Air Hotel. A second later she almost told Nan to cancel it—and stopped herself. No. That would make too much of too little—give the message undue importance. Even as she said this to comfort herself, she surrendered to a feeling of peril. There was nothing to do but wait.

The button on the phone flashed red. Nan was full of good cheer.

"Mr. Lennos had to catch an earlier plane. He left a message for you. Said he'd call when he returned to L.A."

"Thank you, Nan," Christie said, thinking of the message ... of Roger Tysen. How much did Stavros know about her? What difference could it possibly make today? Her face was quiet, her lips tight. Lennos used blackmail. What price did he expect her to pay? And for what? For having had a mother and father?

Chapter 4

IT WAS almost nine o'clock by the time Christie arrived home from the studio. Every time she tried to leave the office, Linda called. Louis had something else he wanted checked. Clearly he didn't want her to go home. Or—more likely—he didn't want to go home. He asked her twice if Tommy and she wouldn't come over for the weekend and celebrate Tommy's birthday at his house. She promised they would. Next year.

Christie packed Tommy's things and her own. They didn't need much in the way of clothes. Underwear and sock changes. Jeans. Swimsuits. Towels. Toothbrushes. Irish fisherman sweaters for the cool evenings. What made it more complicated was the fishing tackle. His and hers. And the water skis. His and hers. They'd be roughing it—Saturday, Sunday, and Monday—her version of roughing it, not Tommy's. It did not entail sleeping under the stars in a sleeping bag. It meant sleeping in a bed with clean sheets and soft pillows in a comfortable bed and breakfast cottage. Tuesday morning they would head home to the town of milk and honey and Mercedes.

About one o'clock, Christie collapsed into bed, and set her alarm for five. They were booked on a seven o'clock plane to Reno where a Hertz rental had been reserved for the drive to Lake Tahoe. At four o'clock the alarm went off. Christie had been dead to the world—the ring startled her. She gazed at the clock, bleary-eyed. In a daze she groped for the clock to shut the fiendish thing off. Damn it! She'd set it an hour too early on a morning when she needed all the rest she could get. Four A.M. She'd meant five. Damn! Damn! It rang again. Her hand stopped in midair. It wasn't the alarm. The telephone was ringing. Still groggy with sleep, she stared at the clock, then at the phone. She shook her head trying to clear it. Who was it? Roger Tysen? She blinked. That was ridiculous. Stavros Lennos? What had she been dreaming? Who the hell was calling at this hour? It couldn't be for her. She could count on the fingers of one hand the people who had her private number. Damn it! It must be a wrong number. But the only way to stop the ringing was to answer it.

She picked up the receiver and said, "Hello?" Irritated.

"Christie?"

"Who is this?"

"Louis." The voice was indistinct.

"Louis?"

"Louis Levy. Remember me?"

Her mind suddenly cleared and she was shocked by the weakness of his voice. "Sorry, Louis. I'm still half-asleep."

"I'm sorry I had to wake you."

"Forget it. My alarm was set to go off any minute."

"I thought so. I waited as long as I could. I knew you'd be getting up about now to grab your early plane."

The adrenaline was pumping through Christie's body. "For Christ sake, Louis, why are you still up? Is something on the burner burning? Are you all right?"

"I'm lousy."

"What's the matter?" Christie waited. There was no sound. The seconds ticked by—had the phone gone dead? "Louis, are you there?" Christie asked. Still no sound. Maybe they'd suddenly been disconnected. "Louis! Are you there?" she shouted.

"I'm here, Christie." Again the strange voice.

"What is it?" A heart attack? No. He wouldn't be calling her if he'd had a heart attack. He'd be in a hospital. What the hell was wrong?

"Could you come over here right now?" he asked in a faint voice.

A chaos of thoughts reeled around in Christie's mind. Tommy? Lake Tahoe? They'd miss the plane to Reno. The Hertz car. Louis knew . . . and was asking her to junk her plans. That did it. "Be there as soon as I can. I have to dress."

"I'm sorry about spoiling Tommy's birthday vacation."

NAKED CALL 55

"Forget it. He's got lots of birthdays. I can rearrange everything."

"Thank you, Christie." He hung up.

Christie stared at the telephone. The onrush of bad feelings was verging on panic, but she pushed them out of her mind. Without allowing herself to think ahead, she slipped quickly into the clothes she'd planned to wear that day—panties, a bra, a T-shirt, jeans, socks, and sneakers. She then tiptoed into Maria's room and woke the sleeping housekeeper.

The pleasant, dark-haired woman opened her soft, brown eyes. They were blank and drowsy. Then she saw Christie and her eyes came into focus. She smiled tentatively.

"*Sí, señora?*"

"Maria, I've just had an emergency business call. Tommy and I can't fly to Tahoe this morning." Her voice faltered. "Maybe this afternoon. I'll call you later and tell you. But I have to cancel your weekend off, for now. Although maybe not. It may all straighten out later. I'll call."

"*Sí, señora.* I make Tom a good breakfast."

"He'll be up at five sharp."

Maria nodded.

"Give him a kiss for me. Tell him I'm sorry. That I love him. Wish him happy birthday. Happy everyday. I'll call later and explain. Tell him I had to see Mr. Levy."

"*Sí señora.*"

"Thank you, Maria." Christie stood for a second not moving, hesitating. She smiled at Maria. The smile was an effort. She didn't want to go, but she had to. Move, she told herself.

While waiting for Christie, Louis Levy pulled himself together and made a call to New York. Although it was still pitch black in California, the sun had been shining in New York for an hour. Louis had his own resources, and among them was the private number of Stavros Lennos' penthouse apartment on Sutton Place. He dialed the number and after three rings, Stavros picked it up.

Louis said quietly as though reading a menu, "Listen, you miserable bastard! Take your fucking stunts and shove 'em. If you ever again come anywhere near me or United, I don't care what it costs, I'll see to it that the SEC sticks it to you, right up your ass." Louis exhaled sharply and hung up.

Lei was standing quietly at the entrance of Louis Levy's home, his face grave and guarded. "Mr. Levy is waiting for you," Lei said softly. "Come."

Following him through the long corridor and down a flight of stairs, Christie noticed a change in the atmosphere of the house. The warmth and glow of the present, the echoes of revelry in the romantic past that she so often felt in the rooms, all seemed to have evaporated. It seemed like a house that no one had lived in for years. The furniture should have been been shrouded with dust covers.

Eventually Lei led her to their destination and bowed himself out of sight. They had arrived—not, as Christie expected, at the library with its impressive wood-paneled walls and leather-bound classics lining the shelves. Instead they were in Louis' library-bedroom-den where he occasionally worked the night through. The room was on the lowest level of the house, set close to the edge of the cliff facing the Pacific. The wall-length window at the west end of the room overlooked Pacific Coast Highway, the flat sandy beach beyond, and still further, the Pacific Ocean.

The rough, pine bookshelves that lined the walls testified to business as usual. There were no leather-bound classics, but an extensive collection of hardcover books—some in their original paper jackets, now dog-eared with use—and paperback novels, their pages yellowing, along with piles of manuscripts, magazines, and one shelf of photographs in folders.

Louis was seated in his George III chair with his shirt open and no tie, his business shirt and pants badly wrinkled, looking completely disheveled, offering a perverse contrast to the elegance of the chair and the rosewood Regency writing table.

Usually this room was one of Christie's favorites in the house. It stood for the hard-working, hard-driving, omniverously curious Louis Levy she knew best. But a glance told her this was no ordinary working session. Louis wasn't being creative. He hadn't been sleeping either. The Napoleon provincial campaign bed was still neatly made up. He'd been walking on the beach. His sandy socks and sneakers were scattered about on the rare Charles X tapestry rug that covered the floor. There was a half empty bottle of Napoleon VSOP on his desk and an empty snifter beside it. Louis was famous for his hollow leg, but it occurred to Christie that through the long night the leg might have been filled. He seemed to be asleep with his eyes open.

I'm here, Louis," Christie said softly.

Louis stared at her with bleary curiosity . . . a man sedated by alcohol. Then his face paled as he came back into the world. "Christie," he said tentatively.

"What happened, Louis?" He seemed in a few hours to have aged more than a decade.

Louis stared at her unseeing. Slowly his face changed, settling into an expression of awful, dawning comprehension. His eyes were the eyes of a man who has seem something ugly and lunatic in a world he thought sane—something too terrible to be described or named.

But it had to be named.

Straining every muscle, he hoisted himself up from his chair. "Come, Christie," he said hoarsely, quickly walking out of the library. "I've something to show you."

Christie followed silently, noting with a chill that he weaved as he went and that he was walking barefoot.

As they walked up the steps to the main floor and through the house, occasional windows let in shafts of the coming dawn. In the distance Christie could see the low surf breaking on the shore. They entered a section of the large house that Christie had never seen before. It was the east wing, and one wall of the corridor consisted mostly of a long, floor-to-ceiling window. When Christie paused momentarily to gaze out the window, she saw that the corridor overlooked a hidden garden of bougainvillea. There were great bushes, red and luscious and full of flowers, massed along the building wall and extending its length, stopping finally beneath a window at the end of the wing. There they presented a whimsical entertainment.

The crimson bougainvillea formed a background for a little clearing of well-tended grass. Here, as though on a stage, were small, bronze, naked statues of dancing fauns and nymphs, and at the center of the entertainment, piping gaily on his double flute was Bacchus, the god of wine and revelry. Christie gazed with pleasure and surprise at the garden. She couldn't imagine Louis creating it. Who did? More unanswered questions.

They approached the closed door at the end of the corridor and, glancing at it quickly, Christie suddenly guessed where they were. Jessie's room. She swallowed hard. Louis opened the door and the odor of Femme drifted out. Christie thought how beautiful the room must be. Louis entered and she followed him, curious and eager to see—wondering why she was there at all.

"Jesus Christ!" She could hardly speak at the sight that met her eyes.

The bedroom had been exquisite. Now it was a wreck ... a grisly horror. There was the four-poster, canopied bed handmade from mahogany that Louis once told her proudly was a present to Jessie from Norma Shearer. The raw silk draperies were ripped and bloody. So was the matching wall covering. The crocheted blanket was in pieces on the floor and the white silk sheets were bloodstained and torn. The lavender silk nightgown was in bloody shreds. The bedside table was overturned. The reed organ Jessie once played was trashed. The large gilt mirror above the red lacquered antique dressing table was shattered. There was blood soaked into the beige carpeting and the chairs with their silk brocade covers were bloodstained, overturned, and some had broken legs. An antique limestone Cupid and Psyche pair had been thrown to the floor and the head of Psyche was cracked. On the floor, Louis' Jahrzeit candle was burning. The scene had the improbablility of a nightmare. Christie couldn't stop shivering.

"Jessie's room," Louis said. The words had the grim finality of a lesson learned on the rack.

"Yes..."

"Ugly sight."

Christie nodded dumbly. She made a small gesture indicating the room. "W-what happened?" she stuttered.

"This is the way her room looked afterward." The coldness of his explanation was, along with everything else in the air, horrifying.

"Afterward?"

"After her murder."

"Murder?" The room was a ghastly testimony to a desperate struggle.

"They found her body—hideously mutilated—near the ocean about two miles up the shore."

"God!"

"God wasn't watching."

"Louis!" Christie scanned the room. There was a pool of vomit near the door. She shivered in revulsion.

Louis followed her eyes. "That's me. The set designer didn't throw up. I did. The bastard did everything else. Even to the blood in the bathtub. You wouldn't like seeing it."

"No." Christie closed her eyes for a moment. "Jessie didn't die of pneumonia," she said at last.

"She didn't die of pneumonia. I wish she had."

"Oh?"

"She was murdered in this room and dragged to the beach. The police never found the killer. I had the whole thing hushed up. Jessie was into drugs, into actors, actresses, everything. She was too beautiful, too passionate, too rich, too generous, too trusting... too everything. But mainly too free. Too much on her own. No father around to say, 'No!' As I told you, I indulged her." There was no defense against his shame.

Christie glanced at Louis and looked away. She was face to face with the victim of a personal catastrophe that could happen in any family. Still, she wished she had been spared this knowledge.

"But why is the room like this now? It happened long ago."

"Stavros recreated it for me."

"Stavros did this?"

"Not Stavros himself. He ordered it done by a couple of his soldiers."

Louis was trembling, but she didn't know if it was anger or pain. "Why, Louis? Why did he do it?"

"To bring me to my knees. To show me his power. Strong-arm me into selling him United."

"You're sure it was Stavros?"

There was a lost look in Louis' eyes. "I'm sure. He did his homework on me. As he did on Michael. A thorough research job. On my life ... on Jessie's ..."

Christie felt chilled by the vicious accuracy of Stavros' perceptions. Jessie's bedroom was Louis' crucifixion. He had been forced to face Jessie's fate again.

"... and on the studio," Louis muttered.

Christie and Louis had a moment of quiet, intuitive communion. "You mean the cash flows?"

"Yes. If he could get the cash flows, he could get anything. From someone. Someone who knows the company intimately. Who knows me intimately. Someone I trust ..." He swallowed. "The same son-of-a-bitch knew about Jessie ... and told him."

"Linda?" Christie asked, a catch in her breath.

"No. Mannie Wolf."

"Mannie!" Christie was shocked. "He's been with you from the beginning."

"He's been with me from the beginning. But I made you president."

"He wanted the job that much?"

"He could taste it."

"But he isn't qualified. He's a numbers man. No feel for scripts, actors, directors—for making movies."

"Tell it to the Marines."

"You made him rich. A multi-millionaire. Didn't he appreciate what you did for him?"

Louis half-smiled. "I suppose so. But gradually he began to feel unappreciated. He thought of all the things he did for me."

"How do you know?"

"Instinct. It's what's I've lived by."

"That's why he retired. Because of me."

"Because of me. He didn't retire. I fired him. My dear, good friend, Mannie, who leaked the cash flows." Louis stared at Christie, and there was a moment of silence between them such as people observe when paying their respects to the dead. "He admitted to leaking the P & L and the cash flows. But not this. This hadn't happened yet."

"But you expected something."

"Michael's experience taught me. The numbers were nothing. I waited for the big bomb."

"And this is it."

"Jessie's room," he said gravely. "Look at it. Look at that damn Jahrzeit candle."

"You didn't put the candle there?"

"In this hell?" There was a hurt look deep in his eyes. "I brought mine to leave this evening . . . and found this inferno by Hieronymus Bosch. Only Mannie knew the truth about how Jessie died. Only Mannie would have thought of that finishing touch—Having them leave a Jahrzeit candle."

Christie said nothing. There was nothing more to say.

"It won't work," Louis said with absolute finality. "At least not for Lennos. I've decided to sell United, Christie. I want no more reminders of how I fouled my own nest. It's time I moved on."

There was a cruel, stunning voltage in his words. Christie knew what he wanted to hear from her, and went numb at what she must give up. But there was only one answer to his appeal.

"I agree. I think it's time to sell."

"Thank you, Christie. I wanted you to say that." He looked at her with searchlights in his eyes. "You mean it?"

"I mean it," she said with stifled soreness. And then to further prove her loyalty she added, "Stavros called me for drinks."

"When?"

"Yesterday. Nan got the message."

"Did you meet him?"

"No. When I called him back at the Bel Air, he'd already left for New York. But he left a message. He said he'd call when he returned."

"He won't call."

"Why?"

"I warned him." Louis' eyes filmed with hatred. "For good measure, I'll have a chat with Mannie Wolf. Lennos should know he accomplished his purpose. He made me hate the work I loved. My studio. Now I want the dead past to bury its dead."

Christie's head was a pounding drum of pain, but her tone was level, neutral. "Who will you sell the company to, Louis?"

"Macleod Brothers."

"Guy Macleod?"

"He'll do."

"You dislike him."

"In some ways he's worse than Stavros. But he has one great natural advantage. He's not Stavros. He's what Stavros longs to be. Stavros will choke on him."

Christie nodded.

"And thank you for holding my hand."

"Louis, please. If you'd like I'll bring Tommy here for the weekend."

"No, dear. I appreciate the offer. But I have to be alone. Go to Tahoe and try to forget the Louis Levy Museum of Horror."

Driving along the Pacific Coast Highway in the early morning sunlight, Christie thought about the lost Jessie, about the raw misery in Louis' eyes, about Stavros Lennos. He had been asembling the jigsaw puzzle called United Cinema. Michael Riordan first, then Mannie Wolf, even herself . . . but primarily, Louis. That was his mistake. He'd tried to force the Louis piece into place and it didn't fit. So now he'd never have the final corporate picture. Guy Macleod would.

Guy Macleod. Finally she allowed herself to think about him, about herself, about the enormous vistas of the future that she once saw before her. How it had all been there like a huge trust fund, an account upon which she would someday draw. Now she was bankrupt. Guy Macleod would own the studio. He would not make her president of United Cinema.

The idea filled her with bleakness and a kind of dry amusement at her heritage. It proved she was her father's daughter. Her luck was like his luck. It was, wasn't it? She remembered Stavros' message. "Greetings from Roger Ty-

NAKED CALL 63

sen." The present dissolved and a flood of memories exploded in her mind. The ghosts of her smothered past washed over her, and she saw again the pale, unappeased face of her beloved father. It was a sight she would never forget.

PART TWO

1971

Chapter 5

IT WAS the night before the world went spinning out of control. There had been warning signals for months. Christie heard them almost every night. She loved her mother and father and she believed they loved her. But that was the beginning and the end of it. They didn't love each other. It was really more awful than that. Her mother despised her father. Her father knew she despised him and didn't care. Not anymore. She'd broken his heart a long time ago.

Tonight her mother had declared war on her father again. Not that you could tell it unless you were in the same room and could see the fury in her eyes. Her mother didn't raise her voice. It sounded courteous . . . kind. But at fourteen, Christie had learned too much, too soon. She had the ears of a night-feeding animal that knows it must listen for larger predators or die. Her mother's calm, composed voice masked a constant, low-keyed rage; icy despair lay beneath her father's reasonable replies.

Christie tried to concentrate on her math homework, but it was hopeless. The equations blurred before her eyes. She couldn't stop herself from listening.

". . . Tom, do you like me in this blue? Not my usual blue-green . . ."

Silence.

"Baby, do you?"

"Yes."

"Good. Don't sulk, you big baby. It's silly to be jealous of Zach. He's only a backer who, fortunately, has backed the hit that rents your old lady's playhouse. For a very whippy sum . . ." Pause. "Now say something. Pretty please."

Christie closed her eyes. In her mind's eye, she could

see her father slumped in his big, brown leather chair, saying nothing, doing nothing.

"Say something!" Her mother's voice became more insistent.

"I'm glad," her father said.

"Me, too." Her mother was bright again. "It's money. Lovely, crisp, green money. Pays the mortgage on the building. Also the taxes. The repairs and maintenance. Even leaves a little over. Mmmm . . . dear Zach's promised to let me produce and direct *Bleecker Street*, his next production." Silence for three beats. "Tom . . . say, 'Good.'"

"Good."

"Say . . . 'won-der-ful!'"

Christie's heart hurt as she heard her father say, "Wonder-ful." He had no defenses.

"The dress works. Don't you think?"

Silence.

"Tom, baby! Don't you think it works?" Her voice was cool and menacing.

"It works," Christie's father said softly.

"Mmmm . . . Zach will adore it." Her mother's voice was lilting again. "But remember, baby, he's just a connection . . . useful in theater. Don't think dirty thoughts. He's taking me to dinner. That's it. He's too old to make it in bed. I think. Anyway, he doesn't come near you." She gave a throaty laugh. "Tommy, darling, you may not believe it, but I married you for love. You were so big and strong and handsome. So educated. So rich. This little street urchin from Staten Island wanted it all. The Lagerfeld dresses, the big apartment, the great fuck . . . And let's not forget the polish you gave me. The education. And theater. I'd never seen a play. Or been to an opera. Or a concert. Only movies. The popcorn princess of Tottenville. I blew the head off the beer." She giggled. "It was good practice. Me, the great American sow's ear. You turned me into a silk purse. Thank you, darling. I am constantly surprised I had the sense to spill the bottle of Femme all over you at Bloomie's. Would you zip me up please . . . thank you. Of course, when I married you, I had no idea that you didn't know shit about making money." The voice became forthright. "Truly, Tom, I was stunned when I discovered that you were a natural-born loser. A high-class bum who lived off his father's *largesse*. Correct?"

Silence.

"Silence gives consent," her mother said cheerfully. "Your pop was a great man. Knute Larsen. Make and lose and make a fortune every other month. A genius! What a shame he died. Worse shame, baby . . . you didn't inherit his genius. Wasn't it a shame, darling?"

Silence.

"Say it was a shame."

"It was a shame."

"A disgusting shame. When he died the shit hit the fan. Didn't it, Tom?"

"It hit the fan," her father said dully.

"So all God's chillun got tossed out of Eden. Weren't we?"

Silence.

"Weren't we?" Again the threat.

"We were tossed out of Eden."

"To live on spit. Like all the beer-swilling damn fools I grew up with." Deep breath. "But isn't it lucky that old Knute left me the Fourth Street building? He must've known I'd turn it into a money-making proposition and you wouldn't. Right?"

"Yes."

"Of course, yes! You don't have what I have, baby. Ambition. I will be rich and famous." Her voice carried a smile. "Well, Tommy boy." Humming and singing off key. " 'Plant you now, dig you later. . . . ' Give my love to Christie if I sleep through breakfast. Things do happen."

Christie heard the door slam and all that remained was the hollow silence in the living room. She wanted desperately to go to her father and comfort him, but she didn't dare. He mustn't know she'd heard the fight. She knew how ashamed he felt. Christie stared into space, feeling desperate . . . exhausted. Money! That was what her mother was raging about. Money. Always money. Why couldn't her father make lots of money? She called him a bum. He wasn't a bum. He was a . . . ? Each time Christie tried to answer the question—what was her father? —the only word that come to mind was . . . "lost." Her father was lost. Abruptly Christie put her face in her hands. She must not cry. Tears would do more than make her eyes puffy. But the tears streamed down her face.

Christie would always remember the next day. April 11, 1971. Her father was standing at the kitchen window looking up 71st Street towards Central Park West. Christie could see what he saw. The morning colors of the city were fresh and green and there was a promise of sunshine and spring in the air. The kitchen and breakfast nook both overlooked 71st Street, and from their windows in the morning and on quiet evenings, they often watched the changing weather of the sky and the city. That's why the kitchen and the breakfast nook were their favorite rooms in the apartment.

When her father heard her enter the kitchen, he turned, grinned, and went back to preparing their breakfast.

"Do you want scrambled or poached eggs? Bacon or sausages?" he asked in his normal, deep, rich voice.

His voice told Christie too much. Usually in the morning he spoke softly.

"Poached eggs with bacon, Daddy," Christie said brightly, trying to match his mood. She watched him for a moment and then started to set the table. She was holding at bay an idea that frightened her . . . a question that she'd never before dared to face. But after she'd laid out the knives, forks, and spoons, the necessity to know overwhelmed her.

"Excuse me. I left my scarf in my room, Daddy. Be right back."

Christie hurried off down the short corridor that led to the bedrooms. But instead of turning right, she turned left and tiptoed to the master bedroom. Her heart pounded as she saw the tightly closed door. Was her mother asleep behind that door in the extra-long, king-sized bed? She offered up a silent prayer that she was. But if she was asleep, why wasn't her father whispering? He always whispered when her mother was sleeping. She stood frozen. She'd never done this before. Finally she put her ear against the door and listened. Not a sound. She waited. She listened again. Still nothing. With the stealth of a burglar, she grasped the knob and turned it. Very slowly, she opened the door and peered in. The room was empty. Only her father's side of the bed had been used. Her mother had not slept at home last night.

Christie had the sensation of falling through space. She closed the door quickly and leaned against it, catching her breath. Now she knew the answer to the unanswered questions she'd been afraid to ask. All those mornings when her father didn't speak softly while he made breakfast . . . those were the times her mother didn't sleep at home.

Steadying herself, she hurried to her own room. She picked up a scarf she didn't need, wound it around her neck, and almost ran back into the breakfast room.

Her father was looking out the window when she arrived.

"Got your scarf, honey?"

"Yes." Christie managed to keep her tone easy. Breakfast was ready. Her orange juice was poured, her poached eggs and bacon were on her plate, and a glass of milk stood next to it.

Her father remained at the window.

"What are you looking at, Daddy?" It was imperative that she maintain her poise.

"The city, Christie. It's magnificent. Come here."

She walked to the window and stood beside him, looking at the city from the fifteenth floor of their building. Together they craned their necks and gazed at the traffic winding through Central Park. Glancing south, Christie saw the skyscrapers of Manhattan silhouetted against the sky.

"It's splendid, Daddy."

"A city I never conquered," her father said softly.

"You will one day, Daddy. You will."

"Maybe. Come eat your breakfast, or you'll be late for school."

That afternoon, when school was over, Christie tried to figure out where to go to avoid going home. A feeling of dread about what she might find there had mounted within her as the day passed. She was certain something awful was waiting for her at home. She thought she might escape by going to a movie. But she'd have to telephone her father and tell him. That would take too much explanation. Walking home along Central Park West from the bus stop, the feeling of dread increased. When the building doorman greeted her, the look on his face made her feel worse.

She took the elevator to the fifteenth floor, and although her feet felt like lead she made herself get off. Taking her keys from her purse, she walked to the door of their apartment—15CW—stopped, and stared. A printed notice was Scotch-taped to the door. Christie started to shake. This was what had been waiting for her. Somehow she'd known it was coming. Her fingers trembled as she pulled the notice off the door and scanned it quickly.

"FINAL NOTICE OF FORECLOSURE." The notice stated that since the maintenance on the apartment had not been paid for nine months and since Thomas J. Larsen also owed interest to the bank on monies he had borrowed using the apartment as collateral, the bank—with the building's consent—had taken over the ownership of the apartment from Christina Larsen . . . !

Christie gasped. Christina Larsen. That was her. What were they talking about? She didn't own the apartment. She made herself read on.

The Larsen family was to vacate the apartment within thirty days. Christie blinked and the tears that had formed in the corners of her eyes overflowed. They were homeless.

She shivered violently as she tried to figure out what she should do with the notice. Should she tape it back on the door, ignore it, and go into the apartment? When she found her father sitting in his chair reading or listening to music, should she pretend she hadn't seen it? She knew how he would feel when he saw the notice. The sense of his shame far outweighed her shock at seeing her name on the foreclosure notice or her fear of not having a home. She wiped her cheeks. It would be easier to leave it and say nothing . . . except for her mother. When her mother came home and saw the notice, she'd make a rotten scene. If Daddy wasn't warned, he wouldn't be prepared. That settled it. She'd give him the notice and tell him how much she loved him. That she didn't care about losing the apartment. They'd find a way. She put her key in the lock and, carrying the notice in her fingers as if it were a horrid, squirming insect, she opened the door quickly before she lost her nerve.

Her father was sitting in the same chair that he'd been

seated in when she left for school. He hadn't gone anywhere during the day. He was staring into space, like a man under hypnosis. The same record he'd put on this morning was still playing on the record player. Frederick Schorr, a great Wagnerian baritone—one of his favorites—was singing Wotan's "Farewell"... over and over all day. Christie closed her eyes. There was nothing to do but give him the notice.

"Daddy," she said quietly. "I think you'd better look at this, please."

Her father looked at her, at the notice, and nodded wearily. "I've been waiting for it, Christie. I thought it would come tomorrow. I meant to take it off before you came home, to spare you the first shock." Everything about him, from his half-shut, blue eyes to the downward curve of his mouth to his slumped position gave evidence of a beaten man.

"Daddy, we're being evicted. And my name is on the notice. It says I'm the owner of the apartment."

"You were, Christie. You owned this apartment." His voice broke. "Until I lost it for you."

"I don't understand."

"Your mother called. She'll be home shortly. I think we should talk first," he said as he reached for the notice.

Christie set her schoolbooks on the floor and settled on a low footrest next to her father's chair. She folded her long legs under her body and waited.

Her father spoke slowly, faltering at every word. "You know... since your grandfather's death... money has been tight."

"Yes."

"I'm no good at making money." He reddened slightly. "Maybe you'll understand why... after I explain. Your mother doesn't."

Christie gazed at him in anguish. "I'll understand."

He smiled, reaching over to smooth her hair and trace the outline of her firm chin. "You look more like your mother every day."

"I do not! I have Momma's red hair. That's all." But Christie knew her face was her mother's. The same luminous skin, the same slanting green eyes, the same wide, full-lipped mouth, the same burned copper hair. Her mother was a beauty and Christie often thought that her face was the one thing she could thank her for. She hoped she would never have her mother's disposition, her temper, her nastiness. She would rather be her father's daughter. "I'm not built like her at all. She's small. I'm tall. I'm built like you. Long legs. Long everything. And I'm not like her. I'm more like you. I even think like you."

"Let's hope not, Christie. With any luck you'll think like your grandfather." It would have been difficult for him to look more disarmed and defenseless. "Grandfather Knute was a hell of a lot smarter than I am. In business. In everything. Although I might be a better boat designer."

"That counts for a lot." This idea prompted her to add, "Grandfather made his money in the shipbuilding business. You designed the boats that he sold. You're a wonderful boat designer. He was lucky to have you."

Her father smiled. He let himself go with irony, with extravagance. "Thank you for the vote of confidence. I am a superb boat designer. Unfortunately my talent ends at the drafting table. It was your grandfather—not me—who supported the family. He sold the designs. He made money with me. He would have made money without me. Boats were in his blood." He glanced at the model of a sloop within a glass bottle that rested on the mantelpiece. "Sailboats, sloops, ketches, yawls... All his life your grandfather rode the waves and loved it. The ocean waves... the money waves. When he rode a big one, we were rich. When the wave broke, he owed everyone... millions... to the banks, business associates, friends. But no one worried. Your grandfather had charm, energy, nerve. Everyone believed in him. He'd come back and repay them with a handsome profit. Which he always did. Until the last time."

Christie sat motionless with lowered lids. "When he died."

"A heart attack. I don't think he ever expected to die."

"I don't think you expected it either. That he wouldn't leave us any money." For a second their eyes met and his pain echoed within her. Pain she hadn't intended. "I mean you loved him so much... you never think someone you love can die."

"I guess that's true." His voice was muffled. His daughter's perceptions were too acute for comfort. Then he cleared his throat. He couldn't stop now, saying things he'd never said to her before, as much for his own relief as for her information. "Your grandfather died in the middle of a money crunch. Two years earlier, his death would have left me a rich man. Two years later he'd have made back the millions he lost and we'd have inherited a fortune. But he died flat broke." A sudden restlessness seized him and, rising from the chair, he paced the room. "The banks, his business associates, our friends who invested—they took everything. The Larsen Shipyards on City Island, the cars, the boats . . . everything."

"You didn't stop them?" Her eyes followed him.

"I couldn't. You see, my name was on the notes along with your grandfather's, so I was equally responsible." He paused, then went on, almost in a whisper. "No one believed that I could run the shipyard. I wasn't my father. As time has shown, they were right. Without him, I'm nothing."

For a second Christie didn't trust herself to speak or to look at her father. Then, "Daddy, don't talk like that."

"It's true."

Christie felt pity for the trouble he was in, but she had to ask, "Daddy, why didn't you fight? I would never have let them take our things . . ." She stopped. His face was withdrawn, warning her of hidden wounds that she had touched too roughly.

"You wouldn't. You're a fighter. I'm not. It's something my father never understood . . . or your mother."

"It's all right, Daddy. I don't care. Let's not talk about it anymore. I'm not Momma. I understand. I'm Christie . . . your daughter."

"My daughter. What luck."

"For me, too. And you've taken care of us, Daddy. We haven't starved."

"I've tried to keep us afloat. Doing everything. Odd jobs around boat yards. All kinds of temporary work. Sometimes your mother contributes from the profits of her theater." His face had grown excessively pale and haggard.

"Why don't you get a job with another shipyard, designing boats? Grandfather's been dead for five years."

"I tried. Believe me, I tried. I called all my father's business contacts. Other boat builders. All his personal friends. Our friends—your mother's and mine—the people who bought boats. Anyone who could recommend me. Many of them regularly lent money to the Larsen Shipyards." He shook his head. "It's been useless."

"But you're a wonderful boat designer."

"No one will give me a commission. No one will hire me."

"That's crazy. I've seen your sketches..." She stopped, mystified, seeing his withdrawn face.

"People don't believe I designed the Larsen boats. They believe my father did. He let them think so. It was good business... made the sale easier." Tom Larsen surrendered to a feeling both humble and stoic. "Your mother still doesn't believe I designed the boats."

Christie stared at him. In the silence that followed, she was discovering more and more the necessity of courage. "Maybe if you did some new designs and showed them to people..."

His face brightened. "That's exactly what I've finally done. You see, I do know everything about designing and sailing boats. I'm a first-class designer. In fact, I've a project in the works that might do something for the family."

"Oh, Daddy!"

"I think I do." But even as he said the words he knew what he was most afraid of—that he would fail her. It was this that made him say, "But I can't count on it. You never know for sure until the money's in the bank. And, Christie, I'll say one thing in my own defense. I did manage to save a little from the disaster after my father died. The building downtown. Your mother's theater. I asked your grandfather to put it in her name, so no one could touch it if anything happened. And this apartment, too. That's why it's in your name. I bought it for you when you were born." His bouyancy vanished. "Then I borrowed against it. I used it as collateral for a bank loan to pay our living expenses when I couldn't find work.

"But now I'm working on something... something I want to do..." His voice trembled and broke as he fought to get the words out. "Something I can do. It could give us a fresh start. I've helped put together a syndicate to build a boat the way Grandfather used to." He longed for Christie not think of him as too old . . . too inadequate.

The sound of the door being opened made Christie whirl around. Framed in the doorway, her lovely face ice cold, was Christie's mother. She still wore the blue silk dinner dress she'd had on the night before and carried her patterned linen jacket.

"Tom, darling," she said in a deceptively sweet tone as she quietly shut the door. "Why did the doorman leer at me sympathetically and say he was sorry? Sorry about what?"

Without a word Christie's father handed his wife the foreclosure notice. She glanced at it and then gave her husband the most merciless look a woman can give a man. It said loud and clear: You eat, you breathe, you occupy space—but you are not a man.

"Darling, how could you let this happen?" she said as if nothing had happened. "Why do I ask foolish questions? You could." She went to a table where she'd set up a makeshift bar, filled a sherry glass with gin, and took a swallow. "Why didn't you tell me this was coming?"

Her father erupted in sudden anger. "You knew it was coming! Don't play dumb. I told you we've been living on money I borrowed from the bank on Christie's apartment." As he spoke, his voice weakened. "How did you think I would repay the loan? Or even the interest on the loan?"

"I didn't," she said without any emotion.

"What would you have done if you'd known?"

"Quite a bit . . . if I'd been reminded in time. I have my admirers . . . like Zach." She gave a low, seductive laugh. "If I'd known what was happening, I might have charged for my favors, to use a quaint phrase. My admirers can afford to pay generously."

Christie's father heaved himself to his feet. He towered over his wife. "Shut up!" He glanced at Christie, who looked at him blank-faced, hoping he'd think she didn't understand her mother's words.

Her mother gave Christie a knowing smile. "Tom, dearest, our little angel is growing up. I'd bet my panties that she knows about the birds and the bees and the mating call of the naked ape . . . and the beast with two backs. I sure as hell did at her age."

"Thank God she's not you!"

"And you're not Zach—heaven help us—you deadbeat. Since we're being tossed out on our asses, where do you suggest we live? In wigwams? Or sleeping bags in Central Park?"

Christie's father answered with effort, "Maybe . . . for a short time . . . with your cousin."

"In Staten Island? Are you out of your mind?"

"She visited us every summer on the boat. She stayed for weeks. And we wouldn't be there very long. Just a month or so. Then we should have money . . . anyway I hope so." He sounded disoriented.

"Maybe I'll take Christie and move in with Zach," her mother said in a soft, steely voice.

Christie thanked God that her father didn't hear her mother. He was too caught up in his hope against hope dream.

"You see . . . I've been putting together a syndicate to build a boat to compete in the America's Cup races. I'm a good designer. One of the best. These men knew my father, and they're interested in backing me."

"They're fools. You are not your father," she said fiercely. "What an asinine way to waste your time. Raising money for a boat you can't design. And if you do design the damn thing, it'll sink as soon as it's launched." She shrugged in disgust and poured another gin. "What a shitty joke. You poor, mad fool—you design a boat for the America's Cup! Spare me your—"

The ringing of the telephone interrupted her mother's venom. Christie rose to answer it, glad to escape.

"Hello?" she said, hoping it was for her mother. "Tom Larsen? Yes, he's here. Who's calling? Roger Tysen? I'll tell him." She held her hand over the receiver and turned to her father. "Daddy, it's for you. A Mr. Roger Tysen."

For an instant her father couldn't find his voice. Then an expression of childlike wonder passed over his face. "Thank you, Christie," he said, taking the receiver. "Hello, Roger." After that he said nothing—he listened. At last he said, "Yes... of course. Yes, I'm delighted. I know I can do it. Yes, I'll see you tomorrow afternoon. Around four. At your office. Good-bye." Very slowly, her father hung up the telephone. He stared at Christie in astonished disbelief. "They've decided to back me. They've actually decided to put up the money for the boat." In a daze he walked over to Christie, put his arm around her waist, lifted her feet from the floor, and waltzed her madly around the room, singing at the top of his lungs, "They're going to back me! Back me! Back me!"

"Tom! Cut it out! What the hell is going on?" Christie's mother shouted.

"I'm back in business. Like my father! At last! I'm going to build a boat for the America's Cup. They're going to back me... back me... back me!"

Christie's mother stared at the two waltzing figures with angry surprise. "You mean those men are actually putting up real money to build one of your stupid designs?"

"Roger Tysen and Company. They formed a syndicate to back me. With very real money! Millions!" her father sang out with authority. Abruptly he stopped waltzing and set Christie's feet on the floor. "Will my daughter do me the honor of allowing me to escort her to dinner tonight? To celebrate the next winner of the America's Cup?"

"Oh, Daddy, yes!"

"Go change."

"What about me?" her mother shrilled.

"I'm sure you have a previous engagement. With Zach."

"I do." Christie's mother nodded as she walked to the telephone. "But I've decided to break it. I love family celebrations."

Chapter 6

CHRISTIE TRIED to curl herself into a small ball and pull the blanket around her. The raw January wind cut through the gaps between the glass and the rotted wooden window frames, freezing every bone in her body.

When they'd first moved into the ground floor apartment in the town house on East 94th Street between Park and Lexington, her mother had been delighted at the idea of the sun porch. The airy porch at the rear of the apartment would be an ideal place for Christie to sleep.

Christie's mother had found the apartment and she adored it. There was a fireplace and exposed brick in the living room that was charming. The sun porch overlooked a small garden in the rear. Beyond these attractions—her mother made this point emphatically—she could invite her theatrical friends to the apartment. Though the rent for the apartment on the East Side was more than double that of a comparable West Side apartment, the East Side had prestige ... the West Side didn't. Her mother considered this fact crucial. She claimed they could afford the East Side. At last Christie's father had a good job—supervising the spending of millions to build a boat for the America's Cup race. And he controlled the bank account. Her mother also insisted that Christie's father must live in a good neighborhood. Plus, he needed an office, and the basement would be perfect for that, just as the sun porch was a perfect place for Christie to sleep.

Her father gave in to her mother. He always did. Christie never understood why.

Now, as Christie shivered, too cold to sleep, she heard her parents arguing again. Tonight was another of their long struggles over money.

NAKED CALL

"I would appreciate it if just this semester you would pick up Christie's tuition at Riverdale. Your theater's been making a profit," she heard her father say. "Say you covered half the cost. $1,750. I'll pick up the second payment."

Her mother's laugh was a taunt. "Don't be silly, Tommy boy. Christie's expenses are yours. You'll pick up both payments. That's a father's role."

"If I could pay it all, I would. Consider it a loan."

"Loan you money? Don't insult my intelligence, darling. Although you'd make a great gigolo. If I could afford you."

The pause between them was prolonged, until her mother gave a nasty laugh.

"Cat got your tongue? Now, now. The truth isn't pretty. Which reminds me, I picked out a new winter coat for Christie at Bonwit Teller's. Three new skirts, two pairs of jeans, five blouses, three cashmere sweaters, two pairs of gloves, two woolen hats. Oh yes, I also bought her two pairs of boots on sale at Sak's. They should arrive this week. We can't have our daughter looking like a ragamuffin."

Again there was silence. Then her father said hoarsely, "I know she needs clothes, but why buy them at Bonwit Teller's and Sak's?"

"It is amazing, but you now have a divine job. The bank account for your boat runs to over six million. Imagine! Six million to build a silly racing sloop. More money than to mount ten Broadway plays." Christie could see her mother shaking her head in disgust.

"But you know they've only given me two hundred dollars a week for living expenses." Her father sounded baffled.

"That's insane. That kind of money could barely cover my cab fares."

"It's supposed to cover our food, clothing, and shelter."

"Fine. Put the rest on your expense account."

"I don't have an expense account."

"My God! You didn't tell me!" Her mother was incredulous. "You really were born yesterday. You mean you didn't insist on an expense account?"

"No."

"Why not?"

"It didn't seem appropriate."

"When will you learn, you fool?" she lashed out. Then she paused, caught her breath, and continued with exquisite mildness. "Well, darling, there's one solution. You must act as if you have an expense account. *Noblesse oblige.* If you try to live on that tight-ass budget, they'll think you're a worm. How can you design a boat costing over six million and be the kind of man who lives on two hundred dollars a week? Please. Now I must get my rest . . . eight hours of beauty sleep." She left the living room.

Christie felt a strong urge to scramble out of bed and rush to her father, tell him they would send all the clothes back. But she couldn't. His pride was at stake. If he knew that she had listened . . .

One Saturday in the late summer, Tom took Christie to City Island to watch the launching of the boat hull. Her mother had other plans. When Christie broke a bottle of champagne against the side of the boat, the long, slim hull slid smoothly down the ways, settling into the water with barely a ripple. The workers and members of her father's syndicate who had gathered for the launching applauded loudly. Christie watched with shining eyes as the eight men and their wives took turns shaking her father's hand.

She overheard one ask, "How's the money holding out? Costs coming in as estimated?"

Her father nodded. "Pretty much so, Roger. We lose a little here and pick up a little there. Nothing to worry about."

"Fine," the man said. "No one expects you to hit every number on the nose. Are the books in shape for our accountant to take a look?"

Her father made a strangled coughing sound. "I've spent so much time here, I've let the paperwork slip."

Roger Tysen laughed and slapped Tom on the back. "Not to worry. You're a boat builder and a sailor, not a bookkeeper. Tell you what. I can't spare her this month, but next month I'll send over my personal bookkeeper. She'll get the books into shape in a day or two. Christ, a man like you shouldn't have to worry about bean counting."

"Great. Or . . ." Tom paused as though a new idea struck him. "We still have a couple of months' work ahead of us

NAKED CALL

fitting her out. Why not wait until we're finished? Then do the whole job at one time?"

Christie watched as an odd expression crossed the man's face, but all he said was, "Good idea, Tom. No need to do the same job twice."

Christie glanced at her father. He was standing absolutely still, but she knew him too well. She could feel the trembling of his body under the surface of his calm. On the bus going home from City Island she waited for him to tell her why he was so afraid. But he said nothing and she couldn't ask. They both knew and dreaded the truth.

Christie was with her father when the telephone rang. He picked it up. "Hello?... Yes, hello, Roger."

Roger was talking so loudly that Christie, standing by the desk, could hear snatches of his voice.

"... time we got those books into shape... next Monday okay for you?"

"I thought we'd agreed to wait until all the work was completed?"

"... don't want to wait until spring..." the voice grew louder, more insistent. "There's only about ninety-seven thousand in the bank account... not enough to finish the job... not concerned... If you need more money, Tom, we'll put it up. We just want to know how our money was spent... Understand?"

"Sure, Roger. Did you say next week?"

"... my girl's name is Emily Landau... call you... Goodbye, Tom."

Christie was never to forget the look on her father's face when he hung up the receiver. His eyes roamed the room blindly like a breathless fugitive. Then his whole body crumbled, shaking with dry sobs and his face dropped forward again into his hands. Christie watched him, unable to breathe. That her father should weep so uncontrollably terrified her. In a state of severe shock she stared at him wide eyed and numb... like someone helplessly witnessing an earthquake.

After Roger Tysen's bookkeeper had reviewed Tom's books, Roger called an emergency meeting in his office at 400 Madison Avenue. Tom, Christie, and her mother were present at the conference room meeting. Three folding chairs has been set up facing the conference table. Christie sat in the middle between her mother and father. She was there because she wanted to be there. Her mother wanted her there, too. She said it would be a learning experience. It would teach Christie the truth about her father and to appreciate the burden her mother lived with.

Her father wore his new, dark business suit, a white shirt, and a black tie. Christie thought he looked as if he were going to a funeral. By way of contrast, her mother wore a bright red wool three piece suit by Geoffrey Beene with a gray blouse and red micro-mini skirt that showed off most of her legs. A mink coat was draped over her shoulders. Paying for that one outfit alone must have cost thousands and thousands of dollars. Christie was dressed as she dressed everyday: a skirt, a blouse, a sweater, a folded raincoat in her lap.

Facing them across the glass covered Duncan Phyfe table were the eight syndicate members. Christie searched their faces for sympathy. Here and there she thought she saw a shadow of regret or disappointment or compassion. These were wealthy men who had invested money they could afford to lose. What they'd anticipated—as had their wives—was being part of the traditional Newport social whirl that went with the America's Cup trials. Now, with the sloop unfinished and the man they relied on to build the boat turning out to be a clumsy thief, they simply wanted to write off their losses and forget the mess. Only Roger Tysen was angry. He'd originally approved Tom and put the group together. He exuded righteous indignation. Tom had betrayed him by stealing, had lost his friends' money, had made Roger Tysen look like a damn fool.

As Tysen passed around each check that her father had written to himself, her mother shook her head with resignation. Christie held tightly to her father's perspiring hand, trying desperately to tell him through her fingers that none of this mattered. She understood and loved him.

When Tysen finished collecting the checks, he asked Tom, "Just how do you propose to repay us? In round numbers it comes to about one hundred seventy-seven thousand dollars."

NAKED CALL

Tom shrugged. It was the gesture of a man who had run out of answers, not one who did not care.

"I don't believe my husband can repay you," her mother spoke up with detached coolness.

"Then maybe you can, Mrs. Larsen? Theater is a passion of mine," Charles Macleod, another syndicate member, suggested. "I've been to two shows you produced. And enjoyed them." His eyes roved compulsively over her mother's crossed legs. "I understand you own the Fourth Street Theater."

Christie took the cue instantly. Knowing her mother, that look was unmistakable. Charles Macleod was another of her lovers. She watched him intently. Listening to him warm to his subject, it struck Christie he was mildly embarrassed by her mother's presence, and their history together.

"Would you consider selling the property to cover your husband's . . ." He became the diplomat. ". . . shall we say, debts?"

Her mother gave a low laugh. "Dear Mr. Macleod, I would not. This is my husband's can of worms. He'll have to bail himself out."

In spite of the intimacy between them, Christie saw Macleod was put off by her mother's callousness. He turned to her. "How old are you, young lady?"

"Sixteen, sir."

"You look older. Why are you here?"

"I wanted to come."

"I wanted her to come." Christie's mother was enjoying the show. "It's educational. I want her to see how her adored father handles other people's money."

"Are there any assets in her name that can be used to repay the monies?" Tysen asked.

"I have a gold watch my grandfather left me," Christie said quickly. "You can have that."

"We don't want your gold watch, but thank you for the offer," Macleod said gently.

"We sure as hell don't. And this is a damn fool meeting." The words were spoken by a tall, heavyset man with a deep tan and a fringe of snow white hair, the only man in the room not wearing a tie. "I didn't fly up from Palm Beach in January to listen to you try to get blood from a stone."

Evan Van Moorlandt and Charles Macleod represented the old money in the group. They were the only ones who would be at the yachting trials whether or not they entered a sloop. Nodding toward Tom, he said, "The man has nothing. The kid certainly has nothing. And as for the woman..." Van Moorlandt permitted his contempt to show, "...meet Madam Defarge. Here to see an execution."

"Evan." Tom spoke for the first time. "I took the money. Not my wife. Leave her out of this, please."

"My God, man, you're even a bigger fool than I expected," Van Moorlandt said and turned to the syndicate members. "Gentlemen, we have three choices. We can toss Larsen to the D.A. and get ourselves a lot of smelly publicity ... a reputation for being stupid asses. Or we can fire him ... hire another builder to finish the boat. Or we can take the bank account away from Larsen and keep him on the job." Van Mortlandt ignored the mutterings of the other men. "I stopped on my way in from the airport to see the boat. I'll give Larsen this much. I know he stole some chicken shit money, but he did build us a damn fine boat. If she handles as good as she looks, he may have designed a winner."

Roger Tysen thought this over. Speaking to the other men, he said, "I think Evan has laid out all our options. Unless someone has something else to add?"

No one had anything to add. Tysen then spoke directly to Tom Larsen. "Will you wait outside in the reception room, please?"

Tom stood up. "Of course. And thank you, Roger."

"And thank you, too, my friend," Christie's mother purred as her eyes locked with Charles Macleod's.

Christie and her father waited side by side, seated on the couch in the reception room, holding tightly to each other's hands. Her mother went downstairs to get a hamburger and coffee.

It didn't take long for the syndicate members to reach a decision. Christie and her father rejoined the meeting, each of them straining to protect the other from the ruin of their lives.

NAKED CALL 87

Tysen spoke carefully. "Tom, this is a very sad business."

Christie watched her father grow paler. He stared straight ahead, saying nothing.

"We're not vindictive men. The hundred and seventy-seven thousand you stole is meaningless. What is sad is you betrayed our trust. You'd have been wiser not to steal. We wish you'd come to us and told us you needed money. Maybe we could have worked something out."

If he would only get on with it. Christie held her breath.

"At any rate, what's done is done. We want the boat finished. When it's finished, we're quits."

Christie's mouth fell open. Tom Larsen look stunned. "You mean..."

"We mean we're not going to prosecute. We want you to get on with it."

"Mr. Tysen... Roger... I... I don't know how to thank you," Tom stammered.

"Don't thank me. Just get to work."

Christie had a sudden, irresistible impulse to speak. "Mr. Tysen?"

"Yes?"

"I have to say something."

"Go ahead, child."

"Yes... well... you see." Christie took a deep breath and the words spilled out quickly. "My father and I appreciate your generous nature. But how can we... how can he do what you want without your help?"

"What kind of help, young lady?"

"My father and I..." Again she made no mention of her mother. "... we have to live between now and the time he finishes your boat. We need money for rent... food... telephone... necessities."

Tysen chuckled. "I admire your courage. Asking for money on top of what your father has stolen."

"I'm not brave, Mr. Tysen. I'm scared stiff. But scared or not, we do have to eat. Besides..." Christie was now going on instinct—an instinct for survival as keen as her mother's. "... my father stole nothing from you. He borrowed some money, which will be repaid from the work that comes into Larsen Shipyards after his sloop wins the

America's Cup. But what about Mr. Macleod? Is he prepared to repay what he took—should I say what he borrowed—from my father?"

"He didn't borrow it," her mother said, laughing as she entered the conference room. "I gave it to him. Didn't I, Charles?"

Charles Macleod at first turned white and then blushed deeply. He stared at Christie in confusion. Christie stared back at him, a stone mask, nonjudgmental. Roger Tysen cleared his throat. He was not one to shrink from a friend's need. He glanced at Macleod with embarrassed sympathy. His eyes said he understood all about men who played around. But the look of disgust he gave Christie's mother said, You are a tramp.

"How much do you need, Larsen?" he asked.

"Daddy, will $350 a week cover our expenses?"

"Yes. That's plenty... more than enough." Tom couldn't believe what was happening.

"$350 it is. You have to live," Tysen said.

Charles Macleod intervened, giving Christie a kindly smile. "I'd like you to know that we're really not bad men—"

"Yes... of course we aren't," Tysen interrupted. "And to prove it, I'll have Miss Johnson draw a check now for seven hundred dollars. That will give you a start, Tom. Two weeks' salary."

"Why not make it out to Miss Larsen, as a gesture of our appreciation? She is a fine advocate for her father," Macleod said, giving Christie's mother another furious glance.

Roger Tysen nodded approvingly at Macleod. He understood that Charles was trying to make peace with Tom Larsen... and his daughter, to disentangle himself from all connections with the wife. He buzzed his secretary and gave her the instructions, then paused. "What is your full name, young lady?"

"Christina Larsen."

"Make out the check to Christina Larsen. And bring it to me." Tysen and Macleod both smiled at Christie. "Two weeks' salary in advance," Tysen said. "To seal our bargain. And show our good will."

NAKED CALL 89

* * *

Christie, her father, and her mother stood in the doorway of the building. A cold sleet was falling, and cars and buses moving up Madison Avenue were beginning to skid a little on the slippery asphalt. Christie held her hand tightly on her purse, almost feeling the outline of the check through the thin plastic. Her father stood beside her, still dazed by the turn of events. His expression was transformed—one she had never seen. Radiant and awed . . . the expression of a man who has seen a miracle. "Now that you're rich," her mother said, "act rich. Hail a cab like the gentleman you are. I want to go home to a scotch."

"We can get a bus," Christie said.

"Think big, Christie. You've been doing it all afternoon. Tom, get us a cab," her mother said.

Her father did as he was told, edging between two illegally parked cars and peering down Madison Avenue. All the yellow cabs were filled. He spotted an empty cab on the east side of the street, ran for it, but he was too late. A lady got in.

"Daddy, be careful. It's slippery," Christie called.

The light changed. "There's one! There's one!" her mother urged him. "Get it! Get it, baby!"

"No!" Christie screamed. She saw a taxi trying to turn up Madison Avenue from 47th Street. Suddenly it seemed that every action was reduced to slow motion. Her father's eyes were intent on the street. He didn't see the rear wheels of the yellow cab spinning out, taking the taxi sideways across the street. Christie could only watch with frozen horror as the space between her father and the side of the cab grew smaller. "Daddy!" she cried out as loud as she could. "Watch out!"

Tom Larsen looked up a fraction of a second before the cab crashed into him. Christie never knew if he realized what was happening. Or if—like so many other disasters that had happened in his life—he saw the accident as inevitable and accepted his fate. To be crushed by a taxi on Madison Avenue . . . even as the great, golden future he had dreamed of for so long was within his grasp.

Blind to the traffic, Christie ran across the street. She cradled her father's head in her hands and felt the sticky wetness that oozed from the back of his shattered skull. She was dazed by the horror.

A woman knelt beside her. Christie sensed rather than saw it was her mother. She couldn't bear to look at her. She knew she would never forgive her. In her heart... in her blood... she felt a direct connection between the woman in the red suit and her father's death. Her mother was responsible. As responsible as if she'd pushed her father in front of the skidding cab.

From a great distance she heard her mother's calm, confident voice saying, "He had a remarkable capacity for failure. And a genius for bad timing." Christie said nothing and the voice continued. "If I were you, baby, I'd hang on to that seven hundred dollars. We'll need it to cover the funeral costs."

PART THREE

1991

Chapter 7

"WHO THE hell is she talking to? I've been holding on for five minutes."

"I'm sorry, Miss Caro. Shall I have her call you back?" Nan Grey asked.

"If it's not Louis Levy, what the devil is taking so long?"

"I don't know, Miss Caro," Nan said tactfully.

You're lying, you bitch, Jo said to herself. "Nan, I am not a director with a hot property looking for a studio. Or an actor with a hot property he wants to direct. I'm not even a student from Miss Larsen's film class at UCLA looking to be another Spielberg. You know me. I'm Jo Caro. Would you cut in and tell her I'm waiting with bated breath?"

"I don't do that, Miss Caro. Except for Mr. Levy. But I would for you, if I could. She's on her private line." Nan's voice was pained and conciliatory.

"It's about as private as a credit card bill collector's line. Why the hell doesn't United Cinema have direct dial?"

"I'm sorry, Miss Caro, I don't know."

"Don't be sorry. Do something. It builds character. Tell me who she's talking to and I'll know how long she'll take."

"I don't know. I was in the ladies' room when the call came in. I only pick up on her private line when she's in a meeting," Nan said primly.

If Jo Caro didn't know better, she would have lost her temper. Christie had the woman log every call she received. "Forget it. Let her waste company time. What I mind is she's wasting my time. Tell your exalted boss to call me when she gets off the pottie," Jo said briskly. "Remind her we have an appointment tomorrow to take measurements."

"I'll do that."

"Remind her, too, that tomorrow is Saturday. That the

Union for Rising Executives frowns upon brazen ambition. Ambition is considered an unattractive quality. Signs of it—like working Saturdays—are looked upon as a personal deformity. I'll expect her in my driveway at 10:30 . . . in Levis."

"I'll tell her."

"Thank you, Miss Grey. It's been my pleasure," Jo Caro said acidly.

"I wish I could be more help, Miss Caro," Nan said, but Jo Caro didn't hear. She'd slammed the phone down.

Nan Grey stared at the receiver in amusement. It wasn't an accident that she was Christie Larsen's private secretary. She was committed to confidentiality. She understood that Jo Caro was Christie's old and good friend. Practically a sister, as Jo once told her. She'd known Christie since time immemorial . . . virtually from diaper days. This made no impression on Nan Grey. Her mother, as executive secretary to that prince of power, Charlie Berenson, had screened every call on his three private lines and the four office lines. No one spoke to the prince—not his nearest and dearest, including his mother, his father, his ex-wives, present wife, current mistress, ex-mistresses, daughters, drug dealer—no one, unless he indicated to Mrs. Grey that he would speak to them. Christie was different in one respect. There were two people whose calls she always took. One was Louis Levy. The other was Tommy Larsen. At the moment Tommy was talking to his mother, and a call from Louis Levy in New York was waiting.

Jo Caro's dream house, for which she was prepared to put down $80,000 cash plus $720,000 from her friendly banker who she regularly screwed, was a splendid anomaly on the edge of Bel Air, one of the most statusy villages in L.A. The house had a strong French accent—an all-brick French country manor surrounded by an acre of landscaped grounds, brick patios, and terraces. The interior had textured plaster walls, high, stained oak-beamed ceilings, Spanish-tiled floors, and two fireplaces. The spacious 4,000 foot layout included a gourmet kitchen—for Jo Caro, who never boiled an egg—an oak-paneled library with built-in bookcases, a formal dining room, and two bedroom suites, plus a master bedroom suite with a Jacuzzi and sauna. Behind the house was a thirty-foot pool and spa surrounded by a brick patio for outdoor entertaining. Christie had been a guest in enough great houses to know that in Hollywood terms this was "a big, small house." But looking around as she and Jo ambled through the spacious rooms, she agreed it was a prize. And to Jo it was a symbol—concrete proof of the distance she'd travelled from a tent home in Bakersfield, California to the Century City offices of Jessup, Overstreet & Stein. In some ways, it was longer and more difficult than a journey to the moon. Now if she could keep up the mortgage payments, meet the taxes, pay the... Christie hoped she could.

"It's beautiful, isn't it?" Jo asked as she measured the length of the living room wall.

"It's wonderful."

"You think so? Honestly?"

"I think it's perfect." What else could she say? To argue against this irresponsible extravagance was a waste of breath.

"You weren't so enthusiastic when I showed it to you Thursday," Jo said.

"They're asking a lot of money for the house."

"You thought I'd lost my mind."

"Something like that. You'll need a live-in housekeeper."

"I think I've found one."

"A gardener."

"Regular pool cleaning."

"A security system."

"I love it!"

"How are you going to handle all the expenses?"

Jo dismissed the problem with a casual wave of her hand. "I don't work at the Safeway checkout counter anymore."

Christie sighed. "You have money to burn?"

"O.P.M. Other People's Money. I told you—I have friends in high places."

Which left her, Christie thought, exactly nowhere. "The house does suit your personality," she said lamely.

"Don't put me on, Christie. It doesn't. But the new Josephine Caro will adapt. People will think I've always lived in the castle. I love every inch of tile on the floor."

"Yes, the tile is magnificent. I saw some just like it at Jenny Lattimore's home."

Jo Caro gave a deep sigh of satisfaction. "Okay—let's blow the joint. I'll put in my bid at Ryan. By the way, I thought Jenny was on location with *Serpent*."

"She is. I saw her about two months ago."

"Is she still the star?"

"As much as she can manage with Franco directing."

"Franco Marconi, the fiend with actresses."

As they walked toward the door, Jo asked too casually, "Is the divine Jenny still seeing that stud, Matt Renault?"

"I don't know. She was then. He called from Manhattan and she was glued to the phone through the salad course."

"Then you've never met him?" Christie shook her head. "Let me fill you in . . . that bastard is one great hunk of male. I've seen him around. But I'm not a star. He doesn't know I'm alive."

"Why not invite him over for tea and some of your famous sesame sex cookies?" Christie teased.

Jo's eyes narrowed. "Actually, in my new incarnation, we'll probably get acquainted. He'll like the neighborhood. And my neighbors . . . Nancy and Ronald Reagan for openers. Aside from them—the singer, Mac Davis. Also Johnny Carson's ex-wife, Joanna. It isn't Coldwater Canyon or the Holmby Hills, but it isn't all bad. Classy neighborhood, wouldn't you say?"

"I'd say." The longing in Jo's eyes made Christie sad. How her friend yearned to be one of the elite of Hollywood. How she dreaded that she never would be.

"You honestly like the house?"

"Honestly." The house was beautiful, a metaphor for Jo's life: ambitious, opportunistic, valiant, preposterous. A live-in housekeeper, a gardener, et cetera . . . lunacy piled upon lunacy. Jo was no bimbo brain. What was she doing? Her salary might just cover heating bills. A cruel, wounding word stirred in Christie's memory—a hateful word: Foreclosure. She shook her head—forget it. Don't remember. With luck she'd always have a spare room for Jo. With or without her job at U.C.

* * *

NAKED CALL

Once it was agreed that United Cinema and Tosca Ltd.—Franco Marconi's company—would start shooting *The Feathered Serpent*, Jacob "Jake" Jakes, Franco's art director, stalked Mexico looking for a town situated near water that resembled the town in the novel, Santo Domingo.

His search led him to Oaxaca, the fertile valley ringed on one side by the Sierra Madres del Sur, considered the heart of the real Mexico. The area, steeped in pre-Colombian and Spanish colonial traditions, was dotted with Indian villages, ornate colonial churches, ancient ruins. He settled on the village, Mitla, for major sections of the film. Not only was the village lousy with atmosphere but it also had "gringo" accommodations in food and in guest rooms and for those in the cast and crew who insisted on Hilton type conveniences, Oaxaca was a short drive away.

For the scenes with the legendary serpent, he chose the Pacific Coast fishing village of Puerto Escondido, a short plane ride or long bus trip away. Besides the spectacular sweep of the ocean and the atmosphere of the beaches, Puerto Escondido had a lagoon filled with wildlife and a mangrove swamp which Jake felt were ideal for the movie, a natural home for the strange visitor from the past.

When Jake returned to Los Angeles, he sketched scenes, frame by frame, from Mitla, with the village site and the surrounding mountains and valleys in the background. He did the same with Puerto Escondido, taking in the ocean, the fishing boats, the lagoon, the beach vendors selling jewelry. Jake was satisfied with his "finds." In the edited version of *The Feathered Serpent*, the two towns would be merged into one. No one—besides the cast and local Mexican Indians hired as extras—would know the difference.

In her office at United Cinema, Christie Larsen almost immediately knew the difference. It proved—if nothing else—that Franco still had a gift for spending money. The final production budget was $20,765,521, rounded out to $21,000,00. Christie had vetted *The Feathered Serpent* budgets from the start. Now that Franco was shooting in two towns, not one, she could see the budget stretching like rubber. Two towns meant time lost packing and moving the cast, crew, and equipment from one location to another. It meant new housing, maybe new catering, new everything. It meant a change in the lighting, the quality and length of daylight hours for shooting time. The longer she stared at the cost of shooting in the second town, the more her experience, instinct, and professional smell disliked it. Taking into consideration the added expenses—and many understated ones like travel time—she guessed Franco was already over budget by about two million dollars, if not more. And he was still shooting.

Franco was working at high pitch, curly hair flying, unself-conscious as a child, with a face that managed to look both boyish and satanic. He laid out in infinite detail for his actors each and every line, each and every minute bit of action. His volatile, headlong manner energized some of the cast to work with greater intensity. Others wished they had never left Broadway.

Jeff Chambers, United's man on location, was production manager. His reports to Christie showed measured restraint, but the between-the-lines innuendos read loud and clear. Day by day the production shooting schedule was falling behind. The budget for *The Feathered Serpent* had always been loaded with minor "ifs." If the leading lady didn't gain weight . . . if the Mexican government isn't overthrown . . . if there's a hurricane . . . if . . . But the big "if" had always been, could Franco Marconi complete the shooting of so complex a script in the six weeks agreed on? Apparently not.

Rereading Jeff's latest report, Christie rubbed her forehead. Time was running away from them. A production scheduled to take six weeks—or thirty-six shooting days—was going to take three months, or eighty-eight shooting days. Or possibly longer. It wasn't Franco's incompetence that worried her. Franco wasn't incompetent. He was highhanded . . . pigheaded. She thought about her earlier conversation with Jeff.

"Franco can do everything. That's half the reason we're running late. If he doesn't like the sound, he takes the microphone apart. That takes time. If he doesn't like the lighting, he resets the lights himself. More time. A genius. A fucking pain in the ass."

"Is he changing the script, too?"

"Every scene. Dialogue. Locations. The Grossmans are screaming. The shooting schedule means nothing."

Christie had hung up the telephone and stared into space. At the rate Franco was shooting, the budget would come in closer to twenty-five million. Okay. They could live with that—but no higher. Enough was enough. She'd fly down to Mitla, have a look. Franco was spending money like a prize fighter on a spree.

When she arrived, she was welcomed by wonderful weather. Bright sun, clear sky, called "grip weather" because most of the lighting was handled by nature. Jeff Chambers almost fainted with relief at seeing her. Christie was authority. They took a six-pack of Mexican beer and sat on a high spot of land overlooking the set.

"Jenny's very quiet," Christie said, sipping her beer.

"On Valium. Franco drives her crazy."

"Conchita?"

"Valium. And Dalmaine. Franco should be a drug dealer. Cast and crew suffer anxiety attacks. Depressions. They rented a plane and flew a go-fer to Tijuana for Doxepin."

"That makes people drowsy. What kind of performances can he get from drugged-out actors?"

"You know the creed—the show must go on. They're fine on camera. Jenny collapses off the set. The constant script changes make her—make everyone—crazy. Insecure. Yesterday Franco barred the Grossmans from the set. They're so pissed they're going to sue everybody connected with the film."

Christie smiled in a tired way. "What about our General? How is Alan bearing up?"

"Alan Lucca? The only Italian matinee idol who is also a *mensch*. Ave Lucca. Unflappable. I figure growing up in Vecchio Roma after the war was even worse than Franco at his most impossible."

One of the key scenes—the funeral march in the plaza—was being rehearsed. It had been run through almost fifty times, not only to give Conchita Supervia a feel for her role as Juanita—a mother and murderess—but to drill the camera and light crews. Franco finally decreed it ready for a take.

"Franco wants shadowed low-key lighting to set a mood of menace. The story's filled with menace," Jeff explained.

Julian Hennesy, the makeup artist, joined them. He was a wiry man with *cafe au lait* skin. Deep lines of exhaustion were etched in the corners of his eyes and mouth. He squatted beside Christie.

"This movie is ulcer time," he said in a quiet interval between takes.

"So I hear, Julian. Give me a for instance."

"For instance, Franco insisted on shooting one scene with Chita six times. Said her breasts needed to be more tan— our olive-skinned Chita needed more tan—to look natural in daylight. Christ! She almost bit off my finger." He waved a Band-Aided forefinger in front of Christie. "I'm maimed for life. Chita hates makeup. Says it ages the skin. Then there's Maureen Corley—she plays Rosa, Juanita's sister— she needs thick body makeup. I could apply it with a shovel, not a brush. Maureen has typical Irish skin. It's like parchment. She doesn't tan, she deep-fat fries. And she freckles. Did you ever try covering peeling skin and freckles with Max Factor 5? Try it some time, you'll like it."

"What else?"

"Alan's beard. A killer. It grows too fast. For the fight with Jasper, he was shaved in the morning. I made him up. By the time Franco was ready to shoot, Alan had a five o'clock shadow. He was shaved again. Made up again. It's been like that every time he's on camera." Julian shook his head.

Christie sipped her second bottle of beer, saying nothing, watching the work in progress.

A sound man was tying a microphone to the end of his boom. The grips were laying the aluminum track on which the camera dolly would roll as the scene progressed. The electricians had finished arranging the lighting. Franco had laid out the setup with Gary Chang, director of photography. He would angle his master shot to take in the small Mexican town with its sixteenth-century church, plaza, and the fine statue of some heroic nineteenth-century revolutionary.

What looked like a family moved slowly across the plaza,

NAKED CALL

led by a barefoot Juanita, in a colorful, striped, ankle-length skirt wrapped around her full hips like a sarong. Above her waist—as was the custom in the town—she was naked. Julian's makeup highlighted copper tones of her lush, rounded breasts, glowing in the sun. Her long, black hair moved with her hip-swaying movements as she glided slowly over the sandy street. She carried a package on her head. Behind her came the bottle-bronzed Rosa—for all his bitching, Christie realized that Julian had performed a miracle. Two women followed the sisters, barefoot and barebreasted, moving with the same, sinuous grace. All were eating bananas and laughing softly, little children at their elbows and a group of men ahead of them. Some ate oranges and spit out the pits on the cobbled stones as they walked.

The package balanced ever so delicately on Juanita's head was no ordinary package, but one covered with white satin, fringed with gold. The package was a small coffin.

Gary Chang was riding the camera dolly, his eyes on the finder, signaling the grips when to push him. Franco moved to the camera and hunched forward on the bucket seat, scanning the scene again and shaping it for composition. Finally he was satisfied. The camera operator climbed into his seat, the assistant director yelled, "Quiet, people!" The funeral march scene in the plaza began.

On Christie's way to the *hacienda* to meet Franco, Jeff persisted in detailing his concern at the cavalier way Franco treated the shooting schedule. And it could get worse.

"There are still sixty-five pages to shoot."

"I know."

At last they reached the *hacienda*, the quarters for the principal members of the cast and crew of *The Feathered Serpent*. What was once the servants' house had been redone as offices for Franco. Here major decisions were made and call sheets for each day's work issued.

Jeff prudently sidled toward the *hacienda* as Christie entered Franco's office. Deep in concentration—marking a script on his desk—Franco didn't look up. When he finally glanced up and saw Christie, his expression became playful.

"I couldn't ask for a more beautiful watchdog." He relaxed, stretched, set his magic marker on the script, and pulled out a bottle of scotch from a desk drawer. "Sorry, no ice. This is Mexico."

Christie pulled up a chair. "I didn't come to drink. I came to tell you that as of today you are two weeks behind schedule. And way the hell over budget."

"Rumors," he grinned. "You know about Hollywood rumors... Mae West was a man."

"These rumors aren't merely rumors. They have a foundation in hard numbers."

His smile became teasing. "We both know I can't be replaced."

"I wasn't thinking of that."

"You don't want to fire me, you want to kill me." His eyes glittered with anger and mischief.

"You're close. Why, Franco? You're no amateur. Why the horsing around—the snail's pace?"

Franco snapped. "You do understand the creative process? This is not *Halloween VI*."

"I hope it makes as much money."

Franco began to gesture. "This script is lousy." He slammed his hand down on the papers.

"Agreed. It's not perfect."

"It's not only not perfect. It's not shootable."

"The Grossmans were too faithful to the novel," Christie admitted. "It won a Pulitzer prize."

"Fuck Pulitzer prizes! Movies aren't books. I've had to rewrite the entire mess. Got rid of the Grossmans, too."

"We'll probably hear from their lawyers. Anyway, let's agree you're a genius." She watched his vanity sit up and salute. "But at the rate you spend money, if *Serpent* isn't a red-hot ticket, United will take a bath. We'll never get our money out, not even with TV rights... video rights... foreign rights."

"How much we in for now?"

"Over twenty million. Going for twenty-five."

"That's not so terrible." He started to laugh. "Art isn't cheap. This picture will be as expensive as it has to be."

The time had come for a little ego blackmail. Christie hunched forward sympathetically. "Franco, it's embarrassing, but Louis insisted I talk to you. I mean... well, he worries that you've lost your nerve. When he agreed to finance *The Feathered Serpent* he was betting on you... your creative talent... energy... your guts. Now he's afraid." She paused for effect. "He's afraid you may be getting too old. It's all the scenes you shoot. Over and over. I understand what you're going for. Perfection. But to Louis it means you're shaky. You are the producer. Maybe you should concentrate on producing. Get a young man on board to wrap up the movie. A director like Spielberg or Lucas, who can work under pressure, who can shoot the rest of the film quickly."

Franco's face had grown progressively paler. "Horse shit! Pure Louis Levy type horse shit! Shitcan it, Christie."

"I'm only the messenger. Don't kill the messenger because you don't like the message. I'll put it simply. Louis worries if you're up to the pace of *The Feathered Serpent*."

"The old fart." Franco stared into space. "Get off my back, Christie. I could do fifty-three setups in a day again, if I had to."

The sore spot was sore enough. "I don't think Louis expects that kind of action. But he wants the picture to come in close to budget. He insists on a Christmas release."

"What do I get in return?"

"Bags of money... great press... maybe an Academy Award. And my admiration." She smiled. "You can't have everything."

Franco laughed. "All right. I'll pick up the pace."

"I'll tell that to Louis."

A young man knocked on the open door. Christie glanced at him and felt a fleeting surprise. He wasn't very tall, yet he had a dark, intimidating presence. His unblinking scrutiny of her made her uncomfortable.

"Matt! Come in!" Franco cried out, glad for the interruption. "Here it is." He pulled out a check from a file folder and waved it in the air like a flag. "Those fucking bean counters in accounting finally sent down a batch of checks to cover the cast's special expenses."

"Hello, Franco." Matt's voice was deep and pleasant. He glanced at Christie.

"I have Jenny's check here. A nice fat check for promotion expenses. Signed by Harry Weiss, United's new controller. And co-signed by Will Weaver, the assistant treasurer. Sixty thousand dollars. You'll like it."

Matt's eyes shifted to Franco. He walked to the desk.

"Here. Take it. Jenny deserves a little something for taking on the media. That's hard work. Blood, sweat, and ... er ... smiles."

Matt carefully folded the check and slipped it into the breast pocket of his loose-fitting, white cotton shirt. "Thank you, Franco."

"You're welcome. Say hello to Christie Larsen. The power behind the signatures on that check."

Matt smiled, his dark, vibrant face lighting up. "A pleasure, Miss Larsen."

Christie nodded, wondering why she hadn't seen him in a film. Having spent most of her adult life among the world's most glamorous men, she was still dazzled by the dark vitality of Matt Renault. Even in his flowing Mexican clothes, she could sense an intense masculinity.

"And tell Chita to stop by for her check to cover that little bungalow expense. The studio is reimbursing her for having a new toilet installed. We want her in good health, but in Mexico one can't be too careful. If Montezuma takes his revenge, at least she'll have a modern toilet. Right, Christie?" His smile was teasing.

"I'll tell her." As he turned to leave the office, Matt gave Christie a long, cataloging appraisal. "I've heard a lot about you, Miss Larsen."

Christie gave him exactly the right smile. "Then you know I don't give autographs."

"Don't worry about it." The laugh lines around his eyes deepened. "I collect baseball cards. But it's been nice meeting you. *Ciao.*"

"Who the hell was that?" Christie asked after he was gone.

"Jenny's live-in stud."

"Is he what the sixty grand is for?"

"For promotion expenses. You heard me."

"He's the promotion."

"A good stud costs money."

"You buried him in the budget?"

"You wanted Jenny Lattimore," Franco said in a pained voice. "Matt Renault goes with the territory."

"At sixty thousand a pop."

"Talent is talent. He wants a new Merc."

"I saw the payroll for the last week of July. It included payments to one director, two stars, one 'also starring' actress, fifteen supporting players, thirty-three extras, one hundred thirty-four crew members, et cetera, et cetera. Over and beyond those expenses—and the actual cost of making the picture itself—there was housing, food, and other fringe benefits. Like Matt." She smiled an old-friend smile. "Wouldn't it have been cheaper to use him as an actor? At SAG minimum? Doesn't he dream of being a star? Instead of a stud? If he swings that way, and a lot of studs do, he could afford his own stud."

"Doesn't everyone want to be a movie star? The first time I met him I thought—why the hell isn't he?"

"Why?"

"I gave him a screen test. He had six before mine. In person he's Robert Redford with dark hair. On camera . . ." Franco raised both hands.

"Flat?" Franco nodded. "No magic?"

"None. Silver nitrate isn't predictable. So he's found his career. He's a natural stud."

"He commands a hell of a price." Christie stood up to leave. "Franco, I respect your talent. But the cost of this movie—including fringe benefits—gives me a headache. It cannot continue."

Franco reached into the jade box on his desk, took out a cigarette, and lit it. "Relax, Christie. You're too nervous." He inhaled and blew a smoke ring towards the ceiling.

Christie realized she had not yet won the match. "By the way," she said, full of friendly concern. "How is your cousin, Paulie? I hear he couldn't finish *Fortune Cookie*. A spot on his lung, I heard. He's in the hospital."

Franco stubbed out his cigarette. "Bitch! Get out, Christie!"

"Bye, Franco. Stay well."

At the door, she gave him a swift backward glance that caught him in the act of dumping the jade box of cigarettes into the wastebasket. "I'll tell Louis you're on the wagon," she said.

"Get out! Or I'll strangle you!"

Walking down the sandy, moonlit path to the *hacienda*, Christie smiled. Maybe there was a justice...blind... honest...impartial. She'd zinged him. If she had, it partially evened the score for every second of misery he'd once given her. Without the misery, she would never have known him. And she did know him...he was exactly the way she remembered. The same chinks in the same armor. Vain as a peacock. Afraid of growing old. Terrified of dying. She'd panicked him. He might even finish the movie within a reasonable time frame, just to prove he could still hack it. A young lion...listen to his roar. A survivor...his words. He had two Academy Awards, proof of how well he survived. What was also true was on the way to the awards he'd left a few corpses rotting in the Hollywood sun. She didn't intend to have her name engraved on another of his tombstones.

PART FOUR
1991

Chapter 8

THE ACTRESS had only half-memorized her lines and glanced frequently at the script.

"Who is she?" a man seated in the nearly empty theater asked.

"Ssssh." The woman sitting beside him dug an elbow into his ribs.

*"Backward I looked at Troy,
But the ship sped on
and Ilium slipped away.
I was dumb with grief."*

"I want to meet her."
"You will. Shut up!"
"When, Irene?"
"Later. Please!"
"Cast party?"
"Guy, this is a rehearsal. I'm having people over later. Now please. Ssssh!"

*"O adulterous marriage!
Helen, fury of ruin!
Let the wind blow
and never bring her home!
Let there be no landing
for Helen of Troy..."*

As Agamemnon spoke his last words, "May all go well in Argos!" the final curtain descended.

"I dislike Greek tragedies. Particularly Sophocles." Guy Macleod slumped in his seat, his eyes closed.

The stunning woman seated at his right looked up from the small pad on which she'd been taking notes. "It's Euripides. Not Sophocles."

"Sophocles? Euripides? What difference does it make? I dislike all Greek tragedies. But the chit playing Polyxena is a pretty thing. Pretty enough to be Helen. Why wasn't she cast as Helen?"

"If you'd come in at the beginning, you'd know that Helen never appears in this play. It's about the Trojan women, not Helen of Troy." The woman leaned forward, fixing her expressive green eyes on Louis Levy, who was seated on Guy Macleod's left. "What do you think of it, Louis?"

"I don't think anything. I'm no judge."

Louis Levy glanced away, not wanting to meet her eyes, and looked around the almost empty theater. Little mounds of cardboard coffee containers, half-eaten sandwiches, and stale doughnuts were strewn around on empty seats or piled in odd corners. The atmosphere on the stage was uneasy. Actors and actresses hung about in silent little groups or chatted with a false camaraderie. The sound of forced gaiety permeated the air. Louis heard the leading actress say to a stagehand, "I think they find a draft and build a theater around it."

"Is this the first rehearsal you've seen, Louis?" Irene Bentley asked.

"On the New York stage, yes."

"You mean they have theaters in Los Angeles?"

"Irene, come off it!" Guy snorted.

"Actually, we have tribal dances," Louis said.

Irene shrugged with good nature. "I deserved that. But Guy told me you dislike theater."

"I don't see enough plays to dislike it."

"He's been in Manhattan five days and he's seen three movies. Eats popcorn and coconut Mounds with the kids. I had to drag him here today . . . kicking and screaming."

"There's a good French movie at the Paris," Louis said.

"Why do you dislike theater? It's the foundation of all the performing arts." Irene gave him a winning smile.

"I don't dislike theater. But every show I wanted to see is sold out for at least the next six weeks. At the movies I just stand in line, wait my turn, go in, and sit down."

"You are not an ordinary tourist," Guy pointed out. "You don't have to go to the box office for tickets. I'll get you tickets to any show in town."

"You'll ask friends?"

"I can get you house seats to any show," Irene added graciously. "They would even be free." She laughed.

"Thank you, but I can get my own house seats. I wanted to see what Just Plain Bill and The Little Woman go through to see a hit," Louis took a deep breath. "Frankly, it's a lousy system."

"He does have a point, Guy." Irene pursed her lips. "It is hideous for Just Plain Bill. That's why I'm interested in films. You reach a wider audience."

Louis heard the woman's velvet tones and recognized the signal. He'd been waiting for it.

"I'm delighted you came, Louis. The smell of grease paint is good for your soul. Although I admit rehearsals are not exciting, not glamorous. They're usually pure hell! But what did you think of what you saw?"

"It would make a great movie," Louis murmured.

"For heavens sake—no! Please! No movie called *Helen of Troy*!"

"Why not? The budget would be outrageous—but the box office could be great. Helen of Troy has sex appeal."

"It's a cute idea," Guy chuckled. "For United Cinema. Lots of gorgeous Grecian queens . . . delicious looking slaveys."

"It's a terrible idea," Irene pouted.

"It's as good as Cleopatra," Louis dreamed.

"Louis, darling, Greek tragedies make rotten movies." She studied him. "But if you're thinking of doing an upscale feature that will also make great box office, wait until I mount *Deirdre*."

"*Deirdre? Deirdre of the Sorrows?*"

Irene's eyes sparkled. "What a surprise!"

"How did you know?" Guy asked.

"I read. Moving my lips," Louis said.

"You're amazing," Irene said.

"You mean for a movie mogul?" Louis gave a small knee jerk of annoyance. "I'm literate."

"Well—yes. I do mean *Deirdre of the Sorrows* by John Millington Synge."

"I don't see it."

"Wait until opening night. *Deirdre* will be a smash. You'll see the name splashed all over the newspapers. The news magazines. On television. It's the agony of young love. The heartbreak kids. Deirdre will be as famous as Juliet. You do know about Romeo and Juliet?" She smiled mischievously. "My production will make history. I'm casting it now."

Irene Bentley wasn't very tall, but she was striking. Her luxuriant red hair was brushed straight back from her forehead and hung to her shoulders. She was not only beautiful in the conventional sense, but she had an uncommon distinction, an individual style of her own, that lent everything she did a special importance. It was a gift that seemed to be peculiarly hers alone. But it struck Louis that he'd seen it somewhere before.

She gave him a quick, conspiratorial smile. "There's no business like show business. Is there? Guy will bring you over to my place later. Twelveish. You'll meet the whole cast, and we'll get to know each other." She slid gracefully to the end of the row, turned, threw them a kiss, and moved up the dark aisle.

Louis watched her go. He was fascinated by the vibrancy and force of the woman, but something about her was disturbingly familiar.

"It should be an interesting evening," Guy muttered. "A change from Wall Street and cash flows."

"I'm tired," Louis said. "I think I'll turn in early. We have a big meeting tomorrow."

"But a friendly meeting. You need entertainment, Louis. Irene will be very disappointed if you don't show."

Either she was Guy's woman or his pimp... or both, Louis decided. "She'll survive," he said, rising to his feet. "I am tired. Give her my apologies. I'll see you tomorrow in the office."

"Spoilsport," Guy called after him.

As Louis edged his way out of the aisle, he glanced at Irene Bentley, who was lecturing the producer. He stared at her, feeling angry, confused, ineffective. Why did he think he knew her? And why had Guy insisted that he meet her? What kind of hold did she have on him? His thoughts veered to Guy Macleod. Why had he accepted Guy at face value? Because of Guy's credentials, that was why. A wealthy, blue-blooded WASP. Actually, he knew more about Stavros Lennos...knew his blood type...Mafia positive. He really knew nothing about Guy. He'd been blindsided by the street kid who lived within him. By his own vanity that he, a boy from the wrong side of the Bronx—were there any right sides these days?—was being wooed by the Oh-So-Social Macleods. He shook his head to clear it. He had no reasonable reason for this sudden attack of the jitters. Only a hunch based on the sight of one woman. He was probably suffering stage fright at selling United. He was... Suddenly it hit him. The shock of recognition. He'd seen that face before—often. Who would believe it? Anyone who had ever made a film in Hollywood, that's who.

By the time he reached the lobby, his head was aching. He, Louis Levy, had made a world-class blunder. He should have shopped Wall Street for a banking house. If he'd been his usual self, he would have. But his nerves were shot and, like a man who had been too long under heavy fire, he broke and ran for cover. Straight into Guy Macleod's arms. Shit! He shut his eyes for an instant in self-disgust. It was Hollywood gallows humor—in the same tradition as the legendary Marilyn's legendary crack, "Who do I fuck to get out of this movie?"

Apocryphal or not, Marilyn's wry quip perfectly described his state of mind.

It looked like any other morning on Broadway and Pine Street. The turbulent, desiring world of Wall Street sparkled and gleamed with energy and color. A runner elbowed his way between people on their way to work, racing to satisfy an early-bird dealer. Two women in dress-for-success suits, each carrying a red leather attaché case, chatted on their way into a building. At the street vendor's fast food establishment, several clerks breakfasted on bagels and coffee. Two cops stared with admiration at a Brink's armored car and its guards, who were unloading dozens of highly insured satchels of money. A construction worker lumbered north toward a half-built skyscraper and two street people drifted along, indifferent to the purpose of these purposeful natives.

At Amando's on the second floor of a twenty-story office building on Pine Street, hair was being styled—not cut—in the newest mode for young men and women on the rise. There was no longer an Amando at Amando's but the business flourished in the shrewd hands of his daughter, Rosarita, and under the nimble fingers of his three sons, Amando the Second, Umberto, and Stephano. Easy cuts were seventy-five dollars. Special cuts started at one hundred dollars. For five hundred dollars you got the works.

Though all the brothers were popular, Amando the Second—known to friends as Secondo—was the house favorite. But since he divided his time between the salon, TV studios, backstage theater, and house calls, Secondo was often unavailable. On this day Secondo was in residence in the salon, but, tragically, his residence had been temporarily shifted from its semi-exclusive position on the small balcony overlooking the shop to the main floor. The balcony was being refurbished. He was forced to dance attendance on one of his regulars in a booth on the main floor adjacent to his brothers, Umberto and Stephano, and other relatives. All were busy with their own card-holding clients . . . naturally American Express platinum.

Secondo's client was Kevin MacIntyre, a senior partner at Macleod Brothers. He and Guy Macleod had much in common, including a taste for raunchy sex, Savile Row clothes, and Secondo. While Secondo snipped a lock here and trimmed a stray hair there, Kevin held forth on his importance in the firm to a new partner, Sherwood Anderson—importance proven by the fact that Guy MacLeod, in his infinite wisdom, with Kevin standing resolutely at his side, was about to take over United Cinema.

"What's the big deal? Why the hell would anyone want United Cinema?" Sherwood asked from his seat in the ringside arm chair one of the sweepers had hauled into the booth to accommodate Kevin's guest. "Movie studios have a multiple of three. The assets drive in and out the entrance gate."

"Use your bean," Kevin said, his mind elsewhere. "Secondo, go easy on top. There isn't much there."

Secondo looked pained. "Mr. MacIntyre, please. I'm nothing if not reliable."

"There's always a first time."

Secondo sniffed arrogantly while Anderson waited for the byplay to end. Then he plunged. "Maybe I took stupid pills, but I don't follow your thinking. U.C. does not own hotels or shopping malls. Christ! MGM, Paramount, Columbia—they used to own real estate. Disney still owns Disneyland! In Anaheim, Tokyo, Florida, Paris..."

"Outside Paris."

"Close enough. That's a property."

"We don't need a theme park, buddy boy." MacIntyre stared at the mirror, following Secondo's scissors. "What about my ears, Secondo? Annabelle—my latest—thinks my beard makes my ears look too large."

"She's wrong. Your beard is the perfect accent. Mmmm ... though I could trim it back just a smidgen. Mmmm ... perhaps it is time to rethink your hair. Yes, when you leave here, your ears will be in perfect balance with your beard. It's a matter of the way your hair is combed."

MacIntyre studied himself in the mirror. He was a ruddy-faced man with a neat, pointed, blond beard, and a round head perched on a thick, creased neck, the result of too much rich food. His face, with its rounded surfaces, had a look of jovial wiliness. His inspection completed, he turned his full attention to his anxious partner.

"You're still not using your bean, old friend. U.C. has all kinds of hidden assets."

"Sure. Like its film library. I'll give you that. But besides the film library, all it has is a movie-making capability. They can make movies and TV features. Nothing else. We'd have to raze the entire studio to sell off the real estate. And what would that amount to? A lousy few acres."

"We're not buying it for the real estate, buddy boy. We're buying it for its multiple."

"Like I said. Three."

"Crap! All they need is a box office winner and the stock can move ten points in a day. Movie studios have glamour." A lascivious glint appeared in his small brown eyes. "Sex appeal."

"Shit! It can go up ten points—or down fifteen if they

make a bomb." Buddy Boy took a deep drag on his cigarette. He had a long narrow head, black hair, and cautious gray eyes devoid of loyalty. "There's no fallback position if they bomb out."

"That's half the fun. It's a pure play. We get to kick the gong around." Kevin grinned. "We can ride it up. Short it on the way down."

"I don't like pure plays. We're investment bankers, not race track gamblers." Sherwood grew short of breath, as though his custom-made jacket, tightly buttoned over his wide shoulders and thick chest, was smothering him. "Guy allowed me the privilege of buying half a percent of Macleod Brothers' stock. That snappy half of one percent cost me three million George Washingtons . . . a nice chunk of my meat and potatoes reserve. So far I don't regret a nickel. We've had a great six months, and I want more of the same. The firm's rock solid, but owning a movie studio—with no assets—doesn't strike me as a rock-solid investment."

"Sherwood, show a little imagination. You need imagination to make money." Kevin paused to emphasize his point. "There's big bucks here. And the money's only the half of it."

"It is? Okay, I'll bite. What's the other half?"

"The perks of the movie business. The broads, you dimwit. The girls with big breasts, round hips, and long, naturally blond hair."

"I'm a married man."

"Who isn't? What's one thing got to do with the other? Listen, Sherwood, why do you work your ass off? For money, sure. Also for a little fun. Yes?" His voice grew oily. "Think of yourself at sixty. A rich man . . . rich enough to own a yacht. But what good does the money do you? Or the yacht? No broad will give you a tumble. You roll in the sheets alone. Or play with yourself. Unless you pay cash on the bureau for it." He made a disgusted sound. "Some future! What does an aging millionaire do for a good-looking piece of ass if all he can offer is money?"

Sherwood's face was suffused with a look of bewilderment. "I'll worry about that when I'm sixty."

"You won't have to worry about a thing. A man who owns a movie studio is a producer." Kevin licked his lips.

"Yeah, a bona fide producer. He can launch a starlet. Maybe even a star, if she's got talent outside the bed. Think about it. We'll be provided for in our old age. And not by bimbos. By genuine beauties. They're doing it for love."

"Ha!"

"The creamy breasts swell. The nipples grow hard. The luscious thighs spread to welcome us. Goddamn! I can hardly wait to retire."

"Mona would divorce me."

"Mona doesn't have to know."

"She'd find out."

"So what? You could marry a starlet."

"It's Mona's money."

There was a moment of silence before Kevin MacIntyre continued more soberly. "I'm glad you told me now. Maybe we can work something out. But keep your priorities straight. The movie business is a money machine . . . a sex machine . . . a fountain of youth."

A man in a chair in a booth adjacent to Kevin MacIntyre was having his hair styled by Umberto. He was one of Umberto's regulars, but unlike most of Umberto's customers, he rarely spoke. The young stylist dared not interrupt his concentration. Umberto knew why he received an occasional thousand dollar tip. It wasn't for his talent at hair styling—this client would have been equally satisfied in a barber shop. It was for keeping his mouth shut, and opening it only when he had a choice piece of gossip hot off the Wall Street grapevine, which was always budding with the fruit of pure imagination, eager rumors, and occasionally twenty-one-karat fact. Umberto had said his say in muted tones, and the man paid little attention. He was listening to Kevin MacIntyre. When Kevin's resonant voice switched from movie money to movie sex the man's eyes grew bored, then concentrated . . . cruel. The man was weighing what he'd heard. It frightened Umberto to think what must have gone into the making of those eyes.

15 William Street was a twenty-five-story brick building that had stood for almost seventy years, making its quiet statement . . . very old money. Unlike 1 New York Plaza,

it was non-glitzy. It did not flaunt its wealth, its megabuck deals, its greed. In New York City, which is constantly undergoing an architectural face-lift, such an ancient relic in another part of the city might have housed a wholesale jewelry company or a detective agency. But in the heart of the financial district, the land on which the building stood was worth about seventy-five million dollars, give or take a few million. And to those who knew, or those with an eye for the sociology of money, it was apparent that the building was a temple of power.

There were two brass front doors, the brass polished to a glossy sheen. The doors did not revolve. Anyone wanting to enter 15 William Street must do what all previous generations had done—pull. Once through the gleaming doors and standing inside the awesomely silent lobby, a visitor might have the impression that somewhere a choir was singing. The ground floor hall leading to the elevator bank was travertine marble and clean enough to eat off, as a banker's wife once remarked. The ceiling molding was decorated with gold leaf as rich as the gold leaf framing Old Masters. When a visitor or native reached the elevator bank, there was always one of the four self-service elevators waiting. And something more: a trim, gray-uniformed elevator man to press the button for the proper floor. 15 William Street was the only building in the Wall Street financial district that still employed elevator men.

Macleod Brothers insisted on keeping the elevator men. The investment banking house occupied the first four floors of 15 William Street and had done so since the day in 1920 when the building first opened. The firm had its own private entrance at the corner of the building, its own private staircase between floors, and, since 1937 when Simon and Guy Macleod's grandfather—Simon Macleod, Sr.—had it installed after his first stroke, its own private elevator and elevator man. Guy Macleod used the elevator frequently. When a partner needed Guy's okay on the price of a stock offering and Guy was irritatingly unavailable, the partner might lurk near the elevator, hoping to corner him. Guy enjoyed the cat and mouse game. When he sensed a partner waiting to corner him, he climbed the stairs. Simon Macleod never used the elevator and was available to everyone, including back office personnel.

The third floor of Macleod Brothers housed two good-sized private dining rooms and one smaller room reserved for use by the Macleod Brothers, Guy and Simon. All three rooms served breakfast, lunch, and dinner with white-jacketed waiters moving silently among the diners. In the Macleods' own dining room, guests sat down to lunch in red leather, gold-studded, Chippendale chairs set around a Sheraton mahogany table. The table setting was Spode Fitzhugh china and Queen Anne silver atop a snowy linen tablecloth that carried the Macleod family crest along its borders, as did the linen napkins. To compensate for the lack of a view, the walls were papered with a handpainted mural of Wall Street at the turn of the century. The gleaming teakwood floor was covered with a large, lustrous, antique Tabriz rug. Charles Macleod, who had supervised the most recent refurbishing, disliked wall-to-wall carpeting.

And perhaps nowhere on Wall Street was the food as good—or as nutritious—as it was at the Macleod dining rooms. The manager of the kitchen, Jean Pierre Bosc, was a graduate of the Ecole Hotelier in Lausanne, Switzerland and the Cordon Bleu in Paris. On his arrival in the early eighties, Jean Pierre quickly adapted to the American obsession with health. It was an obsession especially prevalent among very rich men, often more sheltered from high taxes than high cholesterol or high blood pressure. Jean Pierre soon concluded that the wealthier the man, the more prone to heart attack, stroke, and sundry other medical inconveniences. Countless studies had fixed the blame—the appetizers, entrees, and desserts they were accustomed to eating, dishes that made lavish use of butter, cream, sugar, *et al*. These were the guilty parties bankrupting the body. The shifting tastes of the rich American caused an uproar in *haute cusine* restaurants. Spaghetti—now called pasta—was seen on the finest menus, there was a sushi revolution, and swordfish exceeded filet mignon in popularity and price. The new crop of rich men planned to live forever.

Taking his cue from his brethren in other private dining rooms, Jean Pierre added to his staff, besides his stylish chef, a dedicated nutritionist, whose bedtime enjoyment was reading *Topics in Clinical Nutrition*, *The Berkeley Wellness Letter*, and reports from the National Institutes of Health. She kept abreast with the profit and loss statements on survival. The classic French cuisine at the Macleod dining room was lighter and simpler than Louis Levy enjoyed. The midday meal might consist of a cold watercress vichyssoise, veal chop cordon bleu, stuffed tomato with ratatouille, sautéd snow peas, and fresh blueberries or strawberries for dessert. Pastries were available but frowned upon. Louis understood. The same quest for immortality went on in L.A. As for himself, he would trust his genetics. He'd die at ninety-seven, as had his father before him. He ordered a chocolate mousse for dessert.

Guy Macleod leaned back in his chair, relaxed and at ease. He was in his middle forties—tall, lean, and elegant, with regular features and a head of thick black hair that he parted on the left side and wore just a touch too long. Impeccably turned out, he wore a chocolate-brown, custom-tailored Savile Row suit and handmade brown shoes. In his own way, he was an icon on Wall Street. He had all the cachet . . . a patrician background, a substantial fortune, intelligence, and an eccentric but impressive track record. Actually, everything about him, including his smile and his arrogant manner, seemed monogrammed. His life was grounded on the premise that some men, like himself, were more equal than others . . . that his ideas were brilliant, if somewhat unconventional, and would lead to a glorious future. He dreamed of doing for Macleod Brothers what the formidable J.P. had done for the Morgan Bank . . . of returning to the time when a handshake over lunch at the club was enough to guarantee a five hundred million dollar bond placement. Macleod Brothers would be a unique power on Wall Street . . . and he would be the power behind the power of the bank. It was an article of faith: his destiny.

"You drive a hard bargain, Louis. Eight hundred million dollars is not cheap." Guy smiled.

"I'm told it is. But I haven't shopped the deal."

"I appreciate your loyalty."

Louis thought about the word and decided that it was due

to some higher form of loyalty that he was selling United at all: a loyalty that made it impossible for him to bury his memory of Jessie's blood on the sheets any longer. "Eight hundred million is enough."

"I should think so. You have a seat on the board."

"I'm Chairman of the Board."

"Emeritus." Guy raised an eyebrow.

Louis knew he was being baited and his face remained impassive. "A consultant on all movie deals."

"Yes. But corporate headquarters will be transferred to New York."

Louis sipped his coffee.

"I'll have Sullivan and Sawyer draw up the papers for immediate signature."

Louis said nothing.

It was not Guy's denseness but his acute sensitivity that prevented him from questioning the reasons for Louis' glum face. "By Friday we can have the whole package signed and sealed."

Louis signalled the waiter for more coffee. A hint of irritation showed in his eyes. "Nothing can be signed until we agree on Clause 23B."

Guy gave him a sidewise glance. "The rider you added at the last minute. You still insist on it?"

"You know I do."

"Why? I'm dense."

"I'll sleep easier."

"That's no answer." The good-humored smile.

"It's the best I can do."

"You've been in town two weeks. The contract was finalized. Now this. What happened?" Guy's expression had slowly evolved from friendly sympathy to unfriendly calculation.

"I want to be sure you'll make great movies."

"I want to, also. I mean to employ top people. I have a list of names—"

"Fine. And to help you sift through those names of top producers, let's add that rider. Clause 23B."

"You mean to make it an issue?"

Louis nodded. He was thinking of a rehearsal in a dimly lit theater.

At that moment, Simon Macleod entered.

"Nice of you to come." Guy's normally cold Calvinist eyes lit up with a combination of genuine pleasure and irritation.

"Sorry, I'm late. Lunch is a bitch. My boys are still cleaning house on Intercoastal. It ain't easy to dump 300,000 shares of a company without making a stink. If the odor drifted downwind, Salomon Brothers or Merrill Lynch could sniff it. The stock would fall out of bed before we're clean." Simon pulled up a chair opposite Louis as a waiter appeared with a sandwich, salad, black coffee, and a plate of strawberries.

"What's that?" Louis asked.

"A rare roast beef sandwich. They know what I like. English mustard and no mayonnaise. Usually I eat at my desk."

Louis nodded and decided he liked Simon. He seemed to fill the room with energy. Still, it was his calmness that soothed Louis. He was a few years younger than Guy, as fair as Guy was dark. He was saved from being too handsome by a narrow, straight nose with a scar across the bridge, a wide, thin-lipped mouth, a heavy, square jaw over which the skin was tightly drawn. Like the well-coordinated athlete he was, his movements were both economical and sure, his voice deep and low, displaying an inborn self assertion that had nothing to do with aggression. Unlike Guy, he was no dandy. Conservatively dressed in a three piece gray suit, white shirt, and gray-striped tie, one might have thought him to be the managing partner. He wasn't. Guy was.

Guy interrupted Louis' musing by describing the terms of the United buy out to his brother. "Everything's settled except the rider, Clause 23B. What do you think about it?"

Simon continued to eat.

"Simon!"

"You know what I think, Guy. About this whole Hollywood fandango. Louis knows it, too. Why beat a dead horse?"

"You haven't changed your mind?" Louis asked, sipping his coffee. "Even after seeing the last five years' earnings?"

Simon bit into his sandwich and swallowed before answering. "No. Not even after you said we get annual passes to every new movie, plus free popcorn and chocolate bonbons."

Louis laughed defensively. "If you dislike the project so much, could you suggest another house who would be more enthusiastic?"

Simon's eyes met Guy's and for an instant the air was charged with electricity. Then the storm receded. "I'm sorry," Simon said. "My comment was uncalled for. How I feel does not affect the enthusiasm of the firm for the deal."

"You don't like the idea of owning a movie company?" Louis asked sharply.

"I'm in favor of the firm taking United public. But for us to own a movie studio . . . it's nuts. It's not our business."

"We won't own United. We'll be offering forty-nine percent of the stock to the public," Guy said shortly.

"Forty-nine percent of our one hundred percent. We damn well will own it. And we're damn fools to get into a business we don't understand." He delivered the balance of his remark without emotion, like a police sergeant giving evidence in court. "We're not producers, directors, writers, performers. We're investment bankers, stock and bond traders. We know Wall Street inside out. What the hell do we know about making movies. We know nothing."

"That's why I insist on Clause 23B," Louis pointed out.

"We've been through this before, Simon. Enough!" Guy's voice carried authority. "What do you think of 23B?"

Simon finished his sandwich before looking at Guy. Because he loved his father, he had made him a promise, and now he had to bear the burden of that promise. "I've said my say. Make up your own mind. I won't do it for you."

Guy stirred his cup of coffee and then glanced at Louis.

"This Clause 23B? It's a deal breaker?"

Louis was silent. There was so much he hadn't foreseen . . . *Helen of Troy* . . . *Deirdre* . . . Irene Bentley. At last he spoke. "It's a deal breaker. If you don't agree, other Wall Street houses will. Simon can introduce me and be rid of United."

Guy was silent for a heartbeat. He rose from the table. "I'll think about it, Louis. I'll call you tomorrow."

"Do that." Louis knew that Guy was bluffing. For some reason, Guy had made up his mind to own United. For an instant he worried about what Simon was thinking. He decided it was better for his peace of mind that he didn't know.

Louis rose and followed Guy from the dining room... dismissing the dispute as simply an ordinary disagreement between brothers. He was understandably mistaken, but he could hardly be expected to know the brothers' history. Nor could he have guessed Simon's real feelings. Simon knew Guy, knew his brother was one of the shrewdest investment bankers on The Street. Guy understood that a movie studio without assets was an amateur's play. Why was he doing this? What the hell was going on? If he asked Guy, his brother would look blank. Their father had warned Simon it would be a long, dark tunnel all the way. God only knew what the cost would be at the end. All he could do for now was wait... and watch. Until the bill was presented.

Chapter 9

THEATER 55 was on 55th Street in New York City, between Broadway and Eighth Avenue, the last remaining small Broadway theater in the city. In 1973, Irene Bentley had shown the foresight, optimism, and grit to sell her Fourth Street Theater in the East Village and negotiate for over a year to buy Theater 55. In 1974, when the city faced bankruptcy—and Manhattan real estate hit rock bottom— the owner of the property finally sold the theater to Irene for a fraction of its appraised value. By the mid-eighties, Irene Bentley had received several seven-figure offers for the property. This pleased and amused her. Showing a proper respect for seven figures, Irene dined with all would-be buyers, slept with some, and said a firm, "Thank you but no thank you," to all. Those she selected to take to her bed often became backers. The property never became part of the site of a high-rise office building or a ten-level garage. It remained a theater . . . the exclusive home of Irene Bentley Productions.

The theater was almost empty except for the performers on the stage and a stage manager who slouched in the darkened hall in the orchestra eating a Hershey bar. On the stage two actresses, both in jeans and T-shirts, and five actors wearing chinos or jeans and T-shirts, sat in the semicircle of chairs facing a wooden table. Irene Bentley, in a khaki skirt and cotton blouse, perched on the table swinging her leg.

"Let's take that again, Holly . . . more grasp of who you are. You are not Medea, queen of all sorrows, about to kill your two children." Irene's voice was soft but authoritative. "You are Deirdre, the young, pagan princess of Ireland in the eighth century A.D. At sixteen, your destiny is fixed. You were raised for one purpose—to marry Conchobar, the king of the five parts of Ireland . . . an old man of thirty-two. But you were sunning yourself on a rock and you saw Naoise ride by, bare-assed. Your little clitoris twitters at the thought of him. You forget the prophecy of disaster—that you are destined to destroy the kingdom of the five parts of Ireland. All you think of is Naoise. So pick it up, Holly. More lilt. Save doom and gloom for Act Three."

This was the first reading of *Deirdre of the Sorrows*, the play Irene was mounting for her fall production. As usual, the actors were lifeless . . . nervous . . . twitchy.

Holly's voice was deep and rich. She affected a slight Irish brogue.

"I will dress like Emer in Dundaelgan, or Maeve in her house in Connaught if Conchobar'll make me a queen. I'll have the right of a Queen who is the master, taking her own choice and making a stir to the edge of the sea. . . ."

The cordless telephone on the table rang softly. The reading stopped as Irene picked it up. She did not wait for the caller to introduce him or herself. She spoke as though giving stage directions, and because the telephone was equipped with a voice shield, it was impossible for any of the actors to hear what she said.

"Bring it up after the shooting this evening. Over drinks ... cigarettes ... fucking ... be offhand ... casual. Think out loud. Become enthusiastic. A few seconds of sparkle, then, as soon as he shows real interest, drop it. Change the subject. Do it awkwardly. Talk about Mexican food ... the customs ... landscape. Anything. When he questions you, put him off ... fumble ... stumble around. If you can blush, blush. Finally, unwillingly, say why you're worried. You were told not to mention it. Irene Bentley is temperamental. All creative geniuses are. Isn't he, Franco Marconi, temperamental? Laugh appealingly. Irene will cut your throat if she finds out that you told him about *Deirdre*. They've been driving her crazy with offers. She's been flooded with calls from Hollywood directors panting for an artistic triumph ... with box office pizzazz. A tits and ass classic. Lousy with young sex. It can't miss. *Time* magazine ... *Newsweek* ... *Vanity Fair* ... *People* ... all the dental office mags are doing pieces on it. A sure winner. Yes ... yes ... assume he knows it. He's educated. Knows all about great plays. It simply didn't occur to him. Take a deep breath. Beg him to stay away. Right now, Irene has neither the time nor the patience to think about Hollywood. Then fuck him again. Or say you're hungry. Get up and get out. And shut up." A pause. "Do you understand how I want you to handle it? Yes, that's what I mean. That's what I mean. That's a good thought. Go for it, Maureen. I expect a riveting performance. Good-bye." She put down the telephone, and looked at the waiting cast seated in their chairs, squirming nervously.

"Go on with the reading, Holly." she said calmly.

Holly went on.

"... I'll put on my robes that are the richest, for I will not be brought down to Emain as Cuchulain brings his horse to the yoke, or Conall Ceameach puts his shield upon his arm; and maybe from this day I will turn the men of Ireland like a wind blowing on the heath ..." She paused for breath and glanced at Irene for approval.

Not a single person in the theater overestimated the powers of Irene Bentley ... including herself.

NAKED CALL

* * *

Guy Macleod and Sol Stein did not lunch in the Macleod Brothers dining room. That would start talk. Instead they lunched at the City Athletic Club where Sol was a member. Guy had agreed to the City AC with indifference. He was a member of more clubs than he remembered—including the New York Athletic Club, the Racquet Club, the Union League Club, the Harvard Club. If Stein's name had been Sullivan, they would have lunched at the New York AC where the food was no better and no worse than the City AC. Guy considered all club food pedestrian... Christian or Jewish. But since Sol's last name was Stein, his emblem of business and social status in Manhattan was the City AC.

"This Clause 23B came up out of the blue?" Stein asked.

"It's a whim. Louis is flexing his muscles."

Guy looked across the table at Stein. He saw a lean, bony-faced man in a seersucker suit and a narrow-striped tie, with thinning brown hair that was combed back from a high forehead. A full mustache bristled under his long, straight nose. Dark eyes like wet tar contrasted with his pale skin. He looked like what he was: a smart, Jewish professional. Doctor, lawyer, banker... they all looked somewhat alike. Stein was a lawyer—among L.A.'s best—who had the brains to stay out of the California sun.

"If he's made up his mind about Clause 23B," Stein said into his chicken salad, "he won't change it. Louis is a mule."

"Tell me something I don't know." Guy toyed with the cold roast beef on his plate. "What happens if I don't agree?"

"I beg your pardon?"

"I'll spell it out," Guy said with annoyance. "What happens if I sign the contract as drafted?"

"Including Clause 23B?"

"Yes."

Stein leaned back. Guy Macleod had always been a puzzle to him. The man's mind was a maze. What secret track was he following now? "If you sign it as drafted, that's it. It's a closing."

"And after I sign the contract, I find reason to..."

"... violate the contract?" Sol had a talent as serviceable

as his knowledge of contract law—an authentic instinct for the double cross.

"Colorful word— 'violate.' "

"As your lawyer, I would advise you against it. A contract is a binding agreement."

"You sound positive."

Stein shrugged. "With all respect, Guy, I am positive."

"Contracts have been broken."

"Bad business practice," Stein said stolidly. "You've signed contracts before. You initial the bottom of each page. You sign at the bottom of the last page. It's witnessed. It's got the corporate seal, plus all the rest of the legal shit. Once that's done, the contract is a binding document. To violate it is illegal." He meant to sound stern. "What the hell is this about? Do you want me to renegotiate the deal?"

"Pointless. As you said, Louis won't budge."

"You still want the company?

"Yes."

Sol Stein had flown almost 3,000 miles to have lunch with Guy Macleod, knowing the lunch would be a nightmare. Guy was an irascible but important client. Jessup, Overstreet & Stein had enough California high tech, real estate, aerospace, communications, fast food clients. The problem was Jessup, *et al* had no financial client with clout . . . and no major entertainment client. Guy was the firm's way into both—this big one mustn't get away. The conversation was going poorly, being for Stein a milling confusion of half-perceived suspicions and unstated purposes. He decided on a show of authority.

"To violate the contract is . . . I'm sorry to say . . . to be honest, sheer lunacy."

"Lunacy?" It was Guy's turn to have elevated eyebrows. "I repeat. Contracts have been broken."

"Unless there is a justifiable reason, if you violate the terms you can be sued for big bucks. Louis is the man to do it, too. Unfortunately, I don't think Clause 23B gives you a justifiable reason."

"She's a woman."

"Maybe I'm naive." Stein hoped to sound anything but naive. "But I fail to see that as a drawback."

"It isn't always. It depends on who the woman is."

NAKED CALL

Patience, mystification; Sol clung to them both. "You have someone else in mind?"

"No one."

"Then why not her? I've investigated her thoroughly, as you requested. Her reputation is impeccable. Her business deals are sharp and smart. Her word is good. I wouldn't say she's well-liked, but she is respected. Why not her?"

Sol noted Guy was torn between giving a satisfactory, but possibly indiscreet, answer or seeming childishly stubborn. He did neither; he changed directions.

"Why not well-liked?"

"She's not Hollywood."

"What the devil does that mean?"

"She isn't one of the town's own. She's an outsider. You see Hollywood is . . ." Sol was vamping until ready. "Hollywood is . . . well, I think of it as the ultimate company town. A town of insiders. She's not an insider. And the insider crowd doesn't go for outsiders."

"I'd think if anyone belonged, she would."

"She doesn't."

"Why not?"

"No simple answer. Maybe it's because she's nobody's daughter. She's not the daughter of a famous director, or a performer, or a studio head. So she's not a member of the old Hollywood aristocracy—if there is such a thing. I mean even metaphorically . . . Or maybe it's because she hasn't screwed the right men. No famous actor ever left his shoes under her bed. You see, it's the Hollywood mystique . . . the mores, the *modus operandi*. It's all unclear . . . elusive. Frankly, I don't understand it myself. Maybe it's because she's not part of the network. She doesn't lunch with powerhouse agents or breakfast with high priced writers. She's rarely seen at a big bash—like the star-studded Yulefest Marvin Davis held for five hundred intimate friends. Her one slip into celebrityhood was her reported hot fling with Franco Marconi."

"Marconi? The director?"

"The incomparable, et cetera, son of a bitch. One could almost say Hollywood has never heard of Christie Larsen. One marriage, one divorce . . . no scandal, no mess. She drives a standard American Cadillac Eldorado. Not a

Mercedes, a Rolls, an Excalibur. She doesn't shop at Gelson's supermarket. More likely, she goes to Lucky. She doesn't live in a thirty-room mansion that she can't afford dreaming of Aaron Spelling's 55,000-foot football stadium. Her style is closer to Michael Milken. As you know, Milken's worth close to a billion dollars. Probably could sell Spelling, if Spelling was a junk bond. But Milken lived quietly in a 5,000 foot house in Encino . . . before going to the clink. The man liked his privacy. So does the lady. Home is a house in the West Hollywood Hills. Lives there with her son and one housekeeper. No one else. Not three boyfriends—or three girlfriends for that matter. She keeps to herself. So the industry pretends she doesn't exist. Makes no difference that she's been with United Cinema for twelve years, been at Louis' right hand for eight. Hollywood is obsessed with publicity. Celebrityhood is glamour. Notoriety is glamour. She's not celebrated . . . or notorious. She's not Hollywood. Christie Larsen is still 'Christie Who?'"

Guy's face was impassive as he took this all in. "If she's so much an outsider, how can she function?"

"She has Louis behind her. The Chairman of the Board of the Insider Club. Also, she's smart. That gets whispered around. So she's handled gingerly, at arm's length. I think what really bugs the insiders most is she doesn't seem to notice that they don't notice her. She doesn't give a damn." Stein shrugged. "I say, so what? Her job isn't winning a popularity contest. It's watching the bottom line. She's done that very well. She's honest and very sharp with numbers. She'll give you budgets that make sense."

"Meaningless. Any accountant could do it."

"Nope." Stein concentrated on Guy. "Movies aren't tubes of toothpaste. To make movies that make money, you need shrewd creative judgement . . . box office savvy. She has that, too. Most accountants don't."

There was an awkward silence. At last Guy said, "It's not good enough."

"Why not?"

"She belongs to Louis." Unwillingly, Guy showed a card.

"So?" Stein was still at sea. "You and Louis have the

same aim. To make a big-buck-making movies. Isn't that why you're buying United?"

Guy's answer was slow in coming. "Yes. But movies cost millions. What if we disagree? She could be wrong. One bad deal can really hurt a studio."

"Okay. But keep in mind, movies are her territory. Yours is Wall Street." Stein decided to stand tall. "When it comes to movies, I'd put my money on her."

"You're probably right. I still don't want her."

More wheels within wheels. "You want someone who belongs to you alone?"

Guy paused and seemed to think. "Praying over my money."

"She's honest . . ." Sol swallowed the rest of his remark as he saw Guy's lips compress. "You want a watchdog."

"Something like that."

It was with a little lighter heart than at the start of the lunch that Stein continued the conversation. At last he had a clue as to what the hell was going on. "Let's see if we can find someone to watch over Clause 23B in another department who will be working closely with her."

"That's a thought."

"Better than going for a violation."

"How about production?"

"No. The staff line producers could leave at any time. And a producer who comes to United to produce a film is there on a one or two picture deal. You want a corporate type . . ." Sol took a shot in the dark. ". . . how about the treasurer? Mannie something. . . ."

"Mannie Wolf? Useless."

"A useless treasurer? He signs the checks. He won't let anyone play games with costs."

"Mannie Wolf retired. The new man is Harry Weiss. Louis has known him for years. Anyway, I don't need a numbers man. Weiss will be sending me detailed weekly reports. I can read numbers as well as he can. I need someone who reads people."

"I've an idea," Stein said, hoping he did.

"Yes?"

"Stanley Silver retired last week. He had a massive coronary on the eighteenth hole of the Riviera Country Club, so there's an opening for chief corporate counsel. Counsel works closely with our Lady of the Technicolor. Counsel draws the contracts."

A calm settled over Guy. "Any suggestions?"

"I'm thinking."

"How about you?"

Stein gave him a startled look. "You're not serious?"

Guy laughed for the first time. "No. I won't embarrass you by listening to phony excuses. The truth is I wouldn't pay you enough. Right?"

Stein gave him a weak smile.

"As is, I pay you a fortune as outside counsel." Guy stopped smiling. "Okay, Sol, make some intelligent suggestions. How about Murray Braun?"

"Same problem."

"Eli Wallis?" Guy suggested.

"Also a partner."

"Well?"

"Mmmm . . . I've another idea," Sol said slowly.

"Who?"

He tested the water. "Don't say no until you hear my logic."

"You may not be aware of this but I am considered open-minded, lousy with tolerance. All I require is a reasonable suggestion . . . a possible. Who?"

"Jo Caro."

"Who?"

"Jo Caro." Stein sounded pained. "She handled the Brunswick matter for you when I was down with the flu."

"Was that her name?"

"Come on, Guy. You don't forget your business deals."

"I remember now. Didn't do a bad job."

"Works like a horse. Eli said you were pleased. She walked around Guy-struck for a week."

"My charm."

"Charm, my ass! Or her ass." The climate at the table was steadily improving. "You screwed her ass off."

"I did? I don't remember."

"Bullshit. She remembers."

"What were you thinking about her?"

"She was born to be house counsel. And she's yours.

She still mentions your name in a soulful tone."

"She's not a partner?"

"An associate."

"With high expectations. Why not a partner?"

"The usual. Her resume. No connections. She doesn't have a judge in her background... a Senator... an old family name... East or West coast. She didn't attend one of the classier law schools. Comes from Bakersfield. Ever hear of Bakersfield?"

"Bakersfield where?"

"That's my point. Bakersfield, California. It's okay. But it's not Beverly Hills... Park Avenue... Peachtree Street ... Lake Forest. It might as well be the end of the world."

"She's not partnership material."

"No. But she is house counsel material. Then she's top dog. The buyer. Not soliciting clients. A house counsel doesn't need background... or class. You've got enough class for the whole studio. Your class will rub off on her."

Guy ignored the flattery. He was accustomed to it. "I never take leavings."

"You misunderstand. She's not a bag lady. She's a damn good lawyer. She'd be your woman at United," Stein answered defensively. Suddenly, he gasped. "Shit! She's perfect. I forgot her most important qualification. She's Christie Larsen's best friend."

"Is she?"

"She is." Sol Stein was pleased with himself. "It's her one real claim to fame."

"They came out of Bakersfield together?"

"No. Larsen is a bona fide lady. She gives off the scent of breeding, of good taste, good schools. Expensive dentistry at age nine. I got a nine- and a twelve-year-old. It's something that can't be faked. She's a different cat than Jo Caro."

"How do they know each other?"

"I hear they arrived in Hollywood at the same time." He took his time... he had Guy's full attention. "Anyway, they met. Both young... aspiring. Became buddies."

Guy thought this over.

"What do you say?" Stein asked. "Jo Caro is perfect."

"I'm thinking."

"What's to think about?" He offered his most convincing argument. "Louis doesn't like her."

"Why not?"

"I don't know. Stanley Silver told me. When Dean Jordan retired, Louis talked to Stanley about being house counsel. At the same time, Christie recommended Jo. Louis saw red. He wanted Stanley. Not only that—the idea of Jo made him upchuck."

A moment of silence, then Guy said, "You may have a good idea, Sol."

Sol grinned. "It's a brainstorm. It's what you pay me for."

Guy smiled a benign smile. "It isn't bad."

"What next?" Stein asked, the strain easing out of his body.

"Next we go back to my office, put in a conference call to your office, and speak to Miss Caro."

"Good idea," Stein said as he picked up his fork.

"Forget the salad. Let's get out of here."

Stein signaled the waiter "I'm finished," he said sadly, putting down his fork.

"And when the call is over, keep your mouth shut. Talk to no one about it—not even your twelve best friends."

"Guy, I wouldn't." Stein sounded hurt.

Guy glanced away, thinking that Sol could really be dense. What had taken him so long to bring up Jo Caro's name? He'd been waiting all through lunch to hear it. If the idiot hadn't brought her up, he would have had to find a way to give him the idea. He couldn't bring up her name directly. That would have been a mistake—too obvious. Even for Stein. The man wasn't a complete fool.

Christie settled herself in Seat 3A, the window seat, on the right of the aisle in the first class cabin. Flight 210 from LAX to JFK was scheduled for takeoff in twenty minutes . . . they said. One could hope. She glanced out the window at the brilliant sky. It was raining in New York. Occasionally she missed the New York weather . . . the hot hot, the cold cold. The rain, the sleet, the snow. Then the sudden, glorious blue, crisp, clear, sunny days. For the past few years, she'd been making overnight trips to New York to deal with

NAKED CALL

United Cinema's bankers. Each time she hadn't stayed long enough for any sight-seeing... not even for nostalgia. But the little she did see was an unfamiliar city. Her memories belonged to another time, another life, another city. How she had loved that lost city... the hazy, spring sunrise that had crossed the Atlantic. The vivid fall leaves in Central Park—just about the only place in Manhattan with a grove of trees. Rockefeller Center at Christmas. Christmas carols and the ten-story Christmas tree. The pulse, the struggle, her father's last effort to tame the fabulous city. That ended with a whimper. A time of blackness and grief, filled with her family's grotesque melodrama... senseless tragedy. The tragedy dominated. In the end, there was only the feeling of displacement, of profound loss and shame, stamping her soul with obscene graffiti. She could no longer take the city on its own terms. Instinctively, she made her escape.

A familiar voice roused her, and she glanced up at the passengers filing to their seats in the tourist cabin.

"Christie! What are you doing here?"

Christie smiled. "What are you?"

"Don't ask. Don't answer. We know what we're doing. Flying to New York. I'm parked in 6A." She gestured with her head. "Maybe I can get the seat next to you."

In short order, Jo had twinkled and charmed Christie's seat partner—a bemused tax accountant—into switching seats with her. It was a typical trade. In exchange for the switch, she promised lunch at The Four Seasons—on her. He gave her his card and moved down the aisle. Jo decided, if she called, he would pick up the check. She stared at Christie with the bright, unblinking eyes of a puppy waiting for a pat. "It's kismet that we're on the same plane. Imagine! We'll have lunch together twice in two weeks."

"I wish I could hold out for dinner until we land."

"But you can't. And the meals in first class are only moderately lousy. In tourist, they're the pits. I brown bag it when I fly tourist. Or when I book I order vegetarian. They can't screw up carrots."

While she held forth on the quality of flight food, she studied Christie's black linen suit and white pique blouse. She straightened the collar of her pale blue silk dress, thankful she, too, had gone classic. She'd packed the same number in beige.

"I love your outfit," Jo said, abruptly switching topics in midair.

Christie had been aware of Jo's appraisal. "Thanks. I like yours, too. It's the kind of dress I wear."

"I know," Jo said. "It's not the real me ... more you. But I am learning. I ask myself, 'What would Christie wear?' I mean ... you're my role model." She didn't add, a hard act to follow.

Christie disliked the compliment. It had the ring of jealousy. "Jo, you are not applying for my job."

"No. I didn't mean that. I mean I want your fashion sense." Jo smiled wanly. She had talked too much. She knew it. Christie knew it. What Christie didn't know was how much Jo mimicked her, that by using Christie as a model, Jo had overcome her urge to knock-'em-dead in a skintight, jersey tube job all wrong for a business meeting in New York. The tube job was okay for a business lunch—maybe. Even better for dinner.

"Are you flying in for Jessup, Overstreet & Stein?" Christie wondered why Jo was so keyed up.

"Actually I'm flying in for a job. I'll tell you about it." Jo smoothed her hair, breathed in deeply, and felt a shade more confident. She raised the question she'd been trying not to ask. "You're flying in on United business?"

"Yes. Louis called early. 7 A.M., New York time."

"Seven in the morning!" Jo interrupted. "Does it occur to Der Fuhrer that 7 A.M. in Manhattan is 4 A.M. here?"

"He doesn't care. This is a command performance. He wants me in Manhattan tomorrow."

"Did he say why?" Christie shook her head. "Why do you think?"

"I don't think. Maybe to fire me."

Jo gave her an impatient look. "Is my tower of strength having the shakes? Louis wouldn't have you fly 3,000 miles to fire you."

Christie closed her eyes for a moment. "No, Louis wouldn't do that. Sadism isn't his style. I have my own paranoia. I don't know what he wants."

"Didn't he hint?"

NAKED CALL

"He told me to meet him tomorrow morning in the reception room of Macleod Brothers on Wall Street at eight-thirty sharp."

Jo was quiet, struggling to keep her voice steady. At last she managed to say in a reasonably casual tone, "That's the investment banking house that's buying United Cinema."

"That's them," Christie said dryly. "I wish Louis wouldn't sell." She ran the knuckles of her hand over her forehead. "And what job are you applying for?"

"You'll never believe it."

"Try me."

"Sol Stein called me. Yesterday—from Manhattan. He asked me to meet him in New York." Jo choked out the rest of her answer. "It was a conference call from the Macleod Brothers offices."

The silence was awkward. Finally, Christie asked, "Macleod Brothers offices. Why?"

"Jessup, Overstreet & Stein are Macleod's West Coast lawyers. Remember what a kookie coincidence we thought it was that I work for the firm that represents the buyer of United Cinema?"

"I remember. Stein drew up the contracts for the purchase of United," Christie said in a bitter voice. "Why did he want you?"

"Hold your horses. How much is Macleod paying Louis for United?"

"Eight hundred million. Give or take."

"Whew! That's money."

"When they take U.C. public, they'll sell off enough stock to get back between four and five hundred million. And they'll still keep enough stock to retain control of the company."

"Smart."

"Very. Why did Stein call you?"

"Guy Macleod wants to meet me. Tomorrow at his office."

Christie's eyes widened in astonishment. "You're meeting Guy Macleod? I don't understand."

"Neither did I at first. It's been so fast."

"This happened yesterday?"

"At exactly 12:33. I was having a sandwich at my desk. It gives me chills to think that if I'd been at a taco bar eating chili or salad I'd have missed that call—and ruined my whole career. By the time I called Macleod back, he could have changed his mind."

"About what?"

"About me. It's the biggest thing that's ever happened in my entire life."

"What is?"

"I was going to tell you all about it yesterday. Then I decided to wait until after it actually happened. I didn't want to jinx it. And I wanted to surprise you."

"You have surprised me. What the hell happened?" Christie was running out of patience.

"I thought afterward we might celebrate. You've listened to me bitch so long. For a change, this is good news."

"What is this all about?"

Jo took a deep breath. "Guy Macleod. Guess what he said."

"Stop playing games, Jo! Just tell me."

"Okay. After we spoke for a few minutes about how highly Sol Stein thinks of my ability as a lawyer, and so on . . ." She paused for dramatic emphasis. ". . . Guy Macleod asked me to be house counsel for United Cinema. I'm to fill Stanley Silver's spot."

Christie took this in at every pore. Jo's words in the Bel Air house flashed into her mind. "Friends in high places." She started to ask if Guy or Sol was the friend, then changed her mind. Jo would tell her or she wouldn't.

As though reading Christie's mind, Jo said enthusiastically, "Sol Stein recommended me . . . my friend in high places."

"Good for him." So much for one question. There were more. A whole stack of questions she couldn't ask. Like—how come Louis agreed?

Jo giggled nervously. "Sol and I . . . we've been . . . call it, chummy."

"I didn't know. Not that I should. It's none of my business." Christie's voice was precise and unmarked by emphasis, showing neither surprise nor distaste.

"Christie, please don't be tactful. You're my best friend.

I never mentioned Sol because I know it's tacky . . . sleeping with the boss. Plus he's terrified of Leah finding out. California is community property country. Also he worried about Madeline. That blond bimbo's a terror. She keeps poor Sol on a tighter leash than Leah does.'' Jo giggled again. "But he did manage to squeeze me in. Every now and then."

Christie told herself she should have guessed. But she'd long ago stopped thinking about the infinity of beds Jo visited. For an instant she could see them down the years, like a series of stop-action photos. Sex was Jo's strategy for survival.

"If Sol wasn't my boss, I wouldn't apologize. But fucking him looks like a cheap way to make points. Except it's not. I'd like him if he was my druggist. I think he's cute." Jo was seized with a mania for self-justification. "Besides, he's lazy, and he likes it when I go on top. I like to be on top, too. We have a lot in common." She gave Christie a piercing look. "You never . . . ? I mean you never made it with Louis—did you?"

"No. It never came up."

"Would you if it had?"

The moment had a weird kind of tension. "It wouldn't come up. Not with Louis."

"He's boffed half the stars in Hollywood."

"It's different with us. We work together."

"He worked with them, also."

Christie shrugged helplessly. "True. But it never came up."

"Suppose it had. What would you have done?"

Christie looked at Jo a long time before answering quietly, "Quit . . . I think."

"You really didn't fuck him for the job?"

Christie's eyes were as clear and candid as a child's. "You've asked me the same question over . . . and over . . . and over."

"I guess it's hard to believe."

"Believe it. I didn't. I wouldn't," Christie said with a tired honesty.

"You're a marvel. You really didn't fuck him to get your

promotions?" Jo persisted. In her grim, realistic view of the world, Christie's claim was incredible.

"You know the answer."

"I am dumb with admiration." Jo stared at her friend for a long, bleak moment. "No. I guess you wouldn't. Ever. Not for a job . . . not for an entire career. You're telling the truth. I remember when you didn't have a pot to pee in. You still wouldn't be a 'comes along'. I don't understand you. You can't hock moral scruples. All the virtue in the world won't buy a hungry girl a hamburger at McDonalds."

Christie looked away, hoping to spare her friend her gentle, pitiless appraisal.

Jo smoothed her skirt. At last she said, "I guess it's a matter of values. I don't think my body is that precious. Sol's been good to me. He's my rabbi in the firm. He got me two raises. He thinks I'm a good lawyer. And not because I haul his ashes."

"You're a fine lawyer." Christie was embarrassed for her friend. "Sol Stein is not doing you a favor for services rendered. He would never recommend a dud for a key position like house counsel of United Cinema. If you screw up, it'll reflect on him. He could lose Macleod Brothers as clients. Why would he risk it?"

Jo gave a sigh of relief. "Yes . . . when it comes to business, Sol's prick comes in a poor second. Money—the partnership—that comes first."

"That's why he picked you."

"You should've been a Jewish mother. They insist their kids are geniuses. You must have sent me fifty referrals . . . actors . . . once a whole camera crew."

"Forget it."

"You're my best contact in the entertainment world. Jessup, Overstreet & Stein's best contact." Her eyes lit up with a sudden revelation. "It just hit me. Sol recommended me because of you."

"Me?"

"You. You know as well as I do what makes the world go round. Not love. Contacts. You are my best contact in—"

"Your contact may not be a contact after this meeting."

"Crap. You're a big number, Christie. They're probably

going to pour holy water on you . . . sanctify you . . . or do whatever the boys who buy companies do." Jo gave a tense little laugh. "You always land butter side up. But me! House counsel. Imagine!"

"You deserve it." But it didn't add up.

"I do." Jo cocked her chin. "Jo Caro, house counsel for United Cinema. Imagine *Forbes* interviewing me."

"Imagine *Time*." What about Louis? Christie thought.

"The *Wall Street Journal*." Jo sat straighter in her seat. "I was preordained to have that job. I remember the first time the job was open, how you tried to help me get it."

Christie gave Jo a quick look. There was something in her tone that carried a darker message. "I did try. It didn't work out. I'm glad Guy Macleod sees your value."

"Louis does, too. He must have agreed, or it wouldn't have happened. I bet Louis even helped Sol persuade Guy."

"Mmmm . . . probably." Louis help Sol? The need to say something more became an uncomfortable urgency, but Christie could think of nothing to say.

"I've always thought Louis was one of my strongest supporters. I mean after you. He had good reasons the last time for not offering me the job."

Christie bent her head with a false calm. Her mind had got hold of the memory . . . sticky and unsavory. Jo's humble, hopeful face only a few years ago when Louis was looking for a new house counsel. How insistently Jo had dogged her about the opening. But what could she say? What did she dare say? When she mentioned Jo's name to Louis, at first he was amused. She must be joking. She wasn't. All hell had broken loose. Louis had called Jo a crooked, greedy, conniving piece of ass. You could trust her only as long as she was handcuffed.

Now Jo's voice was a shade too curious as she asked, "But you believed I should have had the job, didn't you?"

"Why else would I have suggested you?"

Jo lowered her eyes, mesmerized by her fingernails. "I am qualified. I am not just a pet chimp that somebody taught how to type a legal brief."

Christie had a sudden flash flood of insight that left her defenseless. It was possible Jo had never believed her excuses . . . had thought she lied . . . believed Christie had never mentioned her to Louis for the job. "You don't have to convince me," Christie said wearily.

"I don't?"

This time their eyes met. "No, you don't."

"If you say so."

"I say so." Christie looked directly at her friend. She could only guess at Jo's suspicions. The curve of her smile never changed.

Jo changed the subject with sudden cheer. "Okay. Now that we've seen my future in tea leaves, what can dear Louis have in mind for you?"

A fragile silence ensued, full of Jo's excitement and Christie's private turmoil. At last she said, "I'll find out when I get to Macleod Brothers tomorrow at 8:30 in the morning."

Jo arched her brows. "The time proves I'm right. I'm due there at 10:30. That means you're in for great news." There was incipient envy in Jo's voice. "Getting canned takes minutes. But they need at least two hours to work out the details of their contract with you. Exactly what job... for how long... and how much loot."

"My contract?"

"Your employment contract. I bet we have adjoining offices." This idea pleased Jo. She started humming, "Yankee Doodle Dandy.

As the plane gathered speed and rose in the sky, Christie had the odd premonition of flying back into her past. It was as though she had spun around a traffic circle and was returning to her history—the heartbreaking, early years of her life. Or to a new chapter in that history that began in the present.

Louis was waiting for Christie in the reception room of the Macleod Brothers office. He was wearing a dark New York suit, pale blue shirt, dark tie. When in New York do as the New Yorkers do.

"Good morning, Christie." He beamed.

"Good morning, Louis." She tried to return the glow.

After the greeting, time became an unreal blur. Full of strange faces, handshakes, smiles, talk. Businessese. Legalese. Filmese. Christie felt as though she were working

NAKED CALL

on the frames of a film in the cutting room at United. On the screen above one editing machine was the master shot of a spacious wood-paneled conference room. On another screen were some close-ups. Louis introducing a man. The sound tape added to the video.

Cut to the "Hellos!"

"This is Guy Macleod, Christie. Guy Macleod, Christie Larsen."

"How do you do, Miss Larsen? May I call you Christie?" A warm handshake, a practiced display of pleasure at the sight of Miss Larsen.

"Of course. How do you do, Mr. Macleod? May I call you Guy?"

He laughed formally. Then Louis introduced her to Simon Macleod, Guy's brother. Their eyes met. Standing motionless, she could feel his warmth as he moved across the room toward her.

"How do you do Christie?" He flushed under his pale skin.

"How do you do, Simon?" Christie noted that he was younger than Guy, as bright gold as Guy was dark. About six foot five, he was big-boned and muscular without being clumsy. He had large, strong features, yet for a face so boldly male his lower lip was surprisingly sensuous. Unlike Guy, his golden hair was cut on the short side and brushed straight back.

"It's a pleasure to meet you," he said softly.

"Thank you." She lowered her eyes, feeling the blood beat hard in her temples. She turned away, hoping she wasn't blushing, trying to master herself.

There was a pounding in Christie's head as the meeting picked up speed, as she watched Guy settle into his chair across the desk from Louis, speaking as he did so and smoking a cigarette, asking her questions. Simon said nothing.

"The budget for *The Feathered Serpent* projected a cost of almost twenty-one million dollars. You mean the budget wasn't accurate?"

Christie faced the firing squad. "As of yesterday, we were about five million over budget."

"You mean the budget is meaningless?" Guy asked with

sardonic good will. Then he put his cigarette down in an original Picasso plate he used as an ashtray.

Meaningless... meaningless... Christie had the art from years of listening to heated business pitches of paying attention with the front of her mind while another, quite separate faculty wrestled with the real implications of what was happening.

"Not meaningless. A budget is a rough estimate... a projection. Sometimes padded... inflated... sometimes optimistically understated. Like most projections, a film budget is rarely on target."

"So the numbers mean nothing."

"They're as close as we can come. The budget is an honest attempt to say the picture will cost this much if...."

"If what?"

"In this case, if the director can shoot the picture in the time allotted." She shot a quick glance at Simon, who seemed to have been struck dumb.

"So this budget is an example of Marconi's incompetence ... extravagance," Guy said in an even, cold-blooded voice.

"Franco is reaching for unusual depth... passion... the vision of primitive Mexico. That's taking more shooting time," Christie said gravely.

"Vision costs money." Louis smiled faintly.

"I may be an amateur at movie making, but numbers talk to me. He has not been shooting his vision on schedule. He's three weeks late... if I read these notes correctly." Guy's nostrils flared.

Franco was late... they could be in a crunch. Christie's mind was haunted by the inescapable bottom line... and no Louis Levy to fall back on.

"Plus, I see hundreds of thousands of dollars for extras. Promotional appearances... housing stars' hairdressers... stars' secretaries... exercise trainers. Feeding them three meals a day—those people eat like pigs."

"What matters is how long Franco takes to shoot the rest of the film," Louis said.

Guy was wrathful... acutely aware of grosses, profits, the pre-tax net.

Louis was concerned. "We have an ironclad release date."

"My motion picture analyst informs me..."

Ah yes. You had a quick course in *The Sound of Music*, Christie thought.

Guy challenged her. "What about exhibitors from the non-blind bidding states?"

"Ready by October, Guy," Christie said, automatically hoping for the best.

Simon refused to enter the conversational vacuum.

"Mid-October," Guy insisted.

"Mid-October," Christie heeled. Franco could kick and scream. The film must be in shape for the non-blind bidding states by mid-October.

"We need a work print for the media..." Guy was enjoying himself.

"To preview in mid-November," Louis remarked with a shrug; it wasn't a serious matter.

It was only life and death. Christie braced herself. "In mid-November."

"We must make the Christmas season. My motion picture analyst informs me..."

Christie fought the impulse to say, "Fuck you!"

"...Christmas is the prime time to release a new movie." Guy stared into space as though considering the implications for society of what he had said.

"On the money," Louis gave her his benevolent leader smile. "Right, Christie?"

"Right. It usually is. But not for *The Serpent*. We'll be out in time for Christmas—but in a limited release. Not full-scale national. As you know, Louis."

"Why not a full release? It's Christmas! My information tells me..." Guy reared up.

Louis' smile was only mildly patronizing. "We don't want to play all our cards at once. Do we, Christie?"

"We don't. You see, Guy, the limited release is just to get us in line for this year's Academy Awards. *The Feathered Serpent* should walk away with at least two major awards—Best Director, Best Actress—and a hat full of minor awards."

"Don't forget Best Film," Louis expanded. "A Mexican *Ben Hur*."

"Best Film," Christie repeated. "We cross our fingers."

"I learn something new every day," Guy said. "But suppose you don't get those awards."

"It's a gamble. But I decided to take it," Christie said calmly. "If things break for us, we're in four-leaf clover. Great U.S. distribution with the major movie house chains . . . UA theaters, Mann theaters, General Cinema, and so on. We'll insist they hold *The Serpent* in house for a long run. A month . . . six weeks. Not just the usual week or two. Better foreign distribution contracts with the theater chains abroad. A better videotape deal. Actually all sub rights deals will be better. We'll hold off on a television mini-series—"

"I repeat. Suppose you get no awards. We miss the Christmas business—"

Christie said, "I repeat. It is a gamble."

"A very risky one, I think."

"The box office will be triple," Louis said.

Guy asked, "You're willing to take the risk, Louis?"

Simon, the great stone face, said nothing.

"Barkus is willing," Louis smiled serenely. "Once we make the limited Christmas release we're off and running. We will make it, won't we, Christie?"

Christie tried to concentrate and not look at Simon. "The editing crew are already working 'round the clock."

"Piecing together the dailies flown up from Mexico?" Louis asked as if he didn't know.

"So that Franco can work on the final editing?" Guy wanted the last word.

"As soon as the final scene is shot." That is, if he ever finished shooting. Christie faced the killing bottom line again.

It was a wrap. Print it.

Once Guy accepted Christie's release schedule, they proceeded to the grand finale; transferring the ownership of United Cinema from Louis Levy to Macleod Brothers. The meeting simmered . . . re-heated. Steam rose from Louis, iciness from Guy. Simon remained silent. In due course,

NAKED CALL

Guy and Louis, with mutual distrust and dislike, arrived at Clause 23B, which, true to the honest tradition of self-serving Wall Street, Guy intimated to Christie was his idea. According to Guy, Guy invented and heartily endorsed Christie as the right person for the job. Sold Christie to a reluctant Louis, who gazed at him in amusement.

When Guy paused for breath, Louis told Christie she could stay and listen if she chose, or she could go to the Macleod dining room for coffee and a croissant. Christie declined with a thank you. Negotiations began. Guy was enthusiastic about the spirit of Clause 23B, but Louis, vociferous... Guy, unyielding... Louis, bullying... Guy, adamant. Other men might have come to blows. Instead, after much justifying, theorizing, and quibbling, they compromised on the length of renewal of Christie's employment contract. Louis wanted five years, Guy, year to year. They settled on three. Next, the money. More locked horns. Louis voted for five. By deductive reasoning, Guy arrived at two. The wheel of fortune stopped at number four... four hundred thousand dollars a year for three years. Simon watched Christie. Christie tried not to react, intensely angry with herself for her awareness of him.

At last it was finalized. Four hundred thousand dollars with bonuses for three years for Christina Larsen, the new president of United Cinema. President!

Simon moved in his chair, creating a field of disturbance around him. The great stone face came to life, wearing a dark, brooding expression. "Now that you're president of United Cinema, Christie, what are your plans for the studio?"

The gentleness in his voice was an indictment of Guy's condescension, but he meant his question to be taken seriously. He didn't want a slick answer.

Christie was almost too poised for comfort. She looked directly at Simon, not past him or inwardly at some thought of her own. Although she didn't know it, he liked that she looked straight at him... that she didn't permit herself the physical relief of even the slightest movement. The intensity in each of them ran like a current into the eyes of the other. Then Christie surveyed the conference table. She spoke to the three men present as one. It was something she had often thought about, and she spoke for minutes without pause. Afterward she remembered only snatches of what she had said.

"I cannot forget them or make them vanish from my mind's eye...

"Seven P.M. in the Fashion Mall of San Diego County. A fragile, gray-haired woman in a wheelchair is pushed into the darkened interior of a movie house by a cheerful young girl. The movie connects the woman in the wheelchair to a comedic sexual adventure, giving her a taste of a life she has never known or will know.

"Oak Street in Chicago. A balding man worries about his job, waits to see a movie about Burma, and wonders why he never did something about his B.A. in Far East Studies.

"Detroit on Grand Boulevard. A black factory inspector takes her daughter to a movie about another black woman who refused to be stereotyped.

"A parent in Des Moines who has real problems with her husband's fidelity is engrossed with the flickering problems of another unfaithful husband accidentally caught in a dangerous liaison.

"Movies accomplish something... ease the chill of loneliness, of feeling defeated, dreamless, burned out. They dilute the fog of ignorance and false authority... nourish the minds and imagination of people, opening up ranges of new possibilities.

"There is enough that is trite and rubbish. The wonder is not how many movies are banal but how extraordinary so many can be... a movie about an emperor who is a simple human being... about a daughter teaching Mom how to mother... about the family life in an office and the lack of it in a home... a priest confused by his own bigotry learns a little from a movie about athletes and religious tolerance."

"A painting or a statue or a book is usually a one-man or woman creation. A movie is the art of collaboration, using the talents of a great many different kinds of creative people. That's only half the collaboration. The other half is the audience. Making them laugh... weep... terrifying them. When a film reaches an audience where it lives, the film has an impact that no other art form can equal..."

A button on the phone next to Guy lit up. He picked up the receiver and listened. "She's expected. Send her in. Thank you, Christie," he said briskly, putting down the receiver. "An informative little speech."

"Let her finish," Simon said.

Carefully, Christie looked at Simon. "I am finished. I believe in movies, and I think good movies can stretch the boundaries of people's lives. I'm proud to be part of an industry that can make movies that make us think twice... about everything."

The rueful lines extending from Simon's eyes and mouth were somehow appropriate. "Okay, Guy, I admit it. I was wrong. After hearing Christie's ideas, I think United Cinema will make an interesting acquisition."

Christie looked at Simon again. Their glances fused and did another dance of intimacy.

At that moment, Constance Neill, Guy's secretary, stuck her head into the conference room.

"Miss Caro is here, Mr. Macleod."

"Send her in," Guy said.

With a start Christie remembered again Louis' words. "... crooked greedy, conniving piece of ass." She looked at Louis in a mute exchange such as is sometimes granted to old friends. Jo Caro was his trade-off for her... her presidency. She would have to live with his brutal assessment of Jo—Jo, her old friend. She hoped he was wrong. Either way, she must make good his bargain with Guy.

Jo scanned the room, assessed the expressions, and finally fixed her eyes on Christie. Her raised eyebrows asked, adjoining offices? Christie answered with a nod. Yes.

They were doing retakes of the gory serpent scenes. Franco allowed Jake Jakes, who had been hyper-critical of the special effects, to have his day in the sun and direct the shots.

The first scene was a shot of eight-year-old Pedro splashing in the shallow water with Jasper, while the serpent, moving slowly toward them, appeared on the horizon. To make it harder for the audience to distinguish the monster's approach, the camera looked as directly into the sun as possible without overexposing the film. Then there were shots from the serpent's eye view, from a distance... always coming closer, watching the boy and the man. After that, a shot of Juanita and Rosa spotting the serpent... Rosa going wild, racing into the water to save her child. Juanita, unmoving, calls from the beach to warn her lover, Jasper. No use. The serpent demands a sacrifice. Rosa and Jasper are caught in a belch of fire from the creature's nostrils while Juanita watches, stoically... and Pedro paddles frantically toward shore.

Next, there was the retake of Helena swimming naked in the cove and the serpent rising from the water, seeing her. Miguel, also naked, diving into the water. The wild confusion as Miguel battles the serpent in a desperate effort to save Helena. Finally, Helena, groggy and exhausted, stumbling onto the beach, turning to stare with horror as she sees Miguel being bitten in half by the serpent.

For these retakes, every camera with every type of lens was used. Jake was confident he'd gotten all there was to get out of the special effects. There would be enough footage to satisfy even Franco's eye for perfection... let alone his.

That evening, the company gathered in the improvised screening room to see the dailies. Franco was silent. Too silent. The cast tried not to squirm. Suddenly he burst into a fierce yell. "By God, this movie has balls!"

PART FIVE
1992 MARCH

Chapter 10

BY MID-MARCH, newspapers in all the major markets across the nation carried full-page advertisements for *The Feathered Serpent*.

An absolute stunner!
8 Academy Award Nominations
Best Picture
Best Director—Franco Marconi
Best Actor—Alan Lucca
Best Supporting Actress—Conchita Supervia
Alan Lucca   Jenny Lattimore   Conchita Supervia

A Franco Marconi Film
The Feathered Serpent
United Cinema and Tosca Films Present...

Magnificent and Moving
A beautifully made, passionate and mysterious
adventure...
Alan Lucca's best and boldest role...
a powerful performance...
8 Academy Award Nominations
Best Picture
Best... Best... Best...

"Are they done?" Christie asked from the doorway of Harry Weiss' office. "We're a little late. I wanted them out before the awards."

"They're done!" The fashion-plate controller, who had replaced Mannie Wolfe, replied. "Vanished in the mail sack this morning."

"All of them?"

"All 238 of them."

"To every one?" Christie asked.

"Every single man, woman, or child who is scheduled to receive a 1099 form for unsalaried income on a United Cinema film, including *The Feathered Serpent*, will receive a 1099 form for unsalaried income, complete with the amounts paid out to him, her . . . or it. There was a dog on the hit list. How could a dog have unearned income? Was a dog used on *The Serpent?* Anyway the total came to over seven hundred thousand dollars."

"And the IRS?"

"Of course the IRS. What am I, a trainee? Two copies of the 1099 went to the 238 lucky winners. One copy went to the IRS. One copy is in our files."

Christie rolled her eyes heavenward and shrugged. "Tsk. Tsk. There will be no joy in Mudville tonight."

"Your first official act, Madam President."

"Not my first . . . my most visible. And most vindictive . . . as they will say."

"Unfortunately, I agree."

"*Mea culpa*. What must be must be," Christie sighed.

"Louis is a hard act to follow."

"Would you swear it?"

"He never sent out 1099 forms on unearned income." Harry started to sing off key, "But the times they are changing . . . the times . . ."

"Harry, you're flat."

"I'm tone deaf. But I love folk songs. I suppose Louis enjoyed playing Big Daddy. He got a kick giving his favorites lush payments for their personal expenses . . . fun and games. An actor, a director, always a few actresses. They never received 1099s. Not only did he give them the extra money, he paid the taxes on that money. Millions of dollars of tax-free income that the little darlings took for granted."

"Louis was a very rich man."

"I know. Everyone knows ... including Louis." Harry closed his eyes. "Louis told me that one year he paid out over three million in gifts to his special friends who worked on *Love Child*, out of sheer affection for his playmates."

"Louis was a very generous man."

"But to give away millions! Weird! I guess it was good for his soul. A private form of atonement."

Christie tried to mop up the blatant jealousy. "Let's forget about Louis' spiritual motives. Keep in mind that United was Louis' show. A private company totally owned by Louis. He could afford all sorts of generous gestures. Now United is a public corporation owned by Macleod Brothers and the shareholders who buy movie tickets. It is our job to send out 1099 forms, or our board of directors could pop a few blood vessels."

"Yeah. Stockholders could instigate a class action suit. Lawsuits are the new wave of income for lawyers. Libel suits, malpractice suits, environmental impact suits. My cousin, one of the kings of malpractice suits, makes more money than ..."

"Thank you for filling me in." Christie started to back out the door.

Harry shrewdly changed lanes. "And for your next official act, Madam President?"

"Hopefully, I'll be accepting the Academy Award for the Best Picture of the year. 'Thank you ... everyone. Thank you so much. What a wonderful and rewarding profession this is for me ... who has been a movie fan since I sat on my mother's lap at the movies ...'"

"I used to wet my mother's lap."

"Poor toilet training. Bye, Harry." Christie closed the door.

Jenny Lattimore, wearing blue-tinted sunglasses and a blue straw cartwheel hat to cover her ash-blond hair, stomped around her heart-shaped swimming pool ... screaming. Her supple, tanned body glowed in the morning sun of Bel Air ... as did the single-strand diamond necklace that sparkled between her remarkable breasts . . . as did the golden sea shells sculptured to follow the contours of her ears and invite notice of her high cheekbones . . . as did the twisted rope of tiny gold chains on her wrist, drooping like a chiffon handkerchief, shimmering with every dramatic gesture. Her hands were naturally expressive. So were her bare feet . . . and mouth. She stamped her feet, she shouted, pouted, paused, and gazed appealingly at Lester Farber.

Lester shifted uncomfortably in the small poolside chair. Beads of sweat trickled from his armpits. His three-piece, gray seersucker suit, white button-down shirt, and gray striped tie were clinging to his body like a straitjacket. Watching Jenny prance around the pool had grown increasingly difficult. His erection was now embarrassingly obvious. He had trouble keeping his mind on business . . . and his eyes off her nipples . . . her buttocks . . . her black-haired crotch. For aside from her sunglasses, straw hat, and jewelry, Jenny Lattimore was naked.

"I worked my ass off on *The Serpent*, Lester," Jenny moaned. "And what thanks do I get? None! Did I get nominated for the Best Actress Award? No! But Alan Lucca gets nominated. And would you believe it, that green-card-carrying Supervia is up for Best Supporting Actress. Get that!" She buried her face in her hands and let out a muffled wail.

"Jenny! Don't take it so hard. You've been nominated four times." He could hardly sit still.

"But I've never won! Suppose she does?"

"She won't. They owe it to Fanny Esen—a pat on the head for decades of good work. For the patience of a saint. Plus she turned in a stunning performance in *No Place To Hide*."

"Fanny won't get it. Supervia will. You idiot, she's not American. It will show how broad-minded Academy members are. If I were a Fiji Islander, I'd have a better chance. I could scream." She did. "And Franco, that foul-mouthed asshole! He's up for the Best Director Award. And that fucking movie will get the Best Picture Award! Watch."

"You're probably right. In the limited release it grossed okay, but it's no gross buster." He laughed uneasily. "Pardon the pun. Anyway, because it's not, it was okay for the

Academy to nominate it. *Serpent* wasn't produced solely for the crude purpose of making money. That's why *Heartbreak House* wasn't nominated. Grosses are too high. What's more, *Serpent* is serious... but not too serious. People have to think, but not too much. They don't have to chew on new ideas, like in *Blue Skies*. Academy members are conservative—"

"Lester, shut up! I know how those lamebrains think."

Lester swallowed, wishing she would shut up, too... and sit in his lap. Sometimes she did. "Don't take it to heart, Jenny. Because, besides everything else, you know—I know—everyone knows—the Academy Awards are fixed. Franco paid them off. United paid them off. You know how it is."

Jenny raised her sly eyes and gazed at Lester affectionately. This was one of their favorite lies... highly prized for its tranquilizing effects. After all, everything in life was a payoff... a kickback. So why not the Academy? Why not? Why...? "Shitsville! I know... I know. But I keep hoping. I just wish I knew who to pay off."

"Baby, it's Hollywood's biggest and best-kept secret. The Big Secret. Where the bodies are buried. Everyone keeps mum."

"Like the Kennedy assassination. Nobody talks." Suddenly Jenny started to giggle. "What the fuck, Lester. If it isn't a payoff, those dumb bastards have their taste in their asses. That's what's wrong." Jenny's voice dropped an octave. "Fuck the Academy, Lester. As long as I get my points I don't give a damn. I didn't get you here to listen to this shit about the Academy Award. What's burning my ass is a little piece of obscenity from her highness, Christina Larsen."

Jenny stopped in front of a round, chrome and glass table. Two crystal glasses, a bottle of tequila, and a tapestry-covered briefcase rested on the table. She opened the briefcase's eighteen-karat-gold clasp and pulled out from among the jumble of papers a printed form about the size of a check.

"You agree I know how to add and subtract."

"If you didn't have such incredible acting talents," he choked the words out, unable to keep his eyes off her crotch, "you could have built a major accounting firm."

From long association, Jenny knew this was Lester's highest form of praise. She swallowed her venom and held out the form. "You see this? It's a 1099. You do know what that is? They did teach you about the IRS when you studied accounting? You do know about 1099s?"

Lester nodded weakly. "They're forms covering any type of earned income that is non-salaried income. They were sent out five, six weeks ago. You must have had the thing over a month. If it upset you so badly, why didn't you telephone me sooner?"

"Because I didn't have a chance to look it over. I was memorizing my acceptance speech for the Academy Award ... and having a dress made. But now I have the time. Lester, look at this—it's outrageous!"

Lester gazed at the form Jenny handed him. "Non-salaried income. Sixty thousand dollars ... hmm."

"Franco Marconi—the bastard himself—had the check drawn for me by United. Sixty thousand dollars for my outstanding promotional and publicity work on behalf of *The Feathered Serpent*. It was a personal expense and United reimbursed me."

"Jenny, you and I know you spent no money—you did no publicity. United gave you the money. It was a freebie, to do with as you pleased. In the past, Franco would have simply buried the sixty thousand in the production budget of the *Serpent*. Charged it off to publicity ... promotion ... cost of living—any damn thing that came to mind."

"That's what Louis always did. Every studio I ever worked for did it.

"Used to do it, you mean. Studio practice for years, making it cushy for the stars ... the cast and crew. What the hell! They wrote it off as a business expense. No more. The IRS cracked down. No more burying personal perks in the budget ... or the IRS gets nasty."

"But United kept on doing it."

"While Louis owned the studio. He probably paid the taxes himself, if he couldn't hide it as a business expense."

"I love Louis."

"I'm glad. Except that Louis doesn't own United now. It's a public corporation. Christie Larsen is president."

"So Christie snitched on me to the IRS."

"She told the truth. The studio auditors must have spotted the check. Sixty thousand dollars isn't that easy to hide. The auditors probably went to Larsen and asked her what kind of actual business you did for the film . . . beyond acting."

"You heard me. I did publicity."

"Jenny, dear, you did no publicity."

"So what? Christie never was such a bum sport before."

"She had no choice. She knew it was a perk. Pure and simple. Louis was still head of the studio when that check first crossed her desk. So she didn't think about the IRS. That wasn't her territory. But now—no Louis. United is a public company doing what all public companies do . . . sending out 1099 forms. It's your turn to pay the taxes on the sixty thousand. Louis doesn't live here anymore."

"Louis was an angel. Christie is a stingy bitch."

"If she covered for you, she'd have to cover for everyone else on *The Serpent* who received extra checks. I'm sure you weren't alone."

"Hell no! That bitch, Supervia, had her cottage renovated."

"And United paid for it. And if Christie covered for you, she must cover for Conchita . . ."

"That cunt had new plumbing installed, a shower, a Jacuzzi."

". . . and for everyone else. Which means the studio would be paying taxes on hundreds of thousands of dollars it laid out to make everyone's stay in Mexico pleasant."

"Pleasant! You're out of your mind. I got diarrhea. I didn't charge them for the Kaopectate."

Lester gave her a tired smile. "You billed them for sixty thousand dollars. The money was not a production expense. It was non-salaried income.

"Shut up! I needed that money for Matt."

"Is that his name?"

"He wanted a red Mercedes."

"I think you ought to dump that parasite."

"Lester, baby, when you make music in bed like Matt, I'll buy you a red Mercedes, too." Jenny sank into his lap and pulled his head down on her bare breasts. "Darling little Lester with the big, big prick... I want you to see what you can do." She nuzzled his ear. "To persuade our good and dear friend, Christina Larsen, to make a special case of me and pick up the tax on that sixty thousand..." Her soft voice wheedled on as she unzipped his fly.

Karen Holzman, overweight, over-problemed, and under-solutioned, sat patiently waiting for Conchita to get to the point. At the moment, Conchita was examining the seven emerald-green boxes—recently arrived from Paris—overflowing with handmade satin, silk, and lace lingerie.

"I love old lace and embroidery. Did I tell you my mother was a seamstress? She could spend six months making a silk peignoir. Even all those years ago, Mama's nightgowns sold for thousands of lira." Conchita wriggled a pair of scarlet silk satin bikini panties over her full hips and buttocks. "With a little practice I could sew as well as this." She held up a pair of yellow satin boxer shorts, trimmed with black lace, and its matching satin camisole. "Pretty, isn't it? They're not that hard to make. If I weren't an actress, I could make a living as a seamstress, working in a design studio."

"How much?" Karen was bored. She paid no attention to her lingerie, as long as it was cotton... white cotton.

"Only two hundred seventy-five dollars each. So beautiful. I love the feel of satin on my skin. Of course, this is a bit more expensive." She slipped a pale peach silk satin bra with rose lace applique over her breasts. "I bought three of these... ice cream shades... expensive. But they are handmade. See—fastened with buttons."

"How much?" Karen asked. She was flat-chested.

"I forget. Six hundred apiece, I think. And look—this cute garter belt—Franco will love it. I think it was four hundred seventy-five dollars. I buy everything so fast I forget to keep track of the numbers."

"Good Lord, Chita! Nobody sees your lingerie. It's your bod they ogle."

"Franco believes in dressing for everything... even sex."

"The hell with Franco. That's ten thousand dollars for

nothing. A dress for the Academy Awards could cost about that much. It has. You are up for the Best Supporting Actress Award."

"I know." Chita pirouetted around, stopped in front of Karen, and grinned mischievously. "Maybe I'll wear my lingerie to the Academy evening. The yellow satin camisole and panties with the black lace. That should impress the *paparazzi* . . . even Franco."

"Stop clowning, Chita. You should send the lingerie back. As for Franco . . . Did you pay by check for the lingerie?"

"I don't remember. American Express? Maybe a check? Which reminds me, *cara mia* . . ." She tiptoed over to the curly-headed blond and kissed the tip of her nose. "We— or rather you, as my agent, business manager, and *darlissima*—have a problem."

"I know. That 1099 form. The money United gave you for buying and remodeling that cottage in Oaxaca. You put in a new toilet . . . a new shower . . . a Jacuzzi."

"It makes a lovely vacation house."

"It cost a tidy eighty-three thousand dollars."

"But the studio paid for it. They are richer than I am . . . and I work so hard in the hot sun I need a little pleasure."

"Chita, my dear girl, when Louis Levy owned United, they used to pay for little items like cottages. But that was last year. No more. Louis sold United and this year it's a public corporation. The IRS won't permit such items to be buried in the budget. Any monies the studio pays you over and beyond your salary must be declared as non-salaried income."

"What has happened to United? It never . . ."

"It will from now on. The IRS ruling applies to all studios. Columbia. Warner. Universal."

"But I couldn't live in that cottage the way it was."

"You could have stayed at the *hacienda*. There was running water. All the conveniences."

"*Darlissima*, you are angry with me. It is Franco—not *la casa*. Please. He has many lovers. All the time. In Oaxaca there was me and that silly Maureen . . . the Broadway actress. Even Christie was his *amore* long ago. Franco and I . . . we understand each other. No strings, as you say."

"Yes, I am angry about Franco, but he's irrelevant. That eighty-three thousand dollars United so generously paid you now comes under the heading of non-salaried, additional income."

Chita leaned over and put her fingers under Karen's chin and ran her tongue around the flush-faced woman's lips. "If you behave . . . maybe I take off my so-expensive lingerie. You must speak to Harry Weiss and persuade him to persuade dear Christie that United Cinema should . . ."

"They won't do it," Karen said gruffly, trying to keep her hands to herself.

"But why did Franco give me the check if . . ."

"Because the damn fool doesn't know tax law."

"Now . . . now . . . *cara* . . . we must talk about this carefully and think what you can do. You know how poor I am." Chita's voice was a husky, inviting whisper.

Alan Lucca stood in front of the three-sided cheval glass mirror that reflected his well-muscled body, his smoky eyes, his tousled black hair that fit his head like a bathing cap. With the right camera man, his magnetism came off the screen in waves. But today Alan didn't see himself in the mirror. He saw a horse . . . lean and muscular as he was, self-confident, proud. He loved that animal. Princeling. A horse that was born to run. It was in his blood. He had high hopes for the horse. He looked right. Right enough for him to pay ninety-five thousand dollars for the horse. That was peanuts for a great two-year-old. He'd missed Seattle Slew—only seventeen thousand five hundred when a colt.

The telephone rang. Lucca picked up the receiver. This was his private line, and he spoke without waiting to hear who it was.

"Sidney? What the hell do those bastards want? You read my message. Answer me. Why the 1099? Is United going broke? I never got one of these things from them before. Can't they pay their own taxes anymore? On a stinking ninety-five thousand . . . that money United paid me was not income! Absolutely not income! It was repayment for my out-of-pocket expenses. For what? Go to hell! For publicity appearances around the country for *The Feathered Serpent*, you fool." There was silence while he listened to the voice at the other end of the phone. But he couldn't contain himself very long. "All right, Sidney. The fact is I tell you too much. So I know you know I made no appearances. I used the money to buy Princeling. You're my accountant. You know I can't afford that horse. How can I? There's Marabelle. And Georgia. And Antonia. *Stronzo!* And seven children. You know that. How can I pay the tax? I'm broke all the time. No money. How would you like to be a friend and lend me a few bucks? You know—a friend in need . . . okay, you bastard! Excuses, excuses. All right—call Christie Larsen—say . . . okay. Call Harry Weiss. I don't give a shit who you call. Just tell him to go fuck himself. In Yiddish. Tell him I said he was a *momza*. Oh . . . you're right. A *gonif*. Sidney, are you sure you're a goy?"

Julian Hennesy, barefoot, wearing a color-spattered smock, carefully picked his way around his studio. It nested on top of his two-car garage, vibrating slightly when a car drove in or drove out of the garage. The walls were marked with scribbles that looked like caveman drawings. The floor—like that of the legendary, French painter Leger—was a fire-engine red. Chaos was the dominant note. Scattered around the floor were large sketches, drawings, the beginnings of posters, all in various stages of completion. Julian had to trot between them to get a beer from the small refrigerator. The place had a lighthearted look with its large unfinished drawings of Madonna, Shirley Temple, Cher, Shirley MacLaine . . . all outlined in eyebrow pencil.

Julian was a talented draftsman but his method of drawing was more inventive than his fine line studies. His palette was cosmetics—the sketches were done in various shades of eyebrow pencil. When more complete, they were filled in with various shades of powder and lipstick and nail polish colors—red, pink, brown, orange. Or tones were applied with eye shadow—green, gray, blue, purple. It depended on Julian's mood and his attitude toward his subject. Only when he was satisfied did he spray a fast-drying, clear, hard acrylic over the work to prevent the cosmetics from smearing. Five or six sketch pads of drawings were leaning against the walls. Nothing was completed. The only finished portrait was hanging near the sink . . . one of his current girlfriend and model, Cindy, covered with white powder and graffiti, a clown's face floating over her head.

"Why the clown?" Cindy had asked when she saw it.

"My alter ego. The comic side of my movie work. Making clowns beautiful. That's why I call it Cosmetic Art."

Cindy, with green hair curling, smeared with green lipstick and green eye shadow, nude beneath a hideous green mink coat, posed holding a green hand mirror and a green lipstick.

"I'm getting stiff," she complained through her teeth.

"Hush, girl. The work is never finished. I got to get a show ready for Castelli."

"The New York man with the art gallery?" Julian nodded. "Are you going to be a famous arteest, Julie? And sign all your drawings?"

"Shut up, baby girl."

"What a gas! You won't have to wait for the name credits in itsy-bitsy type on the screen. Stop staring at me cross-eyed."

There was a knock on the door, and Cindy started to get off the stool. "I'll go."

"Stay still. You know the door isn't locked. Come in," he called out.

Bald, fat, bespectacled, Harvey Hartman sidled through the door. He was carrying a briefcase. He put it down as though it weighed a ton and straightened up, grinning from ear to ear.

"Hello, everybody," Harvey said.

Julian leaned forward. "It's a pleasure, Harvey. Glad you finally made it."

"My pleasure, too," Cindy crooned.

Harvey eyed her appraisingly, then turned back to Julian. He glanced at the sketch of Harrison Ford on the easel, then at the other drawings scattered around the floor, and shook his head in bewilderment. He stared at the bottles of cosmetics, each containing a different shade of powder, lip gloss, nail polish. Jars of hair coloring were also waiting ... Clairol, L'Oreal and other brands all did their part for Julian—and art.

"This could be a beauty salon," Harvey said. "It's all very interesting, Julie. I think you've made a breakthrough.

A new art form. I hear you're going for a New York show. What do you call it?"

"I haven't named it."

"Why not Cosmetic Art?" He rolled the words around on his tongue. "Why not? It should be a sensation. Women love cosmetics. My wife spends a bundle... so do men. And you have authority. You're a makeup artist. You work on the most beautiful faces in the world. Anyone can see where you got your inspiration."

"From the late, late show," Cindy sniped.

Julian gave Harvey a slow grin. "That's a beautiful idea, Harvey. Cosmetic Art. I wish I'd thought of that. Cosmetics inspire me. I see my work on the wide screen... the small screen... every screen. Morning, noon, and night. Every actress, every actor, every director knows the creativity of cosmetics. Now I've taken cosmetics to their logical conclusion... pure art... Cosmetic Art."

"Julian said that ten minutes ago. My elbows hurt," Cindy pouted.

"I know, baby girl. Rest while Harvey and I mammypalava."

Harvey gave up his art lover stance. "Julian, I saw your message on the 1099. Every accountant at Frank & Farber has apoplectic clients choking on that form. This morning Sidney Frank had five telephone messages from people who worked on *The Feathered Serpent*, including Jenny Lattimore, Alan Lucca..."

"I bet. Lucca played a lot of poker and lost. He said he was putting in for ninety-five thousand... to buy a horse."

"Sidney has heard. But there's nothing even Sidney can do to get Lucca off the hook. It's the IRS. The studio's stopped playing Santa Claus. No more spending production money for knickknacks like a new Mercedes, a horse..."

"I told you I didn't. Listen to me, Harvey! I know all about the handouts. Nothing is secret on a set. But I'm allergic to horses. I don't want a cottage in Oaxaca. I'm not Jenny who needs a Mercedes for her man with the big prick. I got my own prick. I'm clean. I take my paycheck and run."

Harvey gave Julian his best cynical smile. "Julian, old buddy, the studio wrote out a check to you for seventy-seven big ones. I don't care what damn fool white lie you told them for getting it. Maybe you said you bribed NASA officials so they'd let you make up the new female astronaut. Then she swore to announce when she landed that *The Feathered Serpent* was a creature from outer space. Beautiful! But it won't play. No matter how much it cost you personally to bribe NASA, you have to pay the tax on the money United reimbursed you for the bribe."

"What reimbursement? What money?"

"I just want you to understand..." Harvey sounded peevish. "...that you have to pay the taxes on the money the studio paid you. No matter what you said it was for. They won't..."

"I may have to strangle you." Julian's voice was low and mean. There was silence for a few seconds. Then he spoke carefully, distinctly. "Harvey, I never put in for any additional expenses." Harvey said nothing, so Julian continued. "I've never in my life put in a chit for phony expenses. Not at Warner. Columbia. Universal. Nowhere." Harvey pursed his lips. "You know me, man. You've been handling my money and doing my taxes for eleven years. Did I ever suddenly acquire a beach house in Laguna that you know I didn't pay for, because you never gave me the money?"

"Hmm," Harvey murmured. "That's true. So why this time?"

"*Dumkopf!* I didn't do it. Not this time. Not any time."

"You sure you didn't?"

"I'm sure. I didn't ask to be reimbursed for anything."

There was a few more seconds of silence.

"Then you didn't buy a horse?" Harvey laughed uneasily.

Julian's voice was cold with anger. "I didn't ask for seventy-seven thousand dollars. And I didn't get seventy-seven thousand dollars."

"But you did get a 1099 form for exactly that much?"

"Exactly. Seventy-seven thousand dollars."

There was another long pause while Harvey stared at Cindy.

"You wipe that mean look off your face, Mr. Harvey Hartman," Cindy sputtered.

NAKED CALL

Julian shook his head in disgust. "Cut it out, Harvey. Baby girl never goes through my mail at night... or my pants. She would—but she never sleeps over. Suppose one of Viola's private eyes should decide to drop in? I'd lose all my visiting rights with the kids. The divorce isn't final yet."

"What about Viola? Spend any time with her?"

"My dear second wife has been in Atlanta with her mama and the kids since June. She didn't fly here on a broomstick to grab that check."

"So what happened to the check? There's a record in the United accounting department of a check for that amount being paid to you."

"I don't give a shit about United's accounting department. I don't give a shit about their records. I never asked for that money. And I never got it."

"Maybe it got lost in the mail," Cindy reflected.

Harvey faced Julian nervously, swaying back and forth on his heels. He had never known Julian Hennesy to lie. If he said he didn't get the check, he didn't get the check. "Julian, I don't understand any of this."

"That makes two of us."

"Strange. All our other clients who received 1099s from United know exactly what monies the form refers to. They admit they got paid by United. They admit what they spent the money on. What outrages Lucca and Lattimore and a few dozen others is that they have to pay taxes on the money. Nobody says they didn't receive the money."

"Tough shit! That's their flap. It's not mine."

"You are the only client of Frank & Farber who didn't receive any money."

"The devil moves in ways as mysterious as God," Cindy intoned.

The men exchanged looks. "There is something going on here that isn't kosher," Harvey said.

"Very unkosher is my feeling."

Whenever Sidney Frank had occasion to meet with Harry Weiss, he felt at a disadvantage. It wasn't their disputes—the polite, low-keyed, but vehement struggles over share of gross, share of net, or the way a film charged off expenses, wiping out any profits for Sidney's clients ... actors, actresses, writers. Through the years, Sidney had grown accustomed to confronting bizarre—even fraudulent—movie bookkeeping. By now he enjoyed the battles, because usually he came away with some kind of win. The greediest producer couldn't function if he was on the hit list of too many accountants.

It was not the battle that made Sidney uncomfortable in Harry's presence—it was Harry. Tanned, slim, natty, Harry reminded Sidney of his paunch, his flabby muscles, his pale skin, his suit. The fact that, as founder of the very successful CPA firm of Frank & Farber, Sidney's net worth was five times Harry's did not always buttress his feeling of confidence.

Today was different. Today the shoe was on Harry's foot. What Sidney told him had shaken his impeccably groomed facade. He had difficulty collecting his thoughts and for a few minutes remained speechless ... very unlike Harry. Finally he found words.

"You do mean a 1099 form? That is what he received?"

"Yes. I brought along a photocopy for you." Sidney opened his briefcase and handed Weiss the form.

Harry's face was pale under his tan. "And he claims he never received the money?"

"He received nothing. After Harvey Hartman told me about it, I saw Julian myself. He confirmed everything Harvey told me."

"Hennesy is Harvey's client?"

'Yes."

"He could be lying."

"He isn't. Harvey's been his accountant for eleven years ... swears by him on all counts. At tax time accountants are like priests. They get to hear all the garbage confessions: criminal evasions, fake expenses, illegal practices that shake one's faith in the survival of the nation. We don't get asked for salvation, no, we get asked for advice on how to cheat the government most efficiently. But Julian is another breed. He's caught Harvey making mistakes twice ... in his favor instead of the government's. What can I tell you? A real stars and stripes patriot. Born in Haiti. Believes he owes his life ... his success ... to the United States of America.

He gets square by paying his taxes in full, no tricks. Julian Hennesy may be the only honest man in Hollywood."

"Fuckin' *meshugener*." Harry had reverted to the coarse, one-of-the-boys style of his blue-collar Brooklyn boyhood.

"I have clients like Alan Lucca. You advanced him ninety-five thousand—"

"Don't tell me that bastard didn't get his check either. I remember signing it."

"Oh, he got it all right. What chokes him up is paying taxes on the money."

"Fuck him!"

"He'll pay. But I repeat, Julian is something else. He never asked for the money. He never got the money. What he got was a form. Knowing Julian, if he'd gotten the money, he'd pay the tax . . . without a peep."

Harry stared at the form with distaste. "I'll follow this up. Apparently there's been a mistake somewhere . . . a misunderstanding in the accounting department." He pushed a button on his intercom. "Elsie, send in Edgardo."

In minutes there was a light tap on the door. "Come in," Harry called out.

A young man in a navy blue suit entered the office. "Yes, sir?"

"Go see Del Fasano and get me the books on the production of *The Feathered Serpent*. I want to see the invoices, the ledger sheets, the checkbooks, the cancelled checks, the works. Understand?"

"Yes, sir." Edgardo turned smartly on his heel and left.

Harry gave Sidney a broad smile. "This will take a little time. I want to look into everything. I'll get back to you in a few days."

"Fine, Harry," Sidney said standing up. "I can wait."

"I'm sure it's nothing at all. Some kind of bookkeeping mistake," Harry said cheerfully. For a few seconds he mulled over this statement, then gave Sidney the earnest, we-understand-things look of one professional to another. "Of course, you'll say nothing about this, Sidney, until we have it all straightened out. Clerical errors—they happen all the time."

"Of course," Sidney said. "And of course Julian can forget about that 1099 form."

For a heartbeat Harry paused, then nodded in agreement. He, too, knew when to bargain and when not to. "Of course. He shouldn't pay taxes on money he never received. I don't know what caused this mix-up, but I'll take your word for it. Julian never received a check for seventy-seven thousand dollars."

"Right," Sidney said with satisfaction. As he left the office he thought about Harry—Harry, who today reminded him of the joke about the amateur robber. He broke into the bank and pulled out a gun, shouting, "All right you mother stickers! This is a fuckup." Poor Harry. It sure was a fuckup.

Chapter 11

HARRY WAITED until he was certain Sidney Frank had enough time to reach the street before he pressed his intercom. "Tell that kid to shake his ass—" He stopped talking as the door was lightly tapped, and Edgardo entered carrying a carton loaded with all the financial information on the production of *The Feathered Serpent*.

Harry hunched over his desk, a sense of foreboding overwhelming him. Grimly at first, and then with hard concentration, he spent the afternoon reviewing the books of *The Feathered Serpent*. As time passed, his feeling of doom lightened. Listed beneath the heading of Extraordinary Expenses, he eventually found the item he was looking for. His spirits lifting, he followed this clue, which led to an exhaustive scrutiny of the invoice file under both paid and unpaid bills. What he located in the paid file was reassuring: an invoice from Julian Hennesy with the notation, "Check 1337," written on it. Harry took a deep breath, full of pride of purpose. His next step was the checkbooks for *The Feath-*

ered Serpent. Hopefully they would not be a disappointment.

They weren't. Actually, one checkbook was a truly inspiring experience. Check 1337 had been made out to Julian Hennesy. So much for Julian's purity of soul. Sidney was surprisingly gullible. With a feeling that amounted to manifest destiny, Harry braced for the final dig: to review the actual checks returned by the Bank of California. If he was right this should be the *coup de grace*.

In took almost an hour, but he found it. Check 1337. Hosanna! Et cetera! Endorsed ... cancelled ... paid to Julian Hennesy! The bastard lied, like everyone else. Harry reached for the intercom button. "Get me Sidney Frank."

But Sidney would not be convinced. If anything, he was more adamant. After their meeting, he had personally reviewed Julian Hennesy's finances.

"Harry, I don't give a damn what your records say. I don't give a damn about that cancelled check or the endorsement. Listen to me—I'm telling you this once and I will not repeat myself."

"Temper, temper, Sid. Bad for the old blood pressure," Harry chided happily.

Sidney's tone never wavered. "Julian Hennesy never sent United Cinema an invoice for any unusual expenses. And he never received a check in payment."

"I have the cancelled check."

"Balls! Frank & Farber takes care of all Julian's bank accounts, pays his credit card chits, his department store bills, his mortgage payments, and his alimony to his first wife. Not a penny has he ever shortchanged anyone. We give him an allowance on which he lives—and lives well. Now hear me, Harry—are you listening?"

"I'm listening. But I have to say—"

"You have to say nothing. Just listen. If you keep up this shit, I am warning you that I am personally going to the criminal investigation department of the IRS and complain."

"Sidney, that's below the belt." Harry was stunned.

"I am going to complain that United Cinema is playing games with their taxes. You have heard of tax evasion?"

"For Christ sake, Sidney—"

"That they are trying to claim phony expenses. Expenses that don't exist so the studio can show less income and pay less taxes."

"But we have the cancelled check! I have it in front of me. I'll photocopy it and messenger it over to you—"

"Shove it up your ass! After I register my complaint with the IRS, the CID boys with their frayed collars and green eyeshades and nasty dispositions are going to swarm over your books like a bunch of army ants. They'll examine every check that United Cinema has written for the last ten years. And if they do that, you and I both know they'll find plenty. Louis Levy was no saint."

"Sidney, you are a bona fide bastard!"

"You get my message? Am I coming through to you?"

"A son of a bitch!"

"Sticks and stones, Harry. Sticks and stones." Sidney hung up.

Harry Weiss was savvy . . . always had been. He was ultra-sensitive to the slow and fast beat of the corporate pulse—aware of the indispositions of clerks and janitors, of the good or bad humors of production executives. But the discovery of this cancelled check surprised him—and, yes—it gave him an unwelcome premonition. As controller he was accustomed to handling the occasional glitches that inevitably arose in a studio where tens of millions of dollars in checks of all sizes were regularly sent out and received. That was business as usual. This wasn't.

Sidney's firmness had unsettled him. So had his threat of siccing the criminal division of IRS on them. Damn! Those boys didn't give a shit about tax avoidance, like buying tax-free muni bonds. All America was into tax avoidance. Disallowed tax avoidance required you to pay up in full with interest and penalties. Period! That was it. Tax evasion was something else. It was criminal. You paid up with interest and penalties. And then you went to jail.

Harry's stomach felt queasy. If Sidney was that convinced that Julian was straight, then maybe something was wrong. Suppose this Julian Hennesy thing was the tip of the iceberg—what iceberg? His mind shied from the word. It might be—it could be—embezzlement. What a stink that would

NAKED CALL

cause. He had to protect his flank, and pass the muck along to the next level . . . Christie Larsen.

"I heard Princess Diana wears his rags. If they're good enough for her, why not me? Madam Mimi copied the dress for beans. What do you think?" Jo had shed her usual "dress for success" office uniform and slipped into a strapless, blue velvet evening gown. "See, it fits like a glove. Mid-thigh."

Christie laughed. "Proof positive that less is more. Minimalist dressing."

"It comes with this jacket." Jo added a black toreador jacket, dripping jet, and waltzed around the office.

"Wow!"

"Eat your heart out," she said, twirling about. The jacket was almost blinding. On the back, blue and gold sequins spelled out the word "LAKERS."

"Good Lord!"

"Double wow!" Jo said. "I ought to get an Academy Award from the Chamber of Commerce."

Christie's intercom buzzed. "Yes, Nan?"

"Harry Weiss wants to see you."

"Damn it! Have him wait," Jo shouted.

"Jo, it's only Harry. He'll love it. Send him in, Nan."

"Christie—you bitch!" Jo tried to wriggle out of her jacket. Harry entered . . . his mouth fell open. Jo changed her tactics. "As always, Madam President, you're right. Harry—for you, a private showing." Jo sashayed by Harry, her smile toothy, her cleavage seismographic, twirling the jacket, tossing it in the air, curtsying, pirouetting, hips swiveling—a parody of a runway model. Christie decided the performance was worth at least one Oscar . . . maybe two Emmys.

"Excuse me for interrupting, ladies." Harry tried to sound embarrassed, which he wasn't.

"You're not interrupting. Don't be shy," Christie said. "Jo has just switched to the Mommy Track. She wants two days off a week to get her closets diapered. Spring fashions are teething . . . just learning to walk. Jo wants them to feel loved."

Jo glared at Christie and quickly removed her jacket.

"Forget what you saw, Harry. I was just showing off what I'm wearing to the Academy celebration, when we dance with all our Oscars clutched to our hearts."

"I understand." Harry was all diplomacy. "But something's come up . . . and if you'll excuse us, Jo."

"I'll excuse you," Jo said, sashaying toward the door. "And I am not on the Mommy Track, Christina Larsen. You are a classic fink. Classic, you understand? Spelled p-h-y-n-q-u-e!"

"What's the matter, Harry?" Christie asked. "You look like you ate something awful. Or it's eating you."

"It's eating me. Those damn 1099s." He placed the folder he was carrying on Christie's desk.

"Harry, breathe deeply. Okay, you knew it, I knew it, we knew this would happen the instant we sent out those forms. I, too, have heard the anguished cries of the boys and girls floating over the telephone wires. The voices of our movie legends who hate to pay taxes. I've had five calls in the last week."

"I know. You graciously passed them along to me. To your five, add the dozen I've gotten directly."

"It was inevitable when there was no more Louis—no *paterfamilias*. So? What's the scoop? You feeling jumpy? Nerves frayed? By now you should have a callused eardrum."

"I have. It's not the usual howls that's gotten to me." He paused to give weight to his next words. "It's Julian Hennesy."

"Julian? Our makeup man?"

"Our makeup man." Choosing his words carefully, Harry Weiss recounted what had happened in his meeting with Sidney Frank. He went on to explain how he'd routinely checked *The Feathered Serpent* books and located the documentation for a payment to Julian Hennesy, living at 11131 Rochester Avenue in West Los Angeles. In short, Julian had received a check for seventy seven thousand dollars. Harry opened his folder and pulled out a cancelled check, which Christie only glanced at.

"Apparently Julian lies. Everyone does," Christie noted impatiently. "What makes his lie so special?"

"Sidney Frank . . . Harvey Hartman! Both of them swear

in blood that he never received the check. Frank & Farber manages his monies."

"You believe them?"

"That's what troubles me. Yeah! I believe them." Harry deemed it wiser to say nothing about Sidney's threat . . . not yet.

Christie paused. For Harry, the remark was so eccentric that she couldn't help but stare. Then she shrugged. "You can believe them. They can believe Julian. I like Julian. I admire his work. But I don't believe him. He's lying."

There was a longer pause. "I don't think so."

Christie remained unmoved. "Why not?"

"A lousy hunch."

That could mean anything or nothing. "Did you examine the cancelled check?"

"You bet I did." Harry's fingers smoothed on the check.

"And?"

"It was drawn on United's *Serpent* account at the Beverly Hills branch of the Bank of California. Payable to Julian Hennesy . . . endorsed by Julian . . . like the endorsements on his regular salary checks." Harry went on to detail the date the check was issued, that it was endorsed by Julian Hennesy and cashed by Julian Hennesy at the Bank of California.

Christie listened to his recitation, her face impassive. All his extensive research had a purpose behind it. Harry was frightened. Her response this time was measured and temperate. "You've done well, Harry. Now probe deeper. Call the bank. That's a sizeable amount. They'll have a record of who cashed it. A teller may remember seeing Julian. But if Julian Hennesy didn't cash the check . . ." She gave Harry a long look. "Get back to me as soon as you can. I need more information on who did what and where they did it. More information than your records give."

Harry slid the check back into the folder. "Do my best, Madam President."

"You've done that already. Now do better."

Harry's brain ran through a maze. "Suppose I don't come up with Julian? Suppose it's a man with a mask . . . someone we don't know?"

"Suppose it is?"

"Seventy-seven thousand dollars is peanuts to United Cinema. We could pay the taxes." Harry said hopefully.

"Peanuts? Maybe. But if you're right, they're poison peanuts. We may be dealing with grand larceny. Embezzlement! Good God, Harry! The press would have a field day if they caught us trying to bury it. They'd eat us alive in the *Reporter* . . . kill us in the *Wall Street Journal*."

Christie watched Harry Weiss leave her office. She wondered what it was she sniffed in the air. Fire and brimstone? Burning at the stake? But who was burning . . . and why?

Angelo Lupo was relaxing in a lounge chair on the flagstone terrace of his house in Amagansett, staring out at the Atlantic Ocean and drinking Clan MacGregor scotch. He liked cheap scotch. He liked family restaurants—a plate of pasta, green salad, a glass of Chianti. And he liked expensive clothes. Although he never played tennis and seldom went out in the sun, he was wearing white sweats made especially for him by Garabaldi, his custom tailor in Roma, Nike tennis shoes because his Napoli shoemaker could do no better, and Persol sunglasses, naturally made in Milano. Although his sartorial splendor never saw a tennis court, it made the point. Since his second triple coronary bypass, Angelo was into excercise. Swimming in his indoor, unheated, ocean-fed swimming pool, cycling on his stationary Life Cycle bike, rowing at his rowing machine. But the trunks he wore for swimming and rowing and cycling were hardly as flattering as the sweats. And Tony had grown vain with age and a sense of his own mortality.

Stavros Lennos repressed a smile, observing that in repose Angelo's face had a deceptive look, suggesting a gentle nature . . . a pit bull who liked children and cats. One might even mistake him for some kind of teacher—not of music or history but possibly a football or wrestling coach. All in all, a nice guy . . . friendly.

Stavros fixed himself a vodka and ice . . . Stolichnaya. The men sat in a companionable silence for a while. Lupo spoke first.

"I'm sorry Louis didn't see things your way. I've always liked him. He was good company."

"That was thirty years ago."

"Forty-six, Stavros. Don't try to flatter me. Even then he was a madman. But committed to making good movies."

"And throwing great parties."

"The best. We had some very good times."

"Why didn't you want me to use your name? He might have been more amenable."

Lupo's words were icy with offended dignity. "He'd have thrown you out, my son. He doesn't trust me. Louis lives in the past. He believes everything he saw in *The Godfather*." He gave Stavros a sardonic smile. "Louis thinks my only interests are prostitution, gambling, drugs, loan-sharking. *Maledetto!* Loan-sharking! He forgets how often he waited, hat in hand, at the New York banks. He forgets that my purse was open to him. The interest he paid on the five million he borrowed from me was less than those bankers—bloodsuckers—would have charged. I always made exceptions for my friends."

"I didn't know Levy borrowed from us."

Lupo said gravely, "Louis borrowed, Sam borrowed, Cecil borrowed. All fuckin' Hollywood borrowed—and still borrows. Some day I'll show you my celebrity ledger. Only Louis got special rates. I really liked the bastard. He played a good game of poker . . . straight . . . didn't mark the deck. But he never gave me proper respect for being an American like him. He ignored my offer of friendship. He was ashamed to be in debt to me."

"He insulted you."

Lupo's eyes were remote, staring into another time. "Yes. He never believed that I was a patriot . . . a Sicilian American patriot. That I, too, want our country to grow bigger . . . stronger. It is good for the Family. For the American people. The media make noise about gambling, drugs, prostitution. Why? If people would be honest, are we not a service industry, servicing human nature, like the laundromat . . . the fast food joints? When human nature changes, our services will change."

Straight-faced, Stavros asked, "How do you see loan-sharking?"

"More human nature. People make bad business judgements. We make repairs. Repairs are costly. Think about medical repairs for the body. Do you know what my bypass cost? Those doctors make more money than we do. I should have been a heart specialist."

"Nice analogy."

"Stavros, my son, understanding human nature is the key. Louis thought I was limited, like Capone, like Luciano. I'm not. I'm a man of vision. Like Moshe was."

"Moshe had a beautiful funeral."

"Fitting. For a great man. He taught me much. That's why I extended our operations. Today we have banking connections, Wall Street connections . . . we sit in the boardrooms of companies—many are in the Fortune 500. You represent us on some."

Stavros bowed his head. "I thank you for the honor."

"It was Moshe's decision." Lupo gazed at Stavros, hard-eyed, full of recognition. "Moshe was right. You have done well for the Family."

"I'm glad."

"Very well for poor Sicilians . . . poor Greeks. Too bad you are a Greek."

"Half. So? Moshe was Jewish."

Lupo almost smiled, his face giving acceptance. "True. We became an American melting pot . . . but your mother had fine Sicilian blood. She was my favorite sister. So you understand me. You understood Moshe. That's why we sent you to Hollywood. Remember what Moshe taught you when all you wanted was to grow up and be Carl Hubbell."

"Dizzy Dean."

"A baseball pitcher." Lupo's tone was indulgent. "He taught you the Family comes first. You work for the Family . . . protect the Family. The Family goes on."

"Moshe once said, 'One generation passeth away and another generation cometh.' We must think about the future."

"The Old Testament. He loved to quote it. Moshe was born Jewish. But at heart—Sicilian. He understood about our children . . . grandchildren . . . the future. His last words before he died were, 'Angelo, be careful. To everything there is a season, and a time to every purpose under heaven.

You are the victim of mass hysteria. The butt of the Mob Commission. You are getting bad press—it is a warning.' *Capice*?" Lupo went on indignantly. "The press has a *festa magnifica* when one of our boys takes a hit. They forget the Colombian coke kings . . . the Jamaicans running crack . . . the Asian gangs!"

"The rise of the third world." Stavros smiled.

"Yes! The third world! Poor, repressed people making their way in the land of opportunity—preying on the American poor and the repressed, who have no choice but to be preyed upon. *Che stronzo*! Maybe once a year this scum is reported on *60 Minutes* or *MacNeil Lehrer*." Lupo sighed. "While we American-born Sicilians—we get no sympathy. We are always news . . . bad news. No one mentions that Carlo's son is a Navy pilot. Alberto's daughter is in the Peace Corps. We do not live off the poorest . . . the homeless. We never go where we are not invited. We keep our distance. A chairman of a corporation . . . a Senator . . . a baseball hero . . . a Hollywood celebrity . . . do we call them? No! They telephone us. What we need is for the media to understand our side."

"It would improve our public image."

Lupo nodded encouragingly. "Moshe taught you well. Our public image is shit . . . un-American. It needs to be changed." Angelo was pleased. He was reminded how much he loved his nephew. He almost wished Stavros was his own son. Stavros was the kind of man who could follow in the footsteps of the genius, Moshe Cohen. He had the brains and the courage to lead the Families into the twenty-first century . . . stronger and more powerful than ever . . . the third world be damned!

Lupo went on in a factual tone. "So you see why the movies are a good place to start. We buy United . . . we make good movies. Sometimes movies about ourselves. The audience leaves the movie house laughing . . . crying. Either way, they know us better. They understand us a little. The movies will show how American we are."

"The movies are a fine way to launder money."

"A good idea . . . practical." There was just a touch of disdain in Lupo's tone and Stavros flushed. He had not meant to mention the obvious. Somehow it had slipped out, listening to all of Angelo's nonsense about changing the image of the Mafia. "I think the movies are an excellent way to build for tomorrow."

"That's the idea. It is everything Moshe wanted for us." He licked his lips. "Have you accumulated enough United stock yet?"

"Not yet. It must not become obvious."

"Go quietly... slowly. I trust you."

"Thank you. Now tell me, knowing how Louis Levy felt, why did you pick United? There are other studios."

"Stavros, you underestimate me." Lupo's tone was a gentle rebuke. "I harbor no grudge against Louis. I chose United because my old friend is getting old... as I am. We are not immortal. I knew Louis would need help soon."

"He didn't think so."

"He always was vain. Now we frightened him so much he makes a foolish mistake. Instead of coming to us—his friends—he goes to this Wall Street house, Macleod Brothers." Lupo made a face of disgust. "Again we must rescue him. Once it was for five million. This time... a little more."

"A lot more."

"We can afford it. And this time we do it for ourselves ... the Family... not Louis. Only a little bit for old times' sake. Tell me, what's going on with this Wall Street *paisano* ... this Guy Macleod?" Angelo Lupo was finally getting down to the real business.

"It's in the works. Your friend, Louis, has given us the perfect opening."

Lupo smiled, his expression benignly abstracted. "Louis and I should be friends. Tell me about it."

"It involves the IRS."

"Ah. The big guns. Very good. The IRS got Capone." Lupo was full of admiration. "Moshe would like it. It's his kind of play. I am proud of you, my son. Don't give me details, just the gist of things."

"It's the new game... the 1099 game."

"Non-salaried income."

"You never needed an accountant."

"I like the numbers. How long will it take?"

"Six months . . . give or take. Then we should be rid of Guy Macleod."

"The government will do our work for us?"

"The government will."

"Who has made the contact?"

"Mario Rinaldi."

"Laura's son. A very fine Italian boy. All the girls like him. He should do fine in the movies. Maybe we use him one day."

"He's doing very well without our help."

"You will tell me about him when the time comes. Not now. But, with you, Stavros, I am very pleased." He smiled a fatherly smile. "Now, what do you think of this Larsen woman . . . this president? How does she feel about the sale of United?"

"I don't know. She wouldn't have dinner with me when I called to congratulate her." His voice took on a metallic edge. "But she did not enjoy telling me that Macleod Brothers had acquired United."

"So? You knew that. What else?"

"She asked me to give her regards to Roger Tysen."

"Is that all? No questions?"

"None."

"Ah. She should have been a man."

"Better as a woman. You should see her."

Lupo laughed for the first time that afternoon. "You always had a good eye for a woman. Will she cooperate?"

"Her contract is for three years. We can make it three days . . . if necessary."

"Is she good?"

"She was the executive producer on *The Feathered Serpent*."

"Eight Academy Award nominations. Not bad."

Stavros smiled into the sunglasses. "Plus a few interesting 1099 forms to her credit."

Chapter 12

IT WAS one of a row of seven little town houses on a side street on Manhattan's platinum Upper East Side, five stories high, designed by a highly regarded English architect. Behind the rose-colored facade of the house there were marble floors, and in the rear of the fifth floor—occupied by the owner—was a terrace overlooking a garden. A soothing spot for Manfried Hauser's clients to relax and sip wine or Perrier water.

Hauser had purchased the house for three million dollars when it was an unfinished shell, a collection of interior spaces dramatically lit by a skylight, but lacking walls, lighting, even bathrooms. He had adapted the first four floors to his needs as beauty arbiter of the Dazzling... and the would-be Dazzlers... who called it—only half-joking—The Shrine.

At nine o'clock in the morning, Irene Bentley and Mona Anderson were sitting side by side in the peach-tinted Image Room. Both had had their faces steamed with chamomile tea to open the pores. They wore matching peach-tinted velour robes while waiting for the specialists to continue the facial ritual.

"My Aunt Laura's doctor had her Retin-A mixed with Complex 15. I'm waiting to see the results before I ask Dr. Murphy," Mona whispered between creamed lips.

"Mmmm... another hot, new moisturizer. What did Woody say about your putting some pin money into *Deirdre*?"

"I haven't told him yet. But I know my doll baby. He loves the theater. He'll love being an angel."

"He wasn't a doll baby when you invested in *Long Live the Queen*."

"That was before he joined Macleod Brothers... and started making real money."

"Mona, Mona, steadfast and true." Irene's smile was kind. "It was also before he knew Guy Macleod had invested in *Deirdre*."

"Guy has nothing to do with it. Sherwood is very independent. He worries about borrowing money from me. He wants me to look up to him." Her tone was impish. "He doesn't know that the money I gave him to buy his partnership was peanuts. Poor baby, he hasn't a clue as to what I'm really worth."

Irene laughed, a short abrupt laugh. "Very smart."

"Don't laugh. I got my money's worth. Sherwood went to Yale, and prepped at Choate... same as Guy. That's why Guy let him buy into the firm. Guy's such a snob. But the Andersons are as social as the Macleods... New York's four hundred... just broke." Mona looked pleased with herself... her tact. She discreetly refrained from mentioning Sherwood's pillow talk. Guy had almost been expelled from Choate. "I know money matters. Momma warned me before she died. She said if I married a man who wasn't equally rich, he'd end up living off me."

"It has been known to happen."

"Sherwood isn't like that. I'm not either. What I mean is I'm not one of those women who will stay in a relationship where I support the man."

"Sound thinking."

"I couldn't live like that. But I feel very protective of Sherwood. My Aunt Laura keeps wondering why I do what I do for him. I said, because he brings out every mothering instinct I have. I just love him to death."

"What if Woody found out how rich you really are?"

"So what? It wouldn't change anything. I'm not naive or foolish. But I'm sure he wouldn't want to live off me, because he really loves me. And he's an independent type."

"Hello, Mrs. Anderson," caroled a white uniform with blond braided hair.

"Irene, I'm booked solid. I squeezed you in because... well... you're you," stated the twin white uniform.

The skin specialists, Inga and Ulla, had arrived. Conversation came to a halt... lip motions would interrupt the facial ritual. First there was the artful extraction of every little comedone—native New York blackheads—that might pepper the elegant skin of their clients.

"Inga, press harder," squeaked Mona Anderson.

"No, no, it would leave a blotch."

"It's big—my husband can see it."

"Mmmm. I got the little bugger."

Neither woman required a scrubber cleansing, so Inga and Ulla proceeded to the masks, appropriate for both clients' skins. During the application and setting of the mud, neither woman spoke. Both were too immersed in the illusion of firming and tightening . . . a feeling they knew was strictly temporary. It was during the peeling of the mud mask—the cleansing with a moisturizer suitable, naturally, for each skin—that Mona's sublime idea took shape.

"Irene! I have the most fantastic idea."

"Mmmm . . ."

"It occured to me under the mud."

"Mmmm . . ."

Boldly, Mona detonated her depth charge. "Did you ever think that *Deirdre of the Sorrows* would make a great film?"

"No." Maintaining surpreme calm. "I don't care much for movies."

"Well, it would. Just think—*Deirdre of the Sorrows* . . . a teenage love story . . . a box office smash."

"Mrs. Anderson, please—relax your facial muscles or I cannot peel the mud properly."

"Sorry. Irene, you know what else?" Mona spoke with lips carefully unmoving.

"What?" Irene sighed from the depth of relaxation beneath Ulla's fingers.

"Did Guy tell you they bought United?"

"United what?"

"United Cinema . . . the movie studio. Macleod Brothers are the major stockholders."

"So?"

"So United Cinema could produce *Deirdre* as a movie."

"I never thought of *Deirdre* as a movie," Irene murmured.

"Irene, don't argue. You'd make a great director."

"Producer-director." It slipped out accidentally.

"Yes, producer-director. My uncle would know exactly what to do to convince Guy to let you make *Deirdre* as a feature. Please, you must meet him."

"The things I do for friends." Irene's newly clean face smiled at Mona. Radiant, blatantly artificial, utterly convincing. "Which uncle? You have so many. Angelo? Stefano? Stavros?"

"We're a big family. I mean Uncle Stavros. He wanted to buy United, but Guy beat him to it."

"Was he... indeed... hmm... If you insist."

"I insist. As a favor. I'll call him—set it up," Mona giggled. "We'll double date."

"Charming. Stavros and I. You and Woody."

"Irene, I've been meaning to mention it. You mustn't be offended, but we're friends so I can say it."

"Say what?"

"I would rather you didn't call him Woody. His name is Sherwood."

"Mrs. Anderson, I cannot cleanse your skin properly if you continue this conversation."

"I, too, Mrs. Bentley. I was solidly booked...."

When the Image Room program was completed, Mona and Irene moved languidly to Close-Ups, the room where lashes were applied and, when requested, eye shadow, eyeliner, and mascara. This morning both women were interested only in lashes. On their way into the eye salon they were stopped by a woman in a blue velour dressing gown who was exiting.

Mona greeted her like a long-lost sister. "Mitzi! How wonderful to see you! Zelda outdid herself. Your lashes are so luxuriant, as Manfried says."

"It wasn't Zelda. It was Monte."

"Monte? He's two hundred dollars extra."

"Tonight we're going to the Jacob Van Vliis benefit for the unsheltered. You understand... the homeless... white tie required." Mitzi, a small, bosomy woman with a short cloud of gray hair haloing her face, gave Mona only distracted attention. Irene was the hallowed presence. "Aren't you Irene Bentley?"

"Do we know each other?"

"I saw *Long Live the Queen*. Wonderful."

"Thank you." Irene was accustomed to celebrityhood among rich, stage-struck New Yorkers.

"I was at a backers' audition. I meant to invest. But there wasn't time to write a check. I was meeting my husband in Milan."

"Pity. You'd have made your money back three times over."

"Irene, come along. Our lashes are waiting," Mona urged.

"Perhaps you would like to come to one of the backers' auditions for *Deirdre of the Sorrows*?" Irene sounded bored. She wasn't.

"I would. Send me a note . . . same address as Mona. My name is Benjamin, Mitzi Benjamin . . . Mrs. Ira Benjamin." And Mitzi was gone.

"Who is Mrs. Ira Benjamin? As a matter of fact, who is Mr. Ira Benjamin?" Irene asked, eyes wide, from the chair beside Mona, while Felix prepared their lashes.

"A trading partner at Macleod Brothers. That's not the investment banking group. Sherwood is in the banking group . . . Guy's group. The traders are Simon's group. They make half as much."

"Woody works for Guy?"

Mona's stomach flipped. "Yes. Kevin MacIntyre is Sherwood's immediate boss." Mona stared at the ceiling. "Do you think I should try double lashes? Mine are so sparse."

"Are you going to a waif benefit, too?"

"No. Tonight is a private celebration. Sherwood and I have been married three years."

"How romantic. You and Woody—"

Some remote Sicilian ancestor took possession of Mona. Her voice grew steadier. She never missed a beat. She made her points quietly. "Me and Sherwood. Sherwood, Irene. By the way, Mitzi has no money of her own. I do. Ira has to give his permission for any real money she spends. Ira hates theater . . . movies. In fact, he was dead set against Guy buying United Cinema."

The maroon Cadillac stretch limousine deftly executed a series of complicated turns through the narrow, crowded streets of lower Manhattan. Crawling through the most powerful financial street in the world, it slid by the building where junk bonds were invented... where the bull rampages... where the rock stands firm... finally braking to a stop in front of 15 William Street, the home of Macleod Brothers, Inc.

Four stories up, in one of the austere but elegant Macleod offices, Sherwood Anderson glanced out his office window at William Street and the maroon limousine waiting for him. The scene faded and in its place he saw again a beautiful green day and the tennis courts of Choate. At Choate he'd played on the tennis team... as had his father before him ... as had other relatives—preparing for life. Those who had not attended Choate had attended Groton... St. Mark's ... Exeter. Sherwood came from a good family—tracing its lineage back to Rupert Anderson, one of Washington's aides, and on his mother's side to Mrs. Denise Hancock, who introduced the Lincolns to society.

Unfortunately, by the time he entered Choate he knew that his good family was having financial difficulties. In his freshman year at Yale—paid for by an inheritance from a grandfather—it occured to Sherwood that what he needed was an heiress... a rich wife. But fortune hunting, like painting, is an art form that requires talent, and Sherwood lacked the gift. Although he was invited to all the right parties, met all the right girls, nothing happened. Some of the right girls were interested for a short while, most not at all. No one fell head over heels in love with him. His credentials were fine but financially frayed.

Once he fell in love with a girl he met at a wedding in Locust Valley. She was pixieish and poetic and related to the Mellons. She invited him to a dance at the Plaza. When he called for her at the family duplex on Fifth Avenue, her father escorted them to the waiting taxi. They rode down in the family's private elevator.

"Are you related to the late Elliot Anderson?" her father asked Sherwood at last.

Sherwood blinked. "My father."

"I went to school with Ellie. Too bad about his accident."

You mean his suicide, Sherwood thought.

"Terrible!" The pixie's father clucked.

After that evening the girl was always busy when Sherwood called. Flunking with the girls and barely passing his courses, he was on a sticky wicket.

When he graduated from Yale, a concerned family friend got him a trainee job on Wall Street. Eventually he became a customer's man, with surprising success. He was smart enough... cagey enough... to understand one of Wall Street's basic secrets. He had a nose for leaks. To add to his research in leaks, he romanced two secretaries who worked for major fund managers. He dumped before the managers dumped, bought before they bought. Between these varied sources he did well for his clients. At thirty-two he was poised to become a partner in a third-tier Wall Street firm. At that moment Mona arrived in his life.

She wore a black, wool jersey, thigh-high, mini-dress that followed her body like a second skin, black stockings, black boots, and carried a fur-lined, wine-colored suede jacket slung over her shoulders in the fashionably casual manner. Her earrings were silver hoops sprinkled with rhinestones. Later, Sherwood learned the rhinestones were fake ... they were actually diamond chips. She wore almost no makeup and had long, black curly hair much like Cher's. While she outlined her financial goals in a distinctly nasal New York accent, Sherwood noted, with dazed appreciation, her round hips and full breasts. Actually it was the outfit that clued him—exactly duplicating one he'd seen in an issue of *Vogue* or *Harpers Bazaar* at his mother's house. He pegged her as a working class party girl who spent too much money for clothes. Sherwood had no idea that within the party girl beat the heart of a Godfather.

He'd been recommended to her by one of his best clients, Frank Amato, owner of a garbage collection company in New Jersey. He'd made a bundle for Frank. Sherwood assumed she was Amato's girlfriend and Amato would bankroll the trades. When Mona gave him a six-figure amount to play with, he dismissed the Amato connection... and the working girl assessment. As her broker, it soon became clear that Mona Montefuoco was an heiress. How much of an heiress she never would say. But judging from her account with him—and Amato later indicated it was only a fraction of Mona's holdings—her net worth had to be substantial. This fact recorded, Sherwood became her teacher.

Mona Montefuoco was not what he had envisioned for a wife. But if she could be molded... Happily, she could. Much to his delight, Mona was an Eliza searching for Professor Higgins. So, dutifully, he played his part and she played hers. He suggested a school for diction lessons, French lessons, art history and music lessons, fashion and cosmetic consultants to groom her. And he himself taught her the niceties of dining and which charity... which benefit ... which dances were worth attending. Mona was a quick study, and she rapidly took on the glaze of the chic women lunching at Mortimer's. She even made a start at social climbing, managing pseudo-friendships with a social decorator, a fashionable real estate broker, a well-connected art dealer who saw Mona as money on the hoof. The art dealer and Sherwood had much in common.

Events moved rapidly toward an announcement of their engagement, although Sherwood foresaw some ghastly moments when his proud WASP mother met the orphaned, heiress Mona... and her Italian relatives. His mother was loftily indifferent to practical matters—marrying for money would offend her. But Mona's money wasn't the whole story. Mona was even satisfactory in bed... almost virginal in her innocence, a grateful pupil who accepted his genteel tutoring. Such virtue was familiar to Sherwood—standard among the few heiresses he'd bedded. Virtue would grow boring in time. But then one memorable spring evening, the real Mona introduced herself to him. The maroon limousine was parked and waiting at his apartment house. Originally he had thought it rented... by now he knew better. He opened the limo door and Mona sat waiting; wrapped in fur, sipping sweet champagne. The car was expensive but the champagne cheap.

"Sherwood, darling..."

"Mmmm..." He sniffed the heavily scented, musky air as he slid into the seat beside her. "Where would you like to go tonight?"

"A secret place," she crooned, licking his ear. Tapping on the glass partition with her emerald ring, she signaled her chauffeur. "Harold, raise the partition. And drive through the park... slowly."

Sherwood tried to compose himself. What was the silly girl up to? "What secret place? Where?"

"It's a surprise for you, darling." She placed the glass of champagne on the built-in bar.

"I don't like surprises. What is it?" he stammered nervously.

"I'll show you," Mona whispered and languidly opened her fur, smiling as Sherwood stared. Beneath the fur Mona was naked . . . except for a black garter belt, black stockings, and black velvet pumps with diamond buckles.

Nothing in Sherwood's history had taught him what to do in such a circumstance. "Mona . . ." he gasped.

"Here," she whispered and expertly took Sherwood's head between her hands . . . placing it between her legs. The silky tendrils of her pubic hair touched his lips. Before he knew what he was doing he was kissing her, his tongue licking her clitoris—he had never done this to a woman before. As he kissed her he felt her fingers opening his belt and unzipping his fly . . . sliding along, gliding, descending, arousing every bit of flesh she touched. Her fingers moved around and over him, finally closing on his penis. This gave him a shock of such intense pleasure he had to fight not to have an immediate orgasm. His own hand went out, blindly fumbling over her body. In a frenzy, he tried to push his penis into her. But she held him gently away, whispering in his ear, "Use your mouth and your tongue, darling . . . your mouth and tongue here." She raised her hips a little. "And your finger there."

After that session, their roles were reversed. There was nothing he could teach her. She knew everything . . . showing him things he had only fantasized, as one Indian love book said, "to follow his bliss." So the relationship was mutually educational and rewarding . . . ending at last in an elopement, thus sparing Sherwood's mother the agony of consent.

Sherwood stared at the waiting maroon limousine. This was their anniversary celebration . . . his personal celebration. Kevin had told him he'd do very well this year. "All the investment group will receive a substantial bonus," Kevin promised. Mona had probably reserved a table at

Lutece or Le Cirque. Tonight he would pick up the tab. He could picture her, wrapped in her sable, wearing something extravagantly expensive by Saint Laurent or Lagerfeld, sipping champagne. The ice bucket in the bar probably contained a bottle of Dom Perignon. He'd taught her what wines . . . what champagne . . . was right.

Approaching the limousine, he sighed. Maroon—Mona still insisted on maroon, not black. A hang-over from her Eliza days. She still had a few things to learn. He paused. She could be spoiled by over-education. Maybe it was wiser to stop now. She was the heiress he'd yearned for, satisfactory in ways that heiresses usually weren't. The original Mona would have met him at home . . . bare-assed for the real celebration. The educated Mona met him in a Lagerfeld.

He opened the limousine door and grinned. Mona was still Mona. Her sable coat was thrown back. She was not wearing a Lagerfeld or a Saint Laurent. She was wearing nothing at all. Quietly sipping champagne, she was as naked as she had been before she learned which fork was the salad fork.

Chapter 13

THE MEETING of the Select Committee to determine the size of the partners' annual bonuses was held, as usual, in the boardroom of Macleod Brothers with Guy Macleod presiding. The most important piece of furniture in the boardroom was a thirty-foot-long, massive oak table that was centered under two large, brightly polished brass chandeliers. The table was ringed by twenty maroon leather cushioned oak chairs. Floor-to-ceiling Elizabethan oak bookcases stood against the north end of the room. They contained all the books and records of the minutes of board meetings since Pierre Macleod had called to order the first meeting of the newly formed Macleod Brothers more than one hundred years earlier. Around the room, in gold-leaf frames, hung portraits of six generations of Macleods. A Duncan Phyfe table on which three multi-buttoned telephones rested stood against the wall behind Guy's chair.

Seated at one end of the table on either side of Guy were Simon Macleod, manager of the trading division, Ira Benjamin Sr., a trading partner, Kevin MacIntyre, a senior investment banking partner, and Jonathan Graham, another senior investment banker and a distant nephew, twice removed, of Ben Graham, the father of the fundamentalist approach to investment. Jonathan Graham felt strongly that traders, who bought a stock a 9:30 in the morning and sold it at 3:55 after a three-quarters of a point rise, were somehow akin to thieves.

Guy had mentally prepared for the meeting. He'd donned his purple mantle of power and adopted his imperial managing partner's voice. Upon calling the meeting to order, he barely refrained from using the royal "we." A half hour later, occasionally pausing to sip black coffee from a translucent Wedgwood cup, he was still reading from his notes.

". . . I believe it was Erich Fromm who said, 'The challenge of the twenty-first century man is to be comfortable with his own ambivalence . . . as well as that of others.' I'm comfortable with my ambivalence. I hope you are with yours. Because I'm aware that some of you will be distressed by my decisions. But do me the courtesy of accepting that I have given each decision long, hard thought in an effort to be absolutely fair . . ."

Ira Benjamin took a deep drag on his cigarette. Bullshit. Pure bullshit! He was a short, chunky man with a broad, fleshy face, a Roman nose, and bright lemur-like eyes which stared out at you with a disconcerting concentration.

". . . You do understand that as the managing partner of Macleod Brothers . . ."

"And the manager of the investment banking division," Ira said dryly.

". . . I often have to make painful, personnel choices, which, in the interest of fairness to the firm as well as to the individual, requires that I keep the big picture in mind."

Neat, organized, the perfect adjutant, Kevin MacIntyre's beaming face was a vote of confidence.

"In considering the distribution of bonuses earned during our latest fiscal year, I've had some difficult decisions to make..."

"We will now witness a virtuoso performance in how well you live with ambivalence." Ira couldn't keep quiet.

"Yes, Ira, I am sometimes conflicted—ambivalent—about how big—or small—a bonus a partner deserves."

"I hate to think of you losing sleep over us."

Guy was impervious to sarcasm. "I have to consider not only what a partner has contributed this past year to Macleod Brothers but what his potential is for the future. I do my best to make the distribution evenhanded."

"Excuse me, Guy, before you make any final decisions I have a request."

"Yes, Ira."

"I want to make a point about fairness. In all fairness we cannot cancel Martha's bonus. It's true her maternity leave was three months longer than expected—but motherhood, too, is highly individual. And she's the best secretary I ever had."

"Knock it off, Ira. You know she'll get her bonus," Simon said quietly.

Guy continued. "As of the end of fiscal 1991, the book value of Macleod Brothers was almost five hundred sixty-five million dollars, before taking into account a provision for taxes and the partners' bonuses. And thanks to our acquisition and the public offering of United Cinema stock, the book value of Macleod Brothers stock continues to grow. As you know, since the Academy Award nominations were announced, United's stock has had a seven point rise. So there will be grounds for rejoicing next year at bonus time. The partners—shareholders in Macleod Brothers—will do even better next year and this has been a fine year."

"All partners stand tall... bankers stand taller," Ira jeered.

Guy consulted the summary of the Peat Marwick financial statement his secretary had typed up. "Last year, Macleod Brothers netted two hundred twenty-two million dollars... before taxes and bonuses. The investment banking group generated pre-tax profits of about seventy-five million, while our trading division can be credited with producing pre-tax profits of one hundred fifty-seven million..."

"I am speechless with self-respect," Ira crowed.

"Since it is my job to render unto Macleod Brothers that which is the firm's—and to the partners that which is the partners'—I have decided that the pool of money to be set aside in 1992 for partners' bonuses will be one hundred thirty-one million dollars."

Simon had been sitting poker-faced, listening to Guy's recital of book value, profits, bonuses. Off-guard for the moment, his face reflected his surprise at the size of the bonus pool.

"I think of myself as a man who recognizes and rewards individual performance..."

"We know that, Guy," Kevin MacIntyre fawned

"...rather than one who regards bonuses as a fixed item. I make the hard choices. At Macleod Brothers we have always had a policy of rewarding the individual...the individual's originality, hard work, dedication. Bonuses are not equal because all men are not equal." It was a considered judgement.

"Some are more equal than others," Ira snorted.

"Naturally. If bonuses are a fixed percentage of the firm's pre-tax income, then talent is ruled out," Kevin said contentedly.

"Not banking talent," Ira muttered.

"True, Ira. I place a high value on individual banking talent. It works to the greater advantage of the firm. Therefore, out of the one hundred thirty-one million dollar bonus pool I mentioned will come substantial bonuses for those hard-working, dedicated banking partners—and, of course, our trading partners."

"I'm about to be given a lesson in living with ambivalence," Ira muttered.

"As has been our tradition in the past, the investment banking division will get two-thirds of the bonus pool, the trading group one-third. Each partner's bonus will depend on the amount of stock he owns in Macleod Brothers. All our partners know how much stock they own and how to do the arithmetic. It does not require new math." The matter was closed.

Simon Macleod had a singular natural advantage, besides self-control—the knack of appearing far more relaxed and less formidable than he really was. Among the greedy, talented, hard-featured men seated at the boardroom table, only Simon's face revealed neither anger nor strain. He sat quietly, looking reflective and intelligent, rather like an innocent surrounded by riverboat cardsharps.

Ira was too shell-shocked to speak. It was about as bad as he'd expected. Then he let fly.

"Seems to me there are one hundred ten thousand shares of Macleod Brothers stock in the hot, sweaty hands of our forty-seven partners. Of that one hundred ten thousand shares, the banking partners own . . . come on, folks, take a guess. Who'll be the lucky Lotto winner? Guess the right number and you win the jackpot. You get to own the U.S. Treasury and print your own money. Don't be shy. Cat got your tongues? All right, I'll tell you. The banking partners own seventy-one percent of the stock. Cry havoc and let slip the dogs of war!"

Simon patted Ira on the shoulder. "Take it easy, friend."

"Easy? Simon, I'm on Easy Street. My heart overflows with the milk of Guy's kindness. The banking partners own seventy-one percent of the stock . . . including Guy's legacy of twelve percent. As for us traders, we know our place in the pecking order. What can crude, cloddish traders expect? That Guy will at least feed and clothe us. So we own what's left . . . twenty-nine percent, of which, Simon—you lucky devil—inherited nine percent. Thank your lucky stars that your father had the good sense to include you in his will or Guy might have included you out. You can't count on blood being thicker than water . . . not when you're a slob of a trader."

"Ira, if you don't calm down, I may have to ask you to leave," Guy said with distant courtesy.

Ira Benjamin took a small box out of his pocket and popped something chocolate into his mouth. He chewed hard. "I'm calmed. I keep a box of chocolate-coated Valium—otherwise known as Raisinettes—to keep me tranquilized for these meetings."

"I realize that the trading group will be distressed by my allotment of two-thirds of the bonus pool to the bankers and one-third to traders. I don't dispute the value of the traders. Last year our traders were responsible for more of the total profit picture than the banking division—"

"More than double, damn it!"

"Ira, think about the quality of earnings. Our investment banking group works with gentlemen . . . leaders of industry . . . people you would be proud to have to dinner and sponsor for membership in any of your clubs."

"I never was allowed to join your clubs."

Guy elected to ignore that truth. "You traders work with . . . other types."

"You mean slobs."

"I mean little people who live on their salaries. They want to make killings on two hundred shares."

"Your leaders of industry don't want to make killings?"

"Or course they do. But they play in The Show, as they say in baseball. I prefer to have a hand in shaping the future of American business than to have Macleod Brothers improving the lot of Ma Perkins—"

"Whose husband could be the research biologist who finds the cure for Alzheimer's. Guy, you're full of shit. You think ordinary people are slobs, and we're slobs to work with them," Ira ranted.

"I wouldn't go that far." Guy's smile said he would. "But if my taste offends you—you're a numbers man. Think about the numbers. Investment banking income is related to fees paid by companies for our professional services. It entails less risk of Macleod Brothers capital than does trading. Am I right?"

"No! We're not a big retail house like Merrill Lynch et cetera. Although we love Ma Perkins, you know damn well we do most of our outside trading for the funds. Your boyhood buddies, the fund managers, routinely cut our commissions to ribbons . . . damn near zilch."

"We also trade for the Macleod Brothers account," Guy pointed out.

"Sure we do—and we make millions."

"You could lose millions."

"There's an old saying—less risk, less reward."

"That's my point. The risk of our capital is higher when we trade for our own account. Isn't it?" Ira reluctantly nodded. "Thank you. You confirmed my position that banking profits are a better quality of income... less risky. That's why bankers should be rewarded with more generous bonuses."

"And traders should get tips. Like maitre d's."

"You're a very fair man, Guy," Kevin sighed with pleasure.

"As I mentioned earlier, after you do the numbers you'll be quite satisfied with your bonuses. This discussion has gone on long enough." Guy glanced around at the men seated at the table. He handed out copies of his bonus proposal. "We'll put it to a vote. All in favor of my bonus proposal raise your hands."

Jonathan Graham and Kevin MacIntyre's hands shot up.

"All opposed."

Ira almost dislocated his arm, while Simon's hand hovered a little above his shoulder.

With an absolutely straight face, Guy said, "I count two votes in favor and two opposed. Which leaves it up to me. I vote in favor of my own bonus plan. The plan is approved." He paused for a second. "The meeting of the Select Committee on partners' bonuses is adjourned."

Simon strong-armed Ira from his seat and out of the boardroom before his friend could open his mouth. The banking partners filed slowly after them, each lost in his own dream of the lovely millions he would soon have to spend.

Alone in the boardroom, Guy stared at a portrait at the far end of the room. Abruptly, he swiveled his chair, picked up one of the telephones on the table, and dialed a number. He waited, immobile, until the phone at the other end of the line was picked up. Without any preliminary, in a voice that was barely polite, he said, "No. I'm calling from New York. Give me a full a report." He listened in silence. Finally he said, "That may be good news. But remember—things can change rapidly unless one is careful." He listened again. When he spoke, there was a taunting edge to his voice. "That's sheer nonsense—if you've covered your tracks. Don't lose your nerve... not at this late date." He was silent, listening, then spoke quickly, his tone frigid. "I'm glad you haven't changed your mind . . . it would have been unfortunate. Let's say—a major career mistake." He hung up in the middle of the other person's reply. He turned his chair and gazed again at the portrait of his father, Charles Macleod. His smile was arctic . . . and obscurely triumphant.

The bar was on a side street of lower Manhattan, off the beaten track, dimly lit, unfashionable. It was a solid, old-time bar, never noticed or patronized by Wall Street power players. It was the private hide-out of the Macleod Brothers traders. They came to the bar to celebrate, to lick their wounds, to exchange gossip. They were usually gone by six. By nine the bar was empty except for a few neighborhood drinkers . . . and tonight, Simon and Ira. They sat in a booth, both silently sipping scotch. Simon was still nursing his first. Ira was on his fourth. Ira was wired . . . Simon impassive.

"The bloody fool!" Ira exclaimed.

"It's the way he sees the firm."

"What the fuck does he think he's doing with his high-handed shit—two-thirds bankers, one-third traders? The boys won't sit still for that crap anymore. It's gone on too long."

"Five years."

"What are you going to do?"

"I don't know." Simon was realistic, sober, baffled.

"He's your brother. Can't you talk to him?"

"I've tried." Simon brushed his hand over his eyes, like a man trying to clear his head. "He's a proud man . . . a stubborn man."

"A stuffed shirt son-of-a-bitch."

It was rare for Simon to allow his anger at Guy to show. He made a strong effort to control it so he could speak calmly, choosing his words. "It's hard for Guy to admit that Wall Street is changing. Investment banking is changing. Macleod Brothers has always been one of the first-tier private investment banking houses. Guy likes that feeling. He has a strong sense of tradition."

"He's wearing blinders. If he continues down this road,

there'll be no Macleod Brothers tradition. It'll end... *kaput* ... a dinosaur that's outlived its time." Ira gave Simon a hard look. "Listen—I did the numbers. Given the amount of money Guy allotted to the investment bankers, do you have any idea how much that king of jackasses will make on this bonus pie?"

"You mean Kevin?"

"Kevin. That fat fool walked away from the board room tonight with a cool fourteen million dollars." There was a jagged pause before Ira went on. "And that Mongolian idiot, Jonathan Graham, whose only claim to fame is a dubious tie with old Ben... he gets twelve and a half million."

"I know," Simon said in a resigned voice.

"Do you know what I get?" Ira waited a moment, then said with stiff sensitivity, "Yours truly gets two point six million. And you know damn well what my contribution has been to the pre-tax profit—the bonus pool!"

Simon was silent.

"We're all getting reamed. Bernie Mefford, Marty Downes, the whole trading division. When the boys hear how Guy's divided the pie, they'll hemorrhage all over The Street. They may take their stock and tell Guy to shove it. Macleod Brothers will lose the best trading team on The Street."

"I know that. You know that. Guy doesn't believe it. Or he doesn't care." This discussion was not easy for Simon. He hadn't been able to protect his traders... not as he should have protected them. He felt somehow soiled, dishonored. His next words were an effort to justify his failure. "I've been arguing with Guy about the split for most of the month. It was no use. Guy is the managing partner. I had to go along."

"We figured that. It's not you, Simon. The boys love you. But they gotta make their bucks. My God! Marty has three ex-wives and nine children to support. And he earned it."

"You all earned it."

"It's a damn shame. I remember when you first offered me a partnership in Macleod Brothers. I thought I was being anointed. My God! Macleod Brothers! What a house! What a history! It was like getting into the right fraternity, the club that had always blackballed people like me. That's how all the trading partners felt."

"But not now." Simon spoke with bitterness.

"Not now." Ira's tone was gentler, even a bit embarrassed. "There's more to it, Simon, that I, for one, don't like. I'll give you a for instance. For instance, if Macleod Brothers was traded on the Big Board today, I'd recommend we not touch the stock with a ten-foot pole."

"Why?"

"Because the stock's a dog. There's not enough equity in the firm for the size of our operation. Guy's gotten famous on The Street for his generosity with bankers' bonuses. Maybe not as generous as Fred Joseph used to be but none of our banking clowns are geniuses like Milken. He was worth the five hundred million. They're worth zip. Zero. *Nada*. So why the bonus bonanza for clowns? Guy's not leaving enough equity in the firm. It's all going into the bonus pool. I wouldn't touch the stock of a firm that isn't solidly financed. Not if I was trading it. Macleod Brothers is no longer solidly financed. If I were you, I'd worry."

"I worry."

"You got reason. What the hell does Guy think he's doing?"

For once, Simon, the most discreet of men, was not at all discreet. "I don't know," he admitted. "It's not what my father had in mind."

"Ira Benjamin. You gotta call," the bartender yelled.

Simon half-smiled. "Mitzi?"

"Mitzi. She could track me in the Amazon. I never should have mentioned this place."

"What happens if you're not here when she calls?"

"She figures out where I am and finds me. Someday I'll tell you the story of how Mitzi found me when I was snowbound in Cleveland without a hotel reservation. I still don't know how she figured out at which bar I'd end up." Ira called to the bartender, "Tell her I'm on my way. Thanks." He shook his head. "I just mentioned a bar in lower Manhattan . . . didn't even give her the name."

"Go home, Ira."

"Yeah. See you tomorrow . . . if I live through Mitzi's mother's cooking tonight."

"Go home, Ira."

Ira weaved his way out of the bar.

Simon remained in the booth, thinking of the days ahead. He signaled the bartender for another scotch and leaned against the back of the booth. Somehow the traders must be convinced to live in peace with the bankers... at least for another year. The traders knew they were being screwed. That was bad enough. But Ira had put into words his own buried fear. Yes, the size of the bankers' bonuses was unfair. Simon could understand this as Guy's elitism. But there was something stranger. Why was the bonus pool so large to begin with? Why was Guy putting so little of the profits back into the financial base of Macleod Brothers? His brother was much too bright not to know that he was short-changing the firm. Did Guy have a motive... some purpose he didn't grasp? The whole messy business reeked of something foul. Suppose Guy had no choice. He had to hand out king-sized partners' bonuses. Why? What was going on?

Simon's questions triggered a host of memories. He shut his eyes, flooded with regret. He thought of the years he played football, of his ex-wife, Kitty. He thought of his father... how much he loved him. He remembered promises made... promises broken.

He had memorized forever the look of the room in the Klingenstein Pavilion of Mount Sinai Hospital where his father was recovering from surgery. The room was white and sunny and filled with flowers. He remembered how his father looked before he saw him. There was almost no color in his face. Charles Macleod's face was more strained and anxious than Simon ever remembered seeing him. At first he was sure it was the bypass surgery and a natural concern about his health. After their talk, Simon knew better.

The nurse was straightening the pillows behind Charles Macleod when Simon hobbled in. She gave him a warm, cheery smile before turning back to his father. "You're coming along fine, sir. Just fine," she said.

"I'm sure I am. Hello, Simon," Charles Macleod greeted his son with sudden animation.

"Your father's doing very well," the nurse said, turning to Simon. Simon got another brand of smile... flirtatious.

"Good," Simon said, unaware of her approval. He gazed at his father, hoping she was telling the truth, wondering how worried his father was about his health.

"We're both casualties of our lifestyle," his father said. "Me, with my bypass . . . courtesy of Wall Street. You with that walking cast on your knee . . . thanks to the New York Giants."

Simon felt better. With the return of color to his father's face, he no longer looked so fragile. "All true. I did get the torn ligaments in Secaucus, playing the Bears for the league championship. But don't thank the Giants. Thank Wendell Roosevelt Corey. It's an old story between us."

"The press says that Corey is the offensive lineman of the year. Without him the Bears wouldn't have made it to the Super Bowl—or won it."

"They wouldn't have made it if I hadn't gotten hurt." Simon's tone was bitter. "Corey rolled into my knee in an illegal crack-back block. That happened once before."

"It did? I don't remember."

"There's nothing to remember. Corey couldn't pull it off. He tried it at a late spring mini-camp practice. That's when draftees show up for the coaches to look them over. They play with helmets, but no shoulder pads, sneakers, no cleats, and hard physical contact is not permitted. By accident—pure accident you understand—all 255 pounds of Corey tripped and rolled into my knee. It was a crack-back block. If I'd been wearing spikes, my foot could have caught in the grass, wrecking my knee. A rookie with torn ligaments and cartilage damage isn't going to be kept on the squad. Corey was after an Ivy League rookie."

"You."

"Me. Some of the guys never forgave me for going to Princeton. And with me out, Corey would have had one less rookie to compete with. But I wasn't wearing cleats, so my foot didn't get caught in the grass . . . and my knee wasn't torn up. Corey was not a happy camper." Simon gave his father a sheepish grin. "After practice, that night I took the bastard apart. Broke his jaw as a matter of fact. No hard feelings intended."

"Hmm . . . I see. That was six years ago. You mean

Corey held a grudge for six years? He didn't forgive and forget?"

Simon laughed. "Corey forget? Fat chance! But I didn't think he'd try the same stunt again." Simon grimaced. "I'd slid away from the tight end and planted my foot to cut toward the runner. Corey led the blocking and rolled into me. This time it worked. I was wearing cleats—they got tangled in the artificial turf. The tendons and cartilage in my right knee stretched . . . tore. And here I am . . . cast and all."

"So much for fair play on the playing field. You were carted off the field on a motorized stretcher."

"How about fair play on Wall Street? When Guy telephoned, he said you were carted here from 15 William Street in an ambulance. Why the bypass? Did someone crack-back block your sale of stocks or bonds?"

"There are similarities, although Wall Street doesn't deserve all the credit. It appears that my fondness for roast beef, ten-year-old scotch, and cigarettes also had a vote," Macleod said in a wry voice. "Did you have as much fun wrecking your knee as I had clogging my arteries?"

"I think so."

"I had a longer run."

"I may still have a run. Arthroscopic surgery can perform miracles. When this cast comes off, I'll be ninety percent as good as new."

"I won't be as good as new."

Simon had no answer.

"And because I won't, we must talk. I have a tricky problem with Macleod Brothers."

"With the firm?" The idea shook Simon.

"Yes. It concerns a man who is as dangerous as Wendell Roosevelt Corey . . . but much smarter."

"Who?"

"We'll discuss him tomorrow. I want you to spend the rest of the day reading some material that my secretary will messenger over to you. You are probably the only All-Pro defensive end who majored in economics, minored in business administration, and made Phi Beta Kappa at an Ivy League School. So I think you'll understand what you read.

Send Kitty out to the movies. By the way, is your wife pregnant yet?"

"She's not ready to start a family," Simon mumbled.

"Still the party girl." Charles Macleod sighed. "And now that the season's over and our Kitty has no football hero to cheer for, I suppose she's bored. You have to entertain her."

"Kitty can entertain herself tonight," Simon said flatly.

"Good. Let her entertain herself at a movie or the theater. I want you to read the material alone, without interruption. Then come see me tomorrow."

"I will, Father. Kitty will understand."

Late that afternoon, a carton from Macleod Brothers arrived at Simon's apartment. The carton contained a half dozen thick albums crammed with pictures and documents that described the history of the Macleod family. Long after Kitty returned from a movie and had gone to bed, Simon poured over the contents of the albums.

The Macleods, originally spelled Mcleod, came to Northern Ireland from Scotland as part of the Tudor invasions in the late sixteenth century. Captain Hugh Mcleod was an officer in the Scottish army that controlled the Lagan Corridor toward Armagh. When he was discharged, Captain Mcleod remained in Northern Ireland and eventually married Elizabeth Tyrone. They settled in County Antrim and began potato farming and sheep raising. Sometime during the next hundred years—although the family remained resolutely Calvinist—an "a" was added to the name and Mcleod became Macleod. When Simon's great-great-great-great-grandfather, Michael Macleod, lost the family farm during the potato blight of 1848, he emigrated to the United States.

Unlike so many Scottish-Irish who settled in New York and Boston, Michael Macleod and family went north, settling in Aroostook County in Northern Maine, because it reminded him of the ancestral farm in Northern Ireland. During the Civil War, the family increased their acreage and became a major supplier of potatoes to the Union Army. After the war, the Macleods sold timber, sand, gravel, and limestone to both the needy south and the rich north. As their business interests expanded, so did the size of their family. The beautiful daughters of French Canadian émigrés who had settled in Maine, just over the Quebec border, were brides for the ambitious Macleods. Numerous children were born, grew up, married, and had more children. In the 1880s, Pierre Macleod, a member of the third generation of Macleods, moved to New York City to act as an agent for the family products. Eventually this led Pierre to join the newly formed New York Cotton Exchange, where he added the brokering of sugar, grain, cattle, and oil to the limestone and other building materials the Macleods initially sold.

With their instinct for the main chance, the Macleods were inevitably drawn from commodities into investment banking. At that time, the old-line New England banking houses like Morgan and Harriman were only making loans to established companies. Pierre Macleod went another route. He contacted the German-Jewish merchant bankers—Lehman, Warburg, Goldman—and with them invented new ways to finance riskier ventures. They sold bonds for new railroads and textile mills from New England to Georgia. These high risk investments paid off handsomely . . . Macleod Brothers flourished.

Eventually they joined J.P. Morgan, helping to organize and finance U.S. Steel and International Harvester. They were leading members of the Lehman combine that underwrote Sears, Roebuck and Co., RCA, and the embryonic airlines. But as the fortunes of the Macleod family grew, the family diminished in size. In 1955—when Charles Macleod's wife, Vera Hastings Macleod, died in childbirth—there were only two children in the New York branch of the Macleods: the boy, Guy Macleod and the baby, Simon.

It was dawn before Simon closed the last album. He understood what was implied in his father's desire that he read the family history. For the last three generations, every New York Macleod had worked at Macleod Brothers on 15 William Street. Clearly that's where his father thought he belonged . . . not in the Super Bowl with the Giants.

"What the hell would I do at Macleod Brothers?" Simon asked himself. "If my father dies, Guy inherits the whole shooting match. The oldest son always inherits. Guy doesn't need me." He half-smiled. "He probably doesn't want me." Simon remembered a boyhood oath he and Guy had sworn, pressing bloody thumbs together. "The Macleods against the world," they'd chanted. But that was then... boyhood heroics. This was now. No heroics... only money and power.

"I won't fight Guy," he said to the empty room.

At eight in the morning Simon arrived at the Klingenstein Pavilion. His father was waiting for him.

"Did you read the material?" he asked. Simon nodded. "What do you think?"

"I had a general idea of the family history. In detail it's fascinating. 'A good read,' as they say."

"I didn't suggest you read it for entertainment."

"I figured that out."

"What's your answer?"

"No."

The disappointment on Charles Macleod's face showed only because illness had robbed him of his usual discipline. "Why the adamant 'No'?"

"Look, I'm not immortal. Neither are you. Eventually Guy will be head honcho at Macleod. That's it. Much as I love my brother, I can't work for him. So there's no job for me at Macleod Brothers.

Charles Macleod pressed the button that raised the head of the bed so he could look his son directly in the eye.

"There is a job for you at Macleod Brothers... a big job." Macleod's expression was frank and open. "That's why I wanted to see you alone... without Guy. The truth is, I've been handling a tricky problem in the firm. If it's mishandled, it could cause all kinds of repercussions. I've had to move with extreme caution."

"What's going on?"

"I indicated yesterday that it concerned a man."

"As dangerous as Corey."

"As dangerous. And, as I said, a hell of a lot smarter. That makes him a serious threat to Macleod Brothers, to the family, to me, to you... even to Guy."

"Who is it? You said you would tell me who. Today."

"I mean to. The who in question is your brother."

Simon could only stare.

"You're surprised. Well, the problem is real enough. With the best intentions in the world, Guy is a dangerous threat to the survival of Macleod Brothers, and, therefore, a danger to himself."

"Why?" Simon's face was tense. "He loves the company more than anything in his life."

"And his love—as love often is—is blind. He refuses to accept change... that the company he loves must change with the times, or go under. Wall Street is changing... investment banking is changing, like the Mom and Pop grocery store... like the family farm. In the same way, private investment banking houses like Macleod Brothers could become an extinct species."

Simon mulled over his father's words. They echoed his own thinking. He'd spent the last five years in football stadiums, but his favorite off-season reading had not been the sports page of the *New York Times*. It had been the business section of the *Times*, the *Wall Street Journal*, *Barrons*, and books on The Street. His response to a need... unconfessed... unforgotten.

He gave his father a peculiar smile. "You mean clients no longer look for investment bankers who play golf at the Creek Club or Piping Rock, or old school friends... relatives... friends from Porcelian or the Racquet Club with whom they can reminisce, gossip, and booze it up."

"Exactly." Charles Macleod was pleased at Simon's insight. "The new crop of CEOs have often gone to the wrong schools. Not Harvard like Guy, or Princeton like you. It could be Ohio State, or Oberlin, or East Texas A & M. They won't listen to our words of wisdom when we have drinks at the Racquet Club or the Union League."

"They couldn't get into the Creek Club or the Union League or the Racquet Club."

"They're not part of the old boy network, and they don't give a damn about the old boys." Charles Macleod's face was flushed as he warmed to his subject. "These men are tough and greedy. They want the highest possible price they can get for any new stock or bond issue. And if the new issue bombs—Heaven forbid, but it has happened because the insurance funds, the mutual funds, the bank trust departments don't like the offering price—what happens?"

"I know what happens. Macleod Brothers—let's say they're the lead investment banker—must drop the price of the new issue and eat the difference." Simon took a deep breath. "That takes a lot of capital."

Charles Macleod nodded, not in regret but in submission to hard reality. "I know it. You know it. Guy will not accept that simple fact."

"Father... precisely what do you want from me?"

What passed between them then was an unguarded look, like two men meeting in secret to decide on some desperate measure.

"I want you to listen and follow my thinking. I'm having my will rewritten. A will such as no Macleod has ever before written. I plan to leave my stock in Macleod Brothers to Guy, to you, and..." He had to catch his breath before continuing. "I'll also leave shares of stock to the senior employees of Macleod. They'll become partners—not merely employees. The point I'm making is, men who have no Macleod blood in their veins will own a piece of the company... of Macleod Brothers. So, along with Guy and you, they'll have a stake in the welfare—the future—of the firm." After a short silence he asked, "What do you think?"

Simon felt as if something was stuck in his throat. Finally he answered, "Guy will have a hemorrhage. He'll hate it."

"He'll have to live with it." Charles Macleod spoke without restraint. "I would like to do for Macleod Brothers what Gus Levy did for Goldman Sachs. And I can. If the partners work together for the good of the firm—traders and bankers sharing the profits according to what they've produced—Macleod Brothers will become a muscular, modern investment bank on the cutting edge of Wall Street, not a private banking house for that vanishing breed that forms the clubby, old boy network. What's more, the firm will have the capital to underwrite the larger and larger stock offerings that I see coming."

Only a small furrow in Simon's forehead showed his doubt. "You mentioned traders... what traders? Macleod Brothers has no trading desk."

"We will have. That's your job." Charles Macleod was like someone with a high-powered electrical wire looking for a socket to plug into. "My sources tell me you've always handled your own investment portfolio. And you've done a hell of a good job . . . better than most of the funds." He continued with a final abandonment of pride that was like the taking off of a uniform at the end of a hard day. "Will you do it, Simon? Start a trading desk and a retail operation at Macleod Brothers? Will you help me save our family business?"

Simon was caught in a rush of conflicting impulses. And nothing in the whole tangle of emotions was more surprising than his awareness of the conflict between his father and Guy. He felt sorry for both of them—for himself, too. At last he asked, "Who do I report to?"

"Me."

Simon studied his fingernails, running his thumb over the edge of each nail . . . searching. But there was no way to avoid the question. "Sorry, Dad," he answered softly. "But I must ask. What about after you?"

Charles Macleod smiled. He would have been surprised—and disappointed—had Simon not raised that question.

"No one," he said. "Guy, as my eldest son, must inherit my position as managing partner of Macleod Brothers. He'll run the investment banking group. But he'll have no control over what you do at the trading desk."

Simon remembered one of his history classes. His father was setting up a Frankish State. Guy would be King, ruling in Paris. He would be the independent Duke of Burgundy. Would Guy work with him on a more or less equal footing, or would they lock horns like a pair of bull moose battling over a cow—Macleod Brothers being the cow. It was one hell of a way to test their boyhood oath. He thought about his father's purpose. Were he and the trading desk his father's way of setting him up as a counterweight to Guy? He almost said, "No." Guy was his brother . . . his older brother. Their boyhood oath had been, "The Macleods against the world." Not the Macleods against each other. How could he oppose Guy? But the laws of his own nature spoke out, giving their verdict. The demand for Simon to agree was inexorable. He bowed to a need long unresolved . . . to dreams too long unanswered . . . to his heritage.

"Okay," he said. "I'm with you."

He held out his hand and his father grasped it, signifying with the time-honored gesture of a handshake that the two men had reached an understanding.

"Welcome, Simon. Welcome home," Charles Macleod's sigh was one of peace. "Unlike Hamlet's father, my ghost will come back and applaud you."

"Why speak of ghosts? You've a long way to go."

"Simon, now I have a secret to share." Charles Macleod smiled.

"Oh?"

"I will not have another bypass."

"Do you need one?"

"Not yet. But I will. I'm seventy-one years old, and I do not intend to change my lifestyle, not one iota. Not my ten-year-old scotch . . . French cigarettes . . . rare prime beef larded with fat . . . nothing! I'm grateful for the years of pleasure I was granted, and I won't trade the short time left to me for a few extra joyless years. It's called the quality of life. So one day I'll need another bypass."

"For Christ sake, Father—"

"Don't argue. I've made up my mind. But after I die, Guy will try to go back to the days of the old boy network banking."

"I know he will."

"You must stop him . . . or he'll take the firm under."

Simon walked to the window and looked down at the cars on Fifth Avenue. After a few moments, he faced his father. "I'll stop him," he said quietly. "I don't know how, but I promise. Somehow, I will stop him."

"If you say you will, you will. I know you," Charles Macleod laughed. "As I said, when I'm a ghost I'll applaud."

Sipping his scotch, Simon thought of the promise he made to his father. What he did at Macleod Brothers was ruled by that promise. He thought of the promise Kitty made . . . and broke. He was glad his father had died before he and Kitty hit the silk. Or maybe his ghost had applauded. When Charles Macleod first met Kitty, Simon had the distinct impression his father decided he'd fucked his brains out.

NAKED CALL 211

Obviously he had. He remembered the scent of her body, of her hair as he buried his face in it. . . .

At the same time the draftees and regulars worked out on the field, auditions were held on the sidelines for the New York Giant cheerleaders. The players made book on which girls would be selected—and who would be the first to score with them. Kitty Kjylteka was a black-haired, twenty-year-old beauty from Lubbock, Texas. She had the longest legs in captivity and was the odds-on favorite. Why she'd chosen New York over Dallas was anybody's guess.

When Simon met Kitty, she shook her long black hair, stretched her long, round arms, and gave him a brief, genteel ogle. "Hello," she said.

"Hello, yourself," he said.

"You're Simon Macleod."

"You're Kitty . . . uhm."

"Call me Kitty. Just Kitty. I hear they expect great things of you."

"And of you. As a cheerleader."

"How nice." Her voice had a slightly amorous quality. It hinted of unimaginable delights.

"Kitty, what are you doing tonight?"

"You."

It was love at first sight . . . or lust at first night. Exactly a month later—the day after Simon was told he'd made the squad and Kitty found out she'd made the cheerleader team—they eloped.

Simon remembered their life together—one long party, a nonstop fanfare, a cheering stadium, autograph seekers everywhere. Simon was a shoo-in for the NFL Hall of Fame. Then he tore up his knee and retired . . . the music stopped . . . a silent war began. He grimaced and called out, "Jake. A double scotch. No ice." Kitty had been the ideal wife for a professional football player cheered by press and public . . . not the wife for an anonymous Wall Street trader. The news that IBM rose one and a half points on historic volume bored her to tears. It couldn't compare to the arc of a perfectly thrown forward pass or the sexual thrill she got at the crunch of massive bodies slamming together. Kitty was a pro football groupie, crazy for the life, the fame, the razzle-dazzle of pro football.

There may be some good divorces, but his was lousy. His lawyer, Murray Lamport, could attest that it was one of the worst. Within a month of his announcing his retirement, Kitty began a series of affairs with his former teammates. He'd found out... hired a divorce lawyer, Murray ... who hired a detective... who videotaped Kitty in action, in glorious full color. Rather than have an ugly court battle, Simon agreed to pay Kitty two million dollars to heal her broken heart. Then, prior to the final papers being signed, Kitty decided two million wouldn't do. It was barely enough for a girl to live on. Not enough to live on and raise her baby... Simon's baby.

"It's not Simon's baby. You and Simon have been separated for months," Murray said to Kitty.

"It sure as hell isn't mine," Kitty's recent live-in running back remarked.

"Simon came by one night, unexpectedly. Things happened. He forced me," Kitty murmured.

"I don't believe it." Murray was adamant.

"Would Simon deprive his own child?" Her smile dissolved into a pleading pout. "Another two million isn't that much. A girl needs money to live on. I owe sixty thousand on my American Express Platinum. The other day I bought a little bracelet... just a platinum and emerald circle. The price was outlandish. Little things like that take a bite out of my two million."

"Simon doesn't have the money."

"Please. I was his wife when his father's will was read. Simon inherited a couple of hundred million. Not as much as Guy Macleod... but still money."

"Simon's money is tied up in Macleod Brothers."

"He can untie another two million." Kitty's lawyer, Sam Halpern, smiled, his glossy face perspiring, his bulging eyes glistening with happy greed. "I'd like it in crisp, ten thousand dollar bills. The smell of new money is sexy." He stopped smiling. "No point horsing around, Murray. A cashier's check will do."

"It won't play, Sam."

NAKED CALL 213

"You don't think the care and feeding of the next generation of Macleods is worth two more million." Sam belched noisily. "I do."

Murray's irritation mounted. Sam Halpern was not the highest paid divorce lawyer in Manhattan because of his character or his good manners. "If Kitty's pregnant, it's not Simon's child. You know it...I know it...Kitty knows it. End of scenario."

Sam laughed and rubbed his palms together. "It isn't. Okay, Murray. What am I offered for rape?"

Murray looked at the man with distaste. There was the smell of garbage in his methods. "You'll never make it stick."

"Enough will stick. Simon Macleod, former All-Pro defensive right end for the New York Giants, gets to feeling raunchy one night. So he pays a surprise house call on his about-to-be former wife. His foot's in the door or she'd slam it in his face. He's too big to throw out so she gives him a well-bred 'Hi there' and fixes him a martini. Cool, straight up, the way he likes them."

"Simon doen't drink martinis."

"I'm vamping till ready. After the martini, she suggests he say 'Bye-bye.' But Simon's prick's got other ideas. Kitty is out of bounds but there's no stopping him. She's no match for Simon and tumbles backward. He breaks the line of scrimmage and is in her in seconds. Great penetration by the veteran end. So now Kitty's eating for two."

"Crap."

"You don't like the extra millions—two is too much? Make me an offer. Rape by Simon Macleod won't look good in the *Wall Street Journal*."

"They won't print it." Murray stood up to go.

"If they won't, the *Enquirer* will. After that, *Confidential*. The beat goes on. I never read a scandal sheet I didn't like."

Simon and Kitty settled for three million. When no baby put in an appearance after ten months, Kitty was queried. She said she had a miscarriage cheering for the Dallas Cowboys.

Simon could afford the money. What he couldn't afford

was the emotional damage. Sometimes it seemed to him that he had separated himself from sunlight and joy forever. The wound eventually scarred over, but the scar tissue was stiff and unyielding. Since his divorce, he'd been unable to settle in with one woman for more than a few weeks. He was too afraid of being hurt again. He detested the fear in himself, but wasn't everyone afraid of something? Often he felt a need to talk to someone about Guy. Was anyone to be trusted? Was Christie Larsen? He wondered what she was afraid of. His mistrust of women was an illness that he hoped would go away . . . if he refused to admit it existed.

He slugged down his drink. After meeting Christie Larsen, it seemed to him that somewhere a window was opened in a boarded-up house. Fresh air was pouring into rooms that had been tightly sealed for a long time. He wanted to hold Christie close. Maybe she could stop his continuous slide into loneliness.

"We're closing up, Mr. Macleod."

Simon shook himself and stood up. "I'm going, Gus. Sorry I stayed so late."

"Uhm . . . Mr. Macleod. I mentioned to my son that you often have a drink here. He asked if I'd get your autograph. He'd appreciate it very much. He plays defensive end—just like you did—on his high school team. Wants to go to Notre Dame."

"Sure, Gus." Simon leaned down and signed the cocktail napkin. "Hope football brings him luck." He didn't add—more than it brought me.

PART SIX

1992 APRIL

Chapter 14

ALTHOUGH IT was dark east of the Rockies, the palm trees and mansions of Beverly Hills still cast their long, slanting, smog-softened shadows in the late afternoon California sun. Over five hundred stretch Cadillac limousines—mostly white—crawled through the traffic, inching their way toward the Shrine Auditorium in downtown Los Angeles. ABC network television—cameras, crew, celebrity interviewers—waited with practiced patience for the VIPs to arrive. Bob Dixon did the voice over for ABC while the cameras ranged over every facet of the scene, from the red carpet leading from the street to the auditorium, to the potted palm trees brought in for the telecast—what would Los Angeles be without palm trees?—to the faces of the crowd pressing against the police barricades, eager to catch a glimpse of the famous, the infamous, and would-be famous as they slipped from their rented limousines. Dixon—radiating enthusiasm—filled time for the more than one billion people watching for the arrival of the first celebrity.

"... And now, live from the Shrine Auditorium, we again celebrate that single night in the year which millions of people all over the world share together. Twenty, four-foot statues of golden Oscars stand majestically beneath the sweeping Moorish arches at the entrance of the Shriners Al Malaikah Temple—known to Angelenos as the Shrine Auditorium. This vast auditorium will be filled by nearly 6,500 members of the Academy of Motion Picture Arts and Sciences and their family and friends, each with an unobstructed view of the entire sixty-five foot by one hundred eighty-five foot stage..."

It was a little after six in Manhattan. In a terraced apartment on the fourteenth floor of The Majestic—the most luxurious of the four twin-towered cooperative apartment buildings on Central Park West—Sherwood Anderson fiddled with the television set in his library while Mona anxiously watched him.

"Darling, please make the picture stop shredding. I can't see anything."

"The glitch is in the cable system."

"We have the most expensive television set Sony makes—a forty-six-inch screen—and all we're getting are jagged lines . . . streaks . . . dots. It makes me dizzy."

"I'm sure the cable people are trying to fix it."

"I knew we should have flown to L.A. for the ceremony. Uncle Stavros said he could get us in—didn't you, dear?"

"Mmm," Stavros said.

"It's only $2,000 for an orchestra seat."

"Mona, I've got to be in the office tomorrow," Sherwood said. "Guy is passing out the partners' bonus checks."

"The partners' bonus checks?" Stavros glanced at Sherwood.

For once, Sherwood could flex his muscles for his rich uncle-in-law. "I did very well this year."

"Yes, he did . . . we thought he would. That's why we bought this nine-room apartment. Do you like it, Uncle Stavros? I love the dark walnut floors. They can't make floors like these anymore. Dark walnut is on the endangered species list. And the view of the Hudson River and New Jersey from the terrace is spectacular. Actually I wanted the apartment Frank Costello used to own." Mona giggled. "But it wasn't for sale."

"This is a lovely apartment," Stavros said.

"It is, isn't it? Look! The picture's coming on. Thank the Lord! It's so exciting—I get goose bumps. I adore watching the Academy Awards. I feel as if I'm up for an Oscar myself," Mona squealed.

". . . Here they come, folks—Hollywood celebrities arriving thick and fast. Thanks to an effective traffic control plan employing over sixty specially assigned police officers, our distinguished audience seems to be arriving on time . . .

for a change. Here come the first of the Academy's famous members, hurrying the sixty feet from their limousines to the Shrine entrance. I see Paul Newman and his wife, Joanne Woodward, both Hollywood legends. I understand Mr. Newman has grown that beard for his next role." The camera followed Paul Newman, who was wearing a single-breasted dinner jacket, and Joanne Woodward, beautifully but conservatively gowned in a free-flowing, dark gray silk Karl Lagerfeld. "And Jennifer West, nominated for the Best Actress award, followed by Alan Lucca, nominated for Best Actor..."

Mona hugged herself with delight. "Academy Award night is like Thanksgiving, Christmas, and my senior prom all rolled into one." She took a sip of her Monbazzilac, rolled the wine over her tongue, and, in appreciation, used her glass to salute Uncle Stavros. He had given her a case of the deep, golden, fruity wine after he'd returned from his most recent trip to Italy. She really liked sweet whites better than dry. In fact she liked this wine better than Chateau d'Yquem—which Sherwood insisted was the finest dessert wine ever bottled. Sherwood didn't know everything. She glanced around the library—it was perfect. The books, the classical records, the statues, the CD player, the VCR. Sherwood, in his brown velvet smoking jacket, sipping his VSOP Courvoisier from a glorious, iridescent rock crystal snifter. Uncle Stavros, in his gray suede vest—imagine, a suede vest—and flared continental trousers, drinking his vintage Bual Madeira. She smiled... $150 a bottle. The only fly in the ointment was the missing Irene Bentley. Irene had promised to come and meet Uncle Stavros... a small *en famille* do with the four of them watching the Academy Awards together. But this morning Irene had called to say that something had come up, something to do with *Deirdre*. Well, there was time. Irene wanted to meet Stavros. Mona could tell. He could be a movie contact for her.

"Oooh, look! I see Franco Marconi," Mona cried.

"... And with us from England, Gil Murphy, a nominee for Best Director, with Franco Marconi, also a nominee for Best Director, hot on his heels." He ignored the pair of toothy blonds hanging onto both men's arms. Big-breasted blonds wearing thigh-high, sequined dresses with plunging necklines were an old Hollywood story. But Marconi and Murphy interested the ABC director and the camera zoomed in on the two directors. Gil Murphy, a symbol of British tradition, wore a double-breasted, black dinner jacket, pinched at the waist, a small black bow tie, and pants with the conventional narrow satin stripe running down the side. His black patent leather shoes glistened under the TV lights. By contrast, Marconi, the American trailblazer, had on a blue plaid dinner jacket, a blue shirt with ruffles, and a butterfly bow tie—pale blue on one wing and white on the other. Faded blue jeans and blue cowboy boots completed the outfit. Dixon had been studying the picture in his personal monitor, and he picked up the director's point. He masked his reaction to Marconi's tuxedo. "Study our directors, ladies and gentlemen. They each personify a viewpoint. We'll learn tonight whether British tradition at its finest or American daring will carry the day..."

"Now that we own United Cinema, I feel even more strongly about the Academy Awards. Sherwood, darling, don't you feel more strongly?"

"No. I feel strongly that it was idiotic for us to acquire a motion picture studio in the first place—idiotic for anyone." He gave Stavros a long look.

Stavros said nothing.

"Sherwood, love. Please. No more wet blanket talk. I don't want to hear it—not tonight of all nights. Especially when you know Uncle Stavros considers it a very fine acquisition. Besides, we're up for eight Academy Awards. Oh, look! There's Meryl Streep!"

The casement windows in the library of Guy Macleod's five-story, gray stone town house on Sutton Place overlooked the East River. Irene Bentley, having showered and powdered and perfumed herself, wrapped Guy's too-large green velour robe more tightly around her body. She sipped her Chablis and turned from watching the lights in Queens to observing her host. He was wearing a long, black silk kimono embroidered with a dragon motif in gold and silver

NAKED CALL

thread, while sipping tea spiked with Bas Armagnac out of a fine, blue Canton porcelain cup. Irene considered the tea and the kimono to be new affectations of Guy's—he was probably fucking some Oriental. She reviewed her approach.

"Darling, now that we've completed the prologue to our mutual satisfaction...," she murmured.

"Very satisfactory, my dear."

"Will you please turn on the TV?"

"Irene, I forget. Tell me again. Exactly why did you want to spend this particular evening with me?"

"I enjoy your company, Guy."

"And what else? I'll put no more money in *Deirdre*. Fifty thousand is enough."

"Quite enough. I told you I thought we might watch the Academy Awards together. I knew you would be watching. My friends won't. They say the Awards suck."

"Why the devil do you want to watch that boring circus?"

"I'll tell you after you turn on the set."

"What makes you think I intend to look at that convention of clowns?"

"Dear Guy, you recently bought control of United Cinema. *The Feathered Serpent* is up for eight Academy Awards. Any major awards that it wins will affect the price of United Cinema stock. You won't ignore your investment ... not you."

Guy's lips parted. It was the satisfied smile of a man who had just dined off an enemy. "Perceptive of you."

"Have I offended your sensibilities with my talk of money?"

"Not at all. But the ceremony is a crasher."

"I agree. A disaster. But hopefully a profitable disaster. Let's watch."

"If you insist."

"I insist," she purred softly.

Guy picked up the remote control and turned on the TV monitor that sat between the shelves of a Georgian breakfront bookcase. Almost immediately the screen lit up, and Guy changed the channels to the Academy Awards presentation.

"... Here's that great acting family—the Bridges,

Lloyd, Beau and Jeff . . . followed by an Oscar winner, Miss Sally Fields. The last arrivals are entering the theater, where we will join them in a moment. Here's Sigourney Weaver with a double barrelled nomination . . . up for Best Actress and Best Supporting Actress. And nominated for Best Original Score, here's . . ."

Abruptly Guy flicked off the monitor. "No, Irene. I don't care who wins an Oscar for the Best Original Score . . . for *The Feathered Serpent* or *Little Women*."

"Guy! Please!"

"And I don't care who gets the Oscar for film editing— the *Serpent* or *Crime and Punishment* or if the special effects award goes to *Rambo IX* instead of *The Serpent*."

"Enough, Guy. We agree that the Academy Awards are a perfect example of the Hollywood tribe jerking each other off, then congratulating each other on the size of their organs. But is Wall Street that different? There's no law that says you boys have to publish tombstones in the *Wall Street Journal*. Morgan Stanley, Merrill Lynch, Macleod Brothers, all of you beating your chests, shouting, 'Oyez! Oyez! We hereby announce how many shares of Wuthering Heights Computers we sold, at what price and so forth.' Why the press releases? Only so the boys can sit around at the NYAC, exposing their genitals and waiting to be congratulated on the size of their pricks."

Guy smiled sourly. "You do have a colorful way of putting it. The fact is I grew up loathing films, snapshots, Polaroids, television, movies. Perhaps it's a genetic aversion to photography."

"If you dislike movies so much, why did you buy United Cinema?"

"You know why. Money. United Cinema was a steal." Guy looked at Irene as if he was serving a search warrant. "Now that I've given you my intimate views on Hollywood, what are your shameful secrets? You detest movies. More than I do . . . if possible. So why are you interested in the Academy Awards?"

"I feel I've been too narrow-minded. I can see their potential for reaching millions of . . ."

"Cut the P.R. The only reaching out that interests you is the reaching out for millions of dollars."

"That, too." Irene was a master at wearing a neutral expression.

"All right, no more games. Don't waste your time trying to outfox a fox. There are reasons for your change of heart. Which award are you waiting for on tenterhooks . . . panting to see? Alan Lucca? Handsome bastard . . . sun-browned skin, spellbinding voice, a muscular grace that speaks of power, the male strength of his body . . ."

"Stop it, Guy." Irene started to laugh. "I did my sampling of sun-browned muscles years ago. Now I'm far too cynical for any such romantic nonsense."

Guy shrugged. "It's not Conchita Supervia—unless you've gone bisexual?"

"I haven't."

"Then who?"

"Franco Marconi."

"Ah, Marconi. The idol of the tabloids . . . up for the Best Director award."

"He's creative, inventive, and a first class son-of-a bitch."

Guy considered her gravely. "You have something in mind for Marconi? He's not a stage director."

"Let's say we have similer tastes . . . fly-by-night sex."

"Then why not catch the Awards at home? Alone. You can play with yourself while watching him. Why play with me?"

If there was one thing Irene disliked it was to show her hand, but she'd known from the start that she would have no choice. "I'd like an introduction to Marconi. From you. It would be worth your while." She tried not to sound as if she was bargaining.

"Why?"

"My idea could make money for United."

"How?"

"I'd like Marconi to direct *Deirdre of the Sorrows*."

"For the movies?" Guy's smile was genial, relaxed, and treacherous. Irene knew that expression too well.

"He's telephoned me twice," she said.

"Then why do you need an introduction from me?"

"You would impress him."

"It's not the kind of thing I usually do." Guy's voice

carried a firm prohibition against any argument, a warning that Irene must play the game according to his rules . . . or there would be no game. "If I make the call . . ."

Irene bowed. "You'll call the shots."

Guy reached for the remote control. "We might as well learn about the movie business, which provides the stimulation for millions of wet panties and wet dreams. And I am mildly curious about the major awards. Bluehorn was right . . . there ought to be an Oscar for bankers."

The screen was charged with excitement as the first host continued his opening remarks. ". . . Ladies and gentlemen, to begin . . . here is the president of the Motion Picture Academy . . ."

In the vast Shriner's Auditorium, Christie Larsen and Louis Levy sat next to each other in the eighth row of the orchestra. In the same row, several seats to the left, Franco Marconi sat between Conchita Supervia and Julian Hennesy. Two rows ahead of Christie and Louis, Alan Lucca sat next to Jo Caro. Matt Renault sat between Jo Caro and Jenny Lattimore. Jo wore her mini-skirted, blue evening gown complete with her rhinestone-studded toreador jacket, and Jenny wore an exuberant, gypsy dress with a skirt foaming excesses of crocheted lace. The auditorium was shimmering with the glitter of sequins, beading, taffeta, lace, silks, blazing jewelry, pasted-on smiles, high-strung bodies. The hum and buzz of heavy breathing, whispered voices, pounding hearts filled the air with electricity.

Christie gazed at the crowd, at the men in black tuxedos, the women in a pageant of colors. She was happy to be at the ceremony . . . it relieved her tension that at last things were coming to a climax. Her relief was interrupted. She caught a glimpse of Jo smiling at Matt and Matt smiling at Jo. She hoped Jenny missed it . . . Jenny had a temper. Christie focused on the stage.

A feeling of peace had settled over Louis. He glanced quickly at Christie and looked away. Only from his unblinking eyes could his excitement be judged. The even line of his mouth never changed. He wondered if Christie understood the depth of his pride in her. She wasn't the daughter of his own blood, of his suffering, but she was more than he deserved. Had she never existed, what would have been the sense of his years of work . . . of striving . . . of selfishness? Now the pain and passion of his life would live on. Christie would see to that. As for the rest—for Jessie—the waters never closed over the head of memory. But at least he could rest.

The president concluded, saying, "Ladies and gentlemen, I'd like to return you to your host for the evening . . ."

Jo tried not to smile at Matt again. She listened without listening to the soothing, formless flow of words from the stage. She supposed there was a kind of freedom in not knowing what would happen next. It was like being in the middle of nowhere. She closed her eyes for an instant. It was hard for her to admit to herself that she was afraid— that she might have good reason for being afraid.

The host went on energetically. " . . . How often have we heard those immortal words, 'Movies are a collaborative art.' So I've asked a number of members of the collaboration to join me in hosting. They represent some of Hollywood's best new talent . . . talent nurtured both in films and on the stage. Now, please welcome two of my co-hosts. Miss . . ."

A grinning co-host remarked while holding up an envelope, " . . . the other immortal words that ring in our ears are, 'You're over budget, behind schedule, and not in a condition that inspires confidence.' But you realize that if you can just keep going, and lash yourself to the mast so you won't jump overboard . . ."

"Simon, can I get you more coffee? No?" Mitzi shrugged and collapsed into an arm chair. "Now that Macleod Brothers owns a movie studio, I think we should go to the next Academy ceremony. Think of the parties afterward . . . the Governors Ball, Swifty Lazar's bash . . ."

"The Governors Ball is for movie celebrities," her son,

Ira, said. "And you don't know Swifty Lazar, Mom. He's a big number."

"We're big numbers. We own a studio. You just watch," Mitzi said.

"I'm getting antsy. We've accumulated over four hundred thousand shares of United since the nominations were announced. And so far we've won zilch. All kinds of nifty little nowhere awards, like soundtrack, special effects, makeup. Who cares? Nothing big. Not even the Best Supporting Actress award. A stock doesn't move on special effects," Ira Sr. griped.

"But the special effects in the *Serpent* were stunning," Mitzi chirped.

"Damn it! Why didn't Supervia win Best Supporting Actress?" Ira fumed.

"I understand the stock market, not the movie business. Anyway, Supervia doesn't matter. What would have mattered is the Best Actress award," Simon said.

"Lattimore wasn't even nominated," Ira Sr. said.

"Lucca was for Best Actor," Ira Jr. said.

"An also-ran doesn't count. He didn't get it—remember?"

"I think Alan Lucca should have gotten the award," Mitzi raved.

"Sssh. This is one of the biggies," Ira Sr. snapped. "We need this one. Watch the screen."

"To present the Best Director Award, we have a director who needs no introduction. What is needed are some adjectives to describe his work, which stands out even in this town which has often seen genius at work. His career has been meteoric, a flaming comet more than a career. And the head of the comet is Mr. Steven Spielberg..."

"Fasten your seat belts," Ira Jr. yelped.

"I'm crossing my fingers, Simon... even if I am Jewish. We need all the help we can get."

Silence reigned for minutes in the Benjamin apartment while scenes from the five films nominated for the highly coveted Best Director Award were shown. Then the hallowed envelope was opened.

"... And the winner is Franco Marconi for *The Feathered Serpent*."

NAKED CALL

"We did it!" Ira Sr. shouted.

"Whoopee!" Ira Jr. yelled.

"I'm so glad," Mitzi gurgled.

Ira socked Simon in the arm. "We bagged one! We really bagged one!"

Simon looked relieved. "Seems so."

"Mitzi, I love you!"

"Ira, dear, you're wrinkling my dress."

"Buy a new one," Ira Sr. grinned. "Hey, there's our bastard. What the hell is he wearing?"

Franco Marconi was inches off the ground, having prepared for the stress by snorting three lines of the highest grade cocaine before leaving for the ceremonies. He floated down the aisle and took the stairs leading to the stage in two bounding leaps. "... I want to thank Addie and Art Grossman for their wonderful adaptation of the novel into a screenplay, Christie Larsen for giving me the book to read, and the whole company of actors..."

Franco Marconi concluded. "... This kind of collaboration encourages creativity as well as box office receipts. Thank you very much."

To the almost one billion people watching the awards, Franco Marconi had put on a masterful performance. Christie lowered her eyes and bit her lip. She could always tell when Franco was high, and his borderline hysteria made her nervous. One of these days he would come apart in public.

A co-host was saying, "... We have, as always, saved the very best for last. And to present the award for Best Picture, there is among us a man whose work and influence in films and in the theater has enriched us all ... Sir John Gielgud, the last of the glorious four knights. I know I share that feeling with you and the nominees for Best Picture Award that Sir John..."

"Come on, baby, the big one!" Ira Sr. gestured at the TV screen.

"Take it easy, Ira," Simon said quietly.

"Over the top, killer," Ira Jr. shouted.

On screen, Gielgud, amazingly energetic for his age and comfortably wearing the mantle of theatrical genius, was speaking. Aided by the microphone, his distinctive voice retained much of the subtle shadings that enabled him to play an incredible variety of roles, from the finest Hamlet of his generation to Henry IV in Orson Welles' lost masterpiece; from Falstaff to the butler in the award-winning *Arthur*; to a small part in the X-rated film, *Caligula*. Mitzi glowed. Imagine if she could meet Sir John. "Dear ladies and gentlemen, thank you so much. I'm here to present the Best Picture award..."

"The *Serpent* can't miss," Ira Jr. said.

"From your lips to God's ear," Ira Sr. said.

Simon said nothing.

"Everybody be quiet," Mitzi called. "I'm having trouble breathing."

Tense silence took over in the Benjamin library while excerpts from the five films up for the Best Picture Award were shown.

"... and the winner for the Best Picture Award is..." The greatest actor of his generation took the liberty of a dramatic pause. "... *The Feathered Serpent*. Accepting for *The Feathered Serpent* is..."

Louis reached out, gripping Christie's hand. She remained for some seconds, feeling the strength of her fingers interlaced with his. Then, sitting up straight, she looked at him. "You really should be the one to accept the Oscar."

Louis made a face. "Kid, go get it! It's yours!"

"But if it wasn't for you..."

"Obscenity! Obscenity! Get your ass up on the stage."

Christie's eyes misted. "Okay. How do I thank you for all that you've done for me?"

Louis thought of the many answers he might give, then settled for the truth. "Or I, you... for all that you've done for this old goat."

She let it rest there.

In the Benjamin home there was silence except for the voice on the television. Simon and Ira listened intently to the heavy applause, watching the camera circle the audience and then follow Christie striding down the aisle and up the steps to the stage. She was one of the most beautiful women to walk to the podium, even on this night of nights in this world full of beautiful women. Everything about her was at once exquisite, strong, fine. She was wearing a black silk evening suit, austere in its simplicity, stunning in its elegance. Her red hair was severely pulled back, intensifying her remarkable cheekbones and eyes. Hers was a face that would last—to be lovely in the middle years and in old age. The essential structure was there.

Simon caught his breath.

"She's a looker. I bet it hasn't hurt her career," Mitzi sniped.

"Smart, too. Simon said she was. Didn't you?"

"She's smart. Louis was right to insist she be made president."

"Guy didn't want her?"

"Sssh, Ira. I want to hear what the beautiful corporate president says," Mitzi announced.

". . . I started going to the movies as a kid. I could get in half price because I was young. Now that I have the good luck to be making movies, I see a lot of screenings for free . . . so this is a wonderful and rewarding profession for a movie fan. First of all, I want to thank Louis Levy for his faith in my judgement to the tune of forty million dollars—in our business that's called putting your money where your faith is—for letting me produce *The Feathered Serpent* at United in association with Tosca Films. I want to thank Gary Chang and his entire camera crew for assisting Franco Marconi in going over budget, running behind schedule, leaving enough film on the cutting room floor to make *Son of The Feathered Serpent*, and at the same time being divinely inspired. And of course I must thank the actors and actresses who recreated the life of these strange, half-primitive, Mexican villagers. And my heartfelt thanks to all the gifted and imaginative craftsmen—Julian Hennesy, John Ellerby, Nick Spink, Amy Lowell, and the many others who brought the *Serpent* from the deep of our imagination into fire-storming life. And my special thanks to my son, Tommy, who first reminded me of my childhood fascination with serpents and dragons and monsters from the past . . ."

When Christie finished her Oscar acceptance speech, the final host took over for the good-byes.

". . . And so, ladies and gentlemen, this is a print. We've gone through one hundred seventy-one nominations from fifty-five pictures to name twenty-four winners. Our congratulations to the Oscar winners and our regrets to all the rest of you lovely people. In an evening with thousands of thanks, our warmest thanks go to you, our audience, the silent partner in everything we do. Thank you for being with us and good night."

About 1,700 invited guests, including many of the Oscar winners and nominees, stayed for the Oscar party. The decorations continued the award's theme of old Hollywood glamour. The Flower Council of Holland had donated thousands of red and white tulips, which matched the five thousand yards of red and white chiffon that were draped around the walls of the room. In the center of the room a bandstand with three giant golden Oscar statues revolved slowly under a tent of still more red and white chiffon. The tables, covered by red and white linen tablecloths, were set in circles around the dance floor. All combined to transform the Shrine into a continuing festivity: the Academy Awards Board of Governors Ball.

"I can't remember what I said," the Best Actress worried, thinking about her acceptance speech. "My zipper broke. I don't know why, but it broke. Somebody fixed it. Wow! Am I hungry!"

"How can I celebrate? I have a rehearsal in the morning for a new film." The Best Supporting Actor grinned. "Don't believe a word I say. I'll dance all night."

But dancing on the floor surrounding the orchestra wasn't easy. The floor was being used to photograph the winners congratulating each other.

Christie saw Louis wave as she moved across the room toward one of the "A" tables. She waved back with her Oscar, and in seconds was surrounded by a gaggle of laughing, yelping photographers escorting her, almost forcefully, to the dance floor.

"Stand between Franco and me," Louis commanded.

"Both of you hold up your Oscars. Then we'll do a group shot with all the technical wizards holding their Oscars."

"I can hold up my envelope. I kept it," Franco crowed.

"So did I." Christie laughed.

When the photo session ended, Christie, Louis, and Franco edged toward their table. Franco's blond followed two steps behind him. Like all professional Hollywood blonds, she knew where to stand. Conchita Supervia and Alan Lucca were waiting to dance. Alan took a quick bite of his dessert before they left the table. "*Delicioso*, this *gateau*. I'm a slave to bittersweet chocolate cake and pistachio nuts. I'm going to have seconds . . . thirds."

Conchita sighed. "If I smile at chocolate cake, I put on ten pounds."

"Louis, the breast of duck is superb. I think the sauce is duck stock and black currant liqueur." Alan gave them his million-dollar smile. "So I didn't win an Oscar. Eating well is the best revenge. Fuck the health freaks. They live forever . . . and enjoy nothing."

"I'll live forever, no matter what," Louis said as Christie and he seated themselves. He gave the hovering waiter his order.

Franco remained standing. "I'm getting out of here," he said. The blond looked for the nearest exit.

"To Spago's?" Louis asked.

"Swifty's party. A great crowd scene. Great pizza. Also, Placido Domingo and Ali MacGraw and Mike Nichols and Diane Sawyer and Meryl Streep and Harrison Ford and Louis Malle and Candice Bergen and me."

"Don't pig out on pizza, Franco. Keep Hollywood healthy is the new battle cry."

"I'm as strong as an ox. I'll see you both later."

"Maybe not me," Christie said.

"Why not you? Why miss the fun . . . the confetti . . . the *paparazzi* . . . the inspiring me?" Franco teased.

"Ah yes, you. I might pop in for a quick see," Christie said. "Then it's beddie-bye. I'm not as strong as an ox."

"You're stronger. Strong enough to catch my late-night revel. You always loved my revels."

"There are some pleasures worth regretting." Christie smiled.

The past was between them—that was the essence of the matter. And it was never so much between them as, when not at work, they found themselves accidentally face to face.

Franco pulled his beard. "Miss Larsen, don't you want to celebrate with me?"

"We had our celebration earlier, at the presentation ceremony."

"That was for show. Are you afraid to celebrate with me?"

"You're putting on airs. And no more significant glances, please."

The waiter arrived with the pate that Louis had ordered. Louis had said nothing through the interchange. After the waiter left, he interrupted. "You heard her, Franco. I'll see you later at Spago's."

Franco shrugged, linked arms with his blond and left.

Louis gave Christie a comforting, affectionate smile. He understood too much and had too much tact to talk about the exchange with Franco. "You ought to try the pate," he suggested. "It's duck liver, country style. But it spreads easily . . . has a lot of garlic. You like garlic." He laughed. "Keeps vampires away."

At that moment the Best Supporting Actress stopped by the table. "Christie, could I have your autograph on the menu? For my daughter, Casey. She doesn't want to act, or dance, or sing. She's the new breed . . . wants to be a movie executive."

It was almost one in the morning—the shank of the evening by Hollywood standards—when Christie unlocked her front door. The house was silent except for the voice of Johnny Carson. She tiptoed into Tommy's room and found his small set still turned on. But Tommy was fast asleep. He'd been watching the Academy Awards with Maria. The housekeeper had probably turned off the set and Tommy had switched it on after she went to bed. Christie turned it off again and stood by the bedside, gazing at her sleeping son. She remembered the day he lost his first baby tooth . . . the time he won first prize at school for a drawing . . . the silly questions he'd asked when first learning to talk. Why is nothing we eat blue? Why do we flush the dead

NAKED CALL

goldfish down the toilet? Why don't we bury them? How high is up? She smiled at the boy and the man he would be. She came from a family that fate had left defenseless, shamed, disgraced. But, with time, she had gained a strength of her own that she carried into battle . . . and often enough she'd been the victor. Tommy's childhood was not like hers. With him, she'd tried to recreate her childhood as it might have been . . . she tried to change her past.

She leaned over her sleeping son, kissed him lightly on the forehead, and left the room. Her last stop before sleep was her study. She would riffle quickly through the mail—her routine before going to bed.

She glanced at the telegrams Maria had placed on her desk. Congratulations, she guessed. She opened them in the order they were stacked. One from Jo Caro, sent before the actual awards were made. One from Nan Grey, sent at the same time. A few from friends and strangers she'd met at parties. One was from Louis. He probably had alerted Linda Loomis to send it immediately after the award. And one was from . . . she stopped. She read the telegram, holding it as though it were something alive. A shudder ran through her. It was as though a pail full of slops had been emptied over her head. She read the telegram again. She read it three times before she fully took the words in.

"Congratulations, Christie. I was always afraid you would take after your father. Tonight you proved I have nothing to fear. You and I can now live happily ever after . . . till death do us part. Your devoted mother, Irene."

Christie saw her mother's cat eyes winking up at her from the telegram. What she saw in them was terrible. She had to force down the bile that the memories brought up. She could clearly hear the strident tone, the hatred, the sounds of her mother slashing at her father . . . at her. She wished she could disinfect her memory. In the fifteen years since she'd left New York, she had heard from Irene twice. Once, twelve years ago, when Tommy was born, full of wrath at her grandson's being named after his grandfather. How had Irene known about Tommy or where to reach her? The second time was after the release of *Labor Day*, the first movie she'd produced for United. Irene had suggested that since Christie was interested in horror, she should be interested in making an upscale horror—Irene's theatrical version of *The Pit and the Pendulum* by Edgar Allan Poe. Christie had answered politely, thank you but no thank you. That was seven years ago. Here she was again. Her mother—the Ph.D. of ruined lives. Irene could give seminars on the subject. What did she want this time? She had to want something. Irene Bentley never did anything or said anything without a purpose. Especially not "Congratulations."

Chapter 15

THE PUB-AD departments, as well as legal and sales, of United Cinema had been panting like dogs on a tight leash until the Academy Awards were bagged. Now they zoomed off in all directions simultaneously, barking and snorting, "Look at us! Look at us! Look at us!" Publicity dined and drank with the appropriate editors of major magazines and newspapers, handing out still shots of the stars and scenes from *The Feathered Serpent*, plus frivolous promises of interviews with anyone connected to the film—splendidly costumed or as naked as the "Nude Maja"—suitably retouched so they'd be printable in a family newspaper. Publicity set off fireworks in relevant industries. Zara Bolton, one of their hot shots, wrote an exuberant memo that Toy World was eager to manufacture a *Feathered Serpent* . . . the kiddie market was a prime *Serpent* target. Bozzie Bozworth, who knew all the classy merchandising gimmicks, had a feathery dress designed by Katya Kerensky, the rising star of Soviet fashion and the grand-niece of Prince Aleksandr Feordorovich Kerensky, to be worn by Jenny Lattimore at the premiere. Advertising sizzled with creativity and simmered with impatience. Three different campaigns were ready to go, each announcing the New York opening of *The Feathered Serpent*. All were on hold, awaiting Christie's decision as to which campaign to run with. "A fuckin' waste of time," the ad director muttered in the privacy of a booth in the men's room. In his heart of hearts, he knew he was far more qualified than Christie to make that decision.

Legal was churning out paperwork covering unsigned distribution contracts and budgets and credit violations, like the misspelling of Conchita Supervia's last name and a lawsuit threatened by an indignant Mexican waiter at the *hacienda*.

As for sales . . . sales, thanks to Christie, was in seventh heaven. With her heart in her mouth, she had refused to sign any contracts with national exhibitor chains, knowing she could make a far better deal if *Serpent* walked away with at least one major Oscar. Before the Awards, sales had sweated, argued, pleaded. Now they were ecstatic.

On a sunny morning two weeks after Oscar night, Christie sat at her desk sipping coffee and grinning at the unused desk at the other end of the room. On her desk was a bronze plate with the engraving, "Christina Larsen, President." The desk wasn't neat—contracts, screenplays, treatments, and messages were spread out, covering its entire surface. The desk at the far end of the room was neat . . . bare except for the engraved nameplate. It read, "Louis Levy, Chairman Emeritus." The desk was there in the odd event that Louis might drop in one day and complain that he had no place to hang his hat. The idea amused Christie.

Earlier that morning her sales director Gordie Berlin had stopped by to thank her for not giving in to his fear. She'd smiled, "That's my job."

"I'm glad it's not mine," he grinned. "I'm a very good salesman . . . maybe too good. To lose a sale eats me up alive."

"Me, too."

"So how come you could take the heat?"

Christie shrugged. "It comes with the territory."

She'd had her reasons. Deep down in the bedrock of her heart she had to prove to herself that her faith in herself was justified. That she had the sheer animal cunning, the instinct, the strength of will to hold her own in the Hollywood jungle . . . to gamble everything on her judgement . . . hers . . . without Louis to shield her. She glanced at the empty desk at the other end of the room and saluted.

Guy Macleod had telephoned twice this morning to check the arrangements for tomorrow night's premiere in New York. Clearly, he enjoyed the excitement. Did Simon? Forget Simon. She went back to reviewing the contracts for the European festivals and trade show—the Cannes Film Festival . . . MIFED, the trade show in Milan . . . the Deauville Festival in late summer. Her reading was interrupted by the buzz of the intercom.

"I have Mr. Levy waiting," Nan said.

Christie picked up the phone. "Good morning, Louis. Have you jogged this morning?"

"You know I don't jog. Jogging kills people. Not to mention what it does to your ankles, knees, and hip joints. But I have had my massage . . . especially my arm. I almost dislocated it patting myself on the back for the Oscars . . . for you . . . for my genius in selecting you. Now let's cut to the chase, kid. Three weeks have passed and I haven't heard a peep . . . a harumph."

"A harumph? About what?"

"A harumph about the box office. Which theater chains have you signed up?"

"None. The contracts are on my desk, just in from legal. General Cinema, UA Communications, The Mann chain, Edwards . . . you know the names."

"The big boys."

"Big, medium, and small. They all think *Serpent* is a hot ticket. I'll sign the contracts when I return from the opening."

"How come you're so late?"

"We didn't start negotiations until after the Awards."

Stunned. "You waited for the Awards?"

Satisfied. "I waited."

Impressed. "Quite a chance you took."

Teasing. "A forty million dollar chance."

Humbly. "Why?"

"Stop the quiz. You know why. Once we had the Oscars I knew I could get more favorable terms from the boys.

And I did... with a vengeance. They almost guarantee commercial success."

Christie drummed her fingers lightly on the table, waiting for Louis to speak. She stared at the phone. She could see him—his careful, stock-taking eyes, judging her as he always did, her value for the studio he loved, in terms of the right scripts she acquired, the right decisions she made.

"I couldn't have done any better myself," he said at last.

"Thank you."

"You've got balls of brass."

"I'll settle for nerves of steel." She laughed.

"If anyone ever tells me again that a woman president sucks, I'll tell them to fuck off." He gave a contented sigh. "Where'd you learn to sweat it, kid?"

"From you," she said aloud. And from hanging by my thumbs most of my life, she said to herself.

"Right! And let's not forget that I taught you everything. Don't talk to strangers, even if you've been to bed with them three times. Wear lace panties to the opening. You want to look sexy if you're kidnapped," he growled and hung up.

Christie bent her head toward the telephone as though taking a stage bow and went back to work. She'd miss the old goat at the opening, but Louis wouldn't budge. He'd been to five hundred premieres, and he didn't like caviar or champagne.

In a few minutes she had completed the entry forms for the European events and buzzed her secretary. When Nan came in to pick up the contracts, she brought with her a pile of articles collected by the studio's clipping service. Christie had been featured in articles published in *Forbes*, *Fortune*, the *Wall Street Journal*, *Time*, and *Newsweek*... all with high praise for her business judgement. Creative judgement. Instinct for... She was relieved when her reading of the eulogies was interrupted by the buzz of the intercom. Jo Caro wanted to see her. "Send her in," she said.

Jo pranced in, full of impatience. She scanned the magazines on Christie's desk.

"I read those articles. Dullsville. You sound so sane, so 4-H Club. So full of the business smarts. Fine. That's good copy—once. Unless you're into competing with Marvin Davis or Donald Trump. A Hollywood divinity-in-training must have a bit of craziness. You're on the verge of sounding too healthy. A little obsessiveness wouldn't hurt. What you need is a cause. Maybe get into fitness, like Fonda . . . or aliens . . . or animal rights. Did you see what-the-fuck's-her-name the other night on television? You know, the blond waif with the big boobs. She was caterwauling about the flagrant abuse of mice by science. How about that?"

"I don't like mice." Christie grinned. "To what do I owe the pleasure of this visit?"

"I need two favors."

Jo never asked favors unless the asking flattered the giver. This had a mixed signal. "Go ahead," Christie said.

"First, can I cadge a lift to LAX with you in the company limo? You being our star VIP."

That was meant to flatter. "I was going to ask if you wanted a lift. What's two?"

"The second is due to the fact that I met a man—"

"Matt Renault. You can't afford him." This was the real favor.

A flash of irritation filled Jo's eyes. "True. I can see you're a born spiritualist. You have psychic powers . . . clairvoyance . . ."

"Also 20/20 vision. I watched you Oscar night. I prayed you wouldn't let your hands wander or there'd be blood on the floor of the Shrine Auditorium. Matt Renault is bought and paid for by Jenny Lattimore. She guards him like a sex-starved Doberman."

"That's why the favor." Christie waited. "I would like to depend on your not calling the police or mentioning it to anyone when . . ."

"When?"

"When I don't come home after the premiere party at the Plaza to share with you our luxurious company suite at the Carlyle."

Christie understood. "You have an old school chum in New York. You want to spend the night reminiscing with him about the good old days in Bakersfield High."

"How well you put it."

"Are you sure Jenny is taking Matt to the premiere?"

NAKED CALL

"I am . . . and I'm taking him to bed."

"My dear friend, you think so deep, I don't always follow you. Jenny, as we agree, is possessive with a tinge of homicidal mania . . . sheer genius at character assassination."

"Right—a genuine killer. Her bite is worse than her bark—straight for the jugular. But she's given Matt the night off." Jo's face was unexpectedly exposed and reckless. "She has other fish to fry."

As she listened to Jo, something struck Christie. This wasn't the whole story. "What other fish?"

"She's tracking Guy Macleod. She sees him as a power."

"He is."

"I know. He's my favorite geek with a hereditary title." Jo giggled. "Anyway, Matt's taking Jenny at her word. If you don't see me until Kennedy, and if anyone should ask . . ."

"You're at a class reunion with an old friend."

"An old friend with a new face." Jo made an elaborate pirouette and pranced out of the office.

A bemused Christie watched her leave. It didn't add up. Jo was behaving entirely out of character. She never put sex ahead of her career, and she had no shortage of bed pals, especially with her new status as United's house counsel. Why take the risk of Jenny Lattimore's discovery—and hatred—Jenny Lattimore, the superstar . . . the superkiller? Why? Jo had always lived by one motto—choose your enemies more carefully than you choose your friends.

The intercom buzzed. In came Harry Weiss, looking like a groomed and dapper corpse.

"Are you all right?" Christie asked.

"No."

Harry placed a folder on Christie's desk. He opened it, sliding a slim batch of expense chits, each clipped to a check, in her direction. Then he crumpled into a chair.

"Read them and weep."

Christie picked up the chits and checks. She counted seven. Glancing at the names on the checks and chits she noted that all were made out to men and women who had worked on *The Feathered Serpent*. The chits covered publicity, entertainment, technical effects, consultants, cosmetic surgery, plumbing, one masseuse, and so forth. All the chits were signed by Franco Marconi. She did a quick mental addition of the checks and estimated the total at a little over four hundred thousand dollars.

She looked up. "Does this have anything to do with the 1099s we sent out?"

"Yes."

"The natives are objecting to paying their taxes on these checks? They thought they were fatherly donations from United?"

"They are objecting."

"It's not all quiet on the tax front?"

Harry fidgeted nervously.

Christie spread the checks and chits out on her desk. "I sense a zinger. Spill it, before your ulcer acts up.

"It's already bleeding."

"Okay. What is it? Accounting screwed up these expenses?"

"No. They entered them correctly . . . too correctly. They entered three of them . . . ahem . . . twice."

"Did you say 'twice'?" Harry said nothing. "Why twice?"

"Because three of those checks were issued twice and attached to duplicate expense chits . . . signed by Franco Marconi . . . twice."

"Franco signed the same expense chits twice?"

"He did."

"How could that happen?"

"It happened because the accounting department thinks Franco Marconi is next to God. Nobody picked up the duplication except Edgardo Silvera, my assistant . . . my personal spy in accounting. He was having a morning coffee with Accounts Payable and noticed the expense chit from Maureen Corley on Accounts Payable's desk. He's got a crush on Corley, and he remembered he'd seen the same chit before."

"How long ago?"

"Ten days. Two weeks. He wasn't sure. It was one night when he was banging Accounts Payable on her desk. The duplication aroused his curiosity. So he asked Accounts Payable to check all the files. For Edgardo, Alicia Montero—that's Accounts Payable—will do anything. They checked the files together. They found Corley's first chit with canceled check attached. Then they found its twin. They found the other two twins." He gestured toward the chits on Christie's desk.

Christie had been sitting straight, patiently listening. Now she spoke with deliberate reasonableness. "Why haven't we heard from the people who received duplicate checks?"

"We have . . . all three. They say they didn't receive the second check."

"Ah. There are seven checks here. Three are double payments. What about the other four?"

"The other four claim they never put in for the expenses . . . and they never received the checks."

Christie remained outwardly composed, but the San Andreas fault suddenly shifted beneath her feet. The answer came too quickly. A bizarre and impossible answer—still it blazed in her mind, the only possible answer.

"Forgeries. These checks are forgeries."

"So are the expense chits."

"Too many to be a mistake."

"Seven checks—$415,691 worth of forgeries." His voice was abjectly apologetic. This was financial mismanagement—and he was financial. "To a studio like United— we gross over five hundred million—one might say this is peanuts, but . . ."

"Harry remember, poisoned peanuts. Forgery may not be the crime of the century, but it is grand larceny." She glanced away, her lips compressed. A frightening landscape of possibilities had opened before her eyes.

"The Penal Code of the State of California would define it as felony grand theft."

"Thanks. Whose names were on the duplicate checks?"

"Gary Chang. Corley. Ted Lord. Sidney Frank called yesterday. Sidney is awash in outraged virtue. Three clients . . . three checks . . . six 1099 forms."

"Addie Grossman and the others never put in for expenses?"

"No. According to their accountants, they're supposed to pay taxes on money they never asked for . . . and never received."

"Like Julian Hennesy."

"Like Julian Hennesy. Sidney also had a few words to say about Julian's integrity, honesty, and decency."

"Spare me."

The Hennessy tax form was something Christie had expected would prove to be a minor clerical error, to be corrected and forgotten as she went on to larger, more pressing matters like distribution deals for *The Serpent*, plus getting two new pictures into production as well as eleven development projects on line. Now, what had looked like a small, drifting ice floe was turning out to be the tip of a giant iceberg.

"These checks have all been deposited?" Christie had the sensation of falling through space.

"Cashed, canceled, and returned to us. Fuckin' weird." Harry faltered. "Christie, I have a dumb question... please?" She looked at him. "In your years of working with Franco, have you ever known him to do anything irregular?" He coughed. "I mean in a financial sense?"

Christie had waited for this question. "No. And why would he do something like..."

"Like stealing money from United?"

"It doesn't make sense. He's a rich man. What's the motivation?"

"I don't know. Maybe he's not rich. What did Baron Rothschild say? Something like there are three ways to lose money: women, gambling, and investing in other people's ideas. Women are the most fun, gambling the quickest, and investing the surest. Maybe Franco's keeping too many broads? Or he's in hock to his bookie? Or he backed too many lousy restaurants?"

"If Franco needed a loan, he could go to his banker. Or the studio would lend him the money. Or he has friends all over Hollywood. He has a hundred sources for money—at least this kind of money." At last she had put her worst fear into words.

"You're saying what I've been thinking. If Franco was going to steal, he wouldn't swipe a lousy four hundred thousand dollars. He'd steal millions."

A sense of dread enveloped Christie. The whole thing was like some wild, Byzantine plot. "I don't want to turn this into melodrama, but we have no way of knowing how big this is..."

"It could be millions."

"...or who else may be involved, or where it all may lead."

"Like to Swiss bank accounts... and multi-millions embezzled," Harry muttered.

"Buried in the budget of *The Feathered Serpent*." Her tone was carefully neutral, unmarked by anxiety. "Harry, while I'm in New York, question Sidney Frank. Question the other accountants. See if you can get to the bottom of this muck fast... before it turns to quicksand."

"Will you speak to Franco?"

"Not in New York. As soon as we return. Meantime, try to deal with these forgeries—if that's what they are— internally. No publicity." Her face was somber. "We don't want United involved in a scandal. If there has been stealing—say millions of dollars—we must handle it carefully. Otherwise the news media will have a field day. The studio will be in chaos. The police could start a criminal investigation."

They looked at each other. Christie rarely displayed emotion, whether the news was good or bad. But her reaction to the possibility of forgery and embezzlement on a grand scale was as acute as if she'd learned the studio was bankrupt.

"Speak to no one but the accountants. Impress on them the need for secrecy. Any loose talk could hurt their clients as well as United."

"I'll do what I can." Harry assembled the chits and checks and placed them in the folder. He backed out of the office, moving as mechanically as a sleepwalker.

Christie watched him go, rubbing her forehead with the tips of her fingers. The idea of Franco and forgeries made the world seem surrealistic. The odds were poor that a simple explanation would surface. Seven checks... over four hundred thousand dollars... maybe more to come. How the hell could she keep this mess under wraps? Four hundred thousand dollars was too much money to bury. Like it or not, they'd passed the point of no return.

Chapter 16

RADIO CITY Music Hall had been leased for the black-tie premiere of *The Feathered Serpent*. Traffic in the area was a nightmare, far worse than the usual eight o'clock, theater-going, New York traffic jams. Fifth Avenue, Sixth Avenue, Seventh Avenue, the cross streets in the vicinity of the Music Hall . . . all were close to gridlock. In Los Angeles, the limo brigade had been white. In New York, it was black . . . the gleaming ebony limos of the really rich, the rich, the famous, the infamous, the social, the *politicos*—a few of whom had actually read the entire novel—plus the West Coast contingent, all tailgating each other like shiny black snakes with skins that reflected the lights of the city.

Eventually each limousine stopped in front of the Sixth Avenue entrance to the movie house. A legendary director and his daughter, holding hands, bolted from their car to the safety of the theater lobby. Two debutante daughters of a polo-playing father followed. A Presidential candidate and his wife . . . a former Presidential candidate and the blond reason he dropped out of the race . . . a movie star and her mother . . . a South American president and his bodyguard . . . a rock star and three former wives . . . a hot property and his dog . . . a notorious movie star and her lawyer . . . two Senators and one wife. It was impossible for a pedestrian to move through the crowd of celebrity watchers, fans, autograph hunters, and the miscellaneous souls drawn together by chance with nothing better to do that evening. Young and not so young, the curious New Yorkers stared at the celebrities filing into the theater, hurrying by the photographers, nudged and directed by anxious publicists. Occasionally a famous name would be hailed by a watching fan. The star would invariably smile—a photo opportunity for the newspapers—and wave a professional greeting to the fan he or she had never met but who looked familiar.

Christie and Jo Caro arrived together. Christie walked quickly toward the lobby, wearing a stunning, long-sleeved, deceptively transparent, black lace evening gown. A simple black wool crepe cardigan was slung, cape-like, over her shoulders. No one recognized her face, but her beauty attracted attention.

"Are you somebody?" a plump teenager yelled.

Christie called back, "Is that a philosophical question?"

Jo, as always less conservatively turned out than Christie, strutted after her in a dramatic pajama suit, a white-sequined silk T-shirt tucked into embroidered red lace pants which were decorated with sequins and beads.

"Who are you?" someone called.

"Her mascot," Jo answered, gesturing toward Christie.

Zara Bolton from publicity appeared out of nowhere. "Miss Larsen, Miss Caro, wonderful to see you. Please go directly to your seats. We've a big night ahead, what with the party right after this . . ." She tapped a very young man standing beside her. "Tommy, show them to the executive section."

Christie and Jo were guided through the crowd milling about in the lobby. The heavy artillery was there: the opinion makers of the media . . . the shrewd, tough fraternity of judges who advised the public on whether or not *The Feathered Serpent* was worth the price of admission, and more than three hours of their time . . . an important audience. All around Christie, heads were swiveling and bobbing with professional gaiety, arms were waving and gesturing, and mouths were contorted, smiling greetings as they passed, full of congratulations and great expectations.

Christie and Jo were the last to arrive in the roped-off section reserved for studio executives, stars of the film, special friends of the stars of the film, the director and friends of the director, and the partners of Macleod Brothers. Jenny Lattimore, sprouting feathers, sat beside Matt Renault. Conchita Supervia sat between Alan Lucca and Franco Marconi, holding both their hands. Guy Macleod and Simon Macleod sat together, a little apart from the rest. For a moment the theater blurred for Christie. She was shocked at her realization that her need was as alive as ever. She had not permitted herself to dream, to think, to wonder if she might meet Simon tonight. Now that he was here, she felt like an actress called upon to struggle through an unrehearsed scene with unfamiliar dialogue.

Guy mentioned for her to join them. She let Jo slide in first and sat beside Guy. She tried not to look at Simon and instead scanned the group in the executive section. Some of the people were unfamiliar, and she assumed they were either guests of the Macleods or members of their firm.

Jo nudged her ribs and she followed Jo's eyes. A few rows away sat a man in a tux—an aging star who had not made a film in years. And beside him—to her surprise—was Stavros Lennos. His eyes met Christie's and he nodded, his lips thinning like scar tissue in his version of a smile. She smiled back and looked away.

"I see you know Lennos," Guy remarked quietly.

"We've met."

"Does Louis know him?"

"Many people know him. Lennos gets around Hollywood," she answered with perfect grace, telling nothing.

"I heard he tried to buy United. There's a rumor going around that the Mafia is looking for a studio."

"Is there?"

"It's fortunate Louis had the intelligence not to sell to that scum."

"How are you, Christie?" Simon interrupted Guy.

"Good. And you?" The great stone face talked.

"Good enough. You must be very proud. This is your night. You deserve a lot of credit."

"It's everybody's night. We all deserve credit."

"Christie the diplomat," Guy murmured.

"Christie knows you can't give credit away. The more you give, the more it sticks to you," Jo said with disarming frankness and a smile for Guy.

He smiled back and Simon looked at Jo curiously.

The house lights dimmed, then went on again.

"They're signaling. Everyone out of the pool. Attention!

Here comes the main event," Jo stage whispered.

The lights dimmed again.

"Play ball."

As the lights dimmed for a third time, Simon glanced sideways, hoping for a last look at Christie. The first time he saw her she had aroused something in him—something unexpected. Now it happened again. It wasn't only her beauty, a simple trick of biological composition—hair, skin, bones. It was something in her chemistry, mingling with his, that shattered his defenses.

The huge theater was dark and the audience of almost 3,000 waited courteously, critically, curiously. The brief overture began and then the screen shone with a strange luminescence as the title uncoiled into the words *The Feathered Serpent* . . . hand-written in Franco Marconi's almost schoolboy scrawl.

Christie stared at it numbly, panic-stricken. Was that the same "T" as in Ted Lord? The same signature as on the forged check? Franco's? She never thought of herself as a coward. Now suddenly, she was afraid.

Everyone and everything about the Plaza ballroom gleamed and sparkled and applauded. The vast hall seemed to be electrically charged. Three hundred people were delighted to be there on this night of nights . . . the premiere party of the new smash . . . the hot ticket . . . *The Feathered Serpent*. A buffet table covered with silver chafing dishes and all kinds of food had been set up for photographers at the far end of the room. All photographers had to have press passes. Some had official ones . . . some were faked. Even so, they were more than *paparazzi*—they were honored intruders.

The tables for the more prominent guests were arranged in two rows around the dance floor . . . thirty tables, ten people per table. The place cards were engraved—ordered by the publicity department—with *The Feathered Serpent* on top and, in delicate calligraphy, the name of the guest below. Nobody paid attention to the place cards. Everyone table-hopped. They took their first course seated at the designated table. Then they roamed, to gossip with friends and possible friends . . . to dance . . . to sit at another table for another course, and chat with another friend or enemy. Everybody was having a splendid time.

Without admitting her purpose, Christie had changed tables three times looking for Simon Macleod. Guy had started the dinner on her right. He'd suggested that when this party wound down he'd take her to a better party. She had hemmed and hawed until saved by Jenny Lattimore who—in a cloud of feathers—swarmed over Guy, freeing Christie to move on unnoticed. Where the hell was Simon?

Jo Caro was working the room. From power broker to major agent to male star to female comer, she was staying in touch. She carried on an animated conversation with Sol Stein, while her peripheral vision concentrated on Matt Renault. He was dancing with Chita, body to body—bastard! Why did Jenny allow . . . ah, there was Jenny, adjusting Guy Macleod's bow tie. Why did his tie need adjusting? What the hell had they been doing, fucking in the men's room? Probably the Fire Exit. Her smile grew more intense, and Sol licked his lips.

"Not tonight, Solly," she said with fake regret. "I'm booked. These days you have to call for reservations."

She watched Matt and Chita head for a table. That boy needed a strong hand. When he belonged to her, he would carry her briefcase.

Franco and Guy stood at the bar, each sipping Chivas Regal, talking and eyeing one another warily, as though they were a pair of pool hustlers . . . which they were.

"You mentioned at the table you were interested in filming *Deirdre*." Guy was making conversation . . . one might think.

"Toying with the idea. A beautiful play—to read it's pretentious . . . all that lyric Irish poetry. But last month I was in New York on business and caught a matinee. Onstage it's a masterpiece. Children seeking and finding life's ultimate meaning: to live in the moment, because there is nothing else, only old age and death. Got rave reviews."

"Theater crtics. The decadent *intelligentsia*."

"No, they smell it. The play is a masterpiece."

"Maybe. But it won't work as a film. It hasn't got—

NAKED CALL

what do you call it—mass appeal," Guy said resolutely.

"You're wrong. It's a natural. But I can understand your reservations. I had them, too."

"It's not makeable."

"Why?"

"First, it's written in poetry."

"*Romeo and Juliet* is poetry. Zeffirelli made it work on the screen."

"That's a legendary love story. *Deirdre* isn't."

"It will be. I'll make it into a tits and ass classic."

"That's my point. The nudity, the sex scenes, it won't work without them. That means an NC-17 rating." Guy had received in-depth schooling by his entertainment analyst. "It's too big a commercial gamble."

"Wrong! I'll give it a purifying influence. I have a vision of something beyond the body, beyond mere sexuality."

Guy chuckled. "You mean a family movie in the raw? Like taking baths together."

"Families see it now. It's playing to sold-out houses."

"Onstage, with the nudity and sex hidden in the wings. Anyway, let's say *Deirdre* sells out for a year in New York ... a very successful run. About 350,000 people will see it. If it's to have a successful run as a film, that's something else entirely. Millions of people have to see it ... including the Mormons."

"I'll handle the Mormon factor. The camera and I have a rare relationship. I'll transcend the optical illusion of nudity and reveal the realities of the soul."

"Have you spoken to Irene Bentley about film rights?"

"I called once ... missed her ... dropped it. I want the financing guaranteed before I waste time talking."

"Have you spoken to Christie about your vision?" Franco shook his head. "Then why talk to me? Christie is head of United."

"I'd like to be able to say you like the idea."

"I make no creative decisions."

"Guy, it's a winner—I only make winners. And you'll win both ways—with United and personally. You're one of the backers of the stage production of *Deirdre*."

"How do you know that?" Guy was surprised.

"Maureen Corley told me. See her—over there." He

nodded toward a young stunner across the room—long black hair, sinuous body, vivid face. "She played Juanita's kid sister in *The Feathered Serpent*. We became . . . let's say, friends. She told me Bentley had her slotted for Deirdre if it's made into a film."

Guy silently congratulated Irene on how astutely she'd set her trap . . . for him . . . for Franco. "Interesting. I promise nothing, but if you would like to meet Irene Bentley, she's throwing a party later tonight."

This time Franco was surprised. "Yes, I would. Can I bring friends?"

"If they're talented, young, and attractive, they'll be welcome."

Franco grinned. "They'll be welcome."

Christie was doing two things at once. Her eyes were searching for Simon—where had he gone after the movie? Simultaneously, she was keeping a record of the pulse of the party and waiting for the news. At any moment, the runners hired by publicity would be returning from the *New York Times* building on West 43rd Street with the early edition of the paper . . . and the review. That review counted.

Suddenly Zara was at her side, whooping with glee. "See . . . see . . . the *Times* critic found it a 'splendid, if sometimes clumsy, shocking movie.' Et cetera. 'It gives us a glimpse of a primitive culture teetering on the brink of civilization.' Et cetera. 'Makes us wonder about the thin veneer that glosses over our own animal nature . . . a sometimes pretentious but always astonishing piece of work. . . . If *The Feathered Serpent* is perhaps overambitious, didn't Browning say: "Ah, but a man's reach should exceed his grasp, Or what's a heaven for?" ' Wow! Christie! See that in headlines! Life can be beautiful!"

Christie looked around the room. It seemed different . . . lighter. She scanned the review.

"It is a good review," a deep voice murmured

Christie gave a start, then stood transfixed, staring up at him.

"Actually, it's quotable," he said.

He was smiling, and all her feeling for him flooded over her.

"Yes, it is."

"I thought you would wait for it."

She tried to look at the review, but she couldn't look away. "You left . . . ?"

"I went home," he said.

"You don't like parties?"

"Not this kind. I came back to find you. Now you can leave."

She gave him a luminous glance that made him draw a long breath. "Yes. I can leave. Zara, will you . . . ?" But Zara had discreetly vanished with extra copies of the *Times* review. Christie shrugged. "It doesn't matter."

Without any more words, they moved toward the exit. Guy caught them at the door. "Christie, Simon, are you two running away? Christie, I have a party for you—"

"No, you don't," Simon said.

"I don't?" Guy laughed. It had almost the sound of human laughter.

Watching the Macleod brothers together, Christie felt that the kinship between them was deeper than brotherhood. It had something to do with a sameness of nature. Both were strong . . . both determined . . . both iron-willed. They were the Macleod brothers, born and bred of the same stock. But there was something in Guy that Simon had escaped . . . a ruthlessness that she had seen in Guy at their first meeting.

"I'll see you Monday," Simon said.

"Buy United at the opening . . ."

Christie made a tiny instinctive move with her hand and head, too small to be noticed. She stopped herself. She couldn't warn Simon not to buy United, not without explaining why . . . that hundreds of thousands had been stolen from the studio . . . that if the theft became public, the price of United Stock would plunge.

"We have enough."

"Simon . . ." Guy caught himself. "I would appreciate it if . . ."

The ruthlessness had flashed . . . then softened. Christie

wondered what savage ancestor had put it there. All that was clear for now was his love for Simon. Simon—and Simon alone—was spared.

"I'll buy United," Simon said.

"Thanks. And welcome back to the human race." Guy bowed to Christie and ambled off. A short distance away Jenny Lattimore waited, smiling so gently and beatifically she could have been nominated for sainthood.

"Let's leave by the entrance on Central Park South," Christie suggested. "The chauffeurs are out front smoking and making bets."

Simon chuckled. "You're a natural James Bond."

Like truant children, they slipped out the side door of the Plaza, Simon taking her hand as they crossed the street to Central Park.

"We could ride through the park in a hansom cab like tourists," Christie laughed, acutely aware that Simon still held her hand.

"You are a tourist."

"Not exactly. I was born in New York . . . lived here most of my life."

Silence settled gently between them. Then Simon asked softly, "Before we take a cab ride I have to know a few things." He smiled, lifting her hand toward his face, glancing at her ring finger. "You're not married?"

"Divorced. One son." She moved their locked hands slowly—as if they were a heavy weight—toward her lips. "You?"

"Divorced. No children."

"Let's pick a cab."

Seated in the hansom cab, listening to the clop-clop of the horse's hooves as it moved at a leisurely pace through the shadows of Central Park, they both struggled to keep to the simple, conversational staples.

"You didn't go to high school in Fullerton and grow up yearning to be a studio president?"

"No. I went to Riverdale Country Day School. I grew up yearning for A's so I could get into Radcliffe."

"Did you?"

"No. Too expensive . . . my father died. I went to NYU

... half paid and half worked my way through ... studied theater."

"To become the president of a motion picture studio?"

"No. I loved going to movies. I never intended to make them."

"So?"

"So, things happen."

"Yes." His voice was hoarse as he leaned toward her. In a quiet, unpremeditated way his arms went around her, their lips met passionately, their bodies clinging together.

When she broke from his arms, Christie gasped with surprise at the strength of her desire ... it vibrated with a violence that made her giddy. Embarrassed, she fumbled for words. "What am I supposed to say now? We hardly know each other."

"Time will take care of that. Look, I have a house in East Hampton—"

"No."

"This weekend I'm giving a small dinner party for friends. No Wall Streeters, no Hollywood types. Just the locals ... the Ford dealer, the high school principal, a real estate agent, a president of a very small bank, an undiscovered mystery story team—married to each other—two minor painters. Why don't you spend the weekend at my house?"

"No."

Simon laughed at the look on her face. "You don't get it. You've had too much Hollywood drilled into you. At Sea Dune—my place—you'll have your own room. Plus a key to the lock ... that works. Spend the weekend with me so we can become friends."

"I fly back tomorrow."

"Tomorrow is Saturday—the studio will survive without you."

"I don't have the right clothes."

"Drive out with me tonight. Now. You can pick up a pair of jeans and a couple of shirts tomorrow at a local store."

"My bags are at the Carlyle. I have to change."

"Okay. Change."

Two solemn green eyes searched his. Of the things they

possessed in common, the most decisive was their almost uncanny pull on each other's heart. It made up her mind for her. "All right. I'll change."

While Simon waited in the lobby of the Carlyle, Christie sat on the edge of the bed and reread the message that had been waiting for her, from Harry Weiss. Her fingers trembled as she held it. He wanted her to call as soon as she returned from the premiere. He'd left his private home number. The questions accumulated. Should she change, pack, and then call Harry? Or not call at all—pretend she missed the message? Or call Harry first? She must choose between Harry and Simon. She picked up the telephone and dialed Harry.

The conversation was rapid and jumpy.

". . . now Sidney says he wants to talk to you as soon as possible."

"Sidney does or Julian does?"

"Julian does. Sidney will be along."

"What does Julian Hennesy want? Did he get another 1099?"

"No. He says he knows who did it."

"You mean who forged his name?"

Christie waited, sitting completely still, like a sentry at a post who has no choice but to listen. Finally she repeated, "Does Julian say he knows who forged his name?"

"Yes. What's weird is he even guessed that there were more checks forged."

Christie inhaled deeply. She knew how desperately worried Harry was . . . as worried as she was. He would snatch at straws for an answer. "You believe Julian knows what he's talking about? Why?"

Harry half-choked. "Because Julian gave me and Sidney a list of the people whose names were forged. Just missed one."

"Who did he miss?"

"Addie Grossman."

"The Grossmans weren't on location for very long. Franco sent them home. The others were."

"Maybe that's a clue. I don't know. I'm no detective. But only you, me, Edgardo, and Alicia know those seven names. If Julian knows six, he must know something."

Christie let out her breath. "Did Julian say it's Franco?"

"No. Julian won't even tell Sidney. He won't name names until he talks to you. You gotta get back here immediately. It's too late for the red eye. Get the early plane tomorrow."

She felt pity for the pinch he was in—she was in—they all were in. "I'll be on the plane," she said leadenly.

Slowly she put down the phone. If Franco was the forger, she could think of a dozen ways he could have pulled it off. Kickbacks . . . endless delays . . . faked production costs . . . the list went on and on. There could be a couple of million dollars stashed somewhere. If—so damn many ifs. If Julian could prove it was Franco, a full investigation would be required. That meant publicity . . . rotten publicity. The studio would be involved in the embarrassing public spectacle of having to accuse the Academy Award Winner, Franco Marconi, of forgery. The silence hummed around her tired ears like a hive of bees. She had stepped out of the radiance of the evening into a maelstrom. There were forged checks in Harry's file in Burbank. There was Julian with a possible answer that meant the police and criminal proceedings. She was afraid she was falling in love with Simon.

When the elevator came to a stop, Christie stood for an instant, looking at the closed door, unwilling to walk to the lobby where Simon was waiting. The world was a dangerous place. The doors opened and she stepped out of the elevator.

"Hello." She smiled at him.

"Hello?" he answered, taking in that she didn't have a suitcase and hadn't changed.

"Something's come up," she said.

"It's important," he said.

"Yes. Very," she said.

"I'm sorry," he said.

"I'm sorry, too," she said.

The words of all partings.

"I have to fly back to L.A. early tomorrow morning."

"Why?"

"Tommy." The rules had changed. Christie, who hated

lies, had invented a fiction. "He fell off a horse—"

"Jesus!"

"They say he'll be all right. Sprained ankle and a deep concussion. I should be there."

"You should." He caught all the nuances of her body, a composite of scents so strong and penetrating—the scent of her hair, the drops of acid-sweet perspiration on her neck... under her breasts, all mingled with the scent of her sex. There'd be no opportunity to prove his noble intentions.

"We'll stay in touch," he said.

"Yes. We'll stay in touch," she said.

Christie felt the sting of tears. The sweet time was over.

A few hours earlier that evening, Addie and Art Grossman had had an early dinner at Guido's, their favorite non-Hollywood-type Italian restaurant. Addie had linguini and clam sauce. Art had lasagne. Both were pleasantly stuffed. Afterward they had driven to Westwood, parked the car, and drifted along the streets, gaping into boutique windows, cafes, book stores. Their tour ended at nine o'clock when they arrived at The Crown movie house, an independently owned Westwood theater that prided itself on showing only foreign movies in their original language ... without subtitles. Tonight the film was *Cycle of Life*, a French film that had received a Golden Globe award years ago at the Cannes Film Festival. Addie and Art had missed it the first time around, and they wanted to catch it before it vanished forever into the warehouse vault... the burial ground of non-commercial films. Although the stories and technique of foreign films often irritated them, they occasionally found ideas and tricks worth adapting. While they waited on line for the next show—the house catered to UCLA graduate students and other Los Angeles intellectuals—Addie ate chocolate raisins and Art ate chocolate creams.

"Listen, you sexy old broad, you keep stuffing your mouth and your belly will be bigger than your boobs," a voice whispered in Addie's ear.

Addie swung quickly, ready to let fly a knee to the groin. The whisperer chortled, and Addie stopped midair, stepped back, and shook her head.

"Julian! You could get yourself castrated pulling a stunt like that . . . and you'd make a lousy soprano." She laughed with relief. "Why are you here? How come you're not slurping champagne in Manhattan?"

"I'm too broken down an old swinger to loop back and forth across the country for one night. I've seen the *Serpent* three thousand times . . . in dailies, in the rushes, unedited, edited, reedited, re-reedited, finished. I don't care if I never see it again."

"He means it," Cindy complained. "I wanted to go. I've never been to a premiere."

"Baby, you got years of premieres ahead of you," Julian said.

"You have to be invited."

"You'll be invited. You got the right vibes. I'm only the beginning. You'll be movin' on. Me? 'I grow old, I grow old. I shall wear the bottoms of my trousers rolled . . . '"

"You read poetry." Addie grinned.

"My secret vice. What I need is peace, work, est, and time to read poetry."

"And no 1099s." Art chuckled.

Julian was all attention. "What 1099?"

"Don't play dumb with us, Julian. We're on your team. Addie got a 1099, too . . . for a tummy tuck she never had . . . never put in for . . . and a check to cover the cost that she never received," Art said.

Julian thought about this. "How do you know about me?"

"This town's a switchboard. Everyone's wired into everyone else. Harvey Hartman told us," Art said.

Addie was only half-listening as she stared around like a tourist. With her inveterate watchfulness, she was always on the lookout for story ideas, plot themes, devices, anything to jog her thinking. Now she watched a white Chrysler Imperial moving slowly toward them. There were two Hispanic types in the front seat, one driving and smiling, the other eating a taco. Somehow they looked wrong.

"You use Harvey Hartman? He's with Frank & Farber. Are they your accountants, too?" Julian asked.

"Yes. At least Harvey is. We've know him since Brooklyn College in New York," Addie said abstractedly.

"He moonlights for us." She couldn't take her eyes off the white Chrysler. It was too conspicuous. If she was writing a murder mystery, that would not be the kind of car she'd use . . . what made her think of murder? Anyway, it was too easily remembered . . . not like a black Ford—a quiet, ordinary menace. And yet, because it was so conspicuous, it made her anxious. It was like a setup, if she was writing a setup. Suppose somebody wanted the car to be conspicuous?

"We've used Harvey forever. When Addie got her 1099, Harvey told us about yours," Art explained.

As the car pulled parallel to the movie line, the man tossed the remains of the taco out the window. Even before she saw the Beretta, Addie dropped to the sidewalk, yanking Art after her. As they fell, she heard the shots. One. Two. Three. Four. The car's tires squealed as it hurtled away from the scene.

Panic broke loose on the line. Women screamed. Two men ran after the car. Art lay on the sidewalk, a dazed look on his face. He stared at Addie, who was sitting beside him.

"Are you all right?" a student asked.

"We're all right," Art said, sitting up and shaking his head.

"Thank God those maniacs were terrible shots, or we'd all be dead. Like them," an old woman quavered.

Addie said nothing as she got to her feet and dusted off her pants.

"We've got to do something about these drive-by shootings!" the young man exclaimed hysterically.

"Call the police," a girl sobbed with fright.

Art stood up. "You saved my life," he said reverently to his wife.

Addie mouth was grim, her voice a whisper. "No. I didn't. Look!"

Art followed the direction of Addie's eyes. A few feet behind Addie, two bodies were sprawled on the sidewalk . . . Julian Hennesy and Cindy. Blood from neat black holes in their foreheads trickled down their faces.

"Oh my God! Julian!"

"I saw the guy shoot as we fell. He didn't want us. He

wanted Julian. He aimed at Julian. Julian is dead. I think Cindy just happened."

"Do we tell the police?" Art asked softly.

"You want to die, too?"

The half-eaten taco lay in the gutter.

PART SEVEN

1992
MAY

Chapter 17

ON PAGE five in the "Calendar" section of the *Los Angeles Times* an article titled THE MULTI-MILLION DOLLAR GAMBLE appeared. It read as follows:

> Contrary to the conventional wisdom which advises early summer or Christmas release for potential blockbuster films, Christie Larsen, executive producer and now president of United Cinema, took a calculated risk and released her Oscar-award-winning film, *The Feathered Serpent*, late in the spring. It opened on 2,435 screens across the country. Winning her dangerous gamble, *The Feathered Serpent* soared through its first record-breaking weekend box office to gross $40,200,000. Top management at the studio predicts megabusiness for this monster hit. Marketing insiders expect *The Feathered Serpent* to pass the two hundred million mark by the end of the Fourth of July weekend...

In the middle of page seventeen of the first section of the *Los Angeles Times* a short, one-column article appeared.

DRIVE-BY VICTIM WAS OSCAR WINNER
Julian Hennesy, the makeup man, winner of an Oscar for his work on the award-winning *The Feathered Serpent*, whose talent with eyeshadow, face powder, rouge, and other cosmetics enhanced the glamour of Jenny Lattimore, Alan Lucca, Conchita Supervia, and countless other actors and actresses for several decades, was shot to death Friday night in a drive-by shooting in Westwood, Los Angeles, while he waited on line to see a movie...

Guy Macleod's voice resonated in the squawk box... venomous... impatient. "Christie, grant that I now have an excellent grasp of the movie business. I do understand merchandising, like *The Feathered Serpent* posters, key chains, feathered hats, feathered pajamas, shirts, pants, costumes, gimcracks, knickknacks. All sorts of rubbish. I hate it. I love it. What I don't love is the article in *Time*. They said the plastic replica of the Serpent was twenty-five feet long. I went to see it at F.A.O. Schwartz. Good Lord! It *is* twenty-five feet long! As *Time* said. Twenty-five feet of vulgarity. The price tag is twenty-one thousand dollars. What the devil is it?"

"It's a motorized Feathered Serpent," Christie said. "It flies."

"What did it cost us to have some idiot make it?"

"About one hundred ten thousand dollars."

"So we lose money to start with. What the hell are we ... a film studio or a high-tech toy company? Why did we build it? What use is it to the movie?"

"It's a promotion, Guy. That's why you saw the article in *Time*. There's an article in *Newsweek*, a spread in *People* ... in *USA Today*. It's been covered in a dozen newspapers nationally and mentioned on the Nightly News. And on and on. It's the Flying Feathered Serpent."

"It's ridiculous. No kid can afford it."

"Kids can't but the right parents can."

"What idiot parent would buy that contraption?"

Christie didn't say, your old school ties... those idiot parents... they'll buy it in assorted colors for their kids to prove the point that they can afford to spend twenty-one thousand for sheer idiocy. Instead, she was reasonable. "Think of it as a rich kid's Cracker Jack box prize. Other parents will get the cue. They'll grab the twelve-inch model at toy stores for their kids. It's only ten dollars... even if it doesn't fly."

"Creating mass appeal."

"We learned it from Wall Street."

"Christie, I'd like you to fly into New York. Tomorrow. Or the next day." He changed direction without missing a beat. "We have to talk."

"About what?"

"We'll discuss it in my office."

"Clue me. I like to be prepared."

"Movie bookkeeping practices."

Harry Weiss, weary with battle fatigue, had been languishing in the chair opposite Christie's desk, waiting for the conversation to end. Suddenly he sat bolt upright.

"Our bookkeeping practices are according to generally accepted accounting principles for the motion picture industry," she said with meticulous confidence.

"I refer to the bookkeeping practices of *The Feathered Serpent*."

"Is something wrong?"

Harry's eyes were fixed on the squawk box.

"There will be if we continue what you call generally accepted accounting principles."

"Sorry. I don't follow you."

"Theoretically, we should gross over two hundred million by the end of the Fourth of July weekend. Correct?"

"Yes."

"Substantial as that gross is, in terms of studio bookkeeping, United Cinema will still be in the red to the tune of about twenty million, even after the Fourth of July."

"It's possible."

"It's inevitable the way you do your accounting. First, there is the portion of the gross that goes to theater owners ... something like forty percent, or eighty million, my entertainment analyst tells me. Second, there is the distribution fee which—unless I've forgotten how to multiply—comes to thirty-six million. Then another twenty-five or so million for expenses like prints, advertising, and promotion, as you call it. Plus the payments to those connected with the film who participate in gross—not net—profits."

"Only Franco Marconi..."

"Fifteen percent of the gross. That's a cool thirty million."

"Alan Lucca, Jenny Lattimore, Conchita Supervia, and the others only get a piece of the net."

"Splendid! How did you convince them to act in the film for only a few million dollars salary and a piece of the net? What net? Add to the house of cards the over forty million dollar production costs Franco ran up, plus fifteen percent of the film's budget for studio overhead..."

Christie met this new twist with only the merest shift of expression. "What are you driving at, Guy?"

"I'm driving at the red ink United Cinema's books will show."

"That's not unusual at this stage," she said with relief. "We'll make a ton of money when the theatrical income that's owed comes in. And beyond the Fourth of July weekend there will still be additional domestic rentals, videotape sales, cable TV sales, a TV network sale, TV syndication. Plus foreign theatrical and video sales and..."

"Christie, I'm not getting through to you. I want to show a profit. Now."

"Now?"

"Tomorrow... or the day after at the latest... we'll discuss how we do it. Call me when you've firmed up your schedule." He broke the connection.

Harry fell forward, limp and exhausted. "Did you think what I thought?"

"I'm afraid so. My paranoia is back."

"I felt like he had a gun to my head. But he didn't say a word. Not a single, solitary word. No leaks yet. It hasn't hit the wire services. Maybe I should kneel and face Mecca. I need a prayer rug."

"Maybe you should call Sidney first. We have to get a handle on the forgeries before the media does."

"I called Sidney at the crack of dawn. I woke him up ... boy was he pissed. Net net... he knows no more than he did when I called you. Lousy luck."

"Julian's luck was worse."

"Sidney invited you to this afternoon's memorial service. Harvey Hartman put the list together. He knows everything about Julian. It's at Julian's studio over his garage. No funeral. Harvey has the will. Julian wanted to be cremated. The poor bastard."

Thinking this over did nothing for Christie's peace of mind. "Did you do the research I suggested before we knew Julian knew something?"

"Yes. It didn't help. The checks were cashed at the Beverly Hills branch of Bank of California."

"Our lead bank."

"Where else? Shows inside knowledge."

"Did the manager remember who cashed the checks?"

"Sure."

Christie gave him a helpless, hopeless look. "Naturally, no one we know."

"No one. A very attractive young man who said he was working for Franco Marconi."

Christie stared at Harry. She knew something was happening that she didn't understand, and she hoped her ignorance wouldn't prove fatal. "He was working for Franco ... in Mexico?"

"In Mitla."

"Good Lord! Whoever he is, he did know a few things about the *Serpent*."

"More than a few. He very politely told the manager what the checks were for. Chang's special lenses ... Corley's promotional expenses, which he explained—always friendly and full of sly jokes—really went to buy a skin peel. Juicy little tidbits like that."

"A meticulous forger ... conscientious ... thorough."

"All those things and more. Will you talk to Guy about this when you see him?"

The question lay between them like a buried land mine. Finally she answered, "I don't know."

"What can you say? Hey, friend ... you see, Guy, baby ... it's like this, buddy ... we just happen to have a small hornet's nest in the studio." Harry met her at eye level. "Offhand, I don't think you should say anything yet."

Christie thought, I'm damned if I do ... I'm damned if I don't. The intercom buzzed.

"Yes?" she said.

"It's Mr. Levy."

"Put him on." Christie snapped off the squawk box.

Harry could tell nothing of what was being said either from Christie's face or from her side of the conversation. Several minutes passed before she said, "Yes, I'll be there. Bye." Harry raised his eyebrows. "Louis wants to see me," she said.

"He's coming here?"

"I'm going there." She stood up.

A dark question hovered in his eyes. "I don't suppose

it's about..." He made a vague gesture. "...this *imbroglio*...this can of worms?"

"Don't suppose anything. You'll sleep better." Her smile was full of insincere bravado.

Swiftly and silently as always, Lei preceded Christie through the long corridors leading to the patio before vanishing. Christie paused in the doorway and appraised the scene. Louis, in cashmere pants and an open shirt, was stretched out in his usual lounge chair contemplating a martini. Seated in a chair facing him was Justine Duval, media gossip monger, sipping white wine and playing with her pearls. The tableau might have been staged for a slick advertisement touting the so-called laid-back California lifestyle. Pure fake, Christie thought. This wasn't laid-back. This was a dress rehearsal for mayhem. Louis' telephone call had prepared Christie for trouble, but the actual sight of Justine pounded home the scale of the trouble. In the media-saturated, celebrity-obsessed company town of Hollywood, Justine was a presence to be reckoned with. Her off-the-cuff remarks—her column was called, "Off The Cuff"—could make or break a designer, a restaurant, even an entertainment lawyer. And made prior to a box office break-out, they could, if she chose, seriously impair or enhance the chances of an actor, an actress—anyone on the make—to make it. Seated on Louis' patio, expensively dressed in her paisley printed silk shift, slender and—thanks to the finest cosmetic surgery praise in her column could buy—looking forty-five instead of sixty-five, she might have been a vapid, well-groomed socialite. She was warm, friendly, and full of gossip... and as much to be trusted as a piranha. When Christie entered, Justine gave her an ingratiating smile.

"Hello, Christie. How are you? Louis and I have been chatting," she said while cheerfully sipping her white wine.

"Hello, Justine. What can I do for you?"

"Well, dear... is it true?"

"Is what true?"

"As Louis explained to you, my sources tell me there's been... let's say... a financial irregularity at United."

NAKED CALL

"Let's say an accounting oversight. Accountants are human. They make mistakes."

Justine cast a professional eye at Christie. "Darling, don't crap a crapper. Excuse the language. I'm here because I value your friendship . . . and Louis'." She gave him a warm look. "My highly reliable informant tells me it's a bit more than a bookkeeping error. It comes under the heading of grand larceny. Or call it embezzlement."

"I repeat . . . accountants make mistakes."

"Bullshit," Louis said succinctly. "Justine wouldn't be here unless she was certain of her facts. What's going on at the store, Christie?"

Christie stared at Louis. Justine Duval peered at her conspiratorially. "Tell me, dear. I've sworn to Louis that I'll keep it under wraps. Providing, of course, that if things turn out sticky, I get the inside news first.

Christie's mind raced ahead. Which of a dozen possible answers should she offer? "There is no news worth mentioning in your column."

Justine shrugged her shoulders as she managed a pout. "Darling, don't be pigheaded. You don't want me to print the half-truth I know without telling me your side of the story."

Christie stared at Louis, mutely wishing they were alone.

"That could be more damning than the whole truth—"

"Justine, that's enough," Louis interrupted. "I want to talk to Christie alone." Movie legends were legends because they had highly developed ESP.

"I'm only doing my job, like everybody else in our business." Justine's pout grew more pronounced. "Only remember, dear, it's not my job to give you fair warning. I did that because I . . . well you do know . . . where you're concerned my generous nature overcomes my good business sense. I could have telephoned Christie first—"

"And she'd have bared her soul?"

"Better to me than to that vulture, Sammy Pepys."

"Justine, you are in a class by yourself." Louis smiled indulgently. "So why don't we reconvene our mutual admiration society tonight . . . at supper . . . here?"

Justine brightened at this. "Louis, you don't get older,

you just get better. I love to listen to lurid tales by candle-light."

"I promise you'll be the first to hear . . . if there's anything to hear."

After Justine Duval sashayed from the terrace, Christie and Louis sat in silence. "Okay! Spill it!" he said at last.

"What did she tell you?" Christie parried.

"That the studio had issued the usual quota of compensation checks to cast and crew of *The Feathered Serpent*. A number of those checks—totaling about a half million dollars—were duplicated. Signatures were forged. The money was stolen. That's what she told me."

"She got it right. That's what's happened," Christie said.

"How long have you known?"

"A little more than a month."

"Since before the Academy Awards. Why didn't you tell me?"

"Nothing to tell. The stench only recently floated downwind. We started trying to flush the rat out of the hole last Friday."

"Who's the 'we'? Besides you?"

"Harry Weiss. He stumbled on the forgeries."

Louis stared at the ocean. "I don't like the smell of it. Have you told Guy about this mess?"

Christie gave a dry laugh. "Men like Guy do not like receiving bad news. They have a tendency to confuse the messenger with the message."

"He won't. I'm on the board. So is Simon Macleod. Very big on supporting women presidents. Tell Guy . . . like yesterday."

"Before I have the answers?"

"Before he can blame you for end-running him. Very suspicious, your keeping this to yourself."

"I'll tell him when I see him later this week. He wants me to fly to New York for a meeting . . . on movie bookkeeping."

Louis gave her a peculiar look. "I thought you said nobody else knew."

"It's not about this mess. He wants to know why *The Feathered Serpent* won't show a profit after the Fourth of July weekend. He wants to show an immediate profit."

"He wants the damn stock to rise. He'll shit a brick when he hears about the forgeries." Louis gave her a sideways look. "Anything else I should know?"

Christie had weighed the pros and cons of confiding in Louis while driving to meet him. Now she led him, step by step, into a thicker darkness. "Let me tell you about Julian Hennesy...."

When she finished her account of the Julian Connection—as she'd come to think of it—her head ached.

Louis said nothing for a moment, then remarked grimly, "That drive-by shooting was no accident."

Christie's smile was tight. "My thought, too. It was premeditated murder."

"Yep. This gives off the stink of cold-blooded murder."

"And something else. High stakes poker."

"And United's the pot. Any idea who's playing?"

"Beside Franco? No."

"I'm not convinced he's involved."

"Neither am I."

"Which leaves us to deal with a no-name, walking time bomb." They stared at each other for a moment. "The explosion could trash the studio."

"It could," Christie said.

"Sometimes I forget that this isn't a sane world." There was the memory of a nightmare in Louis' eyes.

Christie rose to go. "Should I say, get a good night's sleep? Things will look better in the morning. Is that possible?"

"Sure it's possible. Anything's possible. That's what worries me," Louis muttered. "Keep in touch. And keep me informed... no matter who you think is going to take the fall."

The memorial service for Julian Hennesy took four hours.

Jo had begged Christie to take her along. She had a hunch it would be a big-name event. She longed to see and be seen... to prove she, too, was on the "A" list. Her hunch was correct. The studio above Julian Hennesy's garage was packed as tightly as a sardine can. Hollywood big names, small names, ordinary people... men and women of all sizes, shapes, colors were seated on small, hard, wooden chairs, side by side, perspiring. In the limo driving back to the studio, Christie and Jo sat quietly, lost in their own thoughts. Eventually Jo broke the silence. "His Serene Highness, Prince Guy of Macleod, telephoned and said I should get my ass into New York. Are the decks clear here? Can I book a flight for tomorrow?"

"What does Guy want to talk about?"

"About counterfeits. The fake *Serpent* items being sold. You've heard."

"Regularly. Merchandising adds to my list daily. My lists have lists."

"That's the thorn in his side. His Serene Highness expects the P.R. department to throw a press conference and explain why we are confiscating fake items. Ron—our exalted merchandising head—will fill me in. Then together we'll field questions from the press."

"I spoke to Guy this morning. Why didn't he mention it?"

"Guy doesn't believe in chain of command. But give him a small due. He told me to clear my trip with you. You are president."

"Nice of him to remember," Christie said with distaste. "Okay. We'll go together. I'm meeting with Guy Thursday afternoon."

"What's your problem?"

"Same as yours. With variations."

"Guy does lap up the merchandising profits. Did you know Jenny Lattimore's feathered dress is being sold nationally by Fashion Flings? Isn't that a gas?" Jo chortled. "And speaking of Jenny, I saw her in the first aisle at the memorial. Half the golden boys and girls of Hollywood were there. Very little deadwood. It could have been a charity gala for the Richard Burton Foundation, or the L.A. County High School for the Arts Foundation, or the Center for Abused Mothers. I saw Jane Fonda, Alan Lucca, Mel Gibson, Kevin Costner, Sally Fields, Michelle Pfeiffer—"

"Enough. Everyone was there."

"One day I'll be on the right list . . . without your help. You wouldn't think someone like Julian would know so many people."

"I would." Christie wished Jo would shut up.

"Poor bastard. What a dumb way to die."

"At least it was quick."

"Jenny Lattimore says he knew who forged the checks."

Christie almost blinked. Something strange had just happened. "What did you say?"

Jo looked at her with wide, candid eyes. "Jenny Lattimore says that Julian knew who forged the checks."

"What checks?"

"Christie, it's me, Jo ... cut it out. No more sand in my eyes. You know which checks. I only know about the Grossmans. They got a 1099 for expenses they never billed the studio and for money they never got paid. So, we—meaning our employer, United Cinema—got taken.

Christie felt a chill run through her, but she made her voice light. "Have you and Jenny become chummy?"

Jo giggled on cue. "Don't be silly. Matt told me. Jenny told him about the Grossmans."

"Where did Jenny get that cockeyed story?"

"From the horse's mouth. Sidney Frank. Frank & Farber are Jenny's accountants ... also the Grossmans ... also Julian's. Lester Farber—of Frank & Farber—is banging Jenny. He's at the end of a long line, but he occasionally does score. Between bangs, he spills the dirt. Accountants talk more than their clients."

"Thank you for telling me."

"Come off it. You knew."

"I didn't know anyone else knew," Christie said.

"It's a hairy piece of business."

"The whole thing is smoke."

"What does Guy say?"

"I haven't told him yet."

Jo stared at Christie as if Christie were out of her mind. "Are you serious?"

"Why would I lie?"

"Tell him."

"You sound like His Serene Highness."

"Then do what I say. Good news, bad news, no news, garbage ... all kinds of shit travels fast. The fax machine is everywhere. If he finds out from someone else ... Do I have to continue this scenario?"

"You convinced me," Christie said, thinking of Louis

... and Justine. "I'll tell him. The limo will pick you up tomorrow at seven. Sharp."

"Seven! Aaah!"

"We'll make American's nine o'clock flight. I'll book the eight o'clock if you'd like to leave earlier."

"Noooo," Jo drawled out the word. "Seven will do."

Chapter 18

THE ULTIMATE power in Hollywood had originally rested in the hands of aging, pot-bellied, charcoal-gray-suited vice presidents working for the money center banks in New York City and later—as more and more studios went public or were acquired by giant corporations—the slick, greedy, financial power brokers of Wall Street. Unlike Hollywood actors, actresses, directors, and producers, Wall Streeters were not household names. If anything they tended to be invisible... unless criminally charged with insider trading, parking stock, selling unregistered stock. But it was Wall Street, not Hollywood, where film deals were okayed or killed, where executives were made or their heads rolled.

Now that United Cinema was no longer a privately held kingdom ruled by Louis I... the Fount of Bonuses, Percentages Promotion, Publicity Payoffs, and random other legal and not-so-legal perks—the executives at United regularly read the *Wall Street Journal* along with the *Hollywood Reporter* and *Variety*. Christie had always read the *Journal* ... she knew who held the power. She did not look forward to her meeting with Guy Macleod.

The discussion went on interminably. It started with a general back and forth on movie bookkeeping, zeroing in at last on the point of the meeting—the accounting practices used for *The Feathered Serpent*. Could the numbers be presented more favorably, in a way that would improve the profit picture of United Cinema? Yes, Guy was aware that they would be better than merely great—wonderful, stupendous, colossal—in six months. Why wait six months . . . why not now? Now was the time to inspire *bravos*, cheers, forelock-tugging from institutional investors, fund managers, market analysts, tape watchers, maybe even the one hundred share per trade little people . . . the American public. When he said, "Simon would like that," he smiled thinly at Christie.

Christie launched into an explanation of Hollywood bookkeeping . . . how they never booked income until a check was received, deposited, and had cleared the bank. But they always booked expenses from the day an invoice was received, even though they might not actually pay out the money for six months.

"Why?" Guy asked. "What's the point?"

"Interest."

"I'm sorry, I'm not following you."

"You know film companies give away points to actors, directors, the producer . . . once in a while even a writer gets points." For the moment Christie was enjoying herself. She was also delaying facing the music.

"I'm aware of that quaint custom."

"Usually we give away points of the net profit after all expenses."

"But not always," Guy pointed out. "Marconi got a piece of the gross."

"Franco is Franco. Very few directors have as good a track record and that much muscle. Believe me, Guy, it's almost always net profits. Take that as a given . . . movie bookkeeping is keyed to manipulating net profits."

"The studio borrows the money from a bank to produce a film."

"Or from its parent corporation." The corners of Guy's mouth flirted with a small smile . . . he thought he saw what was coming.

"By charging an expense immediately—before we actually spend the money—we can charge the production with the interest on the money—"

"The money you haven't borrowed and won't until you pay the bill." Guy's laughter was loud and genuine. "That's the funniest thing I've heard in years. Your costs include interest you haven't paid on money you haven't borrowed. The higher the phony interest, the lower the net. So everyone who's supposed to get a piece of the net profits gets screwed."

"An ancient Hollywood custom... screwing each other."

"And nobody objects? No gimlet-eyed accountant says, 'Whoa Dobbin. Those interest charges aren't for real'?"

"Everyone knows the rules of the game before they ante up."

Guy tilted his chair back on its rear legs. "It's cute. It's so cute I suspect it was invented on Wall Street."

"Don't underestimate the heads of Hollywood studios."

"Believe me, I don't... I've done business with Louis Levy. But just this once, let's break the rules and play the game my way. Book *The Serpent*'s income when you bill it out and the expenses when you pay them."

"The shock will drive accountants to drink. And we'll show a hell of a profit."

"That's the idea."

"You're the boss. I'll work out the details with Harry Weiss." Christie laughed. "Poor Harry. He may have to take a refresher course in basic accounting." She studied her fingernails. She wished she could continue to postpone bringing up the subject. But the wheels were oiled and running... the time had come. "If we're finished boosting United's profits, there's something I have to talk to you about."

Guy was feeling comfortable in the Byzantine-like labyrinth called Hollywood. "Go ahead," he said expansively.

Cautiously, Christie raised the Julian Connection, outlining in detail every aspect of the forgery muddle. She gave it to Guy straight, as it really was... no evasions, no breezy playing down of the danger. Then she waited, surprised at how calmly Guy took it. Was his calm the calm before the storm? Or were his critical faculties on hold? Maybe he didn't understand the implications of her story?

At last Guy asked, "Are you telling me that someone

embezzled half a million dollars from United Cinema during the shooting of *The Feathered Serpent*?"

"Yes."

He gave her a quizzical look. "How could you let that happen?"

"I didn't let it happen. It happened. We issue thousands of checks a month—"

"And you think Marconi may be at the bottom of this?"

"I don't think anything. There's a suspicion, but no proof ... as yet."

Guy fixed his eyes on her. "Then we keep it quiet. Until we can prove who's doing the number on us."

Days earlier, Christie would have agreed. Not now. "Too many people know," she said. "Justine Duval. Lester Farber. Sidney Frank. Jenny Lattimore. Matt Renault. Jo Caro ... Jo is safe. But not the anonymous leak who informed Justine ... who might inform Sammy Pepys or Nellie Gale." She swallowed. "The *Enquirer* ... the *Star* ... all the checkout tabloids will have a field day." Her head ached. They must make a public statement, up front. "It's too late to keep it under wraps. Too many people know."

"Which means that you have your work cut out for you. You're the president of the studio. I depend on you to handle situations like this ... to make it clear it would be better for all concerned—including that group of gossips you just mentioned—if they forgot this irresponsible slander."

His tone told her how stubborn he could be. "I have influence with some of the people. I have none with the leak."

"Justine Duval has. Louis must persuade her to persuade her source to keep quiet."

"It's too risky to depend on Justine."

"If money is necessary ..."

His words gave Christie a queasy feeling. They struck her as an excercise in make-believe. Guy was too smart to pay blackmail. What was he trying to do? "The situation is volatile," she insisted. "I think it's time ..."

"I don't."

They stared at each other. Guy broke the impasse. "As you know, Jo Caro is in town preparing a lawsuit against manufacturers who counterfeit—I believe they're called knockoffs—who knock off *Feathered Serpent* merchandise. We're wasting time. What we do or don't do isn't really a business decision. It's a legal decision. I want Jo's opinion." He reached for the intercom and instructed Constance Neill to find Jo Caro and have her report to his office immediately.

Christie sat back, saying nothing. Guy riffled through papers on his desk. Their wait was short. There was a sharp rap on the door and Jo entered briskly, seating herself next to Christie.

"You wanted to see me." Her eyes focused on Guy, expectant and questioning.

Guy took his time saying, "Christie and I are having . . . let's call it a difference of opinion. It relates to embezzlement. Christie tells me you're familiar with the unsavory events connected with *The Feathered Serpent*."

Jo nodded.

"A question's come up. It's my feeling that we keep this unpleasant business to ourselves until we know beyond a doubt who is the responsible party."

"The hand that holds the smoking gun," Jo said, grinning.

"A popular way of expressing it." Guy's smile was soft, his eyes hard. "Christie feels we should make the story public immediately."

Jo's eyes shifted back and forth between Christie and Guy. Christie watched her mental acrobatics to avoid getting caught in corporate cross fire. If the matter wasn't so serious, she might have laughed.

"What is your opinion, Jo?" Guy asked.

Jo's face was somber. "I'd like to be more help, but I can't. This isn't my decision . . . or yours." She almost sighed with relief as she put down the burden. "It's one that must be made by the board of directors."

Guy's voice was flat. "Is that really necessary?"

"Yes. This is a corporate matter. Whatever you do needs board approval."

Christie had to admire how Jo got herself off the hook. She wasn't taking sides. The board would do that.

Guy shrugged. "So be it. I'll call a board meeting for tomorrow morning at nine. Thank you, ladies. See you

NAKED CALL

tomorrow at nine." Without waiting for Christie or Jo to leave, he directed Constance Neill to, "Telephone board members . . ." Guy turned to Christie. His smile lacked humor. "Simon has heard that we were meeting. He asked me to tell you to drop by his office on the third floor when the meeting is over."

Feeling strangely helpless, Christie said the usual. "Thank you for the message."

"You're doing wonders for my brother, Madam President. Keep up the good work." Guy's charm was as thick as sludge.

"I'll do my best," Christie said, moving quickly toward the door. Jo followed.

Once in the reception room, Jo gave Christie a sly smile. "I see you hooked the one that got away from me."

"You were interested?"

"I'm always interested in a gorgeous hunk of male who's also rich."

"You're faithful to Matt in your fashion."

"Don't be silly. I'm never faithful . . . I'm responsible to no one. Only to my own conscience. And I have no conscience. In New York I have another stable." Jo preened a little. "But nothing like Simon Macleod. Good for you."

"The luck of the draw."

"Here's to luck. See you tomorrow at the board meeting." Jo waved and disappeared down the corridor.

The receptionist gave Christie directions for reaching the trading floor. Descending the circular stairway, her nerve endings sang with anxiety and elation. Simon was waiting.

The stock and bond trading activity of the investment banking firm of Macleod Brothers was on the third floor of the building. Here Simon Macleod ruled. The elevator opened directly onto a vast room, approximately 10,000 square feet. The place was a maze of cables and wires that ran beneath the carpeted floor . . . the veins and arteries that provided the power that kept alive the ringing telephones and computer terminals hanging from the ceilings and sitting on the dozens of desks.

Christie stood quietly as the oak-paneled elevator doors closed behind her. For a second she felt the frenzied images and sensations of the feverish men in the room pouring over her.

A man in horn rimmed glasses shouted. "Frank! It's a pure play. You could make six mill..."

"Why the fuck a naked call?" That was Fast Eddy.

"Hell! What goes down must go up. I hope."

"Misha, baby... it takes time. This is an LBO—nine hundred million on the hoof. Stay loose. Sit still. You got to do something? Play with yourself. Jerk off. Yeah... masturbate...," smiled a rosy cherub with a Friar Tuck belly.

"You made ten million playing T-Bill futures. Suddenly you worry about gentlemen's 32nds?" moaned a sharpshooter.

"This junk bond isn't junk! There's junk and there's real junk!" screamed a bald youngster of thirty. He put his hand over the phone, "You dumb fuckin' bastard!" Then he took his hand off and said sweetly, "Ishmir, dear, I do not have Michael on the other line... or Ivan Boesky. These bonds have nothing to do with Drexel... Drexel's history..."

There were no partitions—not even glass—between desks. No one would have guessed that the men in the room took home salaries and bonuses in the high six figures. Some took home seven figures. Compared to this bedlam, the organized chaos on a shooting set had a church-like calm. Here there were no breaks, no breathers, the action was nonstop.

"Looking for Simon?" asked a quick, crisp voice. Christie turned to see a shortish man with unblinking eyes trying to be genial.

"Yes."

"You're Christie Larsen. We saw you on television the night of the Academy Awards. Simon and my family... we ate pizza and watched."

"Oh?"

"I'm Ira Benjamin. Let's go. Simon's waiting in the Fish Bowl."

"Fish Bowl?"

"His office. Straight ahead."

Single-file, they moved down the narrow aisle toward what looked like a round glass cubicle in the center of the room. It had been hidden from Christie's view by the men milling around it, waving their hands, talking, shouting. Suddenly she recognized Simon in the cubicle hugging one of the men, slapping his back, and kissing him on both cheeks.

"Simon's our troop leader. When he's pissed, he curses. His obscenity file could flatten a Marine drill sergeant. Now he's giving out merit badges. I think Reilly just made five big ones for the firm. Simon appreciates that."

Christie swallowed. Nothing was less calming, less conducive to reason, than this atmosphere of money, money, and still more money. In the Macleod trading room, multi-zero numbers were tossed around like confetti. Millions changed hands in the time it took to blow one's nose. If Macleod did a fraction of the three to four billion dollars traded daily on the New York Stock Exchange, Macleod handled—she did a fast mental calculation—more money in a week, not including futures, options, bonds, treasuries, and the American Stock Exchange and the over-the-counter markets, than United did in a year. And United Cinema was no small potatoes studio. It did cut one down to size.

"Don't trip, Miss Larsen," Ira said, leading her up the steps to the Fish Bowl. "Simon, look what I found," Ira crowed, interrupting the hosannas. He bowed to Christie. "Welcome to Disneyland on Wall Street." Then he left, pulling Reilly with him and closing the door.

The Fish Bowl was filled with a throbbing silence. Simon stared at Christie. The shock of seeing her hit him in the stomach and he was unable to speak. He'd been afraid she wasn't real . . . he'd invented her out of his need. Now he saw she was real . . . exactly as he remembered. Recovering his equilibrium, he stepped forward quickly. His smile welcomed her. "Hello."

Christie felt a sudden warmth behind her eyes and in her throat. "Hello yourself. How are you?"

"Fine. Your son's recovered?"

Christie fumbled, then she remembered her lie. "Good as new."

"Good. I'm glad Guy asked to see you. How'd it go?"

"It's still going." How much should she say . . . or not say?

"Guy said it was minor . . . a bookkeeping problem?"

"That's where it started." Should she give him a straight answer or let him find out at the board meeting?

"You mean that's not where it ended?"

"That's not." Carefully, she looked at Simon.

"Hmmm. You can tell me about it at dinner tonight."

The telephone on Simon's desk gave a soft ping. Simon picked it up and began talking without waiting to hear who called. "You've been needling me hourly. Enough! If we buy any more stock there'll be none left for the public. The float will be so small the Exchange will delist it. You like that? Right. It's impossible. Bye, Big Brother." He looked at Christie. "Since you came into the picture—sorry, no pun intended—I'm glad we made the United deal. But there is a limit to how much United stock we should own."

"Guy wants you to buy more United stock?"

"More, more, and still more. Does he know something I don't know?" Perplexity flashed across Simon's face. "Is there a new blockbuster coming, a guaranteed winner that will gross hundreds of millions? Is that the real reason you're here?"

"There's no such thing as a guaranteed winner." She was going cautiously. "We are just trying to make some reasonable pictures that don't trade on old formulas or recycled schmaltz. Hopefully they'll be good and make a decent profit. But United proposes and God—the public—disposes. No. That's not why I'm here."

Simon gave her a shrewd look. "I'm a patient man. You can tell me." He waited.

"At dinner?" She gave him a smile that made his heart miss a beat.

"At dinner. Do you have any food preferences? Say black bean cakes with jalapeño relish and seared tuna? Or cornmeal-coated catfish topped with white caviar. Or . . ."

"Enough. Please, no . . . no guru *nouvelle cuisine* tonight. Just good cooking."

"Any restaurant preferences? Le Bernardin . . . The Four Seasons . . . Lutece?

"Pick one, they're all perfect. Oh!" A thought streaked through Christie's mind. "There is a restaurant I loved when I was a student. In the West Village . . . if it's still there.

Students, teachers, working stiffs from the neighborhood went for lunch. And one night a week—Thursdays—they served dinner. I went for dinner. It was so good, and so cheap, I could afford it. I had seconds... thirds for the same price. I think the name was..."

"The Kitchen." Simon smiled with genuine pleasure. "With kitchen windows that are stained glass."

"That's it! The Kitchen! It's still around?"

"It is. I'm a Thursday evening *aficionado*."

"You, too?"

"Me, too." He gave her a long look. Whatever she might worry about with regard to their future, his long looks were one thing she would never get enough of. "Let's go there."

"I'll pick you up at seven."

"It's so small. Can we get in? Once I made a reservation for every Thursday for three months."

"We'll get in." Simon's confidence was contagious.

When Christie left Simon's office she decided the black silk georgette dress she'd packed in hopes of this dinner was wrong. She needed something more casual, yet luscious. She found it at the Giorgio Armani Boutique on Madison. Beige silk and velvet pants and a beige bomber jacket made of thin suede and silk threaded with gold. I have no blouse she thought. Then she noticed an olive silk T-shirt. The ensemble cost a few thousand. Oh well. It was for Simon.

To get to The Kitchen, Simon and Christie left their cab at Washington Square and walked the rest of the way, taking the route Christie took in her student days at NYU. Walking slowly, she stared around with the eyes of a tourist. The Greenwich Village of today was not the Village she remembered. It was a Village reshaped by itself and by the way she now saw it... by the things that had happened to her since she left for California. Once she'd been a very young woman, both more hurt and more hopeful, full of faith and confidence in her dream. What she found was knowledge cross-grained with sadness. Like everyone, Christie had made concessions to life.

Simon broke into her reverie. "Are you feeling nostalgic?"

Her smile was faintly embarrassed. "I think so."

In silence, they continued walking west, through dimly lit, uncrowded streets. They turned left on Greenwich and headed toward the Hudson River.

"I remember it was owned by the Lollini family," Christie said. "Momma and Papa did the cooking. Their children, Aldo and Maria, waited on the customers."

"It's the same," Simon said. "But Aldo is now also maitre d'."

"Still only one entree on the menu?"

Simon grinned. "Still. The best bread in the city. One menu . . . one appetizer, one entree, one dessert, coffee. You remember everything."

They stopped in front of a dark, curtained window that looked like an empty storefront. No sign identified The Kitchen. Simon knocked. The door was opened by a raffish-looking young man wearing a black bow tie, white shirt, sleeves rolled up revealing powerful arms, and a white chef's apron.

"Simon!" he grinned, giving Christie a polite ogle. "You missed the sweetbreads."

"Not my dish, Aldo. Bouillabaise is. And that's what's on tonight."

"We could have seated your table three times. Come."

He led Christie and Simon to a booth with red, vinyl leather cushions reminiscent of a diner. While Simon ordered wine, Christie glanced around the dimly lit, brick-walled restaurant. It seated forty-four people . . . no more, no less. In contrast to its diner-style furnishing, the tablecloths were white linen, the wine glasses lead crystal, and to Christie's seasoned eye the small room resonated with "in."

"Is it as you remember?"

"Yes, but I forgot one thing. The place is a must for celebrity watching." Christie leaned back, smiling. "Some nights it drew them like flies. Celebrities and the hounds. Once I saw Pavarotti . . . once Jerome Robbins."

"The other night I saw Woody Allen. Some things never change."

NAKED CALL

Aldo brought the wine. After he left, Christie smiled . . . a wry, almost sad smile. "Some things do change. Last time I saw Aldo he was a teenager."

Simon was giving the room a quick once-over lightly. Abruptly, he stopped and did a slow double take. He nodded and waved to someone across the room.

"See someone you know?"

"Two someones. Stavros Lennos and . . ."

"Stavros? Here?" Christie followed Simon's eyes. There was Lennos. He nodded, she nodded . . . he smiled, she smiled. She glanced at his companion, a man with small, unfinished features and a conceited expression. She'd cast him for the youngest, untitled son of Lord and Lady Montesque.

"You know Lennos?" Simon gave her a peculiar look.

"He made Louis an offer for United."

"That's what he told me."

It was her turn for odd looks. "He told you? You know him that well?"

"Well enough. He was in Guy's class at Choate and at Harvard. A year ago he wanted to join Macleod Brothers. He offered to pay a lot of money for a partnership in the firm." Simon's tone was as sober as his face had become. "Guy turned him down flat."

"Why?"

"Stavros doesn't have the right bloodlines for Guy, or belong to the right clubs . . . et cetera." Pause. "I've a hunch something more was operating in the case of Lennos. You see, Guy and Stavros were taking out the same girl . . . a very pretty girl named Victoria Manners. She liked Stavros, but she married Guy."

"Guy is married? I didn't know that."

"He's a widower. Victoria died." Simon's voice was flat . . . it said, no more questions about Victoria Manners Macleod.

"You don't feel the same way about Lennos as Guy does?"

"I'm not certain how I feel. He puzzles me. I know the scuttlebutt, but nothing's been proved. All I do know is that he's a brilliant trader . . . he'd be an asset to any firm. He has a wide range of interests, makes good conversation.

Like me, he's a regular here. Occasionally we eat together. I enjoy his talk. He seems decent enough." Simon's smile was rueful. "I don't know how I would have voted if Guy hadn't made the decision for me. I have a streak of unpredictable prudence. When did he try to buy United?"

"The week before Louis telephoned Guy."

Simon took this in. "You have a detective's memory."

"That week left a vivid impression. Louis had Stavros to dinner. Told him he'd never sell United . . . the studio would always be privately held by him. The only change he planned was naming me president." Christie had the feeling of moving through a narrow ravine. "Then something happened . . . Louis changed his mind—Macleod Brothers could take United public." Christie managed a half-smile. "That was not a good time for me. I had no idea who was going to be made president."

"You . . . from the beginning. Louis insisted. That was a part of the deal."

Christie blinked. "Guy objected?"

"He doesn't trust women in business."

"I thought that."

"Louis refused to sign the closing documents. He threatened to break the deal if Guy didn't agree." Simon frowned. "Louis never told you?"

"No. I wondered why Louis had it spelled out in the contract. Clause 23B. Now I know."

"I'm sorry I told you. Louis was right not to." Simon's expression was chastened. "Don't resent Guy. Louis knew he'd change his mind. Guy respects brains, and you're very bright."

Embarrassed, Christie asked, "Did you object to me?"

A less clear-sighted man would have hedged his bets. "As you know, at first I disliked the whole deal. A motion picture studio, no fixed assets, only highly mobile people. I changed my mind after you spoke at the meeting."

Christie sat very still.

Simon hesitated, then asked, "What did Stavros offer Louis?"

"One billion dollars."

"We paid eight hundred million. Why did Louis go with us and not Stavros?"

Christie's troubled expression told him that this was the question she'd hoped he wouldn't ask. "He's Louis Levy . . . he has his reasons."

Simon accepted her guardedness. He had a second thought. "Was Stavros surprised when Louis made the deal with us?"

"I think more angry than surprised. He realized he'd made a mistake. Louis, you see, thinks Stavros did something. If he did, his idea backfired."

A momentary silence settled between them. The word "blackmail" resonated in Simon's mind as though a pedal on a piano was pressing down.

Christie laughed, a low gentle laugh. "Stavros is the reason why Louis made the deal with Macleod Brothers."

"Then I have to thank him for introducing us."

For an instant a recognition took place that was both intimate and awkward. To Christie's relief, Maria appeared with a wicker basket full of garlic bread grilled in olive oil and a *pate Provencale*. By the time each ate several pieces of the garlic bread and pate and washed it down with a glass of wine, Simon's attention was again on the other side of the room. "They're leaving."

"Stavros and his friend?"

"His friend is an investment banker."

"You know him, too?"

"Yeah. What I didn't know was that he knew Stavros," Simon added in a quiet, puzzled voice. "His name is Sherwood Anderson. Sherwood is one of Guy's banking partners. Now can we talk about what brought you into town . . . besides Guy?"

Christie had been running a private debate with herself on just this topic. Simon's question made up her mind for her. She started to speak, gingerly laying out the grimy story of embezzlement. At that point, Maria appeared again and placed two gleaming ceramic bowls in front of Christie and Simon. She was followed by Aldo carrying a steaming pot of bouillabaise.

"Ah, Simon," he murmured, setting the pot on the table. "This is no ordinary fish stew. All the fish are white and firm-fleshed. We use no oily-fleshed ocean fish. The fish stock and olive oil are flavored with saffron, fennel, parsley, garlic, onions, tomato, salt, and pepper. And like a souffle it must be eaten immediately.''

Stavros continued his conversation with Sherwood on West Coast culture as the two men walked the dark streets.

"Yes, the scene is improving. The La Jolla Playhouse is doing *Macbeth*. And the San Diego Opera is mounting *Boris Godunov* in October. They say the Russian playing Boris has a typically rich Russian bass voice . . . he easily encompasses the full range of the part. I'm curious to hear him. Mona would enjoy it."

"I'm sure she would . . . damn it!" Anger leaked out of Sherwood's body. After two blocks of polite cultural chit-chat, he could no longer suppress his fury. "Stavros, did you know Simon Macleod ate at that restaurant?"

"He's frequently there on Thursday evenings."

"Then why the hell . . . ? With a million restaurants in this city, why there? He'll tell Guy he saw us together."

"I imagine he will."

"What's wrong with you? You know Guy dislikes you!"

"He despises me."

"Do you want him to despise me, too?"

"No."

"Then why did we eat there?"

"I want Guy to fear you."

Sherwood paled. His eyes went wide with alarm. "What are you up to?" When Stavros said nothing, he grew heated. "What the hell are you thinking?"

Stavros looked thoughtful. Then he answered with a good-natured smile that made Sherwood's question seem irrelevant, little more than small talk. "I was thinking that the Russian bass in *Boris*—he had an unpronounceable name—is not Chaliapin. But he may be interesting. Mona loves opera . . . not just Puccini. Why not fly out and catch *Boris*?"

The Kitchen served no liquor, only wine. This gave Simon an excuse for suggesting that the best bar for an after-dinner drink and talk was his place. Conveniently, he lived around the corner.

Christie agreed.

NAKED CALL

Simon's Hudson Street apartment was the top floor of a six-story loft building designed by the architect Louis Sullivan, Frank Lloyd Wright's mentor. The unique feature of the building was its cast iron facing, which entitled it to be designated as a "landmark building." It had been built in the late nineteenth century. Originally, it was a palace of commerce, later a rundown sweat shop, still later a desolate haven for drug addicts and other derelicts. Simon and two friends had restored it. The bachelors occupied the top three floors. Two painters and their families occupied the two lower floors, and the Greenwich Village Association for the Homeless occupied the ground floor—fifty homeless men and women ate, bathed, and slept there. Neither the painters nor the Association paid any rent for the space. The building was the first of what Simon planned to be a series of privately financed homes devoted to helping struggling artists and the homeless. New York City was damn near broke and the mayor's office was doing everything it could to try to house the homeless. Simon and his friends were rich . . . they could take up some of the slack.

"I had four thousand square feet of space to work with," Simon said as he led Christie from the small elevator into his apartment. Maybe—when he got to know Christie better—he'd share his ideas about helping the homeless with her.

Christie walked slowly around the apartment. The way people lived often told her all she needed to know about them. This was more than she'd hoped. Simon's lifestyle was discriminating rather than lavish. Her professional eye noted everything, as it would on a sound stage. The seating arrangement in the living room was comfortable and very masculine—two olive green leather sofas flanked by Le Corbusier chairs and a leather armchair by Bellini. Modern pieces and geometrically shaped lamps provided a quirky contrast to the Queen Anne dining chairs set around the mahogany dining table. The furnishings were a mix of European and Americana, antiques and today. His taste in art was eclectic, even eccentric. What could be a Jackson Pollock hung next to a lovely seventeenth-century Dutch landscape by a painter whose name she didn't recognize.

Somewhere there was a bedroom . . . maybe two. She didn't ask.

Simon tried not to stare at Christie. He felt as though somewhere a window had opened slightly and fresh air was drifting into a room that had been tightly closed for a long time. "What would you like to drink? And go on with what you were saying about Franco and the forgeries."

As Christie explained the situation at United, Simon found it difficult to concentrate on her story. If the scandal he had finally wormed out of her became public, United stock would plunge. But his mind kept wandering. She looked so beautiful lounging on his couch . . . jacket off, all long legs, full breasts, and that tumbled, tawny hair.

"There's no way we can keep this problem quiet," Christie finally concluded. "Jo Caro insists that it's up to the board to decide if we make the scandal public. Tomorrow Guy will take a vote."

"I had better show up."

"I think so." She tried to read the changing mood of his face. "And since the meeting's at nine, it's time I got back to the Carlyle. I've notes to assemble."

"Arguments for the board to convince them to vote your way?"

"They must."

Simon watched as she slipped on her jacket and rose from her curled-up position on the couch with a quick grace, not using her hands . . . not a movement wasted . . . just unflexed her long, supple body and floated up. Unexpectedly the rules of the evening were changing, and he stood up to block her way. Facing her, he caught all the nuances of her body, a composite of odors so strong and so penetrating . . . the scent of her hair, perfume mingled with the drops of acid-sweet perspiration on her neck . . . under her breasts. He couldn't let her go.

"Don't you want my vote?"

A fugitive flush crossed her face. "Yes. I hope you will . . ."

"You might try seducing me." Now he was hardly poker-faced.

Half-smiling. "I'm not campaigning."

She tried to step around him, but he reached out and

gathered her into his arms, crushing her body hard against his. He murmured into her hair, "Don't go, Madam President. Let me seduce you into voting my way."

Then he kissed her again and again, his lips taking possession of her eyes, her ears, her throat where a pulse beat. His strong fingers roamed beneath her flimsy shirt. His palm cupped her breast while his thumb expertly tantalized the nipple. His excitement was so strong and contagious that she swayed, her body twisting and melting into his. "Simon, please," she gasped. "No..."

They heard the screech of a police siren on the street below. Her mind cleared and she tried to pull away. "Let me go, Simon. Let me go..."

He choked off her protest with his lips, as though he was drinking her in.

Christie reeled with conflicting emotions. She struggled against her desire for him. His large hand explored the curves beneath her soft pants...fondled her buttocks, pressed her body harder against his, exulting that even as she protested, she clung to him.

"We'll take these things off," he muttered, his voice harsh with desire as he unzipped her pants.

"No!" She panted, writhing in his arms, weakly trying to break free. But even as she struggled, her clothes were slipping to the floor.

"Yes! We're overdessed." Minutes later, she was naked in his bare arms. His mouth roamed downward to her breasts. "Your heart is pounding," he murmured, sucking her nipples, feeling her pulsate with passion.

Christie was beside herself. "No...no...please stop..." But her hands gripped his shoulders...her nails bit into his flesh...every movement denied her words.

Simon made a hoarse sound of satisfaction as he felt her sensuality overcome her resistance. Her hips moved against his while the flat of her palm caressed the hard circle of his nipples. His shudder inspired her hand to drift downward to stroke his maleness.

I want you, she wanted to say, but she could only gasp.

She didn't have to say it. He knew. He had won their silent battle of wills. He dropped to his knees and began kissing her moist thighs. His fingers held her firmly, cupping her buttocks. Quite unaware, she arched her body to welcome him and he buried his face in her tawny pubic hair. His tongue tasted and tormented her, awakening all of her. Christie was coming back to life.

Her body had not been an instrument of passion for such a long time. Once there was Barry... then Franco... then Band-Aid sex. That's what she called it. Was Simon another Band-Aid? She tried to twist away, but old feelings were flooding back, as alive as in the past.

Simon lifted his head. "Should I stop?"

Christie was dazed with desire and conflict. "No... yes ... I don't know. No more Band-Aid sex."

"Sssh. This isn't sex... it's a campaign for votes." He stood up and covered her mouth with kisses. "In the morning we'll go to the Carlyle. You can get your notes and change. Now we'll go to bed... where we belong." With his mouth again on hers, he lifted her up in his arms.

Nothing in the whole tangle of her emotions had prepared Christie for the ardor of her response. Her face was flushed and her eyes blurred with passion. Drugged by her senses, she gave up all resistance as he carried her into his bedroom. On his wide bed she stared, dry-mouthed, at the powerful grace of his body, at his rock-hard sex. She gasped with excruciating need, her body arching upward in longing.

Kneeling, Simon straddled her. She felt the warmth of his breath and the heat of his mouth as he sucked at her nipples... sipped her navel... his lips causing contractions of desire deep within her.

"Simon... Simon... now..." Her nails scraped his shoulders, her fingers tugged at his hair, her knees were drawn back, opening herself to him. Her sexual hunger was rising like a madness, blinding her to everything but having him within her.

His eyes shone with pleasure. This was how he wanted her... mindless with desire, burning to be possessed by him.

"Take me, Simon!" she begged.

A gruff male sound came from Simon's throat. Crouched over her like some great animal, he gazed at her. Then he could hold back no longer. With a hoarse groan he thrust his rigid flesh inside her... filling her... losing himself as her hips rose and fell to meet his every thrust. Her breath came in short gasps. Her pulse raced as quickly as his. Sensations she was powerless to control surged through her body. Soon there was nothing but the throb of his penis in her and the dizzying freefall of her orgasm. Then he took her again, slowly and with such sweet violence that she came in wild, racking shudders. Clinging to him, she felt his sex grow even larger, harder. He roared as his orgasm exploded into her, flooding her. And she felt his pleasure rocketing through him even as if it were her own.

Dawn came before Christie and Simon were ready. Their night of lovemaking was over. As he had promised, a confused Simon Macleod drove an equally confused Christie Larsen to the Carlyle. The meeting of United's board of directors had brought them together. It now separated them.

Chapter 19

THE SEVEN members on the board of United Cinema included Guy and Simon Macleod, Christie Larsen, Louis Levy, Avery Longstreet, Leo Hightower, and Gordon Mugrae. Jo Caro—as house counsel to United Cinema—had been asked to sit in on the meeting and advise the board as to the legal ramifications of whatever acts they took. Constance Neill sat at a small table in a corner of the room. Her job was to take down what was said and enter the minutes of the meeting in the corporate minute book. For over an hour, board members sat silently in the Macleod Brothers Conference Room B—the small conference room—listening to Guy Macleod and Christie Larsen present their views of the problem facing them. Christie's and Guy's views were diametrically opposed. Soon the board would vote.

"... So what we have is a crime but no criminal ... not even a suspect. Nothing can be proved. If the crime becomes public, we are open to a fair amount of unpleasant speculation in the media..." Guy was summing up again.

"But Miss Larsen says that if an outsider breaks the story first, the police will think we're hiding something," Leo Hightower said nervously. Leo was a stout man dressed in a dark, double-breasted suit that did little to disguise his weight. His family's wealth was an American legend.

"As I mentioned earlier, Miss Larsen has agreed that if we vote for secrecy, she'll persuade those few who know of the value of silence to keep their mouths shut." Guy's tone was reasonable.

"But Miss Larsen feels that silence is not golden. It's dynamite. Miss Duval can't be bound and gagged. Neither can the leak. Frankly, Guy, I agree with her. I don't understand why you object to making the matter public." Avery Longstreet had the tone of a man who expected answers.

"I object to washing our dirty corporate linen in public. It's nobody's business until we discover who the actual criminal is. I want to protect us all . . . our privacy—"

Christie broke in. "I'm not convinced that you would be protecting us, Guy, by keeping this matter quiet. We need to start a thorough investigation immediately. The money involved isn't that small. Four hundred thousand dollars is grand larceny. And there could be millions buried in Swiss banks or Tosca accounts."

"And there's the murder." Avery's eyes glittered. "That makeup man."

"I don't believe it's connected," Guy stated.

"I do." Louis sounded as if he'd just awakened. "And I know damn well we can't keep the story under wraps for very long."

"I agree with Louis and Christie." Simon spoke for the first time. He smiled at Christie's look of relief. What did she think he'd do . . . even if last night had never happened? "Stuck is stuck," he concluded.

"Guy, this could be a big scandal," Leo Hightower worried.

"And you're convinced we should make this mess public, Miss Larsen?"

Christie said, "I am, Mr. Longstreet. Otherwise—"

"We'll be caught with our pants down," Louis cut in. "Think of United Cinema as Watergate West."

"You've made too many cops and robbers films. This is real life. You're dramatizing—"

"Crap! What's the matter with you, Guy?" Louis wouldn't be patronized. He was as good as any of them. If they had money and power, so did he. "You're a Wall Streeter. You know the rules. Hiding an embezzlement is not like fixing a spelling bee. I can hear Dan Rather. Financial irregularities at United Cinema . . . closed-door sessions . . . the board slugging it out . . . where are the bodies buried?"

"Exposing our problems could affect the receipts of *The Feathered Serpent*," Guy said sternly.

"Not a chance." Avery laughed. "My advisors tell me the receipts will exceed several hundred million. It's still behind *E.T.*, *Star Wars*, and *Return of the Jedi*. But it's closing in on *Jaws* and *Raiders*. And the total ticket sales on those movies included rereleases. *Serpent* could still move up, up, and still further up. News of the crime will draw bigger audiences. The little people love to hear about dishonesty, crookedness, hugger-mugger in Hollywood. It breaks the monotony of their dull lives. When it happens to someone about whom they've read, it's great fun."

"You keep track of the numbers," Louis said.

"I've seen the *Serpent* twice," Avery smiled.

"Me, six times," Louis smiled back. "The audiences love it. It's an instant family monster."

"Okay. Let's have a hand count. Mmm . . . four to three." Louis stood up and beamed at Avery, Simon, Christie. At his benevolent best, he said sympathetically, "Mr. Chairman, the board's voted. Make the damn news public."

"Louis, I don't think you understand the consequences of your decision." Guy's tone was carefully moderate. "You are acting precipitously."

"Wait a minute, everyone," Jo Caro interrupted. She'd been listening silently all through the meeting. "I've investigated the question and it's not that simple."

"Why not, Miss Caro?" Avery asked. "I was asked here to vote. I've voted. It's settled. My dear young woman, you can add nothing."

"I can add my legal opinion."

"What is it, Miss Caro?" Guy's voice was almost gentle.

"I'm not sure this matter can be settled by a board vote, one way or another. There's a body of SEC law covering the duties and responsibilities of a board of directors when dealing with internal corporate criminal activities. I'd have to study the cases to determine whether or not you must make the facts public. The bylaws of the corporation also have to be taken into consideration to determine the extent of this board's—United Cinema's board's—personal responsibility if the public is not informed."

"Your point is well taken," said Guy.

"No, it's not," said Avery. "It's pure gobbledygook."

"I agree with Guy," Leo said. So did Gordon.

"I don't," said Louis. "And neither does Christie. Nor Simon."

"As I explained, there are SEC precedents. And I'll go over the corporate bylaws carefully. Then I'll prepare a memo—"

"How long will all that take?"

"A month maybe."

"My dear Miss Caro, I'll write it for you now," Avery said.

"Will you?"

"Easily. I've read enough similar memos."

"Legalities are my responsibility," Jo said fiercely. "I run the legal department. Not you. That's what you pay me for. So listen to me! Or fire me!"

They sat in fragile silence for a moment. Then Guy spoke. "Continue, Miss Caro. We're listening."

Jo continued going, pedal pressed to the floorboard. "As I said, I must prepare a memo. It's possible that in the time it takes to research and write it, the criminal may be found. Then this discussion is meaningless." She fixed Avery with a cold stare. "Meantime, two warnings. No loose talk. Not at breakfast . . . not at dinner . . . not in bed. Second warning. Do not sell any of your United Cinema stock. Because of what you've heard here, the SEC would be real upset. They'd think you were acting on inside information . . . and they take a very dim view of trading on inside information."

"Of course, if you are interested in buying . . ." Guy

sounded as if he were picking up a conversation interrupted by a waiter.

"You can buy more stock. But no selling," Jo concluded sweetly.

"All in favor of allowing Miss Caro the time to prepare a memo on what we must do, please signify by raising your hand," Guy said.

Four hands rose. Avery Longstreet had changed his position.

"All opposed."

Three hands rose. Simon had not changed his position.

"The motion is carried. I move to adjourn the meeting until we receive Miss Caro's memo. Do I hear a second?"

"I second the motion." Gordon Mugrae had made his usual contribution.

"All in favor?"

The same four hands rose.

Guy did not call for an opposing vote. "The meeting is adjourned," he said, standing up.

Louis was still talking to Avery when Simon pulled Christie aside. "I can't change your mind?"

"No. I told you. I have a son . . . a job . . . and Franco Marconi. We meet tomorrow to discuss a new project. How can I stay?"

"Hello, Mr. Macleod. Nice to see you again." Jo joined them, giving Simon her best siren smile. Then she turned to Christie. "A round of applause, please. I bought you time to dig up the stinker who raided the cookie jar."

"You know I don't want time. I'd rather break the news now, before an outsider beats us to it."

"Oops! I thought I was doing you a favor. Let's have a chili dog lunch next week and thrash it out." She left before Christie could answer.

"Christie, come on," Louis signaled.

"You're leaving now?" Simon asked.

"Louis is giving me a ride to the coast. He borrowed a neighbor's Lear jet to fly here. I wish . . ."

"So do I. I'll call you. We'll see each other soon. If you're stuck in L.A., I'll play Mohammed to your mountain . . . maybe over the Fourth of July weekend." He made an almost imperceptible kissing movement with his lips.

Christie watched him leave the conference room with an ache in her heart, this semi-stranger, bound to her by only a few slender hours of passion.

In the Macleod limo driving to Butler Airport where the private plane was waiting, Christie's mind was a chaos of thoughts . . . like chips of colored glass in a kaleidoscope they appeared for an instant than sank out of sight. There was Simon . . . what was there to think about Simon? Their future was full of questions . . . so many questions, so few answers. Jo? Something about Jo troubled her . . . she was missing something. What? An inner voice kept prodding her . . . saying what . . . what? Guy . . .

Louis broke the silence. "I was wrong about the embezzlement. We both were."

"Wrong? How? What do you mean?"

"I've just realized we've been dead wrong. It's lucky Guy opposed us. And that silly bitch, Jo Caro, has her memo to write. They saved your skin . . . accidentally."

"My skin? You don't think I took the money?"

"Of course I don't, but Hollywood will." He explained his reasoning with cavalier casualness. "You know and I know what's true. But Hollywood isn't a world of facts. It's a world of perceptions. Some bastard out there has talent with a pen. If the news breaks before we know his—or her—name, the town will perceive you as guilty until proven guilty."

"Me? Why me? All the evidence points to Franco."

"So what? Franco is one of their own. You're an outsider. In the world of Hollywood—which includes the Hollywood Hills, Holmby Hills, Benedict and Coldwater Canyons, Bel Air, Malibu, and a few other locations in the *Thomas Guide*—Franco will seem as pure as driven snow. They'll lay odds your fingerprints are on every check."

Christie felt lightheaded. A hundred protests and objections welled up within her.

Louis sighed, "Sorry, kid. Just be grateful you've got a little breathing space."

"Then I should thank Jo. She did me a favor with her memo."

"The hell she did. I don't know what that cunt is up to,

but whatever it is, it's not for your benefit. And you don't think so either." Christie blinked. There was a detestable truth in his words. "I've the impression you don't trust our Miss Round Heels the way you once did. Why?"

His perception was too acute for comfort. Christie was at a loss. She wasn't ready with a reason. That is, not a reasonable reason. So she settled for an inferior substitute. A white lie. "Jo's busier than ever these days being corporate counsel. We see each other less. We're less close. It happens."

"I never wanted her for house counsel."

An unguarded look passed between them. "Guy wanted her."

"Sol talked him into it. Now he's outside counsel for United. On a very handsome retainer."

"But you wanted me for president." Christie gave him a warm, affectionate grin.

"Simon told you."

"He did."

"He's the first *mensch* you've picked. You're a genius at picking film properties . . . a *schmuck* at picking men."

Christie laughed. "I suppose." Their understanding left them with a certain awkwardness. To change the subject and relieve their mutual discomfort, she reminded Louis of her meeting with Franco.

"He's in a frenzy about this new project. I hope it's good."

"It is," Louis said.

"You know about it?"

"In detail."

"Tell me."

Louis glanced out the window. "You'll find out soon enough."

"Louis, you're doing nothing for my peace of mind. I don't understand . . . why all the secrecy?"

Louis understood too much to answer. Instead he produced a *non sequitur*. "The only chancy part of flying is takeoffs and landings."

On the long flight west—although Christie pressed him hard—she could not coax or cajole another word out of him on the subject of Franco's new project.

Guy caught Simon on the way down to the trading floor. "You stopped buying United. Start again."

"Now? With what we know? You want more?" Simon's tone reflected disbelief. "It's impossible."

"Why impossible? Our house counsel tells us that buying United is not insider trading. Only selling the stock is."

"And suppose someone breaks the story tomorrow?"

"The stock goes into free fall. We lose money. But I'm confident United will be cleared . . . ultimately."

"Then the stock flies again . . . on the *Serpent*'s grosses."

"And we make a killing, Simon. You do like that."

"I do. The SEC won't. They might consider the forgeries a plant, so we can play games with the stock."

"Nonsense. You're looking under rocks."

"That's where you find the slugs. Guy, you are a man of tradition. You join only the right clubs . . . The Creek Club, Piping Rock, The Union League Club. I doubt that you'll like the country club the SEC selects. Ivan Boesky was a member. He had a white beard and white hair . . . an aging hippie. There's Boyd Jeffries. They're members. Am I getting through to you?"

Guy started to laugh. "Yeah. Loud and clear. You convinced me . . . at least for today."

Chapter 20

HARRY WEISS slumped in his chair while Christie questioned her secretary on the intercom.

"Is Louis really playing golf at Three Oaks, or he just won't come to the phone?" She listened and laughed. "Okay. Lei says the dinner party is tomorrow night? Tell him I accept." Christie replaced the receiver shaking her head. "Lei insists Louis is at Three Oaks. He says Louis loves the club, especially the men's locker room. It's the only place where he can see a naked rabbi." Still laughing, she scanned the messages on her desk. Agents, writers, Franco, producers, Franco, Louis. Louis? If Louis was giving a dinner party tomorrow night, why didn't he invite her on the plane? She gazed at the nervous Harry. "Go on with the Sidney Frank story."

"I gave you the drift. Something's bugging him. He'll call back to set up a meeting." Harry swallowed. "I have this eerie feeling it's got to do with Julian and the forgeries. I don't like the vibes."

"Keep me posted." Christie stood up. "Now I have a meeting with our in-house genius, Franco Marconi."

"Genius!" Harry made a sour face. "Hollywood's definition of a genius is that he can make a box office bonanza out of a movie that isn't totally tasteless, and isn't for children of all ages from eight to eleven."

Christie started toward the door. "He's also brilliant and unpredictable. Meaning he can also bomb in a movie that isn't totally tasteless, and is for children of that special age from thirty-five to ninety."

Harry pursed his lips. "Madam President, will you mention to our genius that he is under suspicion of forgery?"

Their eyes met in an unhappy exchange. "No. It's too

301

soon. First I want you to talk to the Bank of California branch manager in Beverly Hills. See if he recalls anything odd in connection with cashing United checks. We might get lucky."

Harry stretched. "Enjoy Malibu. I hear Franco has parking spaces for eighteen stretch Cadillacs."

What did Franco have in mind, Christie wondered as she drove along Pacific Coast Highway. *Foucault's Pendulum . . . Uncle Vanya . . . Doonesbury . . .* what? She turned off the highway onto the Colony lane. The guard at the gate recognized her, smiled, and waved her through. She drove the hundred feet to the road that paralleled the beach and turned left. In a few minutes she arrived at Franco's house.

Franco Marconi had been a Malibu resident for more than twenty years. He claimed his house was originally owned by Ronald Coleman—or was it Clara Bow?—and in the thirties had cost a princely $3,500. Christie shrugged. Real estate values go up and down—in California mostly up, way up. Today, the beach bungalow—with an enlarged living room, three additional bedrooms, a pool, and Jacuzzi—was worth about five million.

Christie parked her car. The guest parking area was large by Malibu standards, but not eighteen limousine large. For an accountant, Harry had a surprising talent for exaggeration. She ambled toward the main house, looking for signs of life. She climbed the steps to the highest sun deck and peered around. Where was everybody?

"Hello, Christie darling."

She heard the voice before she saw the face. But the face was in the voice. The smile . . . the eyes . . . the hair brushed severely back but falling softly to the shoulders. The voice was rich with lovely lies . . . faithless vows. A tidal wave of memory washed over Christie. A field of wild flowers . . . a boat adrift . . . long, dancing days on sunlit water . . . a sea shell marked, Souvenir . . . a man and a woman holding hands . . . two butterflies on her hat, a rose on his . . . the rose kissed the butterfly. An August twilight when a little girl tumbled down a hillside, falling toward a bramble patch . . . warm arms saved her, swinging her in the sunset . . . laughing. "Boo! Mommie found you!" Daddy laughed

NAKED CALL

too... another face... a colored phantom in the air. Another day... an ordinary day... except it rained and then sleeted. Except he died. And sobbing and stumbling to where he lay—miserable and lost—she held him close, but there was nothing there. All that was left was stinging eyes, a mound of dirt and the dust of dead roses. It was one of those moments when the accumulated impressions of years mingled together in a mysterious hymn of beauty and grief. So many good times. It made Christie think that if she hadn't once lived in the sun, she might have done better in the black years that came after. She turned toward the voice ... awkward and embarrassed.

"You're staring at me." A thick, red eyebrow arched.

"I could say the same for you." Christie tried on a smile.

"Actually, I'm relieved. You're not just another pretty face."

"Is that a compliment?" Christie asked.

"Yes. You can thank me for your good looks."

"Ladies, let me do the honors!" Franco came bounding onto the deck wrapped in a maroon beach towel. "Irene Bentley meet Christie Larsen."

"We've met." Irene watched Christie curiously.

Christie stared at her mother in wonder... and admiration that was close to awe. Irene was still agelessly beautiful, as if she'd been airbrushed with eternal youth. She searched for the tiny scars, the telltale signs of cosmetic surgery. No scars... no cosmetic surgery needed. Charm still animated Irene's face. Then it registered that her mother, too, wore nothing other than a maroon beach towel to cover her nakedness. "Yes, we've met," Christie fumbled.

"Good," Franco enthused. "That makes things simpler. Let's adjourn to the living room... and cool drinks." Franco handed Irene a terry cloth bath robe. "Here. Slip into something less comfortable." He gave Christie a crocodile smile. "Irene and I were enjoying the Jacuzzi when you arrived."

Christie tried to smile. She couldn't.

"Isn't Franco delicious?" Irene patted his fanny indulgently. "The kind of man you want next to you when you enter the tunnel of love."

Christie said nothing. Her head was still too full of memories . . . of echoes.

"Come off it, Christie," Franco teased. "You've been in my Jacuzzi. The entertainment center of the house, accommodates seven in contoured seats . . . or two in one contoured seat. Five jets provide a mixture of air and water for a relaxing massage. Remember how it relaxed you? Who can resist it—or me—when we're in it together?"

Christie remained irresolute . . . a mind undone.

Franco snapped his fingers in front of her eyes. "Wake up, sleeping beauty. We have business to discuss."

The deck was turning over . . . Christie felt young and gawky and foolish. Then she made a great effort. "Right, Franco. No one can resist you. Let's have a Gatorade, or Perrier water, or gin and tonic, or . . ."

"A gin martini," Irene said. "I still adore them. Remember?"

"Do you two know each other?" Franco looked puzzled.

"We met years ago,"

"Years and years ago," Christie added.

"Proves a pet theory of mine. There are only thirty-two people in the world. They change places by changing masks," Franco babbled on nervously as he slid open the glass door leading into the living room. He turned back to look at the women, still perplexed. "You two do look a little alike. You could be sisters."

"How nice. Unfortunately, I have no older sister," Irene said.

Christie smiled at the quip. After giving Irene her martini and Christie her white wine, Franco flopped down on the floor. "Okay, Christie, let's dispense with chitchat. We're here to cut a deal. I plan to direct *Deirdre of the Sorrows* . . . my next movie. It will be a box office smash. The critics will love it. The eggheads, the intellectuals . . ." He infused the word with a special scorn that few could match. ". . . will flip their wigs. Plus every red-blooded man and woman from sixteen to sixty will stand in line to see my version of *Deirdre*. It's a natural for the foreign markets. Videotape collectors will put it on their shelves next to *The Feathered Serpent* and *Citizen Kane*."

Christie said nothing.

"Franco is a zealot." Irene smiled.

"Have you seen Irene's production?" Franco hurried on. "Pure magic. Lyrical... sensual... sexual... passionate ... unconventional. The project defies the norm. Audiences will gasp... and love it! It's love in seventh-century Ireland and Scotland. With the nudity, the passion, the violence, it's bound to shock—to challenge—the public mores." Franco was as good a performer as most of the actors he cast in his films. Without warning, he shifted gears. He lowered his voice... bombast was replaced with moonlight and roses. "But I'd stake my life that this will be the movie of the year for card-carrying romantics." He was in fine fettle.

"The *Casablanca* crowd," Christie said.

"Didn't you see that three times?" Irene asked Christie.

Franco blinked. He lived in a completely self-abosrbed space and the remark distracted him. He had a pitch to make and he was bent on making it, enjoying the drama he felt in the room, believing he was the center of the action.

"*Casablanca*. That's just what I mean. Or *Jules and Jim*. *Roman Holiday*. Powerful forces pulling our lovers apart—"

"I adored Audrey Hepburn in *Roman Holiday*," Irene said. "The adorable gamine princess. We saw that one together, didn't we?"

This time Franco frowned. Something was wrong. He sipped his tequila, glancing, puzzled, at the two women. "What the hell is going on? You two old school chums?"

"You guessed our little secret," Irene almost gurgled. "We were at the Actor's Studio together."

Christie smiled her agreement. Now the lie lay between them like an invisible bond.

Franco breathed deeply. That explained their familiarity. The high cheekbones, cat-green eyes, strong—yet feminine—chins, certain nuances in the voice, that meant nothing... pure chance. "Listen, Christie. In all those smash romantic films, the lovers have a necessary illogic..."

Irene picked up the sell. "... A necessary lunacy. A compelling romance must involve the threat of separation and sacrifice... even death. That's why *Deirdre* is a classic romance."

"Like *A Tale of Two Cities*," Franco added. "Like *Wuthering Heights*." He rubbed his hands together in relish. "Come on, Christie, go for it!"

The strained quiet became a subterranean channel of communication. At last Christie asked, "Who do we cast for *Deirdre*?"

Franco glowed. "We use Irene's cast."

"Irene's cast is not bankable."

"The cast isn't. I am," Franco said.

"You are not photogenic," Christie said.

"I don't have to be. I make the world photogenic."

"Maureen Corley will play *Deirdre*. She was in the *Serpent*," Irene said.

"Ah . . . she's good," Christie said. "But she's not Michelle Pfeiffer."

Back and forth—verbal Ping-Pong—their voices went in careful tones, like conspirators against the crown, trusting no one . . . not even themselves. Eventually Christie said, "You have the entire cast for a run of the play contract. And to release them for the film, tell me again what you want?" Christie remembered exactly what Irene had asked. But conscious of what was between them, she postponed. This deal was tricky and exhausting, like trying to walk down an up escalator.

"I'm not greedy. To release my cast I want half a million up front. Plus five percent of gross," Irene said.

"Yes, you did say that. I'll go with the half million up front."

"But . . . ?" Franco watched her, trying to guess what she was thinking.

"Five percent of gross is . . ." She almost said, obscene. ". . . is too much."

"She means five percent of the net," Franco pointed out.

"No, Franco. I said five percent of the gross and I mean five percent of the gross. I know the difference between gross and net."

"That's far too much."

"How much is not too much?" Irene asked.

"Maybe two percent of net," Christie said wearily, wanting to escape her mother's eyes and wishing the meeting was over.

"That's absurd." Irene's tone was dangerous.

Something was struggling to the surface of Christie's mind . . . something she didn't want to remember. Her head hurt the way it did centuries ago. Her whole body hurt, too, as if someone inside her was giving her a bad beating. She shut her eyes to clear it of the vision of Irene kneeling next to her as she cradled her father's shattered head. At last she found her voice.

"I want to be fair. But what you contribute to the film is the cast . . . nothing more. You did not write the play. You directed it—the play, not the film. Five percent of the gross is unreasonable."

"My production has made the play a very hot property," Irene insisted.

"True. But if we decide to film *Deirdre*, we can recast with other actors. That saves the half million up front and any percentages, gross or net. Unless we cast Jack Nicholson as Naoise . . . which I doubt."

"I want to work with Irene's cast," Franco shouted.

"Two percent of the net means two percent of nothing," Irene said. "Movie bookkeeping is a swamp. There are no net profits. They get sucked into the swamp."

"Our books are kept according to generally accepted accounting principles used by the major accounting firms." Christie grimmaced in disgust. The subject of movie accounting had a déjà vu about it. Guy Macleod, where the hell are you, now that I need you? "Two percent of the net will be exactly that . . . two percent of whatever the net is."

"Is that your best offer?" Irene asked.

"Better than my best. It's more than I should offer."

"It won't do." Irene said it clearly, insolently.

Franco jumped in. "Christie, damn it! Don't be a corporate clone. This movie will make more than *The Feathered Serpent*. Let her have the lousy five percent."

"I can't. It makes no sense. I'm sorry."

Irene's eyes were veiled, unreadable. "It makes no sense for me to let United have my *Deirdre* for anything less."

"I won't make it without Irene's cast!" Franco blared.

Christie tried to reason with each of them. She described to Irene the rarity of gross percentages . . . reminded Franco of the risk of using a cast of unknowns. But it was like shaking hands with a glove from which the hand had been withdrawn. So, finally, with a resigned air, she stood up.

"Sorry, folks. Meeting's over. No deal."

Franco and Irene were reduced to glaring at her back as she left the house. Walking to her car, Christie thought about Irene . . . about her father. It had always been difficult for her to face the truth about her early years. The pain was so great she'd tried to block it. She'd used her work to erase all memories. But now she was drawn back to the past by the very success she had used for escape. She now knew that the pain had never ended . . . never would end.

As soon as the door had closed behind Christie, Irene rose, dropped the robe on the carpet, and strode—stark naked . . . Franco no longer existed for her—across the living room to Franco's bedroom. In a few minutes, she was dressed and on her way without saying a word. Franco was at a loss. What the hell went wrong? He'd been so sure he could handle Christie and Irene . . . he was Franco Marconi. Sure, five percent of gross was out of sight. It should have been negotiated . . . if Irene insisted on gross, maybe half a percent or one percent. But those two women were in a Mexican stand-off: Christie, adamant, Irene, high-handed, neither giving an inch. Why?

One might wonder how Franco could miss the connection . . . the similarities in looks, voice, and movement were uncanny. But the world existed for him in the first person singular . . . I . . . I . . . I. He had to find a way to get the show on the road again. Maybe Louis would help. They were invited for dinner. If anyone could handle Christie it was Louis Levy.

Detective Carmella Garcia never let go of a case until it was solved . . . or until superior officers insisted she stop wasting the taxpayers' money. "Nice meeting you, Mr. Weiss. Even if it took seven telephone calls."

Harry had the grace to blush. "I run a large department. But we did finally get together."

"Yes, we did, and I'm glad you have everything under control."

"Everything. Your source is just plain wrong. We know

exactly what happened. A bookkeeping error by the bookkeepers on *The Feathered Serpent*. Human error."

"My source says otherwise." Her voice carried a metallic edge. "My source is absolutely reliable. Something isn't kosher in your bookkeeping department, Mr. Weiss. The forgeries of checks for hundreds of thousands of dollars..."

"There have been no forgeries."

"Forgery is defined as a form of felony, grand theft."

"I know... by the Penal Code of California."

"Hundreds of thousands of dollars—maybe more—are not a simple bookkeeping error," Detective Garcia said. "I hope my visit has alerted you to the danger."

PART EIGHT

1992
JUNE

Chapter 21

JEFFREY MOORE'S office was on the twenty-third floor of the Union Bank building in downtown Los Angeles. Compared to Moore, Michael Milken had been a lazy dawdler who slouched into his office—when he had an office—at 5:30 in the morning. By 5:30, diligent Jeffrey had been working for an hour and a half... he arrived at his office every morning promptly at 4:00.

Besides their absolute dedication to the work ethic, Moore and Milken had other likenesses. Both worked at the limits of the law. However, Milken, unlike Moore, was still revered by many as a visionary genius—the savior of entrepreneurial dreamers, a man of reckless financial zeal bent on ridding moribund American corporations of management deadwood... inept, incompetent, perk-greedy, senior executives... the bunglers... the wasters of corporate assets. Some say his sins—if they were sins—were the sins of a saint, that he was a messiah in the mold of J.P. Morgan, E.H. Harriman, Pierre Macleod, and other nineteenth-century financiers... the men who broke the rules and made America the richest nation in the world, that if there is place in heaven reserved for American originals, a case might be made for Michael Milken at the very highest court of appeal.

Jeffrey Moore was something else... a far less spectacular, far less visible operator than Michael Milken. It's unlikely that anyone would argue on his behalf anywhere. He had none of Milken's breadth of vision. No one benefited from Jeffrey Moore's financial machinations except Jeffrey Moore... and the man for whom he fronted. Moore's was the garden variety of thievery that Milken's inspiration spawned. Jeffrey Moore gave thanks to Milken and kept two sets of books. He was adept at trading on inside information, parking stock for his key associate, using Greenmail to fatten their bank account, always guaranteeing that politicians and security enforcement types got their piece of the pie. But genius or crook, both men had one thing in common... scorn for the safe and sure AAA bonds that paid low interest rates.

Beyond this parallel the resemblance ended. Milken lived with his family in Encino, California, the unpretentious Los Angeles enclave where he grew up, although he ranked high on the Forbes list of the 400 wealthiest Americans.

On the other hand, Jeffrey Moore—who longed to attain the *Forbes* list and was at least a zero away—had a lifestyle appropriate to his fantasy. He purchased a house and two acres of land for six and a half million dollars in upscale Coldwater Canyon. The contemporary house was a three-level testimony to his enormous ego.

There was another difference between Moore and Milken. Not only their lifestyles, but their love styles—which had identical beginnings—developed in different modes. Both men married their high school sweethearts. Moore's was the sweetheart of Theta Beta Tau, Milken's of Sigma Alpha Mu. Years and three children later, Milken was still married to the same prom queen, while Moore stayed married to his wife for five months, subsequently remarrying and divorcing three times. At the moment he was wifeless and childless. A bachelor's life—even a rich bachelor with dollar signs hanging from baited hooks—is feast or famine. Moore was currently suffering through one of his rare famines.

Then Mona Anderson walked through the door of Maxwell, Gluck & Moore. She told Susan Yakamura, the receptionist, that she was meeting her uncle, who was considering opening an account with Maxwell, Gluck & Moore. She sat down to wait. When Moore rushed in from a late lunch, Miss Yakamura told him that his Very Big Client had called... he, too, would be late. Moore slid to a halt. The idea of waiting instead of being waited for irritated him. Moore started toward his office. Then he noticed Mona scanning a magazine. She looked like money on the hoof. Better... she had the smell of high sexuality. Lust ran through his veins, warming him, throwing a flush up into his brain. Suddenly his manhood rebelled. He'd be damned if he'd sit still waiting like a road sign for his client to show up. He had better things to do. On impulse he introduced himself to Mona and invited her to wait for her uncle in his office. "Have a cup of coffee," he said. "We'll have a busines chat," he said. He didn't say he might get lucky. Moore was a virtuoso at the art of seduction. Mona was a sensual woman who evoked his best efforts. The hour passed too quickly.

"Now what is this stock you're so interested in?" he casually asked . . . a conversational ploy.

"My uncle will tell you when he gets here," Mona said. "We're both interested in the stock."

"Does your uncle handle your investment strategy?"

"The big stuff. He's very shrewd, Mr. Moore."

"Call me Jeff." Moore gave her his boyish grin.

Her eyes held no hint of surprise. It was more like recognition . . . acceptance. "Yes, Jeff. You were saying that we should short the stock and buy the futures?"

"That's what I'm saying. Or, depending on the current spread, we could short the futures and buy the stock, Mrs. Anderson."

"Call me Mona." Mona gave him her girlish smile.

"The funds do it every day, Mona. If you like the idea, we can do it, too . . . there's this stock in which you're both interested."

"Jeff, do you remember when the SEC deregulated commissions?" Mona asked with plausible guile.

"Of course. The idea was that the public should be able to negotiate lower commissions . . . people like your uncle."

"I suppose that was the idea, but it didn't happen that way," Mona was charmed by Jeffrey Moore's rich air of fraudulence. "It's the funds that have negotiated lower commissions. The funds have the muscle. They move hundreds of thousands of shares of stock in one buy or sell order, trading on very small stock movements. Why shouldn't they? They pay very small commissions. But the public— the small investors for whom commissions were deregulated—the public gets screwed."

"You think so, Mona?"

"I think so, Jeff, and you think so, too. The public pays through the nose, making up for what the funds don't pay, because the public has no muscle." She shrugged her shoulders... her breasts moved sensuously. "As you said, Jeff, my uncle's the public. I'm the public."

Jeffrey Moore's throat felt dry. She reminded him of a great French porn queen. "You're saying you don't want to buy futures?"

"That's what I'm saying. My uncle's not strapped. Nor am I. Some people think we're rich. He's very rich. But he's not as rich as the funds. Your commissions would eat him up alive."

"Mmmm... that's probably true," Moore said, thinking about eating Mona up alive.

"I'm glad we agree. So I wish you'd suggest this idea to him. My uncle and I think this market's going to break wide open. It's going to be October 1987, all over again. But our stock is going to buck the market... it's going to go up. Try to get him to buy naked calls."

"Mmmm... naked calls." Moore fixed on the phrase 'naked call.' The image of Mona naked, calling to him, floated in his mind. He had to move in... get her phone number for openers. "You know, Mona, talking to you has been interesting. I've seldom met a woman with such a sophisticated grasp of the market. I'd enjoy continuing our talk at lunch."

"Thank you, Jeff. I've enjoyed talking to you, too."

"Maybe next week you could find a free date?"

"I'll check my calendar. It's at the hotel."

"The hotel? You don't live in L.A.?"

"No. I flew out from New York with a friend. She's a theatrical producer. She's here on business." Mona said this with pride. "We're together."

Moore was crestfallen. He didn't go in for long-distance affairs... playing with yourself while you talked to the girl on the phone was childish. Still, she was here for now, with only another woman and her uncle. Much could be accomplished. "Fine. Check your calendar. I'd like to continue this talk. You know, Mona, your mother didn't raise you to be a fool."

"My uncle raised me. He could write books on the stock market."

The intercom button on Moore's phone lit. He picked up

the receiver. "Oh! He's here. Send him in." He turned to Mona. "It's my client. Where are you staying?"

"At the Bel Air." She stood up. "My uncle has a suite there. He's here so much, he ought to buy a house."

"The Bel Air. I'll call tomorrow." Mona looked better and better. Her clothes were stylish but her manner straightforward. No artificiality—just a great piece of ass. He escorted her to the door.

Moore returned to his desk to wait as usual for his client, who, as usual, took his time appearing.

Stavros Lennos was ushered into Moore's office by Susan Yakamura. "I gather you were entertaining Mrs. Anderson," Stavros mumured after the secretary tiptoed from the office. "I met her on my way in." He lowered himself into the deep leather chair where Mona had been sitting. The chair was set directly facing the desk.

"You know Mrs. Anderson?"

"She tells me you're charming."

Moore regarded Stavros warily. "She said she was waiting for her uncle."

"I'm her uncle."

Jeffrey Moore had a sense of turning pale.

"How could you know?" Stavros said.

"I didn't," Jeffrey gulped."

"She's married, Jeffrey."

"Yes . . ."

"Need I say more?"

"Of course not."

"Fine. Now tell me . . . what did you talk about?"

"What do you mean . . . talk about?" Moore stammered.

"How well did you say you know me . . . don't know me?"

"We didn't talk about you. She said she was waiting for her uncle who wanted to open an account with the firm. She didn't say who her uncle was. I didn't ask. As far as she knows I don't know you from Adam," Moore said quickly.

"We'll keep it that way. Now let's get down to business. I want you to pick up some more United."

"United Cinema?" Moore started to scribble on a pad.

"I believe that's the name . . . not United Airlines. United Cinema, Jeffrey."

"Sorry. What do I bid?"

"Buy at the market."

Moore asked stiffly, "Naked calls?"

"Why naked calls?"

"Mona—I mean Mrs. Anderson—said . . ."

"Mrs. Anderson said what?" Stavros waited patiently. He was good at that.

"That I should interest you in naked calls." Jeffrey Moore was way off-balance . . . flustered. "I think she was speaking about stocks in general." *The hell she was.* "Not United Cinema." *I hope not United.*

"I'm glad, Jeffrey. For your sake."

"Stavros! I swear I said nothing. Not one thing."

"Good. I would dislike having to do something unpleasant about you."

"Don't you trust her? She's your niece."

"I don't trust anyone, Jeffrey. You know that. So let's get back to the reason for our meeting. I don't care how you buy United. Naked calls . . . long . . . at the market . . . up, down, or sideways. I want to accumulate more United Cinema stock."

"How much do you want?"

"Buy until I tell you to stop."

"We already own way over five percent."

"Are you deliberately trying to irritate me? Buy as much United as you can. Put it in the firm name. You've done that before . . . you've enough accounts to use as dummies. Give Rita Solieri a daily report on how much stock you've bought and the closing price. She'll know how to get the information to me." Stavros rose. "I'll be in touch." He started to leave, then stopped. "Would you like to join Mona and me for lunch?"

"Thank you, but no thank you. I'd better tell you something I did, for which I'm sorry."

"What is it?"

"You won't like it."

"Try me."

"I told Mrs. Anderson I would call her tomorrow. For lunch." He spit the words out as if they were poison. "I'll cancel out, or not call at all. I can do either. Which would you prefer?"

"What do you think you should do?"

A pulse beat in Moore's forehead. He eyed Stavros closely, trying to decide which way to jump. If he didn't call—or if he cancelled out—Mona could be offended. Not good. She might think Stavros was responsible. Worse. Yet Stavros obviously didn't want them to make contact. Finally Moore figured out what was required of him. "I'll call and arrange a lunch date, then never see her again. Right?"

Stavros nodded pleasantly. "Is the Pope Catholic?"

"I see what you mean."

The warmth of wood, the shine of silver, the sauted *foie gras* resting in its nest of country mushrooms, and the snapper laying contentedly on a bed of couscous . . . Louis' dinner was a gourmet's feast. It should have been filled with a heavenly light . . . but it wasn't. No one except for Louis ate very much. The Black Forest chocolate cake was almost untouched.

Out of sheer deviltry and a sense of survival, Franco made his exit after cocktails, leaving the women to come out swinging . . . convinced that no matter who took the count, he would be winner. For almost three hours over exquisitely prepared, half-eaten dishes, Christie and Louis and Irene bandied opinions on the pros and cons of film versus theater as an art form . . . principles of aesthetics as expounded by Santayana, Whitehead, Rona Barrett, Frank Rich, *New York* magazine. There was a lot of clearing of throats and firmness of tone.

The argument continued into coffee, then brandy, until Louis finally came to the reason for the dinner . . . the filming of *Deirdre of the Sorrows*.

Irene said thoughtfully, "Fortunately Franco understands *Deirdre*. It's a film in which the brutality of the age contrasts with the lyricism of the love. He may be the only movie director who can do justice to the play."

"The sex scenes plus at least five dramatically fulfilling deaths in *Deirdre* make it a Marconi dream," Louis observed. "His best movies center on violence and the romanticism of danger and, finally, death."

Irene's eyes were skeptical with speculation. "That's why he wants to do it. He said if you don't meet my terms, we'll go to Columbia . . . Universal . . . Paramount. He's that eager."

"What are your terms?" Louis asked as if he didn't know . . . a priest performing a rite.

Irene answered his question as if she believed he didn't already know. She pointed out that she had made the culture *Deirdre*-conscious. It had had a spread in *Newsweek*, a *People* magazine feature, a *Vanity Fair* interview. Maureen had appeared on the *Tonight Show* and she had been interviewed on *Today*. The play was a "hot ticket." Irene's take for these good works—including releasing her cast for the film—was worth five percent of the gross.

Louis acted as if he couldn't believe his ears. He placed the tips of his fingers of both hands on the edge of the table. He lifted his chin and smiled forgivingly. Yes, she'd produced a hit, a valuable property. But her terms were absurd. And, like it or not, she'd painted herself into a corner.

"My dear Irene, over dinner you made a fine argument for our case, not yours. Think what you said about film stars while you toyed with your snapper. In films it was personal appeal, not acting, that counted. If that's true, if film actors only need personal appeal, not acting talent, then why shouldn't we use proven box office stars to make *Deirdre*? Thanks to you we have a new wave of *Deirdre* awareness. That works for us. We don't need your cast of unknowns. They may be fine actors, but what we want is screen appeal. If you won't release your cast, we'll choose our own. You'll get zero percent of either the gross or the net."

Irene poured contempt on his logic. "Good try, Louis. But Franco won't touch *Deirdre* without my cast."

"My dear Irene, you won't get a better deal anywhere else. If the film is the winner you think it will be, two percent of the net will come to a hell of a lot of money." Louis' voice had the ring of authority.

"If it's a winner, five percent of the gross will come to ten—maybe twenty—times your offer."

"Apparently you don't believe me." Louis was sorrowful . . . he stopped short of brushing a tear from the corner of his eye. "Why don't I call Katzenbaum at Touchstone... Guber and Peters at Columbia... Pollack at Universal... Diller at Fox? One of them is sure to fall in love with the property. But no one will give you five percent of the gross. It's ridiculous." He pressed the floor bell beneath the table. "Lei will bring me a phone. I'll call whoever you wish right now."

"No." Irene glanced at her diamond watch. "They'll say what you said. Hollywood is an old buddy network." She pushed back her chair. "I'll think over your offer. But if I decide to go to Columbia, Universal, et cetera, I have my own contacts. However, I do thank you for the marvelous dinner."

Louis watched her leave, his lips pursed in distaste. "The beauty of that woman is overwhelming. She is also greedy by nature, corrupt, unscrupulous, and a liar. Talks double talk. You're lucky you only inherited her looks, not her character."

Christie stared at him with surprise, steadied herself, then slowly smiled. "Didn't you believe me when I said I was left on a doorstep by gypsies?"

"Who do you take after... besides her in looks?"

Christie took her time answering. "My father," she finally said. "But he said I took after Knute Larsen." Louis arched his eyebrows. "My grandfather. He died when I was very young."

"Knute Larsen must have been quite a man."

"My father thought so," she said quietly. "How long have you known Irene was my mother?"

"For months. Ever since I made the deal with Macleod Brothers. Guy introduced me to Irene Bentley in Manhattan."

"And you saw the resemblance?"

"Not immediately, but soon. The similarity between you in looks, voice, gesture... it's uncanny."

"That close?"

"That close. She had to be your mother."

He refrained from adding that his first impression of Irene's face was what almost made him miss the connection. In Christie's face was candor... compassion. In Irene's, coldness... craft. She was a mean, scheming bitch who happened to be unusually talented.

"Were they divorced... or what?" he asked.

A momentary silence settled gently between them. Christie felt deeply grateful for the luck of having Louis in her life for all these years. He was more than her employer... he was her best friend. He would take from her in good faith whatever she gave. Talking to him would be a little like thinking out loud. So at last, very softly, she told him the history of her mother and father—of Tom Larsen and Irene Bentley Larsen—and their monstrous passion play. She spoke of them with respect and dismay and heartbreaking sadness. About her father, who was imprisoned by his love for her mother... about her mother who once had loved her father. Christie said when she was very young it seemed impossible that either one could ever live without the other. But they had lived, and a change had come. Her mother had begun the long, dispiriting war against her father ... a war that left him defenseless, humiliated, dishonored.

When she finished, Louis said, "I'm glad you told me."

"Franco hasn't guessed who she is. Neither has Guy."

"Franco sees his Oscars. Guy sees the Macleod name on tombstones. They see nothing else."

"How did you know Irene was flying here to meet Franco to make a deal for United to film *Deirdre?*"

"She called me the morning of the board meeting."

"And you guessed she and I would have a knock down?"

"It was predictable. Then Franco called." Louis chuckled. "I gather you two had quite a scene."

"We've had worse." Christie's terse evaluation was all the more biting for its lack of histrionics. "So you invited us to dinner to calm troubled waters." Louis stared at her mutely. "Is she Guy's friend?"

"Guy has no friends. He thinks she's his plaything. That woman's nobody's plaything. She always has a payoff in mind... a use, some kind of trade-off. She hopes to use Guy for *Deirdre.*"

The merest pink crept into Christie's cheeks. "Is she the reason you insisted on my presidency being written into the contract with Macleod Brothers?"

"No. You've earned the job. You're the best person I

know to keep United ahead of the pack, to build on what I built." He grinned. "Then there was Guy and Irene. If you stood in her way—if Guy had to choose between the two of you—he wouldn't choose you."

"So you meant to protect me from Irene... from my own mother?" What a dreary bit of irony.

"I would cast her as Medea."

Christie said nothing. There was nothing to say.

"There was another reason. It's a little tricky to explain."

"Try me."

"I smelled a rotten egg. Guy is a theater buff. To him, movies are for the little people... whoever they're supposed to be. Guy doesn't give a damn about making movies."

Christie looked puzzled. "Why then? Why buy United?"

"I don't know why he bought the studio."

"If not to make movies..." Christie ransacked her mental files. "And not to make money..."

"How quickly you put two and two together. It's not money. Movies are too dicey... a high-risk investment."

"Lust?" Christie asked.

"No... not Guy. It's something else. Sometimes I wish I'd made the deal with Lennos. He's Mafia, but at least he wants to make movies. United wouldn't be the first Hollywood studio backed by the Mafia. Some films would be garbage, some you'd be proud of, some would be big box-office winners. The Mafia needs big box-office winners to launder big money."

Christie sat up straighter. An orange flag was waving... not yet a red alert. "Louis, about *Deirdre*."

"*Deirdre*?" Louis blinked to attention.

"Irene is greedy, but she's not stupid. She just doesn't understand movie financing. If she did, she'd know that asking five percent of gross is outlandish... a deal breaker. Where do you think she got that number?"

"Five percent?" The words left a bad taste. "More questions... no answers. Franco maybe?" Louis made a face. "Whoever advised her gave her lousy advice."

"Why would Franco do that? He knows it's absurd."

"Still more questions... still no answers."

"I'd really like the answer to that one. I have a hunch

that if we knew who told Irene to ask for five percent, we'd know the answers to a lot of other questions."

Louis' head barely moved. Only one who knew him well could have identified that almost imperceptible movement as a nod of agreement.

"I adore this hotel. The Bel Air is my idea of an absolutely elegant hotel." Mona leaned over and kissed Stavros on the cheek, sliding into the chair beside him. "You angel, you ordered me a martini. How nice."

"Tanqueray on the rocks, right?"

"Right." Mona glanced around the lounge. "This hotel is so understated. Definitely not a showplace. I read somewhere that it's ranked as one of the ten great hotels in the world."

"I'm glad you're enjoying your stay."

"Am I ever. Uncle Stavros, your suite here . . . that's on a semi-permanent basis, isn't it?" Stavros nodded. "You're in the best company. Audrey Hepburn and Grace Kelly lived here for months at a time. Angela Lansbury and Don Johnson and Dudley Moore stay here too."

"You're a mine of information."

"I adore Hollywood, Hollywood people, Rodeo Drive. I was shopping all day. Which reminds me, I'm glad you were late yesterday. Jeffrey Moore and I had a wonderful talk about futures and options, puts and calls, naked calls. He phoned this morning."

"Did he? I gather you got to know each other well."

"We're having lunch next week," Mona caroled.

"Are you?" Stavros was every inch the kindly uncle.

"We'll have lunch on the terrace near the swans. He says I'm a savvy investor, fun to talk to." Girlish pout. "Sherwood acts as if I don't know a put from a call."

"He's your husband. He has that right." There was a bleak note in Stavros' voice as Mona nodded silently.

"What did you and Moore talk about yesterday?"

"Lots of things, but I never mentioned United. If you decided not to open an account with him, it would have been a mistake." For an instant the childlike mask that Mona wore in public vanished. Under the mask was a woman born and bred in an older, more dangerous, world. She grinned,

NAKED CALL

her mask of innocence firmly in place. "I am savvy. What do you think of him?"

Stavros shrugged. "Of Moore? I've no opinion yet."

"I'll tell you what I think. He looks to me like a man who would go to jail rather than part with the suitcase of counterfeit thousand dollar bills he's stashed in his closet."

"You have a vivid imagination."

"Do I?" She laughed. "But that's what I like about him. Now spill it. Did you open an account with him? At lunch yesterday you were still thinking it over."

"I thought it over. I did."

"Good. I told him to tell you to buy naked calls."

"He told me."

"Did you?"

"We worked out a strategy."

"Tell! Tell! You know I love business strategies."

"It's a complicated transaction—"

"Hello, darlings," Irene sparkled as she slipped into a vacant chair at the table. "I hope you haven't waited too long. I broke out as soon as I could from that dismal dinner. Order me Absolut straight, Stavros. You are Stavros, aren't you? Mona talked about you constantly on the flight."

The time passed with this and that. Irene's drink was served and Stavros watched her tongue the vodka. A beautiful woman by the standards of most men. She looked in her mid-thirties but he knew she was fifty-something. The stream of lovers, the booze, the cocaine . . . nothing affected her. He listened to her husky voice as she sipped her drink and smiled and talked about her love of theater, of films. A straight from the heart pitch, well-rehearsed. He wondered when she'd get to the point.

"Theater is my life," Irene said in her low, seductive tone. "But I admit it has limitations. Film is a genuine miracle—a miracle of technical and artistic potentials—only a fraction of which those fools have learned to use."

"You're interested in making movies?" Stavros asked.

"Actually, I am." Irene gave him an unabashed "I have an itch. Would you like to scratch it?" glance. "Stavros . . ." She said it as if tasting his name. "Mona mentioned that you tried to buy United Cinema. You must know the movie business. I need some advice about movies... reliable advice from a friend."

"What's the question?" They were finally getting to it.

"I'm asking five percent of gross to release my cast to make a film version of *Deirdre*. I believe that's reasonable." Her voice expected congratulations... applause.

"If I were producing the movie I'd offer one percent of net... one and a half percent at the most."

Startled. "They've offered me two percent."

"Of gross?"

Faltering. "Of net."

Stavros grew calmer as Irene grew more nervous. "If United offered two percent of net, grab it."

Mystified, she made a face. "But it's my cast. I practically invented *Deirdre*."

"John Millington Synge invented Deirdre."

"Look, before starting talks, I asked advice from an authority in the movie business. I was told that five percent of gross is a reasonable number."

"You asked for my opinion." Stavros spoke slowly in order to let his words sink in. "I gave you my opinion."

Irene sucked in her breath and shook her head. "This is preposterous!"

"Irene Bentley! How wonderful to meet you!" A young woman in beaded silk pants, a cashmere T-shirt, and lots of pearls was beaming at her.

Insolent. "Do I know you?"

"Sorry to interrupt. I couldn't help myself. I saw you on the *Today* show. I saw *Deirdre* last time I was in Manhattan. I loved it."

"Sweet of you to tell me. Now if you'll excuse us—"

"My name is Jo Caro. I'm house counsel for United Cinema. The grapevine says we'll be making *Deirdre* as a film. I think it's marvelous."

"Ah." The welcome mat was out. "How nice to meet you, Miss Caro. I'm so glad you enjoyed the play."

"I adore love stories. I was having a drink with a friend." Jo gestured across the room to where a dark-haired man sat. "And I said, 'That's Irene Bentley! I must tell her I'm a fan of hers.'"

"You think *Deirdre* would make a good film."

"The best. A red hot ticket, a trunk full of Oscars."

"And you're Miss Jo Caro?"

"Jo Caro. Drop by when you're in to see Christie. I'd love to talk to you about theater."

"I will, Miss Caro. I will."

"Good. I won't keep you any longer. It was a pleasure meeting you, Miss Bentley." Jo Caro almost curtsied before she left.

Irene sat up straighter. She looked more collected. She was running an internal debate on percentages.

Mona ordered another round of drinks and Stavros leaned back. He looked at Irene with an impassive expression for what seemed a very long time. Then he said patiently, "In the matter of the percentages, your authority is wrong."

Irene looked at him distractedly, trying to decide. "Maybe you're right. But if I take your advice and you're wrong, I'll end up getting fucked."

Stavros said gently, "I'm about as wrong as a mother identifying her lost child."

Irene smiled but said nothing. The metaphor made her uneasy.

Mona was full of good will and enthusiasm. "I'll bet Uncle Stavros is right. He always is."

"It's possible." Irene's voice was businesslike.

"I haven't convinced you."

"I'm withholding judgement." Irene was thinking of her fan and her thoughts made her spirits rise. "If that foxy L'Oreal blond knows about *Deirdre*, United really wants it. I believe I can do better than two percent of net."

"What did she say her name was?" Stavros asked for the sake of asking.

"Jo Caro... house counsel." The way Irene put it, it sounded as if Jo's first name was Jocaro and her last name, Housecounsel—Jocaro Housecounsel. Not your style, she added to herself.

Stavros understood. Sharks weren't his style. But his mind was elsewhere. After many years of surviving in a world where survival had been refined to an art form, he had developed a remarkable instinct for making connections between seemingly isolated events. He had listened with mild boredom while Irene Bentley expounded her right to five percent of gross. Then he assessed the antics of the Irene Bentley Fan Club as Jo Caro bowed and scraped before Her Ladyship. He was not interested... until he noticed the man with whom Jo Caro was drinking and made the connection. There might be nothing to it, no link between incidents, except that they occurred consecutively. But they started a curious train of thought. At that moment, he was almost sorry for Jo Caro.

Chapter 22

HARRY WEISS was pissed off at Detective Garcia. She was like a hound dog on the scent of something. He knew what she was looking for... but not how to stop her.

Detective Carmella Garcia was pissed off at Harry Weiss. Did he think her a fool... a token female cop with a blow dried brain who he could stonewall. Okay, asshole. The Bank of California was lead bank for United Cinema. She'd drop in at the main branch in Beverly Hills... make a few waves.

"Mr. Dukenfield will be free in a moment. He has a customer with him. Please excuse him," said Miss Johns, the branch manager's private secretary. "I told him you were here."

Detective Garcia thought this over. She would wait.

She sat down in a reproduction of a Regency mahogany armchair facing the secretary seated at a reproduction of a Georgian pedestal desk. "I don't like to interrupt," Miss Johns apologized, torn between her duty to her boss and her fear of the police. "He's with an important customer."

"How long has Mr. Dukenfield been in conference?"

"An hour," Miss Johns said unhappily. "It's a multi-million dollar mortgage default on a house in Holmby Hills." She was about to tell too much when the door to Dukenfield's office opened and an internationally famous blond urchin made a frisky exit. She was so young... so beautiful... so famous... so broke.

Miss Johns jumped to her feet and hurried toward the open door. Detective Garcia followed.

Claude Dukenfield's office was an extension of the ambience in the reception room, completely furnished with antique reproductions.

"Ah, Sergeant Garcia. How do you do?" Claude Dukenfield gave her a carefully measured, aristocratic smile. "I expected a man, but I gather you are Sergeant Rosa Garcia?"

"How do you do, Mr. Dukenfield. I am Detective Carmella Garcia, with the Beverly Hills police department." She showed the banker her badge and I.D.

"Sorry, Detective Garcia. You have business with us?" Dukenfield asked cautiously.

"Yes. And I'd like it settled quickly."

Dukenfield asked no questions, made no offer to be of help. He remained seated, waiting.

Garcia made a mental note... does not want to cooperate. "Have there been any checks drawn on the United Cinema account in the last year that raised any questions in your mind?"

Dukenfield glanced at her, startled, quizzical, but not frightened. Harry Weiss had asked him the same question just the other day. He'd tell the detective what he'd told Harry. That it happened to be the truth was useful. "No. None that I can think of."

"You know of no unusual activity?"

"United Cinema is a substantial account. Each month thousands of checks are drawn on the account and weekly they deposit many hundreds of checks. Unless something extraordinary occurred, it would not come to my attention. Since nothing has been brought to my attention, I assume nothing extraordinary has occurred."

Detective Carmella Garcia sighed. "Okay. We'll do this the hard way. I want to see every check drawn on all the United Cinema accounts in the last twelve months."

"I'm sorry, but that's impossible." He didn't smile. His voice remained smooth, with a distinct hint of superiority.

"Why?"

"To begin with, it's against bank rules. And secondly, we don't have those checks. Every check drawn on a United Cinema account is returned at the end of the month to United Cinema." He gave off an air of patronizing boredom.

"Mr. Dukenfield, once—when I was very young and happy to work for starvation wages—I was a bank teller. I know you don't have the actual checks. What you do have is a microfilm record of every check honored by the bank. I want a printout of the front side and back side of all checks paid out by United Cinema in the last twelve months."

He gave her a safely pleasant smile. "Detective Garcia, be reasonable. That's confidential bank information. If anything strange had occurred, I would know."

"Mr. Dukenfield, you will get me the printouts."

His eyes were intentionally expressionless. "Even the IRS needs a court order to get that information."

"Fine, Mr. Dukenfield. I'll get a court order. And while I'm at it, I'll get another court order to investigate all cash deposits over ten thousand dollars made at this branch. It's called money laundering. Los Angeles, as we know, is one of the money laundering centers of the world. Am I getting through to you?"

For a minute Claude Dukenfield said nothing. He stared at the detective. Then he said quietly, "It will take us a month to get that information."

Detective Carmella Garcia rose from her chair. "Bullshit! This is Monday. You can do it in three days. I'll be back Thursday afternoon. I know Friday is the Fourth of July, but don't leave early on Thursday. And don't hassle me, Mr. Dukenfield, or I will hang your ass out to dry on money laundering charges."

Christie was ready to know the worst... if there was a worst to be known. She watched Harry squirm about. "Okay. So this detective was here, and you think she knows something. How much does she know?"

"Too much. She used the word 'forgery.' That's too much."

"What exactly did you say to her?"

"She was a pain in the neck. She wouldn't listen to reason, wouldn't take yes for an answer. 'Yes, we know about it. Yes, we are looking into it. Yes, it was a bookkeeping error. Yes, bookkeepers are human.'" Harry's body went slack within his raw, nubby silk jacket. "Who the hell tipped her is what I want to know?"

"It could be almost anybody. Too many people know."

"But you warned the Grossmans, Maureen Corley, Gary Chany... the unholy seven whose names were forged."

"And you spoke to Sidney Frank and company."

"Something's buggin' Sid. I wouldn't say he flimflammed, but there's a burr up his behind. We're meeting Thursday."

"You told me... three times. You didn't say about what."

"I don't know about what. All he said was he's doing us a favor."

Christie stared at Harry. She was keyed up, aware of the stillness of the office. What did Sidney Frank know that she didn't? "Do you think one of his clients is the leak?"

"No. We went over that ground. He says his firm's clients are zipped up tight. It's something else. Could be one of them wants special consideration for staying zipped... for a project... a part. Who knows? We'll see Thursday. Maybe you should've nailed Marconi?"

"I want something more before I talk to Franco."

"But what about Garcia?"

"Garcia doesn't matter. A detective trying to get promoted."

The intercom button lit up. Christie picked up and listened and her face changed. She turned pale, as though she'd seen a ghost. "Have them wait a minute," she said, perspiration breaking out on her forehead. "Harry and I are finishing up." Her arm was shaking as she put the receiver down.

"Harry..." Christie looked at him with at him with a strange blankness. "Table this discussion for now. I've some unexpected visitors."

Harry quickly rose, bewildered. He'd never seen Christie so shaken. He almost asked, What is it? Who are you talking to? Who is out there?

"I'll be in touch," he muttered, moving quickly, curious to see who the hell was shaking her up.

Christie pressed the intercom. "Send them in, Nan."

Tommy came racing through the door, yelling, "Mom, Mom, look who's with me! Barry Easton! *Winner's Circle!*"

For a moment Christie was so distraught she couldn't get the words out. "Hello, darling," she managed to say to Tommy. "Barry," she said to the man.

The tallish, well-built man had boyish features, tousled brown hair, baby-blue eyes, a chiseled jaw with a dimple, and an extraordinary smile... reassuring and irresistible. Barry Easton had smiled his way to stardom.

"Hi, Christie." He gave her the smile.

"Where did you get Tommy?"

"Picked him up when he got home from school."

"Maria let you take him?"

"I told a white lie. I said you'd telephoned and asked me to bring Tommy to the office. So here we are." He rolled his eyes and shrugged his shoulders in a gesture that said, I'm a rat... but I'm your rat. Another smile.

Christie was swimming through her confusion. "Barry, what's this about? What are you doing?"

"Building bridges. You forget, baby, your one and only ex has emerged from the slime of anonymity. I've rocketed to stardom... host of *Winner's Circle*." Smile. "Maria worships the ground, et cetera. It took a little doing, but when you became a big wheel at United, it occurred to me that Maria and I should become pals. And when you hoisted yourself up to Numero Uno, I almost dislocated my shoulder patting myself on the back for thinking ahead."

"You've been seeing Tommy?"

"Sure. Maria keeps me posted. On evenings when you work late, go to screenings, or you're out of town on a shoot... you know the drill."

"Tommy never told me. Maria..." Christie choked.

"I would hope not. Tommy promised not to. Maria likewise. It was our little secret. All in good time, I'd surprise you. Didn't I say that?" Big smile at Tommy. Tommy nodded vehemently.

Christie was beside herself with fury. "Barry..." Christie took a deep breath. "Okay. What do you want?"

"I hesitate to be candid, but the truth is I've been thinking about you for a long time. I think we should have a reconciliation."

"He wants us to live together," Tommy said excitedly. "He said he'll take me backpacking."

Christie fought to hold tight to her temper.

"He says we're related," Tommy ran on, wide-eyed. "How, Mom? Is he my uncle, my cousin?"

Christie made herself answer, "No, dear, he's not your uncle or cousin."

"You get one more guess." Barry laughed.

"There's nothing else. Uncles, cousins. You're not my brother? Are you?" His mouth fell open.

"I'm not your brother."

"Then how are we related?" Tommy squealed.

At last Christie found her voice. "I'll explain later, darling. Right now Mr. Easton and I have to talk. How would you like Nan to take you to one of the cutting rooms? Would you like to watch the editing of *The Kiss Off?*"

"Oh, Mom! *The Kiss Off!* Yes!"

"Okay." Christie pressed the intercom. "Nan, put Audrey at your desk. Tell her to hold my calls. You take Tommy down to Mike Galvin. He's editing *The Kiss Off*. I'll meet you there."

"See you, Mom." Tommy left the office at a gallop.

Christie stood up and looked the man squarely in the eyes. "Barry, I repeat, what the hell do you want?"

"This is my first move toward a family reconciliation." He looked straight back at her, giving her his favorite on-air smile . . . ardent, ingratiating. "It's time."

"You're joking." Even as she said it, she knew he wasn't.

"I told you that I want you, Tommy, my entire family reunited. You never did give me credit for family feeling."

"Reunited!" The word was obscene. Disgust showed in each syllable. "You are crazy. Given what I know about your sexual tastes, your boys and girls, your drugs, do you think I would expose Tommy—or myself—to the filth you make of your life?"

Barry gazed at her furious expression and sighed. "You

always were a prude. Hell ... I came to the big city and had a few flings ... sowed a few oats. That doesn't make me a beast or a devil. Truth is, at heart I'm a homebody ... itchin' to settle down."

"For a smart man you are a damn fool!" Christie snapped.

"And you still have a redhead's temper." He gave her a smile that said, let bygones be bygones. "And the fact is, you and I are both successes with a capital 'S'. You're head of United Cinema. And as for your once-needy ex, my contract with *Winner's Circle* is about to be renewed. I'm getting a three hundred percent increase. Plus..." He shrugged as though to make light of it. "... next year I become executive producer. For which, yours truly will receive three points. So, baby, given our private winner's circle, it would be a smart sequel to merge. Tommy needs a father. You need a husband. I need a wife... a family image. Better for my ratings. Better than my being king of sleaze with headlines about my acrobatics and aerobics. It's time I upscaled."

"This is a business proposition?"

"No. Actually I miss you. You were an animal in the sack. And you miss me. You haven't found anyone else. Once upon a time we could spend all day between the sheets. The knack will come back. Add to that, I'm interested in movies. One hand could wash the other. We'd be a very powerful, power couple."

"Go away, Barry."

"Think about it, Christie... think about me."

"I have thought about it. Listen to me, Barry. I'm going to put this in words that a slimeball like you will understand. Get your fucking ass out of here and don't come back."

"Temper... temper." Barry held up both hands. "I'm going, but like General MacArthur, I will return. *Ciao*, baby."

After Barry had left, Christie felt the urge to fumigate the office. This worm, this insect, this swine, this vermin that crawled out from under a rock... this thing was actually her ex-husband... who was asking her to remarry him. She wanted to scream... or at least get very drunk.

Chapter 23

THE HEADLINE appeared on page twenty-four in *Variety*:
A LITTLE SLEIGHT OF HAND AT UNITED?

The article speculated on the rumors of financial irregularities at United Cinema that were unpleasantly reminscent of the saga of David Begelman—the producer of *Close Encounters of the Third Kind*—and the improper dealings that wrought havoc with his career. The article went on to say that no senior executives at United were implicated at this time.

Christie had *Variety* spread out on her desk. Thanks, but no thanks, she said mentally. *Variety*'s statement that no senior executive was implicated at this time implied that one could be at a later time. A dizzying montage flickered across her brain: Harry handing her the forged checks... her recognition of Franco Marconi's handwriting... Justine Duval and the leak... the board meeting... the vote she'd won. Then Jo screwed everything up with her damn memo. Jo's memo... why the hell was she taking so long?

Christie was on the telephone with Louis for fifteen minutes and Harry for another ten. They agreed—tell Guy about the piece in *Variety*. She dialed Jo's interoffice number. Jo's secretary said Jo was in New York filing papers with the court to stop the illegal sales of pirated video cassettes of *The Feathered Serpent*. She was expected back next week. Why wasn't Jo concentrating on that damn memo? To hell with the memo. She might as well call Guy and get it over with. Like it or not, they had to make the mess public—a temporary embarrassment versus a major loss of credibility... and possible criminal charges for concealing a crime.

Guy Macleod was in the middle of an exasperating meeting. When Mrs. Neill told him Christie Larsen was on the line, he refused to take the call. Then he changed his mind. After a curt pleasantry, he listened while Christie read him the article in *Variety*. When she finished he asked, "What is *Variety*?"

For an instant Christie was nonplussed. Then she realized that Guy was being Guy at his most impossible. He knew all about *Variety*. He'd probably read every issue since Macleod Brothers took over United. If he didn't actually read *Variety*, his movie analyst sure as hell did and gave him a capsule summary of everything important. "*Variety* is the major newspaper of show business, the bible of the entertainment industry," she said in the most understanding tone possible. Now what, you pompous ass?

"I see." Guy's voice was condescending, carrying an edge. "I gather you take this item in a meaningless trade journal as a signal to bare our souls to the press."

Christie started to answer, but Guy continued. He sounded as if he was pacifying a retarded child.

"My dear Christie, I am aware there are thousands of newspapers and magazines who fill up space with this kind of muckraking. They're of no importance. None! No one reads *Variety* but actors, actresses, directors, and other such irrelevant people. Let *Variety* print what it chooses. This is Hollywood jerking itself off. As for us, we maintain absolute silence... say nothing, give no interviews. We will proceed—as I assume you are doing—with our own investigation into the matter. Now I'm in a meeting. Good-bye, Christie."

Christie heard the phone go dead. Her eyes, wide open, seemingly focused on a point halfway across the room, were in reality turned inward, watching a slow motion replay of her evening with Simon... of his eyes and voice at the board meeting. She picked up the telephone, dialed Macleod Brothers, and asked for Simon Macleod.

Some minutes later, Simon Macleod insisted that Mrs.

Neill put him through to his brother. Irritated, Guy picked up the phone.

"Mrs. Neill, I told you not to.... Sorry, Simon. Yes. I'm almost finished here. I'll see you at noon."

When Irene Bentley left Guy Macleod's office, she noticed Jo Caro waiting in the reception room.

"Ah. Miss... uhm... Miss Caro? It is Miss Caro, isn't it?"

Jo had been leafing through a magazine. When she glanced up, her eyes held no hint of surprise. She smiled warmly. "Mrs. Bentley... you're back in New York so soon?"

"So soon?" Irene asked in her silky, slurred, worldly voice. "Is it soon?"

"What I mean is, I thought you'd have so many people to see..." Jo was grasping at straws to explain herself to Irene's raised eyebrows. "As I told you, I'm house counsel and I hear everything. I know things didn't go so well back at the store. Christie can be difficult. I want you to know that, personally, I think it's a shame that she lost us *Deirdre*."

"She hasn't lost *Deirdre*... not yet anyway."

"You think it's possible? I thought..."

"What did you think?"

"I thought we'd lost the project so under the circumstances you would go elsewhere." Jo chose her words carefully. "I mean to other studios. That's why I was surprised you were back in New York so soon. You see, I don't believe in trying to cut corners with a property of the strength of *Deirdre*. It will be a big winner, I know it. And the film requires your touch. So you should be kept happy...." She flowed on with an excess of compliments.

"Miss Caro, so much flattery is bad for my business judgement and worse for my character. What are you suggesting?" Irene put a wealth of meaning into the question.

"I'll be in town for a while."

"How long?"

"Until Thursday."

"Hmmm. We might lunch... have drinks. Better, we could have dinner while you're in town."

Jo gave her a wonderful, cunning, affectionate smile. "Marvelous. Let's have dinner... more time to talk."

"Good. I'll check my calendar and ring you. Where are you staying?"

"The Carlyle. United keeps a suite at the Carlyle."

"I'll leave a message." Irene's smile was enigmatic.

"I look forward to our dinner."

Their eyes met in a brief exchange. They were a pair united in a conspiracy, a chancy union since neither knew either the exact nature of the conspiracy or the role they were to play.

Guy was furious at Christie's call to Simon, but he knew Simon better than to let fly at Christie... at least not right away. He began by trying a man to man approach—women are a pain in the ass... except in bed. "That call was standard issue female crap. Like all women, she has a talent for the devious. If she can't persuade me, her next stop is you. The idea is she persuades you, you persuade me, she gets what she wants."

Simon felt distaste at Guy's attitude. Christie had given him back a part of what Kitty had taken away—his genuine fondness for women. "I don't think she's as calculated as you suggest," he said.

"Believe me, Little Brother, she is. Everything she does is calculated. Don't be naive."

"Big Brother, I'm a lot of things but I'm not naive. Besides, calculated or not, I agree with her position."

"You always took women too seriously... almost as seriously as they take themselves. Witness your overreaction to the number Kitty did on you... your former dear, sweet, generous to a fault wife. So now you tumble into bed with Larsen and you think she's Our Sainted Lady of the Silver Screen. Come on, Little Brother, stop frowning. All right ... sorry about the crack. It was juvenile and in poor taste. In any case..."

"In any case, it had nothing to do with my vote at the board meeting. Once I knew about the forgeries, I knew we must tell the public fast, or our asses are exposed. We're asking to be brought up before the SEC on charges of insider trading."

"Jo Caro said that we can buy shares, we can't sell them. All I ask is that you buy."

"Jo Caro is wrong. She's house counsel for a motion picture studio. She knows something about corporate law, and not a damn thing about SEC law. I said it once, I'll say it again. We can't buy, we can't sell. Either way we'd be sitting ducks for an SEC investigation." Simon's mouth remained set. "That's why I want to make the information public now."

"I'm the Chairman of the Board of United, and I say no ... not now. I'm managing partner of Macleod Brothers, and I say we buy United stock. You execute the trades." Although Guy did not raise his voice, there was no question he expected his orders to be carried out.

"And I'm a member of the United board. The board represents the shareholders, and I say you are wrong. I also run the trading desk. Macleod Brothers will not buy or sell a single share of United stock." Simon's tone was equally flat and equally firm. "That was the arrangement our father set up and you agreed to. I run the trading desk ... me, not you. And you're going to live with it."

Guy studied Simon's expression. He knew he was pushing too hard. "All right, Little Brother. Let's not beat a dead horse. I agree we stop trading United. We'll make a clean breast of what happened at the studio ... in time to pass the SEC smell test." Guy became conciliatory, awash with brotherly admiration. Simon was prudent, Simon had vision and foresight ... it was the Macleods against the world.

Listening to Guy, Simon realized that his brother's talk about United was really a preamble to something else.

"Little Brother," Guy said, at last coming to the point. "I want to have a talk with you about women."

"About women in general ... or one woman in particular?"

"One woman in particular."

"Christie Larsen?"

"Yes." Guy's mouth tightened. "To begin with, does Larsen have any idea how close we are? Didn't she think I would tell you about the fishing expedition in *Variety*?"

"You might have overlooked it . . . not important enough to pass on."

"Ordinarily, maybe. That so called newspaper exists on rumor mongering. But since Larsen took it seriously, of course I was going to tell you about it. I tell you everything worth knowing."

Once Simon would have believed Guy without question. Now he wasn't sure. "She thinks of me as a friend," Simon said by way of an explanation. "That's why she wanted to tell me herself."

"Friend? Cut the bullshit, Little Brother. I understand male-female chemistry."

"What the hell does that mean?"

"Come on. We're brothers I know you damn near as well as you know yourself. The woman attracts you. Great!" Guy was being diplomatic. "For a while—after Kitty—I was concerned that you might enter a monastery."

Simon chuckled. This conversation was off the wall. "I never knew you were that concerned . . . I'm not a monk type."

"But now I feel I must warn you."

"About what?"

Guy cleared his throat. "About Christie Larsen. I think you're becoming too involved with the woman."

Simon remained very still. He chewed on the insides of his cheeks.

"And I feel I must say it would be a mistake to get in over your head with . . ."

"What the hell are you talking about?"

"Little Brother, face it. She's a movie type. Not exactly a Hollywood bimbo, but not much more. She wouldn't fit in . . . not with the Macleods, not with the life that you should lead as a Macleod. Didn't marrying Kitty teach you anything? The Macleods made this country. You read our history, you know our heritage. Christie Larsen doesn't belong."

"You mean she should really be another Victoria Manners Macleod?" Simon made no attempt to mask his anger.

Guy heard the anger. His eyes dropped. When he raised them, he glanced at Simon speculatively. Then he shrugged. "I was too young and too wild to take proper care of Vicky.

NAKED CALL

I was careless, which is not to my credit. But if I had it to do over, Vicky would be the perfect wife for me." He let out a great sigh. "That's history. And yes, I would like you to find yourself another Vicky."

"You really dislike Christie, don't you?"

"Dislike is too strong. I don't think about her unless I have to. But I could learn to dislike her quite easily," Guy admitted, "if she comes between us. And I think she is trying to break up the team."

"That's ridiculous."

Guy didn't bat an eye. "I think not. Her calling you about this mud-slinging is the first step. There'll be others."

"Knock it off, Big Brother. You're wrong."

"Maybe. Maybe not." Guy gazed at the ceiling. "And while we're on the subject of United and Larsen, I have an idea that I'd like you to consider . . . even though I know you won't like it, or agree."

Simon asked, "What idea?"

"It may sound Machiavellian but still . . ." Almost a pleading look. "Think it over."

"Think what over?"

"Guy lowered his eyes as if an embarrassing topic had come up. "As I said, you won't like it, but it has occurred to me that perhaps . . . Christie Larsen leaked the news to *Variety* herself?"

Simon stared at Guy as if he were waiting for a cue that this was some kind of joke.

"Think about it. Certainly it was one way to try to force me to make the news public."

"You're wrong."

"No. I think this is only the beginning of her maneuvers."

Simon stared at the floor, frowning slightly, as if the image in his mind held some secret. He looked up at last with a rueful smile. "Well, I've always wanted to play detective. I'm seeing Christie over the July Fourth weekend. The better I know her, the sooner I will know which of us is right . . . and which is wrong."

Christie had Nan check the Ritz Carlton Hotel in Laguna Niguel. The hotel was booked solidly for the Fourth of July weekend. Christie called the hotel herself. An hour later the hotel manager called back. They'd had a cancellation... the Ritz would be delighted to reserve an Ocean Suite for the president of United Cinema and her companion. After she made the reservation, Christie called Simon.

"We're set for the Fourth," she said. "The Ritz Carlton is not cheap—two thousand dollars a night, just for the suite ... meals and drinks not included. What do you..." She hesitated and blurted out, "... think about going Dutch?"

"Sure!" Simon said, laughing. "I like it. It's one of the great contributions of Women's Lib... the Dutch treat."

"That's enough out of you."

They were still laughing when they hung up.

PART NINE

1992
JULY 6–JULY 8

Chapter 24

IT WAS late Sunday after brunch... a shimmering sunlit afternoon. The air was warm and soft with just a hint of moisture carried by the gentle ocean breeze. The secluded terrace was situated high on a bluff overlooking the Pacific. For Christie, the glorious weather was an exhilarating change after the air-conditioned tension of her office. She felt a rush of happiness as she took in the breathtaking view. Along the coastline, golden hills and jagged cliffs sloped or dropped sharply to the ocean, while below them stretched miles of white, sandy beach... miles and miles of California coastline, sometimes called the Orange Riviera. Everything in the world sparkled... the ocean, the sky, the beach.

She was thankful to be alive, despite the chaotic world she'd left behind in Los Angeles. She glanced shyly at Simon, sitting in his white shorts and tennis shirt, sipping iced tea and reading the newspaper. She had reason to be happy. At first, she'd had mixed feelings—nagging doubts—about spending the weekend with Simon. They hardly knew each other. It could be a bad mistake. Christie shook her head, reminding herself that this was just a great weekend, nothing more. Even if the sex was incredible. Astonishing. Forget it. No excuse for mooning like a teenager. Still, the memory of Simon's mouth caressing her body made her flush. Never before had lovemaking approached the lustfulness of her two nights with him... of yesterday afternoon... of this morning.

Simon glanced up and smiled. He observed her tenderly ... the tousled mane of tawny hair, the lines of her shoulders, her long hands, slim ankles, the long legs in white, fringed shorts... a thoroughbred, bred in the bone. Her whole body was a caress.

"What do you want to do now?" He tilted his head. "I think you've had too much brunch to do what comes to mind... for a couple of hours anyway."

Christie smiled... a take on the Gioconda smile. "At the moment I want to do nothing."

"Okay. Do you want to do nothing at the pool, on the tennis court, in Laguna Beach? Because if we stay here, I warn you..."

"I stand warned." She half-rose from the chair and stopped, sat back, and nodded at the paper in his lap. "Why so much interest in the local tip sheet?"

Simon shrugged. "Local newspapers give me a feel of what people who don't live on the main drag think. And they spare me the angst of Tokyo, Washington, and Wall Street."

"Not a word about Hollywood?"

"Sure. What's showing in the Mann Theaters, the Edwards Theaters, and the Beaux Arts—apparently an art movie house, featuring *sex, lies, and videotape*."

"Definitely. A Cannes Film Festival winner. And no mention of my name or United Cinema?"

Simon didn't move a muscle, but he was all attention. "Why would there be?"

"My paranoia is showing. After that leak in *Variety*—'financial irregularities,' they said—the whole thing could explode at any moment."

For two full days Simon had groped for a tactful way to raise the subject of the leak. Now she'd done it for him. "I thought you wanted the forgeries made public. It's happening. Aren't you pleased?"

"Originally, yes—I did want to go public with the story. So did Louis. He changed his mind—and mine—on the flight back to L.A. The news puts me right in the spotlight, where I don't want to be. If we don't find the forger before the story breaks, Louis says my name will be tops on the media list when they dig for suspects. I'll be headlined in *Variety*, the *Enquirer*, the *Wall Street Journal*, you name it."

"Why you?"

NAKED CALL

His question sounded depths within Christie. A full and honest answer was called for. "Because—I quote Louis—to the boys and girls in Hollywood, I'm an outsider . . . not the real thing. I don't drive a Rolls Royce and I still live in the Hollywood Hills, in the first house I bought, not a pricey architectural masterpiece in the Holmby Hills."

That takes care of Guy's theory, Simon thought. He searched her face. "Got any thoughts on who leaked the story?"

"No. Louis is stewing over that. He says I should, too. I guess I am."

"If you hadn't warned me, I'd never have known. Wall Streeters don't read *Variety*."

"I had to warn you. You have a big stake in United. Suppose the leak turns into a sieve?"

Simon's eyes were clear and untroubled. "You play by the rules."

"I do my best. But if the wet smelly stuff hits the fan, the verdict will be guilty long before the trial."

The telephone rang. Simon picked it up. "Maybe. I'll let you know." Then he hung up. "That was von Falkenburg. He wants to know if we still want to browse in Laguna Beach."

Christie mulled this over. "Ahh yes, Herr Kurt von Falkenburg, our own doting, omnipresent concierge. He knows a soft touch when he sees one. You tip him with hundred dollar bills." For the moment, the leak was forgotten.

"Only one hundred dollars at a time."

"Okay. We are now going to play a game called 'Tell The Truth.' How did you swing it? Who did you bribe? I had to pull rank to get an Ocean Suite reservation over the Fourth. How did you mastermind a switch to the hyper-status Club Crown Suite, complete with a personal concierge, a limo at our disposal, one dozen roses in every room, a daily on-the-house bottle of Dom Perignon champagne . . . to say nothing of breakfast, lunch, dinner, or snacks designed to our personal taste and served in the suite?"

"Enough. The price was right."

"At—I believe—four thousand dollars a day? The price was wrong. I can't afford it."

"I said I was exercising Male Lib. I'm affording it."

Christie eyed him curiously. "There are other rich men in America. How did you get this suite for the Fourth of July weekend on such short notice?"

Simon grinned sheepishly and shuffled his feet like a little boy who has been caught with his hand in the cookie jar. "It wasn't that short. I made the reservation the morning after the board meeting."

"After the board meeting!" Christie's brows shot up in surprise. "That's pretty nervy. What made you think I'd be a shoo-in for the weekend? Just because I went to bed with you once? We hardly knew each other."

"I knew you well enough. I hoped I'd know you better ... so I gambled."

"Suppose I didn't accept the invitation."

"I'm a trader. I'm used to taking risks."

Christie's laugh had a sour tinge. "Little did you know what a pushover I'd be."

"You're no pushover," Simon murmured. He wished he could speak more freely. Instead he asked, "Would you like to look around Laguna Beach? See the local art museum..."

"... and watch the boys play volleyball on the main beach. Or maybe we'll do nothing ... just relax by the pool."

"I get the drift. The pool wins. Great! As soon as you slip into something more comfortable ... and more naked ... so I can fantasize about what comes later."

Christie smiled. "You have some fantasy we haven't already acted out? Please! I'm not into pleasure through pain."

"Hmmm. When I was a kid, I read a book about..."

Connie Chung's lead piece on the CBS Sunday night news was, "Scandal has hit Hollywood again. Not sexual scandal ... financial scandal. Informed sources claim that United Cinema, the studio that produced the Academy Award-winning film, *The Feathered Serpent*, has been staggered by losses in the millions of dollars ... losses due to forged checks. The Beverly Hills police are refusing to comment at this time."

NAKED CALL

* * *

Peter Rainer, special editor for the *Los Angeles Times*—hung up the phone. Barbara Saltzman was right. The *Times* had to cover the story... wherever the story led. But this one he'd write himself... make sure there was no lynching by the media as there had been in the McMartin Preschool molestation case. He liked and respected Christie Larsen. She didn't deserve to be put through the wringer. He fingered the keyboard of his computer. "Financial Irregularities at United Cinema?"

Alan Abelson was working on his weekly *Barrons'* column, "Up & Down Wall Street," when the phone rang.
"Yeah. Who is it?"
"Eric Savitz. I just heard a rumor... maybe more than a rumor." He detailed the United Cinema forgery story.
"Very good! *Variety* likes to stick it to Wall Street. Now it's our turn. As the traders say, 'Don't get mad. Get even.' I will."
Abelson flexed his fingers over his computer keyboard. Moving his fingers helped him think. "Hollywood is about to lay an egg... a big, wet, smelly, rotten egg. Not a cinematic egg—they lay plenty of those every year. A financial egg..."

Peter Kann seldom involved himself with the day-to-day operations at the *Wall Street Journal*. As chief executive officer, he rarely had the time. But after turning off the CBS news, he phoned the paper. "I want to speak to editorial first and then to whoever's doing tomorrow's 'Heard on the Street' column."

The pool shimmered like a glassy sapphire. A plump man, breathing hard, was swimming in circles, followed by a splashing, dark-haired child. The pool area was partially deserted. Here and there, sun-bronzed, well-oiled bodies were walking or sitting or lounging, glistening in the sun. In some cases there was too much body to glisten. In others, the bodies deserved a second look.

Christie lay in the white chaise lounge next to Simon, her body relaxed and languorous from the long, slow morning hours of lovemaking and the luscious brunch. Her eyes were closed, shutting out the brilliant blue sky and the sun. But not Simon. She was acutely aware of his closeness. It made her heart pound. If they were alone, she'd...

"Well, well, well. Hello, Christina." It wasn't Simon, but it was familiar. "As always, you look even better without clothes... good enough to eat. I count on that."

Christie's nose took in a remembered smell of soap and shampoo and recent barbering, the spicy scent of Brut, his favorite male cologne. She reached for her sunglasses and opened her eyes, knowing who she'd see. She looked up. There he was—Barry Easton. He hovered over her, grinning salaciously. She grimaced in disgust.

"You're lucky to have her, man, even for a jazzy weekend." Barry shot a swift look in Simon's direction. "She always did provide a full course meal. But eat your fill now—sorry, bad joke—because I'll be moving back in soon."

"Barry!" Christie was filled with pure revulsion.

"Your very own tried and true. Glad to see you're working out, staying trim for me." He glanced at the strawberry blond at his side—a perfect eight-by-ten Hollywood glossy, one of the thousands of clones who haunted the TV and movie casting offices. "This is Heather West."

Christie glared at Barry.

"Ta-ta, Christina. For now." He lifted a brow lazily. "I'll be in touch."

Christie and Simon watched the pair leave the pool area. Neither moved. Neither said anything. It was not one of their compatible silences.

At last Simon asked, "Are you all right?"

His face was impassive. Christie couldn't guess what he was thinking. "I'm all right."

"Who was that?"

Never so much as now did Christie feel the precarious nature of their relationship... this happy, beautiful, untroubled time. It still was so new, so fragile. It hung, at best, by the merest silken thread... at the mercy of any accident that might snap it. Slimy accidents like Barry. Reluctantly she said, "That piece of trash was Barry Easton, my ex-husband."

Simon's expression became rueful. "Since you have a son, he had a father and you had a husband. That's the usual way. Kitty and I—Kitty's my former wife—we never had a child."

Christie lowered her head, exhaled softly, and looked at her hands. Finally her head came up. "I couldn't have made a worse choice. Tommy's the only good thing that came out of it. Thank God, he shows no signs of taking after his father."

Simon made the usual excuses. "You were very young?"

"And stupid. At the time, I was Louis' assistant. He said, 'Don't marry him!' He said, 'You'll live to regret it!' And I've lived to regret it."

"Why did he say he'd be moving back in?"

Christie was ice cold in the sun, her stomach muscles taut and knotted. "He's asked me to remarry him."

Simon gave her a sharp, questioning look.

"I despise him. I want him out of my life."

Simon sat still brooding for a while. At last he asked. "Barry Easton. Is he the host on *Winner's Circle?*"

"Yes."

His brows drew together in concentration. Then his face cleared. "Forget him. I have the perfect solution for our Mr. Barry Easton."

"What?"

"I'll tell you when I've worked out the details. Meanwhile, shall we continue to do nothing here?" Deadpan. "Or how about a shiatsu massage that stimulates the body's energy pathways and relaxes muscular tension through rhythmic pressure?" He started laughing. "A shiatsu massage costs forty dollars. I can get it for you wholesale. If we retire to our suite, you can enjoy a private shiatsu beneath my expert fingers."

Christie smiled, stretching like a contented cat in the sun. "Mmm... so much to choose from. Why don't you decide?"

Simon was ordering drinks when he spied Barry and his girlfriend being seated at a table out of Christie's line of vision. He did his best to keep her occupied, listening attentively while she described the demands of movies made for TV as contrasted with movies made for the big screen. Time passed in animated conversation, and then Simon excused himself to go to the men's room. To his irritation, on leaving the men's room, there was Barry Easton standing in the middle of the aisle, waiting for him.

Barry gave him the Smiling Handshake. "We meet again, friend."

"We're not friends."

"Maybe not. Still, I'd like to do you a good turn."

Simon raised an eyebrow.

"A good turn. I mean it. You see, I thought you looked like an okay guy. So I want to save you some grief... give you the straight dope on my ex." He grinned. "Oh, yes, in case she didn't mention it, Christie Larsen is my ex... my once and future wife. So this is just a friendly tip, friend."

"What do you want?"

"What do I want? I want to fill you in. The straight dope, friend. Just a word to the wise, as they say. I'll take odds she's filled your ear with shit about us. That's her public pose... the Big Deal, high and mighty, above it all. Crap! The woman can't stand anyone knowing I dumped her." He pursed his lips. "The truth is, she's nuts about me... bananas. Poor kid. She writes me letters... hot love letters, real porn. Sends them registered mail to make sure I read them. The fact is, she's been pleading... begging me to take her back." Indulgent smile. "So, finally she wore me down. I said 'Yes'. After all, she's the mother of my son, and I'm a family man at heart. If she didn't have such a lousy temper, I might never have packed up and filed for divorce."

Simon's face was expressionless. "You're a fascinating case, Easton... a psychopathic liar. Payne Whitney could use you as a case study."

I'm only trying to warn you," Barry sighed. He stepped back as if to turn away.

Barry Easton was not a small man. He was a shade over six feet tall and weighed a solid one hundred eighty five pounds. He was also fascinated with the martial arts and had been awarded a Brown Belt in Shotokan Karate... tiger style Karate they called it. He launched a reverse roundhouse kick. He'd executed it perfectly, exactly as his Karate Master had taught him, but incredibly, he missed Simon, who had slid back just far enough to be outside the speeding arc of Barry's foot. Barry tried another tactic—the solar plexus kick. Barry's leg ran into the stone wall of Simon's stomach and the heel of Simon's hand smashed down against his shin. The pain was excruciating. Barry slumped to the floor. When he looked up, Simon was standing over him.

Simon reached down, grabbed hold of Barry's shirt, and hauled him to his feet. He held Barry inches off the ground. With his feet dangling helplessly in the air, Barry no longer felt like a man to be reckoned with.

"Listen carefully, pretty boy," Simon spoke softly. "I took it easy on you. I could have done a lot more. But you are Christie's ex. Get this straight. I'll say it once. Stay away from Christie and her son. Or I will personally beat the living shit out of you. When they find you, it will take a team of plastic surgeons to put Humpty Dumpty together again. And believe me, you won't be as good as new."

Simon let Barry drop. Barry dropped—his legs were too weak to hold him—and slid to the floor.

End of fight.

When Simon returned to the table, the entree he'd ordered was waiting, slices of venison in red claret garnished with green apples and shallots.

Christie smiled at Simon. "The food looks wonderful," she said.

"So do you. And I'm starved. The weekend's been strenuous."

Christie blushed. "You complaining?"

"Noooo," Simon drawled. "That's a *bravo!* I'm thinking what a lucky guy I am."

The last night of their stay at the Ritz Carlton, Christie wore a gold-studded, strapless, slit-to-the-hip evening dress that swirled around her waist, black fishnet stockings, and Arabian Nights-style satin pumps. Simon wore the standard male uniform for formal evenings—black tie, white pleated shirt, black cummerbund, black pants with a black satin stripe, black dinner jacket, and highly polished black leather shoes and black silk stockings. On the dance floor of the Club Grill, people looked and looked again. Especially when Christie gave Simon a lesson in the thigh-to-thigh lambada . . . her skirt was too confining and there were times when she had to raise it almost to her waist. Then the looks became stares of envy and longing. Simon, a quick study, twirled her around the dance floor. A wonderful time was had by all . . . watchers and dancers. Until, at the witching hour of midnight, the flashy couple vanished, taking with them their special light, leaving the Club Grill darker and less exciting.

At midnight, Simon and Christie turned into beachcombers. They drifted like the sand down the long sloping walk to the beach. Simon's arm encircled Christie's waist as they moved beneath the stars. Christie slid off her satin pumps and Simon stepped out of his shoes and socks. The beach was warm and dark and deserted and they slipped off more clothes. Christie took off her embroidered pantyhose and Simon took off his jacket, shirt, and cummerbund. So it went. More and more was slipped out of, unsnapped, unbuttoned. Barefoot and semi-naked, stumbling and kissing, they dragged their clothes along the sand.

The scent of Christie's body, of her hair as Simon buried his face in it, obliterated the world, and between kisses he panted. Swaying against her, he took out his erect penis and Christie stroked it lustfully.

Shaking with desire, Simon dropped his jacket behind Christie and gently lowered her down. Burying his head between her breasts, they lay on the sand, their expensive clothes serving as beach towels, making love. They did it slowly and leisurely, like two dancers well-schooled in each other's movements. Simon loved to caress Christie. Occasionally he would stop and stare at her, overwhelmed by emotions too deep to analyze. She looked so beautiful naked on the sand . . . her hips, her breasts, the tumbled, tawny hair.

Christie savored Simon's lovemaking, the softness and hardness, the powerful hands and the surprising gentleness in his strength. She sighed with delight at the familiar pleasure, fully opened to him, sensing his mounting desire even as she felt her own need. They were both expert at this

NAKED CALL

tantalizing game of playing with each other's bodies... a game that made the pleasure more intense the longer fulfillment was denied.

Until Simon lost control. Aroused by too many seductive caresses, he kissed her passionately and came before she did, leaving her frantic with excitement.

"Please..." she gasped. "Please..." Her vision blurred with the violence of her need.

"Are you never satisfied, darling?" he teased.

"Simon..." Her body trembled, her voice urgent.

His eyes glittered with pleasure as he again kissed and sucked and nibbled on her flesh. "Do you want me?" he asked hoarsely.

"Yes! God! Now!"

Dizzy, trembling, she arched her hips up to meet him, and when she felt him enter her again... a column of hard, hot flesh... a shudder of mindless ecstasy quivered through her body. Her climax came swiftly, even as his did, the heat within both fusing them together.

Afterward they lay quiet, satiated for the moment, stroking each other in a pleasant fatigue. Christie had never been so happy in her life.

Eventually, Simon spoke in a whisper. "You wanted to know how I would take care of Barry Easton?"

"I don't want to think about him now."

"Think about him. I have the perfect solution. Ask me how I'll get rid of Barry Easton."

What the hell... humor him. "How will you get Barry Easton out of my life once and for all?"

"It's simple."

"It is?"

"You'll marry me."

Startled. "What did you say?"

Emphatic. "I said you'll marry me."

"I will?"

"You will. That ends the Barry Easton question. Forever."

Tongue-tied. "Oh!"

"Don't say, 'Oh!' Say, 'Yes!'"

Christie's smile was radiant. She murmured, "My heart is going like mad and yes, I say yes, I will. Yes."

Chapter 25

THE NEXT morning, Christie and Simon waited at LAX for Simon to board the United eight o'clock flight to Kennedy Airport. When the time came, they kissed good-bye ... kissed again ... again. Simon almost missed boarding the plane. Christie stared out the window until the plane disappeared in the morning clouds. She then drove home, showered, told her new housekeeper, Anna, to unpack her bags, skipped breakfast, skipped the newspapers, kissed Tommy, and drove to work.

The moment she entered her office, she knew something was wrong. Nan's smile was brave and artificial ... the way one smiles at a patient whose diagnosis is terminal. "Have a good weekend, Christie?"

"The best."

"I'm glad. I'm sorry you canceled your reservation at the Ritz Carlton. The word is it's heaven."

"It is heaven. I was at the Ritz Carlton this weekend." Christie had a bad moment. "Why?"

"I tried to reach you there."

"I was there."

"You weren't registered."

"Why did you want to reach me?"

"Harry wanted to reach you." Nan's face was grave. "I thought it'd be better if I got to you first rather than he call you out of the blue."

"Why would he call me? What about?"

A few seconds passed in silence.

"I guess you haven't you seen the *L.A. Times* or watched the news on television?"

"No. I glanced at the Laguna Niguel *Sentinel*. That's all."

Nan had nothing to say to this. "I'll call Harry. He'll explain everything."

"Nan, what is this about? I was at the Ritz Carlton... with Simon Macleod. I suppose he registered me as Mrs. Simon Macleod. Is it illegal these days for an unmarried man and an unmarried woman to share a suite?"

"No. Please, Christie. It's just that Harry wanted to talk to you."

"Well, tell Harry to come up here right away!" She wanted to scream, what don't I know? But she didn't.

Once in her office, she sat at her desk and waited. She waited for what seemed a long time. She waited such a long time that by the time Harry appeared, carrying a batch of newspapers, she guessed what had happened.

Harry looked bleary. His white hair was disheveled, very un-Harry-like. He sat down in the chair opposite Christie's desk and slowly, in a strangled voice, proceeded to read one of the headlines. "Financial Irregularities at United Cinema?" Harry sputtered with anger and frustration as he read additional headlines... quotes from articles printed in every major newspaper from New York to California.

"My God! What coverage! Why didn't we sell tickets?"

"And that's only the beginning, folks." Harry choked out a laugh.

In the quiet office, in the sunlight, Christie felt everything go slightly out of kilter. She pointed out, "It had to happen."

"Yeah. Our friendly leak strikes again. Now the press is baying at our heels. You missed all the fun. When they couldn't locate you, I was next. I had at least five calls for interviews... Channel 4, the *Hollywood Reporter*, *Eye on Hollywood*. I forget the others."

"Did you see them?"

"Am I a two-headed monster... some kind of idiot? I said, no comment... fuck off—nicely, of course."

Christie felt unnaturally calm. "The media kicks things out of sight. What they have is pure hearsay."

"I don't think so. In case you didn't notice, that marvelous word, 'alleged,' is missing from the reports. They're damn sure they got the real thing."

Christie had a sudden intuition. "You've heard from the police?"

"Not yet, but we will."

"Why? Detective Garcia has nothing, no concrete evidence. She's in the same position as the media . . . rumors, hearsay."

"You're not listening, Christie. The papers aren't alleging financial irregularities at United, they're stating there are financial irregularities at United. I think I'd better warn you . . ."

"Warn me about what? We've known it was only a matter of time until the media kicked in. The leak had to spurt. It's spurted."

Harry labored to stop twitching. "More has happened."

"Like what?"

"The press didn't light a fire under my ass. The news broke on Sunday. I started looking for you Thursday . . . Thursday afternoon. But you were gone for the weekend when I got back from lunch."

"I left early to meet a friend at LAX. So what?"

"So plenty! Damn it! I don't care when you leave or who you meet at LAX. I don't care if it's Manuel Noriega, unless the bastard owns stock in United. I wanted to talk to you Thursday. Remember Thursday? I had lunch with Sidney Frank on Thursday."

"Sidney Frank? Sidney has a lead?"

"Not exactly a lead." Harry chose his words carefully. "Let's say a would-be lead . . . a lead to a lead. One of Sidney's clients insists on pointing the finger, casting the first stone, accusing, denouncing, disgracing. Do I make myself clear?"

She knew from his tone—let alone his words—that what was coming was a bitch. "Okay. Who is pointing the finger at whom?"

"You won't believe this," he said softly. "I don't. Sidney doesn't. But to cover his ass—he does a lot of business with us—he thought he'd better fill me in, in advance."

"About who committed the forgeries . . . according to the gospel of Sidney Frank's client. What did Sidney say?"

"Jenny Lattimore is going to the police."

NAKED CALL

"Jenny Lattimore, our wound-up toy? Our Jenny is pointing the finger at someone?"

"She sure is." Harry sounded stressed-out.

"At who? Marconi?"

"No. At you."

At first, Christie wasn't sure she'd heard correctly. Then she couldn't think what to say. Too many conflicting thoughts were rattling about in her brain. Finally, she sputtered, "At me?"

"You."

"She's out of her mind."

"Jenny is like an elephant . . . she never forgets. Maybe it's those 1099s you sent out."

"That makes no sense. The 1099s are not grounds for anything as dumb as this."

"Jenny is the reason I was trying to reach you this weekend. I thought you should be prepared."

"Exactly what did Sidney say?"

"He said that Jenny had concrete evidence that you—Christie Larsen, president of United Cinema—had forged a few checks and that . . ."

Christie's intercom buzzed.

"Hold it for a second," she told Harry. "What is it, Nan?"

"Detective Carmella Garcia from the Beverly Hills Police is on line one."

Christie picked up. "Hello. Yes, Detective Garcia? Yes. Now? Of course I can. I appreciate that. It's quite all right," she said, putting the receiver down. What am I talking about, she asked herself. My mouth is out of sync. It isn't all right. It's terrible. "That was Detective Garcia."

"So I gathered. What did she say?"

"She said the police wanted to talk to me." Suddenly, the weekend, during which she'd had very little sleep, caught up with Christie. She felt an enormous fatigue.

"Is Jenny going to be there?"

"I don't know."

"I don't like the smell of this. What do you think?"

Christie wasn't sure what to say. How many ideas could her brain hold simultaneously, each with its own questions?

"I don't think anything. Right now I'll drive over to the

Beverly Hills police station." She stood up. "While I answer questions and, if necessary, swear to whatever I'm asked to swear to on a stack of bibles, call Jo Caro and tell her to stick close to her phone. I want her ready and willing at the other end of the line in case I need legal counsel."

In Beverly Hills, elegant, well groomed criminals steal multi-millions... cars, purses, television sets and drug sales are for the small timers. Stock manipulations, tax shelter swindles, real estate scams, art forgery, and the like flourish among the Beverly Hills mansions with their flower gardens, green lawns, swimming pools, tennis courts and palm trees. Beverly Hills is one of a half dozen or more "paper crime" capitals in the world.

In Beverly Hills the United Cinema embezzlement held little interest for the law enforcement crowd. Compared to the average Beverly Hills con job, this was a chicken shit case.

Detective Garcia did not see it that way. When she hung up the phone after talking to Christie Larsen, she thought about her future... it looked pretty rosy. She had worked in a bank. The embezzlement had fascinating possibilities. It was the kind of case that might lead down paths of glory.

The Beverly Hills police force was not headquartered in an imposing structure designed to pay homage to the blindfolded Goddess of Justice. The location of the station house was so discreet that Christie—who had never before been invited to visit the police station—found her way only by asking directions of passing strangers. Eventually she discovered that the Beverly Hills police headquarters was in the basement of the City Hall. That building, too, could easily have been missed... a matter of mistaken identity. With its mosaic tile dome and landscaping of well-tended lawns and paths, olive, palm, and pepper trees, it looked more like a college library designed by an architect who was conscious of Los Angeles' Spanish inheritance than a building belonging to the city government.

Finally inside the precinct house, Christie gave her name to the sergeant at the desk.

"Detective Garcia asked to talk to me.

The sergeant checked a list. Yes. Detective Garcia was waiting to see Christie Larsen. He motioned to a patrolman who was lounging behind the railing. "Ryan, show Miss Larsen where Room C is. Garcia expects her."

"Sure, Mike."

The patrolman led Christie through a modestly sized room crammed with desks and telephones and people milling around. It looked to Christie like a set from *Hunter* or *Cagney and Lacey*. They came to a closed door. Ryan opened the door and indicated that Christie should enter. She did, and he closed the door behind her. The room was small, grim, windowless, with a low ceiling, stark fluorescent lighting, a dark gray asphalt tile floor, and hard wooden benches set along the walls. It smelled of despair. The room provided a sharp contrast to the two men seated on the benches.

Franco Marconi was sprawled on a bench at one side of the room. He was wearing sneakers, navy silk pants, a white cotton T-shirt, and a baseball cap. Over his shoulder, a loose white sweater was draped. At the other side of the room was a man Christie didn't recognize. In his conservative and meticulously tailored gray suit, he looked highly respectable.

As Christie entered, Mr. Highly Respectable was saying to Franco, "Madeline and I have seen every movie you directed, Mr. Marconi. Actually I've seen most of them twice. I'm a committed Marconi fan. Ever since your first movie, *Vengeance*. That was a remarkable job. Last week I saw *The Feathered Serpent*. Usually I avoid blockbusters, but I trusted you to make it bearable. You did more. That movie was an extraordinary experience."

Franco gazed at the man with affection. "Thank you." He smiled with pretended modesty. "I live for my work." When he looked up and saw Christie standing just inside the room, he sprang to his feet and leaped toward her. "Christie, darling! What is my beloved doing in this hellhole?" He clasped the startled Christie in his arms, kissing her passionately.

Christie squirmed free of Franco's grip. "Let me go, Franco! You're smothering me!"

"Sweetheart! What is it?" His voice was full of mock

concern as he licked her lips. "Brings back memories, doesn't it, Sweetheart?"

"Stop slobbering." Christie pushed him away. "What the hell do you think you're doing?"

Franco dropped his hands and shrugged. "I have to do something to pass the time." His posture drooped as he slouched back to the bench and resumed his sprawl. "I don't know what I'm doing here. I've been waiting for half an hour. *Waiting for Godot*... I never did like that play. While we're at it, what are you doing here?" He glanced at Mr. Highly Respectable. "For that matter, what are you doing here?"

"Frankly, I don't know why I'm here. Detective Garcia called me late yesterday and asked me to be here this morning at ten o'clock. So here I am."

Franco pounced. "Why did she call you?"

Mr. Highly Respectable became flustered. "I can't say I know. I can only assume it has something to do with the photocopies I gave her."

"What photocopies?" Christie asked.

"Photocopies of all the checks issued by United Cinema in 1991." He quickly added, "That is, checks that were drawn on my branch of The Bank of California."

Christie's chest was tight and she couldn't seem to take a deep enough breath. "Are you an executive of The Bank of California, Mr.... er..."

"Dukenfield. Claude Dukenfield."

"You're the manager of the Beverly Hills branch of The Bank of California?"

"I am indeed. And you are Miss Christie Larsen. I read two articles recently on you in the Sunday Calender section of the *Los Angeles Times*. You make women proud of their sex. Few women..."

"Excuse me, Mr. Dukenfield. Have you spoken to Harry Weiss?"

"Yes. We spoke twice."

"Does he know Detective Garcia was in touch with you?"

Claude Dukenfield thought this over. "I don't think so. I believe the detective picked up the printouts of the checks Thursday afternoon. I haven't talked to Mr. Weiss since."

Christie felt as taut as a tennis racket string. "Then Harry

NAKED CALL

doesn't know about Detective Garcia and the checks?"

"Now that you make a point of it, I'm not sure. If you think it would be of interest to Mr. Weiss, I'll call him when we leave here."

"Why are you here, Christie?" Franco was genuinely curious.

At this point Detective Garcia entered, followed by Jenny Lattimore and Matt Renault.

Jenny Lattimore surveyed the room arrogantly. She was a tall, expensively dressed woman who projected the ruthless sensuality of a trained sexual athlete. Even this early in the morning, her jewelry was formidable—heavy gold bracelets, gold earrings, and numerous gold chains. Breathing a little heavily, she paused and stared at Christie. Her look was poisonous and full of obscenities.

Franco jumped to his feet. "Jenny, darling! You, too? And Matt . . . naturally." His voice was full of innuendo. "How are you, Matt? Nice seeing you again. If we had a Jacuzzi we could all sit naked in the hot water and solve the world's problems." He spun around to face Detective Garcia, his good humor erased. "Okay, Madam Policewoman, why the hell are we here?"

"I'm sorry to have inconvenienced you, Mr. Marconi, but I was waiting for Miss Lattimore and Mr. Renault."

"Mr. Renault! How nice." Claude Dukenfield stood up and held out his hand. "We meet again."

"Good to see you, Dukenfield. Sorry the circumstances aren't more pleasant."

"Matt! Quit the crappy mammy palaver. Let's get down to the nitty gritty and get our asses out of here." Jenny glared at Christie with live hatred.

"Yes, Miss Lattimore. I think that's a fine idea," Garcia said. "Miss Larsen, Mr. Dukenfield, Mr. Marconi . . . and Miss Lattimore and Mr. Renault . . . I've brought you all here for a specific reason."

"This had better be good." Franco started to pace. "I have a luncheon appointment. And before that a dentist appointment that they're holding open for me."

"Sit down, Mr. Marconi." Garcia's tone sat Franco down. She continued. "I asked all of you to meet me here because something of a seriously criminal nature has come up in connection with United Cinema."

"Yeah. I read about that. Why isn't Louis Levy here?" Franco's nerve endings were having a field day. "I have a production contract..."

"Please, Mr. Marconi. At the moment the studio itself is not involved. But someone of importance connected to the studio will shortly face serious charges."

Jenny's eyes were balls of fire as she stared at Christie. "I would say criminal charges."

"We're looking at embezzlement... grand larceny," Garcia said, "with extensive ramifications that could run into millions of dollars."

Franco whistled softly. "A real professional job? Well, sorry to disappoint you, Detective. I can't play an embezzler. I might embezzle if I knew how, but I don't."

"Frankly, Mr. Marconi, originally you were at the top of my list of suspects."

Franco's eyes widened. "Me?"

"Yes, Mr. Marconi. I spent the entire Fourth of July weekend—night and day—reviewing printouts of the checks drawn on *The Feathered Serpent* account set up by United Cinema."

"I got an Oscar for that film!" Franco yelped.

"Why concentrate on *The Feathered Serpent*?" Christie asked quietly.

"My source told me that was where the action was."

"Is your source reliable?" Again, the leak.

"Absolutely." Garcia gave Christie a smile. A warm, compassionate smile. She meant it. It gave Christie a chill. The smile was served with the prisoner's last meal.

"You can't make an Oscar film on the cheapo," Franco insisted.

"I was not interested in the budget," Detective Garcia said coldly. "What I was looking for was forged checks."

"Forged checks?" Dukenfield was overwhelmed.

Franco looked baffled. But in seconds his brain began to click. "Only three people could authorize checks drawn on *The Feathered Serpent*. At the home office, the treasurer. That's Harry Weiss. And his assistant—Edgardo Silvera—in case Harry had a stroke. And on location, me."

NAKED CALL 365

"Right! You've named the three. That's why, as I said, I suspected you of the forgeries."

"This is ridiculous!" Franco was on his feet, about to do an operatic performance . . . outraged innocence . . . Iago in *Otello*.

"Mr. Marconi, for the last time, sit down!" He did.

"Why me? Why not Weiss or Silvera?"

"Because the forged checks were signed by you."

Franco stared wildly around the room. "You bet your ass I signed a bunch of checks on location. That wasn't forgery. That was me signing for legitimate expenses." He appealed to Jenny. "You had your promotion tour expenses . . ."

"Darling, I know. Don't worry."

"Chita had a toilet that needed repair." Franco was agonizing with honesty. "Maureen Corley needed . . ."

"I know. Miss Corley's name is on two of the checks."

"Two checks? What the hell are you talking about? I signed one check! You got that? One check! I remember."

"There are two checks made out to Miss Corley."

Franco shook his head. "I signed one check. One, one scraping"

"Mr. Marconi, I don't doubt that you had numerous location expenses. I said that's not my concern. What is my concern is that three checks were actually signed by you . . ." Carmella Garcia paused, enjoying her moment of stardom among the stars. ". . . And three checks were not signed by you. Your signature was forged."

"My God! The bank paid on the forged checks." Claude Dukenfield was aghast.

"It sure did. A forged check was written to Maureen Corley Supervia, another to Gary Chang, and one to Ted Lord. Those forged checks add up to about two hundred thousand dollars. That money was embezzled from United Cinema. We're talking about grand larceny. There may be more checks, but I doubt it. My investigation was thorough, and when I checked with Miss Lattimore, she verified my findings. She told me that three checks were all that were forged."

"Excuse me, Detective Garcia, but I don't follow you."

Christie's voice was steady. "What does Jenny Lattimore know about your allegedly forged checks?"

Jenny was all teeth and fury, a rutting bitch in heat. "I know because you—Christie Larsen—you fucked Matt's brains out to get him to cash them for you."

"I did what?"

"You fucked like a jack rabbit with my Matt. It wouldn't have bothered me so much if you'd really fallen for the guy. A wet cunt has no conscience . . . I know that better than most women. But you're a cold cunt. You only spread for Matt so he'd do your dirty work."

"You're out of your mind. I barely know Matt Renault."

"You know me, Christie . . . very well. Yes, you do." Matt's voice was as intimate as the rustle of sheets. "I took three checks to the bank because you asked me to do it . . . just for you. Dukenfield here cashed them, and I gave the cash to you."

"Mr. Renault, I remember. I did. Oh my! I personally cashed those checks for you. I cashed forged checks." Claude Dukenfield thought he might faint.

"Don't worry, Claude." Matt poured oil on troubled waters. "You're clean."

"You told me Mr. Marconi had okayed those checks. I swear he did." Dukenfield was talking to Matt and Carmella Garcia at once.

"I thought Franco okayed them. That's what Christie told me."

The banker was beginning to resemble a melting candle.

"Relax, Claude. Relax."

"How can I relax? The bank is liable for those checks . . . two hundred thousand dollars. The regional manager will climb all over me. I'll be fired. I trusted you! You're a common thief! A forger . . ."

Garcia thought Dukenfield might have a heart attack. "Mr. Renault is neither a thief nor a forger. He thought he was telling you the truth," she explained. "That is why I suspected Mr. Marconi of the forgeries.

Franco started to choke.

"Then something happened ten days ago that changed my thinking. Like most crimes, successful detective work is a combination of hard leg work and lucky breaks. I did the leg work. The lucky break was Jenny Lattimore's visit. She told me about Matt Renault and the checks he cashed. We combined our information, and here we all are."

"You bet your ass I told you. You think I'd let that Larsen bitch fuck around with my man?" The venom of Jenny's slashing at Christie filled the room. "She promised him a screen career. You know the old gag. Stick with me, kid, and you'll wear diamonds. Everybody knows Matt photographs like shit."

"That's true," Franco nodded. "Remember, Christie, I told you that in Mexico."

There was silence for a moment in the small room. Then Matt cleared his throat. He stared at Christie as if he were about to say one of the most important things she would ever hear in her entire life. "I am sorry, Christie. It was great. You were great. But I discovered Jenny is more important to me than even the chance of a screen career. So when Jenny started asking where I was spending my evenings away from her . . . well . . . I told her. And I guess I was ashamed so I told her why." His smile was almost boyishly bashful. "I can't keep anything from Jenny. She knows me too well. You see, for the first time in my life, I'm in love."

Christie shook off her paralysis. "Jesus Christ! I've had it! Jenny! She'll believe anything you tell her, as long as it's flattering. But you? You're something else again. A paid by the pop stud, a liar, and I don't know what else." Then she asked, as if she really wanted to know, "And where am I supposed to have gotten the checks that you cashed signed by Franco Marconi?"

"Ah, Christie, you know." Matt's tone held a patronizing note. "Come on, Christie, baby. It's me, your Matt. I'm willing to give you the benefit of the doubt, but we know you didn't get them from Franco. You forged Marconi's signature. I only wish you hadn't gotten me into this. You almost ruined my chances with Jenny."

"Oh, you poor baby. I almost ruined your chances with . . . If this wasn't so serious, it would be funny. And as for you, Jenny . . ." Christie crossed the room and stood toe to toe with Jenny Lattimore. ". . . This is what I think of you and your wet cunt." She smacked Jenny across the face with her open hand as hard as she could.

Jenny staggered back. Her legs hit the bench and she sat down—fast! The imprint of Christie's hand on her cheek was clearly apparent, even through the heavy pancake makeup she always wore.

Detective Garcia twisted Christie's arm behind her back. Christie would never forget the detective's next words... the words she had only heard watching television crime stories. "You are under arrest for the forging of three checks drawn on the account of *The Feathered Serpent*—"

Christie blazed, "On the say-so of that slime ball, you'd arrest me?"

"You have the right to remain silent..." Garcia began.

The one phone call Christie was allowed she made to Jo Caro. She told Jo to come to the Beverly Hills police station and have a bail bondsman ready to post bail... a substantial bail. Jo showed up in double-quick time. She took Christie's hand and gave her a long, steady gaze. "I don't know what I thought I was doing, going to bed with a lying bastard like Matt Renault. I'm in this with you for the long haul. You've always been my best friend... you always will be." Her grip was deliberate... firm.

Christie spent a few hours in an unpleasant holding pen while Jo hunted up the bail bondsman. Eventually Judge Miguel Lopez released her on her own recognizance. Driving back to the studio, Christie's mind was clear and perceptive. It didn't add up. Detective Garcia had discovered only the duplicate forged checks... three checks. She hadn't discovered the other four checks. They weren't duplicates, just straight forgeries. Those were written to Jake Jakes, Jeff Chambers, the Grossmans, and poor Julian Henessy. Either Matt Renault didn't know about them or, if he did, he wasn't saying. What the hell was he up to? And why?

The phones in Christie's office rang ninety-seven times that day. Nan took messages from people with whom Christie had worked and those who had hoped to work with her ... agents, directors, producers, actors, actresses, writers

NAKED CALL

... all professionally sympathetic and a few professionally friendly. What they really wanted was the inside info... who did what to whom? Except for Louis Levy. Louis wanted to help, but what could he do besides put out the word that she was innocent?

"Nothing, Louis," Christie said. "You warned me I was vulnerable. I am."

There were the calls from the media. The local NBC, ABC, and CBS channels, the network newsdesks in New York, the Channel 9 news team, the Channel 11 news team, the Channel 5 news team, the *Eye On Hollywood* producer ... everyone wanted an interview. They would bring cameras to the studio and do a live interview with Christie. Nan fielded calls from *Variety*, the *Hollywood Reporter*, the *L. A. Times*, the *New York Times*, the *Wall Street Journal*, *Barrons*, the business magazines, and a host of smaller papers and trade publications. The coverage of the arrest of Christie Larsen, president of United Cinema, on grand larceny charges was national... hell, it was international news. Guy Macleod left a message that Christie was fired. Be out of the studio by the end of the day.

But Simon didn't call. At first, Christie told herself his plane was late landing. Then, maybe the phones were so busy he couldn't get through. After that, maybe he didn't want to speak to her. Finally, maybe he didn't really love her. Men and women say all kinds of things after sex. They propose, make vows, say things they forget or regret in the morning. Maybe it was just his weekend for Band-Aid sex. The one thing she knew now was that Simon Macleod had to call her. First. She was too hurt, too humiliated, and, yes, too proud, to call him.

PART TEN

1992
JULY 8–JULY 16

Chapter 26

IN THE Macleod Brothers trading room, the phones were ringing off the hooks and the decibel count would have drowned out the screech of a subway grinding to a stop.

"Sell my United. Sell it! I want out," Mrs. Rosalie Johnson screamed into her phone."

Ira Benjamin held the receiver a foot away from his ear. He'd read about deafness in teenagers who listened to loud rock music. By the time the market closed today, he might be deaf.

"I can't," he groaned.

"You can! It's my right to sell. Sell! Or I'll sue you! I'll sue the New York Stock Exchange." A fatal urgency was in her voice.

"I know... you'll sue." Ira was patient. He'd been patient with the twenty-five previous calls demanding he sell their United Cinema stock. "Try to understand, Mrs. Johnson. For you to sell your United stock, someone...," He didn't say, some idiot, "... must be willing to buy your United stock. But there are no buyers. The president of United Cinema was arrested on embezzlement charges."

"Ira, sell the stock or I call my lawyers." Rosalie slammed down the receiver.

"Mrs. Johnson," Ira pleaded into the dead line. He turned his head to the man at the next desk. "Bernie! Wake up! The world is ending! Don't miss it!"

Bernie Mefford didn't answer Ira. He didn't answer his ringing phone. He hadn't moved for an hour. He sat frozen, never taking his eyes off the CRT over his desk. United hadn't opened... there was nothing to see. In his mind's eye he saw numbers that weren't there... loses, huge losses, his losses, his equity in Macleod Brothers melting away. A gut-wrenching business . . . his ulcer was eating his stomach, his heart was burning.

"Poor Bernie. He's gone 'round the bend." Ira was dry-mouthed. The trading floor was always bedlam, but this was authentic bedlam . . . St. Mary of Bethlehem type bedlam . . . as in the lunatic asylum in London. The lunatics were yowling, wailing, baying into their phones, at the ceiling, the floor, the walls . . . at customers, at each other, at themselves. Their panicky eyes were leaping wildly about the room, staring everywhere, occasionally at the Quotron Board where each trade ran from left to right in a continuous stream of numbers. The numbers had no meaning. At Macleod Brothers, the single stock the traders watched was United Cinema. United Cinema was not trading.

Ira levered himself out of his chair and trotted down the aisle to the Fish Bowl. He opened the door in time to see Simon slam the phone receiver. The plastic telephone stand shattered. "What's wrong . . . besides everything else?" Ira asked.

"Christie's wrong. I've been trying to get through to her for over an hour. Her goddamned private line rings. And rings. The answering machine doesn't pick up. She must be home, but she won't answer the phone."

"If you were in her spot, would you answer the phone?"

Simon stood up. "Maybe not. But I'd call me."

Ira hesitated before asking, "Simon, the firm is getting killed. How bad is it? Are we dead?"

"It's bad. I'll know more after I see Guy. He's waiting for me. I wanted to touch base first with Christie."

"In up to your ass?" Ira asked.

Simon grunted. "Way over my head." He picked up the receiver and dialed again. He waited. "She won't pick up, damn it. Stay here, Ira. Christie knows my private number. If she calls, you hang onto her and get me. I'll be with Guy."

Simon brushed past Mrs. Neill and entered Guy's office without knocking. He stopped dead in his tracks. Simon had never seen Guy in the office without his jacket on, his Gucci loafers polished to a mirror-like gloss, and his narrow tie tied in the tiniest of knots in the very center of his collar

NAKED CALL

... no garish Windsor knot for Guy Macleod. That is, not until today. Today was a no-knot day.

Guy was sitting at his desk, his coat draped over the back of the chair, his shoeless feet resting on his desk, his collar open, and his tie halfway between his neck and his belt buckle. It startled Simon to see that Guy hadn't shaved that morning. Simon dropped into a chair and waited ... and waited. Finally he asked, "How bad is it?"

"Bad," was Guy's terse response.

"Are we out of business?"

"Not yet. Depends on how far down United opens tomorrow. You know the New York Stock Exchange capital requirements. Over a ten to one debt to equity ratio and we're on the danger list. Over a fifteen to one debt to equity ratio and it's bankruptcy. The Board of Governors will force us into a Chapter 10. We're not eligible for a Chapter 11."

He'd bought much too much United stock with the firm's money. Simon gently pounded his right fist into his left palm. Guy had insisted he buy far too much United stock with the firm's money.

"Give it to me in hard numbers. How much does United have to drop before we go belly-up?"

"Twenty points down puts us on the danger watch. Thirty points down, the game's over." Guy's self-control was almost perfect. Except for the tightness with which his lips were stretched against his teeth and his inability to look directly at Simon, he could have been talking about a football score.

"Humph! It'll open twenty points down for sure. Thirty points ... maybe not."

"Why not? What's to stop the stock from falling thirty points ... forty points?" Guy asked sharply.

"A couple of things. I think you can get Irene Bentley to announce she'll stick with United. I think Louis Levy can handle Marconi. If United announces that Franco Marconi, the Academy Award-winning director, will direct *Deirdre of the Sorrows,* I think Wall Street will listen. The Street lives on dreams. I think the dream of another winner like *The Feathered Serpent* will put a floor under United ... between fifteen and twenty points down."

"Too many 'I thinks' in that scenario," Guy said dryly.

"You got a better idea?"

"Summo National Bank."

"The Japanese bank... bigger than Citibank." Simon saw where Guy was heading.

"I talked to Araturo Takahashi—"

"You speak Japanese?"

"He speaks English. All our yellow brethren speak English... when they want to." Despite his need for Japanese money—or maybe because of that need—Guy was unable to contain his resentment of the Japanese. They were so rich, so powerful... and they weren't his kind.

"I take it Takahashi wanted to speak English. What's the deal? How much money will they put up and what will they get?"

"That's up to you."

Simon stared. "Me?"

"You. The Japanese have one thing in common with Americans: They're sports crazy. Baseball, golf, skiing... big crazes. But Takahashi loves football... the controlled—and not so controlled—violence. The New York Giants are his favorite team. He has videotapes of every game the Giants have played in the last fifteen years. He has a tape of the game where what was his name...?"

"Wendell Roosevelt Corey." Simon's nail traced the fine scar on the side of his knee.

"Wendell Roosevelt Corey blindsided you..."

"Crack-back block."

"... and finished your career. Takahashi thinks you were the prototype of today's defensive end. Do you know what he's talking about?" Never mind. He wants to meet you ... not me ... to negotiate a deal with you... not me. That football hobby of yours may finally be of some use to Macleod Brothers."

"It's my impression I go to Tokyo... Tokyo doesn't come to us."

"On the first plane available. You're expected in the bank's Tokyo headquarters in two days at ten A.M. Tokyo time."

"How much cash am I looking for?"

"Four to five hundred million."

"What are we offering for that kind of money?"

"The usual. A subordinated lender position. Interest at two percent over prime. The loan should be for five years . . . enough time for United Cinema stock to come back. Then the great football fan can take his money and stick it."

"Suppose he doesn't want to be a lender to a banking house in danger of going under? Suppose he wants equity . . . a piece of Macleod Brothers?"

Anger brought Guy's normal color to his face. "Talk him out of it. No equity, Simon. We'd never get rid of the bastard."

"What if he insists?"

"Call me before you make any deal."

Simon rose to his feet. He grinned at Guy. "Relax, Big Brother. The Macleods against the world."

"If not us, who?"

Guy watched Simon leave. Then he sat back in his chair, glad to get rid of his brother. Eighteen hours to Tokyo . . . Simon'd be there a week at least . . . that was long enough. Guy stared into space. How much did he owe his father? Not that much. He was sick of the question. He owed only one person . . . himself. By the time Simon returned, it would be over . . . settled . . . like nailing the lid on the coffin.

Matt Renault drove west on Santa Monica Boulevard, well within the speed limit. He thought about his work. Nothing was ever put in writing. They gave him a long leash. As long as he got the job done they didn't much care how he did it. The payoff was money—lots of money—and more work. If he blew it, he was out there by himself, alone, not a friend in the world. That was okay. He didn't make the rules, but he could live with them. He turned north onto Butler Street . . . only a few blocks to his house. Matt liked the relative obscurity of living in West L.A. Located between statusy Beverly Hills, where perfume granules were sprinkled on the garbage dump, and the rent-controlled People's Republic of Santa Monica, West L.A. was resolutely middle class.

Matt turned left and carefully parked his Mercedes 550SL in the driveway leading up to the small house he rented for eleven hundred dollars a month . . . a steal. Matt liked the house. It gave him a reasonable amount of privacy.

After shutting off the motor, Matt attached a device that locked the steering wheel in place. He preferred the lock to an alarm. Alarms were a pain in the ass. They could be disconnected by a slick thief or go off for no reason, wailing away in the middle of the night, getting him all sorts of neighborly attention which he didn't need . . . alerting the police. He could do without the police. Matt thought about the car . . . Jenny's gift on their six-month anniversary. He suffered a brief spasm of gratitude. It didn't last. He'd worked his tail off for the Merc . . . balled her regularly—sometimes two or three times a day—for the six months. She was a wild woman in the sack . . . on the floor . . . in the Jacuzzi . . . anywhere. She didn't simply spread her legs and fuck . . . not Jenny. She was an actress giving an Academy Award-winning performance in an X-rated film. And he was the supporting cast. Jenny was becoming a crasher. He'd be glad when it was time to close up shop. Soon, baby, soon, he promised himself.

Acting on long habit, Matt slowly slid out of the car. As he closed the car door, he glanced ever so briefly at the cars already parked along the street. All empty? They were. He had good reason for his care . . . the controlled fear of the professional. One day someone might appear . . . some long forgotten enemy, or one of more recent vintage. Someone who—in anguish, or outrage, or fury—would attempt to extract payment in kind for any of a number of betrayals. Betrayals were his speciality.

He walked to the door. The house was dark, the curtains were the same as they had been yesterday evening when he left for Jenny's house. He climbed the step to the front door. There were two locks. One was a Schlage deadbolt. Neither lock interested Matt. They were decoys for the amateurs. The people he wanted to keep out would not be stopped by locks. What did interest Matt was the single hair. Every time Matt left the house, he set a single hair at the top of the door and held the hair in place as he closed the door. If anyone opened the door, the hair would drift, unnoticed, to the ground. Matt didn't want any surprises.

As on all other nights that he'd lived in West L.A., the

NAKED CALL

hair was in place. When he opened the front door, he froze. There was light in the kitchen . . . the light from the open refrigerator. In the patch of light, Matt saw an elegant, black-leather attaché case on the kitchen table. The sound of liquor being poured from a bottle suggested that whoever was visiting knew where everything was . . . knew his habit of keeping vodka and gin on ice. The intruder also knew him well enough to know about the hair held in place by the front door . . . he'd had the sense to replace the hair after opening the door. It was more than likely that the owner of the attaché case was not an enemy, but rather someone with whom he had worked closely.

Softly, Matt tiptoed through the living room to the kitchen door. First he saw the open refrigerator door. Then two Gucci loafers walked around the door. Then Stavros Lennos was smiling and holding a small glass of vodka.

"Stavros!" he exclaimed.

"Congratulations, Matt," Stavros said. "You did very well."

Matt thought about this. He was worth the praise and every nickel he was paid. If that was all this meeting was about . . . "Thank you," he said. "I did my best."

"Very well. Join me in a celebration drink while we discuss your future."

Matt nodded. He watched Stavros take the bottle of gin out of the refrigerator, get another glass, and pour him a stiff shot. Matt snapped on the kitchen light and sat down on a wooden chair at the Formica-topped kitchen table. In the stark fluorescent light, the kitchen looked as if the small house was empty . . . no one lived there. The master bedroom was the only exception. That room was sparsely furnished . . . one wooden chair, a king-sized bed with blue silk sheets and a light wool blanket, a rare Tibetan tiger rug, a nineteenth-century cheval mirror, and an early Grand Rapids bureau. But other than that there was nothing of interest in the room, except for the two closets which were jammed with jeans, tennis outfits, golf slacks, and men's suits, jackets, and pants with Ralph Lauren, Armani, and Calvin Klein labels, all paid for by Jenny Lattimore.

On a job, Matt lived like an ascetic. Only his taste in liquor and canapes, the silk sheets and the tiger rug reflected another side of his nature . . . sybaritic and cultivated. When he chose to exercise it—between assignments—Matt had impeccable taste. His extensive wardrobe was part of his professional gear . . . selected by him, paid for by Jenny Lattimore, who took pride in educating her wild stallion.

"I would like to wind up a few details." Stavros sat down at the kitchen table, placed a glass of gin in front of another chair, and nodded for Matt to join him. "Tell me what you think of her?"

"Cold, congenitally sex-starved, fiercely ambitious. A Napoleonic complex in high heels." Matt shrugged. "But not blinded by ambition or sex. Not as big a fool as I thought she'd be."

Stavros said nothing for a few minutes. "I'm glad you realize that," he said finally. "Be careful."

"Thank you for the concern."

"My concern for you is selfish."

"I know." Matt sipped his drink. "As selfish as my concern for myself."

"And now, no more exercises in penmanship."

"*E finito.* I won't dot another 'i' or flourish another 'M' for Marconi."

"You did seven?" Stavros asked.

"Seven as per instruction. And Garcia couldn't have been more cooperative if she'd been on the take." He went on to describe how the detective had reviewed all United Cinema checks written on United's account in the Beverly Hills branch of the Bank of California.

"And she found three forgeries?"

"The three duplicate checks. It went smooth as silk. She would have had to be on the inside of the United operation to know about the other four. But Christie Larsen is on the inside. That woman is another kettle of fish."

"What do you mean?"

"I saw the lady in action. She's nobody's pushover. She knows she's been framed. I'll bet money she knows exactly how many checks were forged and knows Garcia doesn't have the full story."

"You're a suspicious man."

Matt nodded. "It's why I'm still alive."

"What does your ladyfriend think?"

"Naturally she knows there are seven forged checks," Matt said, a little bemused. He stared at Stavros and frowned. "The forgery charge won't stick to Larsen. You realize that?"

Stavros sipped his drink. "Of course. I never intended it to."

Matt took a sip of his gin. He was aware that he saw only a portion of the puzzle. There were a lot of missing pieces about which he didn't know. His best guess was that it had something to do with control of United Cinema. But whatever was going on was none of his business. He didn't want to know more than was absolutely necessary. The more he knew, the more likely he was to get into trouble.

By the way, Matt," Stavros said, "I've been meaning to ask you. How did you learn to forge signatures?"

"My father. Giuseppe."

"I should have guessed. Exactly how do you copy signatures so perfectly?"

"I get a sample and study it."

"Where did you get a sample of Marconi's signature?"

"From Jenny. I told her a Mercedes would keep me happy. She asked Marconi for sixty thousand dollars. Marconi gave her the check to keep her happy. I studied it for an hour. Then I practiced."

"Tracing it?"

"No! Tracing a signature is too precise. No one ever signs their name exactly the same way twice. I write it upside down and backward... a mirror image."

"Unique." Stavros paused. In the gentlest tone imaginable, he said, "How did Julian Hennesy learn about your talent?"

The question exploded in Matt's ears like a grenade. He'd been waiting for the question... hoping and praying it would never come up, knowing it would.

Still calm, he said, "I was a damn fool, that's how."

"Were you drunk?"

"No. I don't have that excuse. It just happened. In the evening, after a day in front of the camera, Jenny would take a nap before we had sex. That was my free time. Sometimes Julian and I would sit on the *hacienda* porch rapping. He told me all about wanting to be a painter. One evening he brought out a pad of yellow paper and showed me a series of scrawls of his name and asked me what I thought. Which one did I think would look best as his signature on a painting? I pulled a damn fool stunt." Matt's face had grown pale. "I had to prove to Julian that I was more than Jenny's walking, talking vibrator. I studied each signature, took his pencil, and copied them all, one by one. After that, I put together a combination of three signatures and wrote it out. 'That's how it should look. Loose, but legible. Flashy, but not too flashy,' I said. I was a real hero. Julian liked the signature I invented and tried to copy it. He couldn't. He kept trying and kept making lousy scribbles. I said he'd get the hang with practice. He said, 'You didn't practice copying mine?' I told him I had a good eye . . . a kind of gift. He thought about this. Then he asked if I could draw. Maybe I had artistic talent? I said I couldn't draw and didn't have any artistic talent. After that we got off the subject of my talent and his signature and got to talking about women. Later, when the shit hit the fan, he must have put two and two together." Matt's mouth was very dry. The gin didn't help.

"Then what happened?"

"Two and two got plugged into the Frank & Farber accounting network. Julian called Harvey Hartman, who works for Frank & Farber. Harvey told Sidney Frank, who told Lester Farber, who is Jenny's accountant . . . and Jenny told me about Julian Hennesy's private detective work. She laughed her head off. So did I." Matt's face was ghastly.

"And you gave no one else penmanship exhibitions?" Stavros asked gently.

Matt shook his head. He didn't dare say he wasn't that big of a damn fool. He'd been too big a fool already.

Stavros stared at the bare walls. "As I said earlier, you did a fine job."

When Matt spoke, he sounded choked. "You know, even if Julian had accused me, it would have gone nowhere. He couldn't prove anything. His word against mine."

"It would have frightened the fishes."

"Any fish I know? Maybe I could have . . ." Matt stopped himself. He was grasping at straws. He was desperate . . .

NAKED CALL

desperate men make more damn fool mistakes. "I should never have opened my big mouth," he murmured.

"You almost ruined my timetable."

Matt drained his drink but didn't speak.

"I always believed you could be trusted."

"What can I say?" Matt knew better than to beg for his life. "I'm sorry. I acted like a fool."

"Yes, Matt, you did. Because of you we had to dispose of Julian Hennesy. I regret having to order it done. The man was wasted... in the real sense. I despise waste."

Matt stared at his shoes.

Stavros let out a heavy sigh. "Enough recriminations. I will hear from you when the second shoe drops."

"Yes."

Stavros nodded toward the attaché case on the table. "Yours. Next time I hear from you, you'll pick up the second half at Jeffrey Moore's office, Maxwell, Gluck & Moore in Century City. He'll expect you."

Matt felt queasy. "I'll find Moore," he said. So what? He might never live to use the money.

Stavros put his drink down on the table and stood up to go. Matt stood up, too, hypnotized, still holding his glass.

"I have always been very proud of you," Stavros said. He took Matt's head between his two hands. Matt didn't move a muscle. "You did an almost perfect job, Mario." Then he pulled Matt's head toward him and kissed him on both cheeks. There was a heartbeat of silence as he stared into Matt's eyes. He dropped his hands, stepped back, and regarded Matt thoughtfully. "I hope to be proud of you again. Next time, Mario, do a perfect job."

Matt closed his eyes with relief. He was off the hook... forgiven. He wouldn't die for his mistake. "Thank you, Stavros," he whispered. But Stavros never heard him. Stavros Lennos had come, done what he'd intended to do, and left. Matt heard the front door slam.

Afterward, Matt sat for a while in the kitchen staring at the attaché case. He didn't feel like opening it. There was two hundred fifty thousand dollars in that attache case, exactly as promised. Stavros was a man of his word. But if he ever made another blunder like this Julian bit, he'd better get into the FBI witness protection program. Running for your life from the Family would be one hell of a short run.

Chapter 27

WALL STREET, the stock market—why the price of a stock goes up or goes down—is a mystery to most investors. The generally accepted explanations, "More buyers than sellers," or, "More sellers than buyers," are neat, orderly, logical . . . sometimes accurate. When asked why stocks go up and down, Bernard Baruch supposedly remarked, "The market will fluctuate." Clearly, the movement of stocks is a mystery. And of all Wall Street mysteries, nothing is as mysterious as the way the Wall Street Specialist works.

Wall Street Specialist . . . the term reeks of arcane lore half as old as alchemy . . . and almost as efficient. Wall Streeters know that Specialists "make the market" in stocks—they set the price of a stock. But exactly how the Specialists set the buy and sell prices of stocks—how they do what they do—remains more mysterious than the original formula for Coca-Cola.

The firm of Brady, Walker and Kraus had been chosen by the governers of the New York Stock Exchange as the Specialists on United Cinema stock, a gift for which they were truly grateful . . . as long as they were able to raise the price of the stock.

Then came the announcement of the arrest of Christie Larsen, president of United Cinema, on charges of forgery and grand larceny. It was a Specialist's worst nightmare. When they were flooded with sell orders and no buy orders, they did what any sane, sensible Specialist would do. They closed the stock . . . which meant that Mrs. Rosalie Johnson, and thousands of similar United Cinema shareholders were unable to sell their stock at any price.

As Skipper Kraus pored over the books listing the buy and sell orders, he sipped hot, black coffee from a stained, chipped mug. His expression grew more and more disgusted.

"A fuckin' headache. We got sell orders for about three and a half million shares."

"Jesus! What about the buy orders?" Brady was a little frantic.

Skipper rubbed his chin. "We got orders to buy. At forty. That's thirty points down. Yuk!" Skipper rubbed his chin again. "But there's one real weird piece of business."

"Make my day. Tell me the SEC is also investigating United."

"No."

"The SEC is buying United."

"Cut the clowning. Jeffrey Moore says he's ready to buy at whatever price we open the stock."

"Hallelujah! That's Maxwell, Gluck & Moore. They got big dough!" Brady jumped and clicked his heels. "Maxwell, Gluck & Moore has been accumulating United Cinema for months." Walker sucked in his breath and shook his head. "Tell me why. Moore is the original West Coast Shark."

"Moore says he's buying for investors, not himself. He says his investors are Los Angeles types...they love United," Skipper snapped.

"Even after the shitty publicity?" Bobby Brady asked. "You're right, Herbie. I smell a rotten egg."

"How many shares will Moore buy?" Brady asked.

"He says he'll take everything we got. We're talking about three and a half million shares."

Herbert Walker had been working with his calculator. "The stock was seventy-four and a half. Jesus Christ! It'll cost the bastard two hundred seventy-five million six hundred fifty thousand dollars. He doesn't have that kind of money." Walker's jowls shook with irritation.

"He says his people do," Skipper insisted.

"Well," Walker sighed. "We have to open the stock.

So we'll put him to the test. Open the stock ten points down."

"You looking for a funeral home?" Brady asked. "What if Moore craps out at ten points down? We'll be stuck with over a quarter of a billion dollars worth of stock we don't want and can't pay for. Let's say we drop the stock another twenty-five points. Maybe we pick up the real buyers."

Walker's smile was ghoulish. "And we only lose about fifty million dollars we don't have."

Skipper sighed. "It's decision time, boys. Pick a number . . . ten points, twenty points, thirty points down. Makes no difference. I'm getting old and broke too fast and smart too slow. Pick a number—any number—from one to thirty."

Brady opened the center drawer of his desk and produced a pair of gold-plated dice. "I won these at Atlantic City, compliments of the house. I was the biggest loser of the year. I'll roll 'em. Whatever number comes up, we double it. That's how far we drop the price of the stock."

"You mean you roll a seven and we open the stock fourteen points down?" Skipper asked.

"What the hell!" Walker tugged on his earlobe and gave in. He had the look a hangman might see. "I'll go with the dice. It's as good a way as any to go broke with this dog of a stock."

Skipper shrugged. "Okay, Brady. Roll the dice."

Brady shook the dice. "Come on, baby. Don't forget who loves you." He rolled the dice across the desk. They hit a wooden tray, bounced back, tumbled about, and stopped. The partners stared at the dice.

Finally, Skipper said, "Well, it could be worse. Eighter from Decatur is a good number. We open the stock down sixteen points."

"At fifty-eight and a half?" Brady asked.

"At fifty-eight and a half and may God have mercy on our bank loans," Skipper Kraus intoned.

That day, Guy Macleod occasionally glanced at the CRT standing in a discreet corner of his office. Normally it was dark . . . today it was working. United Cinema was trading. It opened at fifty-eight and a half. Guy didn't like it. It should have opened lower. He frowned. How the hell could

NAKED CALL

those damn Specialists hold the price when no one was buying? He'd called an emergency partners' meeting at the end of the trading day. He had no choice. He had to get the ball rolling. If United closed at fifty-eight and a half, he would work with fifty-eight and a half. That was a sixteen point drop—enough to scare the shit out of the clowns.

By ten minutes to six that evening, the forty-seven Macleod Brothers partners were crammed into the large conference room. Only Simon in Tokyo was absent. The elegant conference table and chairs had been removed and in their place were rows of hard, plastic, folding chairs. On a low platform facing the rows of chairs stood a small, rectangular folding table with metal legs and a drink-stained, pressed-board surface. Guy sat in the center of the table. Kevin MacIntyre and Jonathan Graham sat on his right, Ira Benjamin on his left. In deference to the missing Simon Macleod, there was a vacant chair between Guy and Ira. On the floor, the bankers sat facing the bankers on the dais and the traders faced Ira Benjamin.

Promptly at six o'clock, Guy called the meeting to order. "Everyone kindly be quiet," he said in a commanding voice. He waited as conversation trailed off. "Thank you," Guy said. "Is there anyone here who has not studied the memorandum I prepared for this meeting?" He waited. "Good. You've seen it... then you're all aware of the disaster that has struck Macleod Brothers. Our very survival is threatened. But to make sure we understand exactly what has happened, I'll go over the numbers with you." He straightened his shoulders and raised his chin. "As my memorandum says, Macleod Brothers owns about twenty-eight million shares of United Cinema. This morning the stock opened at fifty-eight and a half... sixteen points down." Guy lowered his eyes to view the partners. Beads of perspiration glistened on many heads. "Our firm has sustained a loss of about four hundred twenty-five million dollars."

The whistling sound of breath being sharply exhaled mixed with the hum of men whispering to each other.

Guy's voice was solemn... a religious zealot preaching about hell fire and brimstone. "Every point that United stock drops costs Macleod Brothers twenty-eight million dollars. Logically, that lowers the value of your Macleod Brothers' stock by twenty-eight million dollars."

Kevin MacIntyre whined, "We're in a mess, Guy."

"We are, Kevin," Guy said regretfully. "I'm sorry to say it's going to get worse. I'll be meeting tomorrow or the day after with the Governers of the New York Stock Exchange. There's talk about their putting us on the warning list. All of you know what that means?"

Ira could no longer keep quiet. "You will tell us. Won't you, Guy?"

"Yes, Ira, I will tell you. For those who do not grasp the significance of this warning..." He'd deal with Ira Benjamin when he was ready. Guy's tone became absolute. Silence again dominated the room. "Having our firm on the warning list is one short step from bankruptcy. If United Cinema stock continues to drop, the firm of Macleod Brothers will close its doors."

"What about our stock in Macleod Brothers?" Kevin MacIntyre asked.

"Use your stock to wallpaper your bathrooms." Guy looked as grim as his words sounded. He hoped it was grim enough. "Even if, by some miracle, the firm survives, it will be by the skin of our teeth. Meaning no more partners' bonuses for five years. You'll have to live on your salaries."

"On ninety thousand a year?" Jonathan Graham groaned. "I just bought a co-op on Sutton Place... two and a half million bucks. Ninety thousand a year won't cover the interest on the mortgage."

"Sorry, Jonathan, but that's the way it is." Guy studied the men facing him. He was moderately satisfied. They looked like death warmed over.

The phone on the floor behind Guy buzzed.

Guy reached around and picked up the receiver. "Yes, Mrs. Neill. Good. Put him through." He waved his hand at the partners. "I insist on silence... you, too, Ira. It's Simon calling from Tokyo." He stood up, still holding the receiver. "Simon... I see. No. We can't do that deal. Keep trying. Bye." Guy replaced the receiver. Speaking slowly and clearly to let his words sink in, he said, "So far, Tokyo has declined to become subordinated lenders. They've offered to buy the company for book value. Simon is still trying to cut a deal. If he can't and we sell the company to the Summo National Bank, you'll be working for Japanese bosses."

"No way," Jonathan Graham stated.

"I agree, Jonathan. No way." Guy was even more emphatic. He congratulated himself on his performance, and on Mrs. Neill's good work. She'd earned her bonus. Her call was perfectly timed. If anyone ever found out it wasn't Simon on the phone, it would make no difference. It would be a done deal.

"Guy, I have one question for you."

"Yes, Sherwood. What is it?"

"Originally it was your idea to acquire United . . . a goddamn motion picture company with no assets except the people who work for it . . . like Christie Larsen."

"And you kept buying more stock," Bernie Mefford added.

"That's right. You got us into this mess. How are you going to get us out?" Sherwood demanded.

Guy studied his manicured nails. Thank you, Sherwood Anderson. I counted on you to cut and run. The lemmings will follow you over the cliff. He was silent as the cries, "We're going bankrupt, Guy," "We're going belly-up," and "Do something," ricocheted off the walls.

"Apparently some of you don't approve of the United deal. Others object to the way I've managed my family's business. But since I have no intention of resigning . . ."

"That's right, Guy. I object to the way you managed the company. Buy me out." Sherwood made himself heard over the din.

Guy stared at Sherwood. His face was expressionless. Finally he said, "I can't buy you out. I would if I could . . ." He let it hang there.

Sherwood jumped on the words. "Why can't you buy me out?"

Guy didn't so much as blink. He looked at Sherwood as if he couldn't believe what he was hearing. "The corporate bylaws prevent it. Didn't you read the bylaws before you bought your stock? Macleod Brothers' stock cannot be sold to me or to anyone else." He paused to survey the faces of his partners. "But there is one thing I can do." Another pause. They were as ready as they'd ever be. "Only Macleod Brothers can buy you out..." Calculated hesitation. "...at book value..." Hold for a fraction of a second. "...plus ten percent."

Sherwood did a quick mental calculation. "That'll give me back about thirty percent of what I paid for the stock," he sputtered.

"That's right, Sherwood. You'll lose seventy percent of your investment. Of course, you can sit still . . . and maybe lose one hundred percent of your investment. I don't read tea leaves."

Guy waited and waited and silently cursed Sherwood. Come on, you bloody coward! Let's see that yellow stripe!

Sherwood spit out the words. "You've got a deal."

Abruptly, Guy relaxed. He had them. "Who else?" he demanded. "Who else wants out? Same terms. Ten percent over book value."

"I'll take it," and, "Me," and, "Draw the papers," came from all sides of the room.

"Whoa!" Ira sang out. "Bernie, Marty, David, Peter, Chuck..." He called the names of the entire trading group. "Don't do anything until Simon gets back."

"Simon can't help," David Cohn groaned. "He's blowing it in Tokyo."

"All those who accept my offer, please stand up," Guy said. Of the forty-seven partners present, Guy counted thirty-six sellers. The one surprise was Kevin MacIntyre. He'd been confident Kevin would sell. On second thought, that was short-sighted. Kevin made it a point of pride never to accept the first offer on anything. They'd negotiate, Kevin would chisel a few more points and go away happy, convinced he'd gotten the best of the deal. Ira Benjamin and his block of traders were a different kettle of fish. He'd leave Ira to Simon. When Little Brother found out what he'd done, he'd cheer. At last it was happening . . . Macleod Brothers for the Macleods.

"All those who agree to sell," Guy called out, "bring in your shares of stock in two days . . . Friday. I need the two days to raise the cash. We'll settle accounts in this room at six o'clock Friday. Those who have not yet decided to sell, think it over. My offer is open... until Friday. That's it. Go home. Talk to your wives. Tomorrow is a business day." He watched as the partners slowly filed from the room. Only a few days more and he'd be the Macleod of the Macleods. The oldest son had always been the Macleod of the Macleods, as he would have been if his father hadn't made a lunatic will. That damn will had almost ruined his life.

Sherwood Anderson hurried to his office to phone Mona. When he finished telling her what had happened, he said, "Dress up, honey, any way you like. We're going to celebrate my getting out of Macleod Brothers in almost one piece before the firm goes down the tubes."

Mona listened attentively. When she hung up, she stared at the phone. Then she picked it up. She had to make a call.

Sherwood greeted Mike, the outside doorman at The Majestic, with a jaunty, "Hello, Mike. Beautiful day." So he'd lost some of Mona's money in the Macleod Brothers collapse. Mona was very rich, Mona loved him... she'd forgive him.

"Beautiful, sir." That it was already dark was irrelevant. If an owner of an apartment in The Mighty Majestic said it was a beautiful day, it was a beautiful day. Mike held the door for Sherwood.

"How's it going, Pete? How's the wife and kids?" Sherwood called out to the inside doorman.

"Very well, sir. Nice of you to ask." At a respectful three paces behind, Pete followed Sherwood to the elevator and stood silently until the elevator doors closed.

Although five of the seven passenger elevators in The Majestic were automatic—the two remaining manual elevators were used solely as back-ups for the tower apartments—each automatic elevator was operated by an elevator operator. Rumor had it that when the late Frank Costello—the *Capo di Capi*—lived in The Majestic, he insisted that the elevator operators be retained after the manual elevators were converted to automatic. At that time, no one had dared oppose a convenience about which Frank Costello felt strongly.

Sherwood nodded to the elevator operator. "Evening, Tony."

"Evening, sir." Tony smiled. Mr. Anderson owned one of the few apartments in The Majestic with a large terrace. Among the special people who owned apartments in The Majestic, the terrace made Mr. Anderson a little more special. The elevator doors opened on the fourteenth floor. "Have a nice evening, Mr. Anderson."

"Thank you, Tony." Sherwood grinned as he thought of Mona waiting for him with a glass of champagne in one hand and . . . he didn't know what else. They played a game on their special nights. She might be dressed in one of her Calvin Kleins, ready to go to a restaurant, or she might be stark naked, ready to have sex on the wooden parquet floor in the foyer. Anticipation made Sherwood's groin twitch. His pants felt too tight. He waited for the elevator doors to close before unlocking the apartment door.

When Sherwood entered the apartment, there was no Mona . . . not Mona dressed to kill or Mona naked . . . waiting for him. "Hi. I'm home," he called out. "Where are you, dear?" She was probably still taking a bath.

"Here, Sherwood. I'm in the library."

What the hell was she doing in the library? Vaguely irritated, Sherwood hung up his coat, crossed the foyer, opened the door to the library and stopped. Mona had company—Uncle Stavros. Sherwood quickly collected himself. "Good evening, Stavros." He extended his hand.

"Sherwood."

The men shook hands.

"I have your martini ready, darling," Mona said.

"Thanks." Sherwood accepted the drink, keeping his eyes fixed on Stavros.

"I think I'll take a bath and change for dinner. I made a reservation at La Grenouille. Is that all right, Sherwood?" Mona asked.

"Fine." Sherwood heard the library door close. Alarm bells went off in his head. Stavros and Mona had talked. He didn't know how he knew, but he knew. They had discussed something—whatever it was—without him. Suddenly he was full of resentment. Stavros had power... power that operated on a level far beyond his reach.

"Sit down," Stavros said curtly. "School's out, Sherwood. It's time we had a talk."

Sherwood's resentment grew. This was his home... Mona's and his. What right did Stavros Lennos have to come into his home and order him around? "I'll stand," he said.

"I said, sit down. Now sit!"

Stavros didn't raise his voice, but his words lashed at Sherwood. He slumped into the nearest chair... a deep, ox-blood-colored, leather club chair. Stavros sat opposite him in a smaller, higher, straight-backed chair. Sherwood found himself looking up at Stavros. It was disconcerting.

"Sherwood, you've been married to Mona for three years. What do you know about her?"

"What do you mean, what do I know about her?" Sherwood swallowed his martini in one gulp. He noticed for the first time that Stavros was not drinking. "I know that I love her and she loves me."

"I'm glad. But I didn't ask you that. What do you know about Mona... her history... her family?"

The almost imperceptible pause before the word, "family," gave Sherwood the clue he needed. "Let's see. Mona's maiden name was Montefuoco... Mona Montefuoco."

"Does that name—Montefuoco—mean anything to you?"

Sherwood thought for a second. "No. It's Italian."

"Sicilian."

"Okay. Sicilian."

"What else do you know?"

"Her mother died when she was ten. Her father died when she was a teenager. He was an importer of some sort ... Italian home furnishings, marble, chairs, tables, lamps..." Sherwood's voice trailed off.

"That's all you know?"

"Well, he must have been successful. Mona inherited a great deal of money."

"You married her because she's rich?"

"No!" Sherwood simmered. Stavros was pushing too hard.

"I see. It's true love. You'd have married her if she'd made her living selling housewares at Bloomingdale's?"

"No. If Mona sold housewares at Bloomie's, she wouldn't be the same Mona. She'd be someone else."

Although it wasn't evident, Sherwood's answer pleased Stavros. Buried within Sherwood's pompous ass attitude and peacock strut was a man who had taken a hard-eyed look at himself. He knew what his needs were. Before they were finished, he would have to take another hard look.

"That's all you know?" Stavros asked.

Sherwood shrugged. "More or less. There's no ex-husband and, frankly, I don't give a f—, a damn about her ex-lovers. Mona is a loving, faithful wife. Period."

Stavros chuckled softly. "A fine combination of truths, half-truths, lies, and omissions. Mona has done well... exactly as she was taught. Do you want to learn—as they say—the truth, the whole truth, and nothing but the truth about your wife?"

"Yes! I mean, no!" Sherwood took a deep breath. He could use another drink. "I'm not sure," he admitted. "We're very happy right now. Will knowing the whole truth make us happier?"

"You can go on being happy with Mona even though you know that some of what she's told you about herself are lies?"

"Yes. At least I think so."

Stavros' respect for Sherwood jumped several notches. In choosing to marry Sherwood, Mona's instinct was more on target than his had been. "Have another martini," Stavros suggested. "And pour me a scotch on the rocks."

Sherwood made the drinks. Like it or not, he was going to learn the truth about Mona. And for some reason he felt he'd gained a little respect in Stavros' eyes. It was strange how much that pleased him. He handed Stavros his drink, settled into his chair, and waited.

"First, the truth. Mona's maiden name is Montefuoco. Her mother, Julia, did die when she was a child. And her father, Enrico, did die when she was thirteen." Stavros paused. "So much for the truth. Now the half-truths."

Sherwood sipped his martini. Stavros was the teacher and he, the student.

"Julia died of natural causes . . . breast cancer." A bitterness crept into Stavros' voice. "It seems stupid in this day and age for a woman not to go to a gynecologist, even after she discovers a lump in her breast. Unfortunately, to certain Sicilian women like Julia, it was not stupid. Going to a gynecologist, having a stranger—not her husband—touch her breasts was unimaginable. By the time Enrico felt the lump, it was too late."

"I'm sorry," Sherwood murmured.

"We all were . . . Enrico more than anyone. As for Enrico, it's true he did die when Mona was thirteen . . . not from natural causes." Stavros overrode Sherwood's startled expression. "Enrico was found hanging from a rafter in his home in Glen Cove. The police examined the evidence and the coroner listed the death as suicide . . . a convenient way to close the books on Enrico Montefuoco. The coroner was wrong. Enrico was murdered."

Sherwood swallowed the wrong way and choked on his drink. It was several minutes before he stopped coughing and Stavros was able to continue.

"Enrico Montefuoco. Does the name still mean nothing to you?"

Sherwood read the business news, the sports news, and the international news, in that order. He rarely paid attention to local news, no matter how sordidly sensational the headlines. But now that Stavros pressed him, Montefuoco did have a certain ring. "Montefuoco?" He repeated the name as though the repetition would paint a picture for him. "Montefuoco!" He was startled. "I remember now. Something about a . . ." He looked up at Stavros. ". . . the head of a Mafia Family killing himself?"

"That's close, if not accurate. Enrico was not the head of the Family. Nor did he commit suicide."

"But he was Mafia?"

"Yes. Mona's father was a member of the Family." Stavros sipped his scotch. "And it's true Enrico was in the import business . . . not Italian home furnishings. He imported heroin. At that time cocaine was not so widely used."

Sherwood sank deeper into his chair. Mona's father was a member of the Mafia. He imported drugs. The idea startled him. But that was all. He felt no shame, no outrage.

"Another Family murdered him. They differed over the right to sell drugs in a certain territory." Stavros sounded so reasonable, he could have been discussing a battle between Colgate and Crest over share of the toothpaste market in Des Moines.

"Mona's money comes from the sale of drugs?" Sherwood was surprised at how little he cared, when everything in his background said he should feel disgraced. But all he remembered was the way he'd been put down by the self-righteous snobs with whom he'd grown up. He wasn't good enough for their daughters. He was good enough for Mona . . . that's what counted. "What else do I have to know?" Only the narrow line of Sherwood's mouth hinted at his reluctance to continue to listen . . . and his recognition that there was nothing he could do or say to end the talk.

"Mona's mother's maiden name was Lupo. Does the name Lupo mean anything to you?"

Sherwood now knew in which direction to think. "Yes," he said slowly. "Antonio Lupo."

"Angelo Lupo."

"Antonio Lupo . . . Angelo Lupo . . . same thing."

"Not to Angelo Lupo. Angelo Lupo is the head of the Family. Mona's mother was Angelo Lupo's sister."

"I'm not following this," Sherwood said.

"My mother was also Angelo Lupo's sister." Stavros' tone was respectful.

"I get it. You're all related." Sherwood was aware he sounded stupid, but he was being fed too much new information too rapidly.

"We are all related," Stavros said soberly. "So we take care of each other. More important, her father, Enrico, was my closest friend. We were like brothers. After Enrico's murder, I felt it my duty to take care of his child. So I did. It may ease your conscience to know that Mona's money doesn't come from her father's drug dealing. It comes from me."

"You! You gave Mona millions of dollars?"

"Yes." Stavros smiled. The smile sat oddly on his strongly boned face . . . one or the other was a mask. "I'm very fond of Mona. She's a very intelligent woman who tries hard not to let anyone know how bright she is."

"She is intelligent, isn't she?" That anyone besides him realized that Mona was anything but a ditsy airhead surprised Sherwood. Her act was so perfect. Another truth hammered at him. "Then the rumors are true. You are a Mafia front," he blurted out without thinking. "Oh shit! I'm sorry! I didn't mean to..."

Stavros waved off his apology. "I'm a lot of things. The press embellishes the truth, even when the truth would make a better story. There's another reason why I gave Mona fifty million dollars. Ah! You look surprised. Mona never told you how much she's worth?"

"No. I knew she was rich... anyone could tell that."

"I must compliment her on her discretion... a rare quality even among intelligent people."

"The money?" Sherwood prodded.

"Ah, yes. The money. I gave her the money because in a way her father died in place of me. Moshe Cohen made sure I would live."

"Moshe Cohen!" Sherwood inhaled sharply. "I've heard of him. *Business Week* and *Forbes* did articles on him. The financial genius of the Mafia."

"Moshe Cohen would not like that expression, but now it makes no difference. Moshe is dead... the dead have few rights. In any case, I'm alive because Moshe decided that I would go to Harvard and Enrico would enter the Family business. At the time, I didn't understand why I was chosen and not him. I do now. I would not have done well in the drug business. It's a violent, vicious business without a future. When drugs are made legal, like wine, whiskey, beer, then, perhaps, I'll manage the operation. The Family competed very successfully after Prohibition ended. We should do as well when drugs are legal. Moshe wanted me trained to manage the legitimate family businesses." His tone was both practical and sad. "So I live. Enrico died. And I take care of Mona."

Sherwood studied his drink as though the martini held some kind of answer to a big question. Why had Stavros told him so much? This was what Stavros would call Family business. He wasn't a member of the Family... was he?

"Now you know the whole truth about your wife. Do you have any questions?"

Sherwood was terrified, but it was vital he not show his fear. He looked hard at the man sitting opposite him. "Yes," he said. That the word came out clear and firm pleased him. "You've spilled your guts about Family matters that are none of my business. You want something from me. What?"

If Sherwood was pleased with himself, Stavros was even more pleased. He was aware of the frightening effect he had on most people. He'd spent years cultivating his power, refining it, turning it from a bludgeon to a rapier. He'd terrified Sherwood . . . he'd meant to. But despite his fright, Sherwood had asked a shrewd question. The man had some intelligence, plus his ability to look at unsavory truths.

"What I want is simple. You are not to sell your shares of Macleod Brothers."

For a moment Sherwood couldn't speak. Then he said, "Stavros, that's crazy. Macleod Brothers can go belly-up. If it does, I'll lose everything."

"You'll lose nothing."

"You mean because I used Mona's money to buy my partnership?"

"No! That's not what I mean." Stavros rose and paced back and forth in front of Sherwood. "When you married Mona, you married a Sicilian woman. Her money is your money to do with as you wish."

Sherwood said nothing. He was afraid he might say the wrong thing.

Stavros went on talking, but his tone was so quiet he seemed to be thinking out loud. "Unlike Sicilian wines, Sicilian customs travel very well, even across the wide Atlantic. Sicilians—even twentieth-century Sicilians—are trapped in a love affair with vengeance, vendetta." His soft voice was more frightening than a shouted threat. "Now you are one of the Family. You share our troubles, our triumphs." Abruptly, his voice became businesslike. "When I said you will not lose any money, I mean that I will personally guarantee you against any loss. And you will convince your partners that they should not sell their stock."

"They won't listen to me."

"You'll indemnify them against their losing any money."

"That takes hundreds of millions of dollars. Mona doesn't ... I mean I don't ... we don't ..."

"I do. We are not speaking of your money, Sherwood. We're speaking of mine." Stavros stopped in front of Sherwood's chair, placed his hands on the armrest, and leaned forward until his face was only inches away from Sherwood. "We are Family. You will do this for me. I take things personally, Sherwood. I would take it as a personal insult—an insult to the Family—if you did not do this little favor for me."

Stavros seemed to gather his energy from the air. For the first time his ruthless force was exposed ... naked. Sherwood could almost see the aura of power—like a mantle—that enveloped the man. "But ..." He gathered himself. "What am I supposed to tell my partners? Guy Macleod? That your money is behind me?"

"Guy Macleod knows it without your telling him."

"How?"

"Sherwood, you must learn to remember everything." Stavros paused. "The village restaurant where we saw Simon Macleod ..."

Sherwood hit his forehead with the flat of his hand. "I remember." He stared at Stavros. "Simon told Guy we were together. I told you he would." He shook his head. "You said you wanted Guy to fear me."

Stavros almost smiled. "And now he will."

Sherwood made one last effort to slide out from under. "Look, even if I say that Stavros Lennos is backing me, why should the partners believe me?" He risked adding, "Some of them might not take your money. It's ..."

"Dirty money ... Mafia money ... drug money?" Stavros straightened up, chuckling. "Sherwood, I'm surprised at you. You've worked on Wall Street for fifteen years. Have you ever known a Wall Streeter to turn down money from any source?" Stavros went on smiling, confident his instincts were correct. "When is the next partners' meeting?" he asked.

"In two days ... Friday."

"Very good. Tomorrow I want a list of Macleod Brothers partners, how many shares each partner owns, and the book value of Macleod Brothers before the United Cinema debacle."

A worm of shame ate at Sherwood's pride, but he agreed to do as Stavros asked.

"I'll be here tomorrow evening to pick up the information." He resumed his seat facing Sherwood. "When the partners meet, this is what you must do..."

It took Stavros a few minutes to detail his plan, and a little longer for Sherwood to ask questions. They'd just finished their business when there was a knock on the door.

"Come in, Mona," Stavros called out.

The door opened and Mona posed in the doorway, hand on hip. She wore one of her Geoffrey Beene glitter dresses. Sherwood glanced at his watch. It seemed longer, but less than an hour had passed.

"Will you join us, Uncle Stavros?" Mona asked.

"No, thank you. Sherwood and you have a good deal to talk about. Tell her everything, Sherwood. If Mona has any suggestions, take them as seriously as you would if they came from me. I'll see you tomorrow."

"Tomorrow," Sherwood said as Stavros Lennos left the room.

"Isn't he wonderful?" Mona sighed.

"Wonderful."

Sherwood felt like an innocent bystander caught in the middle of a revolution. When Stavros Lennos and Guy Macleod went head to head, the first to get hurt would be the innocent bystanders. Him.

Chapter 28

THE UNITED Cinema offices had the dumbstruck air of calamity, as if a tornado had swept throught the building, leaving numbed disbelief in its wake. "How could this happen to us?" The guard at the gate, the few people Christie met in the building, seemed staggered at the sight of her ... embarrassed. Some forced out a cheerful, "Hello, ... uh ... Christie?" as if they'd forgotten her name, then quickly looked the other way. Others scurried by, deep in thought. Nan Grey, the good soldier, was at her desk, waiting. When Christie entered she rose and went to her, taking Christie's hand in a warm, steady grip.

"Hello, boss. Everything's ready ... organized. I put all your personal things ... Tommy's and your pictures, your awards, plaques ... the things you asked for into three folders. Easy to fit into your briefcase."

"Thank you, Nan. Thank you very much," she said.

Christie wanted to spend as little time as possible in the office sorting through her files and selecting what she was entitled to take with her. Then she wanted to leave. Fast!

"You're welcome. Now what else can I do to help you?"

"There doesn't seem to be much else."

"Is Tommy okay?"

"Tommy is fine."

"Where is he? Where are you? I was relieved when you called."

"Tommy, Anna, and I are staying with Louis Levy at his home, with a guard at the gate and another patrolling the grounds."

"God bless Louis," Nan said. "The media has been driving me crazy looking for you."

"Tell them we defected to the mother ship." Christie

smiled, trying to get her bearings. There was no quick recovery from the the disasters. "Louis has decreed we remain in hiding."

"He's right." Spontaneously, Nan reached out and hugged Christie. Her hug was as warm and firm as her handclasp, a peculiar, irreplaceable kind of sisterly comfort. Nan's phone rang and a button lit up. She shook her head. "That's Channel 5, or NewsCenter. It could be anyone. Get moving, Christie. The wolves are baying at the door. Someone alerted them that you're in the building. I'll man the barricades. Check the folders, see if I missed anything, and run for your life."

Christie entered her office and closed the door. In spite of herself, she stood for a moment at her desk. Her sense of strangeness had increased the minute she entered the office. She had the fixed, blank expression of a person under hypnosis. Her eyes, although wide open, saw nothing. In her mind a dizzying montage of the events of the last week flicked across her brain. The time with Simon... Barry's appearance... Simon's marriage proposal... kissing him goodbye at LAX. Where the devil was he? Why hadn't he called? Didn't he know how much she needed him? The police station... Detective Carmella Garcia... Jenny Lattimore—smacking Jenny had felt good—Matt Renault, the lying bastard... you are charged with... Guy firing her. Where was Simon? Where was he? Stop thinking about him.

"Can I come in?" The familiar voice hesitated.

Christie glanced at the door. Harry Weiss, complete with a hangdog look... good old Harry.

"Come in, Harry. You're welcome. Everybody's welcome. Christie doesn't live here anymore. I only stopped by to pick up some personal things."

"Tom, that idiot at the gate, called me. He asked me to apologize to you for telling me. He said to say he was only doing his duty. So I'm saying it... technically, you're not allowed on the premises." Harry wiped his sweaty hands on the sides of his pants. "So much for that bullshit."

"Tell Tom I accept his apology." Christie added gravely, "And thank him for letting me in in the first place. There's nothing I can take—except my birth certificate and passport—that your office doesn't have in triplicate... or Eli's office... or Jo's... or someone's office."

"I know. That's why you're not here and I haven't seen you." Harry looked wretched. "I feel so... so... lousy. I wish I could do something to help."

"I've hired a very good criminal lawyer," Christie said as she began putting file folders into her briefcase.

Harry's mind was not on lawyers. "Guy wants me to fly to New York for a meeting."

"Fly to New York, Harry. He's the boss."

"Don't remind me." Harry looked strained.

"In time you may grow to love each other."

There was a commotion in the outer office. Louis appeared in the doorway. Nan, standing behind him, shrugged helplessly.

"Christie! Stop lollygagging. I agreed you could come here to pick up a few things, but this is no time for a class reunion."

"Hello, Louis," Harry mumbled.

"Harry." Louis acknowledged the greeting with a curt nod. "Christie, move your ass. Any minute the dogs of war will arrive."

"Louis! You followed me. Why?"

"Of course I followed you. I don't trust you out of my sight."

"I'm a big girl. I've taken care of myself—and Tommy—for years. When I leave here I am going home to pick up the Disney drawings. Tommy left them in his room."

"You are not going home. Where the hell are your brains? Right now you are hot copy... your house is open to the public. I wouldn't be surprised if the tourist buses have been rerouted to pass it so people can gawk."

"So they gawk. Let them."

"Yesterday I sent Lei over to see how the land lay. There were reporters waiting on your lawn, cameras, camera crews. By today they'll be gone. It's too expensive to keep a crew on location with nothing to shoot except the outside of a house. But the scouts, with their car phones cocked ... those boys remain just in case. One phone call—that's all it takes—and the camera crews will be back. You can't go home... not yet."

"Tommy needs those Disney drawings. He's working on something for his art class—"

"Damn it! I'll buy him a King Kong poster, or one of—"

"Louis, I have to ask you something," Harry interrupted . . . something he would never have dared to do a week earlier.

Louis groaned. "I'm playing golf at Pebble Beach Saturday. Sorry." He gave Christie a sad smile. "By the way, by rushing out, you lost your big chance. Like winning the Publishers Clearing House sweepstakes . . ."

"What are you talking about?"

"Five minutes after you left Casa Levy, you had a call from Tokyo . . . from a concerned friend."

"Simon?"

Louis chuckled. "That question is typical of you. You beat around the bush . . . duck issues . . . ask irrelevant questions . . . procrastinate . . ."

"Can I ask another irrelevant question?"

"Can I stop you?"

"Will he call back?"

"He said he'd call in precisely two hours. Let's go home."

"Yes." Christie closed her briefcase and moved toward the door.

"Louis . . ." Harry interrupted again, his jaw set in his version of Gary Cooper in *High Noon*. "Off the record, I hear that Marconi expects to be made president of United Cinema."

"I heard that also. Hell! Everyone's heard it. Marconi's done everything except rent billboards and make a TV commercial . . . Marconi for president." Louis beckoned Christie to leave.

Christie listened, surprised and resigned. She hadn't heard the rumor . . . proof positive she was no longer in the loop.

Harry's voice carried a quiet appeal. "He's not the man to be president of United Cinema. He's a wild man . . . doesn't understand numbers . . . the wrong image for Wall Street."

"Franco as president has a certain flair," Christie said mockingly.

There was a moment of silence. Then Harry asked, "Would Louis Levy care to comment on how he will vote should Marconi's name come up for a board vote?"

"No comment, Harry. It's against my religion."

For whatever it was worth, Christie knew this was the real reason Harry had come to see her. He wanted her to talk to Louis, to persude Louis to back him for president.

"Come on, Louis, what gives? I'm asking off the record."

"Okay, Harry. Off the record. There'll be a pissing contest... any pisser can enter. If you feel like competing, practice pissing. Distance and accuracy are what count the most."

"If you want the job, I wish you luck, Harry." Christie followed Louis out the door. She paused in front of Nan and kissed her on the cheek. "Thanks again."

"You okay?" Nan asked.

Christie made a clownish smile. "No comment."

As she followed Louis down the corridor she heard Harry's complaint. "With friends like Louis Levy, who needs enemies? Schmuck!"

Christie's suite of rooms—her bedroom, Tommy's bedroom, and a gracious sitting room... Anna had a room in the servants' wing—overlooked the ocean. She'd been sitting for a while, hugging her hands under her armpits, feeling as if she was aleep with her eyes wide open. Why didn't Simon call?

Outside, the evening sky was a rose-gold that reflected in the rose-golden water. Christie saw a solitary evening stretching before her. There was Tommy, and Louis... but why didn't Simon call? When he spoke to Louis he said he would call back in two hours. That was eight hours ago. Maybe the circuits from Japan were overloaded. Maybe a piece of space debris—scientists claimed there was a lot of useless junk flying about in space—had crashed into the AT&T satellite. Maybe... The local lines were working ... too damn well. Local calls were coming in with the rat-a-tat precision of machine gun bullets. She had only herself to blame. They'd never have known where to call if she hadn't broken cover by visiting the studio. Now the press was camped outside the guarded gate. Jo Caro had been interviewed, Nan, Harry Weiss, anyone and everyone she knew or with whom she'd worked . . . with the exception of Guy Macleod. Guy was a professional at avoiding interviewers, better than she was. The media hadn't laid a finger on him. The phone rang again.

She picked up the telephone, knowing it was a mistake. She prayed it was Simon. "Hello?"

"This is the Phil Donahue office. Mr. Donahue himself would like to speak to Ms. Christie Larsen." She heard Louis pick up the extension in his study and she hung up.

The phone rang again . . . and again. She waited for Louis to answer the phone before picking up her extension. She heard the voice on the other end of the line say, "Mr. Geraldo Rivera wants to know if it's true Ms. Larsen worked for United Cinema as Mr. Levy's personal assistant for twelve years before becoming president..." Louis slammed the receiver down a fraction of a second before she did.

The phone rang twelve times in the next half hour. Maybe Simon was trying to call and couldn't get through? She wished she didn't feel so alone, so lost in an unreal world.

The phone rang again. The emotional pull to pick it up was very strong. This time not a muscle moved in Christie's body. She sat quietly, in a fiercely determined stillness. Let it ring. She didn't want to risk another mistake. She got up in a kind of dream state and drifted to the liquor cabinet. She poured herself a very stiff scotch. Everything was hard to do. Everything was in slow motion. There was a light tap on the door. It was Lei. Mr. Levy had sent him to say she had a sinister caller. Should he handle it for her?

"Sinister?" He couldn't mean Simon. "Who is it, Lei?"

"Mr. Barry Easton is the name, I believe."

Barry! What a lousy joke. She was reminded so powerfully of the afternoon by the Ritz pool with Simon—and Barry at his slimy best. Abruptly, she went out of control. She started to sob . . . a short, wild burst of tears. Lei stood still, saying nothing.

She stopped crying as suddenly as she'd started, pulled

herself together, and picked up the telephone.

"What do you want, Barry?"

Lei vanished. Louis remained on the line.

"Chriiissstiiie!" Barry drew out her name. "I want you to know I'm on your side. All the way. Yours truly is shocked at the shit they're throwing at you, kid, and I want to offer my deepest sympathy. It's lousy the way the police treated you, kid ... arresting you, tossing you in the clink ... you, the former president of United Cinema." He was jubilant ... gloating. "At any rate, kid, beyond sympathy, I want you to know that I am sorry I wasted your time a couple of weeks ago, and again at the Ritz Carlton. In fact, I want to make the following point clear ... no misunderstanding between us—"

Christie pictured his pretty boy face, gleefully earnest. "Cut to the chase, Barry. I haven't time."

"You're right, let's not overdo the condolences. The fact is, you can forget everything I proposed. I've thought it over. I now see I am far too fixed in my ways and too unsentimental to enjoy fatherhood, to enjoy raising a son ..." He paused. "... alone, without a wife ... or with a wife in jail." His voice was growing savage. He cleared his throat in an effort to keep a civil tone. He knew Louis Levy was listening. Levy was still a power. "What I mean is, you're facing serious criminal charges with a prison term in the offing. That hard fact made me rethink our future. You are not exactly what a man would want in a wife. So I feel it's the best for both of us not to remarry."

"I agree, Barry. Is that all?"

"That's all. Except I wish you the best. Actually, that bleached blond gorilla—the fugitive from Muscle Beach, the one you spent the weekend with—might still be willing to take you on." He paused. "On second thought, maybe not." His voice grew low and mean. "As I think about it, kid, that type would head for the hills the minute the prison doors closed."

Christie slammed the receiver down. She thought of the death by a thousand blows. Barry could make mincemeat out of people. He was trying to do that to her. You're not good enough for me, kid ... chew on that. You're not good enough for the "bleached blond gorilla" ... meaning Simon. Chew . . . chew . . . swallow. A cold finger touched Christie's heart. Was Barry right? Or wrong? Was she good enough for Simon? Could his love stand the strain? What were its outer limits?

The telephone rang again. Louis picked up. She sat in the chair waiting, head bowed. Where was Simon?

Lei again appeared in the doorway. "It's Mr. Simon Macleod," he said. "Mr. Levy said for you to pick up and he will hang up when you do."

Christie's jaw trembled slightly as she sucked in a breath of air. She picked up the receiver and said hesitatingly, "Simon?" She heard the click as Louis put down the receiver.

"Christie! Darling! Are you all right?" Simon's voice shot through eight thousand miles of air, so clear he might have been in Malibu. Satellite communication was a miracle.

"I'm all right." She had a desperate need to ask, "Simon, do you love me?" She couldn't. Simon had to say, "I love you," without her feeding him his lines. She said, "I'm sorry I missed your call this morning."

"You missed all my calls. I've tried to reach you, at last count, nineteen times. First the office . . . busy, busy, busy." He made what sounded like a rueful chuckle. "Then your home . . . no answer, no answer, no answer. I almost went out of my mind worrying where you were. Finally I used my brain. I called Louis. If anyone would know where you were, he would. Bingo! I found you." His tone was more sober than his words.

"Where are you, Simon?"

"Tokyo. I told Louis."

"I know." Eight hours later and he was still in Tokyo. "I thought maybe you'd . . . Why Tokyo? What are you doing in Tokyo?"

"Seeing bankers. Christie, what happened?"

For an instant, Christie's composure broke. She could think of no easy way of describing what had happened. Then she recovered. "Well, as you must have read, I've been criminally charged with embezzlement and grand larceny."

NAKED CALL

"I know. I read the papers. All Wall Street knows..." He paused.

Christie hung on that for a while. That she expected... but what else? What was he not saying? For a few seconds the satellite transmitted nothing. Then Christie said, "Simon, does your trip to Tokyo have to do with United Cinema?"

"I'll explain everything when I see you."

"Okay." She couldn't hold back. "When will you be here?"

The silence between them was spinning out. Christie waited.

"Darling, I'm stuck in Tokyo... I don't know... three more days... four days, maybe. I don't know. Then I fly to New York. Whatever happens here, I must talk it over with Guy."

"Good!" She was lightheaded with hope. "I'll meet you at LAX. All flights stop at LAX. At least we'll see each other for an hour or two. As soon as you know, give me the flight number and—"

He stopped her. "I'm taking the direct JAL flight to Kennedy. No stopover at LAX."

"Oh... a direct flight..."

"I can't help it. I have to see Guy. It's tied up with why I'm in Tokyo in the first place."

There was a silence in the courtroom of her mind. At last she said, "Then when will you be here?"

"After Guy and I make some decisions."

"How long will that take?"

Simon hedged. "A day... two at the most. Macleod Brothers is in trouble."

"The drop in the United stock?"

In her mind she pictured Simon rubbing his chin as though thinking... actually trying to avoid answering her question. Eventually he said, "Yes."

"Because of my being charged with..." She hesitated.

"Forgery... by Jenny Lattimore's boyfriend." There was a disturbing flatness in his tone. "Somebody named Matt Renault."

"Matt Rennalt." She tried not to sound defensive. "I met the man once. I don't think we exchanged five words.

The first and last time I saw him—prior to the police station—was when Franco was shooting *The Feathered Serpent* in Oaxaca, Mexico."

"Have you any idea why he concocted this story?"

"I haven't a clue." Simon's studied lack of emotion told her that although he didn't want to make judgements, he was shaken. He was probing for answers that she couldn't give.

"What does Louis think?" Simon asked.

Then, just like that, it hit her. She could take no more. He believed in her or he didn't. It all came down to whether he trusted her . . . loved her. "I don't want to talk anymore over the phone," she said in a matter-of-fact voice. "Let me know when you'll be in Los Angeles." Slowly—deliberately—she broke the connection.

Chapter 29

GUY SPENT most of Thursday and Friday soaring on the updrafts of rising expectations. Each hour in his personal Day Timer was crossed off with a thick red marker . . . one hour less to wait until Macleod Brothers was his. The partners who had refused to sell back Macleod stock would sell soon enough. They couldn't live on their salaries. And bonus time was over. That would end any interest they had in remaining partners. Good riddance. At Macleod Brothers there was no room for partners . . . except for a Macleod.

The only tricky moments were Simon's calls. Three times a day, Simon called to report the lack of progress in the negotiations and argue they end the charade. The Summo National Bank would not take a subordinated lender position. "Keep at them. You'll see. They'll come around," he encouraged Simon . . . knowing they wouldn't. Araturo Takahashi would never agree, but he would never break off the negotiations. That wasn't the Japanese way of doing business. They relied on outsitting an adversary. So he'd given Simon strict instructions not to agree to anything until he checked with him. Beautiful! Simon couldn't say, "No," and walk out. So the negotiations would go on endlessly. A final inspired touch was his arranging for Simon to be a guest at the home of Araturo Takahashi himself . . . a rare honor for an American . . . also the one place Ira would not think to look for him. Simon was isolated in Tokyo . . . leaving Guy free to reclaim Macleod Brothers.

If Guy's expectations were soaring, Ira Benjamin was depressed. His hopes of holding traders in line until Simon's return were fading. The traders came in late. They took long lunches in out of the way restaurants and left early. When they were on the trading floor, they gathered in groups, trying to cheer each other up and, incidentally, to discover who was set and where, and who wasn't. Whenever Ira approached a group, the group dissolved. No one wanted to listen to Ira's pleading for them to hang tough. Hang tough for who . . . for Simon Macleod? Simon was an okay guy, but they all read *Forbes*' list of the four hundred richest Americans. Simon was very rich . . . with or without Macleod Brothers. They weren't. On Thursday afternoon, Ira changed his tactics. One by one, he called the traders into Simon's Fish Bowl office. And one by one, he lost them.

"Listen to me, Ira," Chuck Tyler protested. He resented Ira's grilling him. "You don't get it. You don't want to get it. Simon is a Macleod. Nothing will change. Don't you know the family motto, 'The Macleods against the world.'? Get it straight, Ira. They're the Macleods. We—you and I—we're the world." With those words, Chuck left.

Only one thing stopped Ira from following the boys. Guy was pulling this stock buy out while Simon was in Tokyo. Where? His travel agent had called every damn hotel in Tokyo. Simon Macleod was not registered anywhere. He'd tried the big banks. When the Japs didn't want to give out information, no one spoke English. Only four traders agreed to wait for Simon. They weren't happy about waiting, but they were less happy about the loss they'd eat when they sold their Macleod stock back to Guy.

* * *

The Macleod Brothers partners' meeting on Friday—the final partners' meeting—was held in the same conference room as the previous meeting. The chairs and table were the same. The seating arrangement was the same. There was one change. Mrs. Neill sat at a table behind Guy. It was her job to count the stock certificates and make sure they were properly endorsed over to Macleod Brothers. Then Guy would hand the seller a check.

Promptly at six o'clock, Guy called the meeting to order. He wasted no time.

"You all know my offer," he said. "Book value plus ten percent. At four o'clock—after the close of the market—I had our bank certify checks for everyone in the room . . . even for those who, on Wednesday, did not agree to sell my company stock."

Guy did not see the curious look Ira gave him. My company? It's not his company. What's he up to?

"I'd like a count. Will all who wish to sell their Macleod Brothers stock please stand up."

All the bankers except for one man rose. They were joined by all the traders except four. Guy had expected that Ira Benjamin would convince a few traders to wait for Simon's return. But the solitary seated banker startled him.

"Sherwood," Guy called out. "Didn't you hear me? I asked all those who wish to sell their stock to stand up. Get up, man."

"Why?" Sherwood sounded contemptuous. "I'm not selling. Why should I stand?"

Guy was so startled he spoke without thinking. "Of course you're selling," he seethed. "Book value plus ten percent. We agreed. You can't change your mind. You gave your word."

The thread of panic in Guy's quick, staccato phrases puzzled Ira. Why was Guy so upset? If Anderson didn't sell today, he'd sell Monday. Anderson was a lightweight, a guy who got by on his good looks and a family name that once had cachet on The Street.

Guy became indignant. He denounced Sherwood. "You gave your word, Sherwood. You can't go back on your word. Would you rifle someone's wallet in the NYAC locker

NAKED CALL

room and steal his credit cards?" His voice grew somber. No longer the fire and brimstone preacher, he was reading a sermon from the Mount. "Sherwood, on Wall Street that's like stealing the silverware or credit cards. In case you've forgotten, it's called breaking a trade. Money isn't an investment banker's only capital. Keeping his word, shaking hands on a deal and honoring that handshake... that's a banker's real capital." The sober tone softened to a plea. "Sherwood, we shook hands on a deal. You can't break it."

The bankers were hypnotized by Guy's words. They so badly wanted to believe that they were good men... honorable men... men whose word was their bond. They would never break a trade, never! A prospectus, a contract, was invented by the devilish SEC for the sole purpose of providing greedy SEC lawyers with legal fees. Even the cynical traders—even Ira—were impressed. Occasionally, a customer broke a trade and refused to pay for stock he'd bought. His mother-in-law died. He needed money for her funeral. Whatever the reason, the trader was stiffed. He paid for the stock himself and tried to resell it. Guy was right. You don't break your word. You don't break a trade.

Sherwood Anderson was as taken with Guy's sermon as anyone in the room. He was a man of his word, a man who would never break a trade. Until now. Now he was related by marriage to the Mafia. The Mafia had a code, too, simpler and more brutal. Stavros had warned him the Family took things personally. To Sherwood, the translation was clear ... break a trade and live, don't break a trade and die. Slowly, one clap per second, he applauded Guy's speech.

"Eloquent, Guy. You've outdone yourself. What you're really saying is, sell me—"

"Sell Macleod Brothers," Guy interrupted.

"No! Sell you! If this charade goes through as you've planned, you will be Macleod Brothers."

Ira heard Guy's words again... my company, my company. A point for Anderson.

"Incidentally, since Macleod Brothers is on the verge of bankruptcy..." Sherwood half sneered. "... how have you managed to raise the money?"

Guy brushed Sherwood's point aside. "No one has to

sell their stock. But if they don't..." He shrugged. "...They could lose everything."

"And you're buying the stock just to keep your partners from losing everything. Generous, Guy. Generous!" Sherwood jeered. "No." Sherwood finally stood up. Slowly, deliberately—as though he dared anyone to try to stop him—he walked to the dais. In his hand was a nine inch by twelve inch, brown manila envelope. He moved the vacant chair that had been set aside for Simon and set the envelope on the table. "No one will lose a cent. My associate and I will indemnify all of you against any losses you suffer due to the decline in the net worth of Macleod Brothers."

"Oh, Jesus!" Kevin MacIntyre muttered. "What the hell are you talking about, Anderson? You don't have that kind of money."

"Why stop with us?" Jonathan Graham called out. "Call the White House. Tell President Bush that you'll guarantee the budget deficit. Then he can tell the Japs to fuck off."

Ira Benjamin stood up. He banged his fist on the table and shouted, "Wait a minute, everyone. Anderson said something about an associate. I want to know who that associate is."

"Tell us! Tell us!" a chorus started yelling. "Who, is it, Sherwood?...The tooth fairy?"

Guy was rigid with rage. When he spoke, there was a tremor in his voice. "Everyone, please be quiet. I think I can tell you who's behind our Sherwood. Listen to me!" Gradually, the partners stopped shouting. "It has come to my attention that our Sherwood Anderson has some unsavory connections. I didn't mention it before—it's not fair to judge a man by his in-laws—but Sherwood gives me no choice. His wife's maiden name was Montefuoco." All eyes were on Guy. He relaxed. He had them. "Mona Montefuoco is related to Stavros Lennos and Lennos is a key front for the Lupo crime family." Guy's voice gradually rose in volume. By the time he mentioned the Lupo crime family, it was stentorian.

A few partners—besides Ira—wondered where Guy got his information. The SEC and the Feds had been trying to

NAKED CALL

link Lennos to organized crime for years. Nothing had come of their efforts.

"Stavros Lennos is our Sherwood's associate. Do you want to do business with the Mafia? Do you want Lennos—a Mafia front—to own shares in Macleod Brothers?"

"Hold it, Guy, right there." Sherwood's intensity matched Guy's. "You know damn well Lennos won't own anything. You told us at the last meeting—and it's true—that the bylaws of Macleod Brothers prevent us from selling our shares to anyone. They can only be sold back to the corporation. So Stavros Lennos will never own a share of Macleod Brothers, even though he is my associate. Yes. It is his money that's behind me. Whatever Stavros Lennos is or isn't is beside the point." Sherwood stared at the men facing him. "None of you will be doing business with him. You'll be doing business with me. Not actually with me. You'll be doing business with The Bank of New York. The Bank of New York was founded by Alexander Hamilton. Is The Bank of New York clean enough for you?" He waited. "Good." He laughed. It was an open, full-throated laugh. "I probably shouldn't say this, but I can't resist the temptation. I'm going to make you an offer you can't refuse."

"This better be good," Kevin MacIntyre said. "I don't like doing business with the Mafia."

Maybe he doesn't like it, but he'll do it, Ira thought. I hope Anderson can put his money where his mouth is.

Sherwood opened the brown manila envelope and extracted a sheaf of papers. He held the papers in the air. "There's an agreement here for every Macleod Brothers' partner, except for Guy Macleod and Simon Macleod. An escrow account has been established at The Bank of New York's Broad Street branch. Six hundred million dollars is in the account. Don Brenner, senior vice president of the bank, is acting as the escrow agent."

"I know Don Brenner," Evan Saunders, a banking partner, called out. "Any objections if I phone him?" He stood up to leave.

"Go to it. In the meantime, I've made photocopies of the six hundred million dollar deposit slip." He looked down at Ira. "Benjamin, will you help me? Pass out the photocopies of the deposit slip while I explain the deal."

"Sure." Ira glanced at Guy and grinned.

Guy remained standing, his hands pressed against the table, trying to think. Sherwood Anderson! He had to do something about Sherwood. What? Ideas passed through his mind, then shattered against the red haze of fury. That the likes of Sherwood Anderson and Stavros Lennos could affect his future—his birthright—was inconceivable.

Sherwood waited for Ira to step down from the platform before continuing. "The offer is simple. I know how much stock each of you owns and what the book value of Macleod Brothers was before the United Cinema debacle. Figuring out how much your stock was worth was a simple calculation."

"What's the deal?" Jonathan Graham shouted.

"The escrow account has been set up for two years. United Cinema stock should be back in the seventies by then. But if at any time—beginning one year from today and ending two years from today—you decide to sell your Macleod Brothers stock back to the firm, your losses—if any—will be covered from funds in the escrow account."

"What happens if Macleod Brothers goes under?" a trader asked.

"On the day Macleod Brothers goes under, Don Brenner has been authorized to pay you in full exactly what your stock was worth before the company required disaster relief."

"That's a very interesting offer." Another trader stood up. "You're right, Anderson. It's one I can't afford to refuse. I've only got one question. I learned on Wall Street no one gives away money. So tell me. Why? What do you and Lennos get out of this?"

Sherwood had expected the question. It was the single flaw in Stavros' offer. When he'd asked Stavros, "Why?" Stavros had said, "That's Family business. Tell whoever asks that you don't know what I get out of it. It will make no difference," and Stavros had smiled.

"I don't know," Sherwood admitted. "I wish I did, but I don't."

Guy shook off his paralysis. "I do," he thundered. "Stavros Lennos will have your marker. He'll own you.

Angelo Lupo—the head of a Mafia family—will own you. You'll owe the Mafia. Think what that means. At some time—I don't know when, but I do know it will happen—Lennos will tell you to do something. And it won't be an offer you can refuse. It'll be an . . ." He paused. ". . . order you can't refuse."

"You're not agreeing to do anything for Lennos," Sherwood insisted, but his doubts colored his voice.

Guy made a final push. "I'll up my bid. Book value plus fifteen percent for anyone who sells now." He glanced over his shoulder at Mrs. Neill. "You'll have to take my word about the extra five percent until the banks open Monday morning. My word is my bond. It always has been . . . it always will be."

Sherwood was reduced to repeating his offer. "The money is in The Bank of New York waiting for any partner who doesn't sell for one year."

At that point, the banking partner who'd left to call The Bank of New York returned. "It's on the level, fellas," he said in a loud voice. "I just spoke to Brenner. He has the six hundred million in an escrow account."

Guy gave Saunders a black look. "All who wish to sell, form a line at Mrs. Neill's table. Don't push. As I mentioned, Mrs. Neill has checks for everyone."

Sherwood said, "See. It's true. There is an escrow account." His words were lost in the noise of people moving to the front of the room.

Sherwood took a quick count. Of the forty-eight partners, twenty-one lined up to sell their stock. Strangely enough, more traders than bankers stood on that line. Twenty-seven partners—more bankers than traders—were willing to take their chances with the Mafia rather than lose money. Although he'd done better than he had expected, Sherwood was depressed. It said something ugly about the men and women who worked on Wall Street. Stavros had been more right than wrong.

Long after the partners had left, Guy Macleod remained in his office, thinking. He'd taken a big step toward reclaiming his heritage, but he wasn't home free. Not yet. He had to do something to raise the panic level. Too many of the bastards had lined up for Lennos. He could count on some having second thoughts about the demands Lennos might make in the future. Others would have nightmares that the millions in the escrow account might mysteriously disappear. But how many would turn tail and run into his arms? How many? Enough? He didn't know. And there was Sherwood. Sherwood Anderson would try to hold the rabbits in line. It stunned him to realize how much trouble Sherwood was causing him. No! It wasn't Sherwood. It was Stavros Lennos. Lennos again . . . damn him! Harvard, Victoria . . . would he never be rid of the man? To hell with Lennos. First things first. Abruptly, Guy picked up his private phone. He dialed a number.

A voice answered.

"You know who this is?" Guy asked.

The listener knew.

"Sherwood Anderson. You have the name?"

The listener had the name.

"How much?" Guy listened. He made a note. One hundred fifty thousand, fifty up front.

"Anderson's related by marriage to Stavros Lennos and Angelo Lupo."

The listener said nothing.

"That should make it more interesting."

The listener hung up.

Guy hung up, too. He took several deep breaths. For the first time since Anderson had broken his word—broken a trade—he felt content. Little Sherwood would learn that no one breaks a trade with Guy Macleod.

Chapter 30

THEY SAT in Irene Bentley's office, drinking tea... Celestial Seasonings. The office was located on the top floor of her 55th Street theater. It was as much a stage set as an office. Musty, dusty, and ratty, it reeked of theater. Theatrical memorabilia and theatrical furnishings filled the room. The smell of grease paint was everywhere. Outside of an old-fashioned, goose-necked desk lamp, the office was lit by baby spots hanging from the ceiling and other spots half-hidden in the corners of the room. The splintering wooden floor was littered with books and piles of scripts. The walls were hung with posters of plays Irene had either directed or produced... and plays that she wished she'd directed or produced. Frederic March in *Long Day's Journey into Night*... Audrey Hepburn in *Ondine*... Marlon Brando in *A Streetcar Named Desire*... Richard Burton in *Hamlet*. And more recently Dustin Hoffman in *The Merchant of Venice*. Jo Caro stared around the room. Another world... Broadway, off-Broadway, off-off-Broadway... dirty, gritty, grimy. In a way, more her style than glitzy, sunny, smoggy Hollywood.

The windows were completely covered by curtains made from the curtain of one of the many Broadway theaters that had been torn down and replaced by an office building, a tall, sterile rectangle of glass and steel that could pay higher taxes to a revenue-starved city. The furnishings were theater to the bone... a potpourri of stage sets. Irene gave Jo Caro the nickel guided tour. The couch had played in *Watch on the Rhine*. By now the springs were sprung. It took courage and agility to sit in it. Sitting down wasn't so bad... getting up was almost impossible. Large, heavy men often found it necessary to go from the couch to their knees before being

419

able to rise. The hard chair Jo sat in had starred in *The Caine Mutiny*. Another equally uncomfortable armchair had appeared in *The Philadelphia Story*. Every piece had been reviewed and applauded. Their stories would fill a scrapbook. The only non-theatrical furnishing in the office was a modern wall unit that housed sophisticated electronic and computerized video and sound equipment. The keyboard was the equal of anything found in a studio. The console was wired into the theater. Irene could videotape the performance of any actor or actress she wished to study, or tape a live production in its entirety. The Life Cycle bicycle against the wall was another incongruity. When Irene couldn't work out with her trainer, she cycled . . . or claimed she did.

Irene lounged behind her desk—inherited from *Inherit the Wind* with Paul Muni—rereading the Columbia contract for the third time. Jo tried to drink the tea. She wished it was scotch or white wine.

Irene looked up. "Remind me. When was it that we met at Macleod Brothers? I believe we had dinner the next evening?" Apparently, the dinner was too unimportant to remember.

"Yes. Just over three weeks ago. I noted it on my office calendar. I had to be in New York to file papers for a preliminary injunction against those pirates . . ."

"Feathered hats, feathered T-shirts, toy serpents for kids, serpent teeth. Good Lord! What nonsense!" Irene smiled indulgently. "I've no idea what they could do to promote *Deirdre*. Most of the performers are nude . . . half-nude anyway. There can't be much of a market for pubic wigs."

Jo grinned. "No problem. *Deirdre* tents, leather loincloths, spray-on cosmetics for the body, spears, swords, bows and arrows. There are plenty of potential promotion items." Jo rattled her tea cup. "What do you think of the Columbia offer?"

"Interesting. They want to make *Deirdre* as a film."

"They love it. The meeting was a piece of cake."

"Then why only three percent of net?"

"That's one percent more than United offered," Jo protested.

"But it's net . . . not gross." Irene was sullen.

"It's a good deal. Five percent of the gross is not in the cards."

"Guy Macleod told me it was doable. As I mentioned at dinner, we are very old friends."

"I know. But Mr. Macleod never worked in the Hollywood trenches. He's a Wall Streeter."

"He does control United."

Joe said, "True... but... Christie was president and Mr. Macleod believed in delegating authority."

Irene smiled gently. "So I gather. When he originally suggested I ask for five percent, he did mention that Christie Larsen would make the final decision, and that I was not to beat her over the head with his opinion."

"Obviously she didn't feel that *Deirdre* is as valuable a property as you do... or Mr. Macleod." Jo's voice was one of consolation. "But he would never overrule her. Now it doesn't matter how wrong Christie was." Her tone changed to strong congratulations. "Guber and Peters do believe in *Deirdre*."

"I've heard Jack Nicholson got between seventeen and twenty percent of gross for Batman."

Jo focused on a point in the ceiling. "Irene, you're an important theatrical producer—"

"A director, too."

"Director and producer... important," Jo said admiringly. "But on Broadway, not in films. Columbia is being very generous. Three percent of net profits can buy a lot of herbal tea." Jo took a sip.

"If there are any net profits."

"There's a million dollars up front." Jo smiled. "You got lucky. You get the writer's take. *Deirdre of the Sorrows* has outlived its copyright protection. It's a very generous contract," Jo insisted.

Irene was thinking. "It was good of you to put me in touch with Columbia."

"I think your play deserves the best production possible. I told you I saw it three times. It's pure theater magic."

"You don't feel you are being disloyal to United?" Irene asked offhandedly.

Jo took no offense. "No. Why should I? It was my impression you weren't satisfied with Christie's offer."

"I wasn't. I assume you get a nice commission if I take Columbia's offer." The smile was arch, a touch too broad.

"Of course not!" Jo was all innocence. "I'm a lawyer, not an agent. That would be a conflict of interest."

"Sorry. What do they call it in legalese... generally accepted community standards? I don't know the generally accepted community standards of the movie business. I didn't realize that what I suggested isn't done."

"It isn't done." Irene's face had stopped Jo. What affected her in particular were the eyes of the woman... the shadow and liner done by Princess Di's makeup artist, what's her name—if not her, by someone equally costly, tony, and trained—who made Irene's eyes deceptively sultry. Vain, expensive eyes, you'd say. But eyes that suddenly had taken on the glitter of a rattlesnake... an ice cold, level assessment of prey.

Jo's voice grew a trifle defensive. "I consider myself a woman with values. I think the play has many aesthetic and emotional dimensions. It deserves to be seen by millions of people who would never otherwise have the chance."

"I understand. An act of kindness and generosity is so rare that one can misunderstand it." Irene's words had the quality of authentic wisdom.

Jo stared at the woman. Irene Bentley was more of a mystery than she'd guessed... maybe even a danger.

"I did the best I could for the play." Jo placed a premium on maintaining her composure. She smiled weakly.

Irene smiled back. "I know. Thank you."

This tender duet was interrupted by the appearance of Franco Marconi. He threw open the door with a theatrical flourish and tossed his raincoat on a coat tree. Franco flung himself onto the *Watch on the Rhine* couch. It creaked under his weight and sagged even further. Franco might need a derrick to lift him from the couch.

"What the hell is wrong with this city? It's pouring outside and the wind is blowing like crazy. Doesn't anyone know it's not supposed to rain in July?"

Irene shook her head. "You don't understand, Franco. This is July in New York." Without missing a beat, she asked, "How did your meeting with Guy go?"

"That bastard! Son of a bitch! *Che stronzo!*"

"Guy was abominable?"

"*Un uomo maledetto!* We laughed! We joked! It went well. I told him this . . . I demanded that. He agreed. I am worth every penny. We discussed when the announcement will be made. But first there's the formality of a contract." Franco rubbed his forehead.

"Don't stop. The suspense is killing me. What happened?"

"What happened?" Franco repeated the question, growing flushed. "His secretary, that bitch, interrupted us." Franco mimicked Mrs. Neill's New York accent. "'Mr. Macleod, your four o'clock has arrived.' Guy jumped from his chair like a fool shot from a cannon. He said, 'Show him in. Show him in.' He hurried to the door to greet the man. He didn't greet me at the door." Franco ruminated on this shocking truth like a cow chewing its cud.

"Then what happened?" Irene urged him on. She noted that Jo was glaring at Franco.

Franco made an Italian movement with his hands. His eyes rolled toward the ceiling. "A midget happened! A skinny, bald midget in a gray business suit. The midget walked in, smiled at Guy . . . Guy smiled at him. They shook hands. Next time maybe they'll kiss." Franco let fly a few more curses in Italian. "Guy turned to me and said, 'Thank you for dropping in, Mr. Marconi. We'll be in touch. Goodbye.' He took my arm and showed me the door. I, Franco Marconi, I was tossed out on my ass for a midget banker type."

"Why were you meeting with Guy Macleod?" Jo asked.

"We were discussing the terms of my becoming president of United Cinema."

"You, president? Of United Cinema? I don't believe it."

The blood of battle was still in Franco's eye. "I'm the only possible choice. Undoubtedly, we'll work out the details tomorrow."

"Undoubtedly," Jo said in a tone which implied she very much doubted it. "If he sees you tomorrow."

"He'll see me. Before I left I told the broad, his secretary, to tell Mr. Macleod that I was meeting Michelle Pfeiffer for lunch tomorrow. I hoped he might join us."

"Where are you lunching?" Irene asked. "I like Pfeiffer's work. Maybe I'll join you."

"We are not lunching. Pfeiffer's shooting a film for Warner. But she turns men on. Macleod'll meet me tomorrow, on the moon if necessary." He smiled. A political animal, Franco usually knew which buttons to push. "Michelle will send her regrets . . . a script conference. I'll promise future lunches."

"You have no principles." Irene smiled.

"I do have a few. But none struck off in gold."

"Would you try for fool's gold?" Jo smirked.

"That's enough out of you or you'll find yourself back peddling your ass on the Strip for some third-rate law firm. As heir apparent to United, I want to wind up the paperwork on *Deirdre*. Get it scheduled for production . . ."

"You are not president of United." Jo was incensed. "You can't cut a deal."

"Ah, Jo. The blond bimbo fights back." Franco's smile was nasty. "I will be . . . by tomorrow. Irene, I have some thoughts on what we could offer you."

Crocodile smile. "I have an interesting offer from Columbia."

Outraged virtue. "Irene! Behind my back you took *Deirdre* to . . . to . . ." He choked. ". . . Guber and Peters?"

"How can you think that of me, Franco? Of course I didn't go to Guber and Peters. Jo put the gentlemen in touch with me."

Franco gave Jo a corrosive glance. "Bitch, you're fired."

Trim. Bristling. "Get off it, Marconi! You can't fire me!"

Torches of zealotry flamed in his eyes. "It gives me great pleasure to fire you, Jo Caro. I repeat, you're fired."

Up Jo came from the chair, finger wagging at Franco. "You are not president yet, fat boy . . ."

Irene interposed. "I want to ask you a question, Jo."

". . . and you won't be." Jo smiled at Franco, all teeth bared.

"Cunt!" Franco spat.

"My goodness, Franco, you sound so insecure." Jo stared at his bearded, puffy face.

They continued their campaign of cut and slash—neither being able to score a nick on the thick skin of the other—

until Irene repeated, "I've a question for you, Jo."

"Me? Sure. Be my guest."

"Why don't you want me to give the *Deirdre* project to United Cinema?"

Jo actually looked surprised. She swallowed. "I told you. The play is pure magic. It deserves the best possible deal.

When I'm president, you'll get the best deal possible! I swear on my honor," Franco said hotly.

"You wouldn't know honor if it grabbed you by the balls!"

"What if Christie Larsen isn't indicted? Will she be president again?" Irene asked.

"She will be indicted," Franco said with Olympian detachment. "Even if she isn't, Guy Macleod will never make her president again."

"Do you think she forged those checks?"

"Who knows?" Jo said. "It doesn't make sense. Christie is no professional. Forging a signature is tough."

"Was she under financial pressures? Did she need money?"

"Christie! No way! I think she saves supermarket coupons. She has an IRA, Treasuries, CDs. She's already paid for Tommy's tuition at Yale."

"Harvard," Irene said automatically.

"You're right. Harvard. Did she mention it?"

Irene's smile was enigmatic. "She mentioned it."

"Anyway, no money pressures," Jo said. "But Franco always has money pressures. Personally, I think only Franco could forge his own signature. It's indecipherable ... he never learned how to write."

"Are you saying that I forged my own name to duplicate checks?" Franco gave Jo a black look.

Jo made sly noises. "That was a lot of forgery. Seven checks. Maybe I ought to cue the cops."

"The papers said there were three checks," Irene pointed out.

"You're right, there were three checks," Franco murmured.

"Did you count each one?" Jo asked with a hard, cold emphasis.

"I was there. I heard what Detective Garcia said. Three checks were duplicated."

"I was there, too. I got Christie out. I thought there were six or seven checks, but maybe there were only three," Jo said amiably. "Still, suppose the cops are wrong? They should investigate you. You've got all kinds of money problems. United doesn't need another president indicted for..."

"Bitch! Whore! *Putana! Poule!*"

Jo smiled. She'd drawn first blood. "I have always preferred obvious lunatics. Mad people should raise their fists to the sky and curse. Franco does it right."

Irene was so fascinated—it was like watching two great performers trying to top each other... anything you can do, I can do rattier... I can be more ratty than you—she was unaware that someone had opened the door to her office.

"Irene, darling," Mona Anderson trilled. "Sherwood has agreed." Mona paused and surveyed the scene. "You have company. Sorry."

"No. It's quite all right. They were just leaving." Irene smiled at Franco... at Jo. "Dear people, my next appointment has arrived. It's business as usual. We have to discuss my new production of *Lulu*. Why don't you two have a nice, drunken dinner? Kiss, fuck, and make up."

Jo's eyes flashed. "It's more fun to curse the bastard."

"Go to hell!" Franco snorted.

"And join you? Never!"

Franco stared. He was thinking how best to kill her.

"Excuse me a sec, Irene. I have to use the bathroom." Mona left the office. She wanted no part of theatrical tantrums.

Franco struggled from the couch—he was more supple than one might imagine—grabbed his raincoat, and walked quickly to the door. "I'll call you tomorrow, Irene." The door slammed and he was gone.

Jo rose from the chair. "Don't take anything that mountain of ego tells you seriously. He'll never be president. Columbia is another ball of wax. They spend money like it's going out of style."

"Thank you for the advice, Jo. And let me give you something in return. Not advice... information."

Jo nodded expectantly. "Yes?"

"For openers, I don't like you. Not one damn bit."

The cool words hit Jo like a fist.

"But you're the daughter I should have had."

Jo stared. The changes were too abrupt for her to keep up. What next?

"Certainly the daughter I deserved. You and I, we're cut from the same cloth. You have my worst, my most serviceable, qualities. You are merciless in your ambitions, canny and conniving, deceitful. You lie on demand, to protect yourself, aggrandize yourself, for money, power, even just for the hell of it. It's a habit. You are shrewd, flattering, a born killer. If I didn't know better I'd say you were my daughter."

Jo swallowed. The rules of the game kept changing.

"But you're not my daughter. You have everything I have. Except for my talent and luck. Yes, I was luckier than you've been." Irene's manner changed. "I married up . . . a gentleman who taught me many things. And who, a long time ago, I loved." She made a quick motion of dismissal with her hand. "That's past history. What isn't past history is my daughter. She takes after her father, not me. She has his character. Given half a chance, he was decent, honorable, lousy with integrity, capable of dying for love. She's the same. She's a damn fool. But one takes what one gets. She is my daughter. And it recently occurred to me that that is something for which I ought to thank providence."

Mona entered the office. "Oh! You're still busy?"

"Still," Irene said. "Take five." Mona vanished.

Jo forced a laugh. "Another day, another dollar ninety-eight. Thank you for the personal analysis. You're more right than wrong."

"My pleasure."

"And *Deirdre of the Sorrows?*"

"You'll hear when I decide. So will Franco."

"I get the message," Jo said at the door. "Don't call me. I'll call you."

Irene waited for the door to close before making a phone call. Waiting for the call to be answered, her sense of strangeness increased. Why was she doing this? Her business sense, her better judgement, everything she'd based her life on told her not to make the call. She started to hang up but couldn't. She was trapped. There are some emotions that run so deep, one's understanding of them is only on a primitive level, beyond any power of explanation. They form the impulses that ignore common sense, that refuse to be denied. Irene was having such an experience.

Christie sat in Louis' study, trying to read a script he insisted she read, but she felt as if she were asleep with her eyes open. Louis sat at his desk, annotating a script he had already read. He looked up for a moment.

"You okay?"

She smiled. "Okay."

The phone rang, rang a second time. In the middle of the third ring it was picked up. Linda Loomis had moved out to Louis' house for the siege and was taking messages. The intercom button on Louis' phone lit. He picked up the receiver. He listened. He looked at Christie and pursed his lips.

Christie felt a thaw of hope. Simon? "Who is it?"

Louis put a hand over the receiver. "This is your call, kid."

"Who is it?"

"Your mother. Want to talk to her?"

The best Christie could do was say, "My what?"

"I said your mother."

"Irene?"

Louis eyed Christie gravely. "She said, 'Tell Christie her mother is calling.'"

Christie floundered. So many emotions were surging within her at once that she was afraid she might start to cry. Her mother! She hadn't used the word in a thousand years. Until the meeting at Franco's house, it was a non-word. But then the lid had lifted on memory. Now uninvited pictures came and went erratically in her mind almost daily. In a sudden rush they crowded in, leaving no room for any other thought. She saw her father's face the day the eviction notice was posted on their door. She heard her mother singing off-key, "I have rings on my fingers, bells on my toes ... rouge on my nipples ... anything goes ..." Then

NAKED CALL

laughter . . . gasps . . . moans . . . the sounds of passion. The expression on Christie's face changed continuously, like cloud formations.

"I'll take it, Louis." She reached for the receiver. The silence of the years was resonating between them. At last the connection was made. Christie said, "Hello . . . er . . . Mother."

Irene hung up the phone. She'd told Christie why she'd called. The rest was up to Christie. She tapped herself lightly on her forehead. Enough of *Deirdre* for the moment. Mona was a potential backer. It was Irene's experience that backers expect special treatment. They do not expect to be told to, "take five." Irene hurried to the door. She hoped Mona hadn't left. That would be a nuisance. She'd have to call, apologize, make up a silly excuse, start the seduction all over again. When she opened the door, she was relieved to find Mona sitting on the stairs, her raincoat neatly folded under her and her rain hat tied around the banister.

Mona stood up. "Was that Franco Marconi?" she asked.

"The great Marconi, himself." None of Irene's concerns showed.

"You must have had quite a session," Mona said with a smile. "Marconi came down the stairs so fast, he tripped over me. If I hadn't caught hold of his arm, he'd have cartwheeled down the whole flight." Mona entered the office, hung up her coat and hat, and sat in *The Caine Mutiny* chair. She'd had one experience with the *Watch on the Rhine* couch . . . one was enough. "Who was the woman?" she asked. "She was as upset as Marconi. She just didn't show it as much."

"Jo Caro. She's United Cinema's house counsel. She and Marconi went at it pretty good."

"Everyone has troubles, even a great director and a successful lawyer. One way or another, they'll work it out."

Irene found it curious that Mona didn't ask what the fight was all about. It occurred to her that there was more to the rich, luscious Mrs. Sherwood Anderson than her pretty face and designer dresses.

"I told you on the phone I wanted to talk to you about *Lulu* and *Pandora's Box*." Although Mona did her best to sound casual, Irene Bentley was too much the professional to miss the excitement bubbling inside of Mona. "The budget... one and a half million I believe you said."

"That's right. That includes a ten percent reserve for contingencies."

Mona smiled. "There always is the unexpected. And assuming an average house of seventy-five percent, an investor will get her money back in about fifteen months."

"Plus or minus a month." Irene tried not to stare at Mona. She'd tossed out the numbers over the phone, not expecting Mona to focus on them. To most amateur backers, the play was the thing... the bright lights, Broadway, glamour, opening night... not making money.

"I assume you'll direct *Lulu*," Mona said.

"Yes."

"Your salary for directing the play, the rent for your theater during rehearsals, your overhead as the producer... all those costs are included in the budget?"

Irene raised her eyebrows. "Have you ever put money into a theatrical production before?"

"No."

"Then how did you..."

"I know how to read. I spent a few days in the *Variety* library. Everything you ever wanted to know about producing a play—and more—is in the back issues of *Variety*." She laughed. "The only missing ingredient is talent. That's where you come in."

"Thank you." Although Irene's words were cool, her expression was that of a woman who is both charmed and startled.

"Is there anything unusual in the production or operating budget... extraordinary expenses?"

"You mean, have I buried a diamond necklace for the producer in the budget? No. No diamond necklace... no Rolls Royce... not even an expense account at Lutece."

"I didn't think there was, but I had to ask. Sherwood and I had a long talk last night, in between..." Mona was still able to blush. "... er... not talking."

"That's nice. Married people should talk to each other ... in between not talking." Irene did not blush.

"We decided we would like to back your production of *Lulu* . . . with two provisos."

"Why are there always provisos? All right. If I can agree to your provisos, how much money do you want to invest?"

For the first time, Mona looked surprised. "You said the production would cost a million and a half. We'll put up the million and a half."

Irene stifled a gasp. She studied the *Ondine* poster. "I have other investors who won't like being shut out of the production."

"That's their problem . . . and yours. It's an all or nothing deal, Irene."

My God! How the hell did I do it? How could I have misjudged her so completely? Irene tried to lighten the atmosphere. "There's a small male part in *Lulu*. Would Sherwood like to audition for it?"

"Never! Before I'd allow Sherwood to hang out with a bunch of eager actresses, I'd cut his balls off . . . and I love my husband's balls very much."

Irene let out an explosive laugh. "You be careful or I might become too fond of you." After several deep breaths she asked, "What are your provisos?"

"We trust you and believe you, but this is business. I want to sign off on the detailed budgets. Not to second guess you . . . I just want to know where my money is going."

"What else?"

"If *Lulu* is a success, I want an option to back *Pandora's Box*."

"No. You can sign off on the budget. But I can't lock myself into a two-production deal. I can handle my other backers for one production, not two. I'll lose them. Being fond of you is one thing. Being dependent on you for production money is something else." She looked at the young woman . . . a genuine original. "Sorry, I won't risk it."

Mona made a church steeple out of her fingers. For almost a minute, she studied them as though they held an extraordinary secret. When she looked up at Irene, she smiled. "I wouldn't want you to be totally dependent on me for production money either. We'll settle for *Lulu*. When can I see the budget?"

"Now." Irene opened the center drawer of her *Inherit the Wind* desk and slid a manila folder in Mona's direction. "The budget and a backer's agreement. Go over the budget with Sherwood and get back to me with any questions. The backer's agreement is boilerplate, but you'll want to show it to your lawyer."

"It won't take long, Irene. Two days at the most." Mona held out her hand. "Partner."

Irene shook Mona's hand. "Partner."

"May I use your phone?" Mona asked.

"Of course."

Mona dialed a number. It was answered almost immediately. "Sherwood, honey. I've made the deal with Irene . . . one and a half million . . . we're backing *Lulu*. No. She won't go for *Pandora's Box*. You're wrong. I wouldn't if I were in her place. I'll tell her you agree." There was a long pause during which Mona listened, not moving a muscle. Then she asked quietly, "For how long? Four days! Why didn't you tell me? Oh, honey. Please. No more heroics. Promise. What does he look like? Shit! Look, it's pouring. The Rolls is parked downstairs. Harold can take me home and then pick you up. Please wait for Harold . . . please. All right," she sighed. "You're a big boy . . . you can take care of yourself. Just be careful." She giggled. "Me, too. We'll have one of our special evenings . . . martinis . . . I'll light the fire . . . you and me, alone . . . love you." She hung up the phone very slowly and reached for her raincoat.

As Irene walked Mona to the door, she asked, "Tell me, partner, why are you risking a million and a half dollars in my play? The real reason, please."

Mona grinned. She had a marvelous grin. "For fun, Irene. Just fun. Money isn't everything. Fun is two percent. Sherwood needs to have some fun."

Sherwood Anderson stood just outside the doors of the Macleod Brothers offices. It was really raining, a hard, driving rain that turned umbrellas inside out and penetrated raincoats. Stupid not to have Mona send the limousine for him. He glanced up and down the street. No sign of the clown who'd been following him. It was raining so hard he probably took the night off. Mona worried too much. There were no empty taxis in sight. Most Wall Streeters were long gone and the taxis disappeared with their customers. He'd wait a few more minutes, then go back to his office and phone for a taxi. He started to turn, then stopped. A green cab turned the corner. A gypsy cab? Yeah! Sherwood stepped out from the protection of the overhang, waving his hand. The cab blinked its lights . . . the driver saw him. Whew! That was luck. Mona was waiting for him. He wanted to get home. As the cab neared the building entrance, it slowed down. Sherwood stepped to the curb, then onto the street, all the time waving his hand. He was so concentrated on the cab, he didn't see a man leave an alley at the end of the block and run toward him, gesturing wildly with his arms. The rain drowned out the man's cries. "No! No! No!" Sherwood took another step into the street . . . and another. When the cab was twenty feet from him, he stopped watching it and felt for his wallet. Gypsy cabs were expensive. He was so focused on his wallet, he didn't hear the whine of the cab's motor as the driver floored the gas pedal, didn't see the cab pick up speed. When he looked up, the cab was only a few feet away. He stared at the grill, paralyzed. The bumper of the speeding cab hit him, tossed him through the air. He flew ten feet before crashing to the street. Sherwood was dead when he hit the ground, but the driver wasn't taking chances. He turned around and drove back over Sherwood's body before speeding away. Behind the wheel of the cab, the driver grinned. He'd earned his money.

The driver never saw the man who had been crying out and running toward Sherwood. The man stopped in the street. He stared at the cab. Then he took a notebook and pencil from his pocket. Standing in the rain, he wrote down the license plate number of the cab. When he finished, he walked slowly away, shaking his head.

Chapter 31

PETE, THE inside doorman at The Majestic, used the house phone.

"Mrs. Anderson. I'm sorry to trouble you, but there's a Mr. Stavros Lennos in the lobby. He insists on seeing you."

"It's all right, Pete. Send him up."

"Yes, ma'am."

When Stavros arrived, the door was open. Mona was standing just inside the entrance hall, half-smiling. She wore black from head to toe, as her mother, her aunts, and her grandmother had before her whenever tragedy struck the Montefuoco family. But, as in everything, Mona did it her way. She looked like a black exclamation point in an ankle length, columnar, black velvet dress with a turtleneck collar and long, skintight black sleeves. A black silk scarf, tied like a nurse's headdress, concealed her dark hair, and sunglasses hid her red, swollen eyes. The stark black outfit heightened the pallor of her skin, scrubbed as clean of makeup as it had been when she was very young and attended St. Theresa's Catholic School. Judging from the look on her face, she might have been a hurt child, but for two incongruities. In her left hand she held a martini-sized glass of gin... in her right hand, a pistol.

She squinted at Stavros and blinked as though she was having difficulty focusing. "Come in. Am I glad to see you!" She stood on her tiptoes to kiss him on the cheek and then, with head down, entered his comforting embrace.

Minutes passed before Stavros held her away to examine her face. He carefully took off her glasses. "Are you all right?" he asked. "You look ill."

"I'm aces. *Perfetto!*" She kissed his cheek again and backed out of his arms. She drained the glass of gin and sighed. "It's the funeral. Funerals do me in, even the funerals of people I hardly know." She swallowed, at a loss for what to say next. Finally, she made a stab. "Come. We'll sit in the library... his favorite room. It's so right. The club chairs, the Parsons table, the mahogany bookshelves, shelf after shelf of leather-bound books, classics ... at least two nights a week he used to read to me." She spoke in the hushed voice usually reserved for conversations during church services. Once in the library, she placed the gun on the seat of the chair she usually occupied and walked to the bar. "What are you drinking?" she asked. "These days I do the honors."

"The usual," Stavros said.

"I forget. What is it?"

"Scotch. Any brand. Straight up."

Mona made Stavros his drink. She then poured herself another martini glass of gin. Staggering slightly, she handed Stavros his scotch, and then abruptly she lost hold of herself. Her hand began to shake, spilling some of the gin. Her legs buckled and she collapsed into her chair. She was oblivious that she was sitting on the pistol or that she was holding the half-full glass of gin in her lap. Her chest heaved. She appeared to be struggling for tears that would not come.

Stavros grew impatient with the performance. "Stop it, Mona." He was neither kind nor gentle.

Mona wiped her eyes with the back of her hand, laughing with mild hysteria. She took the gun from beneath her bottom and placed it on the side table. "Sorry," she choked. "I forgot it was there. It goosed me." She giggled. "Don't worry, it's not loaded... not yet. I'm not going to shoot myself in my ass. I won't commit suicide. No Montefuoco has ever killed himself." She smiled. "You know what I'd like?"

Stavros' mind was elsewhere. "I'll get Ilsa. She'll wipe up the gin."

"I gave Ilsa the week off. I wanted to be alone after the funeral. We don't have to wipe anything up. Gin doesn't stain. It dries like water." She tossed off what was left of her drink. "What I would like is another gin, please." She waved her hand holding the empty glass.

"I think you've had enough." Stavros loomed over her, his face drawn.

"Uncle Stavros, please. I'm fine . . . shipshape and fancy free. Another drink, sir."

Stavros went to the bar and brought back another glass of gin. He handed it to her.

"How much have you had? The bottle's half empty."

"Thank you, dear uncle." A pulse was beating in her forehead. "Don't worry so much. I am not becoming an alcoholic. I don't have the genes for it. I never heard of a Sicilian drunk. These days I just have a little drink or two before beddie-bye. It helps me sleep."

"And then you wake up."

"Then I drink some more."

"Gin is no answer."

"I have the answer." She patted the gun. "Once it's settled, I'll sleep like a baby. So tell me what gives. I want my suspicions confirmed."

"You're becoming emotional."

"Of course I'm becoming emotional. I'm a woman. Something terrible has happened. When my father was murdered, I wore a black, sackcloth dress and a black scarf on my head like Sicilian women have worn for their dead since time began. I'm older now . . . the newest Sicilian model. My wail is the same wail, I tear my hair the way my grandmother tore her hair over her son, I weep the way Sicilian women have always wept. But I learned at lot from you . . . from Uncle Angelo. I want vengeance as you would . . . vendetta. It is the Sicilian way. So tell me who . . ."

Stavros regarded her for a long moment. "How much do you know already?"

"The hit and run accident was no accident." She tamed her features, lowered her voice. "Sherwood was murdered."

"Why do you say that?"

"There is a fight going on—a vendetta of some kind— between you and Guy Macleod. Guy Macleod! The first time I heard his name I was a kid. It sounded strange. It wasn't an Italian name, or Sicilian, and it was always mentioned with yours. My aunts gossiped. They worried about you. We all did, I more than the others. You were Daddy's closest friend." Her gaze fixed on him. "That's why Alberto was following Sherwood. You knew he was in danger."

Stavros smiled to conceal his irritation. "How did you know about Alberto?"

"From Uncle Angelo. I went to see him the day after you told Sherwood not to sell his stock to Guy Macleod . . . to Macleod Brothers."

"What did you say to Angelo?"

"I told him I worried about Sherwood. I loved my husband, but I knew he was an innocent, a sweet, well-bred boy." She paused for a minute, seeing a picture in her mind. Sherwood's shoulders were heavy and wide, his chest was flat and broad, as hairless as a girl's chest. She loved his hands . . . they were wise with her body. He had a small, brown birthmark on his stomach, like a drop of honey. She stopped the picture. "Also he was weak, soft, no street smarts. He didn't even know there was a street, except Wall Street, which was lucky, because he couldn't take care of himself on the city's slimy, dirty streets. I think I fell in love with his ancestors . . . his belief in his own aristocracy. He thought he belonged, that he, and others like him, were the right people." She'd said it as a challenge, hurled it at Stavros . . . a gauntlet he picked up at his peril. Then she sighed in resignation. "But the right people didn't want him. Once they had . . . not now. He couldn't beat them and he couldn't beat you. He had no balls . . . except in bed. In bed he was the right man . . . all the man any woman could want." Her voice became accusatory. "What you asked of him was beyond him. He tried to do it. He was too frightened of you not to. I was afraid, too. I saw my husband's bloody, broken body sprawled somewhere." She shook her head sadly. "So I told Uncle Angelo I wanted him protected."

"What did Angelo say?" Stavros' face was impassive.

"'Don't worry, Mona. Stavros is protecting your Sherwood.'" Mona's naturally light voice mocked her attempt to imitate Angelo Lupo's rich baritone. "'Your Uncle Stavros is efficient. Nothing will happen to your husband.' Which told me what I wanted to know. Alberto was tailing Sherwood."

"To protect him," Stavros said dryly. "He failed."

"You failed."

"I failed." Mona had never seen her Uncle Stavros so disturbed. Deep circles of worry ringed his eyes. "Alberto is a shadow. He once guarded a president—"

"They shoot presidents."

"Not Alberto's president . . . or Angelo. Alberto is your Uncle Angelo Lupo's personal bodyguard. Angelo released him to guard Sherwood."

"I know. It wasn't Alberto's fault," Mona said dully. "Alberto, the Doberman."

Stavros said nothing.

"Now tell me, who did it? You know who killed my husband."

"What difference does it make?" Stavros asked. "The Family will take care of the matter."

Mona stood up. Sitting down, she felt intimidated. "Sherwood was my husband. I have a right to know."

"The fewer people who know, the better it is. A necessary precaution. In our business, we can never be too careful. You know that, Mona."

Mona shook her head. She was talking to Stavros, but only in her mind. My father wanted a son. I am my father's son. I take vengeance for our Family honor. Out loud she said, almost humbly, "I am not a soldier, but I am a member of this Family. I found my father hanging from the rafter. I found him . . . not Angelo, not you, not Alberto. Me! Tell me who murdered my husband. Which Macleod . . . Guy Macleod or Simon Macleod?"

Stavros was sitting straight-backed with his palms pressed together in his lap.

"I asked you a question." When she received no answer, she said, "Sherwood was smarter than you thought." A jolt of anger surged through her. "You never gave him credit for brains. He was very ambitious. He had a lot of plans."

"I gave him credit." Stavros' answer was a model of bland evasion. "Your husband had intelligence and ability, little of which he used. He loved you . . . you . . ." Stavros allowed himself to stretch the truth . . . it wasn't actually a lie. ". . . not your money. If his life had not been wasted, he would have been—maybe not a better husband—he would have been a better man."

"Wasted? He was wasted. Why was he wasted? You've always claimed you hate waste!"

In the end, Stavros was as fair as most men . . . far more astute, but utterly ruthless. He weighed the contradiction. "He wasn't completely wasted."

"What do you mean?"

"What I said."

"He's dead. Alive, he would have been an asset to the Family."

"He already has been an asset."

"How?"

"By dying. His murder gave us what we want. It opened a can of worms, one that the Family has been trying to open for quite a while." Almost against his will, his face relaxed into a pirate's grin. "Among the worms is United Cinema."

"I don't understand."

"If you think about it, you will."

Mona was certain she'd go mad trying to drag the facts out of Stavros. "Okay. No more questions. I don't care. All I do know is Sherwood would be alive today if he hadn't agreed to help you."

"In the end, we all die," Stavros murmured, thinking about something else entirely. "Meantime, I beg you to remember that you married him. If you hadn't married him, the Family would never have considered using him. He gained a great deal by marrying you."

Mona's frustration spilled out in a gust of anger. "What, besides an early grave? I beg you to remember, I gained a great deal by marrying him. He was the best thing that ever happened to me. He taught me how to dress, how not to wear makeup, how to eat properly. I didn't know there were lobster forks until we were married. He did the Pygmalion number. He made me who I am . . . Mrs. Sherwood Anderson." She wasn't sure she could stand what she was thinking. She stared at Stavros and tried to listen.

"I don't know if the end justifies the means, but Sherwood was a means."

They exchanged a straight, unclouded look. "What was the end?" she asked.

"I told you. The can of worms."

"Why Sherwood?"

"Because you bought him a partnership in Macleod Brothers. Without him, we'd have less than we do." Stavros deliberately turned away from her. "So I have to thank you. Unfortunately, I can't thank Sherwood."

"Without that partnership, he'd be alive."

"You are a Sicilian wife," he said quietly. "You had no choice."

"Yes, I'm a Sicilian wife. I obey my husband in all matters." She sat down hard in the chair. "He wanted it."

"So did you."

"I did." She put the glass down on the table. Maybe the dizziness would pass. "I liked the idea of Macleod Brothers' blue blood."

"Red blood wasn't good enough for you?" His face had an angry straightness she'd never seen before.

"Mine is red. So is yours. We come from a long line of red-blooded killers. I was sick of us... of you... of myself. I wanted something more civilized, a life where differences are settled over a conference table, not with a rifle shot from behind an olive tree. Or an Uzi from an automobile window."

Stavros stood up, took Mona's arms, and pulled her to her feet. He slapped her... twice... harder than she'd ever been hit... once on each side of her face. Then he pushed her down into the chair and stood over her.

"No tears?" he said bitingly. "Ladies with blue blood are seldom struck... and when they are, they weep."

"No tears." She'd already wept herself dry, wept as she had never wept for her frightened, foolish mother... for her violent, loving father.

He held out his handkerchief but she waved it away.

"Forget it," she said. "I don't need it anymore."

"Only blue-blooded killers were good enough for you."

"Something like that. Bad joke on me."

"Very bad joke."

An extraordinary calm came over her. She spoke with soft menace. "He's a murderer. I knew it was him. I pushed you because I don't want to waste the bullets." She made a ceremony of caressing the pistol, as though the barrel was a sexual object. "This is a Glisanti. It's very rare. Once it was the Italian service pistol. In 1934, it was replaced by the Beretta. It belonged to my great-grandfather," Mona explained with a warm, confiding smile. "It uses a special nine-millimeter cartridge. There are only six bullets left. None can be wasted. But if necessary, I will use them all . . . on one man."

Stavros made a mocking sound deep in his throat. "Your father had a taste for melodrama. He called the gun, 'The Montefuoco Executioner.' Whenever he carried it, someone died."

"I honor his tradition with Guy Macleod."

"What makes you so certain he's responsible?" Stavros' tone, like hers, was dangerously flat.

"I haven't told you everything. I wanted to be absolutely sure." Mona's lips were almost colorless. "The night Sherwood was murdered, I called him at the office. He was very upset. He said to tell you that he was being followed . . . had been followed for days, since the argument with Macleod. He didn't tell me sooner because he didn't want to worry me. Worry me . . . with Enrico Montefuoco for a father." Mona shook her head. "Now he was worried."

Stavros' face was as rigid as a mask. "What did you say?"

"I asked him what the man looked like. He described him very well . . . a soldier for one of the Families. I can spot a soldier in a movie line, at a supermarket checkout counter. Anywhere!" She chewed on her lower lip. "When Sherwood described the man, I was scared out of my mind. I wanted to send Harold to pick him up, but Sherwood insisted that he could take care of himself. And I agreed. I actually agreed. Uncle Angelo had promised me he was under the Family's protection. I told him to come home immediately . . . we were going to celebrate."

"We did our best."

"I know that. Who was it? No stories, please. No lies."

"Benvenuto Corsi, a member of the Carlino Family."

"How do you know?"

"Alberto. He got the license plate number of the cab."

"Then Alberto didn't fail entirely." There was a cramp in her neck and a buzzing in her ear like a mosquito circling. "A Carlino soldier? I don't see the connection between the

Carlino Family and Guy Macleod." She shrugged. "I don't have to. But there is a connection. Macleod is the one who hired Corsi."

"Why do you insist it was Macleod?"

"Please, Uncle Stavros. Don't treat me like a fool. Who else could it be? You put my civilian in the middle of a battle of angels... or devils. You and Macleod. In such a battle, the civilians are always the first victims. Sherwood said it could happen. I didn't tell him, but I agreed. You didn't have him killed." She paused. The threat of ancient violence flooded the WASP library. Her lips curled. "No. Sherwood was yours. You don't kill your own. That leaves only Guy Macleod. Guy Macleod had him killed. It was supposed to look like an accident." She picked up the gun ... stroked it. "It isn't a big gun. But that's the thing about guns. They look a lot bigger when they're pointed at you."

Stavros' eyes did not leave her face. "Mona, this is an order. You are not to point the gun at Macleod. We will attend to the matter."

For an instant, Mona was confused. Then she became angry. "Uncle Stavros, you're half Greek, half Sicilian. But suddenly you're all Sicilian. You think women are only good for cooking, cleaning, making love, and having babies. Men run the world. In your world, men kill... and are killed... and men kill again... and are killed. This is not your Sicily. This is my America. Women also run this world... and like men, they can kill."

"I order you to keep away from Guy Macleod."

She started to laugh, a wild, unreasoning laugh. "You order me?"

"Did you hear me?"

Mona spoke with a harsh, male fury. "No!"

"The Lupo Family—your Family—orders you to keep away from Guy Macleod."

Mona clamped her jaw shut and nodded. She continued nodding mechanically.

Afterward, Stavros thought about Sicilian women. We raise them in America, send them to school, give them freedoms they would never have in Sicily. We educate them to be Americans. And what happens to our educated, liberated Sicilian-American women? They acquire the worst traits of Sicilian men.

PART ELEVEN

1992
JULY 16–JULY 18

Chapter 32

IT WAS 12:15 Wednesday evening by the time the Boeing 747 rolled to a stop at the Japan Airlines terminal at Kennedy International Airport. Simon Macleod unbuckled his seat belt and stretched. Fourteen hours in the air. Even first class was too confining for a man of his height and bulk. That he hadn't sold the deal added to the strain. Summo National would only consider an equity position. They would never become a subordinated lender. When he rose to leave, the head of the Japanese negotiating team was surprised. "Don't you wish to call your headquarters for further instructions?" the man asked. "I am headquarters," he'd replied.

He'd broken off talks without telling Guy. Guy would have tried to talk him into staying. Actually, he felt relieved at ending the farce. He was anxious to see Christie. Talking on the phone was a wipeout. Their love was too new, too vulnerable. He couldn't hold her close over the telephone and say, "I love you." The trip had been a waste of time. In fact, the bottom line—net net—was he'd failed his brother, failed his partners, failed Macleod Brothers... failed himself.

Simon was the third passenger off the plane. He glanced at the usual taxi and limousine drivers waiting at the gate, holding signs with names written on them... Yamamuro, Evans, Saito, Gigli, Karasaki, Macleod. Macleod! What the hell? No one knew he was on this flight. Was there someone else on the flight named Macleod? Who? Simon stopped in front of the man holding the sign.

"My name is Simon Macleod. I don't think you're waiting for me."

"I sure am, buddy." The chauffeur was a short, swarthy man of about fifty with a long hooked nose and a thick black mustache. He eyed Simon up and down. "Yeah! The description fits. You're the guy."

"How'd you know I'd be on this flight?"

"I didn't. We got men covering every direct flight from Tokyo . . . been covering all the flights for a week."

"Who's paying you?"

The chauffeur pulled a piece of paper from his pocket. "A Mr. Ira Benjamin. He's already spent about five thousand bucks making sure that you got met."

"Ira?" *What the hell is going on?* "I've got to pick up my luggage."

"I was told to tell you to forget your bags. You can pick 'em up tomorrow. Your office is closed. I'm to drive you direct to 72nd and Central Park West."

"What's your name?"

"Dejerian. Ed Dejerian."

"Okay, Ed Dejerian, let's go."

When the elevator doors opened on Ira's floor, Ira was waiting in the entrance to his apartment. He was wearing a brown terry cloth robe and slippers, his hair was uncombed, and he needed a shave.

"Where the hell have you been?"

"In Tokyo. You know that."

The men walked through the library to a long, narrow, glass-enclosed sun porch overlooking Central Park West. The view of the city—Central Park, the lights in apartment houses on Fifth Avenue and on Central Park South—was one of Simon's favorites and the one thing his loft didn't have.

Ira motioned for Simon to sit in a wicker chair. "I called every goddamn hotel in Tokyo. Where were you?"

"With Araturo Takahashi . . . at his house. Guy said it's quite an honor."

"Guy arranged that?"

"Yes. Why?"

"Figures. Guy arranged a lot of things while you were gone."

"Ira, I'm trying to be patient."

"I've been patient for over a week. Did you close the deal? From the call Guy took during the partners' meeting, it didn't sound like you were doing so good."

"I wasn't. What are you talking about? During what partners' meeting? When I spoke to Guy, I always reached him at home."

Ira started to laugh. "Your brother is a real work of art. He conned everyone . . . including me. Okay, listen. While you were wasting time in Tokyo . . ." In short, terse sentences, Ira told Simon how Guy stampeded many of the partners into selling their Macleod stock. "Sell now or you could lose everything." And how Sherwood Anderson—of all people—screwed up Guy's deal. "Stavros Lennos was backing Anderson. Imagine, that pretty boy was married to Mafia royalty . . . one of the most powerful Mafia families in the United States. Lennos placed six hundred million dollars in an escrow account. Maybe a week's income to the Lupo family."

"What do you mean, 'Lennos was backing,' 'Sherwood was married'?"

Ira had the grace to look embarrassed. "I mean Sherwood is dead. Killed in a hit and run accident right in front of the office. I didn't like the guy much, but it's too bad. He had Guy on the run."

Simon slowly moved his head from side to side. The tension was causing his neck to cramp. A nasty possibility had occurred to him. "Have you gone over the Macleod Brothers books?"

"Me? No. Why?"

"I haven't either. I took Guy's word when he said the firm was in trouble. He's the managing partner. He should know."

Ira ran his fingers through his uncombed hair. He made an abortive effort to smooth it. "Are you smelling a dead fish?"

Simon said nothing.

"Sherwood smelled a dead fish. He wanted to know where Guy was getting the money to pay for the stock he was buying back. That is, if the firm was in such trouble."

Simon Macleod was a man who rarely hid his emotions. You knew where you stood with him at all times. Now, the lack of emotion in Simon's mobile face sounded a warning. Ira knew that battle lines were drawn.

Simon stood up. "It's time we got the facts."

"Where you going?"

"To the office. Tomorrow morning, you see as many partners as you can... except Guy. Find those who have already sold their stock. Call them in the Hamptons, on the Cape, the Chesapeake Bay—wherever they are—and tell them I'm back. I want them to sit tight until they hear from either you or me. Make sure you get to Mrs. Sherwood Anderson. She's not to tender Sherwood's stock to the firm ... not yet. That's important."

"You want Lennos to know?"

"Yeah. I want Lennos to know."

When the car stopped in front of 15 William Street, Simon handed Dejerian a hundred dollar bill. "Wait here," Simon said. He rang the doorbell just to the right of the entrance to Macleod Brothers. Even at two in the morning, someone was on duty. Macleod Brothers paid for twenty-four-hour service seven days a week. In less than five minutes an elderly man in work clothes appeared. Simon knew the man ... Sam Elliot. Before unlocking the door, Elliot peered through the glass at Simon. Simon waved. Suddenly, Elliot recognized him and immediately unlocked both the inside and street doors.

"What are you doing here this late, Mr. Macleod?" he asked.

"Working, Sam. Sign me in."

"Yes, sir. What floor you going to?"

"Second floor. Give me your keys. I'll run the elevator myself."

The second floor at Macleod Brothers was devoted to back office work... buy and sell orders were checked, double-checked, and confirmations mailed to customers. A small staff of proofreaders read and re-read all Red Herrings—slang for new stock offerings—Macleod Brothers' Red Herrings as well as those of other banking houses. All checks received by Macleod Brothers ended up on the second floor, and all checks issued by Macleod Brothers originated on the second floor. Edwin Adams—Macleod Brothers' controller—ruled on the second floor. He took the blame for any back-office screw-ups and he made damn sure there were none. The corporate books were kept in a locked, fireproof safe in his office. Only Adams, Guy Macleod, and Simon Macleod knew the combination. A partner wishing to examine the books had to get an okay from Adams.

Simon made his way to Adams' office. The door was locked. Simon hurled himself at the door. On his third try, the lock broke. He hurried to the large safe. Two complete turns to the right, stop at forty-nine, one complete turn to the left, stop at thirty-two, right to twenty-nine. The tumblers dropped into place, Simon turned the handle and opened the safe.

He adjusted a lamp on Adams' desk so that it spotlighted the safe. The Macleod Brothers books were neatly stacked, one on top of the other, on the bottom shelf of the safe. Each volume was bound, front and back, with a hard, green cover, and each cover had an embossed label . . . Accounts Receivable, Accounts Payable, Assets, Liabilities, Payroll, Taxes, et cetera. One thin volume said P & L/Balance Sheet. That's what Simon was looking for.

Settling himself in Edwin Adams' chair, he worked his way through the P & Ls and Balance Sheets . . . the unaudited quarterly statements and the audited annual statements.

By morning the numbers talked to him. They told a sick, painful story. He replaced the corporate books in the safe, shut the heavy door, and spun the dial. He thought about Guy with despair. If he did nothing, all he believed in would end on the rubbish heap. If he acted, he'd still lose. It would be a Pyrrhic victory over Guy . . . his Big Brother. It took time for Simon to accept that there was no decision to be made. The decision had been made years ago when he'd promised his father, to stop Guy if it ever became necessary. Like it or not, that was now.

The car and driver were still parked in front of the building. Dejerian had fallen asleep at the wheel. When Simon woke him, it took a few seconds for the man to orient himself.

"Where to now, boss?" he asked.

"Sutton Place between 54th and 55th," Simon said. As the driver started the car, Simon closed his eyes. He'd been without sleep for almost forty-eight hours, yet he was so tense he wasn't sleepy. Nothing in his life—not the Super Bowl, not his father's death, not Kitty—nothing had prepared him for this much misery.

Guy was finishing his coffee and reading the *Wall Street Journal* when his combination manservant/chauffeur showed Simon into the breakfast room. Guy dropped the paper and set his cup down with a force that all but shattered the cup.

"Where the hell have you been?" he fumed. "I told you to stay in Tokyo until you closed the deal."

Simon sat in a chair facing his brother. "What deal? There was no deal."

"I left a message for you on your answering machine. Did you get the message?"

"I didn't go home. I went to—"

"You should have called me. Takahashi wants to know why you suddenly broke off the negotiations. You were his guest . . . you insulted him. He was ready to sign—"

"Shut up, Guy!" Simon's huge fists slammed down on the table, making the china rattle. The display of anger disguised his inner conflict. They were brothers . . . the Macleods against the world. Now it was Macleod against Macleod. He hated it.

"You have something to say, Little Brother? Spit it out."

"Drop the Little Brother routine. We've played that game long enough."

"Whatever you say . . . Simon." Guy cocked his head to one side.

"I'm going take this by the numbers, and I want you to listen." It was important not to lose his temper. If he did, he'd lose everything.

Guy placed the forefinger of his right hand over his lips and nodded. He'd known since they were kids that Simon could explode, but he couldn't sustain the anger. The longer Simon kept talking, the better. He'd talk himself out of his rage.

"First, Macleod Brothers bought a movie studio, a business with no assets except for a film library and people. A lousy buy."

"I'm sorry. I know I agreed to listen, but you did go

NAKED CALL

along with the deal." Guy grinned. "Christie Larsen got to you."

"I'm warning you, Guy. Don't push it." Simon swallowed his anger. "Second, we took United public but kept financial control. That took a lot of cash. Why did we do it? Don't say anything. Just listen. Three, we continued to buy United Cinema stock... more and more. And you wanted to buy still more stock, even after you knew about the forged checks."

"I didn't know Christie Larsen forged the checks," Guy said quietly.

"Will you shut up? So help me God, if you don't, I'm going to put a piece of adhesive tape over your mouth. For the record, Christie had nothing to do with the forgeries."

"Who did then? Little Miss Muffet?"

Simon lashed out. "Shut up, Guy. My temper's worn thin. Four, when the United Cinema stock fell out of bed, Macleod Brothers lost millions. You told me the firm was in danger of going under. You sent me to Tokyo to make a deal with the Summo National Bank."

"Which you blew."

"There was no deal... there never was. You sent me to Tokyo to get me out of the way."

Guy said nothing. He quietly measured Simon.

"Five, while I was in Tokyo, you stampeded the partners into selling their stock back to the firm. You wanted only two partners left... you and me."

Guy sipped his coffee. He was too proud of what he'd done to deny it.

"Sherwood Anderson stopped you. By the way, how the hell did he happen to get run over... right after he got in your way?"

"How do I know?" Guy retorted. "Accidents happen. Also, he was backed by Stavros Lennos. When you lie down with the Mafia, you don't always get up with fleas. Sometimes you don't get up."

Simon locked eyes with Guy. He felt some relief. "Okay. Forget Sherwood... for the moment. Sixth and most important, Macleod Brothers never was in danger of going under. Even after the hundreds of millions we lost in United, the firm was solid."

"You figured it out. You really figured it out." The blood ran true... Simon was a Macleod. Guy was proud of his brother.

"When Adams starts ranting tomorrow about someone breaking into his office, tell him it was me. I checked the books. And United Cinema is going up, not down. Someone is accumulating United stock." Simon waited, but Guy merely continued to smile benignly at him. "Okay, Guy, it's your turn. I know what you did, I know why you did it, I just don't know how you did it. How did you work the plunge in United?"

Guy finished his coffee and calmly set the cup in the saucer. "I listened to you. Are you ready to listen to me?"

"I'm ready to listen to the truth."

"Then listen! In spite of what you think, United Cinema was a good buy. You've badly underestimated the value of the film library a huge library of films that, has never been shown on cable or network TV. The videotape market is wide open. None of United's films has ever been available on videotape. The library by itself is worth the eight hundred million we paid for the entire studio."

"Who says so?"

"I thought you were going to listen, not argue. Ron Carson, our entertainment analyst, says so. The studio was a throw-in. Two, you're damn right I wanted to buy more United stock. I figured we'd corner the market. We'd force the price up and gradually unload. We stood to make several hundred million dollars—maybe more—until your great and good friend, Christie Larsen, did us in. However, I thank her for it."

"Christie did not forge the checks." Simon was surprised at how wooden his words sounded.

"I'll come back to that." Guy held up his hand. "When your Miss Larsen surprised me with her helping hand, I grabbed it. The drop in the price of United gave me a chance to get back my own, what should have been mine from the beginning. Yes, I sent you to Tokyo to get you out of the way. I didn't want you gumming up the works with your integrity."

"What should have been yours from the beginning?"

"Macleod Brothers. I think our father was going senile when he wrote his final will."

"He wasn't senile. He knew exactly what he was doing."

"No, he didn't! For over one hundred fifty years, every oldest son has inherited Macleod Brothers. I'm the oldest son. The firm was mine by right of birth."

"Father was afraid your snobbery would ruin Macleod Brothers. You don't see how Wall Street has changed."

"Wall Street hasn't changed that much. All I want to do is run Macleod Brothers as a gentleman would, not like one of your traders. Your Ira Benjamin is an Armenian rug dealer who robs his customer and then moves on to the next sucker. I want companies that will do business with Macleod Brothers for decades. Not for one offering, for every offering. Loyalty, Simon. Loyalty is the name of the game."

"Was the name of the game. The game's changed. Nobody plays Gentlemen's 32nds any more. Price and execution are the name of the game. Guy, your loyal company will dump you the instant another banker promises them half a point more on the offering price of their stock."

"You're wrong. Our father was wrong. But thanks to Christie Larsen, Macleod Brothers is mine. Now we'll do it my way."

"Macleod Brothers isn't yours."

"It will be soon enough. I admit I took full advantage of the forgeries. I told the partners if they didn't sell now, they'd lose everything. I lied. But instead of hammering at me, you ought to give thanks that I did what I did." Guy hesitated for a moment. He appeared to be concentrating on his empty cup. When he continued, there was an odd mix of sadness and envy in his voice. "I don't think I'll marry again . . . no point to it. Besides, I don't know a suitable woman who would put up with me for more than ten minutes. I won't have any children. But you will remarry . . . not to Christie Larsen, I hope. And you will have children. Your oldest male child will inherit Macleod Brothers . . . thanks to me."

"You did this for my children? The hell you did. You did it for yourself."

"You're partially right. Yes, I want Macleod Brothers for myself. I also want Macleod Brothers for you and your children. Don't you understand, Simon, only a Macleod can own Macleod Brothers."

"Sherwood Anderson put an end to that idea."

"Temporarily," Guy said with an unmistakable flush of anger. "Again I got lucky. With Anderson dead—I don't know who ran him down, but I'd like to pin a medal on whoever did it—our partners will sell. They don't have the stomach to deal directly with Stavros Lennos . . . with the Mafia. That says more for them than it does for Christie Larsen."

"Why do you insist Christie did the forgeries?" Simon meant to sound scornful, bemused, disdainful. Instead he sounded doubtful . . . worried. He was disgusted with himself.

"Follow my thinking. Stavros Lennos wanted to buy United Cinema. He couldn't buy the studio, but he could buy Christie Larsen. Look at what's happened. Larsen forges some checks—remember how she wanted to make the forgeries public? The idea was . . ."

"She told me why she changed her mind."

"Did she? Whatever she said, the fact is she only changed her mind after the board rejected her scheme. Anyway she—or someone she hired—leaks the news to the media. The price of the United Cinema stock goes to hell. Then it starts going up. Why do you think the price is going up, not down?"

"More buyers than sellers."

"Stop it, Simon. You know better than that." A tinge of irritation colored Guy's voice. "There aren't more buyers. There's basically one buyer . . . Stavros Lennos."

"You don't know that."

"Yes I do. Skipper Kraus, the specialist in United, told me that only one firm has been accumulating United . . . Maxwell, Gluck & Moore. Have you ever met Jeffrey Moore? He's the managing partner of the firm."

"No. But I know the house."

"Maxwell, Gluck & Moore is backed by Stavros Lennos. I know one of Moore's ex-wives. Moore has a bad habit of talking too much in bed . . . pillow talk. When women change pillows, they also talk too much. Moore does what Lennos tells him to do. Moore is buying the United stock

NAKED CALL

...buying all he can get, holding it in the firm name... for a group of independent investors, Moore says."

"And you think his independent investors are Lennos?" Simon's question was deliberately dull. "And Lennos hasn't filed a 13 D."

"He hasn't and he won't. Lennos is no fool. He would never buy more than five percent of United and not file with the SEC." Guy spoke patiently. He was a philosophy professor instructing a favorite pupil who had missed a step in the logic. "He knows if he didn't file, he'd go to jail."

"You mean he isn't buying in his own name."

Guy nodded his approval. "You got it. Lennos is parking stock with Maxwell, Gluck & Moore." He added, "Very hard to prove."

"Almost impossible to prove... unless someone on the inside cracks." Simon sat rigid, his hands folded on his lap. "Why would Christie go along with Lennos' scheme?"

"I think she started forging the checks because she needs money. Every Hollywood bimbo—"

"Cut it out, Guy!" Simon came to life. "Cut the bimbo shit."

"Sorry. Relax. She's not a bimbo. Every Hollywood lady executive needs money. That better?"

Simon remembered Christie calling herself an outsider because she lived within her income. They'd made love only a few minutes earlier... been as close as a man and a woman could be. He'd taken her word. Did he now, three thousand miles apart? Did she really live within her income or was that a pose? Was she up to her ass in debt?

Guy sensed the doubt eroding Simon's will. He was beginning to bend. "Remember the fight I had with Louis Levy about making her president?" His voice picked up pace, gathered force. "Levy has quite a reputation in Hollywood. He's a generous man and a man of his word. He's supposed to have fucked every woman worth fucking who worked for him. But he pays for favors rendered. Money, a part in a film, a job as a producer... it makes no difference. If Levy says, 'Spread for me, and I'll do this for you,' he keeps his word." Guy took a deep breath. "Including making a beautiful woman president of United."

Simon thought of Kitty and how she screwed around with

his friends. Was Christie another Kitty? "Damn you, Guy! I—"

"I didn't want Larsen as president and she knew it. I planned to get rid of her as soon as I could. I held her to a three-year contract."

Simon clenched and unclenched his fists. Everything Guy said had a terrible logic.

"So she cut a deal with Lennos. She'd see to it that the price of United Cinema stock went to hell so Stavros could pick up the stock cheap. The *quid pro quo* was he'd keep her as president after he took over."

"Wait a minute." Simon's voice regained some of its strength. Guy's logic was flawed. "If Christie is convicted of forging those checks, she'll go to jail. That's grand larceny. She can't be president of the studio in jail."

"Wrong!" Guy shook his head and smiled. "She won't be convicted. From what I've read, the only hard evidence the police have comes from a jealous actress and a man who makes his living off women."

"Matt Renault?" Kitty would have screwed Matt Renault.

"Is that his name?" When Simon nodded, he said, "Who'll believe a Matt Renault?"

"You believe him," Simon said after a long, speculative silence.

"Yes." Another silence followed. Then Guy smiled regretfully . . . a man obliged by his sense of duty to tell the truth. "I believe him because I put together the whole story . . . the connection between Larsen and Stavros Lennos, things that won't come out in a trial." Guy bore down gently. He knew Simon better than to push too hard. Simon would persuade himself. "Listen to me, Simon. Hollywood is its own thing. If, by some chance, Christie Larsen is convicted, she won't go to jail. David Begelman never went to jail and he admitted forging checks. I think he ended up producing films for another studio."

Simon couldn't get Kitty out of his mind. He buried his head in his hands.

"She's going to get away with it. If Lennos wins control of the studio, she'll be president for life."

"What does that mean . . . for life?"

"Stavros Lennos is a killer. Christie Larsen isn't Family. Neither was Sherwood Anderson."

"Are you saying that Lennos had Anderson killed?"

Guy's shrug conceded the point. "The Mafia are not notorious for the longevity of their employees."

Abruptly, Simon stood up. "I have to see Christie. I'll decide for myself what's going on."

"Be reasonable, Simon. I need you here with me. The fight's not over. Many of the partners are undecided. Some of them—like Ira—will listen to you. If you say, 'Sell,' they'll sell. Help me. The Macleods against the world. We always said that. Didn't you mean it?"

"I meant it, but that's a personal thing between us . . . brother to brother. It's not a business commitment." Simon appeared momentarily confused. "It doesn't mean that I agree with your strategy for dumping the partners. You knew I wouldn't or you wouldn't have sent me to Tokyo. You got me out of your way." He was soaking with perspiration. "I won't tell Ira what you pulled. We're brothers . . . I owe you that. But I will tell him that Macleod Brothers is sound. No partner has to worry about losing his money. Some may still want to get out. I won't try to stop them. When the dust settles, we'll see who's left. When I get back, we'll work out once and for all whether you run Macleod Brothers by yourself or you live with our father's will. Right now, Christie needs me more than you do."

Guy watched his brother leave the room. Damn it! He'd lost. Christie Larsen had won. He chewed on the insides of his cheeks. This was only one battle. One battle was not the war.

Chapter 33

THE SOFT light in Louis Levy's guest powder room cast a warm, flattering glow. Christie watched Jo lean toward the mirror. Jo made a point of repairing her makeup every few hours, whether or not it needed repairing. As Christie looked at Jo, a crowd of memories jostled each other in her mind. She heard voices from the past.

"Five card draw. Jacks or better to open."

"I'll take two."

"Fold."

"I'll take three."

"Play these."

"One card . . . luck be a lady."

Her vision blurred, and Jo's reflection dissolved into another time and place. Another Jo looked back from the mirror—the Jo of Christie's first year in Los Angeles.

"Look at me! I'm three years, two months, and five days older than you," Jo snorted. "And I look like your mother."

"You do not!" Christie made a face. "You look my kid sister . . . a teeny bopper."

"I don't." Jo stared at her image unhappily. Her coarse blond hair was teased and lacquered in unbecoming tufts and whorls.

"You do. The question is, why do you want to look like a teenybopper?"

"I want to, that's why." Jo frowned. Squinting, she saw a face she didn't like. Jo was worried about growing old. At twenty-five she saw nonexistent bags and wrinkles. "I look ancient."

"You do not."

"Men like young things. I'm getting long in the tooth."

She shook her head. Even her body was going. "What about my hips?"

Waiting for Christie's judgement, Jo twirled in front of the mirror. She was wearing a skintight, one piece, green merry widow trimmed with red lace and sequins and cut high at the crotch and rear. Her buttocks were mostly bare. The merry widow pushed her bosom up and out, showing off her breasts. Green, fishnet stockings added to the blatantly sexual come-on.

"I have a nasty feeling that some of that pizza—the one with the barbecued chicken and gouda cheese—made it to my waist . . . my hips," Jo moaned.

"Nothing shows." Christie smiled as she examined herself. She saw a very young woman in a similar merry widow. Hers was all black. So were her stockings. "Where did you get that pizza?"

"Sorry—a trade secret. Trendy, isn't it?"

"Mmm . . . I had a slice of the one with terriyaki shrimp and scallions. I won't eat for a week."

"On you it doesn't show. But leave some for the customers. They need food to keep their strength up."

The customers were in the living room . . . Jo's Johns, as she cynically called them.

Jo applied eyeliner. When she finished, she blinked. "Charlie baby, is the walk-away winner tonight. He wants his back rubbed." She regarded Christie closely. "You interested?"

"No." Christie pretended to concentrate on running a comb through her hair.

"He's wants you, not me." Jo lips tightened into a thin scarlet line. "If you say no, you'll disappoint a customer."

"I'm a pill."

She and Jo were refreshing their makeup between serving drinks and pizza to the customers in the living room. Strictly speaking, Jo's Johns were not johns . . . they were dedicated, degenerate gamblers, high-stakes poker junkies who wanted privacy for their game. One night a week, Jo rented her apartment to this revolving group of gamblers. For their privacy—cards, chips, food, and liquor provided—she collected a thousand dollars. Often she was handsomely tipped. The biggest winner of the night got to bed Jo Caro. Next in line was the biggest loser. One or both paid for the privilege. With the income Jo derived from this cozy poker game, she was paying her way through law school. By the time Christie met her, Jo could afford to hire an assistant. She hired Christie, who needed the job. They got along famously . . . except for one boundary dispute. Christie drew the line at her crotch. She would not service the customers.

"Poor Charlie baby. He'll go home with a hard-on and have to jerk off," Jo murmured, struggling to do something with her hair.

"He won't. There's always dial-a-doxie."

"Why lose the business? You should see it as a challenge . . . servicing the customers." Jo laughed, low-down and dirty, spraying still more lacquer on her blond curls.

"I see it . . ." Christie started to say something and changed her mind. ". . . as not for me."

"Where's your business sense? We're the 'comes alongs'. The not-so-free freebies."

"I'm not."

Jo shrugged. "If you won't, I will. Keep the customer happy is my motto. I'll be Charlie's 'comes along.'" She stared at Christie, measuring her. "You are an odd one. I don't have to tell you about Charlie's lech. He pays real good to have it stroked. But you keep your legs crossed."

They lapsed into silence while Christie went on combing her hair.

"Why not give it a whirl? Live dangerously. Charlie said just looking at you gets him hard. That makes him good for five hundred. Five plus the two hundred I pay you comes to seven hundred dollars for a few hours work . . . better than SAG scale." Jo's smile became a touch tight around the edges.

"Sorry. I told you when I started. A one night stand isn't my style."

"What is your style? What are you, a nun? You like to play with yourself . . . or maybe you go for girls?"

"Jo, enough!"

"Come on. Squeeze Charlie in. He's a regular customer. He could be a steady source of income."

"Thanks, but no thanks. Waiting on the table is income enough," Christie said stiffly, "until I find a real job."

NAKED CALL

Jo was outraged. "This is a real job! It pays more than secretarial work. It puts me through law school. If you've got complaints, I can get a replacement."

"No complaints. You hired me as a waitress. Serve food, serve drinks, empty ashtrays, clean up when the game breaks up. I do it. But I said it and meant it... I will not be a 'comes along' for the winner or loser."

Jeering. "Miss Goody Two Shoes is too good for fucking."

"That was not our deal. Maybe we should have had a contract. I repeat. I don't go to bed with strangers."

Leering. "You mean fuck?"

"Okay, I mean fuck. I don't fuck strangers."

Hoot. "You never hit the sack with a passing fancy?"

"Sure... when I want to, not for money."

The word "money" sent Jo into orbit. "Christie Larsen, I could kill you! What are you saying, I'm a Bakersfield bimbo, a madam in training, that I fuck for money?"

"I think you do your best to get by in a tough world. I do my best my way."

"I thought we were friends." Jo glared at Christie. "I'm in my second year at UCLA law school. One more year and I'll be a lawyer. What are you going to be, an executive secretary? Great! I give you a break. You're meeting some of Hollywood's power brokers... agents, directors, producers. One of them might find a spot for you. Take advantage of the opportunity."

"I'll make my own breaks. Thanks for the golden handshake, for hiring me, for being my friend. But—"

"Cut the hearts and flowers. Damn it! You want the job, you help keep our customers happy!"

"If you insist, I'll change and leave now."

A voice called from the living room. "Ladies! I'm starving. My throat is parched. Get your butts out here! Serve the refreshments."

"That's Nick, the pizza monster." Jo's smile was fake friendly. "Get moving, Your Ladyship."

When they entered the room, there were six men seated around the green, felt-covered table.

"Ante up," said Fat Nick.

Each man tossed a white chip—one hundred dollars—into the middle of the table.

Fat Nick dealt the cards. "Seven card stud, no wild cards."

"I'll open for two hundred," said Charlie. He slid two white chips into the center of the table.

"See you."

"See you and raise you three hundred." A red chip joined the white one.

"I'm out.

Two men folded, four stayed. Cards were called for. The betting continued. By the time the last chip was added to the pile, Christie estimated there was about six thousand dollars worth of chips on the table.

The four men turned up their hole cards.

"Black aces and eights. Wild Bill Hickok's hand," Abe Schneider crowed.

"The death hand," Charlie muttered.

"Not tonight." Abe laughed as he raked in the chips.

Jo stepped forward, "Raise one finger if you want a slice of pizza. Two fingers if it's chocolate chip cheesecake. Three fingers if . . ."

Abe Schneider stood up, yawned, and stretched. "Cash me in, Jo. I'm through for the night. I've got to be on the set at six tomorrow morning. One of my lunatic clients is tearing up pages of the script faster than they can write them. If I can't calm her down, she's going to get canned." He glanced at Christie. "Jo tells me you type sixty words a minute."

Incredulous. "Jo did?"

"Yeah, she's a fan. Do you type sixty words?"

Chastened. "I do."

"How many mistakes?"

"Two or three . . . maybe."

"Jo says you were looking for a secretarial job. My girl, Alda, just quit. She's getting married. Want the job?"

Humble. "Oh, yes."

The man reached in his wallet and pulled out a business card. "Abe Schneider, Hollywood Scouts. We're a talent agency. Be at my office tomorrow morning at nine."

That job was Christie's first break . . . thanks to Jo. Louis

NAKED CALL

Levy was her second break...thanks to herself. So the question of Christie servicing customers never came up again, and her friendship with Jo was never threatened again.

"What are you thinking?" Jo asked as she powdered her nose.

Christie came back into the here and now. "Wool gathering."

"Not you, Miss Steel Trap Mind. You were thinking, who did we leave off our list?"

"I was thinking."

"Okay. Back to the salt mines."

The salt mines was the television room...also the screening room...also a workroom of sorts, with a round table at one end where people could sit and make notes and talk about film projects. Jo insisted that if Christie and she put their heads together, they'd come up with the mastermind who paid Matt Renault to lie. Louis had no interest in joining the think tank. Christie sensed he was against the whole idea, but he wouldn't explain why. He slouched in his favorite recliner. His eyes were closed. He didn't turn his head and he didn't say hello. Christie and Jo headed to the round table. There were yellow pads and ball-point pens in front of each chair.

Christie sat down in the chair she had occupied earlier. Scribbled on a pad were notes of what she knew, what she didn't know, who might be behind Matt Renault's lies... a meager list. Jo sat beside her.

"Okay. Let's go for it." Jo put on the granny glasses she'd left at the table. "Read your list again."

"Specifically, who might have paid Matt Renault to lie?"

"Specifically."

"First, Jenny Lattimore. That makes no sense. No motive. She doesn't need the money. Plus it's out of character." Christie felt a stiffness around her jaw. "Jenny was used."

"Agreed. Out of character. Jenny slings shit when she's jealous. Matt decided to make her jealous. The question is, why and for whom?"

"Next we have Franco Marconi."

"Scratch Marconi."

"Why scratch Marconi?" Jo asked. "Originally you thought..."

"Originally I thought Franco was a possible. But the more I think about him, the less possible he seems. If Franco suddenly needed cash, there's not a studio in Hollywood—or a bank in L.A. or New York—that wouldn't lend him a million dollars... two million dollars. Franco is bankable." Christie said it plainly and precisely, the way a good general recalls a battle... the winning or losing is no longer in question, just the general's judgement of the way the battle was fought.

"That's only half convincing," Jo said with her foxy grin. "I remember you mentioned his possibly stashing monies around the world—millions lifted from the *Serpent* budget—in special accounts."

"The books on *The Feathered Serpent* have been thoroughly audited. There are no missing millions. Whoever forged the checks is not laughing all the way to the bank," Christie said, making a half-hearted joke. "They amount to a lousy few hundred thousand dollars... not enough money for anyone to go through the hocus-pocus of hiding it in a Swiss bank account." Christie avoided Jo's eyes. "The checks were not forged for the money. There has to be another reason."

Jo asked, almost under her breath, "What reason? And who else is there? I've run out of ideas."

"I've run out, too. We're back to square one. There is no other reason..." She felt herself sweating. "... that I can think of at the moment."

Louis called out. "How about Harry Weiss?"

Christie asked with some surprise, "Why Harry?"

"Why not Harry? He discovered the forged checks."

"No. His assistant, Edgardo Silvera, did," Christie said, still lost.

"Same thing. Harry's his boss. They could be in this together."

"What's in it for Harry, besides a few hundred thousand dollars? That's not Harry's style... not enough money."

Jo was suddenly alert. "I think Harry's the best idea we've had."

"What am I missing?" Christie shot a sharp, quizzical glance at Jo.

"Honey, you know and I know you were tarred and feathered. Guy called a board of directors meeting. You were not invited to attend. The board voted. One dissenting vote... Louis Levy." She tossed Louis an approving nod. "One missing board member... Simon Macleod. The rest followed Guy in lock step. You were fired. So guess who's now in line to be president of United? Our Harry."

There was a short stillness. "You believe Harry wanted to be president that much... enough to forge checks... commit grand larceny? That's no small crime."

Jo was prepared. "I do."

"What do you think, Louis?" Christie asked in a small voice.

Louis was exasperated. "It's crap! I wanted to see how many dumb ideas you'd accept."

"You're wrong, Louis. I think it's a damn good idea," Jo said with unflappable courtesy.

"I repeat, crap!" Louis said rudely. He fingered the TV remote control. "Let's hear what NBC's local news team, Kelly Lang and Keith Morrison, have to say. I try never to miss the local news. Maybe there's a fish caught up a tree."

The sound came on. Keith Morrison was talking about the film industry. "The wait is over. A lot of interested parties were making book on who would be the next president of United Cinema now that Christie Larsen has resigned. The odds makers made Franco Marconi the favorite..."

"A town full of jerks," Jo hissed.

"... But the odds makers were wrong. It is not Franco Marconi..."

"Naturally," Louis said almost to himself. "Franco is a fine director... no more, no less. As a president, he couldn't find the executive toilet."

"... United Cinema has just announced that Harry W. Weiss will be the new president. Mr. Weiss will begin work at his new post starting Monday."

"Harry?" Christie gazed at Jo with wide-open eyes. "That's your theory. He forged the checks so that... I don't believe it."

"Why not?"

"Gut feeling."

Jo was thinking. "There are two sides to everyone."

"Especially in Hollywood," Christie said moodily. "I don't believe Harry is connected to the forgeries. Do you, Louis?" She waited while Louis thought about this.

Louis flipped off the TV. "I was wondering when that announcement would be made."

This remark produced a nervous response in Jo. She licked her lips, smiled doubtfully, then took a tissue from her purse and wiped her glasses. "You knew?"

"Did you, Louis?" Christie asked.

"Did I what?"

"Know that Harry Weiss would be made president?" Jo demanded, her voice rising in pitch until it bordered on shrill.

Louis blinked and pursed his lips, then answered, "Of course I knew. I'm on the board. I voted for him. Guy Macleod has had worse ideas." His smile had a shrewd familiarity.

"What about Franco Marconi?" Christie asked.

"His name never came up. If it had, the board wouldn't have gone for it."

"You mean Guy had only one candidate?" Jo's voice had a hysterical edge. "What about Monroe Stahr? Oh, sorry, he's fictional. Or Darryl Zanuck? Oops, sorry again, he's in producer heaven. Or..."

"Louis B. Mayer didn't come up, or Barry Diller, or Joe Roth, or Guber and Peters. Dawn Steel is a woman. David Putnam is David Putnam. I can give you a long list of the names of men and women who weren't proposed."

Jo wet her lips and nodded like a mechanical doll.

"So Harry is United's man of the hour," Louis concluded.

Lei entered the room. "A call for you, Miss Caro." He placed a cordless telephone on the table.

"Oh! Thank you." Jo picked up the receiver. "Hello? What!" Suddenly she was short of breath. "You found me. Yes, Sam, you're right. Sorry about that. I'll be there in a few minutes." Jo broke the connection and stood up. "That was Saintly Sam, the spit and polish man. I forgot to leave him his weekly check this morning. I've got to get home and give it to him. You know how it is with cleaning people ... they live from check to check." She forced a smile. "Don't say you told me so, Christie. Between the gardener, the pool man, the mortgage, the real estate taxes, and Saintly Sam to dust and polish and wax, I'm broke." Jo delivered her lines perfectly ... a little self-scorn, a little self-pity, a little laugh.

"I didn't say—"

"You didn't actually say anything, but you thought it." Social smile. "Louis, I hope I'm still invited to dinner? If I don't freeload, I don't eat."

"Dinner is at eight," Louis said. "Sharp."

Jo took off her glasses, put them in her purse, and started toward the door. "I'll be back in plenty of time."

Christie watched her go ... her oldest friend. She sat erect in her chair and began to feel her way through her thoughts. They would come ... oh, yes, the answers would come ... once she put aside her affection for Jo.

"How does she strike you these days?" Louis' voice sounded like a bad connection.

"I feel as if I've been playing a game of cat and mouse. I don't like it."

Louis gave a short smile. "But she doesn't know it. Christie, enough! It's time you told me exactly what Irene ... what your mother said when she called."

Christie's face was tense with indecision.

"Damn it, Louis! I said I would tell you ... at the right time."

"This is the right time. You wanted to wait for the announcement about the new president. The announcement's been made." Louis watched Christie very carefully. "What did she say?"

There was something forlorn about the way Christie studied the yellow pads, like a child expecting punishment and pretending it wouldn't happen. At last, she told Louis about the coincidence of Jo Caro and Franco Marconi bumping into each other in Irene's office. How they fought over everything, whether Franco would be made president, should Irene take *Deirdre* to Columbia ...

"That wasn't Franco's idea, was it?"

"No. That brilliant move was all Jo's." Christie's voice suddenly rose. "Louis, I don't understand. Why would she want United to lose *Deirdre*?"

"I'm putting the pieces together. What else did Irene say?"

"She'd stay at United if I asked her to."

"How touching. Is that all?"

"You mean besides *Deirdre*?"

"Besides *Deirdre*. What did she say?"

Louis had the distinct sense of a barrier, not a faulty memory . . . a determination not to remember.

"You never trusted Jo." A statement, not a question, from Christie.

"What has that to do with Irene's call?"

"Irene doesn't trust Jo either. She said she's more her daughter than I am."

Disbelief. "She called just to tell you that?"

"She said Jo and she are like two peas in a pod."

Bored. "You mean that's all she had to say?"

"No." Christie's breathing had become shallow and rapid. Louis waited patiently for her to go on.

"She doesn't think Larry Willis is the right lawyer for me."

"What else?"

"She talked about the checks."

"The forged checks?"

"The forged checks."

Louis had the impression that every word Christie spoke was tearing at her—that she was bleeding inside—but this wasn't the time to spare her. "What about the forged checks?"

After circling a bit, Christie finally told him the rest. How Irene had picked up Jo's mentioning seven forged checks . . . the news reported only three checks.

Louis prompted gently. "Did you tell Jo there were seven checks involved, not three?"

"I don't think so." Christie hesitated. Then, "No. I didn't tell her," she said softly.

"Who did you tell?"

"Besides you? Nobody. Harry Weiss knows . . . Edgardo Silvera, too. Silvera found the first check." She laughed angrily. "And I think Matt Renault knows damn well there are seven forged checks."

There was a long silence. Finally time began to flow again. Louis said, "You've been close a long time."

"Jo's my oldest friend... my best friend."

"A strange friendship."

"Not so strange. You just never liked her."

"And Irene's been out of your life for years?"

Christie's mind was absorbed by conflicting memories. She raised her eyes to catch the question. "What?"

"I said, Irene's almost a stranger."

"Yes, she is. Why?"

"Because you're thinking, why should you trust her now?"

"Something like that."

Louis recognized Christie was fighting a rear guard action, retreating one agonizing step at a time. "Shall we drop the subject... for now?"

Christie didn't answer.

Louis smiled with possessive fondness. Christie had to work it out with herself, with her mother, with Jo. "I'll make us martinis," he said, getting up slowly. "I don't know about you, but I could use a drink."

And, in truth, Christie's mind was in revolt. A dizzying montage was flickering across her brain. Jo, full of glory in her new house... knowing she'd get the job as house counsel. Friends in high places, she'd said. Who? Irene's quiet statement... Jo mentioned seven checks. How did she know? Jo at the board meeting, blocking the vote to make the forgeries public. Why? Jo insisting on doing a memo. Why? And why was the memo never finished? If the forgery had been made public sooner, would Renault have been able to accuse her? So many ifs. If Jo had never said she typed sixty words a minute, where would she be today? For a second, she nearly lost her grip on herself.

Louis arrived with the drinks.

"So, Christie?"

"So, Christie?" she echoed.

"I'd like to put a thesis to you... a notion about what's been happening."

"Must you?"

"No. There's time. It's pure speculation."

"Speculation or suspicion?" Her voice was detached.

"In this case, they're the same thing."

"Please don't fill me in." Christie shifted restlessly. "I have enough speculations—suspicions—of my own with which I have to live."

"Good. Be suspicious. Survival often depends on just that... an infinite capacity for suspicion." He handed her the drink. "Do you hear me, Christie?"

"I hear you."

Linda Loomis knocked on the open door. "Jed's on the line. Mr. Simon Macleod is waiting at the gate."

Louis told Linda to tell Jed to let Macleod through.

Christie stared at Louis. "You knew he was coming?"

"He called this morning, said he'd be flying out today."

"Why didn't you tell me?"

"Frankly, I wasn't that confident. Does true love always conquer? Isn't that idea a little dated?"

"I suppose you were right not to tell me." She folded her arms across her breasts in self protection. "He might not have come."

"Even movies are no longer committed to happy endings. I was being cautious."

"Stop it, Louis," Christie pleaded. Her hands were over her ears.

He ignored her protest. "Suppose something came up, or he changed his mind, or someone changed it for him?"

"Stop it, please! No more!"

Christie had a picture in her mind of Simon... and a checklist. Among the questions were, would she ever see him again? Now he was here. Another question. What did he feel about her? A third question. First my best friend... now my lover. What if I'm batting zero for two?

Jo drove home with more determination and courage than she had ever possessed. What kept her courage high was her anger. Anger made her mind clear and sharp. All the pent-up bitterness at the things she'd had to do in her life had been transferred from the back to the front burner. When she turned into her driveway, she saw the red Mercedes parked in front of the door. She got out of her car and walked quickly to the house. She wondered why she bothered putting her key in the lock . . . he never locked the door. She found him in the living room, in a dinner jacket, seated quietly, thumbing a book on Henry Kissinger while sipping scotch.

"You moved fast," he said pleasantly.

In the half-glow of the room, a deep, inner fear was now apparent in Jo's face. "Sorry, Matt. Your candidate lost. Your future as a producer is uncertain."

"No sweat," he said. "I don't think I have the drive to make it as a producer. But . . ." He continued in a more practical tone. ". . . what do you do now?"

Jo stared around in black hostility. "I suppose all Hollywood's heard the news."

"Except for Jenny. She's dressing for the Joan and Jackie Collins party. The Collins sisters . . . together at last. I'm picking her up shortly."

"Do that. Get your ass out of here. I'm going to blow the lid off this caper."

Matt asked with an overlay of casualness, "You're sure you're not going to do something you'll regret later?"

Jo put her knuckles in her mouth to stop herself from sobbing. Matt moved forward and put his arm around her. "I've been such a shit," she moaned. "A real shit . . . for nothing."

"A knife in the back goes with the territory," he murmured, kissing her forehead. "Would you like to knock off one for the road . . . a quickie? Good for the morale."

Gradually, Jo's dry heaves gave way to an exhausted sigh. "A farewell to arms? I'd love it, but no go . . . not now . . . maybe never again. I've no idea how this movie will end."

"It could end right here. No one would be the wiser, except for you, me . . ." He smiled ruefully. ". . . and your backer."

"You bet he knows. I ate his shit. Christ! The risks I took—you took—for that S.O.B. Why? For what? For nothing!"

"Not for nothing. You paid me well for my services."

"You were worth every cent. You helped me pull it off. If I'd have tried it myself, I'd have been caught within days." She laughed, not very nicely. "Too bad forgery isn't a legitimate profession."

"I have other talents." He smoothed her hair.

"You sure do," she said, her mind full of erotic images.

He stepped back. "But what about you? House counsel isn't such a bad job."

"I didn't get into this to keep a job I already have." She collapsed onto the couch.

"You had high hopes," he murmured. "We both did."

"And I didn't sink my best friend for Harry Weiss. It's been lousy."

"A bummer. I know how you feel." He tried to console her. "That bastard took advantage of your decency..."

Jo wiped away a tear with the back of her hand.

"... your feelings, your sense of right and wrong. He knew you were vulnerable, not one of those hotshot kids like Larsen who start at the top and work their way up. You're a poor kid from Bakersfield who made good on—"

"Made good how?" Her eyes narrowed.

He stumbled and recovered. "By working hard, using your brains..."

"You got it. My brains... not on my ass. Right! Drop it, Matt!"

"Jo! We're friends."

"We are friends. And if you happen to do a little forging on the side, we're... would you settle for soul mates?"

"Star-crossed lovers." He gave her an odd look. "Remember Marconi's Jacuzzi. Me, the new boy on the block. I said, 'Franco, who's Christie Larsen?' Franco pointed to you."

"I didn't contradict you." She was no longer sure of his good will.

"You went with the flow. We had fun."

"But you still wished I was Christie." Poker-faced. "What if I hadn't told you about my prospects? Would you have dumped me for Christie?"

Wary. "No. We'd have worked out a time-sharing schedule, like with Jenny."

Jo's smile had a coat of malice. "Harry's not gay. You'll have to stick with Jenny full time."

He shrugged. "For a while. Before I go." He reached into his jacket, took out his wallet, and handed her a folded piece of lavender-colored paper. "I thought tonight might be *arrivederci*, so I've a memento for you."

She unfolded the paper cautiously, laying it on the coffee table and smoothing it out. It was a sheet of her personal stationery with her name, Jo Caro, printed at the top. The page was covered with her efforts to imitate Franco Marconi's signature. "Not very good."

"Terrible."

"Where did you find it?"

"On your desk. When I saw it, I knew we had something special going." He gave her a smile. "Burn it . . . or sleep with it under your pillow. Something to remember me by."

Jo looked at him. "I'll remember you. Now get going or Jenny will spank. I have to make a call before I ride slowly into the sunset on my trusty mule."

He kissed her again on the forehead. "*Ciao*, baby," he said as he left the living room.

Jo walked to the phone on her desk. Her gut told her she was making a mistake, but there are some mistakes you have to make. She picked up the phone and dialed his private line. Five rings . . . he picked up.

"Good evening, Jo," he said pleasantly.

She was flushed. She tried to say hello, but couldn't.

"I've been expecting your call." He laughed. "Cat got your tongue?"

She managed to say, "Hello, Guy. You knew I'd call?"

"Of course."

Something had gone wrong with her hearing. "What did you say?"

"I said I've been expecting your call."

"Sure. You've been sitting by the phone."

"I really have." He sounded as if he was congratulating himself. "You've made my day."

"If I believed that . . ." She wanted to scream blue murder, but didn't.

"Believe it. I'm vain enough to enjoy proving that I'm right . . . even if only to myself."

"What are you right about?"

"Human nature. It makes it possible for me to predict

behavior with a high degree of accuracy. And you've demonstrated that I know what I'm doing."

"How?" She was spoiling for a fight.

"The announcement of Harry Weiss's appointment was made at 5:45 P.M., L.A. time. Depending on where you were at six o'clock, I estimated it would take between five seconds and an hour for you to get to a telephone and call me to demand your reward. Actually you took just under an hour. Where were you?"

"With Christie."

"The victim." His glee was transmitted clearly by AT&T long-distance lines.

"You used me!" She felt a shrill rage.

"Of course I used you. And I could not have made a better choice. There were a few others in the company I considered, then dismissed. You were by far the most usable. You're intelligent, energetic, imaginative, ambitious. The perfect choice."

"Perfect! Add a dash of greed, a craving for power. The kind of woman who wouldn't mind a little blood on her hands."

"You were asking to be used. Begging..."

"Foaming at the mouth..."

"I wouldn't go that far. You longed for recognition. You shrewdly pointed out Larsen's shortcomings as an executive in matters of decision making, delegating authority, planning ahead, organizational skills. Didn't you, Jo?"

She didn't have to see his self-satisfied grin. She heard it.

He continued without waiting for her answer. "You even assured me that the phenomenal success of *The Feathered Serpent* had nothing to do with Larsen. It was a combination of Franco Marconi's talent and a fluke."

Jo was trapped in a furious silence.

"Do you hear me, Jo?" Guy asked. "I am explaining exactly how you promoted yourself. You were running for office, and doing it damn well."

Jo hesitated. All her native cunning told her to detour. "And I got out the vote... witness Matt Renault."

"My compliments on Renault. Where did you find him?"

"In a Jacuzzi," she said sarcastically.

"You do have a sense of humor. A Jacuzzi? How typically Hollywood. I'm sure you did everything humanly possible to elicit his best efforts. Even, when need be, in the missionary position."

"You are a charmer."

"Please don't be offended." His laugh was caustic. "Just my little joke. We're not Puritans. We both know the way the world runs."

"I'd say I'm an amateur compared to you."

"Not at all. You're a real pro. I knew, when I asked if you could find a way to rid me of Larsen, that you would find a way... and you did." He spoke with high good humor. "Forging the checks was brilliant."

"Thank you."

"It was inventive, dramatic, effective. It was you at your best... sheer genius."

"And for my sheer genius you made Harry Weiss president?"

"Harry Weiss." He hesitated. "Not the ideal choice. But given the financial mess at United, Wall Street demanded a numbers man. At the moment, Harry is a necessary evil."

"And when he's no longer necessary?"

"I'll replace him."

He paused again. His pauses were becoming more threatening than his words.

"With who?"

"With someone more appropriate."

"Like who?" She had arrived at the forbidden subject. A pinched look came over her face.

"We'll see."

"Like me?"

The silence was like the awful time between screams.

"No, not like you."

She tried frantically to keep her composure. "Why not? What is it? Do I have bad breath or something?"

He was all sympathy. "Try to see it from my perspective."

She was falling and spinning and the dark was getting darker all around her. "I'm curious. Let's hear it from your perspective."

"You are not an appropriate choice for president of United Cinema."

"Why not?"

"You don't convey the right image to The Street... to bankers, fund managers, the Harvard and Stanford MBAs who handle the pensions and trusts. You don't have the right background... the right connections. You're not right. Be satisfied with house counsel. You'll be well-rewarded for your efforts. I'll see to it that Harry gives you a substantial bonus."

A volley of obscenities formed inside Jo. "I was right when you wanted me to do a number on Christie. You promised me—"

"I promised nothing... not in so many words."

"You intimated... in paragraphs."

"You chose to misunderstand. This is important, Jo. I'm a Wall Streeter. I never break a trade."

"What's that supposed to mean?"

"If I had said to you, 'Jo Caro, when Christie Larsen is fired, you will be president,' I would have had to make you president. Otherwise I'd have broken a trade."

"You did say that."

"No. I said, 'When Christie Larsen is fired, there will be a vacancy at United which will require a new president. You, Jo Caro, will profit from that opening.' You believed I meant you would be president. That was not what I said, and not what I meant."

"What did you mean?" She squeezed her lips together to keep from yelling.

"A permanent job—a sinecure—as house counsel of United Cinema... possibly a vice presidency."

Jo's voice had the quiet purity of bitterness. "Silly, naive Jo. She forgot her business law. Our arrangement should have been in writing... a contract, signed, dated, notarized."

"We had no arrangement."

"Checks were forged at your instructions."

"Not at my instructions. Remember, you came up with the forgery idea..."

She tried again, more strident. "... to help you ruin Christie Larsen."

NAKED CALL

"As I said, you did well. I applaud."

"Fine. I've done a good job. Now I want my payoff."

"Your suggestion is absurd."

"A new press release will announce the board has reconsidered the matter. Jo Caro will be named president of United Cinema rather than Harry Weiss."

"Jo, be reasonable. How can a woman of your intelligence—"

"If that doesn't happen . . ." Jo was pursued by demons. ". . . I will pay a visit to the Beverly Hills police department. I will tell Detective Carmella Garcia exactly how I managed the forgeries, that I told Matt Renault to accuse Christie, that I was following your instructions."

"You disappoint me. What will such a foolish action accomplish? Nothing, except to get you disbarred and put you in prison."

"I grew up on the streets, Guy. I can survive in prison . . . as long I know you're doing hard time, too." She glared into the phone. "Take your choice. Caro for president or Macleod for prison."

Guy's reaction to Jo's threat was predictable. He struck back with the full majesty of his position as Chairman of the Board of United Cinema, as managing partner of Macleod Brothers, and, most important, as Guy Macleod . . . the Macleod of Macleods. His voice remained soft, the more deadly for its lack of emotion. "You're irrational . . . unstable. Even if it was possible, you're not presidential caliber. You're not even qualified to be house counsel. You're fired."

Anger swept over Jo like a hot flame. Anger purified her vision. Anger was her one true ally. "Bastard!" she screamed. "When I get through with you, you'll wish you—"

"Do whatever you wish. It's your word against mine . . . the word of a hysterical, jealous woman against the word of a Macleod."

If they'd been in the same room, she would have tried to kill him . . . hit him with a heavy vase. It wasn't possible. With a continent between them, she could only scream, "You bastard! Bastard! Bastard!" Followed by a stream of filth she'd learned before she knew what the words meant.

Eventually, she exhausted herself. Panting, she stopped. The line had gone dead. She slammed down the receiver with a wrenching sense of drowning... water closing over her head. It's going to be laughs all the way, she thought. Hell! I'll lose my suntan in prison.

Chapter 34

SHE'D BEEN listening... she couldn't stop listening. Simon's voice didn't allow that.

"... now I understand that the original attraction of United Cinema for Guy was the instability of the stock. That's why he bought the company."

"Figures," Louis said sourly.

Meticulously, Simon took them through all that had happened at Macleod Brothers since Christie's arrest. His voice was low and deliberate as he detailed his brother's Machiavellian plot to regain total control of the firm.

"... so the embezzlement scandal played into his long-range plan. Guy saw it as a lucky accident."

Christie knew from his tone how much it cost him to speak of his brother's obsession. "Naturally he was delighted with the plunge in the price..."

Beneath his harsh words, Christie could feel the force of Simon's love for Guy. They had been trained in the same school... Macleod Brothers. They shared the same traditions—Macleod traditions... the same values—Macleod values. This truth made her feel inadequate and utterly lonely.

"... and it was easy for him to use the threat of Macleod Brothers going under to terrify the partners into selling their stock in the firm."

Finally the story ended... the story that was an apology to Christie... to Louis. Like the man he was, Simon had returned to make amends for not being close when Christie needed him. He was genuinely sorry. Yet Christie was struck by a sense of wrongness. His concern for her had taken second place to his concern for Macleod Brothers. She was an afterthought. The idea was chilling.

They were seated around the conference table. Christie sat between Simon and Louis. The light showed a web of fine lines around Simon's eyes. Louis, the ageless Buddha, sat with his square hands folded on the table, impassive, yet strangely angry at Simon.

Christie said, "Simon, you didn't have to fly out to tell us about Guy's stunt. Maybe that's how the game is played on Wall Street, maybe not. I don't know SEC law. But either way, it's Macleod Brothers' business... yours, Guy's... not ours. What happened to me was not Guy's fault." She put it as kindly and gently as she could. "That he took advantage of the consequence... the stock plunge ... so be it. You don't owe me any explanation. I don't want to hold you to..."

"To what?"

"To a feeling of obligation because we spent a weekend together."

"That's not fair. I came because I wanted to, not because I felt obligated."

That at least sounded like Simon. No surprise, no suspicions, no remoteness. Just grave and caring.

"I want to help," he said.

"Thank you for that."

She took his head in her hands and kissed him lightly, quickly, on the mouth. It was long enough to know that the chemistry still worked.

"I'm glad you're here. It makes things better," she said ... only to feel him pull back. Humiliated, angry, she stared at his face. It belonged to a sentinel. There was a reluctance in his eyes she'd not seen before. It wasn't lack of desire. It was something else.

Louis slowly raised his head and spoke for the first time since Simon had finished his story.

"I'm suspicious by nature. Coincidences disturb me. Don't you wonder at Guy's good luck? Christie is arrested, the stock plunges, the partners sell... a done deal."

Christie stared at Louis . . . at Simon.

For a beat—no answer. Sounding tired and angry, Simon said, "Guy is obsessive about Macleod Brothers. But what you're suggesting is criminal. Guy is not a criminal."

Louis waited for Simon to go on, but Simon had nothing more to say. Louis asked, "Why didn't Guy nominate Franco Marconi for president?"

"Didn't he? Who was made president?"

"Harry Weiss. You didn't know?"

"I've been living on jets. Guy didn't tell me."

"Franco's on the ceiling. He could jump to another studio . . . leave United and send the stock into a steeper free fall. Does Guy want that?"

"Probably. But what he wants and I want are not the same. When I get back to New York, we have matters to settle."

Simon fell silent, but he didn't relax. If anything, Christie sensed a methodical preparation.

"How good a case do the police have?" Simon asked.

Christie was too disturbed by him to trust herself to answer.

Louis filled in. "It's crap."

"Do you have proof? This Matt Renault says he cashed the checks for Christie."

"Matt Renault lies. That much we do know. What we don't know is who paid him to lie," Christie said. Then she caught a warning in Louis' face.

Simon saw nothing. "Is Renault the government's star witness?"

"Yes," Louis said.

"How well do you know him, Christie?" Simon asked.

"I met him once, on the set of *The Feathered Serpent*. He's Jenny Lattimore's stud." All at once she saw what was troubling Simon, and she was furious. "Listen to me, Simon Macleod. If I want to get laid, I don't need a paid stud. For years I've been flooded with propositions . . . everything from a whippy weekend in Puerto Vallarta to a private cruise around the Greek Isles. Men, women, teenage boys, ten-year-old girls—one at a time or in groups—whatever turns me on. And I wouldn't even have to produce a movie, just agree to consider an idea. Your naivete amazes me. That you would suggest—"

"I suggested nothing," Simon said with the formality of an official visitor. "I'm trying to understand why he accused you."

"I've no idea. I do know that if I wanted to steal from United, I wouldn't announce it in headlines, on TV, beating the drums." She spoke with high disdain. "I am not financially stupid. There are far more sophisticated, damn near undetectable ways to steal money—millions of dollars—than forging checks for a few hundred thousand. Forging checks is so blatantly amateurish I think whoever did it wanted to be caught."

Simon gave a sigh of relief. "That's what I've been thinking." And he meant it. "It is amateurish. Someone wanted to be caught." He wanted to believe her with all his heart. He knew all too well the sensuous mouth, the spellbinding effect of the sea-green eyes. But could she be trusted? He'd asked himself that question a hundred times ... a hundred times it turned his soul to salt. He stared at her hard. "Then let's say for the sake of discussion ..." He spoke as though selecting a remote option. "... that you wanted to be caught." He explained Guy's theory—without giving Guy credit—regarding Stavros Lennos and his interest in Christie.

Louis interrupted, his irritation bubbling over.

"Horse shit! I once told Christie you were a *mensch*. I was wrong. Your trouble, Macleod, is tunnel vision. All you can see is Wall Street ... your company town. You haven't a clue about Hollywood ... my company town, Christie's town. Wall Street makes fortunes for damn fools. So does Hollywood. But Wall Street cuts and runs when its damn fools get into trouble. Hollywood doesn't give a shit if its damn fools get into trouble. It's strictly pay as you go in this town. The box office pays or you go. When the box office stops paying, you bounce off the 'A' list. At Morton's they change your table. A party in Malibu or in the Holmby Hills won't include you in. Make one real bomb, you're suspect. Make two, you're included out. And that, Macleod, is why Christie Larsen is on everyone's 'A' list. Box office smashes like *The Feathered Serpent* and

The Challenger, plus a dozen winners that made millions."

Louis paused for a moment. He was testing Simon with his eyes and thoughts. The silence seemed longer because no one interrupted. When he continued, his voice was filled with still more scorn. "Guy's movie analysts don't know shit from shinola. They've taught him nothing. If Christie Larsen doesn't work for United, it's United's loss, not hers. For the moment she's been dumped into a tub of shit. Once she's cleared, the shit becomes a tub of rose petals. And she comes up smelling like an American Beauty, with offers from every studio in this town. She can write her own ticket. Or she can set up a production company, make a few films, and sell her company to Paramount, Disney, anywhere for a couple of hundred million, and get an employment contract for a million a year at the minimum. Or she might put in a call to Tokyo. She'd get backing faster than a microchip company." Louis' fury was at fever pitch. "What the hell does Christie Larsen need with Lennos? Where are your brains?"

Silence lay like dust around the room. Then, almost reluctantly, Simon spoke. It was as if he was breaking his own rules. "You don't have to tell me how talented she is."

"You got it. She's talented. Her instinct for the bottom line is the best. She picks winners. Anyone who picks winners doesn't need United, or the Macleods, or Lennos. Am I getting through to you?"

"You're saying that Christie doesn't have to worry about her job."

"A miracle has occurred . . . the blind man sees." Louis' sarcasm was scathing . . . so scathing that Christie was puzzled.

Then Simon asked, with studied indifference, "I suppose her instinct for winners is why you made her president?"

The question seemed to be a digression. Christie was confused. Louis wasn't.

"No. I decided to make her president one week after she'd started working for me."

"One week?" Simon asked.

Christie saw his interest tighten like a noose.

Louis said, "It was on her twenty-third birthday."

NAKED CALL

Christie said nothing. She floundered wildly. What was Louis up to?

"You mean you recognized her talent for the business that quickly?"

"I recognized her talent, but not her business talent." Louis chuckled.

"Not business?"

"What I saw was a natural sexual athlete."

Simon swallowed.

"I take it you recognized the same talent?" Louis' crack was not rooted in amusement. His smile was a smirk.

Simon was unable to speak.

"Now ask the question you want to ask," Louis said.

Christie's world, which had shown signs of steadying to the sensible pace of an accepted disaster, was plunging violently. She started to laugh. Her good humor was a deception. Deep within, she felt her anger, far down but rising. "He wants to know if we fucked?"

"Of course he does. Yes, Simon, we fucked. I've banged her steadily for . . . let's see . . ." He tilted his head in thought. ". . . twelve years. First time was her birthday celebration." He grinned at Christie. "You were really something, kid. Special."

"Thank you, Louis. You were magnificent," Christie sighed. "The best fuck I've ever had."

"I would hope so. Girl, I taught you everything you know . . . including how to use the KY jelly." His smile was lecherous. "Christie and I have had some wild times over the years."

"Oh, Louis. We had a ball."

"Is any of this true?" Simon asked.

Louis gave him a furious look. At last he said, "No. It's not true. Yes. It is true. Which do you believe?"

Another pause.

"Did you believe me when I said I fucked her . . . fucked her ass?"

Simon rubbed his forehead. "This is crazy. I'm here to help Christie, not to play Charlie Chan, or write a report on the sexual history of women executives."

"That's half true. You did come to help. But you also came to dig for dirt." Louis pointed his finger at Simon.

"Answer me, damn you. Do you believe me?"

A wary pause. Simon had nothing to say.

Christie stared at Simon, then turned away. Her face showed nothing. No surprise, no sense of outrage, no hurt at the courtroom aroma of the scene. But her thoughts were in chaos. Simon was sexually jealous. She could buy that ... even like it. But there were things she couldn't buy. He thought she might be a thief, a liar, a Mafia tool. Her jaw set.

"Right," Louis said. "You came here because your heart made you come, you miserable son-of-a-bitch. But you came for a second reason... to find out about Christie. Okay. We've answered some of your questions truthfully. Now I'll answer your last question. I'll show you the truth. I didn't boff Christie and never tried, though many's the time I had the itch." He fumbled in his jacket and found his worn crocodile wallet. From it he took a small, dogeared snapshot, one Christie had never seen.

"Look at the picture, Simon."

Simon stared. "Who is it? Christie at fifteen?"

"No. It's Jessie, my daughter, at twelve. At fifteen she looked like Rita Hayworth." Louis took back the snapshot and replaced it in his wallet. "That's why I hired Christie. She reminded me of Jessie when the kid was still my kid. That's why I never tried to fuck her. It would be like fucking my Jessie." His last effort to leer at Christie was a dismal failure. "But Jessie is not why I made her president."

"I've been a damn fool." Simon sounded exhausted.

"Never contradict a man who tells the truth," Louis said.

Christie had nothing to say. Her mind was overloaded. There was the snapshot. It explained so much that she had never understood. There was Simon and all his gnawing doubts. To her unhappy eyes he seemed to be suspended in a kind of limbo, trapped between her world and his own.

Jo Caro was a welcome interruption. She stormed into the room like a fireman bursting into a burning building. Linda Loomis trailed behind her, wringing her hands.

"Mr. Levy, I'm sorry. I wanted to announce Miss Caro, but she didn't give me time."

"Thank you, Linda. It's all right," Louis said.

Linda smiled and somehow managed to vanish.

Jo's eyes swept around the room the way a prowler's flashlight would.

"Hello, folks. I'm back. Come to tell a horror story." Her smile was a thing of furious gaiety. She had a face like mortal sin.

"What's the matter with you?" Christie frowned. "Did you shoot Saintly Sam . . . or step on a spider?"

"Christie, I'll let you in on a deep truth. The world is rigged, and you better watch it."

"Sit down. You don't look well."

"I believe it. I feel lousy." She was talking to Christie as if they were alone. "Look, I've never really been good at dirty tricks, and maybe that's the only thing to my credit."

Christie started to move toward Jo. "I want you to sit down before you fall down."

"And I want you to stay seated. Please!" Jo shouted.

"Okay." Christie sat down. "What's the matter with you?"

Jo stood ramrod stiff, full of the bantam cock combativeness with which she faced her life. But tonight the nonstop battle had taken its toll.

"My history is the matter with me. You know some of the story, Christie . . . bits and pieces. Fairly typical of those who are called the disadvantaged. But try to remember it at some future date when you're feeling pissed at me. Remember that where I grew up there was nothing to do but fantasize. I had the standard, miserable, deprived, lonely childhood. I don't think I ever mentioned that when I was a kid my mother worked eighteen hours a day, every day. And weighed less than one hundred pounds. She was a waitress sometimes. Sometimes a short-order cook, a janitor, a whore. There's no minimum wage for whores. She could have posed for the photograph, 'Migrant Mother.' Once you showed the picture to me in a photograph collection. My mother could have inspired *The Grapes of Wrath*. People who eat three meals a day think hardship builds character. Bullshit. It makes you killing mad. My mother birthed nine kids—five boys, four girls. Six of them died. I'm the youngest. Poverty has a lousy taste. We ate garbage. So I never agonized with integrity." She rubbed her eyes with her knuckles to wipe away the tears.

"Get her a drink, Louis," Christie said.

"No! Don't anybody get me anything. When I finish, we'll celebrate . . . maybe."

"Celebrate what?" Christie asked.

"Me. You. Our being friends long ago."

For a moment Christie was silent. "I didn't know we weren't friends anymore."

"It was lost." Jo shook her head, exasperated. "Sometimes I think you have less instinct for Hollywood backstabbing than half the waiters in the Beverly Hills restaurants."

"What does that mean?"

"It means you were a fool to trust me. Ethics are not my strong suit." She spoke carefully, spitting out her words as though they were watermelon seeds. "I suppose you can call this a confession. I don't like the word confession, but that's what it is." After a lifetime playing understudy, Jo took center stage. "You want to know why Matt Renault said you forged the checks? I'll tell you. Because he got big money to lie. The fact is, Matt did the forging himself. The big money came from me. I got it from Guy Macleod."

Simon sat bolt upright. His huge body lunged forward. "From Guy?"

"From your brother, Guy Macleod. Synonymous with bastard!"

"I don't believe it," Simon said.

Jo laughed feverishly. "Blood will tell. Guy's words exactly. He said no one will believe me. It'll be my word against his." Her voice lost energy. "I don't care whether or not you believe me. The cops will. When people like me—people who are less social, less rich than the Macleods—when we admit to crimes, they believe us. You see, people like me—with migrant mothers—who climb out of the dung heap to live in Bel Air . . . we don't like confessing to war crimes." She made a gesture that dismissed Simon as irrelevant. How could he ever understand? "My family used an outhouse and lived in a tarpaper shack. That makes indoor plumbing and air conditioning worth dying for."

"Go on with your story, Jo." Louis stood up.

"Sit down, Louis."

"I was going to get you a drink."

NAKED CALL

"Sit down." She stared him out. He sat down. "Thanks a bunch, Louis, but I don't want a drink. And you don't want to call the cops. I'll see them when I'm ready." She smiled ruefully. "You think I can't be trusted. You know me because we're cut from the same cloth . . . born in the same sewer, at opposite ends of the country." She looked again at Christie. "You still don't get it, why I did it. Okay, I'll spell it out for you. I did it because Simon's brother promised to make me president of United Cinema. Me, president . . . once you were out on your ass. And since I flunked Basic Morality at UCLA, I had no hesitation putting the whole shitty act together. I found Matt, discovered his talent, paid him to forge checks. It was that simple. Oh! I also paid Edgardo Silvera to find the forged check to Maureen. If I'd waited for the bank to turn it up, I'd have waited forever. Get the name straight . . . Edgardo Silvera, Harry Weiss' assistant. Silvera is the leak to the media you've been looking for. Harry's clean. He floats like Ivory Soap." Jo hastily wiped her face with her knuckles. "I almost committed the perfect crime . . . almost . . . for money and for the presidency. I won't see the money . . . or be president. Funny, isn't it?" She couldn't look at Christie. Instead she looked at Louis. She'd have looked clean through him if she could. She'd have blinded him with her defiant glare. She took a deep breath. "I know I won't set a new standard for loyalty . . . not in Hollywood . . . not even to myself." Another deep breath. "But it does prove one thing . . . the triumph of hope over experience."

"Did Guy tell you to talk Irene Bentley into going to Columbia?" Louis asked.

"Right on. He didn't want *Deirdre* at United."

"And he didn't want Franco to stay at United?"

"Right again. You always were a quick study, Louis. If *Deirdre* went to Columbia, he thought Franco would follow. He wanted that. It has something to do with the price of the U.C. stock . . . that's a guess. He even appointed Harry Weiss president to get Franco pissed. What he didn't count on was how pissed I'd be. Did he, Christie?" She managed a convincing laugh. "So, friend, hail and farewell." She started to say something more to Christie but instead made a slit of a sound to let out the foul odor of shame . . . or guilt . . . or agonizing grief.

Simon stood up. "I know my brother. I don't believe Guy was behind this."

Jo had stopped thinking and seeing. She was running out of words. She wanted to scream at Simon, all the obscenities she'd hurled at Guy, at herself, at the whole painful nothingness of her tangled, wasted life. But all she said was, "You believe whatever you want." Her cheeks were hot. She felt tired and ugly. "I'll give you one tip. Don't try to talk to Guy man to man. He isn't a man."

Christie said, "Jo, please wait."

Jo's vision was blurred. She blinked to clear it. She almost asked Christie for mercy. Then her anger at herself—at the world—provided strength. She backed out of the room slowly, self-consciously, a performer taking bows. She paused in the doorway and put her hand to her ear. "Hark! I hear the sound of police sirens screaming." She turned and was gone.

Christie started to go after her. "Jo . . ."

"Let her go, Christie," Louis commanded. "She's going to the police."

"I know. She needs a lawyer."

"She'll get one. She's a lawyer."

Simon was transfixed, staring into space. He was trying to think logically. Nothing Jo said about Guy fit the brother he'd known all his life. Yet, somehow, everything fit. Guy admitted using the forged checks and the collapse of the United stock to get control of Macleod Brothers. That was the kicker. Guy was not the man to leave a key element like the forged checks to chance . . . not Guy. He'd make sure every base was covered, including masterminding the forgeries. The scheme was as brilliant and unique as everything Guy did.

"Now?" Louis asked. "Are you fully satisfied?"

Simon frowned. "About what? About Christie?"

"What else?"

"I was satisfied before Jo showed up." Simon's mouth narrowed. "Believe me, Louis, I didn't need Jo Caro to sign an affidavit swearing to Christie's innocence. I suppose

I did sound like a world class asshole. I'm sorry, Christie..."

Christie looked away for a moment. "Enough, Simon. Don't say anything you might regret. Like perhaps..." She gave him a remote smile. "...you've learned from this experience."

"I have... too much."

"And now you're going to tell me what you've learned."

"I've learned no one is above temptation... including myself. Only the temptation varies. Mine was ancestor worship. I'm sorry for Jo. A spider caught in her own web. I'm sorrier for my brother—"

Louis broke in. "You waste your time feeling sorry for either of them. Those two are are corruption-prone. It's a degenerative disease... progressive... they go from corruption to corruption."

Simon paid no attention to Louis. "Christie, can you forgive me for..."

"...For distrusting me?"

"I'm only human." Simon turned away to hide the sudden pain. What could he say? He couldn't bring himself to explain how what happened with Kitty had tainted Christie.

"I'm only human, too," Christie said softly.

They stared at each other. Christie's look was deeper and more calculated than ever. She was sick to death of having her integrity questioned by the world and—she felt numb— by the man she loved.

"Does that mean you won't forgive me"

"There's nothing to forgive. We're both only human."

Diplomatic, detached, cool, her words told him everything. She suspended judgement... maybe forever.

"You'll be returning to New York tomorrow?" Christie asked.

"On the first plane in the morning. I must see Guy. He's my brother... he won't lie to me." What would happen between them was his own wretched business, not to be discussed here with Louis... even Christie. He stretched. "And after that, Christie? There's tomorrow...?"

There are some times in life, Christie thought, when you must call on the best God gave you... and the best of what He didn't.

"We'll see about tomorrow... tomorrow. Go quickly, Simon. You have hard things to do." She reached for his hand, clasping it warmly. Maybe that was it, that was all they would ever have... a friendly handshake across the continent.

Simon had enough. His expression firmed. "Once you loved me... till life did us part. Maybe the next time..." He left the room.

Matt Renault sat on the bed in his bedroom and slipped off his patent leather pumps while dialing the phone. It rang once. He glanced at his Rolex. Jenny was expecting him in twenty minutes. The phone rang twice. Fortunately, she was never ready on time, and she hated his compulsive punctuality. Well, this time he would please her... he was going to be late. He had some packing to do before he danced the night away.

On Further Lane in Amagansett, the phone was picked up. "Who's this?" a gruff voice asked.

"Matt Renault."

"Yeah?"

"Is Mr. Lennos there?"

The voice said, "Yeah," and went to find Lennos. Seconds later, Stavros picked up.

"Mario, it's done?"

"Mission accomplished."

Stavros turned to Angelo Lupo, who was playing with an antiquated mechanical slot machine. Lupo disliked the new, electronic models and collected vintage slots. Stavros watched Angelo and smiled in disbelief. Angelo Lupo playing the slots... and losing. "Angelo, it's Mario Rinaldi. I'm putting him on the squawk box."

Lupo grunted, "Put him on," and punched the machine.

Stavros said, "Go ahead, Mario."

"We're home free. My Napoleon in high heels hit the silk. She told Guy Macleod where to head in."

"How do you know?" Stavros asked.

"I was there. I heard the announcement on TV and got her to meet me at her place. When she told me to get out, I figured I'd hang around. So I waited behind the door and listened to her performance with Macleod."

NAKED CALL

"What did she do then?"

"She drove to Louis Levy's house. I followed her. Then I drove home."

"Why did Jo Caro go to Levy instead of the police?"

"To confess her sins to Larsen and get absolution. She carried on like a banshee with me, how she'd done in her best friend." Mario Rinaldi—Matt Renault to most of the world—detailed Jo's conversation, first with him and then with Guy Macleod. He ended by saying, "After Levy, her next stop was the cops. Now comes the fall of the House of Usher."

"Or Macleod," Stavros said.

"Who is Usher?" Lupo asked, still fiddling with the slot machine.

"A fictional family. Mario is showing off the education we bought for him," Stavros answered. "Mario, are you sure she went to the police?"

"Yeah. She's there now. I called Detective Garcia on a pretext. Said I was with ABC News." He laughed. "We did better with Caro than we would have with Larsen. Press the right button and Caro falls into your lap. Gives you all the right answers. I trust my reports about United Cinema—thanks to Jo Caro—have proved useful."

Stavros pursed his lips. "Very useful. Better than I expected. Now we come to the end."

"What's my next assignment? I think Hollywood is no longer a safe place for Matt Renault."

"It isn't. Listen carefully, Mario. Your passport is current?"

"Always."

"Good. Tomorrow morning at six o'clock, go to the offices of Maxwell, Gluck & Moore. Jeffrey Moore will be waiting for you. He'll give you an envelope containing your second payment."

Matt wanted to shout, St. Tropez, here I come. He said nothing.

"Go to LAX and take the first plane to Kennedy. And from Kennedy go directly to Alitalia. A ticket for a flight to Rome will be waiting in the name of Mario Rinaldi. From Rome you fly to Palermo."

For God's sake, Stavros, have a heart, Matt thought. He said nothing.

"You'll be met in Palermo and taken to your Family. You deserve a vacation, Mario."

Some vacation. He felt sick.

"But remember, Mario. The women in Sicily are not American. Be respectful. Stay out of trouble." Stavros added, "You'll live in the village for one year. When we're ready, we'll send for you."

Suddenly the Matt Renault buried inside Mario Rinaldi erupted. "For Christ sake, Stavros. What am I working my ass off for? To spend my money in Castelvetrano?"

"This quiet vacation will make you eager for work." Stavros turned to Lupo. "Angelo, have you anything to add?"

"No. Good luck, Mario. Maybe you get married to a nice Sicilian girl." Lupo had just hit three balls. He'd beaten the damn machine.

"Married? To whom? What wife would put up with my line of work? She'd kill me. I've a better idea. I'll find a young, beautiful girl. Not a Sicilian girl," he hastily added. "I'll train her to be a female version of me. We can broaden my operation to include women who prefer other women . . . even to a man like me. I'll be more useful to you."

Stavros laughed. "Good thinking, Mario. You do that." He hung up.

Chapter 35

IT WAS the end of the line for Simon . . . Kennedy Airport. TWA Flight 840—departing eight A.M. from LAX in Los Angeles to JFK in New York—arrived on time. The thought of what lay ahead left Simon short of breath. He must demand his brother resign from the firm or . . . or what? Guy was his brother . . . a Macleod. How could he threaten Guy? How could he say he'd go to the Board of Governers of the New York Stock Exchange . . . to the SEC . . . to the Attorney General? How could he do that to his brother? Simon rubbed his forehead. Macleod Brothers meant as much to Guy as his life. It was like handing his brother a death sentence. Simon felt hot and cold. He loosened his collar. It would be brother against brother . . . Macleod against Macleod. None of the pictures spinning in his brain bore any resemblance to the life he knew. They were unreal. He was living on the edge of the world.

While Simon waited for his luggage, he tried to reach Guy at the office. When no one picked up the private line, he dialed the main number. He was immediately put through to Mrs. Neill.

"Mrs. Neill, this is Simon Macleod. I'm looking for Mr. Macleod. Do you know where he is?"

"Is it really you, Mr. Macleod?"

"Yes, it's really me. What's the matter?"

"Mr. Macleod didn't come in this morning. The police called."

"The police! What did the police want?"

"Mr. Macleod was mugged last night."

"Guy, mugged! Damn! What hospital is he in?"

There was quiet on the line. Suddenly Simon realized that Mrs. Neill had started sobbing. "He's . . . dead. They killed him."

Simon heard the words, but their meaning didn't penetrate. "What did you say?"

"They killed him."

"My brother? Guy? He's dead?"

"Yes. He's dead."

"Where is he?"

"I don't know. The police know . . . the seventeenth precinct . . . on East 51st Street," she sobbed and hung up.

"No! No! No!" Simon wasn't aware he was shouting and smashing his fists against the telephone. The pain was unbearable. He was also unaware that native New Yorkers—accustomed to living with casual violence—averted their eyes as they hurried by. Just as the phone shattered, a rough hand clamped on his arm and spun him about. Still shouting, Simon drove his shoulder into the man's chest. He half-carried and half-threw the man across the passageway. Only when they crashed against the far wall and the man slumped to the ground did Simon realize where he was and what he was doing.

"Oh shit! I'm sorry," he said to the stunned guard. Out of the corner of his eye, he saw more guards pounding toward him. He took off on a dead run. He had to find Guy. At the taxi stand, he muscled his way to the head of the line. Although he was well-dressed and impeccably groomed, he gave off a static, like madness. No one tried to stop him. New Yorkers respected the divine right of madness.

"Seventeenth precinct police station... East 51st Street. Go by way of the Queensboro Bridge." When the taxi pulled up at the police station, Simon handed the driver a fifty dollar bill and exploded from the cab, not waiting for change.

Inside the station, Simon leaned over the wooden railing and stared at the sergeant sitting at a raised desk behind the railing.

"My brother," Simon panted. "Mrs. Neill said he was killed last night."

The sergeant took in the distraught man "What'd you say your brother's name was?"

"Macleod. Guy Macleod."

"Lemme see. Macleod?" He scanned the names in the precinct registry. Here it is. Guy Macleod. White. Male. About forty-five. Yeah. Mugged last night. On the river side of the East River Drive. Damn fool, walking alone at three in the morning."

It took all Simon's self-control not to shake the sergeant into little pieces.

"What's your name?" The sergeant asked.

"Simon Macleod."

"This is your lucky day, Macleod. Captain Henderson's been—"

"Lucky!" Simon thundered. "You asshole! I'll break your—"

Four beefy policemen surrounded Simon. The smallest—also a sergeant—looked up at him. Pointed, black-rimmed teeth added menace to his twisted grin. He glanced at the desk sergeant. "What's with you, Lombardi? The man's brother's been mugged... killed... and you give him a hard time." The sergeant shook his head. "Okay, Macleod? You don't want to make trouble?"

"No trouble. Where's Captain Henderson? I want to find out what happened to my brother, and where his body is."

"Can do. Lombardi, call the captain. Tell him the mugging victim's brother is here." The sergeant placed his hand on Simon's arm. "My name's Kelly... Sean Kelly. If you need anything, ask for me... Sergeant Sean Kelly. Would you mind waiting over there?" Sergeant Kelly said, pointing to a bench against the far wall. As Simon sat down, he said, "Captain Henderson's been looking for you."

Minutes later, a door behind the desk sergeant opened and a small, dapper, clean-shaven, black man wearing a beige, three-button, vested suit appeared. He was around fifty and everything about him suggested intelligence and efficiency. He walked to the railing and looked at Simon. "Are you Simon Macleod?"

Simon stood up. "Yes. You're Captain Henderson?"

"We'll talk in my office. Lombardi, buzz him through."

Captain Henderson's office was a windowless cubicle about fifteen feet square. In that small space was crammed a desk, a desk chair, a sofa, a wooden chair, and file cabinets. The walls were covered with embossed diplomas.

"Sit down, Mr. Macleod." Henderson gestured to the wooden chair next to his desk. He waited for Simon to settle himself. "Can I see some ID, please?"

Simon handed the captain his wallet. "Take your pick."

The captain glanced at Simon's driver's license and returned the wallet. "Sorry. Rules..."

Simon nodded.

"I've been looking for you since about six o'clock this morning. I called your apartment... got your machine. Called your office... talked to your brother's secretary. I was worried maybe something had happened to you, too."

"I was in Los Angeles. Only Ira Benjamin knew that."

"Who's Ira Benjamin?" When Simon told him, the captain made a note on a legal-sized yellow pad. "When did you get back?"

"My plane landed at Kennedy about four-thirty." Simon placed his large hand on the captain's desk. "I called the office. Mrs. Neill told me my brother is dead . . . he was mugged last night. I don't believe it."

"Neither do I." Captain Henderson took in Simon's startled expression, a mixture of hope and confusion. "I mean, I don't believe he was mugged, but he is dead." Nelson Henderson had made captain because he was smart, tough, and straight . . . a good judge of character. He decided that Simon Macleod could take what he was going to tell him. "At first we were sure it was a typical mugging . . . money and credit cards missing, hit from behind with a blunt instrument, probably a hammer, skull crushed. That's what we told Mrs. Neill. But . . ."

The only evidence of the extreme control Simon was exercising was the whiteness of his knuckles as he gripped the arms of his wooden chair. "But what?"

"Do you know what a Glisanti is?"

"No."

"I didn't know either until our antique weapons expert gave me some smarts. It's an Italian pistol, once used by the Italian *polizia* . . . shoots a special nine-millimeter cartridge. No other bullet will fit the gun."

"Are you telling me my brother was shot?"

"In the back of the head at very close range. There were powder burns on his scalp. Weird. The coroner's done a preliminary autopsy . . . found the bullet. The trajectory of the bullet was down. Whoever shot your brother was a giant . . . or your brother was on his knees."

"Why would a mugger force him to kneel down?"

The captain didn't answer Simon's question. "The murderer tried to make it look like a run-of-the-mill mugging. To disguise the shooting he took a hammer and smashed your brother's skull to cover the hole made by the bullet."

"But it didn't fool you. Why?" Simon spoke in a voice as matter-of-fact as the Captain's. He didn't dare allow himself the slightest freedom. If his veneer of control cracked it would shatter. He'd be useless to the police, to Guy, to himself.

"The man was an amateur. He only took cash and credit cards. He left your brother's driver's license—that's how we identified him—plus a gold Rolex wristwatch worth at least fifteen thousand, and a gold tie clasp, value to be determined. A professional tries to hide the identity of his victim long enough to sell the stolen credit cards. All the credit card bureaus have been contacted. The cards were cancelled... they're useless pieces of plastic." Captain Henderson didn't try to hide his pride at a job well done.

"You're leading up to something, Captain. What?"

"In my opinion, your brother was murdered—not by a random mugger—by someone who knew him..." A deliberate pause. "... and who he knew well. Since you were on the West Coast—assuming that checks out—the unknown murderer wasn't you."

Simon released his grip on the arms of his chair long enough to fish into his coat pocket and toss his TWA ticket at the captain. "Don't waste the city's money on a long-distance phone call."

Henderson glanced at the ticket and returned it to Simon. "Okay. So tell me. Who would want your brother dead?"

Simon frowned. "A lot of people disliked my brother. But enough to kill him? I don't know. Where is my brother?"

"In the police morgue in Bellevue."

"I have to arrange his funeral."

"Not yet. Your brother was murdered. We'll hold his corpse for a few days. I need the coroner's final report and several other reports before I can release the body."

"Can I see him?"

"That's not a good idea."

"I didn't ask if it was a good idea. It isn't. I want to see my brother."

The captain nodded. "I'll arrange it. When?"

"Now."

"In case I need you, where can I find you?"

"At my apartment or in the office. If I'm not there, leave a message. I'll get back to you."

"I don't have to remind you not to leave town?"

"You just did."

"I realize this is a difficult time for you. But if you come up with a name, a possible suspect, call me." The captain held out his hand.

When Simon released the arm of the chair, he had to flex his fingers to restore feeling before shaking hands with the officer.

Simon walked out of the police station into the hot, bright glare of the New York City setting sun. He looked east along 51st Street... no empty taxis. He took a few steps toward Third Avenue when a man called out, "Hey, buddy. Look'n for a ride?"

Simon glanced at the man, a chauffeur leaning against a black stretch Cadillac limousine with dark windows... the kind of windows that allow one to see out but not in. "You off duty?" he asked.

"No. My boss is upstairs... won't be down for an hour. If you're not going too far, I'll take you. You can pay me what you think it's worth."

"Bellevue too far?"

"Nope. Hop in." The chauffeur opened the rear door.

Simon would never again fully trust his instinct for self-preservation. He had no warning... no premonition... nothing told him, don't do this. He was half in the limousine before he saw the two figures in the rear seat. When he tried to back out, he felt a hard object press against the base of his spine... a gun.

"Get in the car," the chauffeur whispered.

"Get in, Simon," the man in the rear seat said. "You won't be hurt. We want to talk to you, that's all."

The voice was familiar, but after the bright sunlight it was hard to see who was speaking in the dark interior. He had to fight his impulse to swing around and grab for the gun.

"Don't do it, Simon," the voice said patiently, as if reading Simon's thoughts. "All we want to do is talk about Guy's death."

Simon sank into the rear seat. The door was shut and the locks automatically clicked. A woman wearing a black dress, a black veil, and a black scarf over her hair sat between him and the man. Simon removed his dark glasses. He recognized him.

"Stavros Lennos," he said in a low, harsh voice. With a quick movement, he seized Stavros by the lapels and hauled him across the woman's lap until Stavros' face was only inches away from his. "What do you know about Guy's murder?"

The limousine moved away from the curb.

"Let him go," the woman said.

Simon was surprised. He'd expected a foreign accent... Italian.

"Stop it, Simon." Stavros sounded mildly irritated. "I'm sorry about this farce, but I want to talk to you in private."

Simon released his grip and Stavros resumed his seat, adjusting his jacket.

"Talk," Simon said. "I'm listening."

"Not here. These matters are too personal to discuss in a car."

"My apartment," Simon suggested. "I guarantee privacy."

"Your apartment. Fine." Stavros pushed the switch that controlled the intercom. "Beppe, take us to 523 Hudson Street."

"You know where I live?" Simon said.

"Of course."

Another question occurred to Simon. "You were waiting for me outside the police station. How did you know I was there?"

Stavros half-smiled. "Guy Macleod died last night. It occurred to me that you would show up at the precinct today ... tomorrow at the latest." The smile faded. "One does a favor where one can and one receives favors in return."

Simon understood. It was the way of the city... of the world. "The desk sergeant... Lombardi? Or the other sergeant... Kelly?"

"It makes no difference," the woman said.

"You speak perfect English!"

"What should I speak? I was born in Forest Hills."

Simon lapsed into silence. The woman was in mourning. Her mourning added to his feeling of loneliness. He was the only Macleod left. Guy was beyond any judgement he might make. At that, he wasn't certain he could have demanded his brother's resignation, no matter what he'd done. It had been the Macleods against the world for too many years.

When the limousine stopped in front of 523 Hudson

Street, the locks clicked. Stavros opened the door and got out first. He gave the woman in black his hand to steady her. Simon followed.

"We're going to the sixth floor," Simon said, leading the way into the small lobby. Simon unlocked the elevator door, waited for Lennos and the woman to enter, pressed the sixth floor button, and stood silently as the elevator slowly rose in its herky-jerky style. It stopped at the sixth floor. Simon opened the gate and unlocked the elevator door that led directly to his apartment.

"Would you like a drink?" he asked.

Stavros shook his head.

"No, thank you." The woman lifted her veil.

Simon was surprised again. The woman was painfully young... lovely. She wore no makeup. There were dark purple blotches—almost like bruises—under her eyes and her face was drawn tight with exhaustion.

"Sit down." Simon gestured to the green leather sofa against the far wall. Stavros leaned back on the sofa, his legs crossed, his hands folded on his lap. But the woman sat straight. She slipped her hand into her purse, as though she drew comfort from something inside the purse. Simon stood facing the couch. "All right. I suppose you want to talk about my brother's murder. If you know something—talk. Talk fast."

The woman looked up at Simon. "Sit down, Mr. Macleod." She removed her hand from the bag. She was holding a pistol. "I'm not a good shot, but you're too close to miss."

Stavros said, "Please sit down. You want to find out about your brother's murder? That's why we're here. But first there are things you don't know that you should know. For your own good... for our good."

Simon sank into a chair facing Stavros and the woman.

Stavros adopted a conversational tone. "We'll start with the introductions. This is Mona Anderson. Mona, this is Simon Macleod."

Simon stared at the woman. "Anderson? Are you Sherwood Anderson's wife?"

"I was Sherwood Anderson's wife. I'm now Sherwood Anderson's widow... courtesy of Guy Macleod."

"What the hell are you talking about?"

"Your brother killed my husband."

"Mrs. Anderson, you are stark raving crazy. Sherwood was killed in a hit-and-run accident in front of the office." Simon sounded feverish.

"And Guy Macleod was killed by a mugger who wanted to steal his credit cards," Mona jeered. Simon was partway out of his chair before Mona said, "Sit down, Mr. Macleod. I still have five bullets that fit this gun. If I have to, I'll use all five on you."

"Let me guess," Simon said as he backed away. "That's a . . . a . . . a Glipari . . . or some such name."

"Glisanti. My great-grandfather once visited Naples. This pistol and a box of many hundreds of bullets were a gift from a grateful friend in the *polizia*."

"A family heirloom." Simon was openly sarcastic.

"That's right," Mona said. "It's a family heirloom."

Simon stood straight . . . immobile. "Guy was killed by a bullet from a Glisanti."

"That's right," Mona said.

"Do you know who killed my brother?"

"Of course."

"If you don't tell me . . ." Simon's muscles coiled into a tight spring. A quick step to the right and . . .

"If you make one move, Mr. Macleod . . ." Mona raised the gun, taking careful aim at Simon's chest.

Stavros Lennos cut through the violence. "That's enough . . . both of you." His tone commanded obedience. He rose and placed himself between Mona and Simon. "Put away the pistol, Mona." When Mona continued to point the gun, Stavros said sternly, "You swore you would not make trouble. Are you a woman who does not keep her word?"

Mona dropped the pistol into her purse. "You're right, Uncle Stavros."

Simon blinked. Uncle Stavros!

"Sit down, Simon!"

Unwillingly, Simon sat down.

Stavros paced back and forth in front of Mona. Finally, he stopped and faced Simon. He stood very still. "I'll start at the beginning. You know Guy and I were at Harvard together?"

"Yes."

"We hated each other on sight."

"So I've heard," Simon said.

"I wasn't good enough for your brother...and I was too good for him."

"What's that supposed to mean?"

"Your brother majored in rudeness and arrogance. He minored in sadism. I was a scared, half-Greek, half-Sicilian kid suffering from an acute case of culture shock."

"Why culture shock?"

"Angelo Lupo had a theory...get your street smarts first and the rest is easy. But if you learn too much from books before you hit the streets, you'll never survive... not in his business. So, from the playground of the streets, I went to Harvard. That was culture shock. Your brother saw a scared teenager and figured he'd make me the butt of his jokes. He was right and he was wrong. I was scared, but not of him. One night I jumped him and beat the shit out of him. I damn near killed him."

"Guy was bigger than you and stronger than you," Simon said in disbelief.

"I knew how to fight. He didn't. Remember, I learned on the streets. I kneed him in the groin, thumbed him in the eye, kicked him in the ribs when he was down. I broke his arm and a couple of ribs."

Simon remembered visiting his brother in the infirmary. Guy was a mess. The doctors said he was lucky he wasn't blind in his right eye.

"Guy said he was jumped by a motorcycle gang."

Stavros shook his head. "Just by me. After that he left me strictly alone. But I was never asked to join a club... not even Hasty Pudding. Years later I learned why. It was thanks to your brother." The memories were crowding in on Stavros...a mixture of pride and bitterness. "When Guy was at Choate, he drank too much, smoked pot, snorted coke, and screwed every girl who would spread her legs. He was almost expelled on several occasions. Tell me, Simon, how did he get into Harvard in the first place?"

Simon recalled his father sitting Guy and him down and reading them the riot act. Guy had crashed his Jaguar XK 150 into the garage door, too drunk to stop the car. As always, their father treated anything Guy did as though they

NAKED CALL 505

both were at fault. "I've had it with you, Guy. You graduate Choate and get accepted at a good college or you will never work for Macleod Brothers. That goes for you, too, Simon," Charles Macleod roared. The threat of losing Macleod Brothers worked with Guy when nothing else did.

What had actually happened was none of their business. "Guy did very well in his senior year at Choate and cracked the SATs," Simon said.

Stavros didn't press him. "Guy wasn't stupid." He gave a faint shrug. "Anyway, Harvard is a large college. In time we learned to avoid each other. Until the Harvard Glee Club gave a joint concert with the Wellesley Glee Club and the BSO ... Bach's *B-Minor Mass*. I had a fine voice. I was the baritone soloist and Victoria Manners was the soprano soloist. We met—"

"You knew Victoria?"

"Very well."

"She was Guy's wife."

Abruptly, Stavros resumed pacing in front of the couch. Even after more than twenty-five years, he found it difficult to talk about Victoria ... most of all to Simon Macleod.

Simon studied Stavros' face, which was suddenly pale and drawn by pain. What was going on?

Mona took hold of Stavros hand. "This is too hard. I'll tell him."

Stavros nodded and sank into the couch. For once his body did not respond immediately to the commands of his mind. He shook his head slowly. It took an enormous effort to compose himself.

Simon watched and waited and nursed his own grief. Stavros Lennos had been infatuated with Guy's girl. Too bad. But Victoria was dead ... ancient history. Simon had no room in his heart for another man's suffering.

"Victoria Manners was in love with Uncle Stavros," Mona said softly.

"Victoria Manners ..." Stavros tried to pick up the story. Again he was unable to continue.

Despite himself, Simon became fascinated. He had discovered a crack in the mask of power that Stavros Lennos presented to the world. One blow with a chisel in the right spot and the mask would splinter.

"You fell in love with Victoria. I can understand that. She was a beautiful woman. But she was in love with Guy, not you." Simon was blunt and absurdly proud. "What has Victoria got to do with this meeting anyway?"

"Victoria... loved... Guy?" Stavros spoke slowly. There was a perceptible pause between each word.

Simon hammered the chisel into the crack. "That's right. Victoria loved Guy. The beautiful Victoria loved Guy and she married Guy. Victoria... Manners... loved... Guy! Now let's drop Victoria Manners."

Stavros did not shatter. Instead, Simon's frontal assault brought out the steel in him. "No! Victoria Manners did not love your brother," he said flatly. "She loved me." His voice fell until it was a whisper. "And I loved her."

Simon had enough. "She married Guy! Cut the shit."

"Her father, the oh-so-proper Rodney Manners, sold her to the Macleod family against her will."

"You're out of your mind." Simon's temper flared. "Maybe Sicilians sell their daughters... for two cows and a pig. Americans don't."

"Sicilians don't. Rodney Manners did. He didn't think of it as selling his daughter. He was providing for her future ... and his. Victoria would marry the right man who came from the right family. That's the way they think of themselves. Not as the good people, not even as the best people. They're the right people."

Simon had no answer. He'd heard this garbage from Guy over and over... the right this, the right that... recently, the right companies.

"Manners made one small mistake. He didn't know Victoria and I were in love."

Simon was disgusted. "Lennos, once I thought you were sane. Maybe a son-of-a-bitch, but smart and sane. What you're saying is nonsense. Victoria Manners was crazy about Guy. She married him... carried his baby."

There was a long pause before Stavros continued. "When Victoria told Guy she was pregnant, she expected him to be happy."

"He was."

"He got drunk. She told me about it afterward. He kept questioning her about me. She lied. At first she thought he might hurt her. But he stormed out of the house . . . stayed at his club for the rest of the week. When he returned home, he was sober. More than sober. He was calm, tender, outwardly happy. But Victoria was terrified of him. She didn't understand why her telling him she was pregnant had set him off." Stavros fixed on Simon with total concentration. "I realized then I had to tell her the truth."

"What truth?"

"Guy was sterile."

"What?"

"Your brother was sterile."

Simon was rocked by the statement. "Sterile? Cut it out. Victoria was carrying his baby."

"No. Victoria was carrying my baby. Guy had mumps when he was eighteen. At that age, mumps can cause sterility."

"How did you know about Guy having the mumps?"

"Long before I met Victoria, I made it my business to know everything about Guy Macleod . . . everything. Finding out that the mumps had made Guy sterile was simple. I spoke to Dr. Grant."

"Dr. Grant told you?"

"For the right price, the good doctor was very forthcoming." Stavros' words slowed to a halt, and Simon had an image of a large, dangerous animal lumbering toward him. "During the week your brother spent at his club, he went to see Dr. Grant, to check if the original diagnosis might have been wrong. It wasn't. That's why Guy never remarried. If he couldn't have children, why remarry?"

Simon let the new information wash over him. Something Guy had said the last morning they saw each other . . . it fit. His children—not Guy's—would inherit Macleod Brothers. Why did Guy say that, unless he know he was sterile?

"I begged Victoria to leave Guy. It wasn't safe to live in the same house with him. I pleaded with her to divorce Guy and marry me. She couldn't do it."

"She loved Guy." Simon tried to regain his footing.

"No. She was afraid to leave him. If Guy was willing to live a lie, so was she. It came down to money. Rodney Manners owed your father a lot of money. Manners had made some terrible stock market investments with money he didn't have based on inside information that turned out to be wrong. Your father covered his losses. The Manners' real estate—everything the family owned—was pledged as security for that debt. Your father wanted his grandchild. The lie must be respected."

"What kind of a man do you think my father was?" Simon spoke with the authority of a loving son. "Victoria could have divorced Guy. My father would not have tried to collect on that debt. When Manners got his affairs straightened out, he'd have repaid my father."

"Maybe your father would be kind but Victoria wouldn't risk it, even though I told her the Family would pay off the debt... go behind her father... with no strings attached. She still said no. She said her father would never accept help from a Mafia Family. She had no choice. She must stay with Guy." Stavros' face was dark, his lips compressed. "I had a friendly chat with your brother. I told him that if he ever laid a hand on Victoria or did anything to hurt her baby, I would kill him... not have him killed ... kill him myself." Stavros lowered his eyes for an instant. "Guy agreed not to touch Victoria, and I was the damn fool who believed him."

"He didn't do anything to her. She died in an accident." Simon was grasping at straws.

"So did Sherwood," Mona said with a bleak smile.

"A lousy coincidence! What the hell are you two driving at?" Simon was furious... and suddenly afraid.

"Victoria died in an accident?" Stavros asked reasonably.

"Yes! She had an accident on a ski slope. I remember." Simon's voice was louder than necessary. Something terrible had happened... something worse was coming.

"I remember, too," Stavros said slowly. "At Mad River Glen. Your brother said she was skiing too fast and caught an edge. She flipped off the trail—The Chute—and hit a tree. Instead of waiting with her, he skied down for help. By the time the ski patrol found her, she was dead. She'd hemorrhaged... the snow was soaked with her blood." Stavros sounded more like a robot than a man. "Tell me something, Simon Macleod. Victoria was an intermediate skier at best. What was a woman seven months pregnant doing on The Chute at Mad River Glen in the late afternoon? That's the steepest, narrowest, most dangerous trail in Vermont. Some expert skiers won't ski down that trail at 4:30 in the afternoon."

"I don't know what she was doing."

"I wanted to kill Guy. The Family stopped me."

Simon roused himself again. "I don't believe you... you and your heroics. Why the hell would they stop you? Those kind, gentle, soft-hearted Sicilian Mafiosi wanted to save poor Guy from you. Come off it."

"No. Not Guy. They wanted to save me from myself. I didn't graduate from Harvard to be a soldier in the Lupo Family. Moshe Cohen insisted I was too valuable to be risked. The Macleods have power. You can't dump Guy Macleod into the Jersey swamp. There'd be publicity and the police would launch a major investigation."

"But you can kill him and dump him beside the East River." Simon's nerves began to sing, a high-pitched scream that threatened to catapult him from his chair. "Now I get it. That's what this Victoria garbage is all about. You're trying to justify your killing Guy."

"Be quiet, Simon. Listen," Mona said softly.

Abruptly, Simon was quiet. He listened.

Stavros was again unable to sit still. He rose from the couch, prowling the perimeter of the room. Like a cat in strange surroundings, he sidled along the walls... always facing Simon. "I didn't kill him... not then, not now. But I threw a scare into your brother. I frightened him so much, he decided he needed protection from me, from the Lupo Family. He arranged for protection."

"Next you'll tell me Guy joined the Mafia." Simon meant to beat Stavros to the punch.

"The Mafia isn't a club. You don't join a Family. Guy wanted Mafia protection. He found it with the Carlino Family. We've had trouble with them before." Stavros stopped pacing long enough to look down at Mona Anderson. Her face could have been carved out of marble. "I'm sorry, Mona." He resumed his restless movements. "The Carlino Family owned several legitimate companies... small then. Today those companies are household names, publicly held companies admired on Wall Street."

"What companies?" Simon asked.

"Not important. Your brother managed an introduction to Umberto Carlino. He arranged for Macleod Brothers to take Carlino's companies public. Besides Macleod's usual underwriting fees, there was a second, unwritten price—protection from me... from the Lupo Family. Umberto Carlino was happy to pay that price."

"I don't believe a word of this. Guy would never knowingly do business with the Mafia."

"He would. He did. Knowingly, providing the senior executives—the men he worked directly with—came from the right families." The look on Simon's face made Stavros laugh. "Do you really think that the name of every Family member ends with a vowel? Like Lupo... Montefuoco... Carlino?"

"No. But—"

"But nothing." Stavros yielded no ground. "When Guy wanted something unpleasant done—a reluctant CEO convinced, a dissenting board member warned off, even killed—he knew exactly who to phone."

Simon sat bolt upright. "Are you saying Guy had Sherwood Anderson killed?"

"We both know your brother wanted Macleod Brothers for himself, with no outside partners. It was his birthright. Nobody stands in Guy Macleod's way... not you, not Christie Larsen, certainly not poor Sherwood." Stavros took in Simon's startled reaction at hearing Christie's name. "That's right, Simon. It took me a while, but finally I worked out what actually happened at United Cinema, and why. Do you want to hear the truth about the forged check caper?"

"No," Simon gasped. He'd heard too much already.

"We have more proof than merely motive." He turned to Mona. "I never believed I'd tell a Macleod about Guy Macleod... about Victoria. Now I have. For your sake." His face softened. "It may help him understand your loss."

Mona Anderson gazed at Stavros, then turned to Simon. She spoke slowly. She sound almost friendly. "Sherwood told me that he and your brother were in a fight. That wasn't true. It wasn't Sherwood's fight. It was your brother and Uncle Stavros who were fighting. Sherwood was trapped in the middle. Sherwood was vain, foolish about many things, not a brave man. I didn't care if he was brave or not . . . he was my husband. He taught me all sorts of things. I loved him very much. I . . .'' Mona's face crumpled. She closed her eyes and bit on her lower lip. Her chest heaved with dry sobs.

"Uncle Stavros tried to protect Sherwood. He failed." She glared first at Stavros and then at Simon. "No one warned me Guy Macleod was a madman."

"And now you're going to tell me he murdered your husband. Sherwood was killed by a gypsy cab. It was an accident." Simon sounded like an exasperated teacher explaining how to count to a dull child.

"No. The car was there to kill Sherwood. The Family has ways of finding out what it wants to know. The car that killed Sherwood was stolen by Benvenuto Corsi. But Corsi was careless. He left his fingerprints on the steering wheel."

"Benvenuto Corsi? Am I supposed to know who he is?"

"No. Corsi is a member of the Carlino Family . . . the Family your brother did business with. Your brother hired Corsi to kill my husband. The price was one hundred fifty thousand dollars."

"How do you know this?" Simon asked.

"From Benvenuto Corsi, who else?"

"I'd like to hear this from Corsi himself, not secondhand."

"Secondhand is as close as you can get," Mona said coldly. "Unless when you die, you go to hell. He's quite dead now."

"You killed him?" Simon heard the shock in his voice at the idea that this beautiful woman was a killer.

Mona pursed her lips in contempt. "No, Mr. Macleod. I did not kill Corsi. I didn't have to. Uncle Stavros informed the Carlino Family that Corsi, one of their soldiers, had taken a freelance assignment. If it had been a stranger, they would have smiled and looked the other way." Her tone became ominous. "But to kill a member of the Lupo Family—even a member by marriage—is not in the Carlino Family's best interests. The Carlino Family does not want a dispute—a war—with the Lupo Family. So they did the honorable thing."

"Honorable thing?" Simon's critical faculties went on hold. "They killed him. You believe it's honorable to kill a man?"

"Yes," Stavros said. "It was the honorable thing. Corsi was not acting for his Family. He could not in all honor expect their protection."

Simon couldn't remember when he'd last heard so much talk about honor. That it should come from two members of a Mafia Family struck him as black comedy.

"After Corsi was disposed of, only one thing remained. We must settle accounts with Corsi's employer, the man responsible for Sherwood's death... for Victoria's accident." Mona watched Simon take this in. "Uncle Stavros insisted this was his right, his vendetta. He had brought my husband into his battle with Guy Macleod. His honor was at stake."

Simon's mind was spinning at a furious rate. He was sick to death of the word "honor." "Did you kill Guy, Lennos?"

"No. I told you I didn't. Frankly, I wish I had," Stavros said quietly.

"Who did then?" Simon glared at them.

"I did." Mona's voice was full of pride. "I used my family's pistol." She patted the Glisanti. "This pistol."

"I don't believe it. You killed Guy? How could you? He was twice your size."

"It was easy. He was so eager." Mona's smile was awful. "I was waiting for him in a car in front of his house. When I wear other clothes, men find me very attractive."

Simon's mouth had gone dry. He wanted to say something, but he felt powerless to speak.

"Your brother—Guy Macleod—was interested... very interested in the pretty, drunken woman in the short, silk skirt and lacy transparent blouse. He was such a gentleman. The little lady wanted to get a breath of fresh air first... he'd love to walk along the river with her. He wouldn't keep his hands off me. Every time he touched my breasts I wanted to scream. But I didn't. When we reached the walk, I sat on a bench and spread my legs. Your brother knelt down. Can you imagine the rest?" She smiled through

NAKED CALL

her sadness. "Now you know how I killed him . . . a man twice my size."

"You shot him while he was . . ." Simon was unable to say what he was thinking. He swallowed hard. "That's why the hammer, the stolen credit cards? You wanted it to look like a mugging."

Stavros was disgusted. "But she's an amateur. She made mistakes. You already know all this."

Simon nodded. "Captain Henderson told me." He stared at Stavros and Mona. Beads of sweat formed on his forehead. It was not what they said. Nothing they said could have convinced him that Guy was a killer. Nothing. It took Guy himself to do that. There were things they didn't know, obsessions that Guy lived by . . . that only a Macleod might run Macleod Brothers . . . all other blood was inferior. If Victoria's baby was the child of Stavros Lennos . . . Simon was swept by an overpowering despair. His brother had a highly logical mind. If Victoria didn't give birth—no baby . . . no heir. Simon remembered that Victoria had had another near-fatal accident. Walking down a long flight of steps with Guy, she tripped and fell. Only her grabbing for the railing broke her fall. Later his father had told him how lucky they'd been. Maybe there were other "lucky" accidents—near misses—he didn't know about, until the one at Mad River Glen. Simon was breathing rapidly and loudly. He glanced at Mona. Guy killed her husband . . . she killed Guy. He ransacked his mind for something to say. "Jesus! What next?" He must have said it out loud, because Lennos answered him.

"Mona says you have to kill her. Then the Family will kill you. Vendetta, vengeance . . . an ancient ritual."

Simon was paralyzed by pain and confusion. "Why doesn't she do it? Kill me? That would end it . . . this vendetta. I'm the last of the Macleods."

A curious, almost dreamy look, came over Mona's face. "No. My father was killed, my husband was killed, I've killed. I've had all the killing I can stomach. I can't kill you. Here." With a trace of a smile, she tossed the Glisanti at Simon. "It's your turn."

Simon caught the gun, held the handle between his thumb

and forefinger. He looked at Mona, bewildered. "You want me to kill you?"

Mona calmly clasped her hands in her lap. "Yes," she said.

"You mean it?"

"I mean it."

Simon slid his finger against the trigger. "You have only five bullets left that fit this gun. Are all five in the magazine?"

Mona nodded. Her cheeks were streaked with tears. Her attempt to smile did nothing to hide her misery.

Simon stared her, amazed. Then he turned sideways and pressed the muzzle of the gun against the back of his chair. He pulled the trigger five times. Although much of the sound was muffled by the cushion, Mona and Simon flinched at each crack.

Stavros Lennos was aware of the smell of human sweat in the room, mingled with burned cordite. He'd hoped for this, but the coin of hope had a second side. Simon was Scottish. The history of vengeance among the Scottish clans was as violent as the Sicilian vendetta.

Simon tossed the empty gun in the direction of Mona. It missed her and landed on the floor. She let it lay there.

Simon's shirt felt clammy. He could taste his rage and despair. "Get the hell out of here, Lennos. You, too, Mrs. Anderson. I'm sorry about your husband. I'm sorry about my brother. I'm sorry about Victoria. I can't change a thing. I would if I could. I'm hip deep in the shit. Just like you."

Stavros and Mona were at the elevator door before Stavros stopped. "One more thing. My associates and I own a substantial interest in United Cinema. We will want at least two seats on the board."

"I'll think about it," Simon said dully.

"Do that. We also want Christie Larsen to be president of the studio."

The words set off alarm bells in Simon. "Why?" he asked.

"The bottom line. Why else? She makes good films which make money for the studio. She's also honest. The Family insists that its legitimate businesses be handled legitimately by honest executives."

Simon felt guilty. What the hell had he been thinking?

"Of course you will not mention this visit to Captain Henderson."

Simon shook his head.

"Good. It will remain another of the many unsolved murders in New York police records.

Simon whispered, "Get out of here. Both of you. This meeting never happened.

Mona smiled at Simon, an odd, forlorn smile. "Thank you, Mr. Macleod."

"Thank me? For what?"

"For killing the chair."

The elevator door closed. Simon sat for a long time. He thought of Guy . . . of his Big Brother . . . of all the love he felt for him . . . of all the harm his brother had done to those closest to him. He went to the library, and on the top shelf he found an album of pictures . . . pictures of his mother and father and Guy and himself. There was one photograph in particular . . . Guy standing in front of the entrance to Macleod Brothers the day he started at the firm. Guy looked so proud. Simon touched Guy's face . . . baffled, loving . . . as a father might touch a child too badly bruised and too ashamed to admit he was hurt. His eyes grew wet as he gazed at the snapshot, like a man assessing all the promises of his past life. Which had he kept . . . which had he broken?

PART TWELVE

1992 AUGUST

Chapter 36

THE BALLOON burst. When the shreds of what had looked like a solid case against Christie Larsen settled on Detective Carmella Garcia's desk, she stoically assembled the facts and listed the winners and losers.

WINNERS
1) Christie Larsen—Reappointed president of United Cinema and a member of the board of directors... the reigning queen of Hollywood.
2) Claude Dukenfield—The bank's loss was covered by insurance. Remained a vice president in charge of the Beverly Hills branch of the Bank of California.
3) Franco Marconi—Cleared of all suspicion... preparing to direct a new film for United, *Deirdre of The Sorrows*.
4) ?...

As far as Detective Garcia knew, there were no other winners.

LOSERS
1) Detective Carmella Garcia—Even if United Cinema pressed charges against Jo Caro—which they refused to do—the conviction of the United Cinema's general counsel did not have the same headline value as the conviction of the president of the studio. This case would not earn Garcia a promotion to lieutenant.
2) Julian Hennesy—The biggest loser of all. What more can one lose than one's life? The murder was

connected to the case. According to Sidney Frank, accountant, Hennesy knew who the forger was. Murderer unknown.

2) Jo Caro—The second biggest loser. Resigned as general counsel of United Cinema. Under investigation by the California Bar Association for possible disbarment.

3) Edgardo Silvera—Fired from his job as United Cinema's assistant controller. United won't press charges. He'll never again work for a studio.

3) Matt Renault—Present whereabouts unknown. An outstanding arrest warrent for Renault...forgery and perjury for openers. If Garcia ever got her hands on him, she'd make him sweat bullets.

4) Harry Weiss—For one brief, shining moment, he was president of United Cinema...seated at the right table at Morton's...his calendar crowded with invitations to parties from people who had never before acknowledged his existence. Resumed his old job as controller at United...a comedown!

5) Jenny Lattimore—Lost one lover...gained one enemy—Christie Larsen. Not good for an aging beauty to have an enemy as powerful as Larsen.

Detective Garcia was aware that her list of winners and losers was incomplete. It dealt only with Hollywood. The murder of Guy Macleod, CEO of United, was outside her jurisdiction. The ringing telephone roused her.

"Garcia," she barked into the receiver and listened. "On my way, Captain." She hung up. Back to the usual grind ...break-ins, stolen cars, prostitutes. Still she'd keep her eyes open. United Cinema wasn't the only studio with dirty linen they didn't want washed in public. All she needed was one lucky break and she'd make lieutenant.

Franco Marconi was getting reacquainted with the star of his new film. He used his usual technique...wine, cocaine, and his magical Jacuzzi. But for the first time in his life, something was wrong. Not with the actress. With him. He couldn't get it up. His mind kept drifting back to how close he'd been to being president of United, king of the hill. He glanced at Maureen Corley lying on one of the jets.

"You're doing it wrong," he said.

"What's wrong?"

"Turn over. Lie on your stomach. It works better that way."

Maureen rolled over and adjusted herself so that the water jet hit her most sensitive spot. In seconds, she was breathing heavily. "Oh, God! You're right," she gasped

Maureen's growing excitement was contagious. It made Franco rethink his values, what was important and what was shitsville. Why the hell did he want to be president... all that fucking paperwork, meetings with bankers, the board of directors, conferences about lousy movies he wasn't directing. Leave that to a paper shuffler like Christie Larsen. He was Franco Marconi, the genius. Jesus! He was as hard as a rock.

"Hey, baby. C'mere. It's working now."

Reluctantly, Maureen lifted herself off the jet. "It didn't work before," she gasped. "I'll kill you if it doesn't now." She straddled Franco, lowered herself over him, and felt him slip inside her. "Oh, yes!" she sighed.

Franco didn't move a muscle. He let Maureen do the work. This was living. A great script, a beautiful woman, booze, coke... what else did he need? He wouldn't be president of United Cinema if they got down on their knees and...

The secretary said, "Go right in, Miss Caro. Mr. Schneider expects you."

Jo Caro posed in the door to Abe Schneider's office. "What do you think, Abe? Could I still make it as a 'comes along'?"

"You sure could, kid." Abe chortled. "Like a great wine, you've aged, not soured. What a sleigh ride, the last twelve years. Me with my own agency, AAA Inc.—Actors, Artists Agency, Inc. You made general counsel at United. Pretty fucking good."

"You know I resigned from United."

"Come on, Jo. Don't bullshit a bullshitter. You didn't resign, you were canned. The way I hear it, you tried to do a number on Christie Larsen. Want to tell me about it?"

"No." A resigned Jo prepared to leave.

"Where you going in such a hurry? Sit and schmooze a little."

"I'd like to, Abe, but what's the point?"

"You need a job. You told me when you called that you wanted to be an agent. Being a lawyer isn't good enough for you?" He looked at Jo with a dawning suspicion. "You going to be disbarred or something?"

"Something. I got a censure. I can't practice law for six months, and the next time I do anything—like spit on the sidewalk—I get disbarred."

"Tough," Abe pursed his lips. "I think you got what it takes to make a good agent. You're smart, you know the movie business, your ass is wired into who's doing what to whom, you got a natural eye for young actors. You also got the morals of a mink. You can lie and cheat, promise 'em anything and give 'em you know what."

Jo chuckled. "Thanks for the compliment."

"It's why I love you, kid." Abe rubbed his chin. "Right now, this town's in love with Larsen, the fucking queen of the May. Will she blackball you in high places?"

"Christie is Christie. You never know for sure what she'll do."

"I'll risk it. I pay a draw against commission. Fifty-fifty . . . you get to keep half of anything you make."

"You offering me a job?" Jo asked. She was having trouble believing her ears.

"Yeah. Five thousand a month draw, plus legit expenses. One-year guarantee. Even if you get back your shingle, you stick with the agency . . ." He hesitated. ". . . and with me, when I'm in the mood."

"You used to always be in the mood."

"I've gotten older. I got a wife. She takes care of me. But once in a while . . . you know how it is?"

Jo nodded. Abe was no Matt Renault . . . that wasn't all bad. "When do I start?"

"Monday morning. Ten o'clock." Abe stood and held out his hand.

Jo accepted his hand. "I got a funny feeling I'll make a good agent." She blinked rapidly. Tears would do a number on her mascara. "Thanks, Abe."

"For what? The way you peddle ass I'm going to make a fortune off you." Jo almost curtsied before leaving the office. As soon as she was gone, he dialed a number. "Christie Larsen, please. Abe Schneider calling." He waited. "Christie, it's Abe. Yeah. She starts Monday. I swear I won't tell her. I swear. You got any problems if she handles Maureen Corley? Good. Go with God. Bye." He hung up the phone, placed his feet on his desk, and leaned back. Great feeling, doing something to help an old friend . . . also profitable. With Christie Larsen pushing, Jo could make a lot of money . . . for herself and the firm.

Jenny Lattimore watched as Lester Farber swam laps in her pool. His swimming style was closer to a dog paddle than anything else. The only parts of him that stuck out of the water were his head and his tail. It seemed to Jenny that his buttocks had gotten bigger and softer. They could have been a woman's fat ass. As always when lounging by her pool, except for a wide-brimmed hat and her jewelry, Jenny was nude. She touched herself. She was wet. "Goddamn you, Matt Renault," she murmured. She needed to get laid . . . but by Lester? She considered her options, and her accountant. How could she fuck him if she didn't want anything from him? If she fucked him without asking him to do something for her, it would change their relationship. He might get delusions of gender. The image of Lester pounding his flabby chest and bellowing, "Me Tarzan . . . you Jane," made her giggle. A possibility occurred to her. Lester could talk to Sidney Frank, Sidney Frank could talk to Harry Weiss, Harry Weiss could talk to Christie Larsen. Everyone said Larsen didn't hold grudges. She hoped "everyone" was right. Jenny felt better. Problem solved . . . Lester's and hers. I fuck you, Lester, and you do something for me. Situation normal. She'd fuck Lester and get the ball rolling . . . give him what he wanted and get what she wanted in spades! Lester had a woman's ass, but his prick was all man.

When Louis Levy stepped out of the limousine on lower Broad Street, he was assaulted by a blast of hot, moist air. In seconds, sweat oozed from his pores. He stood on the sidewalk and looked up at the tall building. Etched deep into the marble above the solid brass revolving doors was the name, The Riordan Trust. Although the Trust only occupied the top four floors and penthouse in the twenty-five story building, no one questioned the Trust's name on the building. It was a small part of the Trust's holdings in Manhattan. The Riordan Trust didn't own a building here, a building there. It owned a square block here, a square block there.

By the time Louis pushed through the revolving doors, he felt grimy. His cotton seersucker suit was wrinkled and sweat had darkened the knot of his tie. Why the hell does anyone live in New York City, he wondered. He made his way to the rear bank of elevators reserved for those calling on the Riordan Trust. When he entered the elevator, he said, "Twenty-five, please."

The elevator operator snapped to attention . . . the twenty-fifth floor was the executive floor. "Yes, sir." He pushed the button marked 25 and the doors closed. In seconds, the high-speed elevator deposited Louis on the twenty-fifth floor.

The reception room was small and elegantly furnished with early American antiques. Early American was not one of Louis' favorite periods . . . the chairs were too hard, the tables and lamps too small.

Louis walked across an old hooked rug and waited in front of the receptionist's desk. The gray-haired receptionist looked up and smiled. Louis didn't recognize the woman. He hadn't visited Michael's office in fifteen years. At some point this gray-haired receptionist had replaced another gray-haired receptionist . . . probably her mother. Positions in the Riordan Trust tended to be handed down from generation to generation.

"Yes, sir. Who do you wish to see?"

"Mr. Riordan."

"Your name, please."

"Louis Levy."

"You can go up, sir. The elevator—"

"I know the way," Louis interrupted. He strode to the far end of the reception room. Half-hidden behind a column was another elevator . . . Michael's private elevator. Louis

NAKED CALL

opened the door and entered the small cab. He closed the old-fashioned iron gate and pressed the up button. The elevator slowly rose to the penthouse. When Louis stepped out of the elevator, he was greeted by another elderly, gray-haired lady. This time he knew the woman.

"How are we today?" Barbara Sweeny chirped. She'd been Michael Riordan's secretary for fifteen years and his father's secretary before that.

"We are splendid, thank you."

"You remember the way?" Barbara Sweeny said.

"Unless you've changed things."

"Here? Shame on you, Mr. Levy. Nothing ever changes here. How can one improve on perfection?"

"Right. Shame on me." Louis smiled as he edged his way past the secretary. The hall was wide and the pine paneling was painted an off-white. Colorful prints depicting the famous battles of the American Revolution graced the walls. The short hall led directly to a huge office at least fifty feet square. The office was furnished with large, heavy, leather chairs and sofas. The oak tables were polished to a high gloss. An eighteenth-century partner's desk—Michael's desk—was set against the far wall. Instead of the usual carpeting, the concrete floor was covered by dark walnut parquet and Oriental throw rugs. There were no pictures on the walls. Instead a muralist had covered three walls with huge, romanticized panoramas of Philadelphia, Manhattan, and Boston as the villages had existed in the early eighteenth century. The Riordan land grants—in Manhattan from Peter Stuyvesant and in Boston and Philadelphia from George I, King of England—were cleverly highlighted. The Manhattan grant seemed to stretch from what eventually became 23rd Street to the horizon. The fourth wall was glass . . . fifty feet of French doors that opened onto a terrace, actually the roof of the building.

Since Michael wasn't at his desk, Louis decided he had to be on the terrace. He opened the French door and stepped into the muggy, clammy Manhattan air. When he saw Michael Riordan, he almost choked. Riordan was going over some papers while sitting at a Salterini table that was shaded by a red-striped awning. He was dressed in a white, three piece suit. His chauffeur, who doubled as a bodyguard, stood behind him, slowly waving an ostrich fan.

"Michael," Louis said.

Michael Riordan looked over his shoulder. "Louis. Come over here and sit down." Michael placed the papers he'd been reading in a large folder. "Tell me again. Why is Simon Macleod selling his stock in United Cinema?"

"He doesn't like the movie business. The stock is too volatile. United was his brother's idea." He tactfully forgot to mention that Simon also disliked being Christie Larsen's boss.

"I'm sorry about Guy Macleod. I wasn't fond of the man, but getting killed by a mugger? Terrible!" Michael shivered.

"Not a Class A death," Louis agreed.

"And why am I buying the stock?"

"You're buying the stock because you like the movie business as much as your father did."

"My father liked getting laid. That's what movies meant to him . . . easy pussy. He once told me the secret of living is getting as much pussy as possible. He died in the saddle."

"A Class A death," Louis murmured.

"What about Lennos? In your note you mentioned Lennos will sit on the board. How the hell can I sit on the same board as Lennos? He's an animal."

"He promised me he'd eat with a knife and fork." Louis grinned. He saw no reason to explain to Michael that Lennos' only proviso was that he have the right to veto any films involving the Mafia, especially a film about Moshe Cohen. The idea of a kinder, gentler Cosa Nostra struck him as funny. Done right, it would make a hell of a black comedy.

"Leo Hightower and Avery Longstreet are also on the board, Michael. You'll feel right at home."

"Yes. I like Avery. Leo is, well, stupid but harmless." He paused as if trying to figure Louis out. "Okay. Lennos sits on the board. But there's his lady friend, Mona Anderson. Why her?"

"Mrs. Anderson is not his lady friend. She was married to a Macleod Brothers partner, Sherwood Anderson."

"I read about him. My father knew Anderson's father. She should be all right. That family has lousy luck." Michael leaned back, balancing his chair on its rear legs. "All

NAKED CALL

right, Louis. You know why I'm buying Macleod's stock." It was a statement, not a question.

"It's a good investment. Same reason the Japs bought Columbia Pictures."

"The Japs make mistakes. I'm doing it for Jane. You got to her."

Louis brought the fingers of his right hand to his chest. "Me?" he said with offended innocence.

"You. You told her Macleod's stock was for sale. She still thinks I own a piece of United. Now I'll own a very big piece, a controlling interest. As the wife of the Chairman of the Board of United, she has visions of chatting with Robert Redford about the environment . . . save the warthog or something like that." Michael checked his watch. "Let's go. The lawyers are waiting."

"Lawyers get paid for waiting, even when they wait on the toilet. Michael, think how pleased Jane will be with you once the deal is signed."

Michael was thinking just that. Jane would be totally occupied wining and dining celebrities with never a shortage of escorts. He sighed with relief as he thought of the freedom he would have . . . and the use he'd make of it.

In another part of town—a dusty office on West 54th Street—another contract was being signed. Irene Bentley and Christie Larsen had agreed that United Cinema would film the Irene Bentley production of *Deirdre of the Sorrows* for the upfront payment of five hundred thousand dollars and two percent of the net. Once the signing was complete, the lawyers for Irene and Christie placed copies of the contract in their attaché cases and rose to leave. Christie also rose.

"Christie," Irene said. "Would you mind staying a few minutes? Please."

Christie hesitated.

The "please" had done her in. She turned to Morty Lembeck, United's new general counsel. "Morty, you go ahead. Louis expects us at Macleod Brothers' offices. I'll join you shortly."

Irene waited for the door to close before saying, "We

haven't been alone in a long time. We haven't really talked. It's time I set the record straight."

Christie's green eyes were wary with suspicion.

"I know I wasn't much of a mother... or a wife. Still, you survived me."

"Good genes." She didn't want to say it, but she couldn't stop herself. "My father didn't."

Irene closed her eyes. It was impossible for Christie to tell what images were imprinted on Irene's lids.

"No, Tom didn't." Irene's face was drained of color. "Do you ever wonder why I never married again?"

"No one asked you," Christie said. A dumb question deserved a dumb answer.

"I was asked often enough. Some of the men were very rich, very powerful. A few still hang around, hoping I'll change my mind."

"So?" Christie managed a faint smile. "Next time say yes."

"I can't." She waited for Christie to say something. From the set of Christie's mouth, she knew she'd have a long wait. "All right, I'll tell you, even if you don't want to hear. I never married because I can't. Your father is the reason... always has been, always will be."

Once again Christie waited. Now she was as pale as her mother.

"Do you remember your father before Knute Larsen died?"

Christie slowly nodded. "Must we have this conversation?"

"We must."

"Why?"

"Because then you remember how much I loved your father. I always loved him."

Christie's face mirrored her disbelief. After a bit, Christie said, "I remember how much you hated him."

"No. I loved him." She stared into Christie's suspicions. "What I hated was the man he became after Knute died. The man who was still dependent on his father. I didn't like or admire that man." Her face was very still. "He never gave me a chance to respect him."

This was too much for Christie. "You ruined the only

chance he had . . . the time he got the syndicate to back his design for a racing sloop." Suddenly she ran short of breath.

"He ruined his chances. He signed the checks. He stole the money."

"You made him do it," Christie erupted.

"Would you have signed the checks?" Irene asked quietly. She was almost unnaturally calm.

Christie looked away, feeling trapped. "No."

"Neither would I. He shouldn't have. Do you understand?" A note of desperation crept into Irene's voice. "All he had to do was say, 'Fuck off, Irene.' That would have been it. But he didn't. The more he let me walk all over him, the more I despised him. But I never stopped loving him."

"I don't believe you." But Christie's stern face was changing to one of uncertainty.

"I can have sex with anybody—man or woman—and enjoy it. But love . . . no," Irene sighed. "Your father was the only man I've ever loved." She was impatient. "If I didn't mean it, you would be the last person on earth with whom I'd play make-believe."

"Okay. You mean it. So what? The damage was done."

"To all of us . . . you, your father, and me." Irene studied Christie. "You've inherited your looks from me. And something else. A perverse fidelity. That ex-husband of yours . . . Barry What's-His-Name. You still love him?"

Christie's laughter rang true. "Jesus, no! Barry's a totally committed, genuine shit."

"But you love someone. Who?"

"I don't love anyone . . . except Tommy."

It was Irene's turn to sit in judgement. "You're lying. There's a man somewhere. And like me, you're a one-man woman. I can tell."

This was too much. Christie stood up to leave.

"All right, Christie," Irene said calmly. "I've had my say. Believe it or not, your father's cowardice hurt us all." She mustered a smile. "But I'm a survivor. He wasn't. I hope the man you love is a survivor. See you on the coast."

At the door, Christie stopped and faced Irene. "Bye, Mother," she said softly. She was careful to close the door behind her before starting down the narrow flight of steps.

* * *

By the time Christie arrived at 15 William Street, the closing had taken place. Louis was waiting in the reception room for her.

"You missed Michael Riordan," Louis said sternly. "He wants to meet you. He suggested dinner tonight at the Pen and Pencil." He smiled at Christie's raised eyebrows. "A restaurant has to be in existence in the same location for at least twenty-five years before Michael takes it seriously."

"Of course. What time?"

"Eight thirty, after the theater crowd leaves. Gives us time to talk." Louis chuckled. "He wants you to introduce Jane around—Jane's Michael's wife—to the 'A' list."

"Miss Larsen?" A brown-haired, woman hurried toward them. "They told me you'd arrived. I'm Mrs. Neill, Mr. Macleod's secretary. Remember? I used to be Mr. Guy Macleod's secretary," she added pointedly.

"Yes." Christie smiled.

"Mr. Macleod would like to see you. If you have the time."

Christie had been hoping this would happen . . . dreading it, too. She hesitated.

Louis urged, "Get it over with."

"Where is he? In the Fish Bowl?"

Mrs. Neill sighed. "No. Mr. Benjamin is in the Fish Bowl. Mr. Macleod has taken over his brother's office."

Christie nodded. "Okay, Louis. I'll meet you at the Pen and Pencil." Turning, Christie said, "I'll follow you, Mrs. Neill."

Simon stared out the window at the brick wall of the neighboring building. He didn't see the wall. He saw his brother's grave. Guy! The loss of Guy was like the loss of a vital organ. Guy, who tried to have the world on his own terms. His life hadn't been easy. Some of it had been very bad. He'd ruined so much . . . repaired so little. Yet, Guy was his brother. And Simon missed him. Even now he could imagine Guy standing next to him, arguing . . . adamant that his way was the only way.

A current of air announced Christie's arrival. He turned and saw her elegant figure standing inside the door. Grief begets its own responses. He went to her, seizing both her hands in his. He'd looked forward to seeing her, like a treat he might decently allow himself. But at the sight of her, his defenses slipped. She meant more to him than a simple treat. Thinking this, he abruptly released Christie's hands.

"I'm glad you stopped by. I've been waiting for you."

Christie took in his retreat from intimacy. "I would have been earlier, but I had my own closing to take care of."

"Ah. You signed the *Deirdre* contract?" She nodded.

Simon cast about for something to say. He settled for the superficial. "Do you like my new office? I had it refurnished, but there still isn't much of a view."

Christie managed a smile. She took a turn about the office and stared at the nonexistent view.

"This was Guy's office." Now Simon used it.

"It was his office."

Christie's secret voice started repeating the same old questions. What if there had been no Guy, no forged checks? Would it have been different? Or would something else have turned up . . . like Barry . . . something to make Simon distrust her? Were Simon and she a lost cause from the beginning? Two people who loved each other . . . why wasn't love enough to hold them together? She'd run out of questions. It wasn't. She tried to be offhand. "It's nice to see you again. But why am I here? I thought I was *persona non grata* at Macleod Brothers."

Simon blinked. "Hardly. You're very *persona grata*."

"But you sold United."

"I had to." He searched for a reasonable explanation. "I don't believe Macleod Brothers belongs in the movie business."

"Louis said you didn't relish being Christie Larsen's boss." She looked hard at Simon. "Am I difficult?"

"No." He felt like a member of her fan club. "You're the best."

"Then why?" She glanced away. "Never mind. I like your office." She took a deep breath. "Okay. Why am I here?"

"Condolences, good will, auld lang syne. How long a list would you like?"

It's over, she thought calmly. Then stubbornly asked, "Why has it been so hard for us?"

"I don't know. Maybe God has a human streak. He punishes saints . . . applauds sinners."

"That sounds like an apology. No thank you. I'm no saint. Neither are you. You believed I slept with Matt Renault so he'd cash the forged checks. And with Louis Levy for whatever reason. Maybe ambition. And don't forget Stavros Lennos."

"I was a damn fool."

"Yes, you were. How could you?"

Simon's face was very still. "I was in over my head."

An extraordinary calm descended over Christie, a clarity of thinking beyond anything she'd ever known. "It was Guy's idea, wasn't it?" Simon didn't answer, so Christie went on. "You had to choose between Guy and me. You chose to believe Guy."

"My mistake. I've made that mistake often enough." He gave a faint shrug. "Anyway, I've been punished."

"You punished?" Her bitterness, so doggedly maintained, was slipping. "I suppose you have been. We've both been punished."

He was standing too close to her to trust himself. But he risked it. "Could we have a drink together? Maybe we could be friends?"

For a moment Christie saw him standing on a sunlit terace with the Pacific Ocean below . . . before the mists of doubt and distrust had rolled in. "Guy wouldn't like it," she murmured.

"Guy is dead," he said with an awkward earnestness.

"Is he?" Christie glanced at the picture in a leather frame on Simon's desk . . . a very young Guy Macleod standing in front of the entrance to Macleod Brothers. He made her feel inadequate and utterly lonely.

"At least give me a chance." Simon sounded almost embarrassed.

"To begin again?"

"To begin again."

Suddenly, as if against her own good sense, her face relaxed into a tender smile. "All right, begin again. But not from the same beginning."

NAKED CALL

Simon smiled with relief. "Let's have a drink," he said.

The market had closed, and it was a five minute walk to the neighborhood bar . . . the same bar patronized by the Macleod Brothers traders. Now it was full of raucous noise . . . winners and losers making jokes, laughing, wailing. Today was history. Tommorrow the game would begin again.

HISTORY-MAKING BESTSELLERS
COLLEEN McCULLOUGH

"McCullough's formula for bestsellers may be that millions of us long to make the acquaintance of upright, virtuous souls." *Chicago Tribune*

THE LADIES OF MISSALONGHI
70458-7/$4.95 US only

"Like a box of chocolates, this short novel is seductive and satisfying; readers will want to devour it in one sitting." *Publishers Weekly*

THE THORN BIRDS
01817-9/$4.95 US/$6.95 Can.

"A heart-rending epic of violence, love, piety, family roots, passion, pain, triumph, tragedy, roses, thorns...The plot sweeps on in truly marvelous fashion to its tragic but triumphant conclusion." *Chicago Tribune*

AN INDECENT OBSESSION
60376-4/$4.95 US/$5.95 Can.

A CREED FOR THE THIRD MILLENNIUM
70134-0/$4.95 US/$5.95 Can.

TIM
71196-6/$4.95 US/$5.95 Can.

Coming Soon in August 1991

THE FIRST MAN IN ROME
71081-1/$6.95 US/$7.95 Can.

Buy these books at your local bookstore or use this coupon for ordering:

Mail to: Avon Books, Dept BP, Box 767, Rte 2, Dresden, TN 38225
Please send me the book(s) I have checked above.
☐ My check or money order—no cash or CODs please—for $_____ is enclosed
(please add $1.00 to cover postage and handling for each book ordered to a maximum of three dollars).
☐ Charge my VISA/MC Acct# _____ Exp Date _____
Phone No _____ I am ordering a minimum of two books (please add postage and handling charge of $2.00 plus 50 cents per title after the first two books to a maximum of six dollars). For faster service, call 1-800-762-0779. Residents of Tennessee, please call 1-800-633-1607. Prices and numbers are subject to change without notice. Please allow six to eight weeks for delivery.

Name _____
Address _____
City _____ State/Zip _____

MCC 0491